THE CRIME BEAT

A COMPLETE SERIES OF NINE NOVELLAS

D.D. BLACK

DARKNESS AND LIGHT PUBLISHING

Dear Reader,

A version of *The Crime Beat* appeared as nine separate novellas under a previous pen name in 2019. This volume makes the entire collection available in one edition for the first time.

It has been revised, edited, and updated.

This is the complete story. There will be no sequels.

Thank you for reading!

D.D. Black

THE CRIME BEAT

EPISODE 1: NEW YORK

1

Sunday

"One bullet will change the world."

As he whispered the words, the old man methodically unpacked the rifle. Muscle memory gained through hundreds of repetitions still lived in his aged and calloused fingers. He laid the base of the weapon on his lap, attached the barrel, locked the takedown pins into place, and affixed the scope. Finally, he rested the spiked feet on the soft tar at the edge of the townhouse roof.

His back ached. Sharp pain pulsed through his right knee. But the pain was worth it. "One bullet will change the world."

Gritting his teeth, he dropped to his stomach and took in the crowd.

Six stories down and across Fifth Avenue, a couple hundred people had gathered on the wide marble steps of the Metropolitan Museum of Art to greet the arrival of celebrities and billionaires with *ooohs*, *aaahs*, and countless photos.

This is what America has become, he thought. A handful of tech elites hoard the wealth and the sheeple snap pictures and praise them for it.

He scanned the crowd and whispered the twenty-nine words in a hoarse monotone. "An international brotherhood, united by General Ki for a singular mission: to end technological oppression, to restore the sovereignty of the individual, to birth a new era of freedom." He'd repeated the words dozens of times each day for a year. Today he would do his part to put them into action.

A blur of faces met his eye through the rifle scope, but Raj Ambani's wasn't one of them.

The ability to stay cool in stressful situations was what made him a great sniper. Fifty years back, he could make a kill shot in less than a second without noticing the bombs going off around him. *Floating in the zone*, he called it. His primal energies focused on the target, his vision like a laser, sound muted so he barely heard the crack of his weapon as he pulled the trigger. Just silence and a man going limp, dead before hitting the ground.

His own life flashed through his mind.

Back in the war, if a bomb or an errant batch of napalm was going to land on his head, it was better to be oblivious anyway. Better to lock in and make the kill.

At his peak, he could touch a man half a mile away. He'd trained on a Remington M40, a modified Remington 700—one of the most popular rifles among hunters and the weapon of choice of Vietnam-era snipers. But this rifle was a custom job, state of the art and heavier than the M40 due to the oversized suppressor. Its barrel was even coated with a polymer-ceramic protectant that prevented corrosion and wear over time.

Not that durability mattered.

He would use this gun only once.

The late afternoon was cloudy and unseasonably warm for mid-December in New York City—between fifty and fifty-five degrees with no wind. His wrinkled hands were more prone to shake now, but the shot would be easy enough. No more than three hundred yards and at an angle that made him almost feel sorry for his target. *Almost.*

Eye in the scope, he moved from person to person. A pair of young girls aimed phones at the crowd. A short fat man craned his neck for a better view. Reporters jostled for space before a velvet rope that protected a red carpet running up the center of the steps. A black limousine—its extra large wheel wells and sturdy tires suggested it was armored—stopped between the rope lines in front of the red carpet.

The man slowed his breathing as he lightly touched the trigger. It was all about control. Any elevation of his pulse could throw the shot. He'd taken metoprolol for his heart for years, experimenting with the dose until he'd found the perfect balance. The beta blockers would have disqualified him from competition shooting, but he wasn't here to collect trophies.

His index finger was sweaty inside the leather glove. Leather was hot and cumbersome, but prints could bleed through latex and cloth often left traceable fibers.

The hairs on the back of his neck tingled and the world around him fell silent as the limo door opened. With a long, slow exhale, he allowed most of the air to leave his chest. A tall brunette stepped out of the limo and waved to the crowd.

The crowd cheered.

The old man inhaled. It was only some self-absorbed movie star, filming herself with a cellphone as she walked the red carpet. Not his target.

Moving his eye from the scope, he glanced up and down the street. A white SUV limousine turned onto Fifth Avenue a block away. It slowed and stopped in front of the Met. He trained the scope on the license plate: *@3COMMA*.

That was it. The custom plate matched Raj Ambani's social media name, and he'd had to look up the meaning. Two commas in your net worth meant you were a millionaire. Three meant you were a billionaire. It wasn't enough to brag about his wealth, Ambani had to promote his social media in the process.

He exhaled slowly, waiting for the rear door to open. Everything dropped away except for his eye in the scope and his finger on the trigger. All sound around him faded.

The rear door didn't open. Instead, a portly driver emerged and waddled around the limo. He opened the rear door, his wide back shielding Ambani as he got out.

The .50 BMG round could easily pass through the fat man and take out the target behind him. But that wasn't part of the plan.

Too risky.

He could wait. It had been fifty years since his last kill. And at seventy-three years old, this would likely be his last.

He wanted to savor the moment.

Halfway up the steps, Raj Ambani turned to face the reporters who'd followed him from the limo. "This evening is *not* about me, but I will take a few questions."

The crowd of reporters shouted questions.

Ambani shook his head, took in a deep breath then spoke loudly. "I'm only taking questions about IWPF. If they're not about the cause we're here to support, I'll head inside."

A young woman shoved an iPhone in his face, its screen displaying the wavy red lines of a recording app. "The deal with X-Rev International? Is that going through?"

Ambani stuck his hands in the pockets of his tuxedo pants. He was thirty years old and slightly built, his black hair slicked back and parted in the center. One of his companies had developed an early version of the recording app the reporter was using, and, despite her annoying question, he had to smile at seeing his work in action. Plus, he was in his element, as comfortable with the press as he was in the boardroom. He turned his unflinching smile on her. "Thanks, Sophie, but—again—IWPF questions only. Please."

"I'm a business reporter," she countered. "I *have* to ask about the merger."

He'd done enough interviews to know he could ignore questions he didn't want to answer. "The IWPF is an organization I'm proud to support. I've teamed with donors from the financial and tech sectors to establish an international legal team dedicated to protecting the wildlife of all nations, and of our precious oceans. The fifty-million-dollar fund will allow IWPF to blaze a trail in international law, creating protections for animals in an increasingly global society. As our economies and production bases become more interdependent, so must our conservation efforts."

A stocky male reporter elbowed his way to the front. "Raj, if we promise to get our science editors to write about..." He glanced at his notes, "...IPWF...or whatever...will you comment on the X-Rev merger?"

Ambani frowned. "It's I, W, P, F. The International Wildlife Protection Fund. And no, not today."

Ignoring a torrent of shouted questions, Ambani stood motionless on the steps. He scanned the crowd for an environmental reporter to call on. His limo pulled away below, and he wished he was in it. No matter how much good he did with his wealth, reporters only cared about how he'd gotten it, and what he was doing to get more.

He raised both hands. "No more questions. It's a beautiful Sunday evening in Manhattan and we're about to give fifty million dollars to an important charity." His white-toothed grin widened. "Come bug me about X-Rev on Monday morning if you must. Inside there's a glass of champagne with my name on it."

The thought of champagne made him salivate. He allowed himself one glass per week, and tonight was the night. Ambani loved New York City around the holidays, and he looked over the crowd to take it in. Across the street, twinkling Christmas lights decorated a red maple tree in front of a beautiful old limestone townhouse. A pair of pigeons emerged from the tree and flew south. He breathed in the cool air, which carried a sweet, smoky scent from a nearby cart selling roasted nuts. Life was far from perfect, but it was beautiful.

The birds disappeared into the evening as an unexpected movement pulled his gaze to the roof of the townhouse. A sudden motion focused his attention on what appeared to be a man with a black rifle.

His forehead was like a target. Wide and brown against the backdrop of cream-colored marble. The world dropped away. Everything except the target and his right index finger.

He let his breath out slowly. He grew still. He was floating in the zone. Ready to kill.

Ambani's eyes widened as he saw him, but it was too late.

The man pulled the trigger once. A hissing *pop* came from the gun.

His target went slack before anyone heard the shot. The bullet had entered clean, piercing Ambani's forehead and turning his brain to jello on the way out, leaving a fine, red-mist plume.

He never knew what hit him.

Before the body hit the ground, the man was taking the gun apart. Shrieks filled the air as the old man's senses returned to him, but the words moved through his mind, drowning them out.

An international brotherhood, united by General Ki for a singular mission:

to end technological oppression, to restore the sovereignty of the individual, to birth a new era of freedom.

A minute later, he slung the rifle bag over his shoulder and hobbled toward the ladder on the back of the townhouse. For the first time, his wrinkled face broke out in a wide grin. He'd done his part. The small part he'd been called on to perform.

He'd fired the first shot in a worldwide resistance that would usher in a new age of freedom.

2

Jane Cole was pissed. She'd been pissed at the world for four years, but right now her boss was catching the brunt of it.

She slammed a fist on his desk, rattling a jar of pens and knocking a wire-bound reporter's notebook off the table. She regretted it immediately, but was burning too hot to apologize.

Max Herr, her editor, grabbed his notebook from the floor, then kicked his feet up on the desk, lacing his hands through his thick white hair. "We're *on* the same side here."

She needed this job, and the two vanilla lattes she'd chugged before the meeting were doing nothing to calm her. The weeks before Christmas were already especially tough for her on a personal level. It didn't help that her boss was all over her regarding her recent story.

From anger, she had only one place to go. With the flick of an internal switch, she sighed and her rage morphed into numbness. Her thoughts became white noise—static with a frequency between the crackling of a radio and the gentle whoosh of the cosmic noise app she used—with half an Ambien—to fall asleep each night. She flicked this switch a few dozen times a day. It kept her sane.

Herr squinted. "Jane, are you okay? The story was good, but I'm catching hell for it. I know you're passionate about this, but—"

She shot out of her chair. "And you're not?" The static was gone. The numbness disappeared. The anger was back.

Herr held up his hands. "I published your article didn't I? Jane, I've greenlit more stories on police brutality than any editor in the city. But do you know what's important to me? Do you know what I'm passionate about above all else? *Accuracy*."

"My story *was* accurate. Every word of it. Robert Warren smashed a suspect's face into the metal grate of his cruiser. That. Is. Fact." She shook her head and flopped into the chair. "Didn't you tell me when I started here that every negative story I wrote about the department would get pushback?"

Herr stroked his bushy white beard, nodding. "I'm getting more than the usual pushback. Warren called twice today, three times yesterday. His name was on the list for detective. He can kiss that goodbye."

"*Good!*" Cole snapped. "Brutal cops shouldn't be offered promotions."

Herr shook his head. "No, they shouldn't."

Going emotionally numb gave her power. The static darkness erased the pain but left her perceptive, it allowed her to see others clearly. His terse answer made her wonder whether he truly agreed with her. She could read most people within three minutes. But she'd never been able to read her boss. It was one of the reasons she took the job. She knew she would never get bored.

He didn't look at the floor when he spoke. He never raised his voice when he lied. He had no discernible tell. His affable smile and white hair and beard reminded her of a kindly old wizard from the movies. His was a face that allowed everyone to believe, *this guy's on my side*. In truth, the only side he was ever on was that of *The New York Sun*, the newspaper he'd run for the last ten years. Today that meant he wanted to send her out to make sure she had her story straight. It was a total insult. There was nothing that needed to be added or retracted. Period.

Since she couldn't read him, she kept pressing. "Max, he *smashed* a dude's face *after* arresting him. What more does the public need to know?"

"All I'm asking is that you flip over some rocks to see what crawls out. I'm sure you got the facts right, but sometimes the facts are different from the truth. Got it?"

Cole relented. "Just because Warren calls three times a day doesn't mean he's innocent."

"Not only Warren. I've gotten calls from two others I trust. They say Warren is one of the good guys, one of the best cops in the NYPD."

She waved a hand dismissively. "Cops protect their own. Always have. Especially against journalists."

Herr sighed. "You know I *am* still your boss, Jane."

"For now." She stopped halfway to the door of his office. "I remember when I could actually *hear* and *smell* the person I was reporting on. Now?" She waved her phone at him. "I'm a damn stenographer. I copy Threads statements, Twitter replies—or X replies, or whatever the hell they're called these days—and hope someone calls me back. We break one story based on actual sources and the entire department comes after us. Makes a woman wonder whether there's any room to be a real reporter. I just don't think there's a point anymore."

Herr looked concerned. "A point to what?"

Through the windows of Herr's office, Cole gestured at the expansive newsroom, where a few dozen reporters, interns, and tech people typed at laptops, scrolled on phones, or talked quietly. "This. Any of it. *Anything.*"

"I worry when you say things like that, Jane." He shook his head. "That and things like the little 'For now' comment you snuck in a moment ago. You survived four rounds of layoffs because you're brilliant and you write well. You're the only woman leading a crime beat at a major New York City paper. I know the last few years have been..."

She frowned at him and he smiled sadly.

"...Difficult isn't a strong enough word," he continued. "I know it's been devastating. I mean, I can't know what you've had to go through. But you *made* it. You're still here."

"Nice pep talk, coach. I need to get back to my desk. My spidey sense tells me a police spokesman might be about to upload a post." She stopped in the doorway and swiveled to face him, but his eyes were on his laptop. "I'm gonna need to be ready to transcribe it *right away, sir.* Copy/Paste keyboard shortcut, don't fail me now! Control C, Control V... Control C, Control..."

"Wait!" he called without looking up, his voice urgent. "Something at the Met. A shooting."

"Who?"

"It's social media so I'm not sure it's true. They're saying…oh, dear God… they're saying Raj Ambani was killed at a charity event at the Met." Herr stood abruptly and waved for her to get out. "Get the story, Jane."

Cole met his eyes. "I'm sorry for… for all the… you're right, I'm still here." The thought of a real story, in the real world, had immediately improved her mood. "Christmas is just hard for me, okay?"

"Go! And call me the second you have something."

3

The Metropolitan Museum of Art spanned four city blocks on the east side of New York City's Central Park. Bordering two police precincts—the Upper East Side's 19th and the special Central Park precinct—the famous museum was a crown jewel of Manhattan's Fifth Avenue.

Cole guessed that officers from the 19th would respond first. After evacuating the Met and securing the crime scene, they'd close the 79th Street Transverse, the road through Central Park that connects the east and west sides of Manhattan. So when she'd told the Uber driver to go farther north and cross the park at 84th, she was betting that the more northern crossing would still be open.

She'd bet right.

As she slid out of the car, two officers were setting up a barricade to block off the road.

"Turn around!" one of them shouted at the driver, waving his arms. "No more cars through here."

The driver pulled a u-turn as Cole approached the cop—an acne-scarred twenty-something Cole thought she could persuade. Most of the young ones weren't yet jaded against reporters, not having had time to develop the *every-one-of-them-is-an-liar-until-proven-otherwise* mindset so common to veteran cops. "The 79th Street crossing was closed, too," she said. "What's going on?"

"Police business, ma'am."

The other officer was older and, Cole assumed, a little wiser. He pulled another barricade off the police truck. "Move along, lady."

She didn't recognize either of them. These two were from the 19th, most likely. But they might have information. Her competitors—mostly cute twenty somethings with huge social media followings—would blow right past these two and not think twice. But low-level cops were often willing to talk.

On the ride from the office Cole had learned everything she could about the shooting, which wasn't much. A handful of blurry pictures had appeared on Facebook and Threads, along with rumors about Ambani's murder, but nothing credible.

So far, the police had released no official statements. No video of the shooting or its immediate aftermath had emerged—a surprise since multiple TV crews had been covering the event, and every person in Manhattan carried a phone with a digital video recorder in their pocket.

She made eye contact with the acne-scarred cop who'd returned to the barricades—large blue sawhorses connected by blue 2x4s and stenciled in white lettering that read NYPD. "I'm Jane Cole from *The New York Sun*. Mind if I ask you a couple questions?"

He stepped toward her aggressively, his face turning cold. "Cole, huh? You the one wrote that hit job on Warren." His New York accent was thick for a teen raised on television advertisements and Saturday morning cartoons.

She stepped back. "I reported a brutal attack against a suspect who had already been apprehended, yes."

His smile wasn't friendly. "Then, no. No you *can't* ask us any questions. And not only that." He took out his phone and waved it in her face. "I'm gonna text every reporter at the *Times*, the *Post*, and the *Daily News* to give *them* a heads up on Ambani. Our precinct captain will sit for an hour on the record with the damn NYU student newspaper just to make sure you fall behind." He spat at her feet. "Rob Warren is one of the best. That story made New York less safe." He turned and muttered, "Damn muckrakers."

Cole grimaced and walked away.

The animosity was nothing new, and she let it disappear into the void as she crossed the street. The Fifth Avenue sidewalk was blocked by police barriers, so she walked east, circled around on Madison, and approached the Met from 83rd, scanning every face she saw. A block ahead, three blue and white police vans were parked sideways across the traffic lane. A large crowd had formed. Necks craned to peek between the vans and a few onlookers sat on people's shoulders, trying to peer over them.

"The shooter was on the roof," a man said as Cole passed.

He had wavy salt and pepper hair and wore a tan wool coat over a custom-tailored shirt. He'd been speaking with a woman who also looked rich. *Local residents.* "Who'd you hear that from?" Cole asked casually.

"Didn't *hear* it." The man's haughty voice matched his outfit. "I know it. I live up there." He pointed to the top of a townhouse on the corner of Fifth Avenue and 83rd. "Furnace was stuck on high again, so I had my window open. Heard the shot, looked out...crowd was already scattering." He pointed to the steps of The Met. "I ran down, but it was too late. I'm a surgeon—trauma isn't my specialty, but still..." He studied the ground. "Never seen a head so... damaged. What was left of it." The doctor raised his eyes to meet hers again. "Anyway, by the time I tried to get back to my apartment, the whole area was on lockdown. Cops said the shots could have come from my building, but I'm pretty sure they came from next door." He pointed up again, this time to the lime-stone townhouse next to his.

Cole studied him. He had shallow lines around his eyes and an even tan. His face was stiff, but earnest. A rich guy, guilty about his wealth, who needs everyone to believe he's an honest, good person. The kind of guy who staved off the darkness by remaining above reproach at all times. The kind of man who still needed to make mommy proud.

He wasn't lying.

The fact that he was telling the truth didn't mean he was right, but it was a good start. She nodded at the townhouse. "That one?"

"Pretty sure."

"What did it sound like?" she asked.

"Kind of a shallow pop, not a huge bang."

The townhouse was five stories of recently resurfaced old limestone. Typical Upper East Side home for millionaires or billionaires, though nicer than average due to the prime location. It was a townhouse that would cost ten to fifteen million dollars on a side street, but was probably worth double that because of the Fifth Avenue address.

She reached into her small hip purse—which her colleagues derisively called a "fanny pack"—and retrieved a business card. She held it out confidently. "Jane Cole, *New York Sun*. Okay if I follow up with you about this?"

The man frowned—a common response when people learned she was a reporter—but he took the card, pulled out one of his own, and handed it to her.

"Dr. Martin Horowitz?" she asked, reading it. "The heart guy?"

"I'm *a* heart guy."

The woman next to him tugged at his sleeve playfully. "You know what she means, dear. You're *the* heart guy. On the East Coast, at least."

Cole stowed the card in the front pocket of her purse. "Didn't you do the mayor's triple bypass?"

The doctor smiled proudly. "I can neither confirm nor deny."

The woman next to the surgeon beamed. "He treats *all* the important people because he's the best." The woman tilted her head and leaned in toward Cole. "But he works on *poor* people, too. Pro bono." Her lips curled slightly at the mention of 'poor people.'

Cole crossed her arms. The work may have been pro bono, but it was all about projecting an *image* of compassion. Again, the need to be seen as good.

"I'm Mrs. Horowitz, by the way," the woman continued. "Pleased to meet you. Martin and I are big fans of—"

"Thank you." She deflected the handshake and cut her off. "I'll follow up on that info."

An officer she vaguely recognized was making his way from the steps of The Met back to the police van barricade. His name escaped her, but she knew she'd seen him at Shooter's. Kenny? Or maybe... Remy?

Too bad she'd been three shots into a bottle of tequila when they'd met.

4

She jogged up to him as he passed between two police vans. "Reggie?" she called, making her best guess. He turned, one eyebrow raised, but didn't say anything. "Jane Cole. From Shooter's. Remember me? The other night?"

He waved off another officer and gestured for Cole to follow him around the side of the van. "It's Benny, and yes, I remember. Patrón neat, right?"

"That's right," she said, hit with a little pang of shame. Lately she'd been drinking a little too much tequila.

"I shouldn't be talking with you."

"You look good in your uniform." She wasn't lying. He was about ten years younger than her, with a clean-shaven baby face that belonged on a boyband poster.

"Thanks, but you were at Shooter's with *Danny*, right?"

She flashed him a warm smile. "It's casual between Danny and me." She wasn't proud of using flirtation as a reporting technique, but most men were willing enough to fall for it. And when she was after a story, she wasn't about to leave feminine wiles off the table, to a point.

Benny narrowed his eyes, then smiled back. "C'mon, that's a lie. You're just working me for a story."

"About me and Danny? Ask him yourself." She kept her smile as bright as a high-beam for another second before letting it fade.

"But you're right. I *am* angling for a story. I don't need you, though. I already know where the shot came from." She pointed at the roof of the townhouse. "Are you reviewing the building's security cameras?"

"Surrounding buildings, too." Benny stepped away. "But I really shouldn't be talking to *you* about it."

"I've been around crime scenes, Benny. I'm not asking for state secrets here. Of course you're checking video." She pulled out her phone and pretended to read from the screen. "A post on *Threads* says the shooting was racially motivated." She looked back at Benny but kept the look on her face open, as though it was an innocent question and not a technique to pry a crumb of information from the guarded officer. "Any comment?"

Benny reached for the phone, but Cole pulled it away. She didn't like lying—she wasn't very good at it—but sometimes that's what it took to get people talking.

He sighed. "Who the hell would say that? We don't even have a suspect yet and——"

"A hundred people on the steps when Ambani's head was shattered and *no one* saw anything? C'mon, Benny, don't piss me off today."

"Ramirez!" An angry voice boomed from twenty yards away. "What the hell you talking to *her* for?"

Benny smiled. "See what you did? Now I'm in trouble." He leaned in close, too close, and inhaled deeply, like he was smelling her hair. "You owe me now. What are you doing tonight? Buy you a shot at Shooter's?"

Cole recoiled internally, but flashed a smile he was too dumb to know was phony. "I don't date sources."

"I'm not a——"

"Yes, you are," she called over her shoulder as she walked away.

On her way back through the crowd, she began composing her story in her head, but a series of shouts half a block south interrupted her.

"Get outta here!"

"Screw you!"

She hurried in the direction of the argument and found a lanky officer, arms folded stubbornly to serve as a barrier to another tall, well-built man, who seemed determined to get past the police barricades. The more solidly built man wore plain clothes, but his bearing suggested he might be an officer as well. He stood taller than six feet and his back and shoulder muscles filled out his blue button-down.

She sidled toward them, careful not to get too close, listening to but not looking at them.

"You're not supposed to be here," the lanky officer said. "You *know* that."

"I can help." His voice was deep, and something about it was familiar.

"Then call the Captain. You know he has your back."

"And *you* know he can't take my calls."

"We *all* have your back, Rob, but until this thing plays out…"

Cole stopped in her tracks. *Rob?*

She held her phone over her head, pretending to look for a signal. From the corner of her eye, she glanced in the direction of the two men. The man in plainclothes had a thick, muscular neck and a gleaming deep mahogany-brown bald head.

It was Robert Warren.

The NYPD officer whose career she'd destroyed.

5

At the sight of Robert Warren, Cole shielded her face with her hand.

A college baseball player turned Marine turned cop, Warren wasn't just a big man, he was a specimen. She'd watched videos of his intense workout routines on Instagram while writing the story about him. Boxing. Weights. Running up hills in the park carrying a log over his wide shoulders. He may have been a brutal cop, but there was no denying that he took care of his body.

It wasn't his size that worried her, though. It was his temper. And, on top of that, the fact that he had more reason to hate her than anyone else in the city. She'd written stories about controversial police incidents before. But her story on Robert Warren was the first involving a black cop and a white suspect. Not that it mattered. To her, a brutal cop was a brutal cop.

She peeked around her hand to get a better look, and the officer noticed. Warren turned. If he recognized her, she'd be able to read it in his eyes. He didn't, and she tried to slip into the crowd.

"That's her." The voice of the lanky officer. "Rob, that's *her*." His tone had shifted from confrontational to conspiratorial.

"Who?" Warren asked.

She didn't want this confrontation, but it was unavoidable, so she changed tack and took it head on. Swiveling on the heels of her leather flats, she strode forward and stuck out her hand. "My name is Jane Cole of the *New York Sun*. I'm the woman who ruined your life."

Warren took a deep breath and let it out slowly. Clearly, he was trying to keep his anger from overcoming him. It was interesting to see someone else's technique. When Jane herself needed to control the demon of anger, she went numb and lived in the static. Allowed pieces of herself to disappear into the background. Warren's technique made him more dominant. He seemed to grow somehow larger—as if that were possible—until he filled out more of his already huge frame.

"Jane Cole?" His voice was deep and steady. "The one who wrote the article?"

"The same one you've been threatening."

"Threatening the paper, with libel. I wasn't threatening *you* personally. If I had threatened *you*, you'd know it." He turned to the lanky officer and sighed. "Anything worse than reporters?"

"Criminals?" the officer offered.

Warren scoffed. "Ask me, *she's* the real criminal."

Jane stood half a foot shorter than Warren and was probably half his weight. And though he was on paid leave, he was still a cop. Not the kind of guy she had any business trying to intimidate.

The harsh light of a streetlamp shone down on her. She wanted to feel its light warming her, giving her courage, but the sun had set and a cold wind blew down Fifth Avenue. At times like this, the numbness served her work. Her life, his life, none of it mattered anyway.

"Mr. Warren," she began. "*Rob*." She slid right in front of him and glared into his dark eyes. "You're a brutal cop and should be behind bars. I have your ex-wife's number. Call my office again, I'll get every reporter in the city to write about the period of your life after you left the Marines and before the NYPD dropped its standards low enough to let a jerk like you in. And to be clear"— she narrowed her eyes—"*that* was a threat."

His face twitched. His right hand clenched at his side. She felt his desire to punch her as a palpable presence. Inside, she was a field of gray static that knew only one thing: she'd gotten the story right.

Warren opened his mouth to speak, but she walked away before he could.

Half a block away, the adrenaline wore off. *What the hell had she just done?* She glanced back at Warren, hoping he hadn't pursued her. He stood there, arms crossed, staring right at her. He'd been watching her walk away.

To her shock, his face broke out in a wide grin.

6

The old man breathed in the greasy, fish-fried air as he slid the barrel of the rifle into the dumpster. Checking the alley one last time, he mashed a bag full of fish skeletons down over the gun barrel, then shoved his gloves through an intake vent in the side of the building. Tomorrow was trash day, so the final pieces of the weapon and the gloves would be in a New Jersey dump by eight in the morning.

He hadn't touched the ammo or components of the weapon with anything other than leather gloves. Killers had been convicted by one strand of fiber, by a speck of clay on their boots matched to a scene by a unique chemical or molecular fingerprint. Every perpetrator brings in and takes out trace evidence at the scene. The less you leave behind, the better your chances of not getting caught.

Exiting the alley, he shot a look through the window of Trần's Fried Fish. He smiled at Duc, the owner, who waved for him to come in. He could go for an order of his lemongrass-fried cod right about now, but he didn't have the time.

He'd spent the last hour stashing pieces of the weapon in storm drains and dumpsters across the Lower East Side. Now he needed to post the message.

He unlocked the faded red door of his apartment building and climbed three floors to his studio, one of two on the top floor of the narrow brick building. He examined the piece of hair he'd stuck to the doorknob plate with his own saliva. It was exactly where it was supposed to be. Had it been missing, he'd have known someone had broken in.

Closing the door behind him quietly, he scanned the apartment. At a metal desk in the corner, he opened a black laptop and checked the security camera log. No activity had been registered since he left that morning.

It was silly, but a twinge of something, an insecure feeling, made him check the four corners of the room. Even though he had the physical and digital proof that no one had been in his apartment, he didn't completely trust the technology. Given that the misuse of technology was one of the things he and his brothers were fighting against, it was ironic how much they relied on it. Each camera stood guard in its place in the corner, resting on a brace and peering down to capture any movement.

He crossed the floor and opened the lone window. Outside, a rusty metal fire escape led down to the alley behind Trần's. The smell of fried fish wafted in, stirring his belly.

He walked to the kitchenette, a small space enclosed by a sliding wooden door. At the movement of the door, Liberty looked up. He had the face and body of a bulldog and the black-and-white spots of a dalmatian. The man unhooked the chain that bound him close to the stove. "Liberty, it's all over. Don't worry. We got him."

The dog lifted his head up and set it back on the floor.

"I'm sorry, Liberty." He opened the refrigerator and pulled out a pack of bologna, then slapped a piece on the floor in front of the dog. "Eat up, boy. It's over now. No more closet for you."

Liberty chewed it a few times half-heartedly, then spat it out.

"Crazy dog. I should have named you *Shackles*."

Liberty moved to his bowl and eagerly lapped at the stale water. The old man refilled the bowl from a half empty glass on the counter as Liberty continued to drink.

Then, scarfing a folded slice of bologna, the man limped over to the desk and sat.

Opening an anonymous web browser through his personal VPN, he navigated to DogLoverSupplies.Com, one of the many websites he and his brothers used. The NSA, CIA, and other government agencies monitored Dark Web chat rooms. Hiding their conversations deep in run-of-the-mill websites gave them several more layers of protection. Not that he was too worried about federal law enforcement or military intelligence. Most of the agencies who'd be after them were incompetent anyway. They'd lost Bin Laden for nearly ten years before finding him by random chance, hiding in plain sight. He'd often joked that the motto of U.S. intelligence and federal law enforcement should be "better lucky than good."

He navigated to the chat room buried deep in the backend of the site, where his brothers would be waiting. Undoubtedly, they'd already heard the news, but protocol required that he share it formally. The chat room was a simple black box with a blinking cursor. As he typed, his words appeared in plain white text on the screen.

T-Paine:

1/9

(NBC's Hero)

X

An international brotherhood united by General Ki for a singular mission: to end technological oppression, to restore individual freedoms, to birth a new era of digital liberty.

(NBC's Hero)

X

1/9

He pressed "Enter" and waited, mashing the bologna around in his mouth. Liberty moved back to the bologna sniffing and gingerly taking bites from the floor.

The expected response came a minute later.

Kokutai-Goji:

2/9

(The Silver Squirrel)

Initiated.

An international brotherhood united by General Ki for a singular mission: to end technological oppression, to restore individual freedoms, to birth a new era of digital liberty.

2/9

(The Silver Squirrel)

Initiated.

The required formalities over, congratulatory responses flooded in.

Gunner_Vision: *Saw it on the "news." Way to go, my U.S. brother.*

Tread_on_This!: *Step one, man, step one.*

He leaned back, lacing his hands together through his thin, greasy hair. For the first time since the war, he was a success. He was a contributor—an actor, not a spectator.

"C'mere, Liberty. Come celebrate your daddy. We did a big thing today, buddy. Come love him. Come on, boy." The dog looked up at him briefly, but didn't move.

The old man looked at the screen, where a dozen new messages had appeared.

No_Surveillance_State: *Cheers from across the pond. BBC running with the story.*

8/15/47: *Had it coming. His parents were deserters.*

As the old man read the messages, he stood and took an old wooden baseball bat out of a glass case on the wall above his computer. Signed by Roger Maris, he'd received it from the player himself during his record-setting 1961 season. Despite the pain in his back, he swung the bat, mimicking Maris's beautiful left-handed swing as best he could.

He felt a stirring in his chest, a feeling he hadn't known since he was a boy staring out at the green grass of Yankee Stadium. It was as though a wide open space had opened inside him, a space large enough to fit any possibility.

Freedom_2025: *It's happening.*

End_the_Digital_Panopticon: *They will know your name.*

He'd done it. Years of frustration had inspired months of planning, and now he'd done it. The world would one day celebrate him. More importantly, the world would celebrate this day as a new Independence Day.

For the first time since he could remember, he was free.

7

After striking out with half a dozen cops and potential witnesses, Cole took a seat on the steps of a brownstone that sat on the edge of the crime scene.

Threads had nothing new on Ambani. Though his name was already trending worldwide—more than 800,000 posts had been made in the two hours since he died—nothing reliable was out there. Nothing story-worthy. On the ride from the office, she'd messaged a few of her best sources.

No one had responded.

A sad irony struck her. Ambani's blood was freeze-drying on the marble steps no more than a hundred yards away. Dozens of cops, detectives, and FBI agents surrounded her. And there she was, sitting on a cold stone step, staring at her *phone* for information and messaging cops through their anonymous burner accounts.

This was the crime beat, 2025.

She decided to look into Raj Ambani himself, hoping some detail from his life might lead to a good source outside the department. His Wikipedia page had already been updated with news of his death. Information travels fast. She kept reading.

Raj Ambani was the sixty-third richest man in the world, valued at $17.1 billion, according to Forbes. One of only a handful of American success stories on the list, Ambani's parents had immigrated from southern India in the mid 1980s, his father driving a taxi and his mother waitressing at Bombay Palace, a well-reviewed restaurant in the West Village.

From the time he was two, his parents knew he was special. Before he could speak in complete sentences, he could do multiplication and division. By the time he entered grade school, he was enrolled in a calculus class at City College.

A 1999 newspaper article showed a six-year-old Raj, encircled by college freshmen, a pencil behind his ear and a serious look on his face. The opening line read, "His classmates call him 'Rain Man,' but Raj Ambani's parents believe he's the reincarnation of Srinivasa Ramanujan, the famous Indian mathematics prodigy of the early twentieth century."

When he was thirteen, Ambani received a full scholarship to Columbia University, where he graduated in three years with degrees in math and computer science. From there, he pioneered computer-based stock trading, using algorithms to predict stock movements in real time. His invention lessened the importance of human evaluations and recommendations in the stock market, ushering in an era of markets ruled by computers.

He became a billionaire on his twentieth birthday. Most impressive to Cole was that he seemed to have made a smooth transition into adulthood. Two years ago, at twenty-eight, he'd married an opera singer and they were expecting their first child any day.

"You've got guts."

Cole looked up from her phone. Rob Warren stood before her, hands in the pockets of his gray jeans.

"I respect guts, but I meant what I said about journalists being the lowest. If the facts won't sell papers, just make something up, right?"

She stood and climbed two steps to meet his eye level. "Lower than cops who abuse their power?"

"I *didn't* abuse—"

"Sure." The corner of her lips turned upwards in a sardonic smile.

"You don't know anything about me, lady." He pressed his hands into his cheeks and blew out a long stream of air. He looked ready to explode.

"I know you beat up unarmed suspects. Or that you did, once.

I know you want to hit me. I understand. Really. This world gives us plenty to be enraged about. Have you checked your blood pressure lately?"

Warren shoved his hands back in his pockets, chuckling. "It's not good."

"And you thought getting in my face would help?"

Warren stepped back. "You don't know as much as you think."

"Let's not do this cops versus reporters thing, okay? It's so cliché."

Warren paced a little square. Two steps right, two steps back, two steps left, two steps forward, two steps right. Military precision.

"Why did you come up to me in the first place?" Cole asked.

"I wanted to explain."

"Explain why you broke the nose of a prisoner? An unarmed man? A man innocent until proven guilty?"

Warren waved the air as though shooing a fly. "I mean the period after I got back from Afghanistan. You dangled it in front of me back there, threatened me, but that wasn't in your story. Why not?"

"Wasn't relevant to the story." It was a lie, but the real reason would weaken her position.

Warren scoffed. "That's a lie."

Now *he'd* read *her*. "Honestly, what you did after you got back from Afghanistan was your business. I never would have put that in a story."

"I appreciate that." Warren walked another square, alternating between deep breaths and the double face-palm that seemed to be his pressure release valve.

She sensed there was something else on his mind. "You wanna tell me the real reason you approached me?"

He returned to his original spot. "I want to tell you what I know about Raj Ambani."

8

They walked east for two blocks, Cole a dozen paces behind Warren and on the opposite side of the street. From the research she'd gathered to write the article, Cole learned that Warren had lost the lower half of his right leg in Afghanistan. He had what most would consider a perfect physique but Cole had to struggle to detect a nearly imperceptible limp.

When he'd approached her, information about Raj Ambani was the last thing she'd expected. In fact, Warren himself had seemed surprised by his words. A second after uttering the name, he'd whispered, "Meet me at the Starbucks on east 87th in ten."

Then he'd walked away.

Cole lifted the collar of her sleek blue coat against the cold wind, following Warren as he turned north. When he passed under streetlights, she tried to make eye contact, but he marched forward, stone-faced, not looking back.

Her piece on Warren hadn't been a hit job. Just a fairly routine story about an NYPD cop abusing his power, and the predictable department cover-up. The initial scoop had come from a direct message on X, which she still thought of as Twitter.

It was her least favorite social media platform but the one that comprised a major part of her job. Exponentially more so every day.

On a Monday night two weeks ago she'd picked up a follow from a user with no profile picture and only a half dozen followers. The user's handle was @NYPD_Watcher_NYPD and the bio read, "I tell the truth about cops."

Cole had followed back and, minutes later, received a direct message.

@NYPD_Watcher_NYPD: *I have information about an officer breaking a suspect's nose. Interested?*

@Cole_Jane_NewYorkSun: *Yes.*

@NYPD_Watcher_NYPD: *I could give this to anyone.*

@Cole_Jane_NewYorkSun: *But you chose me. Why?*

@NYPD_Watcher_NYPD: *You'll get it out fast, right?*

@Cole_Jane_NewYorkSun: *If it's what you say, you have proof, and I can verify it, yes.*

A minute went by before the next message, which contained a three-page PDF file. Cole read the document, an internal report on the incident. According to the report, at least one witness saw Robert Warren park his cruiser, open a rear passenger door, and smash a suspect's face into the grate that separated the back seat from the front. Dashcam video confirmed this.

@Cole_Jane_NewYorkSun: *Are you in the 30th?*

@NYPD_Watcher_NYPD: *No.*

@Cole_Jane_NewYorkSun: *IAB?*

@NYPD_Watcher_NYPD: *Ding ding ding. Boss is slow-rolling it.*

@Cole_Jane_NewYorkSun: *So, why me?*

@NYPD_Watcher_NYPD: *I tried The Times. They've had it two days.*

@Cole_Jane_NewYorkSun: *And?*

@NYPD_Watcher_NYPD: *Crickets.*

Just to be sure, Cole pulled up the metro section of *The New York Times* online. No mention of the incident.

@Cole_Jane_NewYorkSun: *I have to ask: you willing to go on record?*

@NYPD_Watcher_NYPD: *LOL.*

@Cole_Jane_NewYorkSun: *They'll confirm this is authentic?*

@NYPD_Watcher_NYPD: *They'll have to. The pain of a story* *like this coming out is less than the pain of denying it officially, then seeing it on page 1.*

Four hours later, Cole had filed the story, complete with a denial from Robert Warren and a quote from a source in the 6th Precinct, admitting the troubling incident had occurred and assuring the good people of New York City that they would get to the bottom of it.

The Sun ran her story on page A1 of the print edition the next morning and on the homepage of the web edition. By noon, Warren had been suspended, pending an investigation.

⊕

Cole entered the Starbucks a little after Warren, who stood at the counter ordering a double espresso. She paid for his coffee, plus a vanilla latte for herself, then followed him to the back. Warren picked a table in the corner—the least visible spot in the place—and sat. Cole took a chair across from him.

She sipped her latte and raised an eyebrow. She'd let Warren do the talking. There was a chance he was trying to set her up, to discredit and embarrass her by planting a false story.

Payback.

Wouldn't be the first time a cop had tried it. But something in his demeanor told her he was for real.

Every few seconds he glanced over his shoulder at the door. The ceramic espresso cup almost disappeared in his large hands as he passed it back and forth nervously. "I shouldn't have come here."

"I can tell there's something you want to get off your chest," she said, keeping her tone casual.

He shot the espresso in one gulp, then pointed at her paper cup. "Sugar. Lot of sugar in a vanilla latte. Between the milk and the syrup, I'm guessing thirty to forty grams?"

Not what she'd expected. "How the hell would I know? Are you here to scrutinize my coffee habits?"

He couldn't let it go. "That's not coffee. That's a liquid candy bar."

While she tried to pick the best of a dozen different smart-ass replies, his eyes darted down. A pair of officers had just walked in, but she didn't think they'd seen him.

"If I'm seen with you," he said, "and it gets back to my department, I'm screwed."

His face was taut, the skin barely concealing a square jaw and sharp cheekbones. She wrote for a living, so her mind constantly puzzled over how to describe someone in the fewest possible words. If she'd had only one, it would have been *brawny*. If she'd had three: *brawny, but anxious*.

She didn't know what it was, but something simmered beneath his surface. Under that chiseled, carefully cultivated exterior, his anxiety was palpable.

She leaned in. "But you *did* come here, Rob."

Again, she followed his eyes to the counter. The two officers were engrossed in conversation. Hand covering his mouth, he said, "I could be wrong about this, that's the first thing you need to know. If I was sure, I'd... well... I don't know what I'd do. The thing is—"

He paused as a teenage girl walked by on her way toward the bathrooms.

Cole was growing frustrated. "You said you knew why Ambani was killed."

"I didn't say that. I *don't* know why." He sighed and shook his head in a tight arc. "I really shouldn't be here."

"Look. I don't like being screwed around with. If this has something to do with the story I wrote about you, I—"

"No. That story was BS, but... I just saw you there, and I need to tell someone."

"Tell someone what?"

"War Dog!" The officer's voice came from the direction of the counter.

Warren shot up. "I'm sorry," he whispered. "I shouldn't have come."

Hurrying away, he took the outstretched hand of the officer and shook vigorously. Cole couldn't hear their words from her table, but he seemed to be having a friendly conversation. Apparently he had a switch to flip as well. From anxious cop on leave to back-slapping colleague without a care in the world.

She watched in silence, just long enough to get angry. But she didn't flick the switch to turn on the static. Instead, she bolted for the door, past Warren, and waved down a taxi. She slid in, but a hand grabbed the door as she tried to shut it.

"Wait a second," Warren said.

She looked up from the back seat. "Stop jerking me around, Rob. What the hell is this about?"

He glanced over his shoulder, then squatted behind the door. "I don't want to say too much, but if it comes out that the shooter used a fifty-caliber rifle, that the killing had professional written all over it, and that there's no personal motive, call me. If those three things all come out, I may know something. Something I'm not in a position to tell the department, thanks to you. If not, I'm wrong and this conversation never happened."

The taxi driver looked back. "We going or what, lady?"

Warren slowly closed the door.

By the time the taxi rounded the corner, Cole was using speech to text to dictate her story on the murder of Raj Ambani into her phone.

9

***

Monday

Robert Warren threw two quick jabs with his muscular left arm, then a right hook that knocked the heavy bag into his refrigerator. A half-full bottle of Rémy Martin 1738 wobbled on its base, nearly toppling off the top of the rusty fridge.

Warren watched, panting and sweating. Half of him wanted to dive for it, the other half hoped it would shatter on the cracked wooden slats of his kitchen floor.

The bottle was a reminder of where he'd been. It represented everything he was now against—his healthy body the foundation of his increasingly healthy mind—but he left it there to remind him. Of what he'd been and what he'd surely be again if he wasn't careful. The bottle steadied and he went back to the bag as it swung toward him.

Another right hook, then a torrent of jabs. Left, right, left, right, left, right.

Chest burning, he stopped.

The bolts that held the bag to the ceiling creaked and the bag rocked back and forth like a pendulum, slowing and finally stopping.

As he cooled, he stalked from the tiny kitchen through the windowless living room and into the bedroom. He grabbed a tub of grass-fed whey protein from a milk crate—his "bedside table" —and returned to the kitchen. After downing two scoops mixed with organic almond milk for some healthy fat and extra post-workout calories, he stabbed at the screen of his cellphone, which he'd duct-taped at eye level to the top of the heavy bag.

Swipe, tap, tap, scroll, tap. It began to ring.

"Hello." The familiar voice. Bright and cheery.

He put the call on speakerphone. "Gabby, this is Rob."

"Rob who? Rob?"

Gabriela Rojas had been his training officer when he joined the NYPD. Coming from the Marines, he'd been embarrassed to take direction from a younger woman. But she'd proven brilliant and tough, more than worthy of the seemingly unending series of promotions she'd received since. From beat cop to Sergeant, from Sergeant to Lieutenant, all in seven years, almost impossibly fast.

They hadn't spoken much since he'd left Brooklyn, but Warren trusted her. She was one of the most honest people he'd come across in law enforcement. Had she really forgotten him?

"Robert Warren," he said slowly. "*War Dog*." She'd given him that nickname on day one.

"War Dog? What the hell? It's been like—?"

"Two years."

"Two years," she repeated. "Right. How... how *are* you?"

"You mean the thing?"

"Yeah, the *thing*. We *do* get the paper out here in Brooklyn."

Warren jabbed the bag as hard as he could. "It's crap," he shouted in the direction of the swinging bag. "You know how those people are."

"Dude had it coming, huh?"

Warren walked a square around the bag as it slowed, eyes always on the phone. "In front of an IAB Review Board, I regret my actions. And actually, I *do* regret it. I lost my cool and I'm not proud of it. Off the record? In a city full of scumbags, the guy whose face I smashed may be the worst."

"That bad?"

Warren jabbed the bag again. "Worse."

"What's that thudding sound that keeps happening?"

"Sorry. It's my heavy bag. Trying to stay in shape."

"I see," Rojas said. "Well, it's been great catching up and I—"

"Gabby, what the hell? You, too?"

"You know how it is."

"I'm *that* toxic?"

"War Dog, I'm in the office."

"I get it."

He walked another lap around the bag, the silence thick between them. He imagined Gabby looking over her shoulder in the thinly-carpeted office, his former home in Brooklyn's 72nd Precinct. She was probably afraid someone would hear her say "War Dog" and leak it to one of the cop-haters in the Brooklyn press.

He decided to try small talk. "So how is the 72nd treating you?"

"Huh? Oh, right. I still live in Brooklyn, but I'm JTTF now. You didn't hear?"

It didn't surprise him. New York City's Joint Terrorism Task Force was where Gabby was destined to land. The home of the best of the best. But he'd never expected her to land there so soon. "Whose butt you kiss to get that gig?"

She said nothing, but his off-color joke wouldn't have bothered her. It was something else. One thing about climbers like Gabby was that they knew associating with a toxic cop could land them in a boss's crosshairs and blowtorch their careers. He was now one of those cops, and this was one of those times.

"Real quick," he pleaded, "you got anything on the shooting at the Met? Ambani?"

"Screw off, dude, you know I don't. And even if I did—"

"JTTF not in on the investigation?" he asked.

"You didn't even know I was JTTF until thirty seconds ago. Why in the name of Saint Paul would you be calling me for that kind of info?"

He went quiet and let out a long sigh. "If *I* knew something, something about Ambani, where would I go right about now?"

Rojas breathed heavily into the phone. "Dude?"

"I'm saying, *if* I knew something, and I am where I am because of the thing in the paper, what would you do if you were me?"

"Honestly, I'd either walk to a payphone and call in an anonymous tip, or I'd leak it to a reporter, someone you trust. Let them write it and let us pick it up from there. Either way, I'd make sure my name was nowhere near it. We're gonna catch the bastard who shot Ambani—whether it was a terrorist, a racist, or a jealous ex who hired a pro. When we do, we want your name nowhere near it." She paused. "No offense, of course."

She was right, and it confirmed his instinct to talk to Cole. The last thing he wanted was to taint the investigation into Ambani's killer by attaching his toxic name to it. And a messy truth about police work was that sometimes it required leaking to the press to get things moving within the bureaucracy. "Thanks, and one more thing."

"War Dog, I—"

"You've seen cases like mine before, so humor me. Please."

She sighed her assent.

"If I don't beat the investigation into my incident, what are my chances at making detective?"

"Zero."

"And what are my chances of a lateral move, say back to Brooklyn?"

"Lateral move?" she was whispering now. "Low, but not zero. More likely a demotion. Parking tickets, traffic control. I don't know, stadium work, maybe."

Warren stood in the center of the dark kitchen. The bottle on the fridge called to him, but it had been forty-nine months and fourteen days since his last drink, and he wasn't going to let this break him. He'd changed, and that bottle, still there untouched, was proof.

Most recovering alcoholics avoided keeping booze around the house. He put a bottle of his favorite drink where he'd see it every day.

He ran a finger over the curved lettering on the dusty bottle, tracing the R and the E with his index finger. "Parking tickets? Seriously?"

"Someone's gotta do it, right?"

He walked back to the bag. "Sorry, it's just—"

"I gotta go. Don't worry, War Dog. You'll ride this out."

"Yeah. Catch a couple terrorists for me."

He tapped "End," then laid into the heavy bag so ferociously his knuckles bled.

Even if his career wasn't over, it was.

36

10

Cole squeezed her husband's hand as he pulled her forward, snow crunching under her boots with each step.

"Keep them closed, Monkey Tree. Almost there." His voice brought a smile to her face.

It always had.

"Around one more corner," he whispered, his words tickling her ear. "Keep them closed."

Eyes shut tight, she allowed herself to be led forward. He was her rock and there was no one else in the world she would give this much power to. "Where are we going?"

"It's a surprise."

She laughed at his childlike excitement. "It's freezing out here, Matty."

"Just a little further."

She knew they were somewhere in Central Park. She'd figured that out from the left turn they'd made out of their building on West 98th Street. But she thought she might be able to figure out where based on sound or smell. Near the carousel she might smell roasted nuts or popcorn from the vendors. Near the reservoir, she might hear the raspy honks of the ducks.

With her free hand, she pulled her jacket up against the cold breeze. A whiff of Matt's spicy aftershave hit her.

Her freshly shaved husband was her absolute favorite smell.

He tugged on her hand to stop. "Open your eyes, Monkey Tree."

She opened them, blinking rapidly as her eyes adjusted to the twinkling *lights against the backdrop of darkness. She was in Central Park, surrounded by a blanket of fresh snow. In front of her sat a small tree decorated with Christmas lights, ornaments, and old-fashioned silver tinsel. It was nearly as tall as her and had been planted in a green plastic tub.*

Tears welled in her eyes. "How did you do this?"

He didn't respond. She let go of his hand and walked to the tree, running her hand, still warm from her husband's, across the prickly branches. "It's a monkey puzzle tree?"

"It is."

"And you put it here for me?" she asked.

"I did."

Her first trip with Matt had been to the Pacific Northwest, where Cole had fallen in love with a droopy-branched variety of pine tree that grew in the front yard of their rental.

Matt had poked fun at her, calling it "The most ridiculous looking tree on earth," and "God's only mistake." On their last night in Seattle, he'd proposed to her on the Ferris wheel by the waterfront and, after she'd accepted, she'd done a dorky, arm-flailing dance that reminded him of the tree's branches.

Ever since, he'd called her Monkey Tree.

She dove into his arms, then pulled back and kissed him. "Oh. My. God. This is so sweet. But where are we, exactly?"

"North Woods. Somewhere near 108th Street."

"Central Park at night?"

"I figure people can tell I'm a Marine on spec."

It was true. Although forty years old, Matt was built like a tank. Not the kind of guy a Central Park mugger would single out. "How'd you get the lights to light up?"

"Battery buried in the dirt. I petitioned the park for a month, even tried to bribe a guy, but they wouldn't let me actually plant a tree here. Good news is, we can take it home. I thought we'd plan a trip to plant it somewhere upstate, maybe in the spring?"

She kissed him again. "It's perfect."

"Merry Christmas, Jane Cole."

<hr />

"Jane. Your phone. Wake up!"

Cole shot up in bed, the warmth draining from her all at once. Her phone's triumphant, *Ode to Joy* ringtone filled the room but, as usual, provided none of the advertised joy. Especially because right now it was crowding out the lingering pleasantness of the dream.

Danny Ronan sat on the bed next to her, holding her phone in her face. She pushed a tangled swath of hair off her forehead and read the caller ID. "Ugh!"

"Your boss, right? Didn't you say you were on thin ice?"

"Let me *sleep*, Danny." It came out more annoyed than she'd intended, but less annoyed than she felt. They'd been dating for six months and he'd had to wake her up every time she slept over. That was no reason to be pissy with him, though. "Everyone over thirty is on thin ice. If you didn't have a smartphone in your crib, you're always about to get fired."

"C'mon," he said. "It can't be *that* bad."

"That's how it feels."

He forced the phone into her hand. "Then shouldn't you answer it?"

Silencing the phone, she shoved it under her pillow. "Not taking this call won't make or break me. I'm not supposed to be in for an hour. Max probably wants something new on the Ambani murder. Gave him seven hundred words last night, but since I dared take the evening off from posting news McNuggets, I guess he's having a conniption."

"Not that I have much," Ronan said, "but I could give you something on Ambani."

"I told you what the rules are. Rules are important to me."

"I know."

Ronan buttoned the top button of a crisp white shirt, studying himself in the mirror. Cole watched him watching himself. He was smart and kind. Handsome, she thought. Square jaw, short brown hair, good skin, lean and toned. His butt looked good in his black slacks. And he treated her well.

So why wasn't she into him in any real way?

The answer came as soon as the question entered her mind. *Because he's not Matt.*

Ronan looped a red tie around his neck. "*Rules* in general are not important to you." He spoke slowly, like he was choosing his words carefully. "You break rules all the time. Jaywalking. Lying to your boss, lying to sources to get them to talk. One outdated journalistic standard is important to you, and that's fine. Just saying, if you *do* get fired, I can help you."

Cole opened her mouth to argue, but caught herself in time and took a couple deep breaths. "You're sweet. I appreciate it. There are a few rules that matter, and not sleeping with my sources is one of them."

He swiveled as he pulled on his jacket. "You were sleeping with me before you knew I was a detective. So technically you wouldn't be sleeping with me in exchange for information."

"That's a distinction without a difference."

He shook his head slowly. "Look, stay as long as you want. I know lazy members of the institution formerly known as the Fourth Estate can ignore their bosses and go in late, but central has half the detectives in the city pitching in on this Ambani thing and, if you ask me——"

She put a hand up. "Not another word."

He stopped in the doorway. "You free tonight? I thought maybe we could go on an *actual* date."

Her eyes glazed. Pieces of the dream still echoed like a fading memory. The piney scent of the Monkey Tree, the warmth of Matt's hand. Happiness.

They'd never made the trip upstate to plant the tree. The evening in Central Park had been Christmas Eve, their seventeenth wedding anniversary. Matt left for his third tour in Afghanistan the following week. He died a month later. The tree now sat in the corner of her apartment, dehydrated and clinging to life.

"Jane, what about tonight?"

She didn't reply. Part of her wanted to say, *Go to hell, Danny. Next week would have been my twentieth wedding anniversary and there's no way I'm spending any more time with you between now and then.* She wasn't in love with him, would never be in love with him. But he was a decent guy and didn't deserve her mockery. She grabbed her phone from under the pillow and pretended to be lost in the screen, scrolling.

As he walked out, she looked up.

"See you around, Jane," he called over his shoulder before shaking his head.

From the moment they'd met she'd known she would eventually disappoint him. Now was as good a time as any.

11

Max Herr picked up his glasses and pointed them at her. "Try everything. *Everything.*"

"I wrote everything I had last night. You think I didn't try every source before I filed? *No one* broke any news yesterday. Not *The Times*, not *The Post*, no one."

"Find better sources."

Her story had been the best she could do, but it hadn't been anything special. By the time she'd filed, the police had released a statement indicating that Ambani had been killed by a sniper. Every news outlet in the city had quoted it. Cole had included Dr. Horowitz's assertion that the fatal shot came from the limestone townhouse, but no other witness could corroborate his story. She'd had very little information about the actual shooting, so she'd spent much of the piece on Ambani's background in order to fill column inches.

Cole glared at her boss. Lately, this job had been the one thing she was good at and the lecture had put her on edge. "You and I both know that I have better sources than anyone else here."

"Doesn't mean they're good *enough*. The best of a bad lot isn't anything to brag about." Herr stood and walked a lap around the desk, stroking his wizardly beard. "There's gotta be something we can do. Ambani's personal life? His business partners?"

"I'm looking into that, but you think I'm gonna crack this case before the cops? Best chance is we get a leak once *they* have something."

"Has his wife released a statement or spoken publicly?"

She'd read Mrs. Ambani's statement on Facebook just before coming into Herr's office. "Shocked and devastated. Requested privacy in this time of personal tragedy. Pretty standard, but I have a sense of what she's going through. With a baby coming, I imagine it's... well... as bad as something can be."

Herr ignored her sentiment. "Try. Harder." He flopped into his chair and sighed. "I'm sorry, Jane. I know you're doing your best. We need a win. *I* need a win. I need something no one else has." His face became pinched, as though with pain. "I'm not demanding Pulitzers here, just... a win."

He looked defeated, almost desperate. For the first time in a long time, she felt for him. *The Sun* had lost half their staff over the last five years. There were rumors of another series of layoffs. Even though Herr did the firing himself, she knew it gave him no pleasure. From the look on his face, it ate him up.

"You're my eyes out there," he said. "You go to Ambani's office?"

"Last night. Total lockdown."

"Okay, what else? Gotta be *something* else."

Cole thought about it again. On the walk to work from Danny's apartment, she'd played her interaction with Warren over in her mind, and one thing stuck out. The story that got him suspended had come out two weeks ago. He'd called *The Sun* dozens of times since—trying to refute it, arguing for a retraction. When he'd first approached her, she'd assumed it was about the story.

But he hadn't mentioned it. Not until *she* brought it up, at least. If he'd been obsessed enough about Ambani to approach her, obsessed enough to forget his anger about her story...

It had to mean something. Under normal circumstances, she might have run the interaction by Herr for his opinion. But what if Warren was setting her up?

Herr caught her eye. "I can see the wheels spinning, Jane."

"It's nothing."

"What?"

"She nodded at his laptop. "You have X or Threads open?"

"Yeah."

"Anything on the gun yet?" she asked. "I checked on my phone before I came in."

He scanned the screen. "Not that I see, but isn't that something you should get from a source *before* it breaks online?"

"You know how it is on these big murders. NYPD, Feds. Lotta handshaking going on behind the scenes. Max, *no one* is talking yet."

Her phone vibrated. She had a notification from Threads, a direct message from one of her most reliable sources. "Finally!"

Herr walked around to look over her shoulder. "What?"

"Note from a source. Hold on."

@Lebron_GOAT23: *.50-caliber from the rooftop you mentioned. No suspects.*

She couldn't suppress the grin that broke out across her face. The anonymous account belonged to Joey Mazzalano, a lieutenant who, despite being a serial sexual harasser and all-around scumbag, had never led her astray. His confirmation that the weapon was a .50-caliber rifle confirmed Warren's suspicion.

"What?" Herr demanded.

"I fed the rooftop thing from Horowitz to my guy and it checked out."

"*A* rooftop or that *specific* rooftop?"

"Specific. Plus, he confirmed it was a fifty-cal, which I heard from someone else. No suspects."

"Okay, but so what? I mean, go ahead and post it, drop an update on the piece from last night, but that's not enough for a full story."

"I might have something else."

"What?" he asked.

"Too soon to say, but…" She trailed off. She wasn't yet ready to tell him about Robert Warren.

"Cole, what?"

She hurried from his office, already scanning notes on her phone from her story on Warren. She knew he lived in the Meatpacking District, but couldn't recall the exact address.

Minutes later, she was in an Uber headed for his apartment.

12

"Rob, we are never, *ever* getting back together."

Warren called his estranged wife exactly once a month, always asking the same question. And for the forty-ninth month in a row, her reply was the same.

He sat at the cracked formica table in his kitchen, but felt like he was floating outside himself, watching his life from above. He put the call on speakerphone, then muted it as she continued. "I just can't trust you. I have to think about Marina. She is all that matters... to the both of us, Rob."

While she spoke, he pressed his hands to his cheeks and blew out through his mouth violently. He'd read online that breathing this way would calm him down in stressful situations. It wasn't working.

"I'm not blaming you...I can't even remotely imagine what you've been through. And now with this police brutality story in the papers. Marina's not old enough to understand it yet, but the Internet is forever. One day she's gonna see it and..."

He unmuted the call. "They're gonna *clear* me, Sarah."

"Even so, you know how papers are," she said. "They run the story on the front page, A1, then they bury the retraction on C29."

"Please, just let me see her. I know I'm not where you need me yet, but I've been sober a long time." He glanced past the heavy bag at the bottle on top of his fridge. "Blood pressure is down to…"

"Down to what?"

He considered lying, but decided against it. "152 over 95 this morning."

Sarah sighed. "Are you taking care of yourself? I heard you. Were you doing that thing where you blow out air to relieve your stress? Are you still doing that?"

"Sometimes, not usually. But I'm telling you, Sarah, I'm mostly better now."

"What did Marina use to say?" she asked.

Warren flashed back to his daughter running in from the other room when he and Sarah would argue. He could still feel her little arms wrap around his neck. Even the thought calmed him more than his tea kettle breathing. He would swing her up and hold her tightly then puff out his cheeks for her to press in while he crossed his eyes and blew air into her face. He wiped away a tear with his knuckle.

Warren took a deep breath. "She would say, '*be the tea kettle again daddy*'." Warren managed to make out the words without a cry in his voice.

Sarah laughed. "That's right. The way you would get her laughing was priceless. But she stopped laughing with you and I needed to take her before… Look, Rob, I'm proud you're sober. I really am." Her voice was quieter, but also firmer. "I know none of this is your fault. That stuff with your mom's brother. Your leg. You've got good reasons to be messed up. But that doesn't mean it's safe for Marina to be with you unsupervised. I can't just leave her with you. Your apartment is… well… limited, and now you're on leave."

Warren looked beyond his living room through the open door into his bedroom. He could see the corner of the extra-long twin he slept on under a tangle of unmade blankets and sheets. No bed frame, no box spring, just a bare mattress on the floor.

Sarah was right. It was no place for his daughter. "*Paid* leave, and I haven't missed a payment. They won't cut my pay unless I'm found guilty, and that's not gonna happen."

"What if it *does*?"

"I could always move back in with you and Marina."

His wife sighed, and he knew he shouldn't have said that. He tapped "mute," sprang from the chair, and threw a series of jabs at the heavy bag.

"Be serious, Rob, and put yourself in my shoes. You could lose your housing, what little there is of it. If I was with a man like you..."

"What is that supposed to mean?" he asked, his tone angrier than he intended.

"...You wouldn't want Marina around him."

He breathed a sigh of relief, realizing the phone was still on mute.

He unmuted the line. "Are you seeing anyone?" he asked as calmly as possible.

"Not that it's any of your business, but no, nothing serious."

Nothing serious meant she was sleeping with someone. Again, he saw himself from above. This wasn't how his life was supposed to go.

When he'd been honorably discharged from the Marines after losing the lower portion of his right leg, he'd come home a hero. Sarah had gotten pregnant soon after and he'd applied to the NYPD. His life was back on track. The PTSD really got cooking soon after Marina was born. More and more, he'd found himself on edge, though he couldn't have told anyone why.

The merest threat provoked a violent overreaction and afterward, shame. Shame that he'd scared his wife, that he'd terrified his daughter. It was like his internal software was corrupted, and he just couldn't march straight, no matter how hard he tried.

So he drank.

Drinking mellowed the anxiety and blunted his anger too. Only while he was on the bottle. When he wasn't, it made everything worse.

So he rarely wasn't.

But then he needed coke to keep him functioning through the blurry haze of the booze, and that aggravated his temper.

Those days were all in the past—the separation had woken him up—but the thought of Sarah with another man made the Remy Martin look better than it had in months. He didn't know which he wanted more, to drink it or bash it over the head of Sarah's new boyfriend. A boyfriend, he knew, she had every right to have.

All of this was his fault.

The line did a quick double-beep. Call waiting from a 917 area code—a New York City number that wasn't in his contacts. He was happy to have an excuse to focus on something other than his almost-ex-wife. "I gotta go. Work's calling on the other line."

He accepted the new call without waiting for Sarah's reply. "Hello?"

"Officer Warren, it's Jane Cole. How about we give this another shot?"

"Okay, but I don't see how—"

"Rob, I'm willing to talk about a retraction."

This caught him by surprise, but he didn't buy it. Journalists always had an angle. "Why?"

"I'd really like to talk in person, Rob."

"Why?"

"I'm standing outside your apartment," she said. "Buzz me in."

This stopped him. Since the breakup, he'd lived in four different apartments. His new place was a three-hundred square foot sublet, and he was pretty sure there was no official record of his new address anywhere other than with the department. "How do you know where I live?"

"Your wife."

The thought of a journalist talking to his wife made his head feel like it was expanding outward. "You think I'm letting you into my apartment after what you wrote? Please."

"Then come down."

He wanted to say no, but she'd said the magic word: *retraction*. It was the one thing that might give him his career back. Hell, maybe it would even help Sarah forgive him—allow him to feel his little girl's arms around his neck.

He would make Marina laugh again.

13

"How'd you know about the rifle?" Cole blasted him with the question as soon as Warren walked out of his apartment building.

"Don't you journalists have any shame?" he fired back.

She was used to this. The conflict between police and journalists went back centuries.

They walked in silence for half a block, Warren shooting angry looks every few steps. Through his slight limp, long strides carried him quickly. Cole also walked with purpose, like she was late for something important, so she kept up easily. They turned west and headed toward the Hudson River. The sun at their backs cast a sharp light on the sidewalk between them.

She was willing to hear him out on the story she'd written, but first she wanted an answer. "Here's the deal—"

"No. Listen. You said you'd talk retraction. I wouldn't have come down otherwise, and today is really not the day to—"

"*You* approached *me*, Rob. At the Met. You have something you want to say. I was as surprised as anyone that you decided to say it to me, but…" Suddenly, the brick buildings on either side of her seemed to close in. She let out a long sigh. Her mind became a field of gray static. "Oh, what's the damn point?"

Warren stopped a pace ahead, blinking in the harsh winter light.

Without thinking, Cole stopped as well, lost in her internal landscape. She'd been on this street before. Some club opening, or maybe a friend's birthday party. The details didn't matter. She'd danced with Matt in one of these red brick buildings. The memory had come like a flash, but it was too painful. The static was a reprieve.

Warren eyed her skeptically. "What's wrong with you? Sugar crash? If you avoided empty carbs you'd—"

"It's *not* a sugar crash. Has it ever occurred to you how stupid this little dance is? Cops versus journalists. Journalists versus cops. I mean, we're standing on a vaguely spherical ball of rock, a few dozen elements temporarily pressed into shape, spinning through space around the sun. Two insignificant mumbling sacks of meat, arguing over scraps of information, kept alive temporarily by the warmth from a literal ball of fire 93 million miles away. I couldn't care less about you breaking some guy's face, or whoever the hell shot Raj Ambani. And it makes me not give a damn about your paleo-keto-whatever-the-damned diet that *might* prolong my existence on this dirty sphere of oversized wet sand for a few more years but would *absolutely* deny me the shred of comfort I get from a vanilla latte. Or two."

She thought she saw Warren smile, but he turned quickly and kept walking. She followed.

"That's BS," he said. "The kind of existentialist crap rich white ladies say when they don't want to be held accountable for their actions."

This jolted her back into the moment. She didn't like the accusation. "You have proof the dust up was anything other than what I wrote?"

"Strictly speaking, no," he replied. "But I can get proof that will make you understand what happened."

"Did you bash a suspect's face into the grate and break his nose after he was arrested and detained?"

He said nothing.

"Off the record, Rob, just you and me, I swear."

"Yeah, I did, but—"

"Then my story was accurate."

"And circumstances don't matter? Facts out of context are as bad as—you know, they're worse than lies. Why don't reporters—"

"I called you for comment on the story. If you wanted to share

49

circumstances or make your case, you had your chance and blew it."

He scoffed. "Like you would have listened."

"How about this?" She pointed at him. "You tell me how you knew about the rifle. Tell me what you already know you want to tell me, and"—she pointed back at herself—"I promise I'll look at any proof you have, *and* make my boss look at it. *If* it's real, I'll personally make sure we run a retraction."

They walked in silence for a minute. Finally, Warren stopped and reached for her hand to shake. "Deal?"

"Deal," she replied.

His dark eyes met hers as they shook. He looked like he was trying to decide if he could trust her.

"I swear, Rob. Convince me, and I'll get the piece retracted." She leaned away and took in his impressive frame. "You're a strong guy, Rob. You hate feeling powerless. It infuriates you that I have this power, but I do." He opened his mouth, but nothing came out. "Now that we have a deal, answer the question. How'd you know about the gun?"

Without hesitation, he said, "I watched the killer buy it."

14

She grabbed his arm. "You what? Start from the beginning."

He tugged his arm free and they continued, turning south on 10th Avenue. "I was on the list for promotion. Detective." He frowned. "I mean, before you took a wrecking ball to my future." His eyes flashed, but he didn't look directly at her. "Because I was on the list, I got invited to a special program where I shadowed teams in each department for a day. Look under the hood, gain perspective, that kind of thing. About four months ago I did a day with counter-terrorism. Specifically, JTTF. Even more specifically, a two-man unit focused on narco-terrorism and Dark Web communications."

Cole knew the Dark Web was a subset of the Deep Web, essentially a secret internet where people bought and sold drugs, hacking software, counterfeit money, and more. But she had no idea where he was going with this. "Okay."

"This unit was a *Revenge of the Nerds* type thing," Warren said. "I don't know how either of them passed their physicals. The one guy's gut popped out in folds from the bottom of his shirt. Other dude looked like he weighed a hundred thirty pounds soaking wet. And he was *my* height. But they were smart. Spent their days monitoring postings online. Dark Web. Shady stuff."

"What were they looking for?"

"Sales of explosives, passports, safe houses. When they came across kiddie porn or big drug stuff without a terrorism connection, they'd refer it out. One guy monitored public postings. Another did something, I don't know what exactly, but he tried to gain access to TorChats. They weren't supposed to be looking for Arab names, but, c'mon. Even a couple decades after 9/11, we're still paranoid."

"What's TorChat?"

"It's basically a decentralized secure chatroom on the Dark Web. Good place to monitor the conversations of criminals."

"Okay."

"So they're showing me what they do all day and I get hooked into a thread about guns. Now, I'm a gun guy. Tom Clancy could take notes from *me*, okay? I'm on this thread and a dude is looking for nine fifty-cal rifles, top of the line and customized with a certain type of suppressor. Suppressors are legal, but he wanted something extra. And, of course, he was looking for weapons that were untraceable. The way these things work is you post anonymously, then you can choose to move into a private TorChat with someone to make the deal. Just so happened that I watched this particular deal go down. Nine weapons. Got the sense the buyer was an amateur, at least when it came to his demeanor. He said too much. Didn't say what they were for, but he mentioned NBC's favorite billionaire."

"Ambani?"

"Dude is a regular on their stations. *Was* a regular. Political commentary on MSNBC, hosted Saturday Night Live. Hell, he was a guest judge on *The Voice*. Being a good-looking celebrity billionaire genius is a pretty good gig if you can get it."

Cole laughed. "What happened with the chat? I mean, what did you do?"

"They couldn't get a trace on the IP address, and it was clear the dude wasn't going to blow up the GW Bridge or anything. They referred it out."

"To who?"

Warren pondered this. "FBI, maybe. Don't know for sure. Wasn't their area, and anyway, a dude trying to buy nine untraceable guns didn't seem to faze them. They saw worse a hundred times a day. I didn't make much of it. The internet is full of political nuts talking about their plots to kill people. And not just on the Dark Web. You can find that stuff on social media or Reddit. Right out in the open. When Ambani went down, though..."

Cole stopped. "Wait. You said he was looking to buy *nine* of the same weapon?"

"I know what you're thinking," Warren said, "and I'm already there."

"If you saw it, surely the JTTF *Revenge of the Nerds* dudes did, too. They'd be following up, right?"

Warren sighed. "Like I said, they referred it out. To them, it was one of a dozen deals they saw that day." Warren shook his head. "But damn, I hope someone is looking into it. Thanks to you, I'm not gonna know. I'm radioactive. No one will talk to me."

"So you're talking to me?"

"Right."

"I have an idea," Cole said, "but I'm cold. Can we go to your place?"

Warren looked at the ground.

Cole grabbed him firmly on the shoulder. "Rob, look at me. C'mon. I get it. What, your apartment's a dump? *I* don't care about that. And it's not something I would write about either. I don't do that kind of reporting."

Warren looked up slowly, taking in Cole's smile, then gave her an *are-you-sure?* raise of his eyebrow.

"I sleep at my sort-of boyfriend's house half the time just so I don't have to clean my apartment. I may not have washed a dish in four years."

His face softened and he smiled back at her. "No judgments either way, then. But I should warn you, I don't have any sugar or empty carbs in the place. Lean meats, fresh vegetables, and supplements only. You sure you'll feel safe?"

"Yeah. I think I can fast for a few hours."

15

"Jane Cole." The old man whispered her name through a mouthful of bologna as he stared at the image on his screen.

Liberty perked up and let out a little *woof* at the sound of his voice.

"Jane Cole."

The dog breathed heavily as he walked across the room to stand next to the old man. The man ignored him.

He'd read every article about the shooting, but the one with the image of a pretty reporter had grabbed his interest. The picture appeared as a thumbnail above the online version of her story, next to her social media handles and email address at *The New York Sun*. Shoulder-length black hair, blue eyes, creamy skin.

Like the others, Cole's story had exactly what he expected. He assumed she'd filled it with information about Ambani because the police hadn't leaked anything about suspects. This didn't mean they didn't have anything, but the New York City press was ravenous, and not a single rumor about a suspect had appeared yet.

He reached for his dog's head and pet it softly. "They don't know we did it."

He re-read a paragraph near the bottom.

According to a local resident, who declined to be named, the fatal shot came from the roof of a limestone townhouse across the street from the Met.

"Kind of a shallow pop," he said, *"not a huge bang."* He added, *"I was by my window. Heard the shot, looked out, saw a panicked crowd."*

The other stories had been more cautious about the exact location of the shot, and no police sources had gone on the record about it.

Not that it mattered. He expected they'd figure out the exact location soon enough. But he'd been careful to leave behind no trace evidence. The fact that Jane Cole had quoted a neighbor bothered the old man. Had her anonymous source seen more than he'd said in her story? Was he—or she—sharing it with the cops right now? Unlikely, but it was a loose end. Not one he planned on being hanged by.

He searched her name, first on the Dark Web, then on Google. Within minutes he'd pieced together a rough chronology of her life.

Born and raised in New York City, Jane Cole had attended the University of Miami to study journalism. There she'd met Matthew Bright, who at the time served at the Blount Island Command in Jacksonville, Florida. They married soon after she graduated. From there, they'd moved with his transfers: two years at Kāne'ohe Bay in Hawaii and two years in Quantico, Virginia. Finally, he'd been assigned to the 1st Marine Corps District in Garden City, New York. She'd done freelance work as they moved around, and finally took a job at *The Sun*, where she'd worked ever since.

Matthew Bright had died in Afghanistan four years ago, one of the last U.S. troops to lose his life there. In the mainstream press, there was a simple death notice and that was all.

He opened his encrypted email program.

Dear Mrs. Cole,

I need to know who the source was in your Raj Ambani story. The source who claimed to know where the shot came from. Can you help me?

Anonymous

It was a long shot, of course. Reporters didn't give up sources easily. If she didn't tell him, he would use the death of her husband. But her husband had died in service. He preferred to get what he needed without dishonoring his sacrifice. He'd keep it in his back pocket. He opened the chatroom and typed out a message.

T-Paine: *Brothers, I need information on the death of Sgt. Matthew*

55

Bright, Andar district, Ghazni province, Afghanistan. Details. Personal infor-mation. Something I can use to gain leverage.

He wouldn't have to wait long. The free-exchange of informa-tion among his brotherhood was second to none.

If anyone knew anything about Cole's husband—or had the ability to find anything—soon he would know as well.

16

I never reveal my sources, but thanks for reading The Sun.

Cole pasted the reply from the folder of boilerplate messages she used to combat the never-ending deluge of emails she got from readers.

"What was that?" Warren asked as she pressed *Send*.

"Email. Nutjob wanting to know the name of a source."

They sat at the table in Warren's kitchen, a single bare light bulb dangling just above their heads.

Cole eyed the dented and duct-taped heavy bag, but didn't mention it. "Rival businessmen, disgruntled employees, personal grudges, extremists. Those are the four categories of possible suspects the TV networks are speculating about. Here." She set her phone on the table. It was open to a clip from CNN titled, *Hunt for Ambani's Killer Begins.*

Warren glanced at the screen, but didn't seem to want to read it. "So what?"

"The clip mentions those four groups, zero specifics, which means CNN is getting generalities from sources. As am I. They're spending more time speculating about racist-extremist groups, even though there's no evidence of that. Hate sells."

"Means nobody knows anything," Warren said. "Nothing worth leaking."

"Right, and that means *your* information about the weapons

might be more than anyone else knows. We're both jumping to the same conclusion—nine weapons means this could be just the beginning—but let's look at the other options first. Rival business deals."

Warren asked, "Ambani was in tech, right?"

"He was one of those Mark Cuban kind of guys. I heard about him constantly but didn't know much about his actual businesses. Researched him and found out he pioneered high-frequency stock trading. Became a billionaire early, then started a firm that did all sorts of stuff. Tech, finance, international business."

Warren typed on his phone as she spoke, then held it up.

Cole read the headline of an article displayed on his screen. *Critics Say Ambani Deal Would Create Monopoly.*

"I just googled Ambani's name with the phrase *business rivals*," Warren said. "Eight million results, and this was the first one. Something about a deal for X-Rev international." Warren scanned the article. "Hmmm, believe it or not, X-Rev stands for 'Extreme Revenue.' High frequency trading firm working on every major stock exchange. Ambani was trying to buy the company, which pissed off a lot of people. There are quotes from three people arguing that the deal should be stopped. David Swanson from National Investment Strategies, Inc., Ibo Kane from Kane, Inc., Sarah Schwitzer from Gussendorf Analytics. I don't have a damn clue who those people are or what they do, but they sound important, and rich, and they're all quoted in this article saying Ambani shouldn't be allowed to buy X-Rev."

Cole stood and walked a small circle around the table, angling her shoulders to avoid the wall and the heavy bag. "I wonder how a deal like that gets approved."

"I don't know," Warren said, "but you can bet it involves a lot of juice in D.C. An alphabet soup of federal agencies. FTC, DOJ. It's the kind of deal that gets made on the basis of who you know."

"Or how much lobbying power you have." Cole did another lap and let out a long, deep sigh.

Warren said, "No offense, but you look like you need to sleep."

"We said no judgments." Cole stopped at the fridge and pointed at the bottle of Remy Martin. From what she knew, he'd had a bout with alcohol, but was now sober. "Doesn't Cognac count as empty carbs?"

"I keep the half-full bottle there as a reminder of who I used to be. Booze. Other things. Who I'm not going to be again."

By *other things* he meant drugs, but she didn't press him on it. "I'd call that bottle of Cognac 'half-empty.'"

He smiled at the joke. "By the way, what I just said *wasn't* a judgment. Just an observation. You look tired."

"In that case, and no judgement here either, your place is a hellhole." She smiled chidingly, first shaking her head then raising an eyebrow at him. "Just an observation."

"I can't say I don't deserve that."

"My boss is in my head," Cole said, "telling me to follow the money, but I don't know any more about those three people than you do. And you said eight million results. My guess is we could find another hundred business rivals. Each one could take a week to look into and I'd be starting behind all the business reporters who know about this stuff. Then there's the weapon angle. Hold on." She grabbed her phone, which was vibrating in her pocket.

The caller ID read, "The Italian Stallion." She took a deep breath and rolled her eyes.

She shot a look at Warren. "One of my best sources. Been waiting for this call all day." Before he could respond, she hurried through the living room and shut herself in the bathroom. "What's up?" she whispered.

"You free?" His voice was wet and throaty. It was after five, and this meant he was on the third or fourth pull from the hip flask of Amaretto he carried with him at all times.

"I'm in the Meatpacking District," she said. "I'm busy, but if—"

"Got something to show you. You're gonna want to see this. When can we meet?"

"Any way you can just tell me, Joey? Or text it over?"

"You know I only answer to 'Stallion.'"

"Fine, *Stallion*. What is it?"

"It's a video. And no, I can't send it." He paused. "I mean I *can*, but I won't."

"Don't screw with me, Joey."

"You know, Jane Cole, you take all the fun out of things." He coughed loudly into the phone. "I'm on the Lower East Side. Tell

59

me where and I'll meet you in ten minutes. Unless you want me to call one of the other reporters I keep around."

She gave him the address of the bar across the street from Warren's apartment and braced herself internally. Mazzalano was like a drunk, abusive Santa Claus. He smelled bad and she loathed every minute with him, but he always came bearing gifts.

17

Cole sat on a stool facing the entrance of the bar nursing her small glass of house red. She steeled herself as the man formerly befitting the name Stallion waddled through the door.

In his twenties, NYPD Lieutenant Joey Mazzalano had been a decent boxer, and still clung to his fighting persona, The Italian Stallion, as though hearing it enough times would make it a fitting description even with his current physique. After failing at a professional fighting career, he joined the department and rose through the ranks busting low-level mafiosi on the Lower East Side. She'd smelled the corruption on him from the moment they'd met. Now fifty, he was anything but a stallion. Average height, he had a massive square head that was somehow too large for his doughy body. He constantly combed over the few strands of greasy black hair he'd managed to retain, which only brought more attention to it.

He threw his overcoat on a stool and leaned in to hug her. The smell of Amaretto and sweat lingered as he wedged his belly under the bar. "You buying?"

She nodded.

Mazzalano waved down a young bartender. "Negroni. And as soon as you see me take my first sip, start making another one. And if you skimp on the gin, well, I've got a friend at the state alcohol commission who's looking for a few licenses to revoke."

Cole leaned away for a breath of fresh air, but smiled politely. "You really are a bastard, Stallion. You know that kid isn't the owner, right?"

"I enjoy making threats."

She sipped her wine. "You have something to show me?"

"Always business with you."

"When I'm *working* it is."

"And when you're playing?"

She grabbed a peanut from the bowl in front of her and shrugged. "I'm *always* working."

The bartender set down Mazzalano's Negroni—a mix of gin, vermouth, and Campari—a drink he'd forced her to try the night they'd met downtown at a cop bar years ago.

She'd hated it.

Sources like Mazzalano talked to her for one of two reasons. Most wanted something—usually gossip she'd heard on the street, but sometimes information she'd gleaned from within the department. Other sources just liked to talk, to show off how much they knew, or to spread rumors about colleagues. Mazzalano was a combination of the two. Nothing made him happier than knowing something she didn't. He loved to show off what a big shot he was.

But he wanted something from her, too. And it wasn't information.

He eyed her with the wet, dull eyes of a man who'd already had one to many. "How about I show you a good time after I show you what I've brought you?"

"You're a lech," she said.

He'd never let a meeting pass without hitting on her. And she'd never missed an opportunity to call him out on it. He didn't seem to mind being insulted, though.

"You know as well as I do it's never going to happen, Joey."

"Ahem."

She rolled her eyes. "…*Stallion*." She slid his drink toward him. "Drink up, and show me what you have. On the phone you said it was something big." She realized what she'd said only after it was too late to take it back.

Mazzalano let out a hearty laugh. "Something *big*?" He took a long sip of the Negroni, splashing the drink onto the bar as he set it down.

"You're a pig."

He sighed. "I know, I know." He leaned in conspiratorially, sliding his extra-large phone down the bar. He nodded for her to scooch closer.

She did, reluctantly.

"This video," he whispered, "has only been seen by a half dozen people. You're the first in the press. And you will *owe* me."

"What is it?"

He leaned away and gazed at her with droopy eyes. "I said, 'You'll owe me.' Got it, Cole?"

"I always pay my debts."

He pressed play and a video began.

The grainy footage showed ten feet of pavement leading to the side of a building. Attached to the building was a black ladder that stopped about two feet from the ground.

"The alley behind the townhouse," Mazzalano said. "We believe he climbed the ladder to the roof, and that's where he made the shot."

Cole noted that the color of the stone matched the townhouse she'd written about.

After a few seconds without activity, a single dried leaf dropped through the frame, dark brown and twirling slowly until it landed near the ladder. A moment later, a figure appeared from the bottom-left. He walked slowly. Hobbled, actually. And he was bent over at an odd angle, like he favored his low back. He wore a gray hooded sweatshirt and brown pants.

"Moves like an old man," Cole said as he reached the ladder.

"There's not a great shot of his face," Mazzalano said, "but there's something coming up."

One hand on the bottom rung of the ladder, the man adjusted something on his back. "Backpack?" Cole asked.

"*Rifle* pack. Ask me, it's the perfect size for a fifty cal."

With great effort, the man swung his left foot up to the bottom rung, pulled himself up, and climbed. Soon he was gone from the frame.

Mazzalano swigged the rest of his drink and smacked his lips. "Hold on." He scrolled back, pausing the video just as the man pulled himself up with his right hand. "There. It's not much, but it's enough to narrow it down."

Using her thumb and index finger, she zoomed in. The image

was blurry, but it clearly showed the side of a wrinkled white face. A thin, wispy beard partially covered a sharp chin.

"That's him," she said. "That's the man who shot Raj Ambani. Can I have a copy of the video? I'll tell you where my grandma was born."

Mazzalano's eyes widened and he nodded his assent. For years, he'd noted her black hair and prodded her about whether she had any Italian heritage, as he did. He'd do his best Tony Soprano impression, asking "What part of The Boot you from, hon?" A reference to the first episode of the show.

Wanting to keep her distance, Cole had always declined to answer. Now, she said, "My mother's mother came from Sorrento."

"I knew it! But that's not enough. Might give you a copy of the video, but only if..." His meaty hand gripped her knee. Casually, she sipped her wine with her left hand as she tried to brush away his clammy paw with her right.

He held firm and she leveled a glare at Mazzalano. Keeping her voice quiet and steady, she said, "You have exactly three seconds to let go of me before I break your face with this wine glass. One, two..."

He let go, an amused smile spreading across his face.

He stood as though to leave, then reached for his phone, staggering forward and nearly collapsing into her lap. Then he flopped back heavily into his stool.

"Everything alright over there?" the bartender asked.

"Fine," Cole said.

"Fine," Mazzalano said. He held up his hands to indicate he was no longer a threat. "Might'a had one too many." He pulled a black comb from his jacket pocket and made a pathetic attempt to get his greasy hair to cover the expansive bald spot that was the rest of his head. "Sorry. Figured maybe you were just playing hard to get."

Resisting the urge to smash her wine glass over his head, she said, "Joey, I appreciate the heads up on this. Like I said, I *always* pay my debts. But not *that* way. And if you ever try that again..." She shook her head slowly. "*Don't* try that again is all I'll say."

Cole slapped forty bucks on the bar and indicated to the bartender that she'd left it to clear the tab. She jumped down from the stool and began to gather her things, vowing to herself that was the last Negroni she'd buy as long as she lived.

18

Back at Warren's apartment, Cole didn't mention the way her meeting with Mazzalano ended, but she went over every detail of the video.

"I suppose you want to go write about it?" Warren asked when she'd finished.

"Not yet. It's a scoop, but it's not enough." She could win five minutes of fame by publishing a post identifying the prime suspect as "older white man," identifying Mazzalano as *a high-ranking member of the NYPD*, as she always did. But she could get a lot more by finding out who the old man was before hitting send.

"You said sixty-five or seventy? Makes me think..." Warren shook his head. "Nah, never mind."

Cole didn't let it go. "What?"

"We're not supposed to take leaps based on race."

"Cops aren't," Cole replied, "but right now you're not a cop."

"Yeah, you think I need to be reminded of that?"

"We're just talking here," Cole said. "Try me."

"When Ambani went down, I thought about that Dark Web transaction. The nine rifles. The comment from the chatroom: 'NBC's favorite billionaire.' I hadn't given it a ton of thought, but when Ambani went down I realized something. Since that day at JTTF, I'd had a picture in my mind of the kind of guy who'd buy a bunch of specialized fifty-cals."

"And?"

"I pictured a guy like the one you described. Older white guy, probably motivated by extreme views. Unabomber type stuff. The way he decided to do it—sniper-style—it suggests military experience, right?"

"Those are big leaps."

"We're just talking here, right? Plus—"

"Wait." Cole leapt up and pressed her hands into the table. "Going with your theory for a second... the chatroom conversation happened when?"

Warren considered. "Three, four months ago."

"Assuming the guy from the chatroom is the guy from the video, he planned it for months and decided on that particular shot. From a rooftop while Ambani walked into the Met."

Warren looked confused. "And?"

"Maybe the *location* means something. Maybe the... look up how long ago the Met event was announced."

Cole did laps around the heavy bag as Warren went back to his phone.

"Press release from June, so—"

"Six months ago."

"International Wildlife Protection Fund." He scanned the press release. "Huge fund to create international legal standards for wildlife protection." Looking up from his phone, Warren caught her eye. "What are you thinking?"

She leaned on the heavy bag. "If I buy nine weapons from the Dark Web and plan to take out a famous billionaire with one of them, I do it one of two ways. If I'm a certain kind of terrorist, I strap a bomb to my chest and walk up to his limo as he gets out in front of his house, or his office. If, on the other hand, I want to stay alive, I find a time when he'll be in public and I take him out with a rifle from as far away as possible. I make sure I have a safe place from which to take the shot. My question is this: why is the crummy video I saw the *only* video?"

Warren frowned. "You said it was from the alley behind the townhouse?"

"Right, so why isn't there better video from the rooftop?"

"Maybe they didn't have cameras up there," Warren suggested.

"Or maybe they were disabled. My point is, if you were planning this killing months in advance, wouldn't you make certain you weren't going to be recorded? Wouldn't you make sure the building was a safe zone?"

Warren stood as Cole sat. He positioned himself in front of the heavy bag and whacked it with a couple quick jabs. "So the question is, who owns the building?"

⊕

Under normal circumstances, Cole could get building ownership records in five minutes through a simple web search. The owner of the townhouse in question, it turned out, was shielded by layer after layer of anonymity.

A public records search told her that the home had been purchased seventeen years earlier by a company called Key One Research. It took her an hour to learn that Key One Research was an LLC formed in Tortola in the British Virgin Islands. As far as she could tell, the company had no American business operations.

It's only asset was the townhouse.

It was a shell company, and a decade earlier her search would have ended there.

But in 2016, 11.5 million pages of documents had been leaked from Mossack Fonseca, a law firm based in the British Virgin Islands. The documents, which became known to the public as The Panama Papers, provided the most comprehensive evidence of tax evasion and corruption among the ultra-wealthy that the world had ever seen. The database was online, and there Cole found her answer.

Key One Research had been created by Manhattan billionaire Chandler Price. A call to a colleague at the business section convinced her that Price had purchased the townhouse through the shell company for one of two reasons: to hide wealth from the city and state to avoid taxes, or to separate the asset from his personal wealth, half of which he'd lose in the event of a divorce from his wife, Margaret Price.

From there, the connections had been easy to make. Margaret Price was sixty years old and well known on the Upper East Side for her extravagant parties and her taste for old champagne and young men. She and Mr. Price had been separated for years, but had never formally divorced. For now, she still called the lavish

68

limestone townhouse home. If her Instagram feed was to be believed, she'd been out of town during the shooting. A two-day shopping trip to Paris.

Now all Cole needed was her personal cell phone number. And she knew where she'd get it.

"Warren, I know you don't drink and I don't expect you to join me but we need Margaret Price's personal cell number. I know someone who'll sell it to me cheap and he happens to drink at this downtown bar. Are you in?"

"Depends on which bar."

"We gotta go to Shooters."

19

"Tell me again why we're here," Warren said as he unfolded his body to get out of the cramped Prius in front of the bar.

As she followed Warren out of the car, her cheeks stung. The evening was cold and windless, like the air had frozen in place. Reaching the sidewalk, they walked toward a windowless store-front. A red awning over a black door read: *Shooter's Tavern*.

Cole tapped her phone to pay the driver as she spoke. "Because this is where cops hang out."

Warren scoffed. "White cops, maybe."

"You've never knocked one back at Shooters?" she asked.

"When I did drink, I didn't drink here. No one *I know* drinks here."

"Like I said, my cell phone guy is usually here. Cop from the 30th who helps me from time to time."

Cole led the way in and found them a booth near the front door—the last empty table in the bustling bar. The place was packed with men who gave off a cop vibe and small, smiley women in ponytails, racing around with trays of alcohol held aloft. Some carried rows of shots, but despite the bar's name, most trays were laden with giant pitchers of beer and thick pint glasses stacked high.

"See him?" Warren asked.

"Be patient." She scanned the room. "Not yet."

"I'm not thrilled about being seen with you."

Cole had noticed Warren tightening up as they entered the bar, and he'd moved to the corner of the booth, where he was least likely to be noticed.

"Don't worry, he shouldn't be long. I texted him."

Warren folded his arms over his chest. "How long do you want to give him?"

Cole shrugged. "Until he gets here."

Warren drummed his fingers on the table impatiently. "And if he gives you the number, what, you're just gonna call her?"

"That's my job." Cole nodded. "You don't get far in this business if you're not comfortable getting hung up on."

Warren chuckled. "I guess cops don't get hung up on as much as reporters."

"I guess not. But seriously, the questions are: does she know anyone who fits the description? Was it a coincidence she was out of town that day? Does she have a security system? Does that system include cameras? Does—"

"I get it, you have questions."

"Don't *you*?"

"Of course, I just don't see why she'd speak with you."

"I have ways of getting people to talk." Cole slid out of the booth. "We might be here a while. I'm gonna get us drinks."

"Mineral water," Warren said.

Cole ambled up to the bar, ordered a double shot of tequila for herself and a mineral water for Warren. Waiting for the drinks, she glanced left down the bar, toward the pool tables in the back.

When she saw Danny Ronan—and the woman he was with— her heart froze in her chest.

From the booth where he sat, Warren watched Cole survey the room. When her gaze stopped, she seemed to be staring at a man in the back. He had a pool cue in one hand and the hip of a pretty redhead wearing tight black jeans in the other.

Warren watched Cole stare at the couple for a full minute. Despite the fact that he was hardwired to dislike her, he had to admit she was growing on him. She had a quick mind and the concentration on her face was like that of a chess player in the middle of a game. Always thinking, always calculating.

Her straight black hair and bright blue eyes were an unusual and striking combination of features. And he liked watching her facial expressions, which couldn't hide what she was truly feeling.

She dropped a twenty on the counter and, eyes still on the couple, shot her tequila. She returned to their booth without his drink.

"What gives?" Warren asked.

Cole said nothing.

"Is that your cell phone guy? The one with the redhead?"

"*Nope.*" Cole looked up.

"Is something wrong?"

"Yeah. I mean, no. I mean… uh, I need to get outta here."

"Say no more." Warren led Cole through the bar and they stepped outside onto the sidewalk.

"You good?" Warren met her eyes with his brow furrowed in concern.

Cole was breathing heavily but nodded *yes* and then nodded to the side to indicate they should walk down the sidewalk. Cole led Warren a few blocks while she took deep breaths. Warren wondered if this was her version of teapot breathing.

Cole turned to Warren. "Sorry about that."

"Want to tell me what's up?"

"That guy in there gripping the redhead, he's my boyfriend. Sort of. I shouldn't care. I'm the one who brushed him off earlier today."

Cole's phone dinged with a text and she reached into her purse and turned her phone to read it without taking it out. She let the phone drop back into the bag. "There goes our cellphone guy. Damn. You know anyone?"

Warren looked up as he searched his mind. "Possibly."

"Outside you said this was where the white cops hang out. Where did *you* hang out before you got sober?"

"So, you're telling me you want to know where the black cops hang out, huh?"

She nodded.

Warren's shoulders relaxed at the thought of Lady Johnson's. He'd learned in AA that just the thought of alcohol could bring on the physiological state of relaxation associated with drinking.

He'd also learned that the best way to stay sober was to eliminate temptation. Don't go to your old haunts, avoid parties with alcohol and, of course, never keep alcohol in the home. He'd done the opposite. If he could withstand the temptation of a bottle of his favorite Cognac on the fridge, he could withstand anything. But he hadn't been to Lady Johnson's in four years.

"I used to know a guy," he said. "Across town. West 30th."

Cole walked to the curb. "I'll flag us a cab."

The taxi stopped abruptly and Cole slid forward, then turned to Warren. "That guy in the bar... I'm sorry I got like that. He and I aren't serious. I just didn't expect to see him there with another woman."

"Aren't serious, meaning?"

"We hadn't put a label on things."

"But you didn't know he was out with a hot redhead?" As it came out of his mouth, Warren realized that calling her 'hot' was probably not the best way to put it.

Cole sighed. "It's not his fault. He invited *me* out tonight and I didn't even respond. I've been terrible to him, stringing him along, not willing to get serious. He's not a bad guy, but——"

She stopped mid-sentence and looked out the window. Their taxi had stopped in traffic, the blue and yellow lights of Time Square flickering off the window.

"And you're telling yourself you're not jealous," he said, "but inside you're fit to be tied?" She didn't respond, and he knew he had it right. "Lemme guess, you've been single all your life, no kids, career before family, too busy to fall in love because you're on your grind, all that BS people tell themselves?" She closed her eyes again, and he was sure he had her pegged.

"That's not it," she said softly.

A minute passed in silence. The taxi jerked forward, then turned onto an empty street and cruised.

Cole turned to him. "My husband was killed. He fought in Afghanistan."

"I'm sorry." Warren swallowed hard. "Your husband served?"

"Marines."

"I'm sorry. Really. I lost friends there. I know what it's like."

73

Cole wiped tears on the sleeve of her jacket. "Died four years ago."

"How did he die? Sorry, if you don't want to talk about it..."

"No, no, it's fine. I love to think of him. I want to remember him. He was a good man. I don't really know how. Details of his death were sketchy."

"ISIS?" he asked.

"Maybe. You were a Marine, too. I read about how you got your limp."

He nodded. "In Afghanistan, but I got out years ago. Lost my leg below the knee. Honorably discharged."

"I appreciate your sacrifice."

"Thanks," he said. "Wait a second, I limp?"

"Just a little."

"Huh." Warren shrugged and pulled up a pant leg. He tapped at the metal prosthetic with his fingernails. "Still scored in the top one percent on the police physical. First amputee accepted for full duty."

"Didn't you have to—"

"Raise hell? Sure did. They denied me until I threatened to take them to court." He raised his pant leg more, displaying the spot where his muscular thigh connected to a carbon fibre socket around the knee. "Damn thing gets loose three or four times a day now. Thigh got bigger and the VA won't give me a new one. Got eighty grand I can borrow for a replacement?"

Cole smiled, then sat up straight, as though suddenly realizing something. "Wait, any chance you knew Matt? Matt Bright? He was there a few different times."

He'd consoled the widows of friends before, and knew they always wanted more information. "I didn't know him."

The driver leaned on the horn, then swerved around a truck that was blocking traffic.

The flashing lights danced on Cole's pale skin. He'd been wondering about something she'd said earlier. "Your husband dying, that why you seem so, I don't know, depressed?"

"I'm *not* depressed."

"Morbid, then? That stuff you said about sacks of meat and a *literal ball of fire*? Everything being meaningless? Why do you talk like that?"

"That's how things *are*."

"If you ask me, that's pretty damn dark." Warren flexed his biceps inside his shirt, a trick he used to connect with his body, his physicality, before he said something he was afraid to say. "I've been going to church lately, and—I don't know why I'm telling you this—but, well, here we are. Wife tried to make me go every Sunday and I... let's just say if the Raiders happened to be kicking off anytime during the service, I didn't join her."

"That why you two broke up?"

"No. It was because I was a drunk and a coke addict." He'd promised himself to say it out loud whenever possible. Admitting the problem somehow eased the shame. "But what I want to say is, I've been going the last three weekends. Still don't believe anything the preacher says. I'll tell you this, though: the feeling I get there lifts me when I'm down, calms me when I'm angry. I'm down a lot lately. Angry a lot, too. Community. Expressing emotion. It's like a balm for all the wounds in this world, in my life. Ask me, you could use some of that."

The taxi stopped in front of Lady Johnson's, a red brick two-story wedged between much taller buildings. A crowd out front shouted, and a group of smokers blocked the sidewalk. The driver called back to them. "Sixteen-fifty."

"My husband went to church," Cole said. Her hard facade had disappeared, leaving vulnerability and pain. "Lutheran. Loved me even though I never went with him. Somehow he was good enough for both of us."

Warren reached for his wallet.

Before he could get it, Cole handed the driver a twenty. "This is all for my story. I can bill it to the paper."

The professional look returned to Cole's face as she spoke, but now that he'd seen it, Warren could no longer pretend that the pain behind her blue eyes hadn't always been there.

20

"There." Warren pointed to a table at the back of the bar as they entered.

Cole barely heard him over the opening chords of Prince's *Little Red Corvette*, but through a space in the crowd of mostly off-duty cops, she spotted a man with long dreadlocks sitting alone in the corner. Apparently he'd been drinking a while because three empty shot glasses were strewn carelessly on the wooden table, along with two more full ones and half a pitcher of golden beer.

Warren placed his hand on the small of her back, gently leading her through the bar. "Put your arm around me."

"Why?"

"And don't introduce yourself to anyone."

"What?"

He stopped between two groups of boisterous drinkers, elbows jostling from all sides. "We need to pretend we're a couple. Don't want anyone to know I'm here with a reporter."

Cole slid her arm through the crook in his elbow. "Got it, War Dog."

When they neared the table, Warren glanced down at the man, who was staring into a glass of beer. "Davey?"

He said it as though surprised, and Cole went right along with the act. "Who's this, honey?"

The man stood, tossing back his dreadlocks. Short and slight, he looked sickly, with ashy, grayish skin and sunken cheeks. Seeing him up close made Cole glad she had decided to cut back on her drinking. Though she overdid it on the tequila from time to time, which undoubtedly took its toll on her outward appearance, this guy looked downright pickled.

"War Dog?" His slurred words carried a hint of a British accent.

Warren leaned in and one-arm bro-hugged him. The size differential made Cole worry, however irrationally, that Warren might break the drunk man in half. Davey flopped back into his chair. The momentum nearly toppled him over before he righted himself.

They sat across from him, and Warren draped his arm around Cole. "Brenda, this is my old buddy Davey. Davey, meet Brenda."

Davey reached out to shake her hand, knocking an empty shot glass onto her lap in the process. "Charmed."

"So what's a tiny Brit doing in a cop bar?" Cole asked, setting the glass next to the other empties.

Under the table, Warren flicked her leg, a signal she took to mean, *Knock it off*.

Davey shot one of the glasses of brown liquor. "Drinking, obviously." He turned to Warren. "Thought you'd quit booze and —" he glanced at Cole—"the other stuff."

"I did, but I need something for the lady."

"What's your pleasure, madam?"

Now Cole was confused. "What?"

He patted her hand. "Don't worry, honey." Then, to Davey, "Got any molly?"

"Thought you were a skier."

"Have it or not?"

Davey pulled his dreadlocks into a ponytail and secured them with a rubber band he'd rescued from a small puddle of beer on the table. "You haven't come here in years, you show up with a white chick asking for molly?" He eyed him skeptically. "This have anything to do with your incident?"

Warren said nothing.

"Like maybe you think busting me will get you back in some-one's good graces?"

Cole considered chiming in, but this was Warren's turf, Warren's guy.

Warren rested both hands flat on the table. "In thirty minutes, Brenda and me are gonna…" He looked from Davey to Cole and back again. "Well, as my father used to say, we'll be back at her place listening to Al Green, if you know what I mean." He shot looks around the bar. "There are at least two other guys in here who can give me what I need. You got molly or not?"

"Sure do, but from what I hear you may not be protecting and serving the good people of New York City much longer, so I gotta charge full price." Davey looked hard at Warren, waiting for his response.

Warren's eyes flashed. Cole squeezed his thigh, trying to calm him down.

"Fine," Warren said flatly.

Davey nodded toward an exit door between the restrooms, then slid the beer pitcher toward Cole. "Tell you what, sweetie, you refill my beer. War Dog and I are gonna step out back. Tonight, you'll be rolling all the way to the river, washing War Dog in the water." He stood and staggered past the bathrooms and through a door marked "Emergency Exit Only."

Cole braced for the alarm.

"Disabled," Warren said. "Always has been."

"Should I refill his beer? I think he's had more than enough."

"Nah, just meet me out front in three minutes. And order us an Uber."

As they left, Cole read the scroll at the bottom of a TV screen over the bar.

NYPD spokesman Todd Framer announced today that there are still no suspects in the Raj Ambani murder.

Leaders from the Indian American Business Association condemned the killing as "possibly racially motivated."

The President called the killing "shocking," "tragic," and "a great loss for American business."

Mazzalano had said that Cole was the first reporter to see the video. The fact that CNN hadn't yet mentioned it confirmed this. If anyone had reported it, images of the old guy would be plastered on every TV screen in the world. For now, it was safe to assume she was the only one with the information.

But that couldn't last long.

Behind the bar, Warren found Davey leaning on a dumpster. "Well done, mate. Back home we call it Riding the Train to Cranham—it's the whitest suburb in London. What do you call it here? Jungle Fever? Swap the white powder for a white chick. I guess it's cool, but if you ask me the powder is a more reliable way to—"

Warren lunged forward, grabbed Davey by the shoulders, and lifted him a foot off the ground. When their eyes met, he slammed the drunk dealer into the dumpster. A dull, metallic thud filled the alley.

Davey's eyes widened. "I'm sorry… I didn't mean."

Warren let go and Davey collapsed onto the ground by the base of the dumpster.

"Get up," Warren barked.

"You gotta relax, man. You sure going clean was good for you? I was just saying, Brenda's cute."

"Get up!"

Davey braced himself on the dumpster, standing slowly. "I'm sorry. I got nothing against…I've got the pills right here, man." He fumbled in his pocket.

"Shut up." Warren leaned in, his face a few inches from Davey's. "Right now, you're going to call whoever you call to get phone numbers. You're going to get me the unlisted cell number for Margaret Price."

"What the—"

"Don't bother objecting. Just do it."

Davey opened his mouth. Warren hardened his gaze, allowed his eyes to fill with rage. "Now." He said it softly but definitively.

Davey reached into his jacket and pulled out his phone. "No hard feelings. Gimme a minute."

Cole spotted Warren from the back seat as he emerged from an alley.

"Got it," he said.

She smiled. "The drugs or the phone number?"

Warren flashed his phone at her as he shut the door and the car took off in the direction of his apartment. It displayed a number with a New York City area code.

"Who was that guy?" Cole asked. "I mean, obviously a dealer, but, why the hell is he getting wasted in a bar filled with cops?"

"Because he's got the best weed in Manhattan and even cops smoke weed from time to time. He drinks for free, keeps the owner and bartenders supplied, sells to cops. Weed only, unless you were me a few years back."

Cole nodded. "He also has phone numbers?"

"He knows a guy who knows a guy."

Cole entered the number in her phone. "How'd you get him to help you?"

"Crooks are always afraid they're gonna get caught. *Always*. He sold me coke for a few months. Back when I was in the darkness. He could have gotten me in a lot of trouble, and I could have gotten him in a lot of trouble. He just owed me a favor."

Cole gave him a side-eyed look.

"Slammed him up against a dumpster. Happy?" He pointed at her phone. "Gonna quiz me all night, or call her?"

Cole started the call, but it went straight to voicemail. "Hello, Mrs. Price. This is Jane Cole of *The New York Sun*, please call me back as soon as you can. I know you must be receiving inquiries from every reporter in the city right now, but you'll want to speak with me when you find out what I know, what *The Sun* knows. I won't say too much on voicemail because I respect your privacy. Let's just say it involves a popular television dance competition and an evening you shared with a dance troupe from Japan."

She ended the call.

Warren stared at her, wide-eyed. "What the hell?"

"You don't want to know."

"Oh yes, I do."

The car pulled up in front of Warren's apartment. "You want to come up?" Warren asked as they got out. "I need to hear about the dance troupe."

Cole considered this as she followed him out of the car. "That's a bad idea for more reasons than I can count. I'm gonna go home."

Warren stepped back. "I wasn't trying to... I mean, I'm still married, technically, and trying to work it out with my wife."

"I know. That was one of the reasons it would be a bad idea."

"You're damn strange," Warren said. "You know that, right?"

"I used to be *less* strange."

"Think Price will call back tonight?"

"I figured she'd be screening her calls," Cole said, "but Margaret Price is addicted to media attention. She'll call."

"You're really not gonna tell me about the dance troupe?"

They moved under the awning of a deli next to Warren's apartment building as the rain started. "You've seen her on Page Six, right?"

"I have," Warren said. "Always dating younger men."

"And she has a thing for Japanese hip-hop dancers."

"So?" Warren asked. "It's a free country."

"Basically she paid for a whole troupe of Japanese dancers to come audition for one of those reality dance shows. Bought their flights, costumes, put them up in her townhouse, the works. Then, well, *dot dot dot.*"

"*Dot dot dot?*"

"I wasn't in the room," Cole said, "but one of them gave the story to *The Sun*. We ended up not running it, but we all *heard* about it. And well, like I said, *dot dot dot.*"

He grimaced. "Gross."

She sighed. "I may be strange, but if you pay attention to the world, there's a lot of stuff going on that's way stranger."

"Can't disagree with that. You'll let me know if you're able to set up a meeting?"

She leaned in and hugged him, her hands tiny against his arms. "I will." She stepped to the curb to look for a taxi, then turned back. "Next week would have been my twentieth anniversary with Matt. My therapist says I need to move on, but, well, let's just say it's not working. Anyway, I wasn't always this strange."

21

Cole jogged across her apartment, towel wrapped around her wet hair, looking for her ringing phone. She and Matt had purchased the two-bedroom before his death, anticipating that they'd soon need the extra room for a baby. It felt too large without him.

She found her phone on a table next to the droopy, dehydrated Monkey Puzzle tree. She recognized the number. "Mrs. Price, thanks for calling me back."

"With whom did you speak? Shenzo? Damian? Not Uni! I'll murder those little bastards."

"None of them," Cole said, "but I'll be sure to check them out for future interviews."

"Damn you. I thought *The Sun* was a respectable paper." Her tone was haughty, but also loose, like she'd been drinking and was trying to hold it together.

"Look, Mrs. Price, sit with me and my colleague tomorrow morning on the Raj Ambani thing and I'll make sure our gossip guy forgets what he heard about you." The truth was, there was no way *The Sun* was ever going to run the story, but sometimes she had to play hardball.

There was a long silence. "You likely already know I was out of town when that monster climbed on my roof and murdered Raj. I supported him, you know. *Knew* him personally. I hosted a fundraiser trying to convince him to run for governor. Gave a million dollars of my husband's money to his little animal project. Anyway, you must know I was out of town." She paused. "You're looking to do a sidebar, right? Beautiful Upper East Side socialite copes with her twenty million dollar townhouse being used to murder a great American? Something like that?"

Cole shoved dirty clothes off the couch and settled into it. "Something like that."

"I could call Max Herr right now." Her tone was harsh again. "There's no way he'd let you run a disgusting rumor about my personal life."

"He already knows, Mrs. Price. And no, he wouldn't run it. He already squashed this one. But our gossip guy could trade it to *The Post* or *The Daily News. They* would run it." She paused to let the threat hang in the air. "I can make sure that doesn't happen."

"Fine, fine. I have half a mind to let it run, might be good for my Instagram following. You know, *People* magazine says I'm the most-followed woman over sixty. Kids today don't care who you love, but…" she let out a long sigh… "my mother is ninety-one years old and still reads *The Post*. Might stop her heart to learn about Uni or Shenzo. My father fought in the Pacific theater in World War Two, after all. Be here tomorrow at eight AM sharp."

She agreed, then hung up and texted Warren.

Cole: *Be at the back entrance on the alley side of the townhouse at 8:05 tomorrow morning.*

Warren: *Why the back entrance?*

Cole: *I need you there, but there'll be reporters out front. When I break this story, I want you nowhere near it.*

Warren: *Got it.*

She opened her email and read the one from her boss first.

Jane,

You avoiding my calls? 24 hours without a story, without a call, without a message? What the hell?

Max

She typed a quick reply, assuring him she was close to something big and that she'd be in the office tomorrow. There was no way he'd approve of the tactic she'd used to get Margaret Price to talk. Every paper in New York City traded stories for other stories, traded stories for access. But threatening to reveal sensitive personal information when, in truth, she never would have, was a gray area she didn't enjoy spending time in.

She walked to the kitchen and poured herself a full measure of tequila in a Seattle Seahawks coffee mug. Her husband's. Returning to the sofa, she scanned the rest of her emails, stopping on a reply from the anonymous emailer who'd contacted her earlier in the day.

Dear Monkey Tree,

The salutation made her heart skip a beat. No one called her that but Matty. And he never called her that in public. Breath caught in her throat, she read on.

Dear Monkey Tree,

I understand journalists rarely reveal their sources, but allow me to make my case. Your husband, Sergeant. Matthew Bright, died in a firefight in Andar district, Ghazni province, Afghanistan. The details you received were sketchy.

I know something you don't: Matty's body never made it home because it contained evidence of how he was killed. It wasn't in a firefight. The men who killed him were never brought to justice. Deep down you've known this and it's bugged you for nearly four years. Am I right?

I KNOW what happened, and I will tell you. All you need to do, Monkey Tree, is tell me the name of your source.

I can meet tonight.

The Insider

The emailer knew the nickname her husband used—Monkey Tree—and he'd referred to him as "Matty." Could it be someone from his unit? Had someone read their emails or texts? What the hell was going on?

She shot the tequila, then, overcome by anger, grief, and confusion, let the mug and the phone fall from her hands onto the pile of dirty clothes. Her chest tightened and she slid onto the floor, then punched the sofa backrest as hard as she could. Shoving her face into a throw pillow, she let out a scream. Then she pummeled the couch again, her punches growing increasingly frenzied until her left fist, missing the cushion, struck the couch frame. She gasped with the sudden, unexpected pain.

Cole flopped onto her back in the middle of the living room. She lay there panting, staring at the ceiling and massaging her injured hand. Her eyes went soft, a blurry field of white that brought the static to her brain. Outside, the rain pelted the windows. She was empty except for a single thought: *Will this ever end?*

The emailer was right. There'd been no body to bury. Just a

sudden break in communication from Matt on a Monday followed by twenty-four hours of panic and the arrival of a chaplain and a casualty assistance officer on Tuesday.

In her grief, she'd read the self-help books and the blogs. She'd even seen a therapist once a month for the last four years. Following the therapist's advice, she'd prioritized her physical health. At forty, she was still in good shape. No one would mistake her for an elite athlete like Warren, but she walked a three-mile loop through Central Park most days and kept the drinking under control. Most of the time. No more than a couple nights a week, and never too much to affect work the next day.

Her body felt pretty good, but her mind and spirit were a mess. She'd followed the steps prescribed by the therapist. Taken time off, given herself space to grieve, accepted the support of loved ones—mostly through calls with Matt's mother in Seattle. She was the only one of their four parents still living, and the only person who could relate to the pain of losing Matt. The only one who'd loved him as much as she did. The only one who hadn't resorted to clichés—"he's in a better place" or "at least he died serving the country he loved." They'd been angry together, they'd cried together. Through weekly calls, they'd mourned together. But that alone wasn't enough to heal, and the weekly calls had turned to bi-weekly calls, then to monthly calls.

She hadn't spoken with Matt's mother in six months.

Cole had read that grief can creep up anytime after the loss of a loved one. Purposelessness, emptiness, the feeling that you no longer exist. For her, these feelings came with anger. To function, she'd learned to go numb. To embrace the static.

For four years she'd lived between anger and despair. The sudden outbursts of grief were proof that she had no idea what was happening inside her. Proof that the things she'd known she loved about her husband hadn't even scratched the surface. That an entire hidden relationship had formed between them, a web of intricate ties made of routines and smells and unspoken needs and expectations. A relationship that had lived underneath the everyday.

She only became aware of it by its absence, knowing it was gone forever. What people didn't understand was that, despite being an independent woman, a strong woman, when Matt died, a piece of her stopped existing. A piece she hadn't been aware of.

A piece she couldn't replace with positive thinking or a new version of herself.

The death gratuity—the $100,000 the military sent her when Matt died—had helped. She'd spent $70,000 to refinance the two-bedroom apartment his salary had helped pay for. It allowed her to stay put on her measly salary, and she'd tucked $30,000 in an emergency fund. She needed the savings in case she got sick, or got fired. She'd told herself it was the prudent, responsible thing to do. But that was only part of the reason.

For four years, she'd been expecting her crisis to reach its nadir. The emergency fund gave her a feeling that, when she hit her low point, at least she wouldn't end up homeless.

Against her better judgment, she replied to the email.

Convince me you know something I don't, and I'll name the source. Meet me at the Starlight Diner in an hour.

Jane Cole

She forced herself to get up and water the tree.

22

The rain came down in sheets, pummeling her wide umbrella as she turned the corner onto Columbus Avenue. Lights from festively-decorated storefront windows illuminated patches of sidewalk, but the streets were empty save for an occasional taxi splashing by.

Meeting random emailers was sometimes part of her job, and she always did so in crowded restaurants and bars, arriving first to control where the conversation took place. Tonight she had fifteen minutes to spare and planned to take a seat at the bar of her favorite diner, where she'd feel safe.

Chances were, the emailer was a lonely guy who knew journalists were often the only people who would listen. But somehow he'd learned things about her and her husband. The Marine Corps *had* been tight-lipped about the firefight Matt died in, and part of her believed that finding out the details would put her mind, and her heart, at ease.

Half a block from the diner, a shadow stirred under an awning. She turned toward it just as a hand emerged from the darkness and grabbed her arm. She tried to pull away but was spun around, her wrist twisted painfully behind her back.

"Do not turn around, Ms. Cole. And do not scream." The man's voice was gravelly and he smelled of wet dog.

Something sharp pierced her shirt and stung the small of her back as she was pushed forward, then into an alley. He pushed her into the wall face-first, her cheek flush against the wet brick.

"Who was the source?" the voice demanded.

Before she could think, she heard her voice. "I won't tell you."

"Probably one of those rich bastard lawyers who own the Upper East Side?" His voice was full of disgust, loathing. "Name him!"

She said nothing.

"You *will* tell me." He pushed the knife a little deeper.

Cole pressed her belly into the cold stone of the building, but there was no further to go.

"Who!" he barked, coughing spittle onto her neck.

Revealing her source wasn't an option. "If you knew anything about me, you'd know that I'm half dead inside." Her words surprised her as they came out of her mouth. "To be honest, I don't much care what happens to me. What you do to me. A few things still matter, and not revealing a source is one of them."

The pressure of the knife lessened slightly. There was a long silence.

"Well, I… tell me this then. Did he see anything?"

Cole considered for a moment. He seemed to have moved on from his first demand quickly. In her mind, it clicked. This was the shooter. The man who'd killed Raj Ambani.

In the video, he'd appeared to be old, and this man, while strong, had the voice of an old man. He didn't necessarily want to *kill* her source, he only wanted to know if he'd seen anything else, anything she hadn't printed in her story. Anything that could incriminate him.

"You read my story?" she asked, face still flush against the wall.

"I read all the stories."

"And you want to know if he told me any details I didn't print?"

"Yes." He pressed his forearm into the back of her neck, grinding her face against the rough brick. "Now."

"Nothing," she said out of the side of her mouth. "He doesn't know anything other than what I printed."

"How do you know?"

Her instinct to stay alive had kicked in. "It's my job to know. If he heard the gunshot, there's no way he also saw something. I know the window he was standing at and he couldn't have seen anything. Plus, he was trying to impress me. That's how I know he told me everything."

The man was quiet for what felt like minutes. Cole stayed still.

"Fine," he growled at last. "In my pocket I have a gun." He tugged her back slightly, fumbled in his pocket, then held a pistol in front of her face. "See! You are going to walk out of this alley without turning around. If you turn around, I'll shoot you. Understand?"

Cole nodded.

He let her go. "Walk!"

She took a slow step, bracing internally. Part of her wanted to turn around, to demand to know how he'd learned about her nickname and what he knew about her husband. But he'd shoot if she turned. Her life would end in the rainy alley.

She took another step, then another, and another, speeding up as she moved. A dozen paces and she was out of the alley.

She sprinted toward the corner, stopping outside under the bright light of the Starlight Diner sign. She pulled off her jacket, then slowly rotated it, studying each sleeve, then the front, and finally the back. The silver light flickered off the shiny blue fabric. On the bottom hem, below the small hole left by the knife, she saw it. A single hair, stuck to the slippery fabric. She tried to see if the hair had retained its root but in this lighting she couldn't tell.

Carefully holding the strand between pinched fingers, she opened a half used lip balm she carried in her purse. She placed the hair in the empty space left by the used portion of the product before recapping the container and placing the specimen back in her bag.

Next, she called Joey Mazzalano.

23

Tuesday

Cole ran a finger over the patch of rough skin on her cheek, reliving the sensation of being pressed into the wet brick wall. Baggy-eyed and still shaken, she swung her feet onto the seat of the taxi and opened YouTube. She had fifteen minutes to cram for her interview with the townhouse owner, Margaret Price.

She'd met with Mazzalano for twenty minutes the previous night and, for the first time ever, he hadn't hit on her. Mentioning that she had DNA evidence from Ambani's killer was enough to make him focus his energy above the waist.

She'd considered calling 911, but going straight to The Italian Stallion was a sure way to avoid hours of repetitious interviews that lead to nothing. Plus, she'd promised to pay her debt, and now she had. Mazzalano had promised to lean on everyone he knew to get the DNA lab to run the sample quickly, but it would still take a couple days, possibly a week. They made a deal: he could use the information however he wanted, as long as he gave her the scoop.

She'd been home by 3 a.m., staring at the ceiling from the bed that filled most of her small bedroom. She'd considered writing a story on her encounter, but without a description of the man or any update from the police, she had nothing worth writing.

As the taxi crossed the park, she clicked on an interview with Margaret Price, a stand-up on the red carpet of a charity event. A young interviewer shoved a microphone in Price's face. "What inspired you to come out in support of this cause tonight, Mrs. Price?"

"Giving back is very important to me, always has been. And the people at Refugee International are doing important work." Her voice oozed self-importance, as though the listener should be paying by the minute for the privilege of hearing her words.

"I have to ask," the interviewer said with a sly grin, "is it true that you and Troy Murphy are dating?"

Price's head tilted to the side and she touched the lower half of her throat. "Not at all," she said. "Troy is a good friend and I respect the work he's doing with Refugee International. That's all. Find someone else to gossip about."

Cole closed the video and opened another, a sit-down promoting a cosmetics line Price had endorsed in the early 2000s, when she was still living with her husband. Twenty years ago, Cole thought, and her face looked exactly the same. This time, she watched the video on mute, focusing on Price's hands and face. Three minutes in, she saw what she was looking for. A hand to the neck. She rewound the video fifteen seconds and listened to the question.

"Mrs. Price, you've never endorsed a line of cosmetics, you've never endorsed any product at all. Why now? Why Allure Natural Cosmetics?"

"Thanks for asking, Tiffany. I endorsed Allure because I believe in the products. I use them myself every morning and evening…" her hand moved to her throat… "and they've simply revolutionized my daily beauty routine."

Cole shoved her phone into the back pocket of her jeans as the taxi stopped in front of the townhouse. She didn't know whether Margaret Price knew anything about Ambani's murder, but she now knew how to tell when she was lying.

Cole rushed past a small group of reporters lingering in front of the townhouse, then rang the doorbell. A moment later, a young

Asian man in a crisp black suit answered. "My name is Uni. I am Mrs. Price's assistant. I presume you are Jane Cole?"

She considered a dance-troupe joke, but thought better of it. "That's me."

She shot a look at the jealous reporters over her shoulder as she followed Uni into the two-story entry hall. Uni closed the door behind them, then led her into a large living room, nicely appointed with modern blue and white furniture, but not lavish in the way Cole had anticipated. She'd expected an old-fashioned elegance, but the house looked like it had been furnished by an upscale Ikea for rich people.

Margaret Price sat on a chaise lounge in the corner. "Jane, welcome. Would you like something to drink? I'm having tea, but Uni can make anything you like."

Uni looked at her, one eyebrow raised.

Cole waved him off. "I'm fine, but I have a favor to ask. In a few minutes, my associate will appear at your back door. Please let him in."

"Why didn't he come in the front with you?"

"Reporters," Cole said flatly.

"If he's your associate, isn't *he* a reporter?"

"Not exactly. He's a cop."

Price sat up a little straighter. "But why? Surely the—"

"Don't worry, it's not that. No one suspects you of anything. It's for my story. He was nearby on the day of the shooting."

The argument didn't make much sense, but Price didn't question it. "Fine, fine then. Uni, let him through the kitchen door."

Cole sat in a chair across from the chaise lounge and cleared her throat awkwardly as she contemplated the best way to approach Price. "First of all, thank you for seeing me, Mrs. Price."

"Call me Maggie."

"Thank you, Maggie. And I'm sorry for the unusual entry of my friend... oh here he is."

Warren entered, trailed by Uni.

Price studied Warren. "Oh, yes indeed. Men like you inspire me to give money to the New York City Police Foundation every year. If only they'd let me stuff my checks into the back of his trousers."

Cole stifled a laugh. "Please, Maggie. He's a former Marine. Have some respect."

Price growled seductively. "The few, the proud." After an awkward silence, during which her eyes never left Warren as he took a seat next to Cole, she said, "Right then, ask your first question, Mrs. Cole."

Cole launched a pre-planned series of questions about the building. How long had Price lived there? How did she like the neighborhood? Small talk. Questions to which Cole already knew the answers. This was a tactic she used often with tough interviews. Get them talking about easy stuff to lay the groundwork and get a read on them. If she was lucky, Price would lie about something Cole knew the truth about, allowing her to test her tell.

But she didn't lie, so once they established a rapport, Cole shifted gears. "What were you doing on your trip at the time of the shooting?"

"Shopping. Nothing like Christmas shopping in Paris."

Had she tilted her head slightly as she answered? Cole wasn't certain. "Find anything nice?"

Price frowned. "How can this possibly be relevant to your story?"

Cole flicked the internal switch, turning off every part of herself except the amorphous static interior. Her eyes focused on Price like a laser. "Did you leave town because you knew Raj Ambani would be murdered from your rooftop?"

Price gasped. "Good Lord, no!"

She spoke the truth. Cole was sure of it. It would have taken a better liar to respond so immediately and authentically. "Did someone suggest that you leave town at that time?"

She hesitated half a second and steadied her eyes on Cole. "No!"

There it was! A slight delay in her response and, as she spoke, she brushed her neck softly with the back of her fingertips.

"I go to Paris in the winter. Every year. The new styles come out there months before they hit New York and—"

Cole was locked in. "Who suggested those *exact* days?" she asked.

"I just told you." Price's hurt look was quickly replaced by an imperious glare. "No one suggested anything. Uni, please see Mrs. Cole out."

Warren wordlessly placed his body between Uni and Cole.

Cole stood and leaned into Price's face. The socialite's skin betrayed the tightness of a recent botox treatment. Her makeup was a thick shade of tan that looked unnatural close up. The room faded away and Cole's awareness shrank until it contained only Price's well-preserved face, awash in a sea of gray. "Mrs. Price—Maggie—just one more question. Did your husband tell you to leave town on those particular days?"

"Uni, please make them leave."

"Did he?" Cole shouted.

Price's neck flushed crimson and she fanned it with both hands. "Please leave."

Uni maneuvered around Warren and grasped Cole's forearm.

She immediately shook herself free. "It's okay. You answered every question I had." She faced Uni. "We'll see ourselves out."

24

Outside, Cole slipped on a pair of sunglasses as they walked through puddles that steamed and sparkled in the bright morning sun. They passed the Met, open again as though nothing had happened, and entered Central Park at 84th Street.

"How'd you know she was lying?" Warren asked.

Cole didn't respond. She was coming down from the intensity of the confrontation with Price. Her nerves were fried.

"You look shook," Warren said. "Tired. Surely Maggie Price didn't rattle the great Jane Cole. What's going on? And what's that mark on your face?"

"You should see the one on my back."

"What?"

She let out a long sigh. "Last night I met the man who killed Ambani. The man from the video."

"What?" Warren grabbed her by the shoulder to force her to stop walking.

Her hands quivered. "He sent an anonymous email. He knew stuff about me—about Matt. His death." She hadn't told Mazzalano these details and they sounded unreal as she said them out loud to Warren. She sniffled. "He knew details and I—"

Warren's eyes widened. "You're serious? Did you talk to the police?"

Cole didn't respond.

"Jane, tell me what happened."

She began walking again and, for the next ten minutes, she talked through the events of the previous night. "They're not gonna be able to find him from the email," she concluded. "Any guy with a decent laptop can run anonymization the NYPD can't track. And I didn't look back. This lieutenant I know is gonna rush the DNA sample, but..."

"Yeah, that could take weeks, unless he has friends in the FBI."

"He doesn't." She shook her head. "Dammit, I *should* have looked back."

"No, you *shouldn't* have. Remember what I said. This thing had 'professional' written all over it. If that's what he is, guys like him genuinely don't want to kill innocent people. But he would have. You did the right thing."

"I can beat myself up about that later." Cole tossed her head to the side as though the motion would shake out bad thoughts. "Can we talk about Chandler Price? I had a hunch, and Maggie confirmed it."

"Tell me how you knew she was lying?" Warren asked.

"Most people have a tell when they lie. Looking at the ground, over-explaining, offering too many details, shifting their eyes. You can learn all that with a Google search. Takes a while to get good at it, though. Takes a lot of self-control to really be *with* the person, rather than in your own head. I'm a reporter. People lie to me all day, every day. Helps to be able to know when they do."

"So what's Maggie's tell?" Warren asked.

"That's easy. She rubs at her neck. Like this." Cole emulated the motion. "People feel vulnerable when they lie. Some protect vulnerable body parts unconsciously."

"But how'd you know about her husband? Chandler Price."

"There's no way it was an accident that the shooter chose that building. He would have had to have known that it was empty, safe. My read was that she was telling the truth about not knowing Ambani would be shot. But *someone* did. My guess was that whoever that was, they got her to leave town those days." She shrugged. "Chandler Price still owns the building, still pays the bills. My hunch was that he was the only person who could get her to leave the house on those specific days. "

"Pretty sure she wasn't in on it?"

Cole nodded slowly. "I wondered whether her husband had a business deal with Ambani that went bad, or maybe they had a mistress in common."

"Ambani was happily married, from what I've read," Warren said. "Plus, why nine rifles then?"

"Don't know, but let's look into the business angles first. Low-hanging fruit."

They stopped at a bench beside a large muddy field. Cole crossed her legs and folded her heels under her hamstrings. Warren began a series of searches on his phone, combining the names Raj Ambani and Chandler Price. Together they read a few of the links, but the quick search didn't bring up any obvious connections. Warren kept searching while Cole called Chandler Price's office number. The man who picked up told her in no uncertain terms that he hadn't given an interview in years, and there was no chance he was going to change that policy today.

"Should we try for his cell number?" Warren asked.

"Maybe, but my hunch is that he's a lot smarter than his wife, less likely to answer his own phone. And what his secretary said is true. He doesn't give interviews. Even if we get him on the phone, he'll just hang up on us. Maggie craves the limelight. He avoids it."

Warren nodded down the path. "Let's walk."

"We don't have much," Cole said. "So let's do an experiment." As they walked, she did an image search for Chandler Price and held up the first picture to Warren. "Would you say he looks more like an Oompa Loompa or an over-steamed dumpling?"

"You must be a writer," Warren said. "I was just gonna say he looks short, pink, and sweaty. What else do you know about him?"

"His *darling* wife was involved in all sorts of charities, mostly Hollywood stuff. She liked hanging with A-listers."

"From the moment I saw the post about the weapons, I thought it was some ultra-nationalist thing, maybe a racial thing."

"Last night in the alley, the way the shooter asked me whether my source was a 'rich bastard lawyer' made me think it could be a class thing, like a populist revolt type thing. But, I mean, I'm just guessing here."

"So let's run with that," Warren said. "Let's say it's *not* a business thing, but a political thing, a racial thing, a class warfare thing. Someone who wants to make a point about something. Chandler Price wants Raj Ambani dead, he gets this old dude to buy the weapons, then makes sure his wife will be out of town."

"Then he disables the video security on the townhouse, giving the guy the cover he needs to get up to the roof from the fire escape, take the shot, and escape clean." Cole swerved to avoid a rollerblader. "That's it."

"What?"

"You just said it. 'He gets this old dude to *buy* the weapons.' If that's true, there's a paper trail. A *money* trail. It's the oldest cliché in journalism. *Follow. The. Money.*"

"It's a cliché in police work, too," Warren said, "but that's because it's usually relevant." He looked over his shoulder and gave Cole a gesture with his thumb. They turned back in the direction of the Met. "Even if I was still a cop I couldn't access a paper trail showing the financial transactions." He stopped short and faced Cole.

Cole nodded and smiled. "You have something. What is it?"

"I can't access a money trail like this, but I think I know who can."

25

An hour later, Cole and Warren exited the elevator at the 23rd Street entrance of The High Line, a public park built on a one-and-a-half mile elevated rail structure running along Manhattan's West Side. The trees and bushes sparkled with Christmas lights. Red bows were tied around the garbage cans that dotted the pathway every few hundred yards.

"Who are we meeting?" Cole asked.

"Better if I don't say too much."

Cole looked around. "Why are we meeting *here*, though?"

"'Cause this is the last place I'll run into someone I know on a cold December afternoon."

They crossed a frozen lawn and sat on wooden steps that dead-ended at a stone wall. The park was deserted.

"In the summer," Warren said, "this is a great spot for picnics. It's packed. Today it's a good place to get a cold butt."

Cole scooched out of the puddle she'd sat in. "Cold and wet."

"There." Warren pointed at two men approaching from the south.

They were young, late twenties or early thirties, and not in uniform. One was tall and rail thin, the other short and dumpy. Why did she think she recognized them?

"Digital JTTF unit," Warren said before she could ask who

99

they were. "Guys I told you about. Fat pasty dude is Samuel Bacon. Tall black dude is Norris Ubwe."

Ubwe approached Warren, ignoring Cole. Bacon stood behind him, looking around nervously. "What is this about?" Ubwe asked. He appeared to be the leader.

"You remember me?" Warren asked.

"Yes, I do, as I said on the phone. Who is she?" He spoke by-the-book English with a slight Nigerian accent.

Cole extended a hand. "Jane Cole, *New York Sun*."

Ubwe took a half-step back. "You brought a reporter?"

Warren smiled. "She's an expert in breaking stories about critical failings within the NYPD. *And* the JTTF."

Bacon stepped toward them, a look of recognition passing over his face. "Wait, isn't she the one who wrote about *you*?"

Warren grinned. "Ruined my career. So you gotta be wondering why I brought her here."

The two men nodded in unison. "When I worked with you two that day in JTTF, we saw a post about a man seeking nine weapons. Do you remember?" They nodded again. "You refer that one out?"

"Probably," Ubwe said. "FBI, most likely. I don't remember for certain, but that is protocol. I can check."

A cloud passed in front of the sun and a light drizzle started to fall.

"I don't like being cold," Warren said, holding out his hand as though assessing the temperature and level of moisture. "So I'll make this short. We believe the man who sought those weapons used one of them to kill Raj Ambani. And unless you want *The New York Sun* to print a story about how you guys blew it, you're going to help me."

The two men exchanged a look.

"Deal?" Warren held a firm and imposing stance.

Ubwe nodded.

"I'm glad." Warren pulled out a piece of paper. "Here's a name, a couple known addresses, and an email. I need the man's bank records for the last year."

The men were looking at the note, but remained still.

"All of them," Warren added firmly.

Ubwe took the paper.

Warren continued his instructions. "I need them sent to the email address on that paper. Within an hour."

"But that's illegal," Bacon said.

Warren ignored him. "You can get them off the Dark Web, I assume."

"Maybe, but we might have to hack into—"

"I don't care how you do it, but do it from a personal computer, or a disposable one. I don't want you getting the department mixed up in this." He looked from one to the other, his gaze cold as ice, then took Cole by the hand and led her back to the elevator.

When the email arrived, Cole and Warren were finishing lunch at a diner in the West Village. It came in the form of four PDFs, one for each of Chandler Price's bank accounts, ranging from thirty to over three hundred pages.

Warren forwarded the first two to Cole, who opened them on her phone.

"When you have as much money as Price," Warren said, "there are going to be a lot of transactions. Start with today and work backwards. Look for anything unusual. Large cash withdrawals or transfers. If we're lucky, personal checks."

They worked in silence, Cole scanning two of the bank accounts, Warren scanning the other two. After a few minutes, Cole said, "Here's something. A regular payment of $4,000 to Maria Flores."

"Address?"

"No, and there are probably a hundred Maria Flores' in New York City. We could spend a week looking for her."

Warren looked up. "And it's probably a mistress he's paying off, anyway."

"Could be the wife or partner of the killer," Cole suggested. "Maybe they sent the money through her to hide it?"

"Possibly, but if I'm right, this guy doesn't have a wife, doesn't live with a woman. We're looking for a sad old dude in his seventies. Probably ex-military."

"What about this?" Cole said. "Transfer to a guy named

Michael Wragg for $25,000 three days ago. This was from Price's Delaware Trust account."

"That name… I saw that name." Warren scrolled furiously through a PDF. "Here. Michael Wragg. A payment for $99,000 on September first. That's right around when I saw the weapons post."

Cole felt the excitement building in her. "That sound like the price of nine custom, untraceable rifles?"

"Sounds about right."

Cole tapped her phone. "Already searching for his address. Two Michael Wraggs in New York City. One in the Bronx. One on the Lower East Side."

Warren jumped out of the booth and threw on his jacket. "Then what the hell are we waiting for?"

26

Michael Wragg logged onto TorChat as Liberty whined in the corner.

Since his visit with Jane Cole, he hadn't left the house. She'd convinced him that her source hadn't seen him, but someone else might have. He was willing to go to prison for what he'd done, but there'd been a delay in the mission. Now he feared that if he was arrested before it was complete, he'd be tortured until he gave up his brothers.

He scanned the latest comments in the chat window. Two of his brothers were in the middle of a debate.

Kokutai-Goji: *The shot wasn't possible. We didn't anticipate the last minute protocol change. The Silver Squirrel will die tonight.*

Tread_on_This!: *I could have made that shot!*

Kokutai-Goji: *No one could have made the shot. We decided to hire the best, and I did.*

Tread_on_This!: *You screwed this up Kokutai-Goji. Now we're off schedule.*

Kokutai-Goji: *It couldn't be helped.*

Tread_on_This!: *You sure tonight will happen?*

Kokutai-Goji: *The Truffle Pig assured me.*

He wasn't their leader, but he thought of himself as the elder of the group even though he'd never be certain about who was on the other end of the chat. He didn't know the ages or real identities of his brothers. But they seemed young, impatient. Probably millennials. He'd need to be the voice of reason. As usual.

T-Paine: *Brothers, let me explain something to you.*

Liberty yelped at the window. He jammed his nose into the small crack, as he often did when Duc was emptying fish bones into the dumpster below. The smell was stronger than usual today.

"Quiet, Liberty. You're not getting any fish today. We can't go out there."

Liberty clawed weakly at the window and yelped again.

The old man limped across the room, took a slice of bologna from the fridge and tossed it toward the dog. "There." The bologna stuck to the window, then flopped to the floor end over end.

Liberty pawed the meat, sniffed it, and again stuck his nose under the window, whining for the succulent bones below.

Wragg returned to his laptop. He needed to get his brothers back in line.

T-Paine: *We can't allow infighting to derail us. We are very different men, so we are bound to disagree from time to time. Our brother Kokutai-Goji tells us The Truffle Pig was not able to take the shot at the appointed time, and even the lying media reported a change to The Silver Squirrel's schedule. Remember, we hired The Truffle Pig because he's a better marksman than any of us. If he says the shot wasn't possible, it wasn't. Everyone else, adjust your plans by one day. Make it work. Remember why we're doing this.*

He stared at the chat box, waiting for replies.

Gunner_Vision: *T-Paine is right. Stay focused on the mission, adjust plans as needed. This is just beginning.*

No_Surveillance_State: *Just beginning. The world doesn't know yet what we have in store.*

8/15/47: *They will soon.*

Gunner_Vision: *T-Paine, we've all been following news reports, for what they're worth. It seems like you're safe. How does it look from your end?*

T-Paine: *Had a slight hiccup with a potential witness, but it turned out to be nothing. FBI or CIA or NYPD could break my door down any minute, of course, but I believe I'm clear. And even if they do, it won't matter. You all know what to do.*

He was about to compose another message when he heard the scratchy *bzzzzzzzzzzz* of his door buzzer.

27

Cole and Warren waited in front of the faded red door. Warren pressed the buzzer again. A minute passed, then two.

On the ride over they'd done a series of searches for Michael Wragg and found nothing online or in any of the databases Cole could access from her phone. No arrest record, no mentions in the press, and no record of property ownership. Cole always started her research with an internet search and she'd learned that there were a few sharp dividing lines based on age.

Young people were all over the internet, mostly social media platforms like Snapchat, Instagram, and X. People in their forties to sixties and into their seventies often had Facebook profiles, while finding people in their late seventies and eighties was more of a crapshoot. Some had online profiles. Others had no internet presence whatsoever.

That didn't mean Wragg wasn't their guy, of course. If their guess was right—that Michael Wragg was the man who'd purchased the guns on the Dark Web, with money from Chandler Price—he was likely smart enough to not leave any trace of himself online, at least not under his real name.

"What the hell were we thinking?" Warren asked.

Cole mashed the buzzer again. "There was a chance he'd be home. If he had the guts to meet me last night…" She trailed off, studying the entry panel directory.

Warren followed her eyes. "We have the right apartment don't we?"

Cole nodded. "Absolutely."

"Then, what are you thinking?"

"There are three floors, two apartments per floor. As a journalist, there's nothing wrong with me buzzing the other apartments and asking the residents a few honest questions about their neighbor. He's not online, at least not under the name Michael Wragg, but if he lives here we can—"

"Oh, hell no." Warren was shaking his head emphatically, furrowing his brow.

"Why not?"

"Uhh, like ten reasons. You might run into him in the hall. You might tip him off that we're here. Speaking of that, why *are* we here?" Warren paced a tight circle. "What the *hell* was I thinking?"

"Warren, you're right. Get going. *I'm* the one who should be here, you shouldn't. I'm gonna do what I'm gonna do. So leave, okay?"

"You think I'm gonna leave you here alone?"

Cole stepped back from the door. Across the street, she'd seen a bar with a table in the window that looked like it had a good view of Wragg's building's entrance. She nodded toward it. "Buy you a shot while we talk this through?"

He gave her a sideways look.

She raised her hands in acquiescence. "Sorry, I…"

"Sure. A shot for you. I'll have coffee."

Wragg gripped the baseball bat loosely, standing by the door as the echo of the buzzer faded. "They're gone." He cursed himself for not installing a video doorbell. He'd tried to convince the landlord to do it, but he'd been too cheap to pay for it. And Wragg was too broke. He hadn't wanted to ask his brothers to chip in on a surveillance system either. First because he was prideful, he hadn't wanted his brothers to know he was broke—and second because he'd already told them he'd purchased and had the high-end setup installed months ago.

He paced to the window and looked out. The fire escape was

empty. The alley was empty. Wragg hadn't eaten in a day, and the scent of fish bones that wafted up—carried by steam from a vent —made him salivate.

Liberty lay silently on the floor by the window.

"It wasn't the police," Wragg said to the weak and sickly dog. "They wouldn't have used the buzzer. Probably a salesman or a wrong address. A teenager pressing all the buttons."

Back at his desk, he used his cellphone to dial Trần's. "Duc, it's Michael from upstairs...I'll have the usual...Fifteen minutes, yeah...What?...Yeah, throw in a few bones for Liberty." Wragg glared at the dog. "He's been bad, but I can't deny him."

⊕

Cole sipped tequila while Warren warmed his hands by curling his fingers around a coffee mug. They sat on the same side of the table in the window, watching the red door across the street through sheets of icy rain.

"I should call this in," Warren said.

"You mean Wragg, the financial transactions?"

"Not that. Can't tell anyone how we got that information. I threatened those guys but there's no way I'd ever out them on this. We have no good reason to be here."

Cole slid her shot glass back and forth on the table. "That's where cops and journalists are different. I didn't break any laws to get that information. Maybe you did, but I didn't. And the First Amendment protects me. Once the information is stolen, I can legally publish it."

"That's pretty messed up."

Cole shrugged. "Be that as it may, it's the law. At least according to the Supreme Court."

"What about an anonymous tip?" Warren adjusted his hands and moved two fingers in and out of the mug handle. "We call in with the name Michael Wragg and the address, say he's connected to the Raj Ambani murder?"

Cole shook her head. "Fine, but your buddies are getting a thousand tips a day. Maybe they get around to checking him out. Maybe they don't."

Warren swigged his coffee. "That's not how it works. They might already be on to him."

107

Cole shot the rest of her tequila, eyes glued to the red door across the street. "How's the coffee in this joint?" she asked.

"Burnt, which is how I like it." He waved at the bartender, who brought over the pot and refilled his cup.

"You like burnt coffee?"

"Same with my burgers—like a hockey puck."

She smiled, her eyes on the red door. "That's sacrilege. If my husband were alive he would have booted you out of our kitchen if you asked for meat any way other than medium rare."

"I like my meat like I like my enemies," Warren said, using an exaggerated, action-hero type voice. "All the way dead."

She chuckled, then turned to him, watching as the steam from his coffee clouded his face. The Warren she was coming to know was definitely angry, but he was a serious cop, as interested in getting at the truth as she was. "Convince me. About the suspect. The one whose face you broke."

Warren waved her off. "Doesn't matter anymore."

"It does. If I got it wrong, I want to know. *Need* to know." She stretched her arms over her head. The tequila made her disinhibited. "But I don't think I did. You already admitted it."

"You have to consider the context, Jane."

"Can you give me a context that sanctions what you did, *Rob?*"

He sipped his coffee, considering this, then shook his head sadly and shrugged. "There isn't one."

Cole opened her mouth, ready to argue, then realized his admission and held her tongue.

Warren's face seemed to have softened, like all the tension had dropped from it in an instant. He slid his chair closer to hers. "I was wrong. I had reason that warranted but doesn't sanction what I did. But if you want, I'll show you the context."

"Show me?"

"I have video."

"Why didn't you…what?"

He put his hand on hers. "I'll show you, but Jane, this is serious. This has to be one hundred percent off the record, okay? I'm not supposed to have this. The person who sent this wasn't supposed to send it. She could go to jail for sending it."

"Off the record, sure."

He lifted her chin and looked right into her eyes. "Jane, do you swear? I want you to see this. To understand. Maybe it will come out one day, maybe not. For now, no one else can know. "

She swallowed hard. "I swear."

Warren opened his text app and scrolled for a moment, then tapped on a video clip. It was dash cam footage showing a wide angle of an empty police car at night from the interior of the back seat. Blue and red lights flashed through the front windshield that must have been coming from a police car just out of frame. The swirling lights gave the video an eerie feel as the interior of the car brightened and darkened.

A man's head appeared on the bottom right of the screen, through the side window. The frame cut Warren off at the neck but Cole recognized his muscular torso even through his bulky bullet-proof vest and tight police-officer uniform. He moved the handcuffed man toward the cruiser. The door opened and Warren protected the man's head as he pushed him into the back seat.

The man was around thirty, with greasy blond hair, a pock-marked face and a crooked nose that looked as though it had been broken several times. Once he was seated, Warren closed the door, walked around to the driver's side, and got in. In the back, the man wore an odd, serene smile.

Cole paused the video. "What was he arrested for?"

"We had a tip about potential trafficking. When we got to his apartment there was…" Warren shook his head.

"What?"

"You don't want to know."

"Context," Cole said. "Don't I *have* to know?"

Warren's lips quivered and his eyes got hard. "Found a teenage girl"—Warren sniffed—"being held captive. We later found out she was Vietnamese. Father had sold her to American traffickers when she was eleven. Guy in the video, well, he was her captor. Took her a week to say anything, she was so terrified." Warren looked down at the table, like he was trying to hold it together. "This wasn't in Iraq or some brothel in Thailand. This was in Queens, year of our lord 2024. Our city hosts evil men like this— every day this stuff is happening to young people—right in our backyards."

Cole felt sick.

Warren pointed at the top of the screen. "I had my wallet out and left it open on the dash to easily reach my cash. Even cops have to pay tolls." He started the video, which showed him starting the car and turning to look for traffic. "Coming up is the part where my wallet falls open," Warren said. "Had a picture in there of Marina, my little girl. Five years old."

In the video Warren pulled into traffic, but as he sped up his wallet flew off the dash.

The man scooted forward and peered between the headrests. "Hold up." He called out from the back seat.

"What?" Warren asked, glancing up to look at him briefly through the rearview mirror.

The man nodded at the wallet which lay open on the front passenger seat. "That your baby girl?"

Warren folded the wallet closed and wedged it between the palm of his hand and the steering wheel as he drove.

"Can she hop on one foot?"

Warren ignored his questions.

"But she's *not* quite old enough to skip well, right? Cute tho. What is she four or—"

"Shut up." Warren's voice was low and slow.

The man licked his lips. "You can't protect her forever, y'know."

"I said *shut up*." Warren's voice was louder this time.

"When I beat this case, I could give her a job, but not until she's old enough to skip."

Warren jerked the steering wheel and slammed the brakes, stopping the car abruptly. He leapt out, disappearing from view, then appeared at the car's back door. Swinging it open, he grabbed the man by the hair and smashed his face into the grate that separated the back seats from the front. Then he threw the door shut.

His nose bloody, the man stuck out his tongue and groaned, licking the blood.

Cole flipped over his phone. "I can't watch any more."

"I broke protocol, yeah. But you don't know how badly I wanted to flip his off switch. World would be a better place without that guy in it." He passed the coffee cup from hand to hand. "Told myself, 'Deep breaths, Rob, deep breaths. Turn around and get back in the front seat.' Took every bit of willpower I had, but I managed to get him to the station without another scratch."

They sat in silence, watching the cars splash by outside.

"I shouldn't have done it," Warren said finally.

"I understand why you did. I feel sick."

"Did he deserve it? Absolutely. Deserves to die, and a lot worse. If you'd seen his apartment, seen the girl." He doubled over, shaking his head like he was trying to erase the memory. "Hell was built for guys like him. And I believe he'll burn there for eternity. But I shouldn't have done what I did."

Cole said nothing. There was nothing to say.

"Now you know," Warren continued. "But you can't write this. I can't give you a copy, and no one can know I showed it to you. I have to let it play out."

Cole thought for a moment, then said, "Seeing the context of what you did reminds me of a C.S. Lewis quote. I can't remember the exact phrasing, but it has to do with enemies. When you hear about some atrocity committed by your enemy, you get angry, right? But what if you learn that the atrocity wasn't as bad as you'd first thought?"

"I don't get it."

"When you realize the person isn't as bad as you thought, are you disappointed because you can't be as mad, or are you relieved on behalf of humanity because your enemy isn't as bad as you feared?"

"I don't know," Warren said. "This sounds like you being strange again."

"Listen," Cole said. "What I'm saying is that a week ago I probably would have been disappointed to learn the context. Now, I feel relieved. I wanted to believe the worst of you. It's probably why I didn't work harder to get the full story. Now I'm relieved, and it leads me to something else. I *have* to write this. My boss told me something the other day—he drives me crazy but he's usually right."

"What did he tell you?"

"Sometimes the facts are different than the truth. Warren, it needs to be written. People need to know the truth. And I can write it in such a way that it will never get back to you."

"No."

"I don't have to mention the video or that we know each other. I'll call the department and—"

"What? What would you do?"

Cole thought. "I'd give it to another reporter at *The Sun*, so I'm not near it. I'll have *them* call the department. It won't be difficult to find a way to flesh out the context."

"The woman who sent me this video wanted me to know it was circulating within the department. But she wasn't supposed to send it. Plus, you promised."

"I did," Cole agreed.

"And you'll keep the promise. Keep your eye on the door. I gotta take a leak."

Warren disappeared into the restroom. Cole stood to get another shot. As she turned toward the bar, movement across the street caught her eye. The red door opened.

An old man limped out onto the sidewalk.

28

Cole froze.

It was Michael Wragg.

She recognized his limp from the video Mazzalano had shown her. His croaky voice still reverberated inside her chest cavity.

She shot a look toward the bathrooms.

"Ma'am, can I help you?" the bartender asked.

"Tell my friend I went across the street. I'll come back to pay…"

She ran out and ducked behind a van. She'd left her jacket behind, so the freezing rain soaked through her shirt as Wragg limped down the street and into Trần's Fried Fish. A minute later, he exited and walked back to the red door. Stopping under the awning, he pressed his face into the white plastic bag and inhaled.

She glanced into the bar. Warren was still in the bathroom.

Casually, she strolled across the street as Wragg opened the door and entered. He disappeared up the stairwell as the door closed slowly on its hinge. Cole jogged the last few paces, then lunged with her right foot, sticking it in the crack before the door closed. She listened as Wragg ascended the concrete steps.

She had two options.

Follow Wragg up the stairs, or wait for Warren to come looking for her, then confront Wragg together. But Warren might convince her to call the police, and her journalistic instincts had kicked in. She wanted to be first to the story. That wasn't the only reason she was tempted to follow him up. Wragg's email was seared into her mind. He knew something about Matt.

She rubbed the spot on her lower back where he'd pressed the knife. There was a Band-Aid over it now, and it stung. As she pressed into it, the rage rose in her chest. The static followed the rage, overwhelming it but leaving the urge to pursue the man who'd used her own grief against her.

She stepped forward, but something stopped her. Warren's voice in her head, telling her to take a beat.

She had to wait for him.

"Yes," Warren said. "W-R-A-G-G. You got the address?…Yes… Yes…Thank you."

He ended the call and stepped out of the restroom. Cole was no longer at the table.

He ran to the counter. "Where'd she go?"

"Across the street. Didn't pay, either. Can you please—"

Warren sprinted for the exit and saw Cole standing in the doorway of Wragg's building. She waved him over.

"He came out," she whispered, glancing up the stairwell. "Then went back upstairs. Let's go."

She turned to head into the building, but Warren grabbed her shoulder. "Wait a sec. Where did he go when he left?"

"Fish place on the corner," Cole said.

Warren looked down the block, then stepped back from the building and looked up, taking in the size and layout. "Wait here." He jogged down the block, peered into Trần's Fried Fish, and stopped at the alley just past the restaurant.

An old metal fire escape led up to the third floor. Wragg's apartment.

Returning to Cole, he said, "Fire escape. I'll climb it, you creep up to the door and wait until you hear me."

She nodded apprehensively.

Warren put a hand on her shoulder. "You'll wait until you hear me, right?"

"Got it."

She disappeared into the building as Warren jogged back to the alley. He stopped below the retractable ladder, designed to bridge the gap between the alley and the first landing of the fire escape. But the ladder would let out a screech if he pulled it down. He shot a look up and down the alley, then leapt and grabbed a metal slat on the landing. Like a pole vaulter, he kicked his legs up over his head and used his arms to push himself up and over the railing.

As he came to rest on the grated metal landing, his prosthetic foot slipped and then he could no longer move forward. He tugged at his prosthesis angrily, but it was caught. All the wrestling finally pulled the socket loose from its polyethylene spacer and the prosthetic fell onto the landing with a loud clang.

Back pressed into the wall, Cole ascended the first twelve steps, stopping on the second floor landing. She peered up toward Wragg's door. Everything was silent.

Slowly, she climbed the remaining flight of stairs, stopping in front of Wragg's apartment, listening for Warren between her steady, quiet breaths.

In the apartment, Wragg heard footsteps in the hallway. He dropped the bag of fish on the desk and pulled a silenced .22 from the drawer. He was probably about to be arrested, or killed, but he'd take out one or two of them on his way out.

At the door, he looked through the peephole, expecting to see a team of men in suits or tactical gear. He smiled when he saw Jane Cole, the pretty, blue-eyed reporter with straight black hair.

He held the .22 in his right hand, swung open the door with his left, then grabbed her by the hair, and yanked her into his apartment.

Warren crouched to pick up his prosthetic. Luckily, the upper portion was too wide to fit through the slots. Sweat beading on his forehead, he looked up. His left leg was strong enough to hop up the two remaining stories, but what if he had to fight? He *had* to reattach it.

Sitting, he smoothed the cloth sheath that he wore like a large sock over his knee and began to attach the leg.

29

Cole held her breath in the corner.

A dog lay beside her, breathing weakly. He was striking, medium-sized with black and white spots, perhaps some kind of dalmatian mix. But he looked malnourished.

"Did you ring the bell half an hour ago?" Wragg's voice was unmistakably that of the man from last night.

She let out a long, slow breath, trying to calm herself. "Yes. I'm not armed."

"Are you alone?"

"Yes. I'm not police, I think you know. Just a reporter."

"Why did you come here?" Wragg asked.

"I wanted to ask you some questions, that's all." Warren would be looking for her. She needed to stay alive as long as she could. She needed to keep him talking, but couldn't think of a good lie. "You were paid by Chandler Price, correct?"

Wragg spat at her. A thick wad of green phlegm landed between her and the dog. "*Paid?* You make it sound like I'm a hired killer. I'm a freedom fighter. Chandler, too. He's one of our benefactors."

"Benefactors to do what? What is this about?"

Something dinged in the corner and Cole followed the sound to Wragg's desk. A computer with a large monitor. Gun still on

Cole, he backed up slowly. His eyes darted to the screen, then back to Cole. "You'll know soon enough."

Cole let the room fall away. She had tunnel vision for Wragg. His gray-blond hair was tied back in a ponytail, his scarred face pinched and anxious. "Where are the other rifles?"

He flinched. "You know about those?" His computer dinged again. His eyes moved back and forth from the screen to Cole.

"We know everything," Cole said.

"We?"

"Me and...my colleagues. If you kill me, everything comes out." Cole tried to convey confidence, to fake self-assuredness. "You think I'd come here without a plan? If they don't hear from me within an hour..."

Wragg swiveled his office chair and sat, gun still on Cole. "You're lying."

Something important was happening on the screen. Something he wanted to read. It pulled his attention toward it and away from her. Wragg still trained the gun on her, and he could fire at any moment, but his mind was on the screen.

"What's your dog's name?" Cole asked.

"Liberty." He looked back and forth between her and the screen. "I should have named him Shackles." He laughed. "Because he's weak."

"How did you know about Monkey Tree?" she asked. "And Matty?"

He glanced at her, a strange smile on his face, but said nothing.

Cole saw movement at the window. A hand. She looked at Wragg. "Are you chatting with whoever has the other eight weapons?"

He stood, smiling broadly. His crooked yellow teeth filled her view. "You know much less than you think." He aimed the gun at her chest. "A moment ago I told you you'd understand everything soon enough. You won't."

A loud scraping came from the window. Liberty perked up suddenly and yelped. Cole followed the dog's head as it turned.

Warren's feet swung through the window into the apartment. The rest of him followed.

Wragg spun around and aimed the .22. "Liberty, sic him!"

The dog leapt up, but he didn't go for the window.
Instead, he lunged toward Wragg as the old man fired wildly.

30

Warren heard two shots as he swung his head into the apartment. The first missed entirely and the second struck his prosthetic leg and ricocheted into the wall. Cole was in the corner, Wragg standing by his computer, the black and white dog biting at his heels.

Leaping to his feet, Warren lowered his shoulder and bolted toward Wragg. He launched himself over the dog, striking Wragg in the chest before he could get off another shot. They toppled over the chair, Wragg slamming the corner of the desk and falling to the floor. Warren landed beside him.

The computer crashed to the floor. Fried fish erupted from a container, splattering the screen. A baseball bat display case slid off the desk and shattered on the floor. The bat rolled across the wooden floor and stopped at Cole's feet.

Fumbling with his grip on the gun, Wragg rolled toward the window.

Cole grabbed the bat and jumped up.

Warren dove onto Wragg and slammed his wrist back, jarring the gun loose.

Cole kicked it across the room.

A hand on each wrist, Warren pressed Wragg into the floor. Half his size, the old man had no chance of escape. He wasn't even trying.

Cole followed Wragg's gaze to the computer screen, still lit up but speckled with grease and tiny bits of garlic and green onion.

She saw it in his eyes. For the first time, the old man looked afraid.

Thinking quickly, Cole stowed the bat in the crook of her arm and pulled her cell phone from her pocket. Crouching next to the computer, she took a photo of the screen. She wiped away some of the food. Adrenaline coursed through her body and her hand shook as she snapped more photos.

Liberty had grabbed a fish carcass and was devouring it in the corner.

Still pinned, Wragg said, "You stupid bastard." He spat in Warren's face. "Aren't you that cop who broke that guy's face? You gonna break mine too?"

In one deft move, Warren spun him onto his stomach. "Throw me that tape."

Cole tossed him a roll of silver duct tape that had spilled out of a desk drawer. Warren bound Wragg's wrists, then sat him up and stood over him. Cole stood next to him.

Wragg frowned at them contemptuously. "A lying journalist and a disgraced cop."

Cole gripped the bat tight. "Shut up."

Wragg looked at Warren, then to Cole. "Monkey Tree, please tell me you're not dating this guy? What would your dear dead Matty think?"

Warren glared down at him. "Shut the hell up, old man."

Through the static, the rage moved inside Cole. Wragg's head was at the perfect level. Waist high.

"Monkey Tree," Wragg said, "I have a confession to make. I was able to find out a few little things, but I don't actually know what happened to Matty. I do know one thing. When there's so little information about a military death, it usually means friendly fire. Or a cover-up. You know why we were in Afghanistan, right? Your husband was a servant to bankers, oil men, and tech monopolists. Not his fault. He probably didn't know any better. Or maybe he did know better and he went AWOL. Hell, maybe he found himself a nice Afghan wife. Monkey Tree 2.0?"

Cole imagined swinging the bat. She felt strong enough to knock his head off clean with a single swing.

"I'm not saying he was sacrificed, but if you don't believe the people in charge would do it, you're naive." He laughed bitterly. "Or maybe he killed himself to get away from his nagging journalist wife."

She jerked the bat back, ready to strike.

"Jane!" Warren's voice cut through the static. "Jane." His hand was on her shoulder, pulling her back gently. "Jane, you can't."

She let out a long breath and tears filled her eyes.

Warren took the bat.

There was a sudden movement on the floor. Wragg had lunged down and kicked a leg toward the computer. Warren dropped on top of him.

Wragg's front door swung open and Cole looked up.

Two NYPD officers stood in the doorway. "Nobody move!" one of them yelled.

Cole put her hands up. Where the hell had *they* come from?

Warren held Wragg on the ground, his back to the door.

"Up. Get off him," the officer yelled.

"Sir, I am Robert Warren, NYPD sixth precinct. Currently on paid leave. His weapon is there." He nodded at Wragg's .22, a yard away on the floor.

"Stand slowly, hands up."

Cole watched as Warren stood slowly, hands on his head, then stepped aside. As he did, Wragg kicked the laptop screen violently. Once. Twice. A third time.

"Don't move!" the officer shouted.

He kicked again, cracking it. Rolling over, he yanked at the cord, pulling it from the wall, then collapsed on the floor, panting.

"Don't move again," the officer commanded. "We *will* shoot you."

Wragg was still.

"Stand slowly, with your hands up."

Wragg obeyed.

"Turn around."

He turned toward them, a grin across his face. "An international brotherhood united by General Ki for a singular mission: to end technological oppression, to restore individual freedoms, to birth a new era of digital liberty."

He took a tiny step back, then another, inching toward the window. In an instant, Cole knew what he was going to do.

"Don't move!" the officer shouted.

Wragg took another small step backwards. "I'm free." He said it quietly, as though to himself.

"Do. Not. Move."

Wragg spun on his heels and dove through the open window, crashing onto the fire escape. He stood, wobbling, as one of the officers reached the window and swiped at his leg. Before he could reach him, Wragg threw himself over the metal railing of the fire escape.

After a second, Cole heard the meaty *thwack* of his body hitting the pavement three stories below.

31

Wednesday

Cole studied her boss's eyes. She'd never before been able to read Max Herr, but she could now. His hands were folded neatly in his lap. He hadn't stroked his beard once this morning. She didn't know why he was lying, only that he was.

"You had the Warren story right from the beginning," he said. "We're not running a retraction."

"I had the facts right," Cole said, pleading, "but I was missing context. I can't write about the new information I have. But a simple retraction saying something like, 'We may have published with incomplete information and the public deserves to see the outcome of the official inquiry.' Easy."

"I talked to a couple sources in the department and they wouldn't give me any details. They assured me that Warren is a bad apple. A brutal cop. Then I don't hear from you for two days and you want to run a retraction based on a video you claim to have seen?" He shook his head. "Jane, no."

"Max, c'mon, have the decency not to lie to my face. What the hell is going on? First you ask me to continue looking into it, then I do and now you're stonewalling me?"

He stood, flummoxed, then sat back down. "Fine," he sighed,

his demeanor changing suddenly. "But it doesn't leave this room, okay?"

She nodded.

"Local community groups want blood on this, and the police department is gonna give it to them. They're gonna dump Warren around Christmas when no one is looking. We don't need to run a retraction. You said it yourself. Nothing in your story was wrong."

It hit her like a kick to the stomach. She stood, fists clenched. "They're gonna fire him? What about the union, the trial, or whatever?"

He shook his head silently.

"If we raise hell," she continued passionately, "we could save him. I'm telling you, there is context the public needs to know."

"It's over, Cole. His career is over."

"What are we doing here if we're not willing to fight on this?"

Max leaned back in his chair. "Living to fight another day."

There was a long silence, then her boss said, "We need to talk about what happened yesterday. I know you're not going to write about yourself, but you understand we have to report on it. Susan will want to interview you about what happened inside Wragg's apartment."

Cole frowned. "Hope she enjoys hearing, 'No comment.'"

She'd spent the evening with the police, explaining how she'd come to be in Michael Wragg's apartment. In a brief exchange with Warren before they'd been driven in separate cars to the police station, she'd convinced him to lie. "Tell them you heard screaming and climbed the fire escape. Tell them we've never met. I didn't break any laws and I don't have to give up my sources. I'll take all the heat."

And that's exactly what she'd done. She'd gotten the interview with Margaret Price, which had tipped her off to Chandler Price. An anonymous tip had connected Price to Wragg and she'd ended up in his apartment. Nope, she'd never met Robert Warren, but she was lucky he happened to be in front of the fish restaurant when she started screaming. That's what she'd told the police.

She'd called Max Herr from the station, telling him what happened and suggesting that he assign another reporter to follow up on the story. No official statement had been issued by the police connecting Wragg to the murder of Raj Ambani, but it would drop soon.

"Max, please, I can't walk out of here without trying one last time. Just, do this one little thing for me. Run a retraction on my Robert Warren story."

"No."

"Fine." She thought for a beat before speaking a two word phrase she'd never used before. One she wasn't entirely sure she could speak until now. Cole took a deep breath and said in full voice, "I quit."

Without waiting for or speaking another word, she turned and walked out.

32

Cole composed her text to Danny Ronan at the bar across the street from Wragg's apartment. Outside, TV crews were filming and a few print reporters hung around, trying to get information from local residents.

Cole: *I think we both know this isn't working. You're a great guy, but I'm not ready for anything real. I thought maybe I could be, but you probably know better than anyone that I'm not. Let's call it quits before you start hating me.*

Breaking up with someone via text was terrible. She'd spent two days trying to convince herself to do it in person, but the thought of his hand on the redhead's hips made her fear the confrontation. She wasn't sure if she was more worried for herself, or for him.

She sent the text as Warren arrived.

Warren handed the bartender his credit card. "Coffee for me." He pointed at the bar in front of Cole. "Patrón, neat, for her. And leave it open."

"Is one of you planning to sign the check before you run out this time?" The bartender looked back and forth between Warren and Cole skeptically. "FYI, I didn't leave myself a tip. I don't want any trouble with the banks but I did sign your bill."

"Right. We ran out before settling the bill yesterday, didn't we?" Cole made an embarrassed expression. "Sorry about that."

Warren nodded in agreement. "Won't happen again."

"Well, fool me once, shame on you, fool me twice…" The bartender paused for effect. "Fool me twice… well, you can get your alcohol somewhere else."

"Got it," Warren smiled.

"Threat taken," Cole added.

The server turned to prepare their beverages with the sound of Bruce Springsteen's version of *Santa Claus Is Comin' to Town* filling the air. Cole and Warren stared at the muted TV above the bar.

Cole dreaded telling Warren what her boss had said, but she owed it to him to break the news in person. "There's something I need to tell you."

"You gonna tell me that I'm getting fired?"

"What? How'd you know?"

The bartender set down their drinks.

Cole gestured to the tequila and looked to Warren. "You sure you want to pay for this? You're contributing to my consumption of empty carbs, you know?"

"Gotta look on the bright side." Warren winked and took a long sip of his coffee. "At least it's not a margarita."

"The coffee sufficiently burnt?" Cole asked.

"Could have used an extra hour on the burner, but it'll do." He sighed before getting back to the subject. "My old training officer Gabriela called this morning. She got wind of it. They're gonna slide me out the back door around Christmas."

"How do they justify *that*? I mean, I thought the police were supposed to protect their own and all that."

"Usually do." Warren shook his head.

"So how'd you know that's what I was going to say?"

"Your eyes," Warren said, "they speak volumes. You looked like you were going to tell me my puppy died."

"Speaking of puppies, what happens to the dog? Liberty."

"If there aren't any relatives who'll take him, and I'm guessing there aren't, protocol is to take him to the shelter. But I know a retired cop who takes care of animals found at crime scenes. Nurtures them back to health and personally finds homes for each and every one. Already called him about Liberty. Guy is a saint, and will give that dog the life he deserves."

Cole smiled, relieved. "I'm glad he'll be cared for." She looked around the bar. "You know, I like this place. Not a cop bar, not a journalist bar."

"Speaking of that, I want to apologize, for, uh, maligning your sacred profession and all that. You were just doing your job."

"No, *I* should be apologizing to *you*. Threatening to call your wife and drag up all your issues in the past. The incident was newsworthy. The other stuff wasn't. I never would have written about it out of spite. Empty threat, and I shouldn't have said it."

"We were both upset," Warren said. "Now, we're square."

They sat in silence, staring up at the flat screen TV. When CNN returned from commercials, a segment about Raj Ambani started. "They still have nothing," Cole said. "It'll take them another day to connect Wragg to Ambani."

"You think he acted alone?"

"Of course not. He practically confessed to an international conspiracy. I told the officers who interviewed me what he said. They wrote it down, but kinda shrugged it off. What did you make of what he said?"

"Barely followed it."

Cole closed her eyes and let the memory fill the void. "An international brotherhood united by General Ki for a singular mission: to end technological oppression, to restore individual freedoms, to birth a new era of digital liberty."

Warren scoffed. "What the hell does that mean? Sounds like some BS propaganda."

"I don't know," Cole said. "I googled it and nothing came up with that exact phrase. Best I can tell, it's a part of a movement that exists in many countries. Anti-corporate, anti-digital globalization, anti-technology. "

"Like I said, BS. Like the unabomber on steroids."

"Kind of, and there are a lot of other strains of thought mixed in."

"That reminds me," Warren said. "In the apartment, you took photos of his screen. Why'd you do that, and what were they?"

"While he had me in there, he was looking at his screen, something was going down. When it fell to the ground, I don't know, I thought, 'What if it turns off and the data isn't recoverable?' I did what people do now, take pictures and look at them later."

"So, did you? Did you look at them?"

She pulled out her phone. "Only got a few. Screen was

covered with food at first. I got one clear image, but it didn't make any sense." She slid the phone to Warren, open to the picture.

It was a crooked image of Wragg's screen with flecks of food and smears of sauce, but a small amount of text was legible in the center.

Kokutai-Goji:
2/9
(The Silver Squirrel)
Final Notice.
An international brotherhood united by General Ki for a singular mission: to end technological oppression, to restore individual freedoms, to birth a new era of digital liberty.
2/9
Final Notice.

When he'd finished reading, Warren said, "You need to show this to the police."

"Forwarded it to them. Plus financial records from Chandler Price. I gave them everything we dug up. I did my civic duty. Didn't mention you, though. Far as they know, you had nothing to do with anything."

"You know, the First Amendment doesn't protect you on those documents. You can't go to jail for writing about them, but if a judge orders you to tell him where you got them, you'll have to."

"There are shield laws," Cole said, "and I doubt it'll come to that. It's weird, I feel like I've heard the phrase 'Silver Squirrel' before. Ring any bells for you?"

"I got nothing." Warren paid the tab and slid his stool back from the bar. "I gotta get home. Get a workout in and get some rest. I'm seeing my daughter tomorrow."

Cole smiled. "That'll be nice. I'll see you around."

"See you around." He headed for the door.

Cole let her eyes land on the TV above the bar. "Wait, Warren, look! Oh dear God, no."

Warren whipped around and followed Cole's gesture to the television.

CNN had a *Breaking News* banner on the screen. The bartender was fumbling with the remote. The bar grew quiet as every eye fixed on the screen. Warren stood behind Cole as the bartender turned on the sound.

"In shocking news tonight," a male news anchor said gravely, "former Vice President Alvin Meyers has died in what appears to be an assassination-style murder in Washington, D.C. Sources tell CNN there are no known political motivations at this time."

"It's connected," Cole said.

Warren sat. "Maybe, but possibly not."

"It's connected. I know for sure."

"How can you? We don't know that it was one of the other guns. Maybe you know of some connection between Ambani and Meyers that I don't."

Cole shook her head.

"Why do you look like that? Jane, what's going on?"

"The name Silver Squirrel. I remember why it sounded familiar. It was the Secret Service code name Alvin Meyers used when he was VP." She handed her phone to Warren. Together, they reread the message from the picture she'd taken of Wragg's computer screen.

"Two-slash-nine," Warren said. "That could mean two *out of* nine. Nine rifles. Raj Ambani took a bullet from number one. Meyers took his from number two." He ran a hand over his head, letting out a long sigh. "I don't even want to think about what this means."

"I *know* what it means." Cole steadied her eyes on Warren. "It means that this whole thing is just beginning."

—End of Episode 1—

THE
CRIME
BEAT

EPISODE 2: WASHINGTON D.C.

33

Wednesday

Through the din of punk music that filled the crowded bar, Jane Cole struggled to hear the TV anchor stumble over the breaking news coverage.

"Former Vice President Alvin Meyers has been murdered...we're hearing...I've just been told..."

Warren, who was sitting on the stool next to her, waved down the bartender. "Can you turn it up?"

A man rushed from a nearby table and slid onto the empty stool on the other side of Cole, "Did he say Meyers got shot?"

Cole nodded.

The man pointed at the TV and turned to the crowd. "Meyers was shot," he yelled.

The bartender picked up a second remote and turned off the music. The sudden quiet drew more attention. Dozens of eyes locked on the TV above the bar. As the bartender turned up the volume, Cole relaxed, no longer needing to fight so hard to pick up the anchor's words.

The reporter brought his finger to his ear. "I'm hearing that...my apologies...all we can confirm at this time is that former Vice President Alvin Meyers has been killed."

"His poor family," Warren shook his head. "He has two daughters, doesn't he?"

Cole nodded. "Yes."

"Once again," the reporter said, "our former Vice President Alvin Meyers has been assassinated while attending an event at the Watergate in Washington D.C. this evening. Born and raised in Virginia, Meyers served as a US Senator from 1970 to 1992, and Governor of Virginia from 1992 to 2000. He then accepted the role of Vice President. Details are still coming in. Since his retirement in 2008, Meyers sat on the boards of some of the nation's top companies, and became an international ambassador for American business. Stay with us this evening as we bring in expert guests and former colleagues to mourn his death and speak about his legacy. We'll be back with the latest updates on this sorrowful event after a brief break."

Next to Cole, Warren sipped his coffee, eyes trained on the TV. Cole drew his attention when she turned to face him and spoke. "Right now, every news producer in the world is trying to decide whether to air videos of a former Vice President being murdered. That poor anchor has a half dozen people arguing in his ear."

"He's doing a decent job," Warren said. "Given the circumstances."

Cole dropped her eyes to her phone. The shooting wasn't trending on Threads or X yet, but it would be soon. Her feed was cluttered with various versions of "OMG, Alvin Meyers is dead," and "Who bothers to assassinate an ex-VP?"

One message stood out—a wobbly cell phone video claiming to show the moments just before Meyers died. It showed the crowded rooftop of the Watergate Hotel, outdoor heaters spaced evenly to warm up the chilly outdoor gathering place. On the left, two bartenders in black and white poured wine behind a curved wooden bar. Waiters shifted in and out of the shot, setting glasses on trays, then disappearing from the frame. Between the bar and the railings that separated the rooftop from the sky, forty to fifty people chatted in small groups, sipping drinks. Some stood by the railings, staring in the direction of the apartment buildings and hotels that loomed across the Potomac.

"Looks like a typical D.C. cocktail party," Cole said.

"You know what the party was for?" Warren asked.

"Something about a satellite internet access program for developing nations. Alvin Meyers was one of the more *involved* former vice presidents. Boards of directors, international foundations, that kind of stuff."

"After he was VP, why didn't he run for president?"

Cole shot him a look. "Really?"

"What? I don't follow politics."

"There was a leaked email thread showing he personally lobbied to kill privacy regulations—right before taking a board seat at a Big Tech firm. Turns out, he helped them push through mass data collection policies that made billions for the companies. His base wasn't too happy about that." Cole rolled her eyes. "Plus, he made tens of millions as a private citizen. That could be another reason he didn't run."

She held the phone between them as the video that had been uploaded to Threads made a quick, disorienting pan to the right, as though the person holding the phone had been bumped. The shot was now centered on a glass door where Alvin Meyers entered, flanked by two men in black suits. Secret Service.

Meyers was blandly handsome. Tall, with silver-white hair and a constant smile that was probably necessary in his line of work but struck Cole as phony.

For the next thirty seconds, the video followed Meyers as he shook hands, slapped backs, and repeated different versions of the catchphrase he'd used for years: "What's good for the world is good for America."

Then, in an instant, Meyers' hand shot to his neck, like he'd been stung by an invisible hornet. The former vice president dropped out of the frame. People screamed. A Secret Service agent pointed at the railing as he ducked to protect the president. The other agent crouched, also disappearing from the frame. The video jerked, then showed a mix of sky, limbs, ground, and the tops of heads as the videographer ducked with the rest of the guests. A shriek pierced the scene.

A woman shouted, "Meyers is down!"

"It came from over there," a man called.

The video jerked again, a shot of heads and sky, then ended.

Cole scrolled for a few seconds, looking for information or other videos, then glanced at Warren. "No footage of Meyers after he was hit. And no footage of where the shot came from. At least not yet."

"Right away, Secret Service would have had Meyers in the elevator," Warren said, "then in the back of his armored vehicle, racing away from the scene. Protocol, even if they knew he was dead." Warren pressed his hands to his cheeks and let out a long breath. His pressure-release valve. "If he was the President, they'd have had bags of his blood in the limo. Not that it matters. They'd have no way to keep him alive if the shot was on target."

Warren nodded at the TV. The broadcast was back from commercial and the anchor had recovered his composure. "Initial reports from the scene—and please keep in mind that these are *unconfirmed* reports—but initial reports indicate that the shot may not have come from someone on the rooftop. Perhaps a neighboring building, we're being told." The anchor paused, focusing on the voice of the producer in his ear. "For those just joining us, in breaking news, former Vice President Alvin Meyers was shot and killed this evening, and we will be here all night providing special coverage of his death, and his legacy. Stay with us."

"First thing that pops to mind," Cole said. "How does Alvin Meyers connect to Raj Ambani?"

"I don't know much about him."

"Moderate Democrat. Four-term Senator, two-term Governor of Virginia before being picked for VP."

"And he cashed in when he left office?"

"Yup. Hundred-fifty grand per speech, seven-figure book deal, the works."

"So he's well off and powerful, two things he had in common with Ambani. But what do they have to do with each other?"

Cole did a quick search on her phone. She clicked the first link. "I thought so," she said, holding it up to Warren. "Ambani hosted a fundraiser for Meyers, and donated money to previous campaigns."

Warren was skeptical. "Don't businessmen like Ambani donate to all the candidates, Republican *and* Democrat, just to make sure?"

"We need to start somewhere, and that's a connection."

Warren gave a short nod. "Why not start in D.C.?"

She stared at him blankly.

"I have a car."

His meaning hit her suddenly. "You serious, Rob?"

He nodded.

Cole scrolled through Threads as she considered. She'd quit her job on a whim less than six hours ago. She hadn't given it much thought, but now she was hoping for some freelance work to tide her over while she looked for something permanent. And if the Meyers killing *was* connected to the Ambani murder, this was about to become the biggest story in the world.

She was about to ask Warren what kind of car he had when a text arrived from Joey Mazzalano—a scumbag Lieutenant from the fifth precinct, but also one of her best sources.

The Italian Stallion: *Buy me a drink tonight. Antonio's at 10.*

Her first instinct was to ignore him, but she tapped out a quick reply.

Jane Cole: *Why?*

The Italian Stallion: *You said you always pay your debts, and that Wragg tip was a disappointment.*

Jane Cole: *The Wragg tip was spot on.*

The Italian Stallion: *He died before I could get any credit, and you could have called me when you found the apartment. Plus, I have something for you.*

Cole let out an exasperated sigh and went back to scrolling through the breaking news on social media. Her eye landed on another video from the roof of the Watergate, which showed a different angle on the scene. She held it up for Warren to watch with her.

While the video played, she considered Warren's offer again. Until recently, she'd believed he was an abusive cop who should be fired and prosecuted. The dashcam footage had shown that he'd been provoked in the worst way possible. But still, she felt uneasy about hopping in his car for the four-hour drive to D.C.

The new video didn't have a clear shot of Meyers. Just people drinking casually before the shooting, and screaming in panic afterwards. When it ended, Warren plucked the phone from her hand and laid it face down on the bar. He waited until she met his dark eyes.

"Cole," he said. "Right now, I've got nothing else in my life. Nothing but this case."

"You don't *have* this case." Cole reminded him. "You're not a cop anymore."

"I'm the last one who needs reminding of that." Warren held a firm stare in Cole's direction before continuing, "In America you need a special license to drive a taxi, need to pass the bar exam to practice law."

"Yeah, you need a permit to serve hot dogs at the fair," Cole interrupted. "So what?"

"Cops have to pass mental and physical tests, written exams," Warren continued. "My point is, you don't need anything except a phone and a laptop to be a journalist."

She didn't know what he was driving at, but she wasn't up for another fight about cops and journalists. "Right, we're protected under the First Amendment."

"That's what I'm saying. I want to get to the bottom of this. I bet you do, too. We can sit here all night watching the news and looking at blurry video clips of the assassination. But you and I are the only two people alive who know about the guns, about Chandler Price, and the screenshots. If Meyers is connected, we have a better chance of figuring out how than anyone. Let's go to D.C. where we can do what we both do best."

His face was pleading and earnest. She recognized that look. It was the one thing they had in common—that indefinable, relentless need to learn the truth. If they could, it would be the biggest story of her life. She nodded at the bartender. "Can we settle up?"

"Please do." The bartender rushed over and slid their check across the bar.

"So we're going?" Warren asked as he signed the check.

"We're going, but I need to make a quick stop on the way out of town."

"What for?" Warren nodded at the bartender as he tucked the receipt under his glass.

"Gotta meet a source," Cole said.

"Who?"

Cole exhaled sharply as she dug into her purse and pulled out her cell phone. "Nobody you'd know or would ever want to."

"You okay?" Warren asked.

Cole answered with a shrug as she tapped out a quick text to Mazzalano.

"What's the plan?"

Cole hit send before she looked back up. "Don't know yet."

"Want me to go with you?"

"Given your temper, it's probably best if you don't," Cole said. She worried that this comment may have offended Warren, but didn't have time to apologize before her phone dinged. She read the message, looked back up at Warren, then spoke before turning to the door. "Pick me up in Little Italy outside Antonio's in an hour."

34

Cole descended the five stairs from street level and peeled off her coat as she entered the restaurant. A handful of people looked up from dark wood tables lit by large candles that flickered deep gold light across their faces.

Antonio's was an old-school Italian restaurant in the basement of a brownstone just off Mulberry Street. Cole had met Mazzalano there five years ago and since learned that it was the last of a dying breed of restaurants—family owned, with the same menu for nearly seventy years. The night they'd met, he'd called it, "Real red-sauce Italian. None of that frou-frou Northern *spazzatura*."

Every time she went to Antonio's, it was half-empty. The owners seemed to go out of their way not to publicize its existence. Restaurants with few customers were sometimes used as money-laundering operations for owners with other sources of income. Mazzalano had hinted at those *other* sources of income but he'd never come out and named them.

Mazzalano stood behind the bar, helping himself to a glass of grappa, a grape-based brandy Cole loathed. He waved her over to a four-top near the bar. Cole chose to sit in the stool closest to the door. She hoped setting her purse on the stool to her left would discourage Mazzalano from sitting within arm's reach.

She flashed the snarky smile she knew he loved. "You work here now?"

"Antonio is back in the kitchen. He lets me help myself. You know, time was, you could find similar joints all over Little Italy. Now, it's mostly tourist spots. Twenty-four bucks for a bowl of weeds."

She smiled politely as he poured her a glass of grappa. She'd heard this spiel before.

Mazzalano shuffled around the bar and pulled out the chair next to her. As he dislodged the purse that had become wedged between his body and the chair, a wet smile dripped from his face.

Cole pretended to be unfazed. "And what do you provide him in exchange for his hospitality?"

Mazzalano handed the purse to Cole then wiped sweat from his forehead with a white handkerchief and pressed it into his nose, inhaling deeply. "I can always tell what I drank last night from the way my sweat smells the next day. You ever notice that?"

"Gross." She pushed the grappa away wishing she could do the same with Mazzalano.

"It's impolite to refuse a drink from a friend."

"I prefer tequila." Cole hoped to get things with Mazzalano moving. The less she had to be in his presence the better. "What happened with the hair sample from Ambani's killer?"

Mazzalano mumbled something inaudible, then said, "You hear about Meyers? Course you did, you're a news junkie, always on your phone." Fundamentally, Mazzalano was a bully, so instead of lying he often just changed the subject when he got a question he didn't like. But it *was* odd that he didn't want to discuss the DNA test. Normally he'd have taken the question as an opportunity to brag about his clout within the lab.

"You drink, I talk," he said, pushing the drink back towards her.

"If I drink, will you get to the point? I have somewhere to be, and you said this was important."

He smiled. "Would I lie to you?"

"Yes, but… Fine, I'll take my chances." She shot the grappa. The liquor seared her throat and cleared her sinuses all at once. "There. Done." The empty glass clacked loudly as she placed it back on the bar. "Saw about Meyers," Cole said. "Does this have to do with your important news?"

"Perhaps. A second high-profile murder in a week, sniper-style? Got me thinking."

"Thinking what?"

He waved her off with a grunt, as though he'd decided to change the subject. He was drunker than usual, which was dangerous, but also useful. Useful because the drunker he got, the more he talked. Dangerous because the booze hyper-charged his piggish behavior.

"Not relevant any more, *is it*?" His voice was biting, sarcastic, a tone he usually concealed under a facade of pseudo-charm.

"The hair sample, you mean?"

"Wragg is dead. You really screwed me, you know. I showed you the video, you gave me the hair sample, but before I had time to do anything with it, *BOOM!* the former vice president is dead and *POOF!* Nobody needs what I can offer. There's a bigger story and now Ambani's murder is all but forgotten. Even you, Jane Cole, you don't need me now that you have Warren. No glory for the Italian Stallion, is there?"

"I'm sorry about that, but I held up my end of the bargain. You were my first and only call when I was attacked. There was no way I could have predicted how that would go down. The evidence I gave you is not nothing. Once you get the DNA results back from the hair, it'll at least help fill out the file."

Mazzalano looked away.

"You *did* submit the hair, right?" Cole asked.

His cheeks, already red, flushed. "Sure I did." A drop of sweat dripped onto the bar. He dabbed it with a napkin, spilling his drink in the process. She studied him as he walked around the bar to pour himself another shot.

Cole knew that people often sweat when they're nervous or lying, but sweat alone isn't a tell.

She had established a baseline during normal conversation. Booze made Mazzalano red and sweaty even under normal circumstances, but tonight something was different. The one thing Cole liked about him was that he'd always told her the truth. He wanted to be liked, wanted to come across as important so deeply, that he'd never tried to spin her.

Tonight there was spin. He was more red and more sweaty, but the biggest tell was in his eyes. They were shifty. This time Mazzalano was definitely lying to her.

143

Cole was sure of it.

35

Warren arrived early in his '69 Ford Cougar and took a spot across the street from Antonio's. He'd purchased the car for $2,000 the week he got back from Afghanistan, and spent a year and another $12,000 whipping it into shape. Everything had been restored to its original splendor, except the radio, which he'd updated to an MP3-compatible system. His drinking and temper had cost him his family, and now his job. *Blue Lightning*, as he called his beloved car, was the only thing he'd been able to keep through it all.

He had a few minutes to kill and needed to connect with someone. He dialed his wife, but the call went to voicemail after the first ring. She was screening him out. Hoping to hear a friendly voice, he dialed one of his buddies. After a few rings, the call went to voicemail. Next he'd dialed Gabriela Rojas. Hoping it would make her more likely to take his call, he'd used her personal line.

Warren spoke first when he heard the line connect as she picked up the call. "Gabby, it's War Dog. Please don't hang up."

"Sorry, man," Gabby finally offered. "Sorry you're getting thrown under the bus."

He sensed hesitation in her apology. "I'm not gonna ask you to try to intervene, but—"

"I couldn't get it done," she interrupted. "Already tried."

He was glad Gabby had been quick to fill the silence this time.

"Decisions like that are way above my pay grade," she added.

Gabby had been promoted through the NYPD in near record time. Recently she'd been assigned to the elite Joint Terrorism Task Force. This put her in the position of accessing intel none of Warren's other friends in the department could.

"What are you hearing?" Warren made a fist at the top of the steering wheel and silently rapped his head against his hand a few times.

Gabby sighed. "I don't know for sure, but I think it goes high up. Judge assigned to the trafficking case—the guy you roughed up—has clout, that's all I know."

"But why would a judge want to see me gone for roughing up a…" He didn't finish the question. If a judge wanted him fired for roughing up a suspect, especially *this* suspect, it could only mean one thing.

"Yeah," Gabby said, as though reading his mind. "Actually I was gonna call *you*. Rumors on this judge are bad. I mean, *bad*. Has a history of going easy on sex offenders. Positions himself to get the cases on his docket. I hear he's already under investigation but, for whatever reason, he has clout with the right people at IAB."

"Are you saying what I think you're saying?"

"I'm saying back away. Quietly. If this judge is what I think he is, he's gonna get got. But not by you. I'll do what I can."

Warren rolled down his window and leaned out. The thought of a judge protecting scumbag human traffickers like the one he'd arrested made his blood boil, and the cool air calmed him. "Okay," he said softly. "I'll back off. But if the judge is what you're saying, promise you'll get the word out."

"I'll try, but you gotta do something for me." There was silence on the line before she continued. "What happened with Wragg? You know no one buys the whole Superman story. You didn't just happen to hear a woman screaming from below and badass your way up the fire escape. And the woman didn't just *happen* to be the reporter who broke the story about you. Did she?"

"We were looking into the Ambani thing together. I had a couple hunches that turned out to be right."

"War Dog, c'mon."

"I don't want to say too much, alright?"

"You don't trust me?" Rojas asked.

He groaned. "You might be the only person in law enforcement I *do* trust. But you still got a job. You don't want any piece of what I'm getting involved in."

"Involved? Present tense? It's *still* happening?"

Warren looked through the windshield. A young couple emerged from the restaurant and shared a vape pen on the sidewalk. He was impatient for Cole to show, but he *did* trust Gabby, and he had time to kill. "You hear about Meyers?"

"Yeah, but I asked you about Wragg."

He let her statement hang in the air.

"There's a connection between Wragg and Ambani, isn't there?"

Warren let out a long sigh. "I *can* trust you, right?"

Gabby's voice was hushed. "I swear on Saint Gabriel."

Warren didn't know who that was, but he'd heard Gabriela say it once before, soon after they'd first met.

They'd worked together on his second day of training, the same day three officers had been ambushed and killed execution-style one precinct over in Brooklyn. The department was shaken. Warren was shaken. She'd sworn to Saint Gabriel the killers would be brought to justice. And they had been.

Warren took the next few minutes to talk her through how he'd seen the post about the gun purchase on the Dark Web, how he'd connected with Cole, and their investigation into the townhouse that led them to Margaret and Chandler Price, then to Wragg.

She thanked him for the information, but didn't seem impressed.

"I don't suppose you can get me anything on Meyers?" he concluded.

Gabby laughed. "The FBI and the Secret Service aren't famous for sharing their cases."

"You can't play the JTTF card?" Warren asked. "Could be a terrorist connection, right?"

"Wrong. And no. Still can't believe you partnered with a reporter. I just can't see it."

Neither could he. "Gabby, can you help?"

"I should say no, but—and not to flatter you—you're one of very few people in law enforcement I trust, too."

147

"I'm no longer *in* law enforcement, remember?"

"You're not a *cop* any more," she said. "Doesn't mean you can't enforce *some* laws."

It wasn't like her to say that, but she seemed to be agreeing to help him. "Michael Wragg. He doesn't have any other addresses in the public record, already looked, but maybe he's got a registration with the state, or an old address through the DMV. Can you check?"

"Maybe," she said, "but don't go expecting any miracles, War Dog."

"I won't, Gabby. I know better than anyone that I haven't a prayer in the world. And thanks."

"For what?" She sighed. "I haven't done anything."

"You answered the phone. Right now, most people in my life won't even do that."

36

Cole stood at the sink, digging through her purse. She couldn't find anything other than a half stick of gum to cleanse the taste of the grappa from her tongue. After rinsing her mouth out with tap water multiple times, she popped the gum in her mouth on her way back to the table with Mazzalano.

She wasn't sure why he'd lied to her, but she wanted to draw him out. "Can I get the DNA results when you *do* get them?" she asked casually as she returned to her seat beside him.

"What for?"

"Just to be sure, y'know. He held a knife to my back. I know it's the same guy, but it'd be nice to have the DNA back me up."

He waved a dismissive hand. "Sure, but you know how backed up the labs are. Could be weeks. Months."

She was losing her patience, but kept her voice level. "Damn, Mazzalano. Why'd you drag me here?"

"First let's talk about Michael Wragg, how'd you find him, anyway?"

"Reporting."

"C'mon, Jane, give daddy some sugar." He leaned in close and continued in a heavy whisper. "What kind of reporting?"

Cole stood and walked behind the bar where she poured two more shots of grappa. The first shot had warmed her just enough to allow her to tolerate this goon. Despite her better judgment, better taste, and because the gum hadn't done anything to mask the taste in her mouth, she wanted another.

Still behind the bar, she said, "I looked into the townhouse where the shooting took place."

"Maggie Price?" He asked eagerly, walking over and taking a seat at the bar opposite Cole.

"Yes, but no," she said.

"Chandler Price then." Mazzalano mopped his face with his kerchief again.

Cole nodded slowly, then shot the grappa.

Mazzalano sat up straight and threw back his shot as well. He slammed the shot-glass down then let his posture return to its previous slouch as he sunk back into his stool. He was sloshed. "Well I'll be damned." He shook his head slowly. "You sure?"

Cole nodded. "You're the only person I've told. It wasn't something I had solidly enough to write. My editor doesn't even know."

"Why not?"

"The way I got the information was, well…" She shrugged. "But anyway, it led to Wragg. I still don't know exactly what Price did, but he told his wife to be out of town the day Ambani was killed. He set it up so Wragg could shoot Ambani from the roof of a vacant townhouse. I don't know where Price leads, or if you can get to him. Promise me if you do surface anything, you'll let me break the story."

He rested his wide arms on the bar. "Thought you were out of a job."

"News travels fast. How'd you hear?"

He smacked his lips. "You're not the only person I know at *The Sun*."

"I'll be freelancing for a bit. Promise me, though, you find Price, you give me a heads up."

"I will."

"So, what was the tip you dangled to get me to Little Italy?" she asked. "I'm eager to get back to the news."

More quickly than she thought he could move, Mazzalano heaved his heavy body around the bar and stood next to her. Too close for comfort. She leaned away, but the other side of the bar was blocked by a tall table covered in menus. His massive body pressed her into the table, which scraped along the floor.

"Get off me." She said it firmly, and just loud enough to cause a couple at a nearby table to look up.

He squeezed her arms tightly. "I told you I had something for you," he whispered, breathing heavily. In a boozy whisper, he continued. "You know you want this as bad as I do."

She lifted a leg and brought her heel down violently on the top of his foot. He groaned in pain and let go, then cackled with laughter. Stepping forward, she grabbed his right shoulder and kneed him in the stomach as hard as she could. Her favorite move from the self defense class she'd taken in college.

Mazzalano toppled backwards.

Dropping to her knees, Cole slid under the table at the end of the bar and hurried out of the restaurant.

She spotted Warren in the driver's side of a dark-blue muscle car across the street. She darted through a gap in the traffic, looking back as Mazzalano staggered out the door trying to follow.

She slid into the passenger seat. "Drive."

Warren glanced toward Mazzalano.

"Drive," she said again.

37

As the Ford Cougar pulled away, Mazzalano inhaled deeply. He still smelled Cole's perfume. Roses, he thought, mixed with crushed black peppercorn. Sweet *and* spicy.

The Cougar turned right at the end of the block. On his cell phone, Mazzalano dialed Officer William Bowman, who picked up on the first ring.

"Stallion, what's up?"

"WB, I need you to tail someone. You still at the end of the block?"

"Like you said to be."

"She's in a muscle car, heading south on Mulberry, likely they'll turn on Canal. Couldn't get the plates but it's dark blue, late sixties or early seventies. She's in the passenger seat, driver's a black male. Got it?"

"Sure. What do you want me to do?"

"Just tail them for now. I'll be around. I want to know where they stop, and when. Right away. And if you can get an ID on the guy she's with, do it."

"I'll try."

Mazzalano inhaled again, then stumbled back into Antonio's.

38

The sound of a police siren broke the silence while Cole and Warren waited to pay the toll at the Holland Tunnel. Cole looked out the angled back window, but saw no flashing lights.

Warren shifted in his seat.

"I don't see anyone pulling us over, do you?" Cole continued to look out the windows.

Warren handed her his cell phone, which was blaring a police siren ringtone.

She exhaled with relief. "Why the hell would you set this thing up to do that?"

"I assigned it to only one person. An old friend."

Cole looked down and read the text. "It's an address in Nutley, New Jersey. From someone named Gabby."

Warren fumbled in his pocket for cash. "I asked her to help us with Wragg."

"Who is she?"

"Old friend, like I said."

The wailing siren announced another text.

Cole aloud as Warren paid the toll. "She says, '*Ship, Store, and More*. Came up in an address search for Wragg. His business, apparently.' Nutley, New Jersey is about twenty miles north. D.C. is south. Worth the detour?"

"Ask if police have been there yet. She might not know, but—"

"On it."

Cole sent the question and stared at the screen as they entered the tunnel. "Won't get a reply while we're down here."

"What is this, 2011? Reception is actually better *in* the tunnel. We've got eight thousand feet of leaky coax."

Cole had no idea what he was talking about. "Huh?"

"Coaxial cable with holes that leak cell reception into the tunnels."

"Since when?"

"Eight years or so," Warren said. "What are you, some kind of anti-tech dinosaur?"

"No, but do we really need to be sending posts and texts a hundred feet under the Hudson River?"

The siren blared again and Cole quickly muted it.

"What's she say?" Warren asked.

Cole read the text.

Gabby: *Can't promise some enterprising detective didn't find it, but I got it from NYS DOS. Wragg registered the company in 2015. Since he's dead, probably wasn't high priority to get out there.*

Cole was puzzled. "Says she doesn't think anyone has been there yet. Got the address from the Department of State, but I checked there. Wragg's business didn't show up when I searched. I searched everywhere."

Warren chuckled. "You think she's hopping on DOS.NY.GOV?"

"Is there a defunct business list or something?"

"Something like that. Put the address into your maps and let's go."

Cole tapped the address into her phone. They were only thirty minutes away.

As the phone led them north on Route 7 through Newark and Kearney, Cole noticed that Warren drove like a professional. She and Matt hadn't owned a car since moving to Manhattan, but even when she'd driven regularly, she'd never driven like Warren. He weaved in and out of traffic, leaning into his lane changes as he accelerated, like the car was an extension of his body.

They pulled into the small town of Nutley just after midnight and slowed at a sign that read, "E-Z Storage."

Warren pointed. "I thought you said it was called Ship, Store, and More."

"That's what Gabby said."

The parking lot was poorly lit and nearly deserted, but a light was on in the small office. Instead of turning in, Warren drove past and parked a block away.

As they walked back toward the office, Cole gave him a questioning glance.

"I don't know what this is yet," Warren said. "Plus, I saw the company you keep."

"Mazzalano?"

"He's a dirtbag, or worse," Warren said. "We need to have a talk about that guy later."

Behind the desk, a young man sat on a stool, watching a video on his phone. When a bell on the door broke the silence, he looked up and brushed red hair from his eyes.

Cole strode up to the desk and gave it a double-tap. "Whatcha watching?" She'd read his expression right as she walked in—confusion and surprise—and wanted to keep him off guard.

"Um, I, what?" he mumbled. "Can I help you, ma'am?"

Warren stood a step behind her, thumbing through a rack of pamphlets. "You know a Michael Wragg?" he asked calmly.

"No," the young man said, "I don't know any…"

Cole held up her phone in front of his face, which interrupted him. A photo of Wragg. "Take a look," she said. She'd lifted the image from *The Sun's* website, which had published its first piece on Wragg's death only hours earlier. In the photo, Wragg smiled by the side of a lake, holding up a large fish. It was from at least ten years earlier, Cole guessed. But she was just judging by his hairline.

"Has this man been in here lately? Would have been older, less hair on top. Face more withered." She briefly turned the phone to take another look herself. "Probably not smiling, though."

The kid leaned in. "Yeah, I think so. Ponytail? Is that this Wragg guy you're looking for?"

"Yup," Cole said. "When was the last time he was here?"

"Week or so. Why?"

Warren set a pamphlet back on the rack and joined the

conversation. "We're investigators." It was technically true, since they were investigating. If this kid assumed it meant they had legal authority, so much the better. "Did the guy from the photo, Wragg, have a storage container here?"

"Yes, but—"

"Where?" Warren pressed.

"Sir, I can't tell you that."

Cole put a hand on Warren's forearm and pushed him back gently. "Has anyone been here in the last day or two to ask you about him?" she asked.

"No, what? Why?" The young man was clearly ruffled.

"You sure?"

"I was here the last three nights, and Monica would have told me if the cops came during the day. Not much happens out here. At least not that we can tell from outside the sheds." He waved an arm at the rows of storage sheds behind a fence through a large picture window.

"Ever heard of Ship, Store, and More?" Cole asked.

"No."

Cole pointed up at the signage above the counter. "E-Z Storage didn't change its name from that or anything?"

"We were told that this was the address of Ship, Store, and More," Warren added

"No, I mean, I don't think so. I really should call the manager if—" The kid picked up the landline and pressed a button on the autodial panel.

Cole pushed down the receiver and leaned in. The kid was standing a little taller. Cole intuited he was over his initial surprise. "You don't want to do that. My friend here is a police—"

"Cole!" Warren glared at her, a look she took to mean *leave me out of this*.

A half dozen objections leapt to Cole's mind, all starting with the word "But." Warren's look told her they wouldn't do any good. Apparently he wasn't willing to push their bluff that far.

"I'm getting in there," Cole whispered.

She turned from Warren back to the kid at the counter. "The man I showed you is dead. You want to know how he died?" Cole didn't wait for an answer. "Killed himself. After being caught for the murder of the billionaire Raj Ambani."

"I don't know what you want me to do here." The kid held the phone towards Cole and the coiled cord wiggled then stretched allowing the movement. "You can call the manager, but I doubt…"

"Look Kid," Warren said. Even if he wasn't making a threat, the sound of his voice was imposing. "We believe evidence from that murder is in one of your storage sheds."

Cole leaned in closer and squinted her eyes at the young man. "You following us?"

The kid looked from Warren to Cole and nodded.

Cole continued. "What will your boss think when EZ Storage and all its employees are accused of harboring or even abetting a murderer." It was a risk to lie so nakedly but it also might gain them some traction.

"Look lady, I don't know what that guy did, but I do know we don't ask specifics on what people store. They sign a form: *no illegal activity in the units*. That's all I know." The kid shook his head. "I'm calling my boss."

"Please," she said, catching his blue eyes. "I'm a reporter. I want only the truth. Give me five minutes in his unit and I swear you won't get in any trouble." She didn't expect it to work, but if Warren wasn't willing to play the cop card, it was all she had.

Warren sighed, then spoke. "Do you like cash?"

The kid hesitated for only a moment. "Fifty gets you one minute. Hundred bucks, gets you three. Don't do anything that leads back to me. I got a cousin who's as big as this guy, feel me? And, no photos. In fact, everything is…" The kid was thinking hard now. "…off the record."

Warren laughed. "You get that from a movie kid?"

Cole dug into her purse, rummaging for cash. "Fine, fine."

This was the equivalent of talking to a source on "deep background." She might get some good information, but nothing she could print. Cole slid five twenties across the counter.

The kid stashed them in the front pocket of his jeans and ran into the back room.

"Hey," Cole yelled. "Where do you think you're going?" Cole zipped her purse closed as she started after him.

"To get the access code, *mom*."

39

Jane Cole followed the kid through a low gate, Warren tagged along reluctantly. They passed through a metal door that opened into a rectangular building. Inside, fluorescent lights clicked on the moment they entered, revealing a long hallway with units on either side. Cole noted the security camera, which had been bolted to the ceiling over the door, capturing them as they walked in.

She counted as she passed ten units—five on the left, five on the right—each enclosed by a sliding metal door. They stopped at the end of the hallway in front of a door marked "12."

The kid typed a code into the keypad, then paused to look at Cole. "Three minutes," he reminded her.

Cole nodded.

He pushed one last button. The keypad beeped and the kid slid the door up.

The screech of metal on metal jolted Cole. "You gonna stay and watch?" she asked.

"Nah, I need to be at the desk. Boss calls a few times a night to make sure we're not sleeping on the job or, you know, running around letting strangers into the units. Close the door when you leave and it'll lock. I'll be back in four minutes if I don't see you leaving in three." He pointed at the camera.

When the young man was gone, Warren said, "I'll wait outside."

She opened her mouth to object, but he was already wandering away. She watched Warren leave, trying to decide if he was being overly cautious or if her plan was too reckless. Not that it mattered—either way she'd be entering the unit.

Behind a stack of cardboard boxes to the left of the door, she found a switch and flicked it. Jackpot. Now illuminated, Cole saw that the unit was roughly ten by ten, and to her left and right, stacks of unmarked cardboard boxes reached just short of the ceiling. Otherwise, the storage unit was uncrowded. It looked more like an office.

Along the back wall, papers covered an old metal desk. A cork board hung behind it, papers and business cards jutting from all angles were held in place by thumbtacks. Next to the cork-board, a colorful world map hung on the wall, dotted with silver pushpins that marked cities in multiple countries. A single bookshelf stood to the right of the desk. She made a quick scan of the spines.

Ghost in the Wires: Escaping the Digital Prison
Technological Oppression and the Path to Freedom
America 2.0
The Last Sovereign: A Manifesto Against the One-World Order
The Machine's Chains: How AI Will Enslave Humanity

To the left of the desk, a display case held a collection of military artifacts, including an old rifle with a wooden scope and a rusty green grenade. She hoped it wasn't live. Quickly, she browsed the papers on the desk. She didn't have time to read them.

She wasn't going to be able to stick to the three minute agreement. The motive for Wragg's crime was in this room. Quite possibly, so were names of accomplices and details of any future killings. There was no way she was going to leave before getting more of her questions answered.

"Cole."

The faint call had come from outside. Maybe Warren had decided to join her.

"Cole." The voice was louder this time, more urgent.

She froze, listening intently, eyes darting around the unit, trying to soak up as much information as possible. The alarm in the voice told her something important was happening. His call wasn't saying, *Cole, let me in.* It was saying, *Cole, get the hell out of there!*

Had the kid had second thoughts about letting her into the unit? Had he left and called the cops? No, he'd only been gone a few minutes. The cops couldn't have arrived so quickly. Maybe he'd pressed an emergency button under the counter as they spoke in the office. Unlikely, but possible.

She heard banging on the back door. "Cole!"

She shot a frantic look at Wragg's desk. Her instinct was to grab every piece of paper, but Warren's admonition rang in her head. She hadn't yet committed a crime—not much of one, anyway—but stealing from what would soon be a crime scene would change that. She'd promised not to publish anything that would lead back to the kid. She'd take a few photos, just for herself. That would be okay.

She yanked her phone from her purse and trained it on the map next to the corkboard.

Warren banged on the door again. "Cole. I'm leaving."

She snapped photos of the map, then a few of the papers scattered on the desk. Racing from the unit, she busted through the back door where she nearly collided with Warren.

"What's going on?" she asked.

"We gotta get out of here," he said. He pulled her back and she followed him through a winding maze of low, rectangular buildings.

Cole glanced over her shoulder as they passed between two buildings. A car was parked in the front of the lot, high beams trained on the office. "Police car?" she asked.

"Yes." Warren led them past three more buildings and stopped along what appeared to be the back fence. Roughly six feet tall, it was topped with two feet of curled barbed wire.

Cole looked up, then back at the parking lot. "Don't tell me you're going to climb this."

Warren ignored her, shuffling along the fence to a spot where a solid pole connected two sheets of fencing at a ninety-degree angle. He pulled off his leather jacket and held it in his mouth, then gripped the pole and shimmied up, stopping when his head was just below the top of the fence. He steadied himself with his right hand and swung his jacket up with his left, laying it over the barbed wire.

Cole watched in astonishment as he swung his feet up and over. His legs landed on the jacket. Arms still on the pole, he pulled down hard, compressing the barbed wire. Then, pushing himself up, he slid his belly over the jacket and dropped onto the other side of the fence. "Now you."

She latched her fingers through the fence and pulled herself up. A second later, she lay face first on the jacket, pressing down into the partially-flattened barbed wire, her upper body dangling over the other side of the fence.

She tried to swing her legs around, but her pants caught on a piece of wire, ripping a small hole in them before she shook herself loose. She shimmied around and achieved a position where one of her legs was over the fence, avoiding the barbed wire. But she struggled to see a maneuver that wouldn't lead to the total destruction of her body.

Warren extended his arms. "Just fall."

She scooched forward and let herself fall sideways, then landed awkwardly into Warren's arms. He set her down, then leapt up and grabbed his jacket.

They edged along the fence, eyes on the parking lot. "If the kid called us in, they'll head back to the unit. If we were tailed…"

He didn't finish the thought. Cole's mind flashed with possibilities, but she didn't have time to piece them together because Warren was pulling her forward. They crept along the fence through the darkness a dozen paces, then a dozen more.

Warren stopped. "There." He pointed at the office window. The kid had come out from behind the counter and was speaking with a figure in a dark uniform.

They watched in silence as the kid led him through the same gate he'd taken Cole and Warren through only minutes earlier. When they disappeared behind a building, Warren said, "Now."

He took off running and she followed in a sprint across the parking lot, reaching the car.

Warren pulled out slowly, leaving the lights off. After a block, he flicked on his headlights and slammed the gas, which jolted Cole back in her seat.

In shock, she said the only thing she could think of. "Back there you said 'Tailed.' Like someone might have tailed us here. Who? How? What made you say that?"

Warren's eyes were on the rearview mirror. Cole turned. The

road behind them was black. Warren swerved suddenly, following a sign for the Garden State Parkway south.

Cole watched Warren study the rearview mirror for what felt like hours but was probably only fifteen minutes. She helped by scanning all around and using the passenger side mirror to make sure no one was following.

Having convinced herself they were all-clear she sat, eyes to the front, as they passed a road sign that read:

Philadelphia: 89 Miles

Baltimore: 190 Miles

Washington, D.C.: 227 Miles

Warren's shoulders dropped. His hands, which had been gripping the steering wheel, relaxed as well.

"Rob, why'd you say we might have been tailed?"

"Because I saw you at Antonio's, meeting with that scumbag Joey Mazzalano."

"You know him?" Cole asked.

"Only well enough to know that when a lovely lady thinks they're done hanging out with the guy, they can't know whether or not they've truly escaped."

40

Joey Mazzalano was well past tipsy. He'd started on the amaretto at four, then killed a third of a bottle of grappa before and during his meeting with Cole. He'd knocked back a triple shot of espresso before following WB's lead through the Holland Tunnel and into New Jersey, but the effects of the coffee had faded and the alcohol still coursed through his blood.

The key to driving drunk was engaging all the senses. He rolled down the car windows, letting the cold air dry his hot, sweaty skin. Over the stereo he blasted a Perry Como ballad that reminded him of his mother. He gripped the steering wheel so hard his knuckles popped.

When he saw the sign for EZ Storage, he made the right turn a little too early, bumping the curb with his right-front tire. He jerked the wheel to the left to avoid doing the same with the rear tire, causing it to skid along the face of the curb, the rubber shrieking loud enough to cut through the music. That didn't phase Mazzalano. Only one other patrol car was in the parking lot, and it belonged to WB. *His guy.*

He parked sideways across three spots near the office and poked his head in. Empty. He radioed WB. "I'm out front. You back in the stacks?"

His radio crackled, then went silent. Letting his head fall back, he looked up. Thousands of stars shone in the clear night sky, more than he usually saw from the roof of his apartment in the city. Growing dizzy, he slapped his face with both hands, then shook his head, trying to clear the haze. He considered heading back to his car to sleep it off, but WB's voice interrupted his reverie. "Boss."

Mazzalano looked at the radio quizzically, as though expecting to see WB walking out of the little electronic device. He laughed at himself and then looked up. A low gate was sliding open and WB stood there with a tall, redheaded teenager. The boy had a round face and what Mazzalano thought was a stupid haircut.

"Kid," WB said, "this is my lieutenant." WB was well trained. He knew not to identify Mazzalano by name in situations like this.

"Nice to meet you, sir," the boy said.

"That's some stupid haircut." Mazzalano barely understood he had said the insult out loud and his speech had not been particularly clear either.

"What?" the kid asked.

"Nah, nah, never mind kid. Just be glad you have any." Mazzalano ran a hand over his patchy head and nodded, then waved at the rows of storage buildings. "Let's go."

They followed the kid to the unit, Mazzalano intentionally bringing up the rear because he wanted to find his footing without them noticing. As they walked, WB explained. "Been here half an hour. Kid says two people came. White woman about forty, black guy around the same. Showed him a photo of Michael Wragg. Said the woman paid him a hundred bucks for a few minutes in the unit. The man didn't follow her in. They were gone by the time we got back here."

WB had described the events as though he didn't know who the suspects were, probably because the kid could hear. Always best to give civilians as little information as possible.

"You lost them?" Mazzalano asked. He was over-enunciating, trying to sound sober. Problem was, he couldn't tell if it was working.

"Kid led me back to the unit, which was open, and they were gone. But you're gonna want to see what's in here. It's…"

"What?" Mazzalano asked.

"Just wait."

They reached the building and walked down the hallway to unit twelve. The sliding metal door was open.

"Give us a few minutes," Mazzalano said.

The kid retreated down the hallway.

Mazzalano walked to the desk and picked up a few papers, steadying himself on the desk by leaning into it with his hip. He glanced at the map on the wall, the books, and the military arti- facts. "Damn," he said to himself. "Holy damn."

This was worse than he thought. Worse than he knew.

"You want me to bag all this up and—"

"Did they take anything?" Mazzalano asked.

"How would I know?"

Mazzalano inhaled deeply, taking in the dusty, mildewed smell, but said nothing.

"Kid said she was only here three minutes," WB said. "You think she was looking for something in particular? Or maybe they just got a tip about the location and bolted when they saw me? Anyway, you want me to call CSI, fingerprints, the whole nine? What would it be anyway, Jersey? CID?"

Mazzalano's next decision mattered, but his thinking was dull and labored. He needed another espresso. He stared at a business card on the desk, mind churning, towing his thoughts like a tugboat through mud. His next action *had* to be right, could make or break him. "You're sure they didn't make you?"

"Cougar drove past the lot, parked down the block. I watched them enter but kept my distance and called you right away. When I approached the kid, he lied at first, then took me back. When I got in there they'd already gone. By the time I got back to where they'd parked, car was gone, too. They didn't see my face. Couldn't have."

He faced WB, who stood in the doorway. "There are empty duffel bags in my trunk. Bag all of this up and throw it in my car."

"Boss?"

"Do it."

"But—"

"Do it!" Mazzalano barked. "And tell the kid you need the security footage from all the cameras they could have passed," he added. "Double check the route, too. Make sure you have the footage, and that it's erased. And tell the kid not to speak with anyone else. Give him your card. Anyone else shows up, you're his first call. Got it?"

"Got it, LT."

WB disappeared down the hall, leaving Mazzalano in the center of the unit to battle his demons. No matter how hard he tried, his mind couldn't force thoughts that would keep his head from spinning.

41

"So, how'd you come to know that piece of trash Mazzalano?"

Warren's voice startled Cole out of a deep focus. The sound of his voice was unexpected but also a relief—Cole wasn't ready to tell Warren what she'd just discovered.

He'd driven halfway to Philadelphia with a precision that impressed her. His hyper-vigilance had gotten them out of a rough spot at the storage units, but Cole knew that it was a trait that could cost a man a lot personally.

During the drive, he'd seemed distant, deep in his own thoughts, so she'd used the time to write an email to Martin Goldberg, an old acquaintance from her days in D.C. Cole and Goldberg had interned together twenty years earlier and he'd since become one of the most influential lobbyists on K Street. She was fairly certain he'd take the meeting she'd requested for the following morning. Next, she'd studied the photos and taken notes on everything she'd seen in the storage unit. The ones of the desk hadn't yielded much of interest—receipts, shipping orders, and a few handwritten notes that didn't make any sense. But the photo of the map, and its implications, had shaken her. So much so that she wasn't sure how to share it with Warren. So she was happy to answer his question while she back-burnered the reveal.

"Met him at a dinner at Antonio's," she said. "I'd gotten an interview with a crusty old guy named Mikey Patisi, who'd just beaten a parole violation charge."

"I know that guy," Warren said. "He owns that restaurant, right?"

"He co-owns it, yes." Cole turned her notebook to a blank page. "He'd served a few years on a drug charge way back."

"Took the fall for his business partner I'm guessing," Warren added.

"Probably," Cole agreed. "This time he'd been accused of 'associating with known criminals.' He'd hosted a dinner that involved some shady figures. Defense got him off on first amendment grounds, believe it or not."

"Not uncommon." Warren checked his mirrors and changed lanes.

"He was in a celebratory mood and invited me to a party at the restaurant. Hoped I'd write a story about him triumphantly beating the case. I guess my natural inclination is to side with the accused, and I thought Mikey was an old restaurateur who shouldn't be judged for who shows up to eat in his restaurant. Anyway, Mazzalano was at that party."

"A cop in a mob restaurant?"

Cole nodded. "This was maybe ten years ago. Right when I moved to the city. I was green. I had no clue how reporting actually worked in a city like New York. It's... well... different than they taught us in J-School."

"It's the same with being a cop." Warren shook his head. "What you learn from the page is not always what you see on the streets."

"I bet." Cole adjusted the heater, pointing it towards her knees.

"It's the opposite for journalists, right?" Warren kept his head facing the road, but eyed Cole.

She read the levity in Warren's delivery and did the math in her head. "So what you learn on the page isn't always what's happening in the real world? Is that an insult to my profession?"

"I'm sorry." Warren laughed. "Old habits die hard."

Cole rolled her eyes but couldn't stop herself from giggling. She liked hearing Warren laugh. She could tell that he needed it. She needed it, too.

"Anyway, back to Mazzalano," Warren said.

"Right," Cole continued. "Mazzalano was at the dinner, completely sauced. He gave me his number. Things kinda went from there."

Warren's face was pinched, like he was searching for the right words. "How much do you know about him?"

"He's a sleazeball, if that's what you're getting at. But I can take care of myself."

"He hit on you?" Warren asked. "I mean, I assume so, but—"

"You think he's the first male source to hit on me, trying to trade a scoop for sex?"

"You comfortable using your sex appeal for a story?"

"Screw you." She glared at him, but his eyes were back on the mirrors. "I always had a policy: I let men know I was happily married, completely off limits. If they wanted to embarrass themselves by leaking me info in hopes they could win me over, that was on them. Women get accused of using our sex appeal when most of the time we don't need to bother. You have any idea how dumb guys like Mazzalano are? He stumbles through the world, led by his Amaretto-soaked libido. I just sit back at a safe distance while taking notes as I watch the train wreck."

"I guess that's one way to navigate the ethical gray area," Warren said, "while also getting the job done."

"Let's not tit for tat go pointing out each other's gray areas," Cole said with warning in her voice.

"You're right," Warren agreed.

"Like I said, I can take care of myself." Cole was defensive about her relationship with Mazzalano, and she didn't like it. But she'd always felt she could control him, and he'd always delivered. The scoops she'd gotten from him led to at least twenty percent of the stories that had made what was once her career. Lately, his behavior had escalated from creepy to downright abusive, and it was getting hard to reconcile her need for information with self-respect. "Why should *you* care? What's all this focus on Mazzalano when he's obviously in our rear-view at this point."

Warren slowed, allowing a car to pass on the left, then broke a long silence. "Mazzalano raped a friend of mine."

The news stopped Cole's breath. Warren's face was hard, eyes straight ahead. He wasn't the kind of guy who'd lie or exaggerate, but still, she had a hard time believing it. "That bastard. That's awful. Why didn't you tell me first thing? Talk about burying the lead…" Cole realized with the last statement, she'd made the story about herself and quickly pivoted. "Oh God, Warren. I'm sorry for your friend."

"Yeah." Warren bit his lower lip.

His expression gave Cole the thought that if Joey Mazzalano had been near, restrained in the back of a patrol car or not, given the opportunity Warren would beat the living daylights out of him just as he had the last degenerate that he'd been in contact with.

"Do you mind if I ask who?" Cole's voice was solemn. "Or what happened?"

"Off the record?" Warren asked.

"Absolutely," Cole agreed. "Off the record, of course."

"I can give you some of the details but this is so far off the damn record you need to erase your memory when I'm done telling you." He shot her a look to let her know he was dead serious. "I'm talking *Men in Black*, neuralyzer-level forgetting. It's *not* my story to tell, but you need to know who you're dealing with."

Cole nodded slowly. "Got it. Like I said, off the record, of course."

"Colleague of mine—she'd worked under Mazzalano who'd been a captain at the time. One night they were working late, going over photos or something, and he came up behind her while she was standing at a desk."

"Don't finish. I don't want to hear it."

"I think you *need* to hear it, Cole. You need to stay away from that guy."

Cole closed her eyes.

Dozens of interactions with Mazzalano ran through her mind. She'd always been careful to meet him in public places, telling herself that made it safe. For her, it *had*. But she'd also let his sleazy advances go because she could handle them. Now, she pictured all the women who couldn't. Those who worked under him, those with less power than her. She felt a knot grow in her stomach, wracked with a wave of shame. All those times she'd just played along with his leering, grabby pig routine, ignoring it because of what she could get from him…and all those women who didn't have the luxury of doing that. "How did she handle it?" Cole asked. "Did she report it or…"

"Asked her the same question because I could never figure out why he was still working after that. I couldn't get her to elaborate.

She didn't want to talk about it and didn't want word to get out. She told me she'd 'swept it under the rug.' And doing so was what was best for her life. She wanted to move forward." He shrugged. "Not like her to be vague about stuff. You gotta understand, the woman's a badass. I don't know the details, but if she says it happened, it happened. And if she knew she couldn't get justice on it…" He trailed off, shaking his head.

"What?"

"Means he's protected. Plus, way she told it, it was only one of his *many* crimes."

"I got the sense he was corrupt, but he's also a fool." Cole shook her head. "I thought he was too stupid to do much harm."

"Don't be naive, Cole. 'Corrupt' is looking the other way for a buddy's DUI, or accepting a pair of Jay-Z tickets from a store owner for looking out for him. Mazzalano occupies a space somewhere between common thug and straight-up psychopath. You're right that he's a fool, and fools usually get caught. But they can do a lot of damage before that happens."

"Right." Cole sunk in her seat, feeling like, between herself and Mazzalano, she was the one who'd been the greater fool.

They rode in silence, occasionally passing under an overpass or flashing billboard, but the road ahead was dark except for the taillights of a single car far in the distance.

She couldn't think about Mazzalano anymore, and wasn't ready to share the information from the map with Warren. She needed to know for sure that she could trust him. His story about his friend who'd suffered an attack at the hands of Mazzalano had moved her in that direction. Acting on instinct over thought, she found herself about to share something personal that had been weighing on her. "You know much about military records? Military communications?"

Warren glanced over, nodded, but didn't say anything.

"It's something I didn't tell you. Michael Wragg used my nickname. Monkey Tree."

"I heard him."

"But what you didn't know is that *only* Matt called me that." Saying his name brought tears to her eyes. "And not in front of people. I was stupid for letting it lure me, but, when he put it in the email… and Matt and I used to email all the time."

"I get it." Warren said. "You don't need to apologize for anything."

Cole took a deep breath and continued. "What I mean is, we didn't write actual pen and paper letters. Could Wragg have gotten access to military email servers or something?"

"Possible. But do you think he was capable of sophisticated hacking?"

"No," Cole said. "But that means he had partners."

Warren nodded.

"I had no connection to Wragg before I wrote that story. Within a day, he'd found the one thing that would get me to show up and meet him. That nickname. I just…" Cole trailed off.

"Like I said," Warren repeated, "you don't need to apologize for anything."

Cole went quiet. There wasn't anything else to say.

42

Warren glanced at Cole, watching shadow and light dance on her face as they passed under an overpass. At this point in their relationship he still couldn't read her.

He worried whether he'd done the right thing—telling Cole about what Mazzalano had done to Gabby—but ultimately he was glad he'd told her. He was also glad he'd kept Gabby's name out of it. Gabby was JTTF now, and wouldn't have liked finding out Warren had shared information about her to a journalist.

Gabby had shared it with him in a moment of vulnerability. When the OCCB was dissolved in 2016, Gabby did a bit with the Patrol Borough South when they gobbled up OCCB's organized crime cases. She thought she'd be involved with bringing down what was left of the mob. Gabby had been Warren's training officer in Brooklyn a few years before, and he'd respected her deeply. Two months after leaving the OCCB, she was back. No explanation. Just said, 'It didn't work out.' Later she'd shared with him what had happened.

At first Warren didn't know why she'd shared it with him. She had explained that she wasn't looking for pity or support—what she had wanted was someone safe to talk with. At the time she'd told him, *'saying it out loud makes me certain the whole thing was real.'* She'd explained that it made the feelings she had been having make sense. With no one to talk with about it she'd been suffering a type of ambient anxiety she had no way of calming because it had no source. She had told him that she felt that this *ambient anxiety* was something she thought she had seen in Warren too. She wasn't wrong.

Warren's mind wandered back to the present and he looked over at Cole, who appeared to be similarly lost in thought. Asking questions about her dead husband couldn't have been easy for her. But Warren felt that there was something she was keeping from him. She wasn't sharing everything she knew, and he needed to gain her trust to find out what that was.

"I don't know what it's like to lose a spouse, not the way you did. I can't imagine what you've been through." Warren took a deep breath. "But, I'm barely holding it together and all I'm losing is my marriage."

"Why are you separating?" Cole's voice sounded concerned.

"My drinking. Basically, I drove her away." He shook his head. "I'm straightened out now and fine, better than fine. But none of that matters anymore. I'm too late now, she's seeing someone."

"Who?" Cole asked.

"Dunno." Warren shrugged.

"How do you know then?" Before Warren could answer, she continued. "Never mind, I know. You just know, right? I would have known if Matt was, well..." She drifted off and the car held a weighted silence.

Sensing the tension, Warren changed the subject. "What's your background?"

"What do you mean?" Cole asked.

"Did you always live in New York City?"

"Nah. Moved around a bit. Raised in the city, though. College in Florida, year in D.C., then after I got married we were transferred from base to base. We were constantly moving." Cole's voice seemed more relaxed now. "You?"

"Bay Area. Oakland. Scholarship to study criminal justice at John Jay, then 9/11 happened and I joined the Marines. To be honest, I was flunking half my classes and the scholarship was about to go away. But I *loved* the city. And I met Sarah there."

He'd wondered about Cole's background since they met. "Your parents? They New Yorkers, too?"

Cole eyed him. "Mazzalano had a way of asking me that, you

know. The line from *The Sopranos*"—she switched to a bad Tony Soprano impersonation—"'*What part of The Boot you from, hon?*'"

Warren chuckled. "So you're Italian?"

"Mom's parents were. Dad's parents, my grandparents, were German Jews who escaped in 1938. Albert and Avigail Kohlberg."

"Kohlberg, not Cole, huh? Lemme guess. They come through Ellis Island? They changed their name?"

"Nah, I hear a lot of people's names got lost in translation there, but this was a business decision. Grandparents had been married only a year and my grandfather had taken over his father's bookstore when the *Kristallnacht* happened."

"Damn."

"They were lucky to get out. Kohl, with a 'K' was a German name, maybe French-German. At some point the 'Berg' was added, so he figured he'd drop the Berg, but he didn't want to take a German word as his name. So he went with Cole, with a 'C.' He figured he could be whoever he wanted in America. He told me before he died that he regretted it. Wished he'd kept the name."

"Maybe you'll change it," Warren suggested.

"Sounds like a lot of paperwork."

"Not more than moving to America would be." Warren shot her a don't-be-so-lazy side glance. "So, your parents consist of an Italian woman and a Jewish man. Would that have been an issue for your parents? I mean for your grandparents or their community, a Jewish guy marrying an Italian woman?"

"I don't really know. Not a huge thing, I don't think. Mom's parents were lapsed Catholics, and my mom wasn't practicing. Might have been a bigger issue if she was. I mean, it was the seventies by then. Bigger issue was the Brooklyn versus Lower Manhattan thing."

"The Italian thing, that why Mazzalano leaked to you?" Warren asked.

"To me he was a source. A sleazeball of a source, but just a source. I don't know what I was to him. For all the crap journalists get these days, I don't think people realize just how much we have to put up with."

Warren checked the gas gauge. Just over half a tank. "I wanna stop soon."

Cole leaned over and checked the gauge. "We have like two-thirds of a tank left."

"Had a run-in with a cop in Nevada once that started when I ran out of gas. Don't like falling below half, especially in this gas guzzler. Half a tank in this thing won't take us a hundred miles."

"Still, we can probably wait. What was the run-in about?"

"Don't want to talk about it."

He'd been on his way to college, with a stopover in Las Vegas. A city kid who didn't quite comprehend how far apart gas stations can be in the vast empty spaces of the West. He'd run out of fuel on Route 15, seventy miles outside of Vegas, and had been stranded before a highway patrol officer rolled up and approached him—gun *drawn*. He'd stood in the blazing sun for twenty minutes while the cop checked and double-checked his ID. Finally, he'd been cleared and dropped at the nearest gas station. Before driving off, the highway patrol officer offered a weak apology. "You understand, kid, we don't get a lot like you out this way. You look like a guy wanted for a robbery 'round here."

For the first week afterwards he'd been pissed at the world. Later, the interaction had crystallized Warren's desire to become a cop himself. As his dad always told him, *don't complain about the world, fix it*.

"Tell me this," Cole said, "why D.C.? I quit my job and need to write, need to track this story. But you seem like a by-the-book guy."

"Try to be."

"Driving a crazy reporter lady to D.C. isn't exactly by the book."

"I guess not." He opened his mouth, but nothing came out. He was still in the Nevada desert all those years ago.

"That's it?" she asked.

Warren chuckled. "I'm a man of few words."

"I'm not, so lemme guess." She eyed him for permission and he nodded, cracking a slight smile. Cole prided herself on being able to read people, but he had a pretty good poker face. "I was thinking about it when you wouldn't come into Wragg's storage unit. You believe in the law. Despite the fact that I screwed you, my paper screwed you, then the department screwed you, you respect the law. Am I right so far?"

Warren gripped the steering wheel tight, then relaxed his

176

hands. She was right, but he wouldn't admit it. He offered a non-committal sideways nod.

"My guess is, like most cops, you figured out pretty quick that the world isn't split into good guys and bad guys. There's a lot more gray area than you used to think, than you'd *like* to think." Matt said that about the Marines, too. "Take your interaction with that bastard whose face you smashed. If we took a poll, half the people in New York City would say you should have blown that guy's head off. No trial. Just execution. Instead, you gotta cuff him, sit back, and chauffeur him to jail as he makes those disgusting comments about your daughter. Now he's eating meals paid for with your tax dollars. Same time, you lost it for *five seconds* and a nosy reporter—namely, me—wrecks your career. My hunch is, despite all that, you're still a believer. You gotta believe that the department is good, the Marines are good, even though you see the bad."

A quick glance at the speedometer showed they were going nearly ninety now. He'd lost track of his speed and eased off the gas. Something in what Cole said was right, but something was also way off. He couldn't put it into words, though. "Interesting theory."

"That's it?" Cole wore a squint that said it wasn't.

The gas gauge needle now stood nearly flush with the halfway line. A sign indicated gas and food at the next exit.

"That's *not* it," Warren said. "I'm just... I'm trying to figure out how to say it." He took the exit and slowed, following a round-about to a brightly-lit gas station. "It's not that I *have* to believe, despite all that I see. I *do* believe. Yeah, I've had a lot of disillusionment. But this system—screwed up though it is—is literally the best thing we've got." A sigh leaked out of him, like a tire going flat, and he turned into the station. "I figure, if you see a problem, you're gonna do something—quit, complain, or try to fix it. I try to play by the rules and bend those that don't."

"So, you're the *fix it* type then?"

"I guess so." Warren shrugged. "I'm not one to complain and even if I wanted to, I can't quit. I have a little girl."

"That's a good reason to keep pushing."

For Warren, that was one of the *only* reasons to keep pushing. "We need gas. Was hoping we'd make Philly on one tank, but..."

"I could use coffee anyway."

"Real coffee, or a liquid candy bar?" Warren hoped the joke would break the tension.

"Call it whatever you want. There's something I need to tell you, but I will be needing sugar first.

43

Cole waited in line to pay for snacks, watching through the window as Warren filled the tank.

But this system—screwed up though it is—is literally the best thing we've got. His words echoed in her mind. He'd been talking about the thin blue line between violent criminals and their potential victims, a line she'd wanted to believe somehow existed *a priori*. What Warren meant was that it had to be drawn every day, by flawed individuals. She'd always considered journalism at its best to be another kind of line, a line that connected governments, corporations, and other institutions to the people they claimed to serve. Lately, sifting through the sea of digital detritus that made up the modern information landscape made her wonder whether this was still true.

Returning to the car, she found Warren standing at the open trunk, mixing a white powder into a large bottle of water.

"I got you a protein bar," she said. "And nuts."

He held up the milky-looking drink. "Got protein. Jane, don't you know those bars are just candy."

"Everything is candy according to you. If you don't eat candy, what's left?"

He answered by downing the quart of protein drink in four impressive chugs.

He slid into the driver's seat. Cole got in and they pulled to the side of the station, where a single light flickered between dented bathroom doors. She pulled up the photo of the map and adjusted the contrast on her phone to make it more readable. Warren killed the engine and she handed it to him.

He gave it a glance and handed it back. "Wondered when you were gonna tell me what you saw in there."

"I almost didn't."

Warren stared, expressionless, inviting her to explain.

"You gotta understand about reporters." Cole shifted in her seat to face him. "We scramble for scraps of info. It's our business. I just walked into the lair of a man who may be the orchestrator of a major serial killing, or a terrorist attack. It's not in my nature to share."

"Especially since, you know, technically, you were breaking and entering." Warren grabbed the food bag and pulled out a pack of almonds. "Talk me through what you saw. We'll get to the map later." He popped a few almonds in his mouth and smiled. "Thanks for these. Only thing I'd eat from that joint."

"I'm just sorry they didn't have any in powder form for you."

"Very funny."

"So, there were books, military artifacts, papers. No computer. Probably planned, or maybe *helped* plan, the Ambani killing from there, then got lazy and began working from home. Or maybe he worked on a laptop from the storage unit that he took with him. Look again."

She held up the map. Warren squinted at the screen. "What am I looking at?"

"World map, zoomed all the way out."

The map had been large, maybe five feet wide by three feet high. The individual states in the U.S. portion were colored in pale shades of yellow, orange, and light brown, as were the Canadian provinces and other countries. Cole zoomed in on the east coast of the United States, then pointed at a tiny silver pin in the map, stuck into the little black dot that marked "New York City." Next, she scrolled down the east coast slowly, reaching another pin on the black dot for "Washington, D.C."

"See what I'm getting at?" she asked.

Warren took the phone. His cop instincts had taken over. He worked through the map methodically, zooming out to get a wide view until he found a pin, then zooming in until he could read the name of the city. From Washington D.C. he scrolled further south to a pin in Miami. From Miami, he scrolled far west to a pin in Los Angeles, then north to San Francisco and back east to Las Vegas.

"Five U.S. cities." He didn't look up.

He continued scrolling, first all the way down through South America, where there were no pins, then east to the bottom of the African continent. Methodically, he zig-zagged north through Africa, hunched over the small screen.

Cole had stuck every pin to her memory while in the unit, but she followed along with him.

Finding no pins in Africa, he scrolled north into Europe to pins in Paris and London. Next, he moved slowly east through Asia. Cole stopped him when he landed on the only pin on that continent: Tokyo.

He regarded her, his face lit in flashes by a flickering light on the side of the gas station. His eyes were wide, his mouth half open.

"Nine pins," Cole said. "Nine cities." She put her phone in her hip purse. "New York, D.C., Miami, LA, San Francisco, Vegas, Paris, London, Tokyo. Nine cities. Nine rifles."

Recognition registered on Warren's face.

"What is it?" Cole asked anxiously.

"Read that mission statement again." Warren leaned over to look at Cole's phone.

Cole read it from her notes app: "An international brotherhood, united by General Ki for a singular mission: to end the technological oppression, to restore the sovereignty of the individual, to birth a new era of freedom."

"*International,*" Warren repeated. "An *international* brotherhood."

"I looked up 'General Ki,' by the way. Top hit was an aikido school in Cedar Rapids. Not a mention of anything resembling a real guy anywhere online."

"Probably a code name known only to a handful of these guys," Warren said. "In my mind, I was thinking of this as a bunch of guys like Wragg. Older, ex-military, angry with the changes brought by social media, feeling left behind by capitalism and tech. Not the kind of guys with access to Paris and London, and definitely not Tokyo."

"So?"

"I don't know. Could be bigger than we thought."

Cole watched Warren. The look on his face betrayed a mind racing with the implications. She'd already decided what they had to do next, but sharing it went against her instinct, which was to guard information until she could write about it.

Cole briefly tensed when a man appeared under the flickering light by the bathrooms, fumbling with a key attached to a long wooden stick. Warren watched him carefully until he disappeared into the bathroom.

Finally, she broke the long silence. "We need to get this map out there. If it means what we think it means…"

Warren shook his head. "Mazzalano. You met with him tonight. My guess is he had you tailed. It's the only way that guy could have shown up right after us. Followed us from Little Italy into Jersey, then hung back to see what we were doing at the storage unit. If Mazzalano had you tailed, it means he now knows about the stuff in storage. If that's the case, he'll be on TV by tomorrow morning taking credit for finding Wragg's dungeon."

"But if he's corrupt—"

"There's no '*if,*' Jane. Mazzalano *is* corrupt, but he's also power hungry. Corrupt cops do all sorts of regular police work, too. You said yourself he likes to be in the know. If Mazzalano has the map, he'll use it to his own advantage, sure, but that will mean taking credit for it within the department."

Cole popped the cap off her iced coffee. "So you're saying we don't release the map?"

"Not yet."

By two in the morning, Cole had paid cash for a room with two double beds in a motel ten miles from D.C. They'd stopped at a 24-hour Wal-Mart and grabbed a few items each, and she stuffed the duffel bag and clothes into a drawer, then flopped onto one of the beds, which was so springy it nearly bounced her onto the floor. Warren unpacked clothes and arranged his water and protein powder by the sink.

"Be careful," Cole said. "The beds are crazy. Like all springs and no actual mattress materials. Why are you unpacking?"

"It's just what I do. I like to keep things in order."

He sat on his bed, detached the prosthetic lower portion of his right leg, and stashed it under a pillow.

"You sleep with it?" Cole asked.

"In case we need to get out of here in a hurry."

"You snore?"

"Not sure," he said. "Been sleeping alone a long time."

"Matt snored sometimes," she said, mostly to herself. She'd been annoyed by it while he was alive, but would give anything for one more night of his snoring.

Warren grunted something inaudible and went about his evening routine, which was much longer than Coles. Her's consisted of rubbing soap over her face then rinsing it off before rubbing toothpaste over her mouth and rinsing it off.

When Warren finally offed the lights and Cole closed her eyes, the videos of the Meyers shooting appeared immediately, as though they'd been playing in the back of her mind the whole night. If it was true that the shooter hadn't been on the roof of the Watergate, he must have been on one of the surrounding buildings. This matched the M.O. of the Ambani killing. Plus, the picture of Wragg's computer screen indicated that Meyers—"The Silver Squirrel"—had been the next target. She felt certain the murders were connected. But she'd been wrong about things she'd been certain of before. "Rob, how confident are you we're on the right path? I mean, what if we're wrong?"

He didn't reply.

"Rob?"

She listened closely. His breathing had changed. Longer, slower, more audible breaths. He was already asleep. At least he wasn't snoring.

She tried to relax into sleep, but Warren's breath and her swirl of thoughts made drifting off even more difficult than usual.

44

Thursday

Warren sat up in bed and looked around the room. Cole was already wide awake, leaning against the headboard, eyes on her phone. She had a look on her face he was coming to recognize. Her eyes wider, her lips pursed. The look implied laser focus. "Cole, what is it?"

"Threads is saying the murder of former VP Alvin Meyers has been solved."

He rubbed his eyes. "Read me what you're seeing."

"It's a thread of about six posts. Hold on."

Warren turned in the bed, propping himself with one arm to face her as she scrolled.

"Here, I'll read them," she offered. "'According to multiple sources within the Metropolitan Police Department, a gunman believed to have killed former Vice President Alvin Meyers was found dead on the roof of the Virginia Suites Hotel in Roslyn, Virginia. The shooter, yet to be identified, was spotted when a news helicopter passed over the hotel on its way to the Watergate, which sits across the Potomac River from the hotel where the body was found.'"

Warren wanted to hear the rest, but couldn't get past a key

detail. "Wait, it said the shooter was on the roof of a hotel *across the river?* How far is that?"

"The story addresses that. Lemme keep reading. 'The body of the alleged gunman was found next to a sniper rifle, and multiple sources say the shot—approximately one mile as the crow flies— would have been difficult but not impossible. According to one source with knowledge of the situation, *A good sniper can make that shot. Wind was low, and he had a favorable angle. It's not easy, but it's a long way from impossible.'* Police sources believe the shooter may have rented a room in the hotel and found a way to access the roof. Multiple sources believe the suspected shooter may have been killed by a self-inflicted gunshot.'" Cole let out a long sigh. "The reporter goes on to say that details are emerging, she'll update the original thread, blah, blah, blah."

Warren watched her scroll. Something about the report didn't sound right and, judging by Cole's concerned frown, she agreed. "Looking for more information?" he asked.

"Always."

"Here's the thing: I don't buy it."

Cole set down her phone. "Me neither. But it *sounds* like good reporting."

"Why take out a guy from a mile away if you're just gonna kill yourself?"

Cole frowned, but said nothing.

"If you're going to kill yourself right afterwards," Warren continued, "why not walk right up to him on his way into the Watergate? The shot would be a whole hell of a lot easier."

"Maybe he hadn't planned to kill himself but someone came to the roof and he thought he'd been caught."

"Possibly." Warren wasn't convinced, and something else didn't sit right, but he couldn't articulate it.

Cole stopped scrolling and locked eyes with him. "People online are debating whether the shot was possible."

Warren reached under the pillow for his prosthetic, attached it, then paced the room, stopping every few seconds to shake out his right leg. It always took a few minutes to get comfortable. "That was my first thought. But if the reporter is right and it *was* a mile, it's possible. I'd want to look at the angle and check the exact wind conditions, but with a good weapon—a custom fifty-cal, for example—and a great shooter, a mile is doable."

"They're also debating motive, they're even arguing about whether the reporter's Threads account was hacked."

Eyes still fixed on her phone, Cole kicked off her blankets and sat cross-legged. Warren imagined she'd done a lot of kicking through the night because her bedding was in total disarray. Warren had woken up—same as every day—having slept in total stillness, his sheets looking like the maids had visited and remade the bed over the top of him.

"Do they think the report is fake?" Warren asked.

"I don't know her, but it's a verified account." Cole scrolled. "I'm guessing it's real and…wait…another news organization just confirmed it."

"Who?" Warren asked.

"CNN, and now Fox News. Plus…yeah everyone is saying it now."

"Secret Service? FBI? They'll be all over this case and I'd trust them more than some unnamed source."

"Right." Cole scrolled for another minute, then said, "They're not even 'no-commenting.' Metro police, too. Radio silence from all official sources. But everyone else is confirming."

"Probably the same two damn sources in every one of those reports," Warren said. "Just because everyone is saying it doesn't mean it's true."

She gave him a look.

"I'm not saying they're making it up, but haven't we seen enough Threads and X and Facebook stories go viral that turned out to be total crap? Isn't that enough to remind everyone to chill a minute."

"If this many sources are saying it, though…"

"I'm not saying the journalists are lying." Warren was growing heated. "I'm saying maybe the sources are *wrong*."

"Wrong about a dead guy on the roof?" Cole asked.

"I'm sure there *was* a dead guy on the roof, it's just…" He didn't know how to finish the sentence. His gut was wrong about a third of the time. Maybe this was one of those times, but he doubted it. "Your guy email you back?"

"Yes. Meeting at his place, K Street lobbying firm at eight."

"What's his name?"

"Martin Goldberg. Me and my cohort of interns used to call him Goldilocks because he had long blond hair—like eighties-

186

metal-band hair—except he was no rock star. We were interns together twenty years ago. Kinda dorky and the last guy I'd have picked to become one of the most powerful lobbyists in the city. They say D.C. runs on information. Figured he'd have some."

Warren checked his watch. 7 a.m. "Then let's go."

45

Cole sat between Warren and a row of large windows that looked down on Farragut Square. They were sitting in a sleek lobby and the small park below was bustling with activity, despite the freezing weather. Watching people hurry to work, Cole discreetly pressed the back of her hand against the cold glass, as if she were checking for a fever at the White House, which was framed against a light gray sky four blocks to the north. She remembered this weather from her one year in D.C.—"pre-snow" they'd called it. In the center of the park, a statue sat atop a stone pillar. She assumed the bronze man was the "Farragut" for whom the square was named, though she didn't know who he'd been.

"Damn the torpedoes!" Warren said. "Full speed ahead."

His voice startled her. "Huh?"

He took a sip from a mug engraved with the logo of *Goldberg & Plotts Government Relations*. "The Battle of Mobile Bay during the Civil War." He pointed at the statue. "That's David Farragut, first admiral of the U.S. Navy. That was his famous line at the Battle of Mobile Bay."

Cole searched her memory, but came up empty. "Interesting. Didn't know that."

"No one knows whether he said *exactly* that. You newspaper folks got stuff wrong even back then. Historians now think he may have said something like, 'Damn the torpedoes. Four bells.' Not as catchy because no one knows what 'four bells' means."

"What *does* 'four bells' mean?" she asked.

"It means *full speed ahead*." It was the familiar voice of Marty Goldberg, who'd bellowed out an answer before Warren had the chance to.

Goldilocks looked nothing like the awkward twenty-something she remembered. His hair was dyed dark brown and cut short, and instead of a wrinkled, off-the-rack suit hanging loosely from a lanky body, a slim-fitting navy suit displayed a muscular physique. He was surprisingly handsome.

"They rang four bells," he continued, "to signal the engine room to give the boat full power as they navigated through a field of mines, which back then they called 'torpedos.' Crucial battle of the Civil War." He held out a hand to Warren.

Shaking it, Warren said, "You a war historian?"

Goldberg chuckled. "Nah. Memorized that to impress clients." He waved an arm in a sweeping gesture toward Farragut Square. "It comes up a lot."

Turning his attention from Warren, he took in Cole—face, then a full body scan, then back to her face. "Good to see you, Jane. You look amazing."

"You too, Goldilocks," she said. Cole accepted a hug that began to last longer than she felt was comfortable. "And, thanks." Cole gave him a pat on the back and pulled back to cut things off. When they released she'd realized why the hug had lasted longer than she'd anticipated then braced for the inevitable condolence.

"I was so sorry to hear about Matt."

She nodded. "Thank you." She could feel him search for her eyes but she didn't look for his. She kept her focus out the window on the White House.

"Quite a view, right? It's even more impressive in my office." Goldberg waved them forward.

Cole and Warren followed Goldberg to his corner office and sat across from him at a large desk. His back was to the window and, from her seat, Cole had a direct line of sight to the White House.

"You weren't kidding about the view," Warren said.

Goldberg nodded, then crossed his right leg over his left before turning to Cole. "They don't call me that anymore, by the way.

Goldilocks, I mean." He said it with a forced casualness, like he wanted her to think it was no big deal.

"Now that you've gone brunet," Cole said, "the name no longer works for you."

"Phoniest town in America. Gotta look the part. But you get a pass on old nicknames." He smiled warmly. "What can I do for you? I've got a busy morning ahead."

"Right." Cole cleared her throat. "We're looking into the murder of the former V.P. Did you know Meyers?"

"I didn't. Had drinks at the Watergate last week, though. Got an invite to the fundraiser he was at when...well...I could have been there." He looked down and shook his head. "I spoke with him on the phone a couple times for various projects. But no, I didn't know him outside of business dealings."

"What kind of projects?" Cole asked, trying to sound disinterested.

Goldberg smiled. "Seriously, Cole, that's how you're going to come at me? Hoping I'll casually drop something to *The New York Sun*? I'm sure you think I've sold out, but at least respect the fact that I'm *good* at it."

Cole returned his grin. It was nice to talk with someone who knew the game. "Too big time for me, huh? Got your name on the coffee mugs and everything. Anyway, I'm freelance now. I quit *The Sun*."

Goldberg turned to Warren. "You a reporter, too?"

"Research assistant," Cole said quickly.

Warren crossed his arms over his chest.

Goldberg studied Warren's powerful physique, and Cole wished she'd picked a different lie. "A research assistant, huh?" Cole got the feeling he wouldn't be doing her the courtesy of pretending to believe it.

She scooched to the edge of the chair, placing her hands on the desk. "Look, Marty, I'm here on the Meyers murder. You got anything on that? Anywhere you can point me?"

"Didn't you hear?" Goldberg said. "Looks like that murder was solved."

"The dead guy on the roof?" Cole asked.

"So you *did* hear."

"I heard, but..." She trailed off, eyebrows raised, inviting him to share her skepticism.

Goldberg seemed to be considering, then he leaned across the desk so their faces were only a couple feet apart. "Don't know if this is out there yet," he whispered conspiratorially, "but I'm hearing it was an extremist group. Meyers was Target-1 of young, online, disillusioned types, both on the right *and* the left. He sat on the boards of an oil company, a bank, and a private prison company. If you could kill a guy with social media memes, Meyers would have been dead years ago. "

"I know all that." Cole shook her head tightly. "But…"

"They *hated* him," Goldberg continued. "Turned him into the symbol for everything wrong with American politics. Not a shock some nutjob went too far." He leaned back in his chair, lacing his fingers together behind his head. "Ask me, the far left and far right have gone—and I mean this literally—totally insane because of social media. Leaves guys like me—the guys who do the deals that actually keep this country running—wondering what the hell is going on in the world."

"Where are you getting that?" Cole asked.

"Can't say."

"Can't or *won't?*" Warren asked.

"I will not be answering that question either." He held up a single finger when his phone vibrated on his desk. "Hold on." He worked briefly, then passed the phone to Cole, who leaned toward Warren so he could read with her.

"Story dropped ten minutes ago," Goldberg said. "They dug through the killer's old social media posts."

According to the report, the shooter had been identified as Baker Johnston, a former school teacher who'd been fired for refusing to make his students recite the Pledge of Allegiance in class. Screenshots of his social media accounts showed him ripping Meyers and other politicians of both parties for caving to corporate interests.

"From Threads it'll filter up to the networks," Goldberg said. "Looks like you and your *research assistant*"—he shot Warren a quick look—"wasted a trip to D.C."

Cole glanced at Warren, wondering whether he believed the article, but his face was expressionless. "Can you connect me with anyone on Meyers' staff?" she asked.

Still leaning back in his chair, Goldberg closed his eyes, then opened them. "No, but it just occurred to me why you're here. Raj Ambani. You think there's a connection, right?"

"We…" Cole faltered.

"Couple days after you get involved in the Ambani and Michael Wragg thing you show up in D.C? I feel a little insulted. Did you always think I was stupid—a dumb blonde?"

She regained her composure. "It's my job to think there might be a connection, but it's just a hunch. Sounds like the guy who killed Meyers was a lone nut." She didn't believe the loner theory, but it wasn't a good idea to press Goldberg. Or to let him know how much information they already had.

The view of the White House from her seat was no accident. Marty Goldberg set up his office to impress and intimidate guests —to show them he was connected, had power in this town, and that they were out of their league.

She shifted gears. "I wonder if you can help with something else."

"Will if I can."

"You work with the DOD sometimes, right?"

He nodded.

"You know anyone who knows about military records, emails, how communications work from troops stationed overseas?"

"That's kinda out of left field," Goldberg said. "Never thought about it, but yeah, I'm sure I know people who know about that. Hell, I helped get votes for the ninety-billion-dollar spending bill that upgraded the communications equipment of the entire military two years ago. But what are you getting at? Something about Matt?"

He lowered his voice when he said her husband's name, trying to sound compassionate, mournful.

It unnerved her that he'd guessed what she was driving at so quickly, and there was no way she would share that Michael Wragg knew about her husband's pet name for her. "It's nothing. I lost all the emails from an old account. The one Matt would send emails to. Was hoping they were still on a server somewhere and…never mind. We've taken enough of your time."

Goldberg leaned toward them. "You guys want to know a D.C. secret?"

Cole looked at Warren, who nodded.

"Well, you know the Watergate is famous for the DNC break-in that brought Nixon down. Most people don't know, though, that Nixon was set up by the CIA."

"C'mon," Warren said.

"Seriously. Don't get me wrong, Nixon was guilty, but the only reason we *know* about it was because the CIA made it happen, leaked it. Forty-five years later and we all go to sleep at night telling ourselves the fairy tale of how two dogged reporters— Woodward and Bernstein—brought down a president."

Cole felt a knot in her stomach. Woodward and Bernstein had been heroes of hers since Journalism School. She had no idea whether Goldberg was BS'ing them, but she decided to play along. "Why are you telling us this?"

"No reason." He smiled strangely. "Cole, how about a drink tonight? I'm sorry I can't help you more on Meyers, but let me buy you a drink."

"No. I'm good," Cole said standing and gesturing toward the door to let Warren know she was ready to leave.

"One little drink and I'll tell you everything I know about D.C., and it's a lot."

"Thank you for your time," Warren's voice had a tinge of warning in it.

"I might be able to find whether emails from deceased military personnel are available somewhere. If I do, would you like me to share with you how I'd go about getting them?"

Warren moved his mouth to speak but Cole beat him to a response. "Yes," she said. "Do that, and I'll have that drink with you."

Warren frowned and shook his head.

Goldberg stood. "Consider it done. I'll text you later."

46

The first snowflakes drifted to the ground as they walked the circular path around the statue in the center of Farragut Square. Cole felt the air shift into a deeper chill and opened her phone. "It's supposed to be three inches before nightfall," she said.

"Where'd you get such a precise weather prediction?" Warren asked, his voice full of skepticism.

Cole turned her phone towards him, open to the weather app.

"Burrr…" Warren responded.

"Burrr… indeed," Cole nodded and re-holstered her phone. "Let's get somewhere warm."

They crossed the square and Cole stood in line to buy coffee while Warren secured a table in the back of the crowded café. When she joined him, Warren was in deep focus reading something on his phone. She slid one paper cup of coffee across the table and nibbled at the sugar rim she'd had the barista add to hers.

"Thanks," Warren said, but he didn't look up.

"They said they didn't have any burnt coffee. Store policy to dump it out after sixty minutes." Cole noticed a concerned look on Warren's face while he continued reading. She finished her thought quickly. "I got you a dark roast—best I could do."

"Thanks anyway. I'm sure it's fine."

"Well, what is it?"

"Text from Gabriela. Says Mazzalano is being investigated."

A combination of guilt and fear washed over Cole. "For what? I mean, which of his many crimes?"

Warren shook his head. "Looks like he's been providing police protection to dropgangs in the city."

"What the hell is a dropgang?" Cole allowed herself to breathe normally again.

"New kind of crime that's sprung up recently. If you want to buy drugs or weapons—usually drugs—you can do it using Bitcoin or other digital currencies, all anonymously online. But you have to pick up the drugs somewhere, right?"

"So, dropgangs?"

"Right." Warren took in a mouthful of coffee.

Cole laughed. "That bad huh?" He was drinking the coffee like a little boy who has to eat his peas before he gets dessert. "You don't *have* to drink it," she added.

"Gotta get the caffeine in." Warren rapped his chest with a fist as though it would help the coffee go down.

"I prefer my caffeine with pleasure."

"And by pleasure you mean sugar?"

Cole's smile broadened, but she didn't speak.

Warren kept Cole's eye with a *watch this* twinkle in his and chugged the rest of the coffee. "Anyway, dropgangs are the criminal version of Uber or TaskRabbit. Each member handles a piece of the overall transaction, then someone leaves the drugs in a location in the city—often a child is the last leg of the drop. For example, in an empty soda can in a particular bush in Central Park. It's pinged with a GPS tracker so the buyer can locate it using a smartphone. No one ever meets. And the key for the gang is that each person handles a different part of the transaction, and no one knows everything, so it's much harder to track. Almost impossible to prosecute."

"How did I not know about this?" Cole asked.

"Like I said, it's pretty new. The internet has made shopping and everything else we do anonymous and faceless. We went from forgetting the name of our local cow to forgetting who our local farmer is to forgetting who our grocer is to not really knowing where our grocery store is and now, some people might starve without access to a faceless internet entity. Do you know that thousands of cows contribute to a gallon of mass produced milk? We are so far removed from the food that we eat, why should we care who sells us our drugs and guns?"

Cole stood and walked a lap around the table, sipping her vanilla latte. "So if Mazzalano is being investigated for providing protection, he...what? What does that mean, exactly? Maybe he makes sure certain areas are unpatrolled for drops?"

"Maybe, or it's even possible he has a larger role—a more direct role."

"Like what?" Cole asked.

"Coordinating with a leader, leaking information about investigations, making sure they know in advance about busts—though busts are rare in this game. Or..." He trailed off, his forehead wrinkled.

"What?" Cole asked.

"Michael Wragg. The JTTF guys. Nah..."

Cole saw where he was going. "You think Wragg's purchase of the nine weapons could have been a dropgang thing?"

"Possibly. If I was going to spend a hundred grand on nine weapons online, I'd want them dropped in a secure location, and any buyer or seller would want extra protection for a purchase that big."

Cole agreed. Wragg had purchased nine rifles, and used one to murder Raj Ambani. But that left a major question. "If Wragg bought nine weapons and picked them up in New York City, maybe with protection from Mazzalano or someone in Mazzalano's crew, how did he distribute the other eight weapons? Assuming the nine cities on the map are all going to host murders with one of the nine rifles, he'd have to distribute those weapons somehow. So how? Another dropgang?"

"Probably not," Warren said. "Dropgangs tend to operate only within cities. Not interstate and not international. Once Wragg had all the weapons, he likely distributed them himself. Possibly through the mail. On one hand, it's riskier. On the other, if he'd paid the seller to deliver the rifles to their final destinations, and the seller had been caught, the seller then could have blown up the whole plan."

Cole considered this. It was still hard for her to believe Mazzalano provided protection for the delivery of the weapons, but it explained why he'd avoided talking about the DNA test results from Wragg's hair. Twenty-four hours earlier she'd thought of him as a creepy but harmless source, now he was something much worse. "So we have two threads here. Track the actual weapons, or investigate the killing of Meyers."

"Why not both?" Warren stood. "I'll call the two guys from JTTF, the Dark Web guys we met. You see what's happening with the Meyers investigation."

Cole gave her latte a swirl. "You weren't buying what Goldberg was selling, were you?"

"Under normal circumstances, I'd say it was possible. Dude had motive. In this case, seems like a misdirection or frame job." He waved his phone at her. "I'm gonna do my cop thing. You use your reporter magic to read through the lines of what's out there and figure out what's actually going on."

After Warren left, Cole opened Chandler Price's financial records on her phone. In New York, they'd found the payment to Michael Wragg fairly quickly, but she hadn't been back to his records since. She scanned for unusual transactions. Maybe she'd get lucky and find something that stood out, like a large payment to someone in D.C., Vegas, Miami, or another of the cities on the map.

She looked for transactions over a thousand dollars, wire transfers, suspicious purchases. Nothing struck her as out of the norm.

Price spent a lot of money, but most of it was on travel, shopping, and everyday stuff. They'd found the Wragg transaction quickly because it was unique. Chandler Price had paid Wragg for the rifles, but if his financial statements were any indicator, he hadn't paid anyone else. It was possible he wasn't aware of the entire plot. As far as Cole knew, he was out of the country. Chances were low he'd be in the U.S. any time soon.

Next, she scanned social media for news on the murder of the former VP. Suspicions were surfacing that it was connected to Raj Ambani's assassination, but they were still rumors. Nothing official. On X, there were rumors about almost everything. There were equally-credible theories connecting Meyers' assassination to the killings of John Kennedy, Robert Kennedy, Tupac Shakur, and Sharon Tate.

She studied the helicopter footage of the body on the hotel

rooftop, the body of the alleged killer. Next to his still form was a black, stick-shaped object—likely the gun—but there was no way of telling whether it matched the gun used by Wragg. Local TV news had reported that "police sources" said the shooter had "probably used a fifty-caliber rifle." That fit with the weapons they knew were out there, but was far from proof. And it wasn't clear whether the reports were based on eyewitness accounts, or just speculation that it *must have been* a fifty-caliber judging by the distance of the shot.

Additional cell phone video clips had been released, and she'd watched them all. The great thing about social media was that it was often hours ahead of the news networks, even the police response lagged the online community's understanding of what evidence was available—realtime videos and the motivations and opportunity of a suspect would be gathered, replayed, and analyzed before the police even knew a crime had been committed.

The terrible thing was that much of the "information" on the apps couldn't be trusted. Half of the clips claiming to show the shooting were fake, leading subscribers to random YouTube videos or advertisements. Many of the others didn't reveal anything new. One was a blurry five-second clip from the street below, showing people looking up after hearing screams from the rooftop. Another was from a few minutes before the shooting, according to the message that accompanied the post, and showed the guests, including the former VP, mingling at the bar. Cole saved the post to study later. It might be useful to put together a list of everyone who attended the event.

She was about to stop scrolling when she found another video. It was shot from the window of an apartment building near the Watergate and, for the first few seconds, the Potomac was visible. The videographer walked past a yellow leather couch in the fore-ground then stepped through a glass door onto a Juliette balcony, which opened up the sound and view of the cityscape.

The video zoomed in on a long, narrow boat on the river, crewed by four women. After following the boat for a few seconds, the video scanned up to a tall building with black mirrored glass. Signage on the front read *Potomac View Hotel.* The video panned up around twenty stories, then scanned to the right where a small group of birds took off in unison. A second later, faint screams rang out and the video began frenetically searching areas on the near side of the river for the source of the screaming. Cole realized the birds must have taken off in response to a gunshot. The screams were in reaction to his assassination.

She rewound a few seconds.

Just as the video hit the top of the *Potomac View Hotel*, visible for only a few seconds, Cole could see someone.

The blurry head of a person in a window was briefly visible before quickly withdrawing.

Cole rewound and watched again, this time confirming that the head retreating from the window was in sync with the birds taking flight.

She watched again, focusing on the head, the blurry face. She thought it was a man, but the shot was too blurry to be sure.

There was one thing she *was* sure of. This person was the killer.

What she didn't know was whether he was also the dead man who'd been found on the roof.

Outside, Warren pulled up the collar of his leather jacket against the snow. He dialed Norris Ubwe then walked toward the middle of the block, away from the stream of people coming in and out of the café.

Ubwe answered right away. "What?"

Ubwe was the more assertive member of the two-man crew he'd shadowed at JTTF. Back in New York, Warren had convinced Ubwe to get Chandler Price's bank records by using a threat. That information led to Michael Wragg and had cracked the case wide open. He didn't expect that the Dark Web expert would be happy to hear from him.

"It's Robert Warren. Remember me?"

"I know you, yes."

Warren paced to keep warm. "I owe you thanks, Norris. Your help led us to Michael Wragg and, well, you probably heard how that went."

After a long pause, Ubwe said, "I do not know what you are talking about." Warren's guess was that he'd studied English for years before moving to the United States because he spoke impeccable, by-the-book English with a slight Nigerian accent.

"Chandler Price?" Warren reminded him. The line was silent. Warren had screwed up. Of course Ubwe wouldn't want to confirm that he'd pulled Price's bank records. "Look," he continued, "I need your help again."

"So you say." Ubwe's tone was noncommittal.

Warren assumed that even though Wragg had accepted a wire transfer from Price, he likely would have used cash or a cryptocurrency like Bitcoin to send the other eight weapons around the world. But it was worth a shot. "Can you get me the financial records of Michael Wragg, the dude who shot Raj Ambani?"

"No." The word was clipped and firm.

"From your surveillance of the Dark Web, can you tell *where* and *how* a transaction is going to go down?"

"Sometimes."

"Can you elaborate?" Warren asked.

"Once a transaction begins, it often moves to a private chat room. In general, different pieces of a transaction are handled by different members of a crew, each digitally walled off from all the others. So it is difficult to track. Not that I would do so."

"But it's possible?" Warren asked.

"Sometimes, but it is only done for important cases."

"Are you saying the sale of rifles I witnessed was *not* one of the important ones?"

Ubwe was silent. Warren knew he wouldn't want to say anything to acknowledge their earlier interaction. Maybe Ubwe was being paranoid, or maybe someone was listening. Either way, he respected the man's caution. "So, theoretically, let's say I buy a pile of weapons on the Dark Web. I'm then routed to another person who takes the payment via Bitcoin, then another person who works with me to arrange a drop-off. Then yet another who actually does the drop. And if we assume I have an NYPD officer on the take, might such an officer, *hypothetically*, be used to protect large transactions?"

"It is possible," Ubwe replied.

"So, to be clear, a JTTF unit could—*theoretically*—have watched those transactions go down. And if they'd diligently followed leads derived from the sale, couldn't they have been able to prevent the circulation or use of those weapons? They may have prevented or still could prevent future assassinations, right? I'm just spitballing here—but having knowledge of the sale and not following those leads—that would be a huge oversight or even *criminal*, wouldn't it?"

Ubwe cleared his throat. "Mr. Warren, my understanding is that you will no longer be a member of the NYPD in a matter of days. This conversation is over, do not contact me again."

The line went dead.

Threatening Ubwe had been a risk, and Warren felt bad for doing it. He hadn't thought it would work anyway, and Ubwe had called his bluff. Word was circulating through the department that Warren was on his way out. Any clout he'd garnered through many years of public service was gone.

He stared across the street to the square, where snow was accumulating on the statue. Warren hated the cold. He'd grown up in the Bay Area and hadn't seen snow in person until he'd moved east for college.

A car slid across a lane of traffic, almost hitting a man crossing the street. Horns blared, then traffic continued.

As he walked back to the café, he noticed a white man with a neatly trimmed black beard reading a newspaper in the front seat of a gray SUV parked across the street. He wasn't sure, but he thought he might have seen the same SUV circling the block while he was on the phone.

He should have been more alert. He was sure they hadn't been tailed after leaving the storage unit, but it was possible a tracking device had been placed on his car, or that they'd picked up a tail since arriving in D.C. He stared at the man, who seemed engrossed in the newspaper. But, who reads a newspaper anymore?

After a minute, he returned to the café.

Cole had the video ready the moment he sat down. He watched it twice, then leaned back. "What are you thinking?"

"We agree the guy everyone thinks is guilty didn't do it, right?" Cole asked.

Warren nodded but his face showed skepticism.

"And we think there's going to be another shooting, right? And this shooting happened differently than the last."

"How so?"

"Wragg shot Ambani, then disposed of the weapon and went home. In this case, the shooter took out the VP and, assuming the dead guy isn't really the shooter, the fact that he died right around the same time means only one thing." Warren was shaking his head, which made her pause. "What?"

"It *doesn't* mean only one thing," he said. "I can think of a half dozen things it *could* mean."

"Can I finish?" Cole asked. "My *guess* is that it means, for whatever reason, the person who killed the VP wanted everyone to fall for a misdirection. He or she left that body on the rooftop, throwing the cops and the press off the scent. That's what makes it different from the Wragg killing. Then, whoever it was started leaking the extremist politics stuff on social media."

"I'm betting you have an idea about why one might have done that."

"Because whoever killed the VP is going to make the next kill as well, maybe all the rest. Maybe Wragg killed first because it was on his home turf, and because he was a lead organizer. I don't know. Maybe they knew it would get harder after the first one."

Warren went quiet. Cole watched him watch the video again. When it ended, he said, "So you think this head in the window dude killed the VP and set up the dead guy on the roof as the patsy?"

"It's a theory," Cole said. "And it's even possible the dead guy on the roof *did* kill the VP, and right afterwards"—she tapped the phone to indicate the video—"the head in the window guy killed him."

"If that's true," Warren said, "in either of those scenarios, police will figure it out from an autopsy, ballistics will be definitive."

"But that information will not be released to them for a day or two. Plenty of time for the window guy to disappear. To Las Vegas, or Miami, or Los Angeles. Even to Paris or London."

"Or Tokyo, or San Francisco." Warren filled in the last two cities they'd seen indicated on the map from the storage unit. He pulled out his phone.

"Who are you calling?" Cole asked.

"If your guess is right, we need to prove it. Has anything on the weapon found with the dead man leaked yet?"

"Nothing solid," Cole said. "Just anonymous police sources speculating that it was a fifty cal."

"My hunch is that FBI, Secret Service, everyone fighting over jurisdiction on this mess will have the same hunch as you. If they don't already have the video from the post, they will soon. And they won't leak the type of gun."

"So who are you calling?" Cole asked.

"I know a guy in Quantico."

47

Not wanting to drive the Cougar through streets growing increasingly treacherous with the deepening snow, Warren stashed it in a nearby long term parking garage.

Cole ordered an Uber to drive them to the FBI headquarters in Quantico, Virginia, then turned off her phone to let her mind rest while Warren made arrangements to meet a classmate from the police academy. He'd explained to her earlier that Bakari Smith had been in the NYPD only two years before the FBI recruited him as a ballistics expert.

When they arrived at the headquarters, Cole followed Warren into Smith's office. She realized immediately that she'd had a false assumption that all FBI agents looked and acted a certain way. She'd imagined a clean-cut, athletic man. All business. In reality, Bakari Smith was short and a little dumpy. His blue suit was too tight and his wide, jovial smile caused his wire-rimmed glasses to bow outwards even as they pressed deep grooves into the flesh between his temples and ears.

Warren took the lead, so Cole studied the office quietly as the two men caught up on old times. A small, triangular room, it had a single window looking down into a courtyard. She watched as wind whipped snow around in violent flurries. The chaotic weather was in contrast to the tidy state of Smith's office, not a speck of dust and everything in its place.

On a ledge behind the desk, a framed photo depicted Smith standing proudly before the Great Pyramid in Egypt. Another showed him on the field level of Yankee Stadium, holding up two hot dogs and pretending to take a bite. A frame laying face down caught Cole's eye. The collapsed frame seemed out of place, like it had been intentionally obscured. She felt her brow furrow with curiosity, wondering what it might display.

Cole tuned back into the conversation when Smith said, "I don't have a lot of time this morning. It's great to see you, War Dog, but what brings you out here? I mean, I was surprised to hear from you."

"Came to get you back into shape. Man, what happened?"

"Don't think we can take care of that in the next ten minutes before my meeting." Smith laughed, patting his round belly. "Desk job, and Ben's Chili Bowl. They say the body is seventy percent water. I think mine might be thirty percent half-smokes."

"What are half-smokes?" Cole asked.

"Spicy local sausage. Half pork, half beef, smothered in chili."

"Ya gotta skip the bun," Warren chimed in. "Empty carbs. Want me to send you some info?"

Smith nodded enthusiastically. "Hell yeah, War Dog. Hit me up with some links."

"You bet. Just to be clear, you mean health-promo links, yeah? Not half-smoke links?"

"Whichever will get me a physique more like yours, bud."

They were smiling and laughing but their interaction felt odd. Smith was being overly friendly, trying too hard. It might have just been his personality, or maybe he was uncomfortable around Warren since they'd gone through police academy together and Smith had since fallen out of shape. Simply being in Warren's presence was enough to make all but elite athletes feel out of shape. But something didn't feel right, and Cole wanted to get to the point of the visit. She inched her foot toward Warren's and gave it a tap.

He didn't look over, but he seemed to get it. "The Meyers killing," he said casually. "The VP. You in on that?"

"Nah, and neither are you, so..."

"Cole's a reporter, like I said on the phone, and since I'm about to be unemployed, I'm helping her out. Kind of a

205

consulting thing." He gestured toward Cole. "Show him the video."

Cole slid her phone across the desk. Smith watched the video the news helicopter had taken of the dead man on the roof, next to what they assumed was a rifle.

Smith handed her the phone. "I've seen this half a dozen times. So?"

"Can you tell what kind of rifle that is?"

"No, and even if I could, I wouldn't tell you." His face softened. "Look—and I'm not breaking any news here—only a few types of guns can make an accurate shot from a mile."

"Fifty-cal?" Warren asked.

"Or a .338 Lapua Magnum. That thing was designed for long-range sniping. Craig Harrison has a confirmed kill from 2.47 miles using it. Also, the .408 CheyTac. A .300 Winchester Magnum is great, but it's accurate only to about 1,000 to 1,500 yards. There are some weapons that would get the job done, and" —he pointed at the phone—"I assume the weapon in the video is one, but I can't tell just by eyeballing it."

Cole slid forward on her chair. "But you do have equipment here to zoom in—digitally enhance or whatever, right?"

"Zoom-and-enhance, like this is a TV show?" Smith asked. "You know it doesn't work like that."

"C'mon," Warren said. "Help us out."

"You gotta be kidding me. No." Smith stood and paced behind his desk, pausing to stare at the pictures. This drew Cole's attention back to the face-down photo. The office was spotless, neat and tidy. Why would one of the photos be face-down?

An ex-girlfriend?

Or maybe a *current* girlfriend? Someone he didn't want just anyone to know about.

Warren tried another approach. "I get it, ballistics are your thing, not photo analysis. Probably couldn't ID it anyway."

Smith laughed. "Playing to my ego? If I zoom in on that video, of course I *could* ID it." He held out his hands, palms up. "War Dog, the problem is—sharing information with you, I could lose my job."

The statement hung in the air. Warren's eyes shifted from Smith to Cole, who broke the long silence. "Obviously it's asking too much for you to help. We'll go. But Bakari—quick thing—when was the last time you were in New York City?"

"Couple years ago." His eyes darted left. "A conference. All the best ballistics guys from around the country."

"That when the photo was taken?" She pointed at the shot of Smith at Yankee Stadium, the one with the two hot dogs.

"Yes. Why?"

"Those half-smokes?" she asked, smiling.

"Regular...regular..." he stuttered. She was trying to make him uncomfortable, and it was working. "Regular ballpark dogs," he finished.

Cole frowned. "But the Yankees signed Martinez, the third baseman standing off to your right, in March of this year."

Warren gave her a long, puzzled look. She met his eyes briefly. He wasn't following.

She turned back to Smith. "How were you at Yankee Stadium after March of this year if you haven't been there since the conference a couple years ago? Who were you with?"

He looked at the floor. "I forgot. I went up there for opening day." His face grew red, then redder. "By myself."

Like most people, he was much less in control of his responses than he believed. Flushing, like most body language tics, originated in the limbic system, the mammalian part of the brain not controlled by conscious decision-making. Being anxious causes some people to release adrenaline, which temporarily dilates blood vessels in the cheeks, causing the reddening.

"You flew to New York City for a single ballgame by yourself and ate two stadium dogs? That's a lot of hot dog. If you don't remember when you were there, I'm sure your digestive system does." She softened her tone to seem less like a shark, less like a reporter out for blood. "Must be a real fan."

"You can take a man away from the Bronx," Smith offered, "but you can't take the Yankees out of his heart."

"Who took the picture?" Cole asked.

Smith raised his hand defensively, looking at Warren for help. "What's her deal? I've got stuff to do."

"What's in that frame there?" Cole asked, pointing at the face-down photo.

"Get outta here, lady. War Dog, c'mon."

Warren stood and walked around the desk.

Cole shot up from her seat. "Warren, don't!"

It was too late. Cole watched Warren pick up the photo. The back of his neck tensed. The vein on his temple popped. He set the photo down calmly, then pressed his palms into his cheeks, expelling a long breath.

She took him by the arm and led him back to his chair. "Sit down before you do something you regret, Rob."

She picked up the photo and, as she'd suspected, it showed Smith with an attractive Latina woman. Warren's wife. A selfie taken outside Yankee Stadium.

"I was with Marina that day," Warren said quietly. "That was the last time I got to spend a whole day with her. Sarah asked me to watch her. Now I know why."

"Everybody calm down," Smith said.

Warren looked anything but calm.

Cole put a hand on his knee and pressed firmly. "Rob, don't say anything. Look at me." His face shook. Sweat rolled from his forehead down the side of his nose. "I need you, Rob. If you do something dumb, you'll be arrested. Or worse. I shouldn't need to remind you that we're at the"—she clearly enunciated every letter—"F-B-I right now."

Warren closed his eyes and took a deep breath.

Cole turned to Smith, who sat back down behind the desk. "I don't know how long you've been seeing Rob's wife, and I don't care. What I *do* know is...you're going to help us."

"Why would I do that?" Smith asked. "I want you out of here."

"How do you think your colleagues are going to react to the fact that you're sleeping with your friend's wife?" Cole asked.

"They've been separated for—"

Warren moved to stand, but she pressed him down.

Cole leveled her gaze on Smith. "Trust me, you don't want to finish that thought. And you don't want me to let go of this guy. Rob was a good cop, but I think even he'd admit he has some anger issues. How about you help us for ten minutes, then we leave in peace?"

Smith looked at Warren, then back to Cole. He gave a short nod. "Okay, but get him out of here first."

The situation was tenuous, so Cole walked Warren into the hallway, promising to find him something to punch once she'd gotten the information they needed from Smith. And once they'd gotten Warren outside of the bureau's camera range.

Five minutes later, Cole was behind Smith's desk, peering over his shoulder as he zoomed in on the helicopter video. He'd found the clip on his computer, downloaded it, and opened it in a program she'd never heard of.

"What can you see?" she asked.

Smith ignored her. He tapped his keyboard and the video switched to a photographic negative, making the gun appear like a white stick on the roof, which had been silver but now took on a gray tone. "Not a fifty-cal."

"You sure?"

"Pretty sure. Hold on."

He paused the video, zoomed again, and rotated the image. He pointed at the barrel. "This is a thirty-cal. Barrel length compared to stock."

"And a thirty-cal can't shoot a mile, correct?"

He paused and sighed. "It's possible, but unlikely. No one would *choose* a thirty-cal for that shot. No one who knew what he was doing."

"How can you tell it's a thirty-cal? Assume I don't know anything when it comes to guns."

"A fifty-caliber round is about three times the size of a thirty, so the frame and barrel have to be larger. *Much* larger." He pointed at the barrel of the gun on the screen. "This gun looks like a thirty-ought-six. Range of around a thousand yards, little over half a mile. A fine weapon—great deer rifle, which is what most people use it for—but no way a pro would attempt *that* shot with *that* gun."

Cole had no reason to doubt his expertise. Still, it was hard to believe he could distinguish different types of rifles from a blurry video taken from a helicopter hundreds of yards over a rooftop. More importantly, it didn't seem as though the significance had struck him. If he was right, the dead man on the roof hadn't killed the VP. The story the cops, the FBI, and the Secret Service were running with was false. The implications were massive, the proof right in front of their eyes, but he was acting like he'd spotted a minor typo.

Cole sometimes noticed this with experts. As good as they were at their jobs, they often missed the larger implications of their work. Perhaps it was better that he *didn't* grasp the implications. She changed the subject abruptly. "Is it serious with Warren's wife? What's her name again?"

"Sarah."

"Is it serious?"

"I…"

His eyes dropped. He seemed uncomfortable, like he didn't know whether it was serious.

She took the opening. "For whatever reason, Warren listens to me. And he just found out you're sleeping with his wife. Can I offer a…trade?"

His face showed confusion. "That *was* the trade."

"I think you know that if you're serious about Sarah, Warren can make that unpleasant in more ways than you care to think about."

He nodded.

"Here's the deal. I'll do everything I can to convince him to move on and not harass you, but I need something else."

He raised both hands defensively. "Not promising anything, but what?"

"The VisionKey system used in most hotels. I've read that hackers created a master key that gets them into any hotel. My bet is the good people of the FBI have it as well. I'd like one."

Smith held up both hands. "You're kidding, right? I'm a ballistics guy."

"We're sitting, quite literally, in the most powerful law enforcement agency in the history of the world. You're telling me hackers created a universal hotel key card reader and the FBI doesn't have one?"

"I'm telling you I don't know."

Cole stood. "How can you not know?

Smith shrugged. "Not my department."

"That's the problem, isn't it?" Cole leaned toward him, shaking her head as she spoke. "Organizations like this have plenty of branches but you can't count on fruit if you aren't connected to the main trunk. Find out if you can get us one."

"Just…" Smith let out a long sigh. "Keep Warren away from me."

She gave a noncommittal shrug and left.

Cole found Warren in the lobby, sipping a paper cup of water that looked ridiculously small in his large hand. He stood when he saw her. "So?"

"It's not the gun. My theory was right."

Warren looked torn between wanting to ask follow-up questions about the gun and wanting to ask whether she'd found out anything else about Smith's relationship with his wife.

"He's finding out how we can get a universal key card reader."

"For what?" Warren asked.

Cole smiled.

"No. *Absolutely not.*" Warren sounded like a father whose teenager was begging him to borrow his '69 Cougar. "Cole, *no.* We're not breaking into hotel rooms."

"*I* am. You can come if you want."

"How'd you get him to help us, anyway?"

"I don't think you wanna know." Cole raised her eyebrows and took a deep breath.

Warren frowned. "Probably not, but try me."

"Told him I'd convince you to move on from Sarah, free him up to date her." She said it with a wry smile, but Warren didn't pick up on it.

"You said *what?* It won't work. I—"

Cole smiled again. "I know, and don't worry, I'm not *actually* going to try to do that. Quite the opposite, I think you should try to win her back."

"Why?"

"They're not serious. I can tell." She was lying. No man has a photo of his girlfriend in his office if they're *not* serious, but she needed to get Warren out of Quantico and that would be a lot harder if he got himself into a fistfight.

Smith appeared from the far side of the lobby, flanked by two other men, both about Warren's size.

Warren stepped forward. "For real? You brought security?"

Cole put a hand on his forearm. "Lemme handle this. Please." She stepped in front of him. "You get what I need?"

Smith handed her a notecard. "Address on there is a gray hat we've worked with. He'll help you. Probably."

Cole took the card. The address was in Alexandria, just across the river from downtown D.C. "*Probably?* What's that supposed to mean?"

"He doesn't work for us. I mean, he does and he doesn't. He's not on our payroll. I can't *make* him help you. Take it or leave it."

"You'll call him?" Cole asked. "Let him know what we need?"

"Already did." His eyes were on Warren as he spoke. "He's expecting *you*, but I don't know what *you* can expect, is all I'm saying."

Warren had the look of a rodeo bull in the chute. Cole could see his muscles tense. She wanted to press Smith further but instead thought it best to get out of there before the situation deteriorated. "Fine. Let's go, Rob."

48

The snow crunched under Cole's feet and the soft gray of twilight lit the flakes as they fluttered down past the restored stone town-houses painted in bright shades of red, blue, and green. Many bore black plaques designating them as "Historic Buildings," some with dates indicating they'd been there nearly three hundred years.

It had taken two hours for the Uber to navigate the slippery roads thirty miles from the FBI headquarters in Quantico to Alexandria, a historic town where many of America's founders had lived. They'd passed the modernized King Street shopping and restaurant scene and turned into an old neighborhood with original cobblestone streets and historic churches, before stopping on a side street in front of an old apothecary that had been converted into a tiny museum.

"I feel like I'm in a movie," Cole said as Warren tipped the driver.

He gestured toward the large window of the apothecary. "Martha Washington used to buy her opium here."

She raised an eyebrow. "What?"

"Seriously, I read it," Warren said. "Opium was legal and used for pain, the flu, damn near everything. Our founding fathers, and mothers, were straight-up high."

"So the opioid crisis was built into the country from the beginning."

"I never thought of it that way," Warren said, "but I guess you're right."

Cole double-checked the address on the card and held it up for Warren to read over her shoulder.

He pointed up the street. "A few more blocks I think."

They walked a block to the North and then turned west onto Queen street.

A blue brick townhouse crammed between two larger red ones belonged to the address. It was no more than ten feet wide and appeared somehow added to the scene, like it didn't belong.

"Is it just me, or is this house ridiculously narrow?" Cole asked.

"It's the Hollensbury Spite House." Warren brushed snowflakes from his jacket.

"Okay, so what's a Spite House?"

"When someone was angry with their neighbor or community, it was not unheard of to build something that would block a view or prevent passage. This one's an Alley House."

"So, what was Hollens-what's-his-name spiteful of?"

"Mr Hollensbury was a brick maker who got tired of wagons coming through colliding with and leaving gouges in his walls, not to mention his frustration with their horses leaving excrement in the alleyway. So, he laid bricks and built an addition wedged between these two buildings to prevent access."

"How do you know so much about this town?" Cole asked.

"Took a walking tour through D.C. that took me by this area —before my deployment. I'm a U.S. history buff so the tour was right up my alley."

"Not up this alley."

"Ha Ha. Actually thought I might be a historian when I got back from overseas. When we had Marina, I figured eight more years of schooling wasn't in the cards."

Cole realized they were stalling. The townhouse was dark and though she wasn't claustrophobic, just looking at it made her feel cramped. Something felt wrong, and neither wanted to knock on the door. "Why aren't we knocking?"

Warren took the notecard from Cole and studied it. "It's the right address, but...I don't know."

"Think your old friend might be setting us up?"

"Possibly."

"Were we sent on a spite quest?"

The buzzing of Cole's phone interrupted them. A text from Marty Goldberg.

Goldilocks: *Got some info for you. Meet for a drink?*

She held up the message for Warren, then nodded toward the door. "Let's try this first."

Warren cast a skeptical look at the townhouse, as though assessing for danger, then banged on the black wooden door. His heavy knock carried through the deserted streets, a deep bass echo above the high-pitched whistle of the wind through leafless trees.

They waited.

Warren knocked again. Nothing. Without looking back, he said, "Tell Goldilocks you'll meet him at Tivera on King Street. Three blocks from here. I'll stake out the house."

Cole tapped out the message. "You sure you got this? You know what we need?"

"I can handle it."

By the time Cole found the Italian wine bar, Goldberg was halfway through his first glass of Barolo. "What took you so long?" He stood and offered an awkward hug. He smelled of fresh cologne, something spicy and overdone.

"Got lost," Cole said. "Never been to Alexandria."

"Where's the cop?"

Her face tightened. She'd told Goldberg that Warren was an assistant, and though she'd known it would be easy to figure out he wasn't, she hadn't anticipated that he'd bother to check. Or that there'd be a follow-up meeting in the first place. Pondering this, she ordered a tequila and slid into the stool next to him. "You researched us?"

"This is the most two-faced town in America, maybe the world." He moved his wine glass in a small circle, following the pattern on the brushed-steel bar. "It's my job to know the real reason people contact me."

"Okay, so what's your take on the *real* reason?"

"You think there's a connection between Ambani and Meyers."

"We've been over this," she countered. "It's *my job* to think there's a connection between everything and everything else. Until I know there isn't. Plus, I'm freelance now. I can follow my gut."

"You and Warren an item?" he asked, casually. Other than a single stray hair that managed to escape the dye-job, his appearance was perfect. Neat, powerful, in control. But it was all a facade, a con designed to hide the old Goldilocks. Under the dyed hair and the $3,000 suit, he was still the insecure Congressional staffer with an innocent crush on her.

The bartender set down the tequila, which gave her the beat she needed to ignore the question. "You said you had some information regarding my husband?"

"Nice dodge."

She smiled. "Thank you."

He let out a sigh. "Fine. I said I had information, but not about your husband."

"Meyers then? The VP?"

"His assassination *is* what you came here to research, right?"

A bell clanged and a shout came from the kitchen. "Order up, table six."

Cole's shoulders tensed, rising toward her ears.

"You gotta relax, Jane." He took a sip of his wine.

Cole reached for her tequila. "Tell me what you know." She downed the drink and waved the empty glass at the bartender.

"First, tell me what *you* know," Goldberg said. "You wouldn't be here if you didn't have suspicions, and my bet is those suspicions are based on something up in New York."

"*You* texted *me*," she replied. "You go first."

"Fine. But really, you do need to relax." He eyed her over the top of his wine glass as he sipped. "I talked to a reporter at *The Post*, guy I leak stories to when I'm trying to get a deal through Congress or pressure an agency. I give big stuff to him exclusively, he gives me a heads up, not only on his big stories but anything the paper is going to run. Paper has a piece tonight questioning whether the dead guy on the roof was the shooter. I got it right before I texted you. It'll post soon and run on the front page in the morning."

Cole's head burned, like a flare had gone off, but she played it cool. She already knew this, but she was hoping no one else would figure it out so quickly. "What's the evidence?"

"Source at the FBI. Ballistics expert, apparently. No idea why this hasn't already come out, but the gun on top of the roof couldn't possibly have made the shot across the Potomac."

Cole cursed Bakari Smith in her mind, cursed herself for not knowing he'd leak it.

"At least, that's what *The Post* is writing," Goldberg continued. "Don't know if the dead guy on the roof was involved, or whether it was a random coincidence. But they've been looking at the wrong guy."

Cole stood suddenly. She wanted to get out of there, to get back to Warren, but Goldberg caught her arm. "Back in my office you asked why I told you the thing about Watergate, the CIA-Nixon set up story."

"Why did you?"

"Think of it as a cautionary tale. I like you, Jane. But reporters often forget to ask themselves an important question. Sometimes in their madness to get the scoop, they miss bigger picture elements."

"Oh really?" she asked. "And what are those?"

"They don't ask themselves 'Why am I being leaked to? Who benefits from this story?'"

"We ask ourselves those questions all the time." It came out more forceful than she'd intended, but she wasn't keen on sitting through a journalism lecture from a D.C. lobbyist.

"Hey, hey. Don't get defensive. I'm just saying, half of the big stories that leak are misdirections from another, bigger story."

"So what's the bigger story?" she asked.

"If you look at the actual crimes Nixon got busted for, they weren't in the top five worst things he did. None would crack the top ten list of the things the CIA did. And I'm no politician here —I don't pledge allegiance to *either* party. Oh, the stories I could tell."

He laced his hands behind his head and leaned back, elbows out, as he had in his office. In her study of body language she'd learned this was called "Hooding." It's what king cobras did to intimidate other animals, and it's what men often did when they felt comfortable and powerful. Goldberg had given her nothing. He'd steered the conversation from the moment she'd walked in, and now he was...what *was* he doing? "Marty, what are you driving at?"

"You're in D.C. now, Jane. I know, New York is New York, but the spin down here is next level. New York is checkers. D.C. is chess. With social media alongside the papers and news networks, it's now speed chess."

"I'm not here to play games," Cole said, but she wasn't as confident as she was trying to sound. Goldberg wasn't only warning her. He seemed to be threatening her.

"Watch yourself here in D.C. Cole. Relax, okay? All I'm saying is don't get in over your head."

As the sky darkened from gray to black, Warren paced the street to stay warm, passing occasionally under the single streetlamp a few doors from the townhouse. Wind shook snow loose from the tree branches overhead, giving the scene the feel of a lonely forest more than a rich suburb. After five minutes, he banged on the door again, louder this time.

No response.

He leaned on a snow-covered car and used his phone to open Google Earth and entered the address. It showed the building in daytime, but no other useful information. Next he entered the address into Zillow, where he learned that it had last been purchased for $1.2 million in 2012 and was now valued at $3.1 million. Two more searches turned up interesting historical information, but not the owner's name.

A creaking sound came from behind him and he turned quickly. He didn't see anything. Had it been a tree branch buckling under the weight of snow? A rooftop?

The night was silent again. He stared up at the sky, and Sarah appeared in his mind, standing in front of Yankee Stadium in a yellow dress. Bakari Smith appeared in his mind next to her, and he shook them loose and turned to study the house again. The ground floor had no windows, just the black door in the center. The upper floor of the two-story house had one small window. As he stared at it, a light turned on. A figure appeared.

Warren stood motionless, watching the fog of his breath in front of him.

The window screeched open. A head emerged, backlit so Warren couldn't make out a face. "You Cole?" It was a man's voice. Some accent he couldn't identify. Maybe European.

"Yeah, I'm Cole," Warren said.

The man eyed Warren up and down. "Thought you were supposed to be a woman."

Warren shrugged. "You have what we need?"

"Smith didn't say anything about 'we.' I don't like what I'm seeing or hearing. What gives?"

"Why didn't you open when I knocked?"

The man ignored the question, turning his head to peer up and down the block. His head disappeared back into the room. Warren contemplated. From the sound of the guy's voice, he was older. Warren could bust through the wooden door if need be, but he'd promised himself he wouldn't commit any crimes. Not if he could help it. He didn't need to make a decision. An arm emerged through the window, then the man's head.

"Catch." The man threw a small black bag through the air. Warren caught it up against his chest as the window screeched shut. Within seconds, the room went dark.

Warren opened the bag and pulled out a device. Three flat computer chips, each the size of a credit card, were stuck together with narrow screws that left about an inch of space between each layer. A six-inch wire ran from the chips to a single plastic card the size of a standard hotel keycard.

Snow crunched behind him and he swiveled.

It was Cole. "Smith leaked our meeting. Everyone in the world is about to know what we told him. How did you fare?"

"Just got the reader." Warren held up the wire and plastic for Cole to inspect. "I think."

"If we want to be first, we need to get there now. When this news drops, everyone will be in a rush to do exactly what we're about to."

Cole opened the Uber app, but Warren stopped her before she entered an address. The gray SUV he'd seen earlier still hovered in the back of his mind. "Get them to take us to my car. It's only a few minutes out of the way, and if Smith leaked the story, he could…"

"What?"

"I don't know. Earlier, when we were at the café, I saw a suspicious SUV. Had me thinking about Mazzalano's guys. And now Smith. You know he can track us through the Uber app and, I don't know…"

Cole ordered a car to take them to K Street, where they'd left the Cougar that morning. "You can drive in this? Rear wheel drive, right?"

"Snow has almost stopped. I don't know what happens next, but we need control over our movement."

49

Warren struggled to keep the '69 Cougar between barely-visible paint lines as he navigated the George Washington Memorial Parkway. After a few harrowing minutes, during which the car fishtailed twice, a plow pulled onto the road at an entrance a quarter mile ahead of them. He settled in about forty yards behind the plow, driving slowly along the newly-cleared road.

In the glow of her cell phone's flashlight, Cole examined the keycard device. "Ever seen one of these?"

"Never."

"Think it'll work?"

"No idea."

As they passed the Pentagon, Cole stared at the Potomac, a wide black patch flecked with silver moonlight. She plugged her phone into the charger sticking out from the cigarette lighter and opened the official Threads account of *The Washington Post*. The article Goldilocks told her about had posted seven minutes earlier.

"Smith leaked it." She scanned the story. "He screwed us."

"Can't exactly blame him. We walked into his place of business and threatened him."

"Technically *I* threatened him," Cole said, "but yeah."

Warren glanced over, trying to see the screen.

"Keep your eyes on the road. I'll read it out loud, but it's probably just a summary of what we told Smith. The gun on the rooftop, as seen from the helicopter, can't have made the shot. Probably—"

She closed her eyes when she saw her own name. She opened them for an instant, then closed them again when she saw Warren's.

"Damnit!" She struck the glove compartment with her free hand.

"What?"

"Smith didn't just give them the story. He gave them *our* story. Our names and all."

"What do you mean?" Warren's eyes flashed back to the road after briefly trying to read over Cole's shoulder.

"I'll read you the part." She let out a long breath and read. *"'According to the source, the FBI was alerted to the discrepancy in the appearance of the rifle by Jane Cole, formerly a reporter with* The New York Sun, *and Robert Warren, an NYPD officer currently on paid administrative leave for striking a handcuffed suspect. Though the source declined to say whether he believed Cole and Warren to be involved in the murder, he did say, "If you ask me, a disgraced cop and a fired reporter shouldn't be down here getting in the way of the FBI and the local police as they investigate this appalling crime." It's unclear what involvement they have in the case, the source concluded, or how they initially came upon the information.'"*

Warren shook his head. "He just made us suspects."

"It won't work," Cole said, though she wasn't sure she was right.

"Probably not, but you can bet the cops are reading that and are, at least, wondering about it." He nervously changed his grip on the steering wheel. "I'm glad we aren't in an Uber right now."

"Reporter went with a single source because he wanted to be first."

"In all fairness," Warren said, "Smith is a *damn* good source. That's why *we* went to him. But why leak it right after we left?"

"Payback. Also, it's a genuinely huge scoop. Reporter is gonna owe him big."

Cole returned to her phone and checked her go-to politics accounts. Five minutes ago, the official CNN account announced "MAJOR BREAKING NEWS" coming up. Probably a report on the story from *The Post*, likely featuring an interview with the reporter who'd broken the story.

She pulled up the CNN live news feed. "There's breaking

news on CNN. Probably a recap." She turned the volume up all the way and held the phone so Warren could hear. The anchor was already halfway through a report.

"…Unclear at this time what impact this will have on the investigation. But to repeat, stunning breaking news tonight…"

The video and audio froze. Cole shook her phone, then held it up to the window.

Warren chuckled. "You think shaking it will help?"

"Shut up. I don't know. Come to think of it, you don't know either."

After a long silence, the video kicked in and the anchor's voice filled the dark car.

"*According to sources, the coroner in charge of the body of the dead man from the roof said he could not have taken his own life. The angle of the gunshot indicates he was shot by someone else. This upends the version of events we've been hearing since Vice President Meyers was killed. Further, a new story from* The Washington Post *cites an FBI source who claims that an analysis of the helicopter footage shows that the rifle by his side could not have made the fatal shot. What does all this mean? Put simply, the real killer of former Vice President Meyers is still on the loose. Stay with us and, after the commercial break, we'll bring in our panel of experts and commentators to discuss what is quickly becoming the biggest news story in years.*"

The video froze again. Cole shook her phone. Nothing.

"Try rebooting it."

Cole restarted the device.

"I know how this works." Warren spoke as the phone restarted. "Police will say they were looking into the possibility of multiple shooters all along, as well as the possibility that the dead guy on the roof wasn't even involved."

Cole shook her phone again. "They'll cover their asses."

"Sure, and chances are, at least some people *were* looking into other options. It'll probably take police half an hour, maybe an hour, to put two and two together and get to the hotel, but not longer."

"Then let's hurry." Cole watched the screen light up. "No whammies, no whammies," she chanted into the phone.

"Don't worry. If the shaking and rebooting doesn't work we can give it CPR." Warren pulled around the snowplow, which had slowed to five miles per hour, and increased his speed.

50

Cole scanned the valet area in front of the Potomac View Hotel, then studied the vehicles parked up and down the block. "No police cars."

"At least none that are marked." Warren corrected.

"You think there could be detectives here or—"

Warren shrugged. "No way of knowing until we go in. If they put the news reports together with the video, they'll show up with black-and-whites, SWAT. Hell, they might send in the National Guard."

"We'd better hurry then."

Warren turned into an underground parking garage, took a ticket, and found a spot near the elevator. "Got the reader?"

Cole held up the small black bag. "If it doesn't work?"

"Let's not go there yet."

"The man I saw in the video was on the top floor," Cole said. "I think I'll be able to tell which room once we're inside."

Warren gave her a skeptical look that translated as *Really?*

"Got any better ideas?" she asked.

He shook his head.

Cole pointed at the elevator panel as they entered. "Damn." Instead of taking them onto the floors where the rooms were, the only options were the other parking garage floors and the hotel lobby.

"I was worried about that," Warren said.

"Never mind. When we get to the lobby, follow me." Cole reached for the panel but Warren grabbed her hand before she could press the button.

"Maybe you should go up alone," he said.

"No." Cole maneuvered out from his gentle grip and tapped the "L" button. "I need you up there. Like it or not, you're in this now. That story in *The Post*, the piece about us...if you were trying to stay on the periphery, it's too late."

The elevator stopped to pick up a man dragging two large suitcases. He got on and pressed "L" even though it was already illuminated. Cole eyed Warren as the elevator ascended, trying not to make eye contact with the man, who seemed to be staring at her.

When they reached the lobby, she hung back as the man exited. "So?" she asked Warren, grabbing his forearm. "You in?"

He met her eyes and offered a single, firm nod.

She looped her arm through the crook of his elbow and put on a smile. Guiding him confidently through the lobby, she nodded at the front desk manager and waved a credit card in his general direction as though showing her hotel keycard. He nodded back, pretending to recognize her. She'd once read that "People see what you tell them to see." It was usually true.

Inside the elevator, Cole opened her phone to a series of screenshots she'd taken from the video. When they reached the top floor, she navigated the hallway to the section of rooms facing northeast, the only ones with windows facing the Watergate. She stopped before a row of three doors—rooms 2010, 2012, and 2014. "Which one do you think?"

Warren looked nervously up and down the empty hallway. "You mean you don't know?"

"I said I knew *about* where it would be located." She glanced at the screenshot again, then closed her eyes, imagining the internal geography of the building they'd walked through and comparing it to the view from the exterior. "The one on the left, 2010," she said, handing Warren the black bag. "I'm thinking there's no chance the shooter is still in the room, right? But that he would have booked it for multiple days to give himself more time to escape. So if there's anyone in the room, that's not it."

Warren pulled the keycard device from the bag. Cole held her breath as he slid the single plastic card into the slot. The lock clicked and flashed green.

It worked.

Exhaling, Cole turned the door handle and pushed slowly.

"What the hell!" A man's voice, surprised and angry. "Who's there?"

She pulled the door shut quickly.

"Housekeeping at night?" he called. "What the *hell?*"

"Sorry!" Cole called through the door, trying on a terrible European accent. "We thought you'd checked out."

"Damnit!"

"Sorry," she called again, moving to the center door, 2012. Then, to Warren, "Better be this one."

Warren moved next to her. "Think he'll call the front desk?"

"Hope not." There was a *Do Not Disturb* sign hanging on the doorknob of room 2012. Cole tapped the door gently. No answer. "Try it," she said.

He slid the card in and, again, it worked. Slowly, Cole pushed the door open only a crack. "Housekeeping," she called quietly.

No answer.

She opened it another crack. The room was dark.

Stepping in, she held the door open for Warren to follow. "Hello?"

No response. Empty.

They stood in the entryway, a bathroom to the left and a closet to the right. The entryway led into a large room, with floor-to-ceiling windows that looked across the Potomac and, to the east, the roof of the Watergate Hotel where Meyers was shot.

By the window, a rolling office chair sat neatly under a desk. To the right, another small closet and an armoire of faux-wood. All in all, it was a typical hotel room. She stepped past the threshold that divided the entryway from the main space, then froze.

The bed was neatly made, a paisley bedspread smooth across the top. On the bedspread sat a rifle.

Warren bumped into her when she stopped suddenly. He put a hand on her shoulder. "Don't. Touch. Anything."

51

Together, they took in the weapon.

It sat on tripod legs, facing the window, as though ready to take out another target across the river. Matte black, it was larger than she'd imagined. Long, with a large scope and a thick barrel that grew even thicker at the end. Actually, it wasn't that the barrel grew thicker. It seemed to be some sort of attachment.

Warren leaned in, careful not to touch the bed. "Custom fifty cal suppressor. Won't silence the weapon, but it'll dampen the sound."

She took out her phone and snapped a picture, then walked around the bed and snapped more from every angle.

"There likely aren't any identification markings," Warren said, leaning in and inspecting the rifle without touching it. "They would have shaved off any serial numbers, but this is one of the nine custom jobs. I'm sure of it."

"There's something about the room," Cole said, stowing her phone and looking around. "It's *too* clean."

Warren walked along the wall beside the bed, moving his head from the floor to the ceiling methodically with each step. He went into the bathroom and knelt over the tub, inspecting the drain. Using a piece of toilet paper, he pulled the drain stopper out of the sink. "No hairs. Everything smells faintly of bleach. This guy was a pro."

Exiting the bathroom, he used his elbow to open the closet, inspected it, then continued around the perimeter of the room to the windows. He knelt and, again using his elbow, cracked a low window that opened outward on a hinge. It opened only a few inches before stopping. A safety feature.

Next Warren lay flat on his belly and scooched back, extending his left arm outward and cocking his right elbow back. The shooting position. He pivoted his head and the angle of the invisible rifle to the right, then back to the left then inhaled abruptly.

"What?" Cole asked.

He stood. "Lay there and take some pictures of that view."

Cole dropped to her belly and took the position. From the floor, the shooter would have had a perfect angle to the roof of the Watergate. She took a few photos.

"Now pivot to the right," Warren said.

She did. To her right was another building, slightly lower, maybe three stories below them. It was the rooftop of the Virginia Suites Hotel, where the dead body and the rifle had been found. She snapped a few photos and stood.

Warren pressed both hands to his face, letting out a long sigh. "This had to have been planned for weeks, months. Shooter knew he could kill the VP from here, and he set up some poor schlub to be on the roof next door. Maybe the dead guy was part of the plan, maybe he was a random unlucky victim." He pressed his face again, sighed, and let his shoulders drop. "Kill the VP, then kill the patsy."

Cole silently nodded.

"Your guess was right," Warren said.

He looked under the bed, in the garbage can, and in the drawer of the desk. "Guy wasn't dumb enough to leave a trace."

"You mean other than the murder weapon?"

He smiled for a half a second, then his face grew dark. Standing over the gun, he said. "You didn't touch it, did you?"

Cole joined him next to the bed and stared down at the gun. "Of course not."

"The weapon from the Ambani killing, Wragg's rifle, still hasn't been located. And this guy just leaves his here. Why?"

"Quick escape, maybe? I'm guessing he checked in, booked the room for a few extra days, then made the shot, left the

228

weapon, and escaped, leaving the 'Do Not Disturb' sign on the door. Probably figured that would give him enough time to get out of the country."

"Maybe. But why leave the weapon?" Warren asked. "This thing can be taken apart and packed into a bag slung over the shoulder like the one you saw in the video Mazzalano showed you."

"What are you driving at, Rob?"

"Most killers want to destroy the murder weapon. This one didn't even bother taking it with him. He left no trace in this room. Bleached it. You can bet there'll be no traces on the weapon. Combine that with the fact that he went to the trouble of setting another guy up to confuse the investigation for a day or two and..."

Cole saw where he was going. "You think he's going to kill again. He wanted to make the escape in order to buy himself time. And he left the weapon because he has another, or will get another."

"Nine rifles, right? Nine cities. You got clear pictures of the weapon?"

"Every angle," Cole said. "Why?"

"Because if we ever run out of money you'll be able to sell them for hundreds of thousands to *TMZ* or *The National Enquirer*. Second to John Wilkes Booth's single-shot derringer, that's about to become the most famous gun in the world." Warren stood up straight, as though every inch of him was alert. His eyes were wide. "We need to get the hell out of here. Now."

52

"Plug in my phone," Warren said. "It's about to lose power and we might need it. What's yours at?"

"Forty percent. I'm good."

She plugged in his phone as he pulled out of the parking garage. Red and blue lights flashed in front of the hotel. Three police cars were parked in the valet area. Warren turned right, away from the police.

"You think they're here because of the story, the video?"

"It's possible."

As she stowed his phone between the seats, Cole noticed it lighting up with a new text. "Who's Samuel Bacon?"

"Remember? Partner of Norris Ubwe. Dude who helped us with Price's records. The quiet, chubby one."

"He just texted you," Cole said.

"Swipe it."

She did, but it was locked. "Face ID?"

"Sorry." Warren turned.

She squared the phone on his face and it unlocked, then she read the text aloud. "'Overheard your call with Norris. He won't help you because he knows we screwed this up. Doesn't want to get blamed. I can't stay quiet. It's not solid, but peeking around the deepest alleys of the Dark Web, I found evidence that one of the rifles may have been left in D.C. for'"—she slowed as she tried to pronounce the name—"*Maiale da Tartufo*. Two days ago.'" The phone nearly flew from her hand as Warren swerved around a car that had stopped abruptly.

"*Maiale da Tartufo*?" he asked.

It sounded as though Warren knew what that meant. "Who's that?"

"You don't want to know." His eyes were on the mirrors, as they had been much of the last two days. "Keep reading."

"He says, 'Dropgangs were used to leave it for him in a park near DuPont Circle. Worse, another one was stashed in Miami only yesterday. A wet drop.'"

"Miami?" Warren asked.

"That's what he wrote. And that's where the next shooting will be."

Warren's eyes darted from the rearview mirror to the road ahead, then back again. He seemed to have stopped listening. "Hold on."

"What?"

"Hold on to the seat."

Suddenly, Warren slammed the gas, turned the wheel to the left and then pulled and released the handbrake. The back of the Cougar pitched to the right, fishtailing on a patch of ice. Cole's head rocked back into the headrest, then shot left, colliding with Warren's shoulder as he jacked the wheel to pull the Cougar out of the fishtail.

The car straightened. Cole shot a glance through the rear window, but couldn't make anything out in the darkness. Warren lay into the horn, which screamed an old fashioned, high-pitched wail as he gunned it through an intersection. Cars from left and right slipped and skidded to elude the Cougar. A violent crash erupted from her right and Cole turned to see the aftermath of a rear-end collision in the intersection.

Warren made a sharp right turn.

Cole pressed her feet to the floor, bracing herself. "What the hell?"

"We're being tailed."

Cole looked behind her. She didn't see anything.

"Keep looking," Warren said, his voice tight. "Tell me if a gray Ford Explorer, or maybe it's a Yukon, appears around the corner."

She trained her eyes on the corner and, as Warren slowed at a stop sign, a large SUV pulled around it. "I can't make out the color in this light, but yeah, an SUV. Police?"

"I don't think so."

"Then who?"

"I say it's Mazzalano."

Cole turned to look behind her. "What?"

Warren eyed the mirror. "Or his guys, more likely."

Cole could see the SUV keeping pace with them, about a block behind.

"Think about it," Warren explained. "Mazzalano easily could have set himself up as the hero who tracked down Wragg's storage unit. That alone might launch his corrupt ass from lieutenant to captain. He hasn't. Why?"

"Because he's involved," Cole said. "The gun thing. He gave protection to whatever crew arranged for the delivery of the guns."

"That's what I'm thinking."

"You think he sent someone after us—"

Warren veered right suddenly to merge onto the George Washington Parkway toward the Arlington National Cemetery. His eyes moved again to the mirror. "I think he sent that SUV after us. Either to make sure we don't have any evidence about his connection to Wragg, or to put us down."

It made sense. Cole believed Mazzalano had never given Wragg's hair sample to the DNA lab. And being the man who located Wragg's secret lair would have been the biggest win of his career. The only reason he *wouldn't* have made it public was because he was somehow involved. "Why aren't they approaching us, then? Why'd they let us get into the hotel and come out?"

"Maybe they only grabbed our tail as we came out."

Cole's head was swimming. "That doesn't make sense. The only way they could have known we were at the hotel was by following us. And if they'd followed us, why would they have let us spend time inside? Plus, you said you were sure we weren't tailed from New Jersey. How the hell could they even know we're in D.C? That article only came out an hour ago."

A quarter mile ahead, Warren saw a sea of red brake lights appear in the darkness. "Damn."

"There." Cole pointed at an exit and Warren slammed on the gas, swerving between two cars.

"We're lucky these roads have been plowed," Warren said. "But if we get onto unplowed side streets, this thing isn't going to be able to outmaneuver the gray behemoth behind us."

At the bottom of the exit ramp, Warren took a soft right past a gas station and a couple fast food restaurants. Cole watched through the back window, struggling to differentiate the cars and trucks in the shifting headlights behind them. For a moment, it appeared they'd lost the SUV. But when Warren turned onto a wide road heading west, traffic thinned and the SUV reappeared.

"Where are we going?" Cole asked. "I thought you'd want to stay on the large roads."

"Gonna try heading into Arlington, into the town. Maybe lose them in an underground lot. They're not even trying to hide that they're following us anymore, which worries me."

They traveled west for a few blocks, the SUV still comfortably behind them, then stopped at a light. Ahead, only brake lights. The intersection was stopped-up with cars. Eyes on the mirrors, studying the doors of the SUV behind them, they watched as the light changed from red to green, then back to red. No cars moved.

They sat through the light again. No movement. And again.

Warren jumped out of the car briefly, looked to the distance, then hopped back in. "Road is closed." Again, he trained his eyes on the SUV.

Cole took in a breath, and held it. She spun around on her knees, looking through the low back window of the Cougar. The top of the SUV was visible about six cars back. "What do we do?"

Warren didn't respond. He stashed his phone in his pocket and contorted his large, muscular body to put his leather jacket on. She turned back to the SUV and her heart tightened. The passenger door was open. A man got out, lit from behind by the headlights of the car behind him. He was large, maybe Warren's size, and he was coming for them. "Rob, he——"

"I see him," Warren said. "Hope you're wearing your running shoes."

53

Cole followed Warren through the intersection, walking briskly and catching him only once looking back longingly at his abandoned Cougar. He favored his right leg, but he picked up the pace as they turned onto a side street. Warren was right, she'd needed to jog to catch up.

The man was only a hundred yards back.

"Where are we going?" she asked.

"We're only a quarter mile from Arlington National Cemetery."

"Isn't it closed?"

Ignoring the question, he picked up the pace. At the end of the block, traffic was stalled on another large road.

"C'mon," Warren said. "He's waiting for us to get out of public view. Doesn't want a scene."

Cole followed across the intersection onto a dark side street. "Then why are we turning here?"

"Because I think we can disappear if we reach the cemetery. If he was sent by Mazzalano, he's likely a rogue NYPD cop. If he's got a badge, your average Joe is going to help him, not us. If we're visible, we're vulnerable. We have to disappear." He glanced back again, then said, "Let's go. You lead."

He gave Cole a gentle shove and jogged beside her. She picked up the pace, running as fast as she could, not looking back.

They reached the intersection of Arlington Blvd. A steady stream of cars passed, shooting salt and mushy snow toward them. They waited for a break in traffic, then bolted. A car blared its horn, another braked hard and swerved across a lane. Pausing at a divider, Cole looked back. The man was closer now—only twenty yards from the road.

The traffic thinned and they broke into an all-out sprint, crossing a large field, perfectly blanketed by virgin snow. Warren stayed behind her, occasionally stepping up to subtly correct her direction. He seemed to know where he wanted to go. They crossed a small side street, then another that jutted out at an odd angle.

Moments later, they reached a low wall.

Cole gazed across the wall into a vast open space, fields covered in snow, dotted with trees. Far in the distance, spaced every few feet with perfect symmetry, the tops of gravestones peeked out above the snow. "I don't want to go in here," she said.

Warren had already climbed over the wall. "Hop up."

"No, I mean, I *don't* want to go into the cemetery. It's not…"

Warren shot an anxious look at her. "Cole, now."

She glanced back, considering, then hoisted herself up, grazing her backside on the snowy ledge on the way over.

The man was about a hundred yards back. "If I'm right," Warren said. "He's not here to kill us. He wants to track us. Maybe relay location back to the driver, just keep tabs on us."

"And we're going to lose him here?"

He took her hand and pulled her forward. "That's right."

Through the snow they trudged across an open field, toward the first patch of graves and something that looked like a tall stone wall far in the distance. "How are we going to lose him here?"

"Head for that wall. That's where we'll lose him."

"How?"

Warren didn't reply. They continued until they reached the curved wall, which rose about ten feet high and was topped with a low stone railing. "Wait here," Warren said. "Don't move or make any tracks." Cole hugged her body close to the Women in Military Service Memorial.

Bounding to his left, he hung tight to the wall, a half-circle enclosing the memorial. A moment later he appeared from the other side, breathing heavily. "Now, go right, around the wall. I'll be behind you."

She walked around the wall. Warren followed on tiptoes, landing in the center of her tracks, heels up like a ballet dancer, trying not to make additional imprints in her track. Looking back at their trail, it was as though a trail of two people had hit the wall, then split up, with Warren going left and her going right. A misdirection. About forty yards on, they came to a crevice where the main wall ended and connected with another.

Warren crouched, his hands cupped. "Up."

Cole looked up. "I can't make that."

"Up," Warren repeated. "Grab the railing, pull yourself up, and lay flat once you're up there."

She stepped onto his hands and he boosted her. She braced herself on the side of the wall. Extending his arms, he held her above his head as she reached over the short fence and pulled herself atop the wall. It was roughly two feet wide and covered with snow. She lay flat, peering down on Warren, who now took one large step into the crevice where the walls met.

From her perch above, she gazed into the black space before her. Below, the fields of snow took on a dark gray hue. Barely visible in the distance were hundreds of tiny headstones. In the silence, she thought about the hundreds of thousands of men and women who were buried here. And she thought about Matt.

After what seemed like minutes, footsteps crunched in the snow. A light flashed on. Not too bright, it might have been the flashlight of a phone.

Now she understood Warren's plan. He'd circled around the wall, leaving his own set of tracks diverging from hers. He figured that the man would follow the larger set of tracks. Warren's tracks. Matt had always told her that in any combat situation, you take out the most dangerous opponent first. After being led around the wall in vain, he'd picked up her tracks.

Now he was walking right into Warren's trap.

She sucked in her belly and pressed her cheek into the compacted snow, trying to make herself as small as possible. She slowed her breathing and peered down as the light approached, accompanied by louder and louder steps.

The wind picked up, screeching through the trees and blowing snow into her face. The light stopped moving. Everything went silent.

She held her breath until the footsteps resumed. One, two, crunch, crunch. One, two, crunch, crunch.

The light was right under her now. One, two, crunch, crunch.

A grunt and the whir of movement below. *Thwack.* She lifted her head for a better view. Warren had leapt out and struck the man, who now staggered backward, holding his face.

He looked up at Cole as he stumbled, then leveled his eyes on Warren and, like a bull, charged him.

Warren waited, perfectly still. When the man was a foot in front of him, Warren tried to jump left, but his right foot slipped on the compacted snow and he hit the ground, face down.

The man fell on him, battering the back of his neck with a clumsy punch. Warren rolled onto his back, hands reaching for the man's throat. The man threw a right hook, connecting with Warren's temple, rocking his head back into the ground.

Warren shouted in pain, then let out a long, deep yell as he again reached for the man's neck. Grasping his throat, Warren absorbed a right and a left to the face, both glancing blows.

Cole sat up and scooched to the edge of the wall. The man had Warren pinned, but Warren's hands around his throat were keeping him from landing any solid punches. Cole draped her legs over the wall, directly over the man's head.

Then, she jumped.

54

In an instant, her outstretched legs connected with something. Maybe the man's neck, maybe the top of his back. When her feet hit the ground her knees shot back toward her chin and she rolled to the side, striking her head on the bottom of the wall.

Warren rolled on top of the man, battering him with three short, vicious punches to the head, and for a moment their assailant didn't seem to have control of his limbs. In that instant, Warren's thick arm closed around the man's neck and began to squeeze. The man tried to twist in his grip, to punch or elbow Warren, but his strength was draining. Within ten seconds, he shuddered and went still.

Panting, Warren rolled off him.

"Is he dead?" Cole asked.

"Unconscious."

Warren stood and patted the man down. For the first time, Cole noticed his face. He was tanned, with a solid jaw and a diagonal red scar across his left cheek that looked like it had been made by a large cat, or a small knife. She didn't recognize him. "He have any ID on him?"

"No weapon, no ID. Must've left everything in the SUV."

"Phone? I saw a light."

Warren gestured to a small flashlight in the snow. "No phone, which doesn't make sense. If he wanted to track us, he'd need a..."

"What?"

Warren checked the man's pockets again, then held up a small black disc the size of a poker chip. "Tracking device. Likely pinging the driver's phone."

"Why use that instead of a phone?"

Warren gestured down at the motionless body. "In case *that* happened. Now we have no idea who he is. Phone or ID or anything else, and if we got the jump on him, as we did, we'd know who was after us."

"You still think it was Mazzalano's guys?"

Warren ignored her question. He tossed the GPS chip onto the unconscious man's chest. "He'll be down for a few minutes. Let's go."

He nodded toward a road that led from the memorial, barely visible in the snow. A faint set of tire tracks, likely left by a maintenance cart because they were narrow and close together, traced down the road and around a curve.

They followed the tracks until they saw the main cemetery entrance and a wall much too tall to climb. Warren jutted left. Cole followed.

A couple hundred yards from the entrance, they escaped the cemetery over a low stone wall. They walked along the cleared road to avoid leaving tracks, then turned right and walked onto Arlington Memorial Bridge, which led into downtown D.C.

The streetlights that lit an arched trail across the bridge were shrouded by a low fog from the Potomac, taking on the appearance of cloudy yellow orbs floating every twenty yards. It was nearly midnight and the bridge's wide sidewalks were empty. At the halfway point, where the bridge hit its crest and sloped down toward the Lincoln Memorial, Cole looked back at the massive stone entrance to Arlington National Cemetery.

She wasn't sure why she hadn't told Warren that Matt was buried there. She tried to tell herself it was because they were in a hurry. But she feared it was her own guilt.

Since Matt's funeral, she hadn't visited his grave. Not once. Instead, she'd visited their favorite places in New York City—the north end of Central Park, a hole-in-the-wall noodle place in Hell's Kitchen, a Seahawks bar where Matt watched the games with other Seattle expats. Sometimes, to make it through a difficult day or month, she'd chosen not to think about his death at all.

"Where are we going?" she asked.

Warren slowed until she caught up. "Train."

"What about your car?" Cole asked. "Our stuff?"

"You want to head back there?"

"No," Cole said.

"Me neither."

They passed under a streetlight and Cole caught the side of Warren's face. His mouth was half-open, like he was trying to decide whether to say something.

"I can see you thinking, Rob. What is it?"

"I need to tell you about *Maiale da Tartufo*."

55

Half an hour later they sat side-by-side on the floor of the grand lobby in Union Station. Octagonal insets rimmed with gold dotted the high, curved ceilings, and the black and white marble floor gleamed from a recent waxing.

Cole had used cash to purchase two one-way tickets on the next train to Miami, which left in six hours. She'd withdrawn $500 from her checking account—the maximum allowed—and used $400 on the tickets, figuring it was better to be broke than to leave a credit card trail of where they were headed. She'd wanted to purchase toiletries and cell phone chargers, but, aside from an automatic coffee machine, everything was closed.

That left them $100, two dying cell phones, and the clothes on their backs.

Warren slid a coffee across the floor, but she ignored it. "There's something I don't get," she said. "Why would Samuel Bacon text you about *Maiale...da...Tartufo*?" She said the name slowly, poorly attempting an Italian accent.

"Feels guilty, probably. Saw the gun transaction go down in real time and just stood there."

"I get that, but why not tell his bosses, or the FBI?"

Warren considered this. "Complicated, but I see two options. One is, he *did* share it with his bosses. But the JTTF is NYPD *and* FBI, two groups who don't always get along. It's supposed to be butterflies and rainbows, sharing and caring, all for the greater good. Doesn't always work out that way. JTTF team members like Bacon, who come from within the NYPD, leak stuff when they don't think the FBI side is handling it right. Or, he *didn't* report it to his superiors because he's worried it'll come back on him and his partner. If he admits they saw the post about the sale of the weapons and didn't follow up, not good."

An uneasy feeling settled in Cole. She didn't like not knowing whether the FBI was following the same lead she and Warren were. "Earlier, why'd you say I wouldn't want to know who *Maiale da Tartufo* is? And what does that name mean, anyway?"

"*Maiale da Tartufo* isn't a name. It's a nickname. It means The Truffle Pig."

"Huh?"

"The Truffle Pig."

"Odd," Cole said.

"It's not odd, it's terrifying. *Maiale da Tartufo* is one of the most notorious hitmen on earth. Came up in the old school mob in Italy. Said to have a hundred murders under his belt. First one at age eleven. Decade ago he killed a boss for no apparent reason, then escaped to the U.S."

"No apparent reason?" she asked.

"I'm sure the reason was apparent *to him*. I'm saying *I* don't know it. After three years, he resurfaced. Rumored to be responsible for at least six murders in the U.S. since then, though of course we don't really know."

"What's his real name?"

Warren shrugged. "No one knows."

"Why do they call him The Truffle Pig?" Cole asked.

"He's from northern Italy, near the French border. Before he was taken in, he and his family hunted and sold truffles. Now, it's the connotation. Even if you're literally buried underground, he'll sniff you out. No matter what, if your number is called, he'll find you."

Cole shivered. "And *that's* the guy we're following to Miami?"

Warren didn't reply.

She took a long swig of coffee, expecting a cup of burnt black crap. It was sweet and creamy. "Thanks for not foisting your black coffee nonsense on me."

"Obviously your body hasn't yet been fully destroyed by sugar.

You were able to get the drop on whoever the hell that was back there." He looked at her, and for a moment she locked in on his dark eyes. "Thanks for that."

His face was scratched and a few grains of dirt clung to his forehead. She brushed them away. "You would have gotten the upper hand on him eventually."

"That's true."

Cole leaned back and shot him a look. "That's not what you're supposed to say."

He looked at her, side-eyed.

"You're supposed to say, 'No I wouldn't have, Jane Cole, you saved my ass.'"

"You *did*, but I would have rolled him in another few seconds. I don't say that to brag. I know what I'm doing in a fight."

"He *did* land a couple shots on you," Cole said.

Warren rubbed a swollen spot on his right temple. "Barely. But seriously, listen. I've got Marine Corps and NYPD hand-to-hand training, but that guy...he was big, but he was an *amateur*. Hadn't been trained in anything. Makes me think."

Cole followed his eyes across the station, waiting for him to continue. In the far corner, a young couple sat on a large back-pack, giggling under the twinkling lights of a thirty-foot-high Christmas tree. Across from the couple, a man in a filthy coat sat on a bed of garbage bags, mumbling to himself. And in the center of the cavernous station, a couple in evening wear slow danced, tipsy and oblivious to the world around them.

"Mazzalano would have sent cops, or ex-cops," he said finally. "Cops would have been trained. That guy was unarmed, untrained. He wanted to follow us, to keep an eye on us, but he had no intention of killing us. That guy wasn't sent by Mazzalano."

"So you think Mazzalano had us tailed until we hit Jersey, but someone else picked us up in D.C?"

Warren nodded.

Cole leaned her head on his shoulder. She was tired and increasingly confused. "Who?" she asked quietly. "And why?"

Warren let out a long sigh. "I have no idea."

—End of Episode 2—

THE
CRIME
BEAT

EPISODE 3: MIAMI

56

Friday

Marco De Santis eased the eighteen-foot runabout through the misty bay, guided by the blinking blue light on his phone. The water glimmered as the sun appeared in the east, a speck of orange across miles of dark water. His phone beeped every few seconds, keeping time with the light of the GPS marker.

He was only a thousand yards from the weapon.

It was barely five a.m. and already the air was sixty-five degrees. De Santis was comfortable in his black speedo and plain white t-shirt. Knowing he'd have to swim, he'd tucked his clothes and keys in a duffel bag. He'd noticed that, in most of America, men didn't wear speedos as European men did.

But everything was different in Miami.

A fit sixty-year-old man in a speedo wouldn't even draw attention. It didn't matter anyway. He wouldn't run into anyone out here. Not this early.

He navigated the boat around a small island the shape of a crescent moon. According to his phone, he was still on course. The dead drop location was four hundred yards away.

He slowed the boat, enjoying the thick, salty air. For ten years he'd toiled, working to stash away three million, almost enough to retire. Three and a half was his goal. Tomorrow, he'd have it. The money he was about to pick up—plus the additional $250,000 he'd receive once the job was done—would give him three and a half million plus enough for three or four plastic surgeries. Enough to ensure his anonymity and safety long term. He'd always been proud of his nose. When he was a boy, his mother called it a "Roman nose." She'd said the prominent raised bump in the center was the mark of a "true Italian." It was too distinctive, though. Flattening it would be his first surgery.

Hell, maybe he'd make Miami his place of retirement. Going home to Italy was never in the cards. He'd planned to go to a small country where his olive skin would blend in—Latvia, or maybe Crete. But a day in Miami had made him reconsider. Maybe he could retire in the States.

He had fifteen more good years, maybe twenty, and he vowed to spend them in the sun. A good surgeon could sculpt a few Cuban features, allowing him to blend in with the community in Miami. He could learn to speak Spanish.

But even if he achieved an impeccable accent and the perfect bulbous tipped nose through rhinoplasty, actual Cubans would know he was a fraud. For De Santis, a fine Italian vintage was a matter of necessity. He hated rum. And in Miami Mojitos and Daiquiris flowed like wine. With less than a week until retirement he could almost taste the Brunello. Maybe not Miami, then.

Tied to a dinghy fifty yards from the tip of the crescent island, a rowboat bobbed in the water. De Santis killed the engine, drifted, then threw the anchor. A second later it landed with a light tug against his boat. He was still in shallow water.

He put on goggles and pulled an exacto knife and a diving light from the duffel bag, then folded his t-shirt neatly, flicked on the light, and slipped silently into the water.

The water was warmer than the air, an odd sensation. The lakes of Northern Italy had never been this warm, especially in December. He swam easily—his taut, wiry body a coiled spring—and found the bottom of the rowboat.

The package was there. Three feet long and maybe a foot deep, it was held in place by duct tape. With four deft strokes of the knife, he cut it loose, expecting it to drift down into his arms.

It didn't.

He tugged at the package, which held fast.

He came up for air holding the side of the boat emptying

droplets of water from his goggles. Across Biscayne Bay, a boat moved through the orange dawn. Judging by its lights, it was roughly the same size as his runabout.

He dunked back under the water, moving swiftly to the bottom of the rowboat. He held the light up to the spot where the package was attached. A makeshift loop of duct tape had been hooked to a short length of rope tied to a metal ring on the bottom of the boat. Extra protection. The men who'd hired him were cautious.

With a swipe, he cut the loop. The package fell free, floating down into his arms.

He swam back to his boat and, treading water, hoisted the package over his head. It weighed about fifteen pounds, just what he'd expected. All U.S. bills weigh roughly one gram. So 2,500 hundred dollar bills would weigh five and a half pounds. The rifle, assuming it was the same model he'd used in D.C., weighed another six. The ammo and the case, another two. All the water-proof bags and tape added another pound. He tossed it into the well of his boat and climbed aboard.

The other boat was moving toward his. It was a small fishing yacht, maybe twenty-five feet, and it had already covered half the distance between him and the shore. He looked to a wooden dock jutting from the center of the crescent island. He allowed himself to hope that the boat was heading for the dock.

If the vessel didn't get any closer, he wouldn't have to do it.

The boat kept coming. "Damn," he said quietly.

Judging by its speed, he had only a minute until it reached him. Using the exacto knife, he slit open four layers of heavy-duty plastic bags. Inside the fifth bag, in shrink-wrapped plastic, he found the money. Always find the money first. Without the money, nothing else matters.

Next, he unwrapped the black rifle bag. Since coming to America, he'd had a policy: always make the customer provide the weapon and ammo.

The process of acquiring these was one more way to get caught. He only worked for top-tier customers who knew the best weapon for the job, and how to get it. This job had been unusual. The men had the weapons before contacting him. He couldn't complain. The custom fifty-calibre rifles were the finest he'd ever seen. He stowed the weapon and the money and pulled a beretta from the duffel bag, placing it under his hamstring as he sat.

The boat pulled alongside. A handsome man around his age waved, smiling. He wore white shorts and an unbuttoned pastel blue shirt, his large round belly leading the way as he waddled to the edge of the boat. "You alright?"

De Santis waved toward the rowboat. "Fine. Saw this old boat tied up and thought I'd check it out. That's all. It's anchored."

"Odd. Abandoned, you think?"

The Beretta pressed into his hamstring. "Guessing so."

Two fishing poles were propped in their holders off the back of the man's boat, which had the words *Marlin's Tomb* stenciled on its side. He gestured at the poles. "Fishing?"

A woman appeared from a small cabin. She was younger, maybe late thirties. Black hair, with a pretty round face. "Let's go, *papi.*" She stood next to the man on the side of the boat, wrapping an arm around his waist.

De Santis felt a twitch of conscience. She was pregnant.

The man said, "Alright then. Wanted to make sure you weren't stranded."

"Thank you," De Santis said.

As the man turned, De Santis stood, sliding the Beretta from under his leg and disengaging the safety in one deft motion.

When he was a boy, he'd hated this part. As a teenager he'd resented it. By his early twenties he'd gone numb to it. Now, well, he'd woken up this morning telling himself he had one kill left.

Now, counting the baby, it was four. So be it.

He squeezed the trigger, striking the man in the back of the head. He crumpled instantly. The woman spun and opened her mouth to scream when she saw the gun. No sound came out. She glanced back at the cabin.

"Don't move," De Santis said coolly.

She turned back and he met her eyes. She opened her mouth again, stammering, "I…I…a baby…I have a baby." She ran a hand over her belly, swollen like it contained a perfectly round melon. "Please. You were a baby once."

"Once I was a baby, baby Marco. For the last fifty years I've been *Maiale al Tartufo.* Do you speak Italian?"

She had a slightly Italian look, but spoke without an accent.

Miami was diverse enough that she could have been from anywhere.

She shook her head. "My parents were from Barcelona."

"Born here, then?"

She nodded.

"You live in Miami?"

She nodded again.

"Where would you recommend a new resident live?"

Her eyes flicked left and right. Desperate. Confused. She began to shake.

"No recommendations? I hear Coral Gables is nice, but I might move to Little Havana just for the food. Last night I had chorizo *croquetas* and…what do you think a two-bedroom on the beach costs these days?" He shook his head. "But I'm worried no one will believe I'm Cuban if all I drink is fine Italian wine."

She didn't respond, just hugged herself, shaking.

De Santis sat, holding the Beretta by his side. He started the engine and let the runabout drift toward the side of the fishing boat. As one boat glided past the other, he stood and shot the woman in the heart.

Leaning forward slightly, he put another bullet in the man's head—just to be sure. Then one more in the woman's round belly.

The echoes faded.

The morning was silent, and De Santis aimed the boat at the shore.

57

Jane Cole floated above a rocky mountain in Afghanistan, watching Matt navigate a Jeep over a dusty road. He wore his Desert Sand Cammies, the light tan of the uniform setting off his dark brown hair. She'd always loved him in uniform.

Two fellow Marines sat in the back seat, watching as Matt maneuvered the Jeep around twists and turns up a one-lane mountain road, then down the other side. The ride seemed to go on forever. His hair blew in the wind, dust circled behind the Jeep. No one spoke.

He stopped at a small town, where children played around a stone well. He waved at a child, who ran up to the Jeep. Matt reached out to the boy.

Suddenly, one of the men jerked forward violently, wrapping a cord around Matt's throat.

"Remember the video I showed you?" Warren's voice entered her dream, drowning out her husband's choked gasps. "Back in New York?"

Her eyes shot open. She drew a sharp breath, as though she were the one desperate for air.

Warren placed a hand on her shoulder gently. "Sorry. I didn't realize you were still sleeping. You okay?"

She blinked, trying to erase the dream. She'd had it at least one other time. Maybe the night in the hotel in D.C. Maybe her last night in New York. She wasn't sure. "I'm okay. Bad dream. What? Were you saying something about New York?"

"The video I showed you."

She scooched up in her seat. "I'll never forget it, or what you told me you saw in that guy's house."

"I haven't followed the guy's case since I was put on leave, but chances are he'll get ten to twenty for what he did. He…" Warren trailed off and stared out the train window.

His face was pinched—the look he got when he wanted to say more, but couldn't bring himself to say it.

They'd boarded the train while D.C. was still dark, and Cole had fallen asleep soon after. Now the bright sun sliced through the windows and glimmered off the snow-covered branches that flashed by outside.

Cole rubbed her eyes. "Where are we?"

"Georgia."

"We passed through North *and* South Carolina?"

"You nodded off somewhere in Virginia."

She was beginning to realize that Warren had a well of emotion and thoughtfulness just under the surface. But it was as though he tightened his face and the rest of him to keep it at bay. "Rob, what's up?"

"Just thinking. Raj Ambani *donated* to Alvin Meyers, right? To his campaigns?"

Cole had learned this with a simple Google search. "Multiple times, why?"

"As a cop, I took down guys like that sick pedophile. That's an easy one. That guy deserves something worse than death. You believe in hell?"

Cole considered this. Matt had been religious, but she never had. "I think hell is the suffering we create for ourselves on earth. Hell is thinking we shouldn't be locked in these bodies, but knowing we are. And I believe locking guys like that pedophile away makes our hell a couple degrees cooler while we're living in it."

Warren studied her, taking in what she'd said. "I think hell's a place. A place people go for the stuff they do on earth. That guy will end up there, to be sure. But I wonder, will Alvin Meyers and Raj Ambani be there with him?"

"What makes you say that?" she asked.

"While you were sleeping, I looked them up. Both are upstanding citizens, pillars of their communities. At the same

252

time, Meyers was VP as the U.S. expanded its drone program. At the president's direction, he *oversaw* the program. We took out tens of thousands of people with machines from the sky, all on his watch. Don't get me wrong, I believe our cause is just, but..."

"But?"

"We took out civilians, too. Kids." He closed his eyes. "Maybe I'm not as convinced of our righteousness as I used to be, as I *wish* I was."

"What about Ambani?" Cole asked. "Helluva guy, by all accounts."

"Not to everyone. You been on Reddit?"

She nodded. She'd used the online message board community for research a few times. Like most of the internet, it was a great resource that was also riddled with misinformation and toxic craziness.

"Hundreds of threads about Ambani's death there," Warren said. "Talking about digital globalization, individual freedom from digital tracking, corporate overreach, and so on."

"Extremists?" Cole asked. "Saying that their ideas justify the murder?"

"Some, sure. But—and this was weird—I found myself agreeing with some of the other commenters. The ones who talked about the way companies like Ambani's are taking over everything. Guys like him are powerful, maybe even more powerful than governments and..."

He didn't finish the thought, but it was clear where he'd been headed. "You think the world is better off without him?" Cole asked.

"Didn't say that."

Cole wasn't comfortable with where this was headed. As a journalist, she faced a tension between reporting the world as it was, and judging the world for what it should be. As much as possible, she tried to report the facts and leave her beliefs out of it. She wasn't prepared to consider whether the men who'd killed Ambani and Meyers had legitimate grievances. All she cared about was cracking the case, breaking the story. "Speaking of donations. That reminds me."

Warren leaned in close as she tapped her phone. He didn't resist her attempt to change the subject, so she continued. "The only certain connections are the donations Ambani made to

Meyers. Where my mind wants to go next is connections between those two and prominent Miami residents."

Starting with "Ambani" + "Meyers" + "Miami," Cole ran a series of Google searches. Nothing came up.

Next she tried searches with only one of the names, plus "Miami." This led her to a series of dead ends. Both men had Miami connections—from political fundraisers to board meetings to well-publicized vacations. Ambani's wife had even done a special performance at the Miami opera house.

Cole set her phone on her lap. "Rob, I…" Pieces of the dream still clung to her. Her mind was foggy. She wanted to tell him about it, but something didn't let her.

She dreamed about Matt often. Usually the scenes were connected to digital photographs he'd emailed her. Her favorite was the shot of him in the Jeep, which had been taken sometime during his first week in country. In the image, there was a man in the passenger seat. His buddy Bryce. In her dreams, she'd often seen them driving peacefully around the countryside in Afghanistan. That wasn't how war *was,* but her therapist had encouraged her to simply enjoy the dreams, that they were just her mind taking something real—the image—and using it to create a pleasant, harmless fantasy.

The dream this morning had been anything but pleasant, and she decided to banish it from her mind. "Rob, gut instinct, where do we start when we get to Miami?"

"You know, before your story about me, I was set to become a detective."

A wave of guilt hit her. "I know."

"Already studying for the exam."

"Something in your study prepared you for this?" she asked.

"Not at all," he said. "Far as I know, there's never been anything like this."

"You're not making me feel any better."

"Not trying to," he said. "At first, I thought we needed to look at this like a serial killing, but it's more like a terrorist attack. In either case, we have two threads. When we get to Miami, I think I should pull one. You pull the other."

"Two threads?" Cole asked.

"The killer and the next victim."

Cole nodded. "Go on."

"I have an old informant in Miami. One of my best sources while I was NYPD. Kind of guy who might have heard if something was gonna go down in Miami. Maybe he knows something about the rifle. About *Maiale al Tartufo*, if he came to Miami after D.C." He sighed. "It's a long shot, but it's the best thing I can think of."

"He *did* come to Miami. I know he did."

Warren offered a weak nod, but didn't seem as convinced as she was. "The other thread is the next victim," he went on, "and that's where *you* come in. You know research better than me. I've known that since that first afternoon in my apartment."

"You think I can magically figure out who the next victim will be?" she asked.

"I'm guessing Google isn't the extent of your research abilities."

Cole thought for a moment. Truth was, there were a hundred possible connections between Ambani, Meyers, and various bigwigs in Miami. Through a combination of online research and checking with sources, she could narrow it down. Her guess was there would be dozens of possible victims. "What time do we arrive?"

"Half an hour. Ten a.m. local time."

For the first time since she'd woken up, she looked directly at him. The flesh under his dark eyes was puffy and a small swelling rose from his cheek. "You've got a lump from the fight, and you look exhausted. Didn't sleep?"

"Nah."

"So we check into a hotel, you sleep for a couple hours, I research."

"Don't you need to sleep more?" he asked.

The thought brought her back to the dream. She closed her eyes.

"Cole?"

She shook her head. "Don't want to sleep."

"What is it?"

"Nothing...bad dream. I'm fine, really. You watched over me while I slept. Once we get to a hotel, I'll make a list of potential victims while you get a few hours of rest. Then we go from there."

58

A palm frond tickled the glass of the second-story window. Cole looked up from her phone. Outside, the light blue sky was visible through a crack in the turquoise curtains. Over the bed, an elegant watercolor of a silver-blue marlin decorated the pale yellow wall.

Warren had fallen into a deep sleep moments after shutting the door of their hotel room in Little Havana. His prosthetic leg stuck out from under his pillow. He was barely breathing. Dead to the world.

She'd made good progress in her search. Using news databases, online searches, and a series of text exchanges with former colleagues, she'd compiled a list of six prominent Miamians with ties to both businessman Raj Ambani and former Vice President Alvin Meyers. They were political donors, business people, bankers, and others who pulled the strings of power in South Florida. They all had connections to Ambani and Meyers, and they all had threads connecting them to other powerful people around the world.

She'd organized her list using nothing more than instinct. Trying to put herself in the shoes of an anti-corporate, anti-technology extremist, she'd asked herself, "Who in Miami would *I* want to kill next?"

She'd written her list on a clean sheet of *Hotel Marlin* stationery:

1) Alejandro Hernandez, former mayor of Miami.

2) Frank Johnston, CEO of South Beach Investments, LLC.

3) Maria Brown, owner of Coastal Exporters.

4) Ana Diaz, financier, Bank of South Florida.

5) Bernard Erickson, Chairman of the Board, Gulf Labs, Inc.

6) Benjamin Patrick Riley, III, Owner and CEO, Tropical Cruises, Intl., and primary shareholder in three local sports franchises.

At noon she woke Warren with a gentle shake of his shoulder. He sat up and quickly put on his leg in one smooth motion. Like Matt and other military men she'd met, he was used to springing into action after too little sleep.

She handed him a Cuban coffee and a *pastelito*, which she'd ordered from room service. "I asked for the coffee without sugar and they treated me like a crazy person. The pastry is guava and cheese."

Warren took a small sip of the coffee. His eyes shot open like he'd been hit by an electrical current. "Whoa!"

"I know, right? I've had two and now I'm thinking that may have been a mistake. If they aren't already, they should be classified as schedule two narcotics. It's like my heart is hugging my brain."

Warren chuckled, setting the flaky pastry on the nightstand. "What'd you find?"

"Some potential targets," she said, taking the opportunity to grab the *pastelito*, "but nothing I feel solid about. There's—"

"Wait." He downed the rest of the coffee in one swig. "There's something else we need to talk about first. Mazzalano. The map."

Warren had a moral compass, a black-and-white sense of right and wrong. He'd exercised restraint by letting it go this long. She offered a noncommittal shrug and continued eating the pastry.

"You been online yet?" he asked.

"Nothing yet about the map or the storage unit."

"You said he'd make a thing out of it right away."

"I thought he would." One thing about Mazzalano was that he was hungry for the limelight, and for promotions. If he'd had them followed to Wragg's storage unit in Jersey, he'd found the map, just as she had. He'd also had the time to go through the rest of the unit. She'd been sure he'd announce the find publicly to bask in the glory.

Warren narrowed his eyes. "You *know* what I think we should do, right?"

"Release the map?" cole asked.

"And everything else we have, yeah. It doesn't mean we need to stop our pursuit, but it's not right to hold onto it."

"Gimme one more day," Cole said.

"Look, the map could—"

"*Could,*" Cole interrupted sharply. "We don't know what releasing the map will do. What if Mazzalano did the right thing and passed everything to the FBI—the map and the rest of Wragg's storage unit? Maybe they're not releasing it yet for good reason. Maybe they don't want to let the killers know they're on their trail? If we release the map, we could be blowing up their spot."

Warren looked skeptical. "You're grasping for straws because you're greedy about information."

He was right. Information was currency, and all journalists jealously guarded their scoops. But there was something else. Something she couldn't quite figure out.

"What?" Warren asked. "I see your mind working."

She closed her eyes. "In D.C., the two guys who followed us. You were sure they weren't Mazzalano's guys because they were amateurs. Mazzalano would have sent crooked cops or whatever. Trained pros."

"Yeah."

"I'm not buying that. There's no one else who knew we were in D.C. No one with a reason to have us followed." Warren tried to interrupt, but she held up the half-eaten *pastelito* to ward him off. "Lemme finish."

He leaned away from the flaky carbs like they were poison.

Cole continued holding the pastelito in her fist as though it were a speaker's rod. "And it goes with Mazzalano not releasing the map," she said. "He's in on it. Somehow. He tailed us to the storage unit, destroyed the evidence, then had us followed all the way to D.C."

Warren's head was shaking in disagreement before she finished. "If that's true, he would want us dead. And he wouldn't have sent *those* jokers. He would have sent someone to *end* us."

"Agree to disagree," Cole said. "In either case, give it one more day. Please. We take until tomorrow to find The Truffle Pig, or the next target. If we fail, we release the map. But if we succeed, this is over."

"And you get the credit?" His tone was slightly mocking.

"*We* get the credit. You think the NYPD might look twice at your resumé with this on it?"

Warren walked a lap around the room, shaking his leg like he was trying to get his stump to settle comfortably in the prosthetic. "Okay. First thing tomorrow we release the map."

She smiled, then stared at the list in her lap, ready to move on. She felt his eyes on her.

"Jane."

She looked up.

"Why are you doing this? I mean, I get you want the story, but—"

"I *need* the story." She said it without thinking, as though it was the most obvious, truest thing about her.

"Okay, I get that. I do. But there's something else."

"Michael Wragg, back in New York. He knew something about my husband."

"That's not it either."

Her skin tingled uncomfortably. Her eyes dropped to the pastel green carpet. "What are you getting at?"

"I don't know. Something about Matt." He frowned. "I never really knew myself until I lost Sarah. I mean when she left me, which she had every right to do. That kind of pain takes us places we didn't know we had in us, forces us to grow. I can't imagine if I'd lost her like you lost Matt."

She quickly wiped away the tears forming in her eyes. She loved remembering Matt, but on her own terms. Not in dreams and not in conversations like this. "I don't know." She said it firmly, trying to end the conversation.

"You're willing to do things—immoral things—to get this story. I want to know why and I think there's a reason you're not telling me, maybe a reason you don't even know."

Steeling herself, she looked up. "I need to get to work finding these people."

Warren raised an eyebrow, then shrugged, letting it drop.

"Call your CI," she continued, waving her list at him. "I'll pull these threads and you start pulling any that you can. Maybe we'll meet in the middle."

"It's weird," Warren said. "Never been to Miami, don't know much about it other than that Will Smith song. SG—that's what I called my CI—he moved down here when he sobered up. Sometimes in my dreams I'd be down here, asking him for information on a case." He smiled. "Weird, right?"

"You think he might know something?" Cole asked.

"Probably not, but it's worth a shot."

59

The midday sun warmed Cole's face as she took in the sights and smells of Little Havana. A brightly-colored rooster sculpture welcomed her to *Calle Ocho*, the wide central road lined with palm trees. Yellow and orange awnings shaded windows of cozy restaurants and bars that were lively despite the lunchtime hour. Yesterday she'd stood in the snowy gray of Washington, D.C., surrounded by stately marble and granite columns.

She had to admit, the weather, the food, and the bright colors made it harder to fall into existential brooding in Miami.

She bought a Cuban coffee, sat at an old metal table on the sidewalk, and took out her list. The rich smell of tobacco drifted from a cigar shop, making her wish she smoked. She'd tried a cigar in college, and, after throwing up for an hour, had vowed never to do so again.

When she was trying to read someone, she let everything drop away, tried to allow even herself to fade into the background. The goal was to experience her subject as objectively as possible. She tried doing that with the list. Staring at the names, she let her eyes go soft, hoping for some direction, some inspiration. Nothing came except a vague sense that #1 on her list, former Miami mayor Alejandro Hernandez, wasn't a good place to start. Frank Johnston was #2. CEO of South Beach Investments, LLC, Johnston was connected to Ambani through an online payment system in which they'd both invested. He was connected to Meyers through a Board of Directors they'd served on in the early 2000s.

She called the listed number for South Beach Investments, where she was told Mr. Johnston was unavailable. After she pressed, his secretary revealed he'd left that day for Japan. She wondered whether he'd left the country after getting wind that someone was after him.

Using Google Translate to search the Japanese internet led her to an article from two weeks earlier, announcing Johnston's attendance at a conference of Japanese investors in the American tech sector. Clearly, it was an event that had been planned for months. She'd missed the announcement in her initial search, but had to believe the killers they were chasing would have known about it. She'd put her list together in under an hour, whereas the killers had been planning this for months, maybe years.

She crossed Frank Johnston off the list and took a satisfied sip of coffee. Thick, strong, and sweet, it was even better than the ones in the hotel. Twice as strong as any espresso she'd ever had and sweeter than the vanilla lattes she drank at home. She could get used to this.

Maria Brown was next on her list. According to the records Cole had found online, Brown was the sole owner of Coastal Exporters, a company that served as the middleman between many of the state's citrus growers and Canada, which purchased $150-million worth of Florida citrus per year. A profile of Brown had reported, "If you've eaten an orange in Canada, you have Maria Brown to thank."

The connections to Ambani and Meyers were numerous. Brown was one of the most influential political donors in the state, and a search of campaign contributors showed she spread her money far and wide. When Meyers had campaigned for Vice President, Brown hosted a fundraiser for the ticket. Meyers attended, praised Brown, and, most importantly, championed a loosening of agricultural review standards that benefited Brown's exporting business. *The New York Times* had run an article, questioning the obvious *quid pro quo*, but nothing came of it. Typical political corruption, Cole thought, but a possible motive.

Unable to find any personal contact information for Brown, she called the Coastal Exporters main number.

"Who's calling?" a pleasant male voice asked when she requested to speak with Brown.

Cole considered various lies that might bring Brown to the phone, but went with the truth. "This is Jane Cole. Until last week, I was a reporter for the *New York Sun*."

"And what is this call in reference to?"

She didn't want to say too much, but she also needed this gate-keeper to feel the urgency the situation demanded. "Ms. Brown was close with former Vice President Alvin Meyers who, I'm sure you know, was shot a few days ago. I have reason to believe Ms. Brown could be in danger as well and—"

"I'm sorry, Ms…Joel, was it?"

"Cole. Jane Cole. I really need to speak with Ms. Brown."

"I'll level with you, Ms. Cole," the man said. "Since Vice President Meyers was murdered, we've been called for comment by every journalist in Miami, and most outside Miami as well. To use a made up threat against Ms. Brown as a way to get an interview is shameful. You're one notch above the reporter who followed her into the women's bathroom at her gym and shoved a recorder in her face. But barely. Goodbye."

The call ended. Cole called right back, but it went straight to voicemail. Just in case, she left a polite message with her phone number.

She took in her surroundings, which appeared even more colorful now that the coffee had hit her bloodstream. The palm trees were decorated with twinkling Christmas lights, and she couldn't wait to see them at night. Locals and tourists came and went, many carrying bags of Christmas presents. A woman rode a bike wearing a Santa Claus-styled bikini, handlebars in one hand, vape pen in the other.

Across the street, a young man tried to get the attention of every woman who passed. He wore long black shorts and a white t-shirt, which he strategically took off, displaying a shaved, muscular chest as each new woman walked by. Christmas in Miami made her smile.

Her next target was Ana Diaz, a prominent Miami financier. Her connections with Ambani and Meyers were more tangential than some of the others, but she rose up the list because of her vast wealth.

Cole ran a series of searches for Diaz, looking for recent news, then read through the website of the Bank of South Florida. It was one of the last of the small Florida banks, independent and locally owned. A phone call got her an empty promise from a secretary: Ms. Diaz would get back to her when she was available. Another call, this one to the corporate offices, got her a shred of information. Ms. Diaz was appearing today at a small business entrepreneurship conference—an event encouraging young minorities to form local businesses, and, of course, to do their banking with the Bank of South Florida.

"May I attend?" Cole asked eagerly.

"Are you a Miami resident?"

"I'm a journalist," Cole replied. "I'd like to write about the event."

"I'm sorry, no press allowed."

"I have a cousin who's a Miami resident who might be interested." The lie came out before she knew what she was saying. "Can you give me the location?"

The woman paused, then gave her an address in Little Haiti, about fifteen minutes north of Little Havana. "Your cousin will need a valid Miami ID—driver's license, high school ID, or military ID—to get in."

"I understand. Can she bring a guest?"

The woman sighed. "One guest per attendee."

Cole hung up. She needed a Miami resident.

The man across the street was repeating his mating ritual. As a woman in a tight red dress walked by, he tore off his shirt and flexed his chest muscles. A gold "305" medallion around his neck glimmered in the sun.

The woman passed without a glance.

305 was the area code of Miami. This guy was a local and proud of it. He was also full of himself and desperate for attention.

Perfect.

60

Dressed in a pink, floral-print shirt, dark sunglasses, and a cheap sun hat, Marco De Santis walked down Ocean Drive. Carrying the black duffel, in which he'd stowed the rifle and the money, he looked like any other tourist. It was nearly eighty degrees, but the breeze off the ocean made it feel like seventy-five. The more he thought about it, the more he saw himself retiring here.

His shot on the Vice President had been the most difficult of his career. A mile away and across a river. Distance meant time: the .50 caliber round had been in the air for over two seconds. And rivers meant wind. In addition to the two-inch vertical sag he'd adjusted for, the wind had pushed it half a foot to the left. The hotel room had been three stories above the roof of the Watergate Hotel, giving him high ground and a solid angle, but still. It was a once-in-a-lifetime shot. He'd never get credit for it, but he took pride in the fact that it would be discussed in sniper circles for years.

But that shot was behind him and it no longer earned him money. This next, his last, would be relatively easy.

The estate was on the east side of the street, facing the ocean, but the perimeter didn't look like the pictures he'd been sent when he accepted the job. The massive beachfront house was caged by a stone wall about six feet high. That much he'd expected. But another layer of fencing had been added awkwardly on top of the stone wall. In haste, he thought. And recently. Aluminum poles had been drilled into the rock every six feet, chain link strung between them and barbed wire angled toward the street. The wall now stood over ten feet high. All that was visible through the chain link fence was the roof, a few windows, a balcony, and the tops of a dozen palm trees.

Walking slowly up the street, he studied the angles between the homes and apartment buildings and the target. He needed height, but most of the buildings across the street were single family homes.

A black Land Cruiser pulled around the corner and turned into the estate when a metal gate opened. Two men jumped from the back seat and guarded the gate as it swung smoothly back into place. Good security. Above average.

It was not the car of a financier, though. That was a fourth-level bulletproof Land Cruiser. Extra-thick doors, bulletproof glass, completely dark so he hadn't even glanced the target, if she'd even been inside. Even the tires were reinforced to take multiple, perfectly-placed shots before they'd flatten. And even if he took out a tire, the car was still drivable. He'd known she rode in a Land Cruiser, but not that it had been armored to one step below a presidential limo.

Walking casually away from the estate, he ran a hand over his smooth face and squeezed his jaw to make sure he wasn't developing jowls. He worried about his age showing, wanted desperately to have a life once he retired. He hadn't been with a woman he hadn't paid in fifteen years. It wasn't fair to bring a woman anywhere near his line of work. But once he retired, maybe he'd have time for love.

He walked north, toward downtown Miami. One block, then two.

The buildings grew taller the further he got from the estate. A block ahead, a small hotel, maybe six stories, sat across the street from the beach. He let his eyes move slowly up the face of the building. It was a creamy off-white, and each room had a balcony. If he could get a room facing the target's estate, he'd have an angle.

Yes, this would do nicely.

266

61

Cole finished her coffee and crossed the street, careful not to look directly at the shirtless man. Around five foot five, the same height as her, he had thick, muscular calves that poked out from the bottom of his shorts, which bore a Miami Heat logo: a flaming red basketball cresting a rim.

She leaned on a parking meter and pretended to stare at her phone, then followed his gaze to another woman, this one coming from the other direction. She had black hair and wore black jeans and a bright yellow bikini top.

The man repeated his routine. Shirt off. Flash a smile. Flex. From her new vantage point, she saw that his shaven, muscular chest was oiled up.

He slung the shirt over his shoulder as the woman passed, again flexing and this time adding, "Hey, *mama*."

The woman slowed long enough to laugh and say, "*Poquito!*"

He put his shirt on as she disappeared down the block.

Gathering her snark, Cole approached. He spied her from twenty yards away and, as he began to pull the shirt over his head, she called, "Don't bother!" Extending her hand, she said, "Jane Cole. I'm a reporter from New York City."

He stepped back, looking her up and down. "Bro, I *knew* word about my music would get out." He spoke quickly, with a slight

267

hint of a Cuban accent. "Didn't expect *The New York Times* to send a reporter down to talk to me for at least another year."

She stared, stone-faced.

After a long look, his face broke out in a wide smile. Apparently he'd been joking.

He took her extended hand in both of his. "I'm Pipo. I rep the 305, I run Little Havana, and soon, the music industry. I'm the next Pit Bull, baby."

She looked up and down the block, then said, "You don't seem to be running much of anything around here today. And by the way, I don't work for *The New York Times*. I'm freelance."

"So you came up just because you liked what you saw?" He lifted his shirt, exposing the bottom half of a bronze six pack.

Cole pulled his shirt back down. "I'm twice your age."

"Then why are you up on me?"

"You and me is never gonna happen, but I saw you taking your shirt off and I figured you're the kind of guy I need."

He smirked. "You said it, I didn't. But yes, I am the kind of guy every woman needs." He broke into a slow, crooning singing voice. "*Soy el chico que necesitas.* Lemme buy you a mojito." He flashed the smile again. Cole had to admit, he had a certain charm. Most men concealed their intentions. They lied, obfuscated, gaslighted. Pipo had what she thought of as innocent narcissism. He was full of himself, sure, but at least he wasn't lying about it.

"I'll take a rain check on the mojito—I'm a tequila woman, anyway—but I'll pay you $200 to help me for the day." She scanned the area. "Looks like no more ladies around anyway. You seem to have free time."

"I've got a studio session scheduled this afternoon. Wasn't kidding about my music." He yanked a phone out of his pocket and, before she could stop him, he blared a rap song with a catchy Latin beat behind it.

"That you?" she asked.

"Damn right. It's on YouTube."

Unable to stop himself, he began rapping along with the track, gesturing and pointing at Cole like he was in a music video. She didn't understand most of the words, but he had a decent flow. She raised a hand to stop him when he rhymed "*Mi amor*" with "Show the ho the door."

"Excellent," she lied. "Help me for the day and I'll send links to some music reporters I know."

He considered this, then nodded.

"I assume you're a Miami resident?"

"Told you, I run the 305."

"Right, right. And how do you feel about local entrepreneurship?"

62

A rusty bell clanged as Warren walked into the dingy bait and tackle shop. The man behind the counter looked nothing like the one he remembered. His face was round and flabby, his chin connected to his thick chest by a triple chin. Warren wondered whether he'd gotten some bad information.

It had taken him all morning and into the early afternoon to track down his old CI. He'd been hung up on by two buddies in the NYPD, failed to find him through a public records search, and had finally resorted to texting Gabriela for help. As usual, she'd come through, tracking SG to a bait shop fifteen minutes from the hotel in Little Havana.

Warren walked to the back wall, where three old drink fridges hummed, fighting to keep cool. He shot a look at the counter. The man's eyes were glued to his lap, where he fiddled with a plastic price tag gun.

Warren cleared his throat loudly. The man looked up, his eyes flashing a brilliant light green. SG's eyes were unmistakable, but they hadn't registered any recognition when landing on Warren, which gave him a moment to plan his approach.

He'd met SG through another informant, a weed dealer from Brooklyn who Warren had busted his first month on the job. In exchange for looking the other way, the dealer had connected Warren with a half dozen potential informants. The best of those had been SG, which stood for Sea Glass. Not only did he have bright green eyes, when they'd met he'd been an addict so they often had a glazed, glassy look to them. They contrasted so strikingly with his dark black skin they looked like they were trying to escape his face, which, at the time, had been scarred, hollow, and bony. Warren had known he was an addict right away, and used that to his advantage. He'd followed SG for a few hours, watched him buy a bag of heroin, thrown him up against a wall, then made him promise to keep an ear to the ground for him in exchange for letting it slide.

Some cops had some hesitation about using confidential informants who were themselves criminals. Warren never had. Though he'd taken an oath to enforce the law, he was a libertarian when it came to drugs. He enforced drug laws when violence was involved, but couldn't bring himself to care one iota about a broken young man choosing to kill his body with substances. In retrospect, he wished he'd taken drugs more seriously. Maybe his laissez-faire approach had just been foreknowledge of his own coming issues.

Warren approached the counter. "Not where I expected to find you, SG."

SG looked up, studying Warren's face. "What in the hell? Rob?"

"It's me."

SG waddled out from behind the counter like he was going to give Warren a hug, but instead walked past him to a small rack of Miami fishing guidebooks. Back to Warren, he began putting price tags on them. "Not where I thought I'd end up," he growled.

"What do you call this part of Miami?"

"Overtown."

The name rang a bell, but Warren couldn't place it. "Tell me something about the neighborhood."

"People think Miami's all beaches, or maybe cigar shops and *pastelitos*. This is the *real* Miami. Spot we're in used to be called 'Colored-Town.' Designated section for folks who looked like you and me. A little gentrified now, but still poor as hell." He set the price gun on the bookshelf and sat heavily on a stool, breathing hard. He squinted at Warren, studying him. "Don't tell me you brought your in-shape NYPD ass to Miami for a history lesson."

"You aren't glad to see me?"

"You used me to bust my friends," SG said.

"I could have arrested you."

"Maybe you should have. Might have cleaned me up earlier. You never cared what happened to me." His tone was bitter. Warren didn't know why he'd expected anything different. The cop/CI relationship was a complicated one, and it shouldn't have come as a surprise that SG's memories weren't as fond as his.

Warren smiled, trying to keep it light. "I thought Florida was supposed to mellow people out."

"What can I say? I guess the drugs made me more fun to be around." He patted his massive belly. "Skinnier, too." He turned back to the books.

"Better sober than nice, I guess." Warren paced the store, picking up a book on local wildlife, then putting it back without turning a page.

He was about to ask for help when SG spoke first. "Heard you had some trouble back home."

Warren had hoped to use his place in the NYPD to get cooperation. That SG knew about his suspension made his task more difficult. "Reporter screwed me. Still hoping to get reinstated."

"What? I was talking about Sarah. Marina."

"I…" Warren faltered. The air left his chest. "What?"

"Heard she dropped you."

SG hadn't heard about his suspension, but he'd heard about the separation. As much as this pissed him off—the conversation with his old friend Bakari Smith still burned in his chest—it confirmed that SG was still the gossip he'd always been. "You were my best CI. I bet you still keep an ear to the ground."

SG walked slowly back to his seat behind the counter and pulled off his hooded sweatshirt. His t-shirt read: *I thought I was in a bad mood, but it's been a couple years. I guess this is who I am now.* He folded his meaty arms across his chest. "I don't owe you."

"You don't," Warren agreed, "but I bet you *want* to help me."

The bell clanged and a young couple entered the store. Warren thought they looked lost and he backed away from the counter as they approached.

The woman asked, "You got pinfish today?"

Wordlessly, SG walked to the far end of the counter. Grabbing a net from a shelf, he dug into a fish tank that looked like an old

272

brown bathtub and pulled out three fish, each about the size of a hand. In a surprisingly deft motion, he scooped up a plastic bucket and dropped the fish in it, then topped it off with water from the tank.

Pulling out his wallet, the man asked, "Where the amberjack biting these days?"

"Sugar Bear Reef is usually good this time of year. Fella told me last week he got a forty pound Jack at Belzona Two. Been there?"

The man smiled proudly. "Pulled a forty-five-pounder there last year."

"He sure did," the woman added. "And I pulled a thirty-pounder." She stretched her arms out wide, exaggerating the fish's size. "Guess they didn't learn their lesson."

Warren studied his old source as he rang up the bait. SG had always been a gossip. Someone who got off on knowing—and sharing—everything about everything. Then again, he'd always been high. Now that he was clean and sober, he'd changed. But Warren didn't believe the gossip in him had died out completely.

The bell on the door clanged as the couple left.

"You're allowed to have a tub of live bait behind the counter?"

"Technically not. It's my private stash. Only people who know about it can buy."

"Pinfish?" Warren asked. "What's it for?"

"Wreck fishing. Bottom fishing. Pinfish are the best for that. Tougher than most other small bait fish."

"Sounds like you know your stuff." Warren knew nothing about fishing, and didn't especially care, but he wanted to keep SG talking. "What's wreck fishing?"

"The larger fish, like Amberjack, search out the deeper reefs where they can find food. The deeper the water, the bigger the fish. Deep enough, they find shipwrecks. The shipwrecks offer the Jacks just what they need: cover to hide in while they dine on the smaller fish."

"Seems like you still keep an ear to the ground. Least when it comes to fishing."

"Does it now?" SG asked.

"Sure does. My bet is that, even though you're well out of the game, you still hear things from time to time."

SG offered up a wry smile, a smile Warren recognized. His bright eyes flashed and twinkled.

Despite SG's changed appearance, his old CI was alive and well.

63

Cole and Pipo waited in line in front of a small convention hall in Little Haiti.

Cole gestured at a small banner hung above the door, marked with the logo for the Bank of South Florida. "What have you heard about Ana Diaz?" she asked.

"She's the jefe supremo, bro. *Chica* has so much cash they call her Money Bags."

"You really comfortable calling one of the most powerful bankers in America '*Chica*'?"

"Settle down, lady. What are you, the friggin' PC police?"

"So what do you know about her?" Cole asked.

"She's the richest Cuban-American business-lady in Miami."

"Looking for stuff I can't get from a Google search. Do you know much about how she got to where she is?"

Pipo shook his head, but it was clear he'd stopped listening. He nodded toward two beefy security guards in yellow shirts who were checking IDs. "Lemme do the talking when we get up there."

As they inched closer, Cole grew nervous. The men were intimidating, like bouncers at a bar. The worst that could happen was they'd turn her away, but something in her was concerned. The level of security seemed unnecessary for a local event about minority entrepreneurship.

When they reached the front, Pipo put his arm around Cole's waist. "*Dale*," he whispered.

They stepped forward together. "*Qué bolá asere.*" Pipo spoke like the security guards were old buddies as he handed over his ID.

"I don't speak Spanish," the man said, inspecting the ID.

"Bro, you live in Miami. *Qué bolá asere* is like the national anthem around here." He was talking fast, congenially. "Came down here to learn how to get my music studio off the ground." He pulled the "305" chain out from his shirt and held it up, then raised a hand to fist-bump the guy. "I'm the next Pitbull, bro. 305, right?"

The man ignored him, wrote his name on the clipboard, and looked at Cole. "ID, please."

Pipo interjected quickly. "Bro, this is my aunt from New York. Brought her down because she's gonna help fund my music studio. Why you think I'm here?"

The man glared at Pipo, unimpressed.

"Technically she ain't from Miami but the 305 runs in her veins."

"No," the man said simply.

"We thought you could bring a guest."

"Policy change. Miami residents only. Please step aside, ma'am."

The guy was like a mountain. Huge and immovable, both physically and emotionally. She imagined Pipo could talk his way into many places in Miami, but this wasn't one of them.

She pulled him out of the line. "If you can't get me in, how about you help me find out where she lives. We'll meet her when she gets home."

⊕

For the next two hours, Pipo led her on a wild-goose chase through Miami, always promising the answer lay at the next stop. They toured Coconut Grove, West Miami, and returned to Little Havana to visit Pipo's uncle. Finally, they wandered into the lobby of a hotel on South Beach where Pipo claimed he "knew a guy."

Cole waited as Pipo searched the lobby, looking in vain for his friend. It was fairly typical for a mid-size hotel: a check-in area, some plants, a few chairs and a small table with newspapers laid

276

out. The main difference between it and any other hotel were the colors—bright oranges and whites, with a floor of textured cork tiles in soft yellows, greens, and teals. He took her hand and pulled her outside to a circular bar at the pool.

To her surprise, Pipo *did* seem to know someone there. A tall, lanky man sat on a stool, staring at his phone and sipping absent-mindedly from a giant red drink that had an upside-down can of beer in it. Various fruits garnished the edges.

When she caught up to Pipo, he was saying, "Dude, bro, when are you gonna get my jams on the radio."

"Mike makes those decisions." The man's demeanor was surly and standoffish. Cole figured Pipo had bugged him about getting his music on the radio.

"I was with you before your show got huge, man, now you're gonna do me like this?"

The man looked up at Cole and extended a hand. "I'm Ben. I work for a radio station upstairs."

Cole shook it. "Jane. There's a radio station at the hotel?"

He nodded, then looked down at his phone. Clearly, he wasn't interested in chatting.

"Quick thing, bro," Pipo continued, still full of confidence. "Then we'll be gone, I swear."

Leaning over the glass, Ben took a long pull from the straw. "What?"

"You know where Ana Diaz lives?" Pipo asked.

For Cole, fear was one of the easiest emotions to read, especially in non-criminals. Like most animals, humans try to take up less space when they're afraid. At the mention of the name "Ana Diaz," Ben's shoulders tensed and pulled in toward his ears. His neck muscles tightened. But even if they hadn't, his mouth and eyelids told the story. Mouth shut tight, his jaw popped. The patch of skin below his eyes grew taught.

Cole saw the reaction as if in slow motion.

After a few seconds, he shook his head, not saying a word.

But his body had said plenty.

"Dude," Pipo said, "that's *caca* and you know it. You guys did a live spot from her bank, and I know you were producing that segment."

"Why you keeping track of what segments I produce?"

"Bro, I'm like the biggest fan of your show. I didn't want to have to go here, but you owe me. You know what I'm talking about."

Ben looked up and down the bar, which had started to fill with bikini-clad women, oiled-up men, and a few pasty-faced tourists. He leaned across the bar, grabbed a napkin and a pen, and scrawled an address. He handed it to Pipo. "Shred this when you get there, or eat it. I could get fired for giving you this."

His words said he could get fired, but his face betrayed what he really thought. It was something worse than fired.

⊕

The address was less than a mile north on Ocean Drive. On the east side of the street, it was a huge beachfront estate surrounded by a stone wall about six feet high. Aluminum poles had been drilled into the stone every six feet, chain link strung between them and barbed wire angled toward the street.

Walking confidently, Pipo rang a bell outside an imposing entry gate.

"You really think they're gonna let us in?" Cole asked.

"C'mon, *mama*. Pipo can talk his way into any house in Miami."

She was about to make fun of him for speaking about himself in the third person when two men emerged from a large garage. The larger of the two, who was the size of Cole and Pipo combined, marched up to the gate. He wore a cream-colored linen suit with a bright white shirt. "What is it?"

"What up, bro?" Pipo extended a hand through the gate.

Ignoring the gesture, the man said, "You have exactly five seconds to tell me why you're here." Beside him and standing about a yard behind, the other man took off his sunglasses, folded his arms, and glared at them. He wore a similar suit in powder blue and his gleaming bald head matched the first man's.

"Bro, my friend here needs to talk with Ana Diaz. It's urgent."

"She doesn't live here," the man said.

Cole tried to read him as he spoke, but sunglasses hid his eyes and his chiseled face didn't quiver. If he was lying, she couldn't tell.

"Bro, c'mon. She lives here."

"Time's up." The man turned.

278

The other shot a cold look at Cole, then at Pipo. He put his sunglasses on and followed the other back into the garage.

Cole pulled her wallet out of her hip purse and held out two hundred dollars.

"No hurry, *mama*, you can pay me after we get drinks. Tequila, tequila."

She shoved the money into his hands. "I'm gonna have to take a rain check."

She needed to get back to Warren, and fast.

64

"I can't tell you exactly why I'm here," Warren said, "but let's say someone is going to get killed." SG shot him a look. "Someone *big* in Miami. Ring any bells?"

His old CI thought for a moment. "It might."

"What can I do to jog your memory?" Warren asked.

"Well, everyone is pretty pissed at the owner of the Marlins, you know, the baseball team." He chuckled. "They've sucked for years."

"And that's probably true of half the sports franchises in the country." Warren knew how angry he'd gotten at the owners of his favorite teams, but there *had* been a sports connection on Cole's list. "You heard anything specific on that?"

"Nah. I was just talking."

"Let's try an experiment," Warren said. "Don't think, just answer: who runs Miami?"

"Since the Trafficante family fell apart, things have spread out. They say *Lady Chicharrón* is running most of the coke now, but who knows?"

"*Lady Chicharrón?*" Warren asked.

"Money bags. Young woman. Cuban and Italian. Niece of someone from one of the New York families…maybe Vegas. I don't know. Just a name you hear whispered."

"Real name?"

SG shrugged.

"But you're saying," Warren pressed, "that if someone big is about to get taken down, she'd know."

"Or would have ordered it. Look, I don't know, but from what I hear, no organized crime goes down in Miami without her blessing."

"Thanks, SG. Any other ideas?"

"Shouldn't even have told you that."

Warren walked to the door, pulling out his phone to order an Uber.

"Rob."

Warren stopped and turned, hand on the door. "What's up?"

"I'm not SG anymore. My mother named me Harold Jackson. That's what I go by now."

Warren leaned on the old brick of the bait shop, happy to take a little weight off his prosthetic leg while the hot sun warmed his face. Before he lost his leg, he could run for miles without fatigue. Now he was a fast-twitch guy. Boxing, a few sprints. He could climb a sixty-foot rope in just over thirty seconds. But the run through Alexandria and the Arlington National Cemetery had left his leg sore.

He Googled *Lady Chicharrón, Miami,*" not expecting to find anything. He shook his head in disbelief at the first listing.

In 2025, even mob bosses had Wikipedia pages.

It quickly made sense why SG had mentioned her. He had no way of knowing if it was true, but according to Wikipedia, *Lady Chicharrón* ran much of the crime in South Florida.

Maria Battle, *(aka Lady Chicharrón), born February 3, 1982 (age 43), is an American businesswoman alleged to be involved in organized crime such as gambling, money laundering, and murder.*

Early Life

Rumored to be the illegitimate daughter of famed Miami organized crime leader Jose Miguel Battle, Sr.—who ran Miami's largest organized crime family known as The Corporation—Ms. Battle grew up in Miami, attended elite boarding schools in both New York and Boston, then received a bachelor's degree in economics from the University of Miami.

She financed a variety of films in the early 2000s, with money rumored to come from her father.

Career

After leaving the film business, it's unclear what legal businesses she engaged in, if any. Though she is the registered owner of three properties in Miami, it is believed she travels often and is no longer a legal partner in any U.S. businesses. It is also believed by some in law enforcement that she laundered money for many lower-level drug dealers using low-budget films. Her expertise in finance, plus her connection to her father, allowed her to make the transition into the Miami drug world.

Personality

Known to have a violent streak, when bored as a young woman, she would say: "I have to fight someone." She allegedly stabbed a rival gang leader in 2011, and drove a car into the shop window of another enemy in 2008. A big soccer fan, she's rumored to be a secret shareholder in at least two MLS teams and has often bet on and fixed games.

Cultural References

She was mentioned by her nickname, Lady Chicharrón, in the 2019 rap song, "305 'til I Die," by The Young Palms.

It was one of the worst Wikipedia articles he'd ever read, and it was marked with a note: "This article's factual accuracy is disputed. It needs additional citations for verification." Even for a site on which anyone could add information, it was sloppy and incomplete.

Still, it was *something*. He needed to get back to the hotel to reconnect with Cole. He texted her.

Warren: Heading back now. You get anything?

As his Uber pulled up, his phone dinged with a message.

Cole: Tell you when I see you. Meet at the Cuban restaurant on the corner by the hotel in twenty minutes.

65

They were halfway through dinner—matching plates of white rice, black beans, smoked pork, and crispy fried plantains—by the time they finished recounting their days. Cole caught the waiter's eye and held up her empty mojito glass.

"You sure you want another?" Warren asked. "We need to stay sharp."

"What we need is creative thinking. I thought I was a tequila gal, but those are delicious! One loosened me up. Two will make me *brilliant*."

Warren laughed. "If you say so. But, for real, the guy at the hotel, the security at the Diaz estate...what does it mean?"

"Ana Diaz is the next victim, and I think she knows it. No listed address, no listed phone number. And security that rivals a president's. I think she's hiding out. And maybe the guy at the hotel was afraid because she's more than just a banker. Ambani, Meyers. You said yourself that they were involved in some shady stuff, despite their stellar resumes. Maybe Diaz is, too."

Warren moved the beans and rice to the corner of his plate and took a bite of the meat. "Let's say you're right about Ana Diaz. And let's say that Lady Chicharrón ordered the hit. How does that add up?"

Cole considered this as the waiter set down the mojito. "Maybe whoever is ultimately behind these killings went to Lady

Chicharrón for permission, paid her crew to allow the hit. This is her territory, right? If they're gonna let The Truffle Pig down here for the hit, they'd need her blessing."

"Could be," Warren said, "but I don't know how they'd get access to her."

They dropped into silence. Cole watched him finish the meat. She spooned half of her meat onto his plate and helped herself to some of his beans and rice. The restaurant was growing loud and the lights had dimmed.

Ever since their sprint through Arlington National Cemetery, she'd been haunted by an ambiguous guilt. A feeling that something was wrong, that she'd *done* something wrong.

She leaned across the table. "Earlier you asked what's driving me, and I think I might know. Matt was a good guy. A *genuinely* good guy. For the first couple years of our relationship—and I'm not proud of this—I used to nitpick him, try to get a rise out of him. Maybe it's because my mom used to do that to my dad, or maybe I just wanted to bring him down to my level. Maybe I—" Her voice cracked and she closed her eyes. Gathering herself, she said, "Never mind. After a couple years, I stopped. I think it took me that long to realize he loved me as I was." She sighed. "I don't know. I didn't feel worthy. And I know that's stupid, but it's how I felt. Now that he's gone, it's like I'm chasing a ghost. No, that's not it. It's like a ghost is chasing me. A ghost of goodness, pushing me on, trying to make me do something good, something worthwhile. The alternative is too terrible."

"What's the alternative?" Warren asked.

"Death."

Warren gave her an odd, side-eyed look. "Huh?"

"Not literally, but—"

"If you keep drinking those booze-shaped candy bars, it might be."

"Lemme finish. I think I'm afraid that if I don't keep racing forward, keep writing the next story, I'll crash and burn. Hole up in my apartment and fall into a tequila nightmare."

"Been there." Warren shrugged. "I mean...for me it was Courvoisier and coke."

"I know. I guess I'm afraid I'll crash. Depression. Like you said back in New York."

"One thing I learned in rehab is that you can't outrun this

stuff," Warren said. "Whatever's in you—one way or another—it's coming out."

The sentence hit her like a slap to the face. *Whatever's in you—one way or another—it's coming out.*

She'd been denying this for four years, and she wouldn't be able to deny it much longer. "If I'm honest, I don't know if I care whether whoever is behind these attacks kills everyone on their list, assuming there's a list. I want to make Matt happy. To prove I'm worthy. Michael Wragg knew something about us, and *that's* what's driving me."

The dream hit her like a punch to the chest, like a traumatic memory from long ago returning all at once. She could see Matt, gasping for air, choked out by a fellow Marine. She opened her mouth to tell Warren, but nothing came out. She was afraid it would make the dream more real than it already felt.

They were silent for a long while. Finally, Cole put on her peppiest voice and said, "Well, that was a bit of a downer. Do something for me: tell me your best military story."

"What do you mean?" Warren asked.

"Funniest story. Matt didn't ever tell me about violence, about the hard stuff. He told me about the funny stuff—the down time waiting for something to happen. He always said the real motto of the Marines was, 'Hurry up and wait.'"

"I can confirm that."

"I wrote words for a living, so he always tried to entertain me with stories. Once he told me about the captain of some aircraft carrier who woke up hung over and wandered down to breakfast. Sitting there, drinking his coffee, the sun was in his eyes, exacerbating his headache. Dude sent a message to turn the ship a few degrees, just so the sun wouldn't be in his eyes anymore."

Warren chuckled. "Heard that one. Not sure it's true, but it's a damn good story." He rubbed his chin, thinking. "Frank Undercroft." His face lit up, an irrepressible smile Cole had never seen from him. "Dude was the single greatest liar I ever knew. And handsome as hell. Looked like Tom Cruise's better-looking younger brother. Every damn word out of his mouth was a lie, but he was so entertaining, no one cared. He lied about little things and big things and everything in between."

"Like what?" Cole asked.

"Dude was your size—no offense—and said he played linebacker at Notre Dame. Told us his grandfather was Quincy Jones. He was a white dude from Maine. Said he'd won the World Series of Poker, twice. His lies were so sincere, and so bald-faced, you couldn't tell if he was nuts or if he was just messing with everyone."

Cole smiled. Matt would have liked that story.

"About three months in country, Frankie got captured in Kandahar. Took us three days to get him back."

"How'd you get him back? Prisoner swap?"

Warren nodded, smiling. "We rounded up ten of their guys and made the swap."

Cole swigged her mojito and chased it with coffee. "So what's funny about that?"

"His lies saved his ass. *Saved. His. Ass.* So, Frankie gets back to base and for a few hours he's saltier than the Dead Sea. 'Why'd it take us so long to rescue him?' Saying things like that. But by dinner, he's back to his old self, telling stories."

Cole had never seen Warren so enthusiastic, other than during workouts. But that was a more intense enthusiasm. His boyish glee in talking about his brothers in the Marines was something she'd never seen.

"Over dinner Frankie tells us about the three days as a POW. His captors knew better than to torture him, but he tortured the *hell* out of them. One of them spoke broken English—probably from movies and YouTube videos—and Frankie spent the whole three days feeding him lies non-stop. Dude spun a river of crap so deep he nearly drowned the Taliban. He was a movie star, Tom Cruise and Meryl Streep's secret love child, sent to Afghanistan to research a role in the next *Mission Impossible* movie. A songwriter, he'd written hits for Celine Dion and Britney Spears in the nineties, and keep in mind, he would have been like six years old then. An accomplished chef, he'd invented the hamburger and was in the Guinness Book of World Records for making the largest falafel in world history. Apparently, this last one got the attention of someone in the crew, and by the third day he was cooking their meals." Warren shook his head wistfully.

"You miss him," Cole said. "Miss *it*."

He nodded. "Routine. Structure. Camaraderie. Marines gave me that. Once I lost that, things didn't go as well." He smiled. "Speaking of mottos, you know what Marines say after we transition back to the normal world? 'You hate it when you're in. You miss it like hell when you're out.'"

"Where's Frankie now?" Cole asked. "In Hollywood writing screenplays, I hope."

"Dunno. When I got injured and sent home, our unit got folded into another unit. Last I heard he was in Vegas doing private security or something."

"I bet he——" Warren's shoulders had tensed, stopping Cole halfway through the sentence. He was staring over her right shoulder. His eyes flashed and he looked at the table.

"Don't turn around," he said. "Two guys at the table behind you."

"What?"

"I'm not certain, but I think they followed us in."

Everything in her wanted to turn and look for herself, but she didn't. "The guys from D.C.?"

"Not the one I fought." Warren waved down the waiter and handed him a credit card. When the waiter came back, Warren signed the bill without looking at it. "Walk toward the bathroom casually," he said, "then through the door that leads into the kitchen. There'll be a back door. I'll be right behind."

66

Loose from the mojitos but not yet wobbly, Cole strolled toward the bathroom as casually as possible. She couldn't stop herself from glancing at a large mirror hung on the brick wall. The specials of the day were scribbled in bright marker: chorizo tamales, ham croquettes, codfish empanadas. She saw a man's head turn. He had shoulder-length white hair and a pale, saggy face. Their eyes met in the mirror. He looked away immediately. Across from him sat a handsome younger man, maybe twenty-five. Bald, with bronze skin and a square jaw.

Turning the corner, she paused at the bathroom door, then cut into the kitchen.

A man in an apron blocked her path. "The restrooms are behind you, ma'am."

She glanced back. "No, I—"

Warren busted through the door beside her.

The waiter said, "Sir, this is the kitchen. You can't—"

But Warren was already pushing past. Cole followed him through the narrow space between the wall and the workstation that divided the kitchen. They were at the back before the waiter could object again. "There," Cole said, pointing at a screen door.

The door opened suddenly. A teenage boy appeared, dragging a dolly stacked with boxes. The dolly caught on the lip of the door, throwing boxes of cilantro and lettuce to the floor. Cole tried

288

to step over, but slipped, tumbling sideways into a giant bag of shredded cheese.

Warren stepped through the doorway and reached back, yanking her up.

Following Warren, she stepped through the screen door into a dark alley.

From the kitchen, the delivery guy was cursing in Spanish while picking up cilantro. The waiter was cursing in English, both at Cole and Warren and at the delivery guy.

Cole froze when she saw the younger of the two men from the restaurant standing next to the delivery truck. He must have run through the front entrance and around the side of the building into the alley. Most of his face was shadowed, but he held a gun pointed at Warren's chest.

The man held the gun low and cast furtive glances left and right. As he did, the gun moved with his body. Cole got the sense that he was waiting for his partner. They had seconds, likely, before he arrived. For now, they outnumbered him.

The kitchen got quiet. The argument ended. Then someone shrieked, "*Pistola!*"

The young man shot a look over Cole's shoulder. Warren took the opening and bounded forward, a sudden leap that closed the gap instantly and ended with a kick to the man's knee. The man collapsed, grunting in pain.

The white-haired man appeared at the screen door as Warren grabbed Cole's hand and pulled her forward. The alley before them was long, painted with colorful murals of Miami sports and music stars. Cole spotted a ladder leading to the roof of a low building. She darted in front of Warren and hoisted herself up. Without a word, he followed.

When they reached the roof, she glanced down the alley. The white-haired man was in a full sprint toward the ladder. The younger man limped behind.

They ran across the roof, crossed onto another, then another. Below, the two men followed them. There was a gap of about a yard between two buildings, leading to a L-shaped roof that ran away from the alley and toward the main road in Little Havana. Cole leapt the opening, careful not to look down at the empty space below. Warren followed.

Reaching the front of the building, Cole looked down. Five

feet below, a white and yellow striped awning jutted out. About seven feet below that, a crowd gathered in front of a bar. Hip-hop music that reminded her of Pipo blared from the bar. She squatted and, holding the edge of the roof, lowered herself onto the awning, careful to use the cross bar to support her weight as she slid down it and dropped to the sidewalk. The crowd around her noticed, but didn't seem to care.

Warren followed, but his weight bent the bar, collapsing the awning. He cascaded awkwardly to the ground, landing on his prosthetic and tumbling backwards into the crowd. He fell on his butt. A man kicked him, then backed away when he saw Warren's angry look.

Warren jiggled his prosthetic into place. Cole helped him up, then walked away briskly, Warren on her heels.

After a few blocks, the crowd thickened until they were no longer easy targets to find. "What's the deal?" Cole shot a look behind her.

A giant stadium rose in the distance ahead. It looked like a spaceship, silver and curved in odd places, surrounded by palm trees. "Not the season for baseball," Warren said. "Concert, maybe. Could be good. We can disappear in the crowd."

Salsa music wafted toward them and a band played on a small stage outside the venue. Cole looked back again, but the crowd grew thicker with each step as people converged on the stadium. "Do we even know they're following us?"

Warren turned, his height allowing him to peer overtop the crowd. "They're a hundred yards back."

Staying near the edge of the throng, they made their way around the stadium, the salsa music fading behind them. The crowd thinned. "I recognize this area," Warren said. "This is near where I was this morning. I passed through here in the car on the way to the bait shop."

The men were keeping their distance behind them. "They're waiting," Cole said, "until we get to a less populated area. That guy in the alley—the one who looks like an underwear model—he wanted to shoot us. Was *going* to shoot us. He was waiting for the other guy."

Warren nodded.

"You think they're Mazzalano's guys?"

Warren didn't respond. He studied the buildings and street

signs. They'd left Little Havana and entered a less colorful area. There were no murals and the streets were dirtier, the buildings duller. Not a tourist section. "This is Overtown," he said, as though reading her mind. "And I know where we can hide."

They turned a corner, and Warren took off in an all-out sprint.

67

After two more turns, Warren saw the lights of the bait shop a block away. "That's where I met my CI. He'll help us." They crossed the street and slammed through the door, Warren casting one last look back to make sure the two men were still behind them.

SG was behind the counter, cashing out the register. He didn't look up. "We're closed!"

"Need help," Warren said. "This is Cole."

SG looked up. "What the hell?"

"You got a piece?" Warren asked, jumping behind the counter. He scanned the shelves under the register.

SG grabbed his shoulder. "What in the hell?"

"Two guys," Warren barked. "Following us."

"I don't keep a gun here."

Warren leapt back over the counter and jogged across the store. Poking his head out, he saw the two men about a block away. They were turned, each looking into the window of a different storefront. He pulled his head back inside, pretty sure they hadn't seen him.

They had two options. Assuming they'd lost the men, he and Cole could hide in the back and let them pass. But something in him wouldn't accept this. He turned to Cole. She had that hard-

thinking look he'd come to recognize. "Let them go or lure them in and find out who the hell these guys are?"

A slight smile moved across Cole's face. "I'm tired of running away."

"L-l-lure them in?" SG stammered. "What in the hell?"

Warren took Cole by the shoulders, then nodded toward the door. "Make sure they see you, then get back in and stay behind the counter. SG, I recommend you head to the back."

SG shook his head and muttered, but he headed to the back of the shop.

Cole moved to the door.

"Wait." Warren grabbed a large spool of thick fishing line, the kind used for deep-sea poles. Reaching a length across the doorway about a foot off the ground, he secured one end to a display rack and the other end to a bait fridge.

Cole stepped over carefully and leaned out. The night was quiet and dark.

The two men moved methodically down the block, checking the doors of each business, most of which were closed. Her heart raced.

The white-haired man noticed her and froze. Once he'd gotten the other's attention, they took off for her. She shut the door behind her and slid across the counter, crouching.

She held her breath, then let it out slowly, not wanting to make a sound. She peeked over the counter. Warren took position behind the bait fridge. His large frame was concealed from view from the outside, blocked by a display rack.

"Get down," he called, and she did.

Warren heard the door creak as it opened a crack. Then it swung open all at once with the clang of the bell. A bald head emerged, then disappeared as the man tripped on the fishing line and toppled into the store.

Warren leapt out, kicking the gun out of his hand while simultaneously throwing a vicious punch into the gut of the white-haired man right behind baldy.

The white-haired man staggered back, but Warren caught him by the hair and threw him into the bait fridge. The glass shattered, spilling styrofoam containers onto the floor.

The younger man had recovered and rolled toward the gun. Warren jumped, landing a heel on his outstretched hand. The bones and knuckles cracked and Warren fell on him, elbow first, striking his cheek.

Screaming, the man threw a series of short punches from his back, connecting with Warren's temple and neck. But Warren gained position atop him and pummeled his face with a series of forearms and elbows.

As soon as the man went limp, Warren looked back. The white-haired man had been knocked out cold by his collision with the bait fridge. A long brown worm wriggled on his pale cheek.

There was shuffling, then Cole stood over them, holding the gun.

She waved it at the white-haired man. "Is he dead?"

Warren reached for the man's neck. His pulse was live. "Just knocked out. Back of his head broke the fridge."

"These two aren't Mazzalano's," Cole said.

"How do you know?"

"I assume these two were connected to the two dudes in D.C."

Cole handed him the gun, then leaned over the younger man, whose face had already swelled. Blood trickled from his lips and one of his eyes had closed like a boxer's in the twelfth round. She reached into his pants pocket and pulled out his cell phone. She swiped, then held it to his face.

Brilliant, Warren thought.

She frowned and tried again. "You busted his face so badly, his Face ID isn't working."

Warren slid himself over and took the phone from her. He centered it on the guy's broken face and tried. The phone shook and displayed, "Face ID Unsuccessful."

Cole was already trying it with the white-haired man. She swiped and held the phone up to his face. It vibrated and unlocked.

Warren stood and leaned over her shoulder.

"What should I look for?" she asked.

"Recent calls, maybe."

She checked his call log. A dozen calls to the same number over the last twenty-four hours.

"D.C. area code," Warren said.

"And I think I recognize the number," Cole said.

SG appeared from the back. "What the hell did you do to my store?"

"Sorry," Warren offered.

Cole walked to the corner, staring at the phone.

Warren went through the pockets of the white-haired man and found a business card. It read *Beltway Investigators*, a private investigation firm out of D.C.

He watched Cole tap the phone. She was calling the number. He wanted to stop her, to discuss how to approach it, but it was too late. He watched the side of her face as she listened.

After a few seconds, Cole's eyes opened wide. "Put him on the phone!" she demanded. She listened for a few seconds, then the phone dropped away from her ear. "Oh, God."

Cole stared at the phone in her hand, her mind leaping between memories of the last few days. Everything was happening too fast. She turned to Warren, who'd been watching her.

"What?" he asked.

She let her eyes drop to the two men on the floor, then shifted her gaze to SG, who stood, arms out like he was asking, *Who's gonna clean this mess up?*

"Cole, what is it?" Warren asked. "Who *was* that?"

"Marty Goldberg's assistant."

"Marty Goldberg sent these two?" Warren asked. "Why?"

Cole's memory flashed again. Her first meeting with Goldberg when they were bright-eyed, optimistic interns together—a night at the bar, the evening of the 2006 midterm elections.

"I don't know why he sent these guys after us," she said. "But now he's dead." She swallowed hard, trying to keep her composure. "They found Marty floating in the Potomac River about two hours ago. Didn't show up for a cocktail event. Assistant couldn't reach him. Went to his apartment and found his phone, but no Marty."

Warren stepped toward her, hand out, but she backed away. "I...who?" was all she could say.

"Suicide?" Warren offered weakly.

She shook her head. "I doubt it, but—" The scene snapped into place suddenly. The broken glass from the shattered fridge. The worms. The two men on the floor. SG. They needed to get out of there.

"Can you make this right with SG?" she asked. "Tell him we'll send him a few grand or something. Ask him to come up with a story. We need to get out of here. Now."

"We can't leave these guys in his shop," Warren said.

"No, you sure as hell can't," SG interjected.

"We're gonna send you money just as soon as we can get it," Warren said. "Couple grand. And I'll deal with these guys."

Warren moved swiftly, dragging the younger of the two men outside and leaving him in the doorway of a shoe store. He covered him with some old cardboard to make him look homeless. Next he carried the white-haired guy through the back of the shop and leaned him against a dumpster.

"How's that gonna help SG?" Cole asked.

"It will," SG said.

Warren locked the back door and surveyed the store. "Right. The card said they're private security from D.C. They illegally pulled a weapon on us. They're not the kind of guys who are gonna call the cops."

SG nodded. "And they're not gonna come back here. Guys like that just disappear when they take a hit like that."

68

Saturday

It was two in the morning and Cole was hungry again. She shoved a bag of popcorn from the mini-bar into the microwave and pressed the "baked potato" setting.

Feeling Warren's eyes on her, she turned. "What?"

"Not only are you microwaving a bag of empty carbs, salt, and fat, but you're using the wrong setting. Why in the name of all that is holy would you use the baked potato setting for a bag of popcorn?"

"It was the top button."

Warren frowned. "There's a popcorn button less than an inch below it."

"Does it matter?"

He shook his head in feigned disgust.

"Look," she said, "I listen for the popping to slow down to one kernel every two to three seconds. That's the only guaranteed way to get the perfectly popped bag."

"But why would they have the popcorn setting, then?"

"Because they're evil." She smiled. "Different popcorn bags are different sizes and therefore require different amounts of time. Sometimes, the 'Popcorn' setting leaves too many unpopped kernels. Sometimes it burns it. My technique is the only way. Plus, can we agree that I know more about the proper preparation of empty carbs than you?"

"I'll give you that," Warren agreed.

Cole listened to the hum of the microwave and the popping. She was exhausted. For two hours they'd gone over what they knew, and they were nowhere. They assumed Marty Goldberg had hired the private security firm to tail them from D.C. to Miami. They didn't think they'd been followed into the train station, but they weren't certain. Maybe the old dancing couple or the young backpackers had been watching them. Maybe the homeless guy was paid by Goldberg to keep an eye on everyone coming in and out of the station. Unlikely, but possible. More likely was that he'd tracked them through their phones. They'd tried not to leave a paper trail, but each of them carried one of the most trackable devices on earth in their pocket. Cole's bet was that Goldberg had bribed the right person at the cell phone company to get a location, and they'd been picked up at their hotel in Little Havana.

The bigger question was why Goldberg had wanted to track them in the first place.

Cole took her popcorn out of the microwave and opened it slowly, then plopped on the bed.

Warren said, "Can you think of anyone who wanted him dead? Goldberg, I mean."

"No...I can think of a *hundred* people. When you're as powerful in D.C. as he is, you make a lot of enemies. Locally, but also international. Foreign governments lobby in D.C. constantly." Cole munched a handful of popcorn, considering. "But it's not a coincidence he died when he did."

"I don't think so either."

Cole held the bag out to Warren, who turned away. "But why?" she asked. "If he had us tailed, why? And how in the hell could that lead to *him* getting killed? Someone protecting *us*?"

Cole's phone pinged with a new email. She swiped it open, then froze. It was a Google alert containing a news story. About *her*.

Years ago she'd set up alerts to automatically email her when news stories about certain people and subjects were published. These days she usually heard about stories on Threads before the alert arrived. But she'd been off her phone all night.

Two more emails arrived. Two more Google alerts containing articles with her name in them. She scanned the pieces one by one, then waved the phone at Warren. "We're famous."

"Huh?"

"The hit pieces have started," she said.

Warren was in the process of taking off his leg. "What?"

"You know how I said that speculation would start online and in the press that the murders are connected?"

"Yeah."

"Well, it's started," Cole said. "And apparently *we're* suspects."

Warren sat up straight, setting his leg on his lap.

"Here's one from Crime-Scene.Net," Cole said. "I'll skip to the punchline. 'Though it's too early to claim a link between the deaths of Raj Ambani and Alvin Meyers, certain coincidences jump out. One is that Mr. Ambani donated to the campaign of Senator Meyers on three separate occasions. The other is that Meyers and Ambani both served on the board of directors of Sen-Jen Private Equity, the only two Americans to serve on the board of the prestigious Japanese firm.'" Cole stopped reading. That was a connection between the two she hadn't found before. She knew little about Americans serving on Japanese Boards of Directors, but she filed it away for further research. "'A third connection,'" she continued from the story, "'is more tangential, but no less real. In New York City, suspended cop Robert Warren and crime reporter Jane Cole were both seen at the apartment of Michael Wragg, the man now believed to be the shooter in the Raj Ambani murder. Only days later, Cole quit her job at *The New York Sun* and, sources say, traveled to D.C. with Mr. Warren. Are the two connected to the murders? It's too soon to say, but Crime-Scene.Net will be keeping an eye out.'

Cole dropped her phone on the bed.

Warren's mouth was open, his eyes wide. "Can we now agree that journalists are the worst?"

"These aren't *journalists*. There are two other similar articles, also on insignificant blogs. They read like all three came from one or two sources, calling around and trying to get the story out there."

"Why?" Warren asked.

The stories were pathetic attempts to smear them. Truly amateur. She doubted they'd gain much traction. The stories themselves didn't worry her, but the fact that someone was out there planting them did.

She lay back in bed. "Tell me again everything SG told you about *Lady Chicharrón*. There's gotta be something we missed."

Warren laced his hands behind his head. "I told you everything."

"Tell me again."

He sighed. "Said she runs the coke in and out of Miami. Said if a hit was going down—something organized like we're tracking —she'd know about it. Might have given the okay for it. But no one really knows who she is, or how to find her."

"And her wiki?" Cole asked.

"Like I said, it's got some background stuff that could be true. But not a real name. And, can we pause for a second and notice how crazy it is that she has a Wikipedia page? Probably has a publicist updating it to build her myth without giving up anything that could get her busted. Probably helps her street cred. Soon there'll be a Pitbull song for her, 'Old Money Bags *Chicharrón*.'" Warren yawned. "I need sleep. At least a few hours." He tucked his leg under the pillow.

"My mind won't shut up," Cole said.

"That's 'cause you keep feeding it sugar." His eyes were closed and his voice was slow and sleepy. A minute later, gentle snores came from his side of the room.

She was out of Ambien, so after an hour of tossing and turning, Cole took a bathrobe from the closet and left the room. The hotel was still and silent. She turned down a long hallway, following signs to the outdoor pool.

The night was balmy, the courtyard deserted and silent except for the sound of the occasional car passing on the far side of the hotel. She tried her keycard on the pool's metal gate, but it blinked red. The pool closed at ten. Using the gate's handle as a step, she climbed the fence, dropping easily into the pool area. After a quick scan, she stripped to her bra and underwear and eased herself into the pool.

She swam a quiet lap, then floated on her back, staring at the starless black sky. She became still, feeling only her long, slow breaths and the cool water.

Closing her eyes, she compared the blackness in her mind to the blackness of the sky. Eyes open, she was pulled into the seemingly infinite darkness, as though leaving her body to go to a quieter, more peaceful place. Eyes closed, her mind folded in on itself, her history collapsing to a point of infinite darkness. It was as though she was disappearing.

Warren had said, "Whatever's in you—one way or another—it's coming out." It hit her hard. She closed her eyes again. Whatever was there, she didn't want it to come out. What she'd told Warren about Matt was a lie. She wasn't driven to get the story to please some idea of Matt. It was to keep herself busy. To keep the darkness at bay.

Another aspect of their conversation pushed her musings to the side, and she replayed it in her mind. Something didn't sit right. *Lady Chicharrón* never would have allowed a hit on Ana Diaz just out of kindness. It had to serve her interests as well. More than that, would the men behind the murders of Ambani and Meyers have sought permission to murder Ana Diaz from *Lady Chicharrón*? She didn't think so. Whatever they were doing was bigger than a coke kingpin from Miami.

She wondered about *Lady Chicharrón's* Wikipedia page. She should have read it herself. Warren wasn't the researcher she was, and she—

Her eyes popped open. "Money Bags."

Cole let the door slam as she entered the room and flipped on the lights, her hair dripping pool water on the carpet.

Warren shot up in bed, fists clenched. "What?"

"You called her 'Money Bags.'"

"Why are you in a robe?" Warren asked. "What happened to your clothes?"

"You called *Lady Chicharrón* 'Money Bags.'"

He rubbed his eyes. "SG called her that. I guess it's another nickname. Any drug kingpin has to have at least a couple. And a *Chicharrón* is a damn fried pork rind, so who wouldn't want a different nickname. I mean—"

"Rob, listen!" She sat next to him. "Ana Diaz *is Lady Chicharrón*. Pipo, the guy who took me to her estate, called Ana Diaz 'Money Bags.' Ana Diaz, the reclusive financier, is *Lady Chicharrón*, the notorious drug kingpin. They're the same person!"

Warren took his leg from under the pillow and passed it from hand to hand. "Holy hell. It's so damn obvious now that you say it. She uses the bank for legit business and to funnel coke money. She's the most powerful person in Miami. And if Ana Diaz is connected to Ambani and Meyers, it means they may have had their toes in the drug game, too."

"Connections to it, at least," Cole agreed. "Whether they were aware of those connections is...well, it's something I wouldn't be comfortable speculating about. Yet. What SG told you, he was close, but a little off. *Lady Chicharrón* didn't sanction the next hit, she *is* the next hit."

An orange-pink light crept through a crack in the curtains. Dawn.

Cole stood. "We need to get back to the Diaz estate."

"Fine," Warren said, "but what do we do when we get there?"

This stopped Cole in her tracks.

Truth was, she had no idea.

69

A sliver of sun appeared over the ocean, bathing the beach in salmon-colored light and backlighting the palm trees that led down the street to the Diaz estate. Marco De Santis had pushed the mattress onto the balcony and now studied the property through the rifle scope, making incremental adjustments from his belly.

He'd never failed to deliver a job on time, but Ana Diaz had the best security he'd ever seen. Better than Antonio Greco, the mob boss who was his first sanctioned hit back home, and better than Alvin Meyers. An interesting commentary on America, he thought, that a financier and drug kingpin should have better security than a former Vice President. Made him wonder who runs the country after all.

Despite her security, Ana Diaz had one weakness: the sun. As it set the night before, she'd stood for a moment on a west-facing balcony to admire it as it dipped behind a hotel, disappearing for the last time. He'd made the mistake of taking a bathroom break at the wrong moment. Her head had disappeared from view the moment he'd put hand to weapon.

Now, two men appeared in front of the estate, pacing the street. He studied their linen suits through the rifle scope. No bulges for weapons. Just patrolling. He moved his sight back to the upper floor, where he suspected the bedrooms were.

He'd never been one to brood on the past, but only hours from retirement, he allowed his mind to wander. He'd grown up on a little farm near the French border in Northern Italy. As a boy, he'd hunted rabbits and deer, which his father had taught him to skin and his mother—bucking tradition—had taught him to cook. His mother, he believed, was the best cook in the world. And since she had no daughters, she'd been insistent that little Marco learn how to properly sear venison loin, and braise rabbit in wine and herbs from their kitchen garden.

At twelve, his father had allowed him to enter his first shooting contest, a local event where his biggest competition had been an old man who'd fought in World War II. He'd won easily. The next year, at thirteen, he'd won the competition for the state of Aosta. He dreamed of representing Italy in the Olympics, and had been saving up for a competition rifle when his mother died. What happened next was his sharpest memory, his worst memory, but it was as though the memory had been chopped apart, the pieces tossed into the air. It came to him in fragments. Two men had come to his father's farm. He'd overheard them shouting at his father about money. Something about his mother owing them. Something about an uncle he didn't know.

A few days later, he was lying on his back in the barn, staring through a crack in the slatted wooden roof when he'd heard a gunshot. Running out, he crashed straight into the arms of one of the men. Before he knew it, he was in the back of a car. He never saw the farm again.

He still wasn't entirely sure what happened. He'd been able to piece together that his parents owed money to the men who'd taken him. Or, more likely, to the boss of the men who'd taken him. They'd killed his parents and taken little Marco to pay the debt.

Between the age of thirteen and his escape at age thirty, he killed sixty-five men and two women for the Fidanzati family in Northern Italy. For most of that time, he'd been treated like a member of the family. He'd become a legend. But he'd always known he was a captive.

On the second floor of the sprawling beachfront home, a door opened. A woman appeared on a balcony that faced the ocean. Eye in the scope, he moved his finger to the trigger.

He exhaled.

Not Ana Diaz.

The woman's pale white skin and red hair gave this away immediately. He took his eye from the scope to get a wider view. She was young and wore a brown uniform. A maid or servant of some kind. Moving around a potted lemon tree, she set orange juice and a plate of fruit on a small metal table. Next she set out an iPad, a napkin, silverware.

Setting out breakfast for the queen.

From his vantage point, he saw the tip of a metal chair facing the ocean and the rising sun. He trained the rifle about six inches above the spot where the chair back ended.

Assuming this breakfast was for her, Ana Diaz's head would appear soon.

70

Cole spotted the two security guards as she hopped out of the taxi. They wore different linen suits today—the smaller one in pale green and the larger in salmon orange—but their bald heads and sunglasses made them unmistakeable.

Warren hung back as she rushed up to them.

The one in the green suit recognized her. "We told you to stay away, lady."

"Ana Diaz is in trouble." The other approached and she put a hand on his shoulder. "Lady Chicharrón," she continued. "Money Bags. Your boss. Someone is trying to kill her."

They exchanged looks. She had their attention now. "Who the hell are you, lady?"

"That doesn't matter right now. Raj Ambani, Alvin Meyers, the assassinations. You've seen them on the news, right? Or on socials? Your boss is next."

"Our boss is safe inside these gates," the guard in the salmon-colored suit said. "Ain't no one getting by us. And if they did, there's four more inside."

Cole turned on her heels, waving wildly at the row of hotels lining Ocean Drive. "Sniper killed Ambani and Meyers. Could be up there *right now*."

Warren wasn't behind her. He was half a block away, wandering toward the hotels. She followed him, pausing only long enough to say to the guards, "Just make sure she's safe in there."

⊕

Given the security at the estate, Warren knew that a shot from distance was *Maiale al Tartufo's* only option. His eyes had landed on the hotels immediately. He was no sniper himself, but he knew how they thought: height and angle. What spot would get the best view of the estate from above and give a shooter the most possible angles?

He settled on a section of three hotels a couple blocks up and took off at a jog, leaving Cole behind. The hotel in the center was off-white, and each room facing the beach had a balcony. Five stories up, he saw it.

He almost missed it at first because the mattress was only barely visible on the balcony. But on the mattress was a man. And the man had a rifle trained on the estate.

⊕

De Santis saw her black hair first.

He had the shot as she emerged onto the balcony, but opted to wait until she sat. She was short and a little younger than he'd expected. And she walked with the confidence of the most powerful person in Miami, moving around the table and sipping her orange juice as though the beach and the sun and the cool breeze had been created just for her. Next, she reached her hands to the sky and stood on her tiptoes. Some kind of yoga pose, maybe.

It was rare, he thought, for a woman to amass so much power so young. Never would have happened back home.

She sat and began reading something on the iPad. She leaned forward slightly so, from his angle, the front of her head disappeared behind a gutter. Only the back portion of her head was visible, but it was enough.

Legs spread to help absorb the shock from the fifty-cal's recoil, De Santis clicked off the safety, took a last breath, and let it out slowly.

Time was, he had to consciously settle himself down before a shot. Not anymore. Just a deep breath in, a long breath out, and stillness filled his body.

He pulled the trigger, heard the click of the striker like his senses were on fire. A fraction of a second later, Ana Diaz's brains splattered onto the potted lemon tree.

He'd taken off the back of her head.

Cole heard screams from the estate.

She turned. The security guards raced through the gate.

More screams. She hadn't heard a gunshot, but Warren's head was aimed up. Up at the balcony. He was a block ahead of her, sprinting toward the hotel, and she followed.

De Santis set the rifle on the mattress and pulled it back inside the hotel room. Next he stowed the weapon in his duffel bag, closed the sliding glass door, and walked out.

Riding the elevator to the ground floor, he pulled a flip phone out of the bag and sent a text to the only number programmed into it: *It's done.*

He broke the phone in half as he stepped out of the elevator. Avoiding the main lobby, he ducked out a side door next to the bathrooms. Screams came from the direction of the estate a few blocks away, but they made little impression on him.

He dropped the phone in a storm drain and unlocked the door of a red Toyota Camry.

Warren raced through the lobby of the hotel. The shot had taken place less than two minutes earlier, and he had a choice. Take the stairs, ride the elevator, or hang in the lobby. De Santis would be out of the room by now, probably executing a planned escape.

A red Camry passed by a glass door that led to the parking lot. There was something about the man driving it.

Warren dashed through the door, then slowed and walked casually. The Camry was stuck behind a couple with kids dragging suitcases across the parking lot. The man driving it was alone. He was tanned, with short black hair and a couple days worth of stubble. It was the man from the balcony.

"Rob!"

He turned, startled. Cole was beside him.

An airport shuttle van was parked across the lot, idling, doors open. A uniformed man strolled across the lot toward the hotel, whistling and staring into a styrofoam coffee cup.

The Camry turned onto Ocean Drive.

Warren nodded toward the van. "Let's go."

71

In the stolen airport shuttle van, they followed *Maiale Da Tartufo* across the Biscayne Bay Causeway into Wynwood. It was early still, but traffic was beginning to pick up.

Warren said, "Call the police. 9-1-1. Next we'll call the FBI." He shook his head. "I never should have let you talk me into keeping what we knew private. That ends now."

Cole opened her mouth to object, but nothing came out. He was right. They had to release the map and tell the FBI everything they knew.

While Warren navigated the Christmas shopping traffic, careful to stay two to three cars behind the Camry, Cole called the police. When a voice came on the line—"9-1-1, what's your emergency?"—she didn't know where to begin.

"Ana Diaz was just shot at her estate on Ocean Drive. My colleague and I were nearby at the time and we believe we're on the tail of the man who killed her. He's driving a red Toyota Camry and, hold on..." She turned to Warren. "Did you get a plate number?" He shook his head and Cole continued. "We don't have a plate number, but we're on Northwest Twelfth street, heading north." After a minute on hold, Cole gave the dispatcher her phone number.

"My guess," Warren said, "is that they'll already have a bunch of units heading to the estate. May take a minute for them to get here."

"Call the FBI?" Cole asked.

Warren maneuvered around a double parked delivery truck. "Yeah, but not Bakari Smith."

"Goes without saying. I'd rather not just call the tip line, though."

"Don't you have any contacts there?" he asked

"Don't *you*?" she replied.

"Bakari *was* my contact there." He considered for a minute. "What about Bacon and Ubwe? The JTTF guys. They're NYPD but they'll know how to get someone fast." He held his phone up to his face to unlock it, and handed it to her.

She found Ubwe's number and dialed, but it went to voicemail. "This is Jane Cole. I met you with Robert Warren at The High Line in New York. We need an FBI contact ASAP. Someone who can actually make things happen. Call back."

"He's probably avoiding us," Warren said. "I wonder if he knows Bacon gave us the tip that took us to Miami."

They had entered into a more industrial area, where storefronts turned into larger warehouses and an occasional liquor store. The Camry turned onto US-41.

"I know this road," Cole said. "Leads across southern Florida. Miami to Naples."

"If he's as good as people say, he knows he's being tailed. My guess is he wasn't planning to leave via the airport anyway. Probably planning to drive to Georgia or somewhere, catch a flight from there."

Cole agreed. "Why do you think no red and blues have shown up?"

"Probably all responding to the Diaz shooting. They'll call you back soon."

Cole had something else on her mind. "In D.C., when Bakari leaked the story to *The Post*, do you think that could be connected to the stories about us that came out yesterday?"

"Doubt it. He probably just did that to get back at us. Those blog hits were different. Aimed at making us suspects."

Like most journalists, Cole hated being the subject of journalism. And even though the stories had appeared on insignificant blogs, she hated that they were out there. Someone *wanted* them to be suspects. She didn't think it was Mazzalano. But she couldn't see what Marty Goldberg could have to do with it either.

Traffic had thinned and the Camry was a couple hundred yards ahead of them, navigating a long stretch of US-41 past signs promising various nature sites ahead.

Cole's phone buzzed. She hoped it was Ubwe calling her back, but it was a Breaking News Alert from X. Not one, but three. Then a fourth, then a fifth.

Her phone kept buzzing and buzzing. A dozen major news outlets were breaking a story at the same time. A group had taken credit for the murders of Raj Ambani, Alvin Meyers, and Ana Diaz.

And they'd released a manifesto.

72

Signs appeared as they entered Big Cypress National Preserve. The map on Cole's phone showed a massive patch of green that took up most of southern Florida. Big Cypress bordered Everglades National Park to the south and tens of thousands of acres of federally protected land to the west.

The manifesto had been published by dozens of news agencies within the same ten minute span, and Cole read it aloud as Warren followed the Camry.

"Dear World,

In the last four days, we murdered billionaire Raj Ambani, former Vice President Alvin Meyers and financier Ana Diaz, also known as drug kingpin Lady Chicharrón.

When we killed Raj Ambani, he was at a charity event, the stated mission of which was to circumvent sovereign nation states and create "international laws" protecting wildlife. For billionaires like Ambani, protecting a rare bird inside the borders of someone else's country is more important than the freedom of the PEOPLE within that country. And all of it was a front, a distraction from the real aim: to control the people within that and all other countries with algorithmic surveillance technology. He was part of the Digital Panopticon Agenda, and he had to go.

When we killed former Vice President Alvin Meyers, he was glad-handing with corporatists, K-Street scum, and globalists, making plans to further enslave humanity to a small consortium of international banks and technologists. He had to go.

When we killed Ana Diaz, she was on the verge of signing a deal to launder money for some of the most corrupt politicians and business leaders the world has ever known. She had to go.

Wake up, world.

The Digital Panopticon Agenda is the grand scheme of tech giants and corrupt governments to enslave humanity under total surveillance and control. Every move we make, every word we speak, every click we make online is recorded and analyzed to build detailed profiles on us. Tech companies are in bed with global politicians, creating a massive network of data collection that invades our privacy and erodes our freedoms. They sell us convenience while secretly compiling dossiers that predict our behavior, manipulate our choices, and stifle dissent. It's not paranoia if it's true. The surveillance state is real, and it's here, watching our every move and waiting to strip away our last vestiges of personal freedom. Wake up! They aim to create a one-world government where every citizen is monitored, controlled, and subdued by an omnipresent digital eye.

The people who control your world number in the hundreds, and today three are gone. Three fewer scumbags running our world.

Soon, that number will be nine.

Our methods may seem extreme, but look into the records and legacies of the people we killed and you'll agree: the world is better off today than it was four days ago.

Our prayer is that the people soon to die will only be the first nine. We wish to inspire an international movement of the people.

We're doing our part. Do yours. Join us.

The new era of freedom begins today.

We do not have a name, only a purpose. Our words are simple, and are spoken around the world. Who are we?

An international brotherhood, united by General Ki for a singular mission: to end the technological oppression, to restore the sovereignty of the individual, to birth a new era of freedom.

Until the individuals of the world are free, the masters—and anyone choosing to remain subject to them—shall live in fear."

The letter was unsigned, but Cole had no doubt it was authentic.

"Damn," was all Warren said.

Under the letter were links. Cole clicked the first, which led to a video. She recognized the face immediately: Michael Wragg.

She studied him for a second or two. His eyes were warm, almost sparkling with life. Then he started speaking. "We do not have a name, only a purpose. Our words are simple, and are spoken around the world. Who are we? An international brotherhood, united by General Ki for a singular mission: to end the technological oppression, to restore the sovereignty of the individual, to birth a new era of freedom. Until the nations of the world are free, the masters—and anyone choosing to remain subject to them—shall live in fear."

The video ended. Cole clicked another link. This one was similar. A close up of an Asian man's face, a window behind him and the bright neon signs of Tokyo in the background. She couldn't understand the words, but recognized the language as Japanese. The video was similar in length to Wragg's and, based on the tone, the man spoke the same words.

The next one was an Indian man, maybe sixty years old, with jet black hair. It was taken on a rooftop with Bombay in the background. Again, same length, same tone and, she assumed, the same words.

The fourth video was a black man, younger, standing in front of Dodger Stadium in Los Angeles. He spoke the exact same words as Wragg.

"There are a dozen more videos," Cole said. "Likely all the same."

She quickly checked the homepages of the major news organizations. CNN, Fox News, *The New York Times*, Yahoo News: all had published the manifesto. The BBC in England. *The Times of India* out of Bombay. *Yomiuri Shimbun* out of Tokyo. Even *News24* out of South Africa had the story.

Men around the world had gathered together to unleash a coordinated attack. Their plan had the scope of a terrorist attack and the precision of a serial killing. Their operation was better funded and better coordinated than anything since 9/11.

She'd been saying for days that this would become the biggest story in the world. She hadn't known the half of it.

Ahead, a car veered into a rest area and she caught sight of the Camry, which brought her back to the moment. Not only was this the biggest story in decades, but she and Warren were at the center of it.

A long, low patch of wetlands appeared in the distance. "You sure we want to follow him deep into the preserve?" Cole asked.

Warren frowned. "No. But we don't have a chance if we don't. How's your cell reception?"

Cole checked her phone. "Zero bars. If the FBI is trying to call me back, or track my phone, they're out of luck. Same with Miami police."

They stayed two cars behind the red Camry. Whenever she lost sight of it, Cole's heart skipped a beat. Her mind raced. If Warren was right that The Truffle Pig knew he was being followed, he could be luring them to a remote area to kill them. She shifted in her seat uneasily, hoping Warren knew what he was doing.

Short boardwalks jutted from scenic areas on the side of the road, leading to marshes populated by giant white herons, red-shouldered hawks, and owls. Alligators sunned themselves along the banks of the marshland. She'd been all over America and never seen anything like it. The landscape was unique, and stunning.

She sighed. The drive on US-41 was one she and Matt had always planned to take together. One of the many things they said they'd do, but never did.

In Ochopee, they passed a tiny white shed adorned with a U.S. flag and marked with the sign: "World's Smallest Post Office."

Just past the post office, the Camry pulled off to the side of the road. Fifty yards off the road, a decrepit wooden church sat in high grass. Both the building and the yard looked like they'd been neglected for decades.

"I'll drive by, then circle back," Warren said. "Don't want to make it obvious we're following him, if he hasn't noticed already."

As they passed the church, Cole tried to catch a clear glimpse of The Truffle Pig, but he was looking the other way, so all she saw was the back of his head. Shifting her gaze to the side mirror, she caught a glimpse of the Camry's red door as it opened.

73

De Santis stuck the Beretta in his waistband as he stepped from the car. After grabbing the duffel bag from the trunk, he crossed the grass and paused on the rotten, crumbling steps of the church, checking for the airport shuttle through dark sunglasses. It had been behind him for at least an hour—probably more—though he was only ninety-percent sure it had been following him.

It didn't make any sense. Law enforcement—both local and federal—would have stopped him if they thought he'd been involved in a shooting. And they wouldn't be in a shuttle van. Perhaps whoever was in the van had been hired by his employer to ensure he got out of town safely. Either way, his money was inside and the Tampa airport only a couple hours away. He'd disappear to Toronto for a month or two, get the first couple surgeries, then return to Miami as a flat-nosed blond man. The beaches were sublime, but in the end, the food made him settle on Miami. The combinations of salt and lime and spice were addictive. So what if Miami would be under water in thirty years? He wouldn't be around that long anyway, and he liked to swim.

He'd even settled on a name: Hector Alvarez. An ode to his mother, who's maiden name had been Hannah Alfonsi.

The old wooden door of the church was unlocked and he walked through the vestibule and into the nave. Pews were covered with moss. Vines grew through broken windows, encircling the crossbeams of the vaulted ceilings. The old missionary church had been abandoned for decades.

In the pulpit, a large cross still hung on the wall. He took it down, revealing a patch in the sheetrock. With a single sharp punch, he busted through the sheetrock and reached into the wall. As expected, it contained a package wrapped in plastic. It was around three and a half pounds. As it should be.

He returned the cross to its place of honor, though it only partially covered the hole he'd left in the wall. He stowed the money in the duffel bag and took the back door into an overgrown graveyard.

After turning the car around, Warren stopped at a turnout a hundred yards from the church. "Don't want to get too close."

The Camry was still parked out front. "Think he's inside?" Cole asked.

"Assume so."

Cole lowered the window, eyeing the door. "Don't want to go in after him?"

"Better just to watch. Chances are it's a pickup. Best thing we can do is stay close until we're back in cell phone range."

"What if he knew we were on him and ditched the car, disappeared through the back of the church and into the woods or the marshland? Or, worse, got picked up by another car while we were turning around?"

"Unlikely," Warren said. "I'm guessing it's the final payment." He waved a hand toward the empty road and expansive marshland in every direction. "I doubt he's meeting anyone, or would try to escape from here. There's nothing. No one."

Cole sighed and interlaced her fingers, twisting them to crack all her knuckles at once. "Then we wait."

After a long silence, Warren said, "That CI I met. I called him SG, short for Sea Glass, because of his bright green eyes."

"I noticed them."

"He said something when I left, the first time I met with him. Something…" He let out a long sigh. "Never mind."

"What is it?"

"Said his mother called him Harold Jackson, and that's what he preferred to be called now."

"And?" Cole asked.

"Don't know. Stuck with me."

"Why?"

"When I knew him in New York, dude was an addict. Not a killer, not a rapist. Broke the law, but never hurt a soul, far as I know, other than his own. Years later I'm still calling him 'SG'— like he's still the same guy. Still just using him to get what I need."

"Using him to get the info we needed. To stop a crime." She caught herself. "Well...*try* to stop a crime."

"I guess I'm thinking about whether any of us can escape our past," Warren said. "He's years sober, a new life in Florida, and I'm still calling him 'SG.' I'm *still* trying to outrun some of the stuff that happened in Afghanistan, and now I'm gonna be known —forever—as a brutal cop. Talked to Sarah about it and what she said was right. Even if the video leaks showing why I did what I did, the version of me you wrote will be etched in most people's minds."

Cole held up a hand, ready to apologize and defend herself at the same time.

Warren didn't let her. "I'm *not* trying to get into that again. It's true of you, too. Your husband died and, you said it yourself, that's what drives you now. And The Truffle Pig—just like SG— has a name, a past, a future. To us, and to the world, he's just *Maiale Da Tartufo*. Always will be."

They watched the door in silence until Warren said, "Something else SG said has me thinking. 'The deeper the water, the bigger the fish.'"

"And?"

"He was talking about wreck fishing. Deep sea fishing. Ana Diaz was one of the most powerful financiers in Florida— respected, honored in her community—*and* at the same time, the most powerful drug kingpin in the region."

"Don't go there," Cole said, shaking her head.

"Where?" Warren asked.

"You were headed back to the 'Maybe these terrorists are on to something' argument."

Warren raised his voice. "Ana Diaz was a killer, a criminal. I'll shed exactly zero tears for her, but that's not where I was going. I—"

Warren cut himself off as a line of tour busses passed, blocking their view of the church temporarily. As the last bus disappeared, he cleared his throat. "Like I said, zero tears for Ana Diaz, but that's not where I was headed. The manifesto promised *six* more murders. And we've already seen the murders of one of the most powerful businessmen on earth and a former VP. I'm not saying I *agree* with the manifesto, or maybe... well maybe I do. I mean, I'm not saying I agree with their methods. I..." he trailed off, sighing deeply. "You just *know* it's going to turn out that they're all connected somehow. I mean, you *know* it, right? What the hell does that say about our world?"

"You're saying the water is going to get deeper. And the fish are going to get bigger."

"Exactly. We have no idea how big the fish are at the bottom of this ocean."

⊕

Sitting cross-legged on the graveyard's mossy ground, De Santis pulled the rifle from his duffel bag. Next he took out a 4-inch hand grinder with a metal cutting blade. Weapon resting across his thighs, he began to saw. First he took off a 5-inch piece of the barrel. Next, a chunk of the stock. The high-pitched screech of the saw filled the graveyard, causing birds in the surrounding trees to take flight.

After cutting the rifle into eight pieces, he stowed the grinder in the bag and dug a small hole in the dirt beside him. He buried a piece of the rifle barrel.

He stood and moved methodically around the graveyard, burying the pieces one by one.

As he did, he read gravestones. Most of the names were too eroded to make out, but he assumed they belonged to members of the Seminole and Miccosukee Tribes, who'd lived in the region for centuries. When missionaries came in the 1930s, the tribal members who converted had worshipped, and been buried, here.

One headstone he *could* read struck him because the date on it was only a day away from his birthday: June 18, 1964. The name was Viola Davis, and she'd died just before her first birthday, May 31, 1965.

His mind jumped to the morning on the boat. Why had he shot the woman in the belly when she was already dead? He didn't think of himself as sick or vindictive. He was all business. He'd been forced into this life by circumstance, never killed for any reason other than necessity. Just doing his job—a job he'd never applied for. And yet, that shot had been unnecessary. A cruel exclamation point.

But why? Maybe it was about the happiness he imagined the woman and her husband were feeling at the upcoming birth of their child. Or had it been a mercy? Perhaps the child would have suffered more, dying slowly as the mother bled out. He didn't know, and he didn't like where his reflections were taking him.

He buried the last piece of the weapon and walked around the side of the church.

Warren pointed.

"That's him," Cole said.

It was their first good look at *Maiale Da Tartufo*. Short and wiry, he was deeply tanned, and his black hair matched his sunglasses. In his white Bermuda shorts and red floral shirt, he looked like a typical tourist.

"Is that a duffel bag?" Cole asked. "Do you think he was out back the whole time?"

Warren shrugged.

The Truffle Pig stowed the bag in the trunk and got in the car.

"What now?" Cole asked, taking out her phone.

"We keep following him."

As Warren started the van, she took a few photos of the church, capturing the red Camry as well. They were crummy shots from far away, but something told her she needed to remember this place.

The gas light illuminated when De Santis started the car.

He'd been so preoccupied with his last target and his retirement, he'd screwed up. He hadn't filled the tank yesterday. A rookie mistake he'd never made before, but not a big deal.

He'd grab some gas at the next station and be in Tampa with plenty of time to have a glass of Chianti at the terminal before his flight to Toronto.

74

Giving the Camry plenty of space, Warren followed until it pulled off at a small gas station—probably the last one in the park. He stopped at a turnaround on the other side of the highway.

"How's our gas?" Cole asked.

"Still three-quarters of a tank."

"So we just wait?"

Warren nodded. "I assume he's headed for an airport. Tampa, or maybe Atlanta. We're almost out of the park. Cell coverage will pick back up."

De Santis started the pump and walked inside, checking the airport shuttle van in a window reflection as he walked in. No movement. He *was* being followed, but it didn't matter much as long as they left him alone. If they dared approach, he had the Beretta at the ready.

He used the restroom and bought a bottle of unsweetened iced tea. He checked the airport shuttle van through the window as he paid. It hadn't moved.

He allowed himself a smile. Must be guys hired by his employers. More an escort than a tail. They probably wanted to make sure he got his money and left the state safely. This had been one of the best operations he'd ever worked for. He had no idea why they wanted Alvin Meyers or Ana Diaz dead—that was none of his business—but he'd been paid well and on time.

Despite the nagging feeling about the woman he'd shot in the belly, he felt blessed that his last job had gone so well.

Warren pressed his hands into his cheeks and let out a long breath.

"Stressed?" Cole asked.

"I'll feel better when we hear from the FBI and get the hell away from this guy."

The Truffle Pig came out of the gas station. Sipping from a bottle, he strolled toward his car like he didn't have a care in the world.

The hot sun warmed De Santis's face as he crossed to the gas pumps. He crouched to pretend to tie his shoe, checking under his car just to be sure. No one.

He replaced the pump, wondering how soon he could safely return to Miami. He could almost taste the *Bistec Empanizado*. He'd ordered the dish from room service last night and it had forever changed the way he saw food.

His mother would roll over in her grave if she knew he'd eaten a deep-fried steak. Steak, she'd taught him, should be seared medium-rare and topped with a subtle sauce. White truffle butter, or a red wine demi. Tougher cuts of beef were to be braised. One *never* deep fried beef.

But the thinly-sliced sirloin, marinated in sour orange and doused with adobo, then breaded and fried, had been a revelation. And he couldn't get enough fresh lime juice on it. The thought of it was enough to push away the lingering thoughts about the woman, the child in her belly, and what it said about him that he'd put an extra bullet through both of them.

One last look: the airport shuttle van hadn't moved.

As he opened the door of the Camry, he caught his reflection in the tinted window of a large silver SUV that was pulling up to the pump opposite him. Before it had stopped, a man leapt from the back seat.

De Santis's hand dropped to his Beretta, but he was too late.

He knew it in an instant. Distracted by the airport shuttle van, the thoughts of food, and his reflections on the woman and the baby, he'd missed something.

The last thing he ever saw was a young man in a black suit holding a silenced Glock 19.

—End of Episode 3—

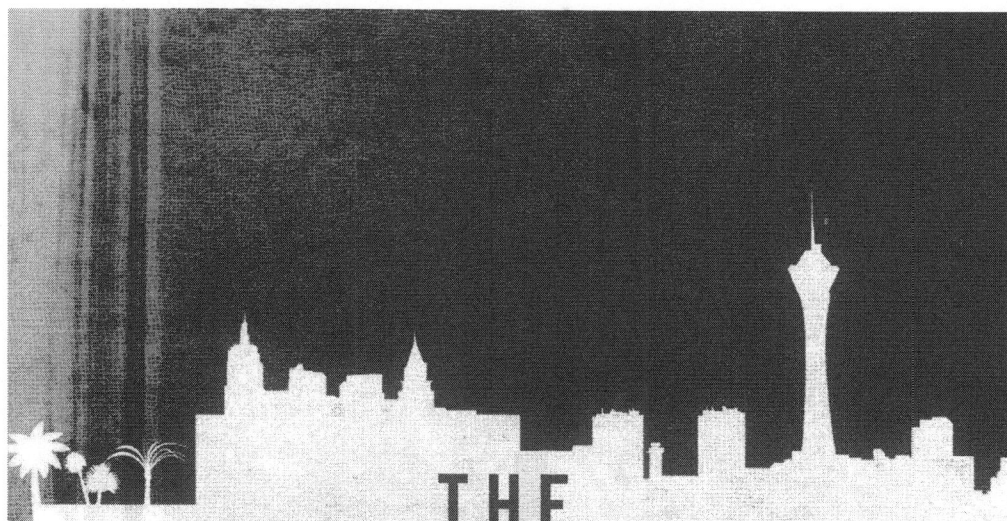

THE
CRIME
BEAT

EPISODE 4: LAS VEGAS

75

Saturday

Cole's hands shot up to cover her mouth, a scream caught in her throat. The Truffle Pig fell, his bottle of iced tea shattering beside him on the oil-stained pavement.

A man had emerged from a silver SUV and stopped ten feet from the gas pump. He'd taken four large strides toward the assassin, then shot him once in the chest and once in the head. It happened in a surreal instant.

Still sitting in the passenger seat of the stolen airport shuttle van, Cole froze. She stared at the blood that streamed slowly from the dead man's chest, pooling around the broken glass.

Warren opened the door suddenly.

"Wait," Cole said, grabbing his forearm. "No."

He closed the door.

Thirtyish, the man who'd shot The Truffle Pig was tall and handsome in a black suit with a white t-shirt underneath. A large gold cross hung from his neck. After standing over his victim for only a moment, he slid into the back of the SUV before it pulled out of the gas station and turned right.

The gas station attendant ran out of the store and stood over The Truffle Pig's body. A woman a few yards away filmed the scene on her phone, narrating like a reporter. Another woman spoke into her phone rapidly. Still another walked in circles around her car, talking to herself.

Cole had seen plenty of crime scenes, plenty of dead bodies. She'd been to gruesome murder scenes within hours of the crimes, but she'd never seen anyone killed in front of her. It was all so fast, it didn't seem possible.

The man they'd tracked from Washington, D.C. to Miami, then found only minutes before the fatal shot on Ana Diaz, had walked out of the gas station holding an iced tea—the same brand she drank. Now he was losing blood by the pint. He was gone, just like that. She'd never forget the sound of the gunshot, followed by the shattering glass. Never be able to unsee the pink brain matter splattered on the gas pump. Her mind went fuzzy—spinning—the gray static ready to take over.

She pressed her feet into the floor to steady herself. "We have to follow. We'll be back in cell range as soon as we exit the park." She turned to Warren, whose eyes darted back and forth between the body and the SUV as it disappeared around a curve a couple hundred yards away. "We have to follow," she repeated. "I don't think they noticed when you opened the door, but I have to think that, if they were following him, they noticed us following him as well."

Warren shifted the van into gear and turned right, allowing it to drift out over the center line. "They're up there. Maybe five cars ahead."

"The hell?" Cole said. "I mean, you're a cop. What the hell is going on?"

Warren opened his eyes wide. Steering with his knee, he pressed both hands into his face and let out a long breath.

Cole had seen him do this before. It was his pressure release valve, his way of getting his emotions under control. Surely his mind was racing with the possibilities, as hers was.

All he said was, "Cell signal?"

"One bar." She tried calling 9-1-1, but it wouldn't connect.

"Gas station attendant probably called 9-1-1. There were enough people there that I'm sure someone called. You did the right thing telling me to stay in the car. Instinct was to run at the guy who fired. Without a weapon, he'd have taken me down. What the hell was I thinking?" He sighed. "When you get the bars, call Gabby."

"Why?" Cole asked.

"Just call her."

They passed another gas station, then a series of signs for locations in southwest Florida, and finally a sign thanking them for visiting the park. The bars on Cole's phone moved from one to two. She dialed Gabriella Rojas, Warren's former training officer who worked for the Joint Terrorism Task Force in New York City. Though they'd never met, Cole trusted her. Mostly because Warren trusted her, but also because of their shared loathing of Joey "The Stallion" Mazzalano.

"Put it on speaker," Warren said as it rang.

"Hello." Gabby answered right away, but sounded out of breath.

Cole held the phone between them.

Warren tilted his head, eyes still on the road. "Gabby, it's War Dog."

"Hey...I'm jogging...what's up?"

"This morning, The Truffle Pig killed Ana Diaz. A few minutes ago, he was gunned down at a gas station in the Everglades. We're on the tail of the killers. I need your help. Fast."

Rojas breathed heavily into the phone, then said, "Rob, seriously, what the hell are you doing?"

"Please, Gabby."

For a few moments, all Cole heard on the line was Gabby's breathing. When Gabby spoke at last, her voice was back to normal. "I heard about Diaz right before I left for my run. What can I do?"

"That was hours ago," Warren said.

"I go on long runs."

"The dude who shot The Truffle Pig looked like a professional. Plates on the SUV were Georgia." He let the car drift left again, squinting to see the license plate number. "Hold on." Waiting for a gap in traffic, he pulled out and passed two cars, then changed lanes so the airport shuttle was now two cars behind the SUV. "Got a pen?"

"Told you, I'm running, but I'll remember it."

"Georgia plates." Warren gave her the plate number. "Get back to me ASAP, okay?"

"I'm two miles from my house. It'll be twelve minutes."

"You can run two miles in twelve minutes?" Cole asked.

"Ten minutes, but it'll take me an extra two to get upstairs."

When they hung up, Cole dialed 9-1-1 and reported what they'd seen, recited the plate number, and assured the woman on the phone they weren't putting themselves at any risk by following it.

They merged onto Interstate 75, heading north up the west coast of Florida. After a few miles, a black sedan overtook them, then pulled in front of them, still two cars back from the SUV. "Local police," Warren said. "Undercover."

"How can you tell?" Cole asked.

He pointed at the rear window. "See the bars between the front and back seats? And the two disc things that look like hockey pucks on the roof? Antennas."

Through the window, Cole saw heavy-duty crossbars that separated the front and back seats. She never would have noticed the black antennas had Warren not pointed them out. "Why aren't they pulling them over?"

"Waiting for backup, probably. Likely got three calls in five minutes. They know these guys are armed and dangerous. Can't exactly blame them."

Cole grew uncomfortable as they rode in silence for what felt like an hour. It was probably five minutes. As a crime reporter, she'd spent most of her time either in the courthouse watching trials or trying to get police, witnesses, and suspects to talk, often by text or social media messages. A week ago she'd yearned for excitement—anything to pull her from her routine and off the internet. But now she was genuinely terrified. As ridiculous as it was, she kept imagining the SUV pulling over and the man hopping out and shooting her.

They passed an exit dotted with fast-food restaurants and Cole broke the silence. "I'm hungry." She hadn't eaten a bite since the half bag of microwave popcorn at 2 a.m. in Little Havana.

Warren said nothing.

Cole's phone rang. "It's Gabby." She held it to Warren as she accepted the call.

"Rob, Cole, you want the good news first, or the bad?"

"The good news," Cole said quickly. She needed something positive.

"Local police and FBI are all over the car. I don't know the details, but, apparently, the FBI was already on the SUV."

"Wait," Warren said. "If they were already *on* them, why'd they let them kill The Truffle Pig in broad daylight? That doesn't make any sense."

The line was quiet for a long moment. "That I'm not sure about," Gabby said. "Could be...well...could be a lot of things. But let me finish. FBI is on them, and now local police are, too."

"Black sedan is tailing them," Warren said.

"That was the good news?" Cole asked, impatiently.

"Means you're off the hook," Gabby said. "Back away slowly from this thing, Rob. You too, Cole. Let the professionals handle it."

Warren sighed. "Which brings you to the bad news?"

"Right. Plates were registered to a woman in Atlanta named Wendy Bluth. She's the aunt of Peter Bluth of Las Vegas, who runs Club Blue and some other nightspots."

Warren let his foot off the gas slowly, as though all the energy had drained from his foot. A line of cars changed lanes and pulled around him.

"What's Club Blue?" Cole asked.

"One of the hottest clubs in Vegas," Gabby said, "and it's owned by Sunny Lee." She paused, allowing the name to hang in the air as though it should mean something to Cole. It didn't. "Either they're NVM or they stole a car from an NVM member's aunt. Would be a helluva coincidence."

"Sunny Lee?" Warren asked. His face held an odd expression. Eyes wide, lips pursed, jaw tight. Cole couldn't tell if he was shocked, confused, or afraid. Maybe it was all three.

"What's NVM?" Cole asked. "And who's Sunny Lee?"

"I gotta go," Gabby said, "but get the hell *away* from this thing, Rob. I'm serious. I had to press a friend in the Florida FBI to get the info, and...anyway, I gotta go."

The call ended.

Warren's face went blank.

He was only going forty miles an hour. Car after car passed them on the left side of the two-lane highway.

"Who's Sunny Lee?" Cole asked. "And what the hell is NVM?"

76

Cole put a hand on Warren's knee. "You're only going forty."

He glanced at the speedometer and accelerated.

She wasn't much for physical contact, so she was surprised by her own action. The ridiculousness of their situation had hit her all at once. What were they doing? "Rob, pull over."

Warren gave her a side-eyed glance, but didn't reply.

"Gabby said it," Cole pressed. "Local police and the FBI are tailing those guys. We're in western Florida in a stolen airport shuttle van. The story we were chasing is now"—she raised her hands like she was throwing confetti—"out in the world. We're *nowhere*. This is out of our hands." He ignored her, seemed to be in some kind of trance. "*Rob*, pull the hell over!"

He snapped back to attention as she waved at a turnout. He took it, stopping the van behind a tour bus that was letting passengers out in front of the restrooms.

"I want you to tell me what NVM is," she said, "but first…"

Cars sped by on the highway. Tourists emerged from the tour bus. Yesterday, she'd argued for Warren to give her one more day before releasing the map she'd photographed in Michael Wragg's storage unit. She'd been selfish and wrong, and she knew it. But she couldn't say it aloud.

"A day." Warren's words broke the silence. "You're thinking about the day we waited."

"Might have made a difference if we'd released the map like you said."

"It wouldn't have." He shrugged. "It might now."

Cole recoiled internally. Every fiber of her being guarded scoops jealously. Even now, when she had to let it go, something in her didn't want to.

"You know I'm right," Warren continued. "You want me to *make* you do it, but I won't. You want—"

"I get it, okay? Just"—she squeezed her eyes tight—"gimme a minute to think."

As much as it hurt, she had to release the map. But other things were nagging at her, things that made her uncertain, paralyzed. Someone had planted articles linking them to the murders. There was no evidence, and she didn't think the articles would make a splash, but *still*. Who had planted the stories, and why? Plus, Marty Goldberg's death was still fresh in her mind. Just a day after meeting with them, he'd ordered men to track them to Miami. At least she thought so. She'd been calling to confirm this when he'd been found dead in the Potomac River. None of it made sense.

Even with all the unanswered questions, she couldn't justify holding onto the map. It was the only huge clue they had that the rest of the world didn't.

Opening the Signal app on her phone, she created a new message. Next, she attached the photo of the map decorated with pushpins in nine cities: New York, Washington, D.C., Miami, Las Vegas, San Francisco, Los Angeles, London, Paris, and Tokyo. She wrote a brief message, explaining its origin. Finally, she attached additional photos from the unit which, though they contained little new information, provided context. She sent the message and put her phone on her lap. "It's done."

"Who'd you send it to?"

"Jon Baker. Crime reporter at *The New York Times*. He's my biggest competitor. Well, he *was* my biggest competitor when I was at *The Sun*."

"Why him?" Warren asked.

"If I won't get credit for the scoop, I want to be as far away as possible. Sent it anonymously through Signal." She held up her phone so he could see the app's icon. "End-to-end encryption.

Untraceable. It's the gold standard for reporters who need encryption. Most don't, but…"

Warren nodded his approval. "You trust him?"

Cole leaned back and her shoulders dropped. Her conscience was finally clear. "Can't stand the bastard. Arrogant as hell. But he's gone to jail to protect sources. Multiple times. He'll get it out there, and it'll have the weight of the *paper of record* behind it. It'll be leading every single news report in the world by tomorrow."

"Why'd you have me pull over?" Warren asked.

The tourists were still spilling out of the tour bus, some taking pictures, some sipping bottled water or staring at phones.

"We needed to slow down, get some distance. We were too close. *I* was too close. With the manifesto, and now the police and the FBI on those guys, this thing is about to get huge."

"Or it might be over by the end of the day," Warren said. "The FBI will nab those guys soon. Interrogate them. I'm assuming they hired The Truffle Pig, waited for him to kill Meyers and Diaz, then took him out to cover their tracks. Planning for someone else to make the next kill like Wragg made the first one. But not if the FBI gets them talking."

Warren smiled strangely. A look Cole couldn't figure out. "What?"

"It just hit me. This could be over by the end of the day, and the fact that we were there might have caused it. We aren't sitting there watching, maybe no one gets the plates, maybe the SUV disappears."

"Maybe." Cole wasn't entirely convinced. "Gabby said the FBI was already trailing the SUV. Doesn't make any sense."

"No," Warren said, "it doesn't."

She crossed her legs in the seat and turned toward him. "What's NVM?"

"New Vegas Mafia."

"I probably should have known that."

"No reason you would," Warren said. "Like the name says, they're…*new*."

"Your foot eased off the gas when Gabby mentioned them. Fear?"

Warren frowned. He didn't like the fact that she could read him.

"It's not just you," she continued. "Humans are hard-wired to avoid danger. It's why we're pessimistic as a species. We're actually pretty good at avoiding trouble. Some researchers think it's why we took over the earth in short order. We thrive at avoiding danger. Avoiding predators. Your response tells me those dudes are predators."

Warren grimaced as if to object, but shook it off. "In the eighties and nineties, the last holdouts of the Vegas mob got taken down. Big business moved in. Corporations took over." He shrugged. "Mostly. But criminals always find a way, and NVM sprang from those ashes. Some are cousins and nephews of the old mobsters, but the new thing is less family-oriented. They let outsiders in, so it's more diverse. Women, non-Italians. A real rainbow coalition of organized crime."

"The *mob* is getting more diverse?" Cole asked. "That sweet."

Warren chuckled. "Seriously, though. It's not an Italian thing anymore. And it doesn't resemble *The Mob* as most people think of it. This isn't *The Godfather*. It's more like a loosely-held-together criminal family that exists about eighty percent online."

"Online?" Cole asked.

"You know how in all the movies, bosses won't talk on phones or use emails or anything?"

Cole nodded.

"NVM is a dozen steps ahead of law enforcement when it comes to technology. They embrace tech instead of avoiding it."

"Dropgangs?"

Warren nodded. "Not only that. They have their own cryptocurrency, advanced facial recognition software in their clubs, stuff most people don't even think about."

"Like what?"

"One I heard about? They leveraged a few people at the DMV for driver's license numbers and photos. It's hooked into their facial recognition software so they always know who's in their clubs."

"Seriously?"

"Gives them leverage against *everyone* in their clubs," Warren said. "Especially when cops or others in law enforcement are stupid enough to end up there. Drugs, prostitutes…" He shook his head. "They're tracking every single person who comes in from the moment they enter and they're using every piece of information they can to screw you."

Cole shook her head, half impressed, half in disbelief. "And Sunny Lee? Who's he?"

"*She's* the bastard daughter of one of the old mobsters. Birth name's Sofia, but they call her Sunny because she was always happy. A little ray of sunshine. Her dad got locked up, mom gave her up for adoption, and she was adopted by a Chinese family in Vegas. Bankers, I think. Got the last name Lee and eventually followed in her father's footsteps. They say she was one of the driving forces in creating the NVM. They're young, tech-savvy, and utterly ruthless."

"And taking over Las Vegas?"

"No, those times are gone," Warren said, shaking his head, "and they're not coming back. When big business takes over, not even organized crime can compete. And that's allowing for a distinction between the two that doesn't always exist. NVM is picking up all the pieces. Consolidating the criminal side hustles."

The tour bus driver emerged and began corralling the people back into the bus. "Assuming you're right," Cole said, "and the FBI stops those guys, interrogates them—either they get info that stops this thing or, more likely, they don't. Either way, we should head to Vegas."

"Why?"

Cole tapped on the dashboard. "Because that's where the next murder's gonna be."

"You don't know that."

Within minutes of sending out the map, her journalistic instincts had kicked back in. She no longer had that piece of the scoop, but she had to keep chasing. "I *feel* it. And, even if I'm wrong, that's where the story is headed. C'mon, we gotta get rid of this van. You hop out and pop the hood. Pretend to look at the engine. I'll get us a lift."

Before Warren could respond, Cole got out of the van and jogged up to a young couple straggling behind the group of tourists. "Where's the bus heading?"

The couple glanced at each other. "Back to the hotel," the woman offered, looking over Cole's shoulder at the airport shuttle van. "Were you...on the tour?"

"Nah. Looks like our shuttle van needs to be taken in for service," Cole lied. Sometimes she feared how easily she lied.

"There were a few empty seats on the bus," the man offered.

The woman gave him a cold look. Cole wasn't sure whether it was because he was flirting, or because he was offering up seats on their tour bus to strangers on the side of the road.

"You'd need to talk to the driver," the woman said.

Cole waved at Warren, who shut the hood and began walking over. She turned back to the couple. "That's exactly what I'll do."

77

The plane had been in the air for half an hour when Cole gave in and decided to pay for the in-flight Wifi. She needed to know what people were saying about the shootings.

The tour bus had taken them to a hotel. From there, they'd taken a taxi to the Naples Airport where she'd dipped into savings to purchase two one-ways to Las Vegas. Warren fought her on it at first. He wanted to get back to his daughter in New York and work on getting back into the NYPD. But she suspected he wanted to chase this crime just as badly as she did. She'd assured him she'd tucked away enough from Matt's death benefit to cover them for a while. Plus, she'd be able to make money writing freelance anytime she needed. Warren was a big part of getting close to the story. She needed him. His opposition melted at her merest push-back, lending truth to her suspicions. He was addicted to the chase, just like her.

On the tour bus, Cole heard whispers about the assassinations and the manifesto. Snippets of news coverage had been playing on the TV in the hotel lobby. The airport had been no different, though all the TVs were muted. Now she needed Wifi to continue tracking the story.

She tapped in her credit card number and opened X.

"I thought you weren't gonna buy the Wifi," Warren said.

She gave him a guilty frown. "I can't *not* know what's happening."

She'd stuck Warren with the center seat, a harsh move given his long legs, but he hadn't complained. One-on-one he could be surly, but in group settings, he turned on the charm and became affable, so he didn't seem to mind sitting next to the stranger in the aisle seat. In fact, he'd been chatting with the guy since they'd boarded. Cole had been leaning on the window since the moment she'd shoved her bag under the seat in front of her, silently fighting the urge to get online.

Warren frowned. "What happened to, 'I need to sleep, clear my head.' What happened to that?"

"I have to admit what I am."

He furrowed his eyebrows at her, amused. "And what's that?"

"A junkie. A *news* junkie. You know you want to see what's going on, too."

As if reading her mind, the man in the aisle seat asked, "You heard about the nine murders, nine cities thing?" He was an old man in a collarless button-down—his accent was Indian, but his vowels were round, like he'd lived in the midwest most of his life. A long gray beard and a purple turban completed the look.

Cole shrugged, pretending not to hear him. The last thing she needed was a random guy's thoughts on the case.

"Little bit," Warren said. His eyes narrowed when he answered, his affability briefly gone before it came back again in a flash. "Damn shame what's happening. What do you think about it?"

Cole shot him a scolding look, then turned her attention back to her phone.

The man beamed, clearly glad to have been asked. "I've got a theory. I'm no detective—I'm in insurance sales, actually, only a year from retirement—but I've watched a lot of CSI, Law and Order, every single episode of Monk, so I know how they think."

"And you've got a theory?" Warren smirked at Cole. "Let's hear it!"

Warren was messing with her. Punishing her for being too weak to stay off the internet. She wanted to read stories from journalists, professionals, official sources, and *he* wanted to subject her to a random theory from an aging insurance salesman.

"Talk loud," Warren added, "so my friend can hear you." He nodded toward Cole.

The man leaned in conspiratorially. Warren put his seat back to make more room. Cole turned her phone face-down on the tray table.

"I was in Miami last week," the man began. "Stayed only a few blocks from where the shooting happened."

"That part of your theory?" Cole asked.

"No, just saying."

Cole rolled her eyes.

"Be nice," Warren whispered. "Aren't journalists supposed to talk to real people?"

She sighed. "What's your theory, Mr…"

"Asan," he said, "but call me Gill. Top life insurance salesman in Nevada, 2017, 2018, and 2020 through 2023."

"What happened in 2019?" Cole's voice was still full of snark.

"Let the man tell us his theory," Warren said.

"Okay, so you know the Unabomber?" Gill asked. "He had a political ideology, and killed the people he believed to be against it, right?"

Warren nodded. "Pure *loco* crazy, wasn't he?"

"Not really," Gill said, frowning. "He was a Harvard grad. Mathematics. Smart."

"The two aren't mutually exclusive," Warren said.

Cole didn't know a lot about the Unabomber case; she'd been a teenager when his manifesto had been published. "Wasn't he anti-technology and industrialization?" Cole asked. "These guys are anti-digital globalization, they're against digital tracking, the surveillance state, global corporations, and so on. They seem to have a beef with the financial system and—"

"Can't really blame them for that last one," Warren interjected.

Cole had looked into their ideology more closely as the tour bus drove from the edge of the park to the hotel in Naples. "They believe the tech giants and corrupt governments are working together on something they call 'The Digital Panopticon Agenda.' The idea is that they're building this massive surveillance system where every little thing we do—every word we say, every click we make online—is being tracked and analyzed. It's all about control. These companies are basically in bed with politicians, using all our personal data to create profiles on us, predicting our behavior and pushing us in certain directions. They sell us the idea of convenience, but behind the scenes, they're using all that data to manipulate us, stifle any pushback, and, ultimately, create a one-world government where everyone is monitored and controlled by this all-seeing digital eye."

Gill gave Warren a look, as if to say, *What's her deal?* "You seem to know a lot about this," he said to Cole. "Anyway, I wasn't saying it was the *same* ideology. I'm saying the Unabomber killed for *an* ideology, like these nine murders people are." He moved his hands when he spoke, as though he'd been bottling up all his words for weeks and dramatic hand gestures were a key part of releasing them. "Now, a big thing for the Unabomber was having his manifesto published. Back then there wasn't an Internet like we have it now, so getting his stuff published in the major papers was the only way to get his ideas out there. Not saying these people have the *same* ideas, but they're killing for their ideas, right?"

Cole agreed. Where was he going with this?

"Okay," he continued, "so why would they announce there are going to be six more killings? Why would they announce it in *advance*? Surely that will send people into hiding?"

"Because terrorism is the point," Cole said flatly.

Warren agreed. "They'd have to know that simply killing nine people—no matter how powerful those people are—isn't enough to stop whatever they're trying to stop. She's right. Terror is the point. Plus, they want to enlist others in their project. They're assuming some mass of people will rise up when they read that manifesto."

Gill shook his head. "But they *do* want to kill these other people. Won't everyone go into lockdown now?"

"Maybe," Cole offered. "Increased security, sure."

A woman in the seat behind Warren stood and leaned between the seats. "You talking about the manifesto thing?" She had to yell to be heard over the persistent roar of the plane. "I got a theory. One word: China?" She was a young woman, no more than twenty, with a large textbook under her arm.

Gill waved her off. "What? You think China is behind this?"

"Watch," the young woman said, "you'll see. Ain't no Chinese person been killed yet. We all know they've been amassin' power. This is their *takeover* move. Watch! Not *one* Chinese elite will be taken out. That'll be your proof. Book it!" She snapped her fingers and, satisfied she'd made her point, sat down, and returned to her textbook.

Gill shook his head and returned to his theory. "China!" he scoffed. "That's insane. Here's what's happening, here's the theory: another shoe will drop. A twist. You don't hatch a plan like this, then announce it, then carry it out. It *never* works that way."

"You mean on CSI or Monk?" Cole's voice dripped sarcasm. In the last ten years, she'd seen a steady rise in conspiratorial thinking among everyday Americans. It seemed every person she met had a different—usually odd—set of beliefs about how the world worked. She couldn't exactly blame them. Some of the craziest conspiracy theories she'd researched had turned out to be true.

"As the lady said, book it!" Gill mimicked her finger-snapping exclamation. "Something else is going on here. Maybe a government's behind this whole thing and they're using these assassins as patsies. Doubt it's China, but I wouldn't put it past them. Maybe it's someone taking out business rivals. But something isn't adding up."

A flight attendant passed, carrying a tray of cups. "Water?"

They all shook their heads, but the woman leaned in, her voice a loud whisper. "Ask me, the whole thing is a cover-up. Everyone who's been killed knows the truth about Area 51. *Aliens*." With that, she continued down the aisle, handing out water.

Warren shook his head. "Business rival was our first thought as well. When it was just Raj Ambani. But there's no way all these people tie together in a business framework. And the killers have stated their motive pretty clearly."

Gill shook his head, then stroked his beard in a way that annoyed the hell out of Cole. "If I'm wrong—which, you know, I'm not—a different motive will reveal itself in time. You don't simply announce all your intentions before the deed is done."

She'd seen Monk too, and she didn't know if the guy was stealing his line ironically, or if he was truly this proud of his theory. Either way, it was her cue to get back to her phone.

Cole sorted through a few dozen emails. Former colleagues had written her about the stories claiming she and Warren were involved in the murders. Most assumed they were false, and she didn't blame them for trying to get a statement on the record. This story had tentacles everywhere and would dominate headlines for weeks, months, maybe years. Until it was over. It had connections to politics, finance, organized crime, international trade, and business.

She deleted the emails without replying.

Next, she checked the homepages of a dozen news websites. The only real advancements in the story were reports from around the world that the police, intelligence agencies, and even militaries of multiple countries had been enlisted. Even though all the killings had taken place in the United States, the promise of international assassinations had woken the rest of the world. The map hadn't yet been published, but it would be soon, which would allow the police and intelligence services to focus on the target cities.

There wasn't yet any news about The Truffle Pig or the men who'd shot him. Marty Goldberg's death was still being treated as a suicide.

Most of the online coverage was about the manifesto—analysis of everything from the political ideology to the writing style. As usual, debates were taking place about whether to report on the radical ideology or ignore it. Some argued that reporting it only amplified the message, but the promise of more killings swayed most newsrooms—the publication of the manifesto might lead to a break in the case. In fact—Cole shot a rueful look at Gill —that's how the Unabomber had been caught. Once his manifesto was published, his brother recognized some of the writing and turned him in.

Cole's phone dinged. Even though she'd been browsing for twenty minutes, it felt odd to receive a text at thirty-thousand feet. It was addressed to Warren, from Gabby.

Gabby: *Rob, I called and texted you but no response, so trying Cole. You still roaming the earth with her? Anyway, I got a call from Alan Takigawa, Vegas FBI. Smart dude. Got wind of the NVM connection, somehow learned you were involved and called me because of the JTTF connection. Knew I was your TO. Wants to talk.*

A second text had Takigawa's number.

"What do you think he wants?" Cole asked.

"Let's find out."

She sent Takigawa a text, explaining she was there with Warren and asking what was up. He responded immediately.

Takigawa: *Can I call?*

Cole: *Airplane. Can't really talk.*

Takigawa: *Airplane where?*

Cole: *Halfway to Vegas.*

Takigawa: *When do you arrive? Pick you up at the airport? If you're OK with that.*

Cole looked at Warren, who'd been reading over her shoulder. He nodded.

"What would he want from *us*?" Cole asked. "You think our theft of that airport shuttle is finally catching up with us?"

"Probably just following up. Maybe after they apprehended the NVM guys, they sent them to Vegas. Maybe he wants us to ID them."

Cole: *Arrival is 8 PM. We'll meet you curbside.*

78

Special Agent Takigawa met them at the McCarran Airport. He'd texted Warren a picture of himself, which struck Warren as odd. But as they greeted each other, it all made sense.

Takigawa was one of those guys Warren had come to know as a BTBB, a By The Book Bastard. He dressed neatly, followed every rule, and covered his bases to the point of overkill. The kind of guy who annoyed the hell out of officers like Warren, who were sometimes willing to bend a rule to get something done.

He stood about six feet tall and wore a boring brown suit. With his short black hair and glasses, he looked like he belonged at an accounting convention. He stood straight and square on the curb and didn't smile as they shook hands. "Mr. Warren, come with me," was all he said.

Warren said, "This is Jane Cole, formerly of the *New York Sun*."

Takigawa shook Cole's hand and opened the back door of his black sedan for her. By the book, Warren thought.

Cole slid into the back seat and Warren took the front.

As he pulled away from the airport, Takigawa said, "I'll be taking you back to the field office, unless we can cover everything on the ride over."

"Not much to tell," Warren said.

"As I said in the texts," Takigawa began, "Rojas filled me in a little, but I'd appreciate if you'd start from the beginning. I've been working on NVM, and specifically on Sunny Lee, for two years. This is a nice break for us." He'd said Sunny Lee with a hint of disdain, the first piece of emotion or personality he'd shown.

Warren glanced back at Cole. "You wanna tell it?"

She waved him off, then turned her attention to the billboards and casinos in the distance. She was mesmerized by the sparkling skyline. On the plane, Cole had mentioned that she'd never visited Las Vegas. She and Matt had traveled widely, so this had come as a surprise. He was used to it, but it wasn't like anywhere else. Love it or hate it, it was hard to look away from the bright towers and glimmering gold signs rising out of the desert.

Takigawa tapped his fingers on the steering wheel. "Mr. Warren? How about we start here: How'd you end up at that gas station?"

Warren didn't have much in common with him, but he trusted Takigawa nonetheless. As they cruised toward Vegas, he told him the story. With each new revelation, his conscience cleared a little. Starting with the day Raj Ambani was killed, he told the truth. He'd raced down to the Met as soon as he heard about the shooting, desperate to tell anyone who would listen about the sale of the nine rifles he'd seen on his day shadowing the JTTF. When no one would listen, he'd approached Cole.

Takigawa asked him a few questions for clarity, but mostly listened respectfully. Though he said little, the questions he asked gave Warren the impression that the man had a sharp mind. Probably didn't smoke, drink, or stay up past ten.

He told how he and Cole had tracked down Michael Wragg, how they'd known the Alvin Meyers assassination was connected to Ambani because of the photos Cole took of Wragg's screen. Finally, he told Takigawa how they'd ended up in a hotel room with The Truffle Pig's rifle. "From there," Warren concluded, "we headed to Miami where we got to Ana Diaz's estate a few minutes too late. I think Rojas filled you in on what happened from there."

"Wait, how'd you know Miami would be the site of the next killing?"

Warren wasn't willing to give up Samuel Bacon and Norris Ubwe, the two JTTF guys who'd helped him. He opened his mouth to lie, but it would destroy the good feeling he'd gotten from telling Takigawa the truth so far. "I'm not going to tell you that. At least not yet."

Takigawa gave him a side-eyed glance. "May I ask why not?"

"Got the tip from someone in law enforcement. I'm on a ledge here, and I don't want to pull them out on it with me."

Takigawa signaled, changed lanes to pass a truck, then signaled again and merged back ahead of the truck once he was a respectable distance past. It was the most by-the-book lane change Warren had ever seen, and it made him miss Blue Lightning, the Cougar he'd left in the snow back in D.C..

"If they gave you a tip they didn't share with their superiors," Takigawa said, "that's a crime."

Warren shook his head. "I didn't say they shared it *only* with me. I don't know what they did, but...look, you know how it is. Sometimes we help each other out. If you want to blame someone, blame me. I'm not outing them."

Takigawa drummed his fingers on the steering wheel. "We can return to that later. How'd you find The Truffle Pig? You know, FBI has had him on their most wanted list for nine years. And you found him in two days."

Warren nodded toward Cole, who leaned against the window in the back seat, eyes closed. "Mostly her. Found a local, figured out the most likely next target. From there, I was lucky to spot him."

"Every detail, please, Mr. Warren."

Takigawa drove slowly, sticking to the right lane. Warren took a few deep breaths, trying to calm himself. The way Takigawa drove made him crazy.

Warren told him the story of how they'd found The Truffle Pig, then followed him across southern Florida. He told him about the church he'd stopped at, then the scene at the gas station and their calls to local police and the FBI. "When Gabby told me the plate belonged to a woman connected to NVM, well, that's where you guys came in."

"Did you get much of a look at the men?" Takigawa asked.

Cole leaned forward, sticking her head between the seats. "Only the shooter. Thirty, maybe late-twenties, handsome, clean-shaven. Black suit. White t-shirt. Gold chain."

"Kinda generically handsome, if that makes sense," Warren added. "Maybe Italian background, but I don't know."

"In the glove compartment there's a stack of photos," Takigawa said. "See if he's one of them."

Warren opened the glove compartment and found an envelope with about twenty photos. He thumbed through them, Cole looking over his shoulder. None was an obvious match for the man they'd seen.

Cole shook her head. "Sorry. Don't think it's any of those guys."

They rode in silence for a minute. On the right, the major casinos on The Strip loomed large. The big glass pyramid of The Luxor, the faux-Roman architecture of Caesar's Palace, and the twirling roller coaster of New York, New York. Warren watched the scene, glancing occasionally at Cole to gauge her reaction. The more he thought about it, the more he thought she'd hate Las Vegas. She was too much of a brooder to enjoy the anything-goes vibe of Sin City.

Takigawa gave him an odd look.

Warren puzzled over it for a moment, then shot up in his seat. "Oh, God."

Takigawa didn't react.

"Why'd you bring those photos?" Warren asked.

Takigawa didn't respond.

Warren shot Cole a worried look. She looked confused. Warren fumed. He knew why he'd brought the photos. It was the same reason Takigawa had texted them in the first place. Something had gone wrong.

"What is it?" Cole asked.

Warren turned to Takigawa. "Please tell me you didn't lose them."

"Mistakes were made," Takigawa said.

Warren closed his eyes. His head dropped to his chest. After a second, his eyes shot open and he struck the glove compartment with his fist, just once, as hard as he could. It hurt his hand and dented the plastic.

"Please don't damage FBI property, Mr. Warren."

"Wait," Cole said from the back seat. "I recognize that passive-voice BS. 'Mistakes were made.' What the hell happened?"

Takigawa squeezed the steering wheel so hard his knuckles cracked. Warren recognized the move. He'd done the same thing out of frustration a hundred times. "I showed you the pictures because I was hoping the men who shot The Truffle Pig were men we already knew, already had locations on."

"And they did that because someone screwed up," Warren said.

"I don't get it," Cole said. "We passed them off. Local police and FBI were on them when we left."

"Mistakes were made," Takigawa repeated blandly.

"You're *not* saying you lost them," Cole said.

Warren sighed. "That's exactly what he's saying."

Takigawa raised his voice for the first time. "A minute ago you wouldn't throw your buddies under the bus." He narrowed his eyes. "I think you can understand why I won't, either. Mistakes. Were. Made." Takigawa sighed. "Let's leave it at that. The question I have for you two is whether you're willing to help us fix them."

Warren tried not to let himself get too high or too low—either extreme could lead him back to the bottle—but he'd been hoping this might be over soon. Had things broken right, the NVM members might have given up others involved in the nine murders. From there, the masterminds might have been caught. He and Cole would be heroes. Maybe big enough heroes to get him back on the force. But now...

"Will you help?" Takigawa asked.

"How far's the field office?" Warren asked. "And do you have coffee?"

79

The Las Vegas FBI Field Office was housed in a gray box of a building, as boring and nondescript as Takigawa's brown suit. He led them past a front desk guarded by two security guards, flashing his ID per the procedural manual, though it was clear they recognized him.

Cole hung a few paces behind Warren, still in disbelief that *mistakes were made.*

They sat in a large cubicle in the center of an open room that bustled with activity. Takigawa—all business—offered them chairs on either side of a desk and opened a laptop. "In the car I had photos of our main targets, but here"—he pushed the laptop across the desk—"take a look." Cole leaned in as Takigawa opened a series of photos on the laptop. "Let me know if any of these men are the man who shot The Truffle Pig."

He opened a photo, waited until both Cole and Warren shook their heads, then clicked another, then another. Interestingly, each photo had a very different quality. Some were posed like professional portraits. Some were square, like Instagram photos, and some were grainy or slightly out of focus, as though taken from a great distance. Surveillance photos.

"Nope," Cole said as another face flashed by.

"Who are all these guys?" Warren asked.

"I've been on NVM for two years," Takigawa said. "Working

like hell just to keep up with them. They use technology better than any criminal organization I've seen and—frankly—better than us. We've got a team of interns combing social media for links between known NVMs and others in Vegas. We cross those folks with photos and info from traditional surveillance, and what we come up with is what I'm showing you." He clicked and another image flashed by. "Our NVM *Person of Interest* file."

Warren shook his head, crinkled his nose, and frowned.

A look Cole recognized as his disgusted face. "What?" she asked.

Warren waved her off and gestured back to the screen, which was on a new image. "What about him?" he asked. The photo was of a young man—could have been a teenager, even—wearing a gold chain and a blue suit over a white t-shirt. He held a heavy-bottomed tumbler and his cheeks were red, likely from a night of partying. Her first reaction was that he was too young. The shooter had been around thirty. This kid looked only a couple years out of puberty. "Why didn't you arrest him for underage drinking?" Cole asked.

Takigawa frowned.

"Seriously, though," she continued, "these photos go back two years?"

"No. I've been working NVM for two years. When I asked our interns to get good at tracking these bastards through social media, I told them to pull in everything, including older photos."

Cole examined the image. Looked like the typical photo a dumb teenager would put on Instagram, but there *was* some resemblance between the kid and the man who'd shot The Truffle Pig. "When was the photo taken?"

Takigawa clicked it, revealing a "Notes" section that read: "Instagram story of Sunny Lee, June 23, 2017, Subject not tagged."

"What does that mean, 'Subject not tagged'?" Warren asked.

Cole and Takigawa began answering at the same time, but Cole relented and let him explain.

"Means this photo was pulled from Sunny Lee's Instagram. This was just a random photo—probably taken in one of her clubs before she rose to where she is now. Whoever this is, his Instagram account wasn't linked to the photo, so we don't have his name. But we know he was in a club with Sunny Lee, and, look"

—he pointed at a circular bar in the upper left corner of the image—"that's the famous bar at Club Blue, one of the hottest spots in Vegas. Owned by—"

"Sunny Lee," Cole said.

Warren leaned in. "I can see it. The ears. If this was taken in 2017, I think the age is about right. Chances are, the shooter was someone in the NVM orbit for years, being groomed. Maybe The Truffle Pig was his coming out party?"

Takigawa wrote in a small notebook he'd pulled from an inside pocket. "Level of certainty?"

"Sixty percent," Warren said.

"Eighty," Cole said.

Warren stood. "So we head to Club Blue?"

Takigawa frowned. "*I* head to Club Blue. I appreciate your help, Mr. Warren and Ms. Cole, but this is where our collaboration ends."

Warren took a deep breath and crossed his arms. "There's something you're not telling us."

"Told you," Takigawa said, "I'm not gonna get into how we lost the shooters. I thought you understood that."

Warren shook his head in a tight arc. "No, something else." He put his hand on Takigawa's neck and pulled him in so their foreheads almost met. "C'mon, man. We tracked these bastards from New York to D.C. I left my car there. I *loved* that ride. Then to Miami where we almost got taken out. Now we're here. Gimme *something*. Please."

Takigawa pulled away. Warren leaned back.

Cole stood as well so they formed a tight triangle. Takigawa looked torn, but Warren was right. He wasn't telling them something. "Please," she said. "I swear we won't tell anyone."

Takigawa sighed. "Look, the last week or two, we've been hearing about a 'Retirement Party' for Sunny Lee. Couple things on social media, confirmed by a source within NVM. Until yesterday, we were operating under the assumption it could be a rival gang member looking to take over her clubs, or, well...could have been a lot of things. Once we heard Ana Diaz went down, we started to wonder. When we got the call about The Truffle Pig and his connection to all these assassinations, we perked up. We believe Sunny Lee is going to be killed. Maybe tomorrow. I don't know how, but I think it's connected to the nine murders." He waved an arm in their direction. "This damn thing you've been chasing around the country. We're gonna loop in with field offices in New York, D.C., and Miami, but for now, we're gonna keep an eye on Sunny Lee. I think she's going to be the fourth victim. If she *is*, we're, well...we lost these guys once...it *won't* happen again."

He leaned back and folded his arms. He wasn't going to say anything else.

Warren extended a hand. "Thanks. We'll stay out of your hair, but I think you understand we need to stay in Vegas to see how this plays out. Keep us in the loop?"

Takigawa offered a noncommittal nod.

Cole didn't expect him to keep them in the loop. "Let us know if we can help."

Takigawa led them to the door and saw them out. A minute later, they stood on the curb. "What are we going to do?" Cole asked. "Where are we gonna stay?"

"I miss Blue Lightning."

It took Cole a moment to remember *Blue Lightning* was the name he'd given his '69 Cougar. They'd left it in a snowy traffic jam in Washington, D.C. "Yeah, sorry about that."

"I wonder if she's okay."

"Probably got towed to a lot or something. If you want, I'll make some calls. Find out. I'll ask Marty G——" she swallowed the rest of the name. She'd forgotten he was dead, only for a moment, only long enough to get half of his name out of her mouth. "I'll make some calls to impound lots."

"Thanks." Warren looked concerned. "We need to talk. Debrief. We've been going and going for days."

A taxi rolled by and Cole waved it down. "Let's find a hotel."

80

"Toward The Strip," Warren said to the taxi driver.

"Where exactly?" he asked.

"Dunno yet."

The driver shook his head, but took the freeway entrance, running right into stop-and-go traffic. "Rush hour."

"Never thought Vegas had a rush hour," Cole said. "Not sure why. Just pictured it as somehow immune."

"People *do* work here," Warren said.

Cole was on her phone, looking up Marty Goldberg as Warren watched over her shoulder. There were a handful of stories, but none more than a few paragraphs. As Goldberg's assistant had told her, he was found in the Potomac River around seven in the morning. Toxicology reports indicated he'd taken two dozen sleeping pills, and the empty bottle by his nightstand confirmed it. Everyone seemed to agree: Marty Goldberg had finally become disillusioned with the corruption on K Street and the life of a D.C. lobbyist. He'd taken the sleeping pills and walked into the river.

Cole turned off her phone. "I know you're gonna say I'm being paranoid, but I don't buy that Marty Goldberg took some pills and went all Virginia Woolf."

"Exactly wrong." Warren chuckled. "I was gonna ask how he

got to the river? He took the sleeping pills at home, then drove there? Caught an Uber? How far away did he live?"

"Don't know where his apartment was. Maybe it was close?"

"Still, why not take the bottle with him?" Warren asked.

Cole squinted. "Devil's advocate—he could have had them in his pocket?"

"Maybe, but why not just put the *bottle* in his pocket?"

Cole nodded. "Not a bad way to stage a suicide. But there's a problem. Assuming it *was* a murder, someone had to be in his apartment, make him take the pills, then get him to the river. There's gotta be surveillance footage of his apartment building, visitor logs, something. Someone would have seen someone breaking in."

"Maybe it was a regular visitor. Someone he knew."

"Still. Would have been a record. *Surely* police would be looking into that."

Warren shook his head. "You see that on Monk?"

Cole's eyes narrowed.

He laughed. "Not 'surely,' but maybe."

After a long silence, Cole said, "Humor me. Assuming he was killed, and assuming he sent those two guys who followed us to Miami, maybe he was killed as part of a cover-up. Maybe someone got to him, knew we were chasing the story, got him to hire those guys...then killed him."

"It's just one of a dozen possibilities," Warren said. "More likely had something to do with some shady lobbying deal."

Cole sighed. "Ugh. We're not going to figure this out. It's like we're always a step behind, one position away from seeing this thing clearly."

"I can call around and see if I can find anything out, but Bakari was my best contact in D.C. and, well…"

"Yeah."

Warren pointed at a sleek dark tower in the distance. "Wanna stay there? One of the nicer joints in Vegas."

"Expensive?" Cole asked.

"Yeah, but I have a discount card. Used to come here a bit when I was in my dark period. Never gambled, but you'd cry if I told you how much I blew on coke there."

Warren called and got them a room with two queen beds. "They have good restaurants. Quite a few, actually, and I need to eat. Was tempted to pre-order an entire cow, grilled burnt, and have it delivered to my room."

Cole laughed. "How manly of you."

"Speaking of 'manly.'" Warren rolled down the window and pointed at a billboard: *Jack's Shooting Center.*

The billboard advertised *Vintage Firearms: Machine Guns, Tommy Guns, and Sniper Rifles, All at Affordable Prices.*

"Ever shoot?" Warren asked.

She'd asked Matt to take her once, but he'd waved her off, telling her, "I've shot enough guns for this lifetime, your lifetime, and ten others."

"Never," Cole said.

"Not hunting? Nothing?"

"Never, and nothing."

Warren tapped on the glass divider, getting the driver's attention. "Take us to Jack's Shooting Center, please."

The driver shook his head in irritation. "We *just* missed the exit."

"Can you take the next one?" Cole asked. "We're tired and hungry, so it's definitely the right time to play with lethal weapons."

81

Jack's Shooting Range was a wide, one-story building a few blocks from The Strip. The decor surprised Cole as she followed Warren through the glass door. Whatever she'd expected, it wasn't this. Firearms lined the walls—everything from long rifles to handguns and, as the billboard promised, vintage weapons she'd only seen in movies. Red and green Christmas lights decorated the walls, along with white stars and snowflake cutouts. Behind the front desk, along with various warning signs and legal notices, hung a large poster of Santa Claus, pointing an AR-15 at a sketchy-looking dude in a ski mask who appeared to be robbing his toy factory.

"Ho ho holster." The man behind the desk greeted them wearing a Santa hat and a fake white beard. "Holster," he repeated. "Ho ho *holster*."

Cole humored him. "I've been good this year and I want a handgun for Christmas."

After a couple minutes of back and forth, they signed forms and watched a ten-minute instructional video, despite Warren's assurances that he was more than capable of skipping it. Store policy.

After the video, the clerk handed them heavy-duty earmuffs and goggles. "What are you looking to shoot?"

Cole had been hesitant at first, but her blood warmed at the thought of shooting. "Magnum," she blurted without thinking.

The clerk looked at Warren, eyebrows raised.

"Don't look at *him*," Cole said. "It's not up to him."

"Magnum could break your wrist," Warren said. "Not a good place to start. I can already see us waiting in urgent care tomorrow morning."

"You don't think I can handle it because I'm a woman."

Warren leaned in, stern but not angry. "Trained my two brothers to shoot last time I visited Oakland. Together they are four hundred and fifty pounds of pure muscle. *They* didn't start with magnums."

"Fine," she sighed, pointing at a 1928 Tommy gun on the wall. Its circular bullet holder reminded her of old mob movies. "How about that thing?"

"How about a nice twenty-two?" Warren said. "Optic sight."

She nodded. "Fine."

"For you?" the clerk asked.

"Nothing for me. I'm going to help her get going. I've shot enough guns for this life. For *ten* lives."

The man took a .22 from behind the counter and led them back to the shooting area. "Standard Ruger," he said. "Ten rounds in the mag. Those are included. Extra mags are ten bucks each. Pick a target." He waved at a row of paper targets that lined the wall. Cole picked a red and black zombie. Warren mounted it and pulled a lever that moved it about twenty feet back in the shooting alley.

"Eye and ear protection first," he said. "They on tight?"

Cole nodded.

"Like the video said, keep the gun pointed down and away from people. Finger off the trigger until you're ready to shoot. Posture. The key is, don't lean back." He took her hips and moved them back slightly, then adjusted her back so she had a slight forward lean. "Keep your collar bone in front of your waist. Keep the red dot on the target until well after you pull the trigger. When you fire, you want a smooth, steady motion. You won't need to press hard."

Cole picked up the gun, flicked off the safety, and aimed. A red dot appeared on the chest of the zombie. The optic scope. Was it really that easy? She set the gun down and pulled the cord, making the zombie recede another twenty feet.

She picked up the gun again, aimed, closed her left eye, and fired once. She'd been tensing her shoulders, and the recoil was less than she expected. She fired again, then a third time, and a fourth.

She set down the weapon, took off the earmuffs, and pulled in the target.

"Not bad," Warren said.

She'd hit the zombie once in the chest, once in the head, and twice in the stomach. "Well, I was aiming for the head all four times, so…"

"Seriously, good job."

She took off the safety goggles. "You want a turn?"

He shook his head. "While you were shooting, I was thinking. Miami. Ana Diaz was involved in drugs—running them and also financing operations for others. Working the legal, respectable side and the overtly criminal side at the same time. Sunny Lee is similar. Finance. Organized crime."

"So what are you thinking?" Cole asked.

Warren walked a little square, eyebrows twitching pensively. Two young men took shooting positions a few rows down from them and began firing. The shots echoed in the space, but not loudly enough to make Cole put the earmuffs back on.

Warren stopped pacing. "I miss my car."

"That's not what I expected. Thought you were about to pull a Gill on me. Guy from the plane. Bust out a whole elaborate conspiracy theory."

"That's just it. Damn well right this is a conspiracy, but I don't *have* a theory." He shook his head and grimaced. "I can't believe they managed to lose the NVM guys. How is that even possible?"

"How *is* that even possible?" Cole repeated.

"Somehow, all these people are gonna turn out to be connected, and it's gonna be ugly. Makes me wish I was back in New York. Job or no job, suspended or not, I could be driving Marina to the park in Blue Lightning. I was supposed to see her last week. You know, when we left for D.C., Sarah didn't even call to ask where I was. When I was drinking, using, I'd miss my days with Marina and, at some point, Sarah stopped following up. Probably thinks I'm back on the sauce. I should be home, taking her to see the tree at Rockefeller Center." He sighed. "I don't know."

Cole put a hand on his arm. "I get it. I do. You'll be home soon. And if you help me crack this thing, that's gonna go a long way to getting your life back."

"Maybe."

The *crack crack crack* of an M-16 about ten feet away startled her. It was hard not to view gunfire as a threat. "You know what I've been thinking?" she asked. "What if all the targets aren't connected in any *real* way, just connected in the warped minds of the killers."

Warren frowned. "Then we have an even worse chance of figuring it out."

Cole put the goggles and earmuffs back on and emptied the clip into the zombie target. Six more shots. When she pulled back the target, she'd hit various places, including three in the center of the forehead. She tugged at Warren's sleeve. "You sure you don't want to shoot? Might cheer you up. I'll buy the bullets."

Warren turned and walked away. Something about his look told her not to follow. He wouldn't just leave her there, she told herself. He'd said he didn't want to shoot, but maybe he'd changed his mind. Then it hit her. He'd said it in almost the same way Matt had. *I've shot enough guns for this life. For ten lifetimes.*

She turned back to the firing range and tried to read the techniques of the other shooters. She doubted she'd ever shoot a gun again, but found it interesting anyway.

Warren returned carrying a rifle. Long and matte black, it had a large scope mounted above the chamber. It looked like the weapon she and Warren had found on the hotel bed in D.C. Wordlessly, he locked in a paper target—a generic-looking man in a ski-mask—and moved it as far back in the shooting alley as it would go, roughly a hundred yards. He loaded the weapon and rested the tripod legs on the counter, then donned his goggles and earmuffs and leaned in.

Cole put on her earmuffs and watched from behind, mesmerized. His shoulders dropped and his whole body went still. He fired a single shot. A *crack* exploded from the weapon.

Warren took off his goggles and earmuffs, then retrieved the target. The shot had left a hole the size of a quarter in the paper. Right in the center of the man's head.

Cole looked at him. "Is that a fifty caliber rifle?"

Warren nodded.

"Let's go," she said. "We need dinner. Tomorrow I'll try to find out what happened to your car."

82

They checked into the hotel—a modern black tower on the north end of The Strip—and ate a fancy but joyless dinner at a steak-house off the lobby.

Warren had turned cold at the shooting range. The loss of the NVM members had hit him hard. He prided himself on doing the right thing and he defended law enforcement whenever he and Cole argued. He'd been in the right place at the right time, had caught The Truffle Pig, then caught his killers. He'd passed them over to the correct law enforcement agencies, and they'd blown it. Cole didn't know how much of his sourness to attribute to this, and how much to the fact that he missed his daughter, but she didn't take it personally.

After dinner, they took the elevator to their room and got ready for bed.

Checking her phone one last time while sliding under the covers, she had a notification from the Signal app, a message from her former rival at *The New York Times*. She'd expected him to do his due diligence, figured it would take a day to get out a story on the photo. But his response took her by surprise.

I was unable to get a second source to confirm the map. No one at the storage facility would talk, and no one in law enforcement would confirm its existence. I trust that you're not trying to screw me, so I shared it with the FBI. But the Times won't be running anything.

She read the message aloud to Warren, who sat on the side of the bed, detaching his leg and stowing it under the pillow. "You think he's part of the coverup?" he asked.

"Are you serious?" Cole asked, rolling her eyes.

"Maybe. I don't know."

Cole walked to the window and stared out at the traffic on The Strip, thirty stories below. "You know how the public is so quick to assume evil intentions with police? Same is true of journalists. I don't agree with his decision, but this is no cover-up. It's journalistic standards at work. He probably fought like hell with his boss to get them to publish the map. But he's not gonna tell me that."

"What are you gonna do?" Warren asked.

Cole paced and clenched her fists, but said nothing.

"Seriously, Cole. You're worrying me."

She was sick of dancing around, waiting, wondering. Half a dozen times in her career, she'd been forced to hold or bury a major news story because she didn't have enough sources, or because her boss *told her* she didn't.

A key piece of evidence—the map—wasn't out there. Meanwhile, the rest of the world was running with the story. Every cable news show was wall-to-wall with "experts" offering all sorts of wild speculation. On social media, everyone had an equal shot at shaping the narrative. An amateur journalist with three followers had a voice just like Cole, who had half a million. A lunatic's opinion—if reposted enough—had as much weight as the President's. The world had gone crazy, as far as she was concerned, but Matt had always told her to see the world as it was, not as she wished it to be.

She stopped pacing and smiled. "You don't want any piece of what I'm about to do. But check the Internet in ten minutes and you'll know."

"Where on the Internet?"

"Doesn't matter." She walked to the door. "It'll be absolutely everywhere."

⊕

Cole took the elevator to the business center on the second floor and logged onto a computer. Next, she created a new email address through Gmail and created a new Threads account using the new email address. Kids and criminals called fake accounts "Burners," and used them for all sorts of reasons. Celebrities used them to try to shape their public narratives or respond to journalists anonymously. Kids used them to track girlfriends and boyfriends without being seen as stalkers.

She was going to use her burner account to leak the most important photograph in the world.

She hadn't been on Threads in twenty-four hours, and the first thing she saw surprised her, though it shouldn't have. The assassinations were trending under two different hashtags. The first was general news and opinion and used the name the media was running with: *#9Murders*. They'd taken the threat of the manifesto and turned it into a branded crime. Just as the killers wanted, she imagined.

The next hashtag—*#9MurdersTheories*—contained theory after theory related to the killings. The story was the biggest in years, and everyone had an opinion.

A buzzing sound came from the corner, startling her. She whirled in her chair. Just the cooler of a drink machine switching on. She took a few deep breaths. Relaxing into the chair, she locked onto the screen like it was a subject she was trying to read. She was going to do this. The photo was a burden she had to release.

For the next hour, she followed every journalist she could think of, then every news organization, then every celebrity. By the time she was finished, she'd followed over a thousand accounts. Only three had followed her back. But the algorithms were designed to show the posts of new accounts to people who might be interested. And the hashtags alone would get her post a lot of visibility.

She considered adding a profile picture to her account, but decided against it. As much as she loathed social media, there was something cool about designing a viral post from an account with a generic avatar.

After a few moments of consideration, she composed her post:

@Ambani_Meyers_Diaz_Truther: The attached image is real. It was taken in the storage unit of Michael Wragg one week ago. The NYPD and FBI have this photo. They've chosen not to release it. #9Murders

#9MurdersTheories #9Murders9Cities #9Murders9CitiesTheories

She hoped her two additional hashtags would create new worldwide trends. She emailed the photo from her phone to her new email address, then attached it to the post. Finally, she made sure that location detection was turned off so no one would be able to see where the post had originated.

She looked nervously around the business center, then closed her eyes and pressed "Send."

Needing something to distract herself, she turned to another task—her promise to Warren. It took her half an hour to find every tow company and impound lot in Arlington, Virginia, where she and Warren had left his beloved Blue Lightning. All were closed, but she printed the list of numbers to follow up on later, then checked back on her photo.

It already had 13,000 views, plus a few dozen reposts and a handful of replies. She checked the reposts, most of which were from accounts with few followers. But the most recent repost was from Danny Chubb, a former child actor who now hosted a politics podcast.

His repost came with a comment.

@Danny_Chubb_TruthEagle: Haven't confirmed this yet, but it would be just like the NYPD and FBI to cover this up.

From there, his followers began arguing in the replies. And then the reposts blew up. A few real journalists sent it out, then actors and even some athletes. Within an hour, the photo itself had begun trending under its own hashtag: *#9Murders9CitiesPhoto*.

No one knew for sure if it was real, but everyone was talking about it. Cable news would pick it up soon—they'd have to—and the FBI and the NYPD would be forced to make statements.

There was no telling what would happen then, but she'd done all she could.

83

Sunday

Warren woke early, attached his leg, and took a few quiet steps around the hotel room. He'd fallen asleep while Cole was at the business center. He remembered her promise that he'd see what she'd done if he checked the Internet, but he couldn't stand the thought of going online.

His mood had lifted overnight. He was still furious at the FBI for losing the NVM members who'd killed the Truffle Pig, but instead of stewing, he'd made other plans.

He slid into his jeans and black button-down, put on his leather jacket, and slipped out of the room without waking Cole. It made sense that whoever had hired The Truffle Pig to kill Alvin Meyers and Ana Diaz would want him dead. If he was caught, he could bring down the whole operation. But what didn't make sense was why the New Vegas Mafia would have anything to do with it in the first place. He was no expert in their beliefs or tactics, but the massive, ideological battle promised by the manifesto didn't connect with the NVM business plan.

NVM was about one thing: money. So why would they take part in an elaborate international plan to kill political and business leaders? It was possible they'd been hired by whoever was ultimately behind the plot. Possible they'd hired The Truffle Pig, then taken him out, for a fee. A sort of middleman for world terror. But then why would Sunny Lee herself—the head of NVM—be the next target?

None of it was adding up.

The hotel lobby was decorated with a large Christmas tree, strung with sparkling playing cards, silver poker chips, and some traditional lights and bulbs. He'd never been to Vegas around Christmas, and he hadn't noticed it the previous night. Classy.

He stepped onto the curb and got in a taxi. "Club Blue, please."

"It's six-thirty in the morning," the driver said. "They closed at four."

"I know," Warren said. "I'm not going to party."

Pacing between the side entrance and the back entrance of Club Blue, Warren pulled up his collar and balled his hands into fists in his pockets, bracing against the chilly morning.

The famous nightclub was the largest, most-popular stand-alone joint in Vegas. In the 2000s, most of the top hotels and casinos had gone to war with one another, creating larger, fancier, and more exclusive nightlife to lure in young people. They hired the hottest musical acts and DJs and fought to get celebrities in the club.

It was eight in the morning by the time someone showed up. He was a huge man, Warren's height and maybe a hundred pounds heavier, practically pouring out of his black Escalade, which he'd parked next to a dumpster behind the club. His shirt was untucked, his eyes covered by large sunglasses. His face showed a couple days of stubble. Warren assumed he was a manager. In the club business, things got crazy at night, and most of the big clubs employed business managers and accountants to go over the receipts in the morning. To count the money, to look for theft. This guy looked like he'd been at the club until four, grabbed a couple hours of sleep, and returned before showering.

As the man unlocked the back door, Warren approached.

The man turned, startled.

"You work here?" Warren asked.

368

The man nodded, glancing side-to-side like he was making sure Warren was alone.

"Don't worry, I'm not here to rob you. Just want to talk. I know this is an NVM club, but I don't care about NVM. I want to talk about The Truffle Pig."

The man had turned back to the door, so Warren couldn't tell if he'd reacted to the name. "Who's that?" he called over his shoulder as he swung open the door. There was a bulge on the left side of his jacket, and Warren took a chance. "That gun licensed?"

The man turned, standing in the doorway. The scent of night-club wafted through the doors. Booze and bodies.

"Who the hell are you?" the guy asked.

"Robert Warren, Marine, NYPD cop, sort of. I'm here with the FBI on the nine murders thing. We believe you and this club are connected."

"I'm Skinny Pete, and I don't know anything about anything. I do the numbers."

"Peter Bluth, right? Got an aunt Wendy in Georgia, I hear. So what's with the"—Warren pointed at the bulge in the man's jacket —"firearm?"

"In case assholes like you show up to rob us."

Warren took a step forward. "It registered?"

"Up yours, pal. You think anyone cares?"

He had a point. Cops often frequented clubs like this. He wouldn't be surprised if the man had worked out an arrangement. "I'll level with you. You've heard of the nine murders thing, right?"

Skinny Pete smirked. "Who hasn't?"

"I don't think you have anything to do with that," Warren said.

"Anyone said I did?"

"No one—but the FBI is monitoring this club, I can tell you that. I imagine you've got back-scratching deals with local police. But if the FBI thinks you guys are involved in the nine murders thing…" he shook his head…"that's game over."

The man ran his thick hand over his stubble, thinking. "You know we don't have anything to do with that. You just said it."

"But your aunt Wendy's car was in Florida yesterday, carrying a dude who murdered The Truffle Pig in broad daylight, so the

FBI *thinks* you do. Gimme five minutes inside and I'll convince them you don't."

Warren was on thinner than thin legal ice. In fact, he was drowning in frozen water. He'd tried the only thing he could. Now he hoped Skinny Pete would feel threatened enough to want to talk.

The massive man studied him for a long moment, then nodded. "I'll buy you a drink."

Warren followed him past a couple offices and a banquet hall, through a kitchen, and into a large space with the famous circular bar in the center. Skinny Pete walked behind the bar and poured two shots of whiskey. He slid one across the bar to Warren, shot the other one, then refilled it.

Warren put his hand around the glass, but didn't drink.

"In the old days," Skinny Pete said, "if a man refused a drink" —he squinted—"it meant you couldn't trust him. The alcohol loosens the tongue, you see, makes it harder to lie. So if a man doesn't drink...he's got something to hide."

"I'm an alcoholic," Warren said. "I take this shot and I'll be in the club for a week, doing blow off your bathroom counters until, eventually, I'll get hauled back to rehab. You want that?"

"This is Vegas. Wouldn't be the first time that happened. Long as you paid for the booze, hell," he shrugged, "it's still a free country. Kinda." He shot his second whiskey, then took the glass back from Warren and sipped. "Now"—he placed the shot glass on the bar—"why would the FBI think this club has anything to do with the nine murders thing?"

"The Truffle Pig escaped Italy and did a bunch of hits in America. Killed Ana Diaz in Miami, then got greased at a gas station in eastern Florida. Guys who shot him were seen in this club."

"*Everyone* is seen in this club," Skinny Pete said. "It's where people come to *be* seen. Prince partied here before he died. Backstreet Boys. Hell, the NFL champs came after they won the Superbowl. You saying they're all in on it?"

Warren smiled. "You never know with NFL players."

Skinny Pete smiled, too. "I like you. Sure you don't want a drink?"

"Nah, man, but seriously—bit of a coincidence, right?"

He shrugged. His face had reddened from the shots and he sat heavily on a stool behind the bar. Warren understood. At his lowest point, he'd needed a shot or two to get going in the morning. He'd be able to get what he needed from this guy. All he needed to do was keep him talking, and keep him drinking.

"I've *seen* the photos," Warren repeated. "From 2017. The guy who shot The Truffle Pig was here."

"You said you were NYPD, and that's the best you can do? A guy was snapped in my club. So what?"

Warren had tried various angles, like a boxer throwing jabs, trying to soften up his opponent. Nothing had worked. He'd focused on Skinny Pete's aunt in Georgia for ten minutes, but the man hadn't given an inch. He'd tried small talk and threats, then finally returned to the man who'd been photographed in Club Blue. Nothing.

Warren had taken this guy for a hungover dunce. A fool. But he'd outflanked him for the last half hour. "Do you *like* working for Sunny Lee?" he asked, his frustration clear.

"Club Blue is owned by Vegas Nightlife, Inc., which is owned by Epic Entertainment Group, LLC."

"C'mon," Warren said. "Sunny Lee runs the club."

"*I* run Club Blue. I'm here counting the money."

"And skim—what?—twenty percent off the top to hand to Sunny Lee in cash before you report it?"

Skinny Pete smiled. "I'd *never* do such a thing." He sipped his whiskey slowly. "You were a good cop—I can tell. You ever wanna relocate, we can get you...maybe eighty grand a year? Plus benefits."

"To do what?"

Skinny Pete's smile grew crooked. "We'd call it *club security*. You're smart, I can tell. Most cops come in here when they want something. They threaten us. You're working the angle."

"Don't patronize me." Warren tilted his head. "Know anything about a *retirement* party?"

"Hosted a few in my time." Skinny Pete's voice was now loose, his delivery sloppy.

"For Sunny Lee, I mean."

With great effort, he turned and took a glass from the shelf.

371

He filled it with water from the bar sink. "What you heard about that?"

"Your first non-denial."

"I take an interest in all activity in Las Vegas," Skinny Pete said. "You happen to know something I don't, it would be irresponsible not to find out more."

"Don't know much, but rumors are floating around that someone's going to take out Sunny Lee, a 'retirement party.'"

Skinny Pete downed the water in a few long gulps, filled the glass again, and set it on the counter. "Hydration is important."

Warren eyed him. "No thoughts on Sunny Lee?"

"Told you. Don't know her. I work for Vegas Nightlife, Inc."

Warren needed some breakfast. He slid the stool out from the bar and stood. "Thanks for nothing."

"You give up too easy." His smile was wet. "Remember the OJ book, *If I Did It*?"

"Heard of it," Warren said.

"Few years ago, OJ wrote a book about how he did the murders, but it was all hypothetical. A confession and not a confession."

Warren eyed the man, who took off his sunglasses for the first time and set them on the bar.

"If The Truffle Pig was who you say," Skinny Pete said, "a hitman for the Italian mob, and he escaped to America, maybe—just maybe—Italy never forgot. Maybe they'd been looking for him for years. Maybe they paid top dollar to an organization that could locate him in America. Maybe The Truffle Pig died a tragic death because he betrayed the people closest to him. Maybe he got what he had coming, and his death had *nothing* to do with the nine murders." He put his sunglasses back on. "Again, just hypothetically speaking, of course."

84

Cole spotted Warren at a table in the corner of the restaurant, where he was already halfway through an omelet. On the table across from him was a plate of waffles, bacon, eggs, a muffin, and a foamy coffee she assumed was a vanilla latte.

She sat, raising an eyebrow at the food.

"I ordered you the exact opposite of what I'd eat," he said. "Hope you don't mind. We gotta go soon."

She sipped the drink, which was in fact a vanilla latte, though weaker than she was used to. "You did well, but what's the hurry?"

"I set up a meeting."

"With who?" Cole asked.

"We'll get to that." He ate the rest of his omelet in two giant bites, then slid the plate away. "First, I gotta tell you about my morning."

"Yeah, you do. Why didn't you wake me up?"

He ignored the question. As she ate, he told her about his meeting with Skinny Pete, spending extra time on the last part of their conversation. "He was definitely trying to tell me something without telling me something."

"Sounds like he told you *point-blank*," Cole said, "killing The Truffle Pig was unrelated to the nine murders. His former Italian paymasters tracked him down and paid NVM to take him out."

Warren ran a finger around the rim of his glass. "Ridiculous, right? Problem is, I think it was the truth. But why tell me?"

Cole frowned. It wasn't ridiculous that the Italians would track him down, and it wasn't ridiculous that they'd hire NVM to kill him, but it seemed far too coincidental that they'd shot him only hours after he'd killed Ana Diaz. "Let's just say it's true. The Truffle Pig could have been heading to another job. He did the last two. If he was killed by NVM, unconnected from the nine murders, he could have been on his way to do a third."

"He wasn't gonna drive to Vegas from Florida. That's 2,000 miles. And the other U.S. cities pinned on the map are even further."

"Could have been headed to an airport. Paris, or London, or Tokyo."

Warren shook his head. "There's something we're missing."

Cole finished her waffle and picked at the muffin. The food was lukewarm and bland. It made her miss the bright colors and exciting flavors of Little Havana.

"Oh my God!" It was a man's voice behind her. A thick southern accent. She turned and followed his eyes to a TV screen above the salad bar.

The muted TV showed a gray-haired news anchor. Text scrolled at the bottom of the screen. "Deputy Crown Prince of Saudi Arabia, Mohammad bin Muqrin, assassinated at OPEC meeting in London. Details still emerging. Stay with CNN for ongoing coverage."

Cole grabbed her latte and waved at the server. "Can you turn the sound on, please?"

She trailed the server across the restaurant. Warren followed, and together they stood a few yards from the TV, their necks craning to hear as the server turned up the volume. The old man who'd been behind her joined them, as did a young man with a baby strapped to his chest in a harness.

The news anchor said, "If you're just joining us, disturbing news this morning, as Mohammad bin Muqrin, the Deputy Crown Prince of Saudi Arabia, was assassinated as he entered an OPEC meeting in London. Speculation has already begun that his death could be connected to the nine murders manifesto and…" She pressed a finger to her ear. "Yes, we have word now that responsibility has been taken for this killing online. We can report that this appears to be the fourth in the string of assassination-style killings that gripped America, and now grips the world." Again, she pressed a finger to her ear. "CNN was in London covering the OPEC meeting, and we go now to Brian McNeely, live in London. Brian, what can you tell us?"

The shot switched to a young man in a tan raincoat, standing under a red CNN umbrella. Behind him, police barricades blocked off a large glass building. Other reporters could be seen doing stand-ups nearby and, behind the reporters, a gray, rainy sky drenched everything. "Thank you, Olivia. The scene here in London is total chaos, but I'll do my best to fill you in on this shocking day. What we know so far is that this morning—which marked the third and final day of the OPEC meeting in London —Mohammad bin Muqrin exited his limousine, waved to the crowd gathered outside, and began walking toward the hotel where the meetings have been taking place." The camera panned to the large glass hotel with a red carpet leading from the curb to the sleek entryway. "He was at the end of that carpet when he was shot through the neck from behind. From what I've been told— and details are still coming in—he was in an ambulance within minutes and was pronounced dead when he arrived at Charing Cross Hospital. That was only about fifteen minutes ago. As of this moment, we have no footage of the shooting, though with the intense media scrutiny of this OPEC meeting, we expect some will emerge shortly."

Dazed, Cole set her latte on the edge of the empty salad bar and returned to the table. Warren followed. She picked up her phone, planning to get online to see what else she could learn.

Warren took her hand. "Wait. Can we just talk for a minute?"

"We had the wrong city."

"I know."

"I was *sure* the next murder would be here," Cole said.

"There's still the retirement party. Maybe we just had the wrong order. London, then *Vegas*."

"I know. Of course I know that." Her head spun and she wriggled her hand free and unlocked her phone. She immediately looked for news about Mohammad bin Muqrin from before he was killed. He was an important world figure, but she knew next to nothing about him besides that.

A quick scan of a few articles and Cole learned that he was

the sixth richest man in Saudi Arabia, a hardliner who argued against the Kingdom's relationship with America. A year ago he'd been accused of using oil money to fund terrorism against Americans, Europeans, and Israelis. Ever since, he'd been in a power struggle with the Crown Prince.

"What?" Warren asked. "What are you reading?"

"I know next to nothing about Saudi Arabia," Cole said, "but it sounds like there could be a hundred people who'd want him dead, including the people above him in government."

Warren stared at her. "This is getting *way* too big for us."

She nodded slowly. They'd likely gone to the wrong city, and, if Warren's source in the NVM was correct, they'd come for the wrong reason. She felt utterly hopeless.

"We still have the retirement party piece," Warren said. "Even if the NVM guys killed The Truffle Pig as a paid hit, there's still Sunny Lee. There's no way it's a coincidence she's going to get taken out tonight. I have no idea how she connects to Mohammad bin Muqrin or Ana Diaz or the others, but it *can't* be a coincidence. There's just no way. So we had the order wrong. The fourth killing was London, but the fifth is coming tonight."

Cole was skeptical, but nodded slowly. "Think you can convince Takigawa to let us come?"

"I'll try."

Warren had said they had to leave soon when she sat down. "Where do we have to be?" Cole asked.

"What?"

"When I sat down, you said there was somewhere we had to be?"

"Remember Frankie Undercroft?"

He was the Marine buddy Warren had mentioned. The one who always lied. He'd sounded like a good laugh, but she was in no mood for stories.

"Well," Warren said, "he's in Vegas now, and we're going to meet him."

85

Their Lyft dropped them in a residential neighborhood fifteen minutes south of the hotel. It was only a few blocks from the historic section of Las Vegas, where the original casinos still stood. Historic Vegas had been cleaned up and was now a major tourist attraction, but Undercroft's building was a crummy six-story residential, its beige stucco chipped and peeling.

They passed through a small courtyard and reached an elevator. Warren stopped short, examining the graffiti sprayed on the elevator door. "Stay down here, alright? It's been a few years and I don't know how he is. I'll text you."

Cole understood. Matt had told her once that the connections he forged with Marines overseas were unique and difficult to explain. If Warren needed time alone with Undercroft, she'd give him that.

She took a seat on a rusty metal chair next to an empty swimming pool in the courtyard. She took out her list of impound lots in Arlington, Virginia, and began calling. Six times she repeated her story—where they'd left the car, when they'd left it, and the make and model. Six times she was told that no vehicle like Blue Lightning had been found. On the final call, she asked whether there were any unlisted lots, or what else might have happened to a vehicle abandoned in a snowstorm. She was told to try the government impound lot, but they wouldn't be open on Sunday.

When she asked how a car would end up in the government lot, there was a long pause on the line. Finally, the man said, "If a car is suspected to have been used in a crime, they claim it and, after four weeks, auction it off." Cole took the number of the government lot and thanked him.

The sun was out, but the day was cool. She walked a lap around the courtyard in an effort to warm up. In D.C., two men had been following them. When they'd abandoned Blue Lightning, one chased them through the snow and eventually into Arlington National Cemetery. The other had stayed behind. Perhaps the one who stayed behind had searched the car, then called it in to the police. Whatever had happened, she'd need to call about the car on Monday. If it got auctioned off to the highest bidder, Warren might never get over it, and she'd never forgive herself.

The photo of the map was still the biggest story on social media. Two anonymous sources from the storage facility had confirmed its authenticity, and three different NYPD sources had been quoted admitting the photo was real, while at the same time defending the decision not to release it. Despite the buzz, no one had linked her to the photo.

She still hadn't heard from Warren, so she sat and checked her email. Messages had come in quickly over the last few days. Friends and colleagues wanted to know what happened at the *Sun*. Matt's mom asked how she was doing. Her therapist wanted to reschedule an appointment, which was fine because she'd forgotten about it anyway.

She also had job offers. In the journalism world, word spreads quickly. Some heard she'd quit—others that she'd been fired. A small newspaper in California offered her a full-time job as its lead crime reporter. The pay was terrible and she wasn't about to move to California, so she deleted it. A prestigious magazine offered her fifty cents a word to write a story about Michael Wragg and how she'd ended up in his apartment. She could write 10,000 words on that in a couple days, but she wasn't that desperate for money *yet*.

She stopped scanning when an email caught her eye. It came from an online magazine called *The Barker*, based in Seattle. She'd written a couple freelance pieces for them once during a transition period between jobs. The pay was bad, but they had good reach and gave her a lot of leeway as to style. The email wasn't from

Bird, the managing editor, with whom she'd corresponded in the past. It was from Alex Vane, their semi-retired founder.

Dear Jane,

We know you're on this story. **IN** *this story. We'll pay you $1/word for anything you send us. No questions asked. We'll clean it up and publish it within an hour. Our social media team will have it trending worldwide an hour after that.*

Newspapers are dead, but journalism isn't.

We can help you get this story out; our speed and reach might be able to help us change how it ends.

Sincerely,

Alex Vane

A dollar per word was a lot more than they'd paid her last time. And he was right about their ability to promote. *The Barker* published a lot of crap, but it had a reputation for being able to shape national coverage faster than any newspaper or cable news show.

It was the only job offer she didn't delete.

86

The scent of rotting trash hit Warren as he knocked on the door. A white garbage bag leaned against the wall in the middle of the hallway, leaking liquid from a hole with a syringe sticking out of it. Someone had made it halfway to the garbage chute, then abandoned the effort. Warren knew quite a few Marines who'd fallen on hard times after retiring, but he'd always thought Frankie Undercroft would be a success.

Last Warren had heard, Frankie worked as a security guard at a bank. But Frankie's Facebook bio said he was a content moderator for an online video company called STREAM3R. Whatever 'content moderation' was, it didn't seem to pay well, judging by Frankie's accommodations.

There was shuffling on the other side of the door, then a dull thud and what might have been the sound of two frying pans being dropped into a metal sink. Shortly after the burst of noise, Frankie emerged. He was as short as Warren remembered, but everything else about him had changed. His hair was long and greasy and he wore University of Nevada sweatpants, gray with a red logo. His blue t-shirt had a large brown stain in the middle; Warren hoped it was coffee. His friend's face, which Warren remembered as round, healthy, and always emitting cheerful lies, looked ashen, pale, and dull.

Warren knew an addict when he saw one.

"War Dog." Frankie's faint smile harkened back to better days, as though he'd been lifted for an instant from the squalor of his situation. "Good to see you. Come in."

Warren followed him in.

"Sorry about the mess," Frankie said. He spoke slowly and without the spark Warren remembered. "Surprised you messaged me. Been a while."

Frankie shoved an iPad and a few dirty napkins off a chair. "Have a seat."

Warren sat as Frankie flopped onto a couch across from him. The words wouldn't come easily, but his own time in recovery had taught him one thing—sugar-coating and BS weren't helpful. It was their shared experience in Afghanistan that gave Warren permission to skip the small talk. "Frankie, it's good to see you, but what's going on? I saw on Facebook you're doing content moderation—whatever that is—but, seriously, how *are* you."

Frankie stared at the floor. "You know, don't you?"

"Is it opioids, Frankie?" Warren's drug of choice had been cocaine, and he was thankful every day he'd put those dark days behind him.

Frankie lifted a coffee mug from the floor, looked inside as though it contained the answer to some silent question, then set it back down. "H."

Warren's head dropped to his chest. He lifted it quickly and met Frankie's eyes, trying to be strong. There were so many Marines hooked on painkillers. Injured overseas, they'd come home to VA docs happy to prescribe opioids. For some, the switch to heroin didn't take long.

"Doc won't refill my Oxy, can't afford rehab, so…" He looked down at his lap. "Was actually doing alright when I was in security."

"I thought that's what you *were* doing."

"Company shut down," Frankie said. "Bank merger, you know the story."

"So what's *content moderation*?"

Frankie shook his head in disgust. "Company called Streamer, except they spell it with a three. It's Youtube crossed with Facebook, that's how they pitch it."

Warren shrugged. Didn't ring any bells, but that didn't mean much. He was no expert in video apps.

Frankie grabbed his phone off the arm of the couch and passed it from hand to hand. "You know how you can report posts on social media sites? Like if something is offensive, or illegal, or indicates suicidal thoughts or hate speech or whatever?"

"I guess. I have accounts but I don't go on them much. Unless I'm trying to find an old buddy." He tried to sound light, but Frankie's eyes were far away, like he was locked in his head, in his own world. "Used to post on Instagram sometimes, but that was mostly because I wanted to show Sarah how well I was doing when I got in recovery."

"You used?" Frankie asked.

"Coke, booze..."

Frankie nodded. "Streamer pays me $39,000 a year, no bene-fits, to sit in a windowless room and judge whether something is appropriate for the site. Lucky me, I got the animal violence job. Anytime someone posts a video that gets reported as showing violence against animals, it comes to me and I check the post. If it violates Streamer's rules, I delete it."

Warren shook his head. "Damn, I never thought about that. Can't believe that's a job."

"How else they going to deal with it?" Frankie asked. "Remember the Christchurch shooter? He broadcast his murders live on Facebook. People watched it until a moderator like me, sitting in a windowless room somewhere for nineteen bucks an hour took it down."

Warren pressed his feet into the floor. "Eight hours a day screening videos of violence against animals?" He felt sick, full of rage. More than a decade in the Marines, and this was the life Frankie had come back to.

"Photos, too. Sickest stuff you can imagine. And probably some things you...*shouldn't*." He smiled down at his lap and let out a weak laugh. "I'm just glad they didn't give me the child abuse cases. Guy I know killed himself after six months on that beat."

"People really post stuff like that online?" Warren knew how ignorant he sounded as it left his lips. He didn't spend a lot of time online, but it *was* the Internet. *Of course* people posted terrible things. It was simple statistics. To him, the Internet—especially social media—was one giant mistake. Just gave people a forum to broadcast the worst of themselves for all to see. "They offer therapy?"

"Therapy? That's a surprise, coming from ol' *War Dog*."

Warren sighed, then frowned. "Helped me sober up."

"We get nine minutes of 'Wellness Time' per shift. Watch disgusting people do disgusting things to their animals for eight hours, and *process* it for nine minutes."

"That's..." Warren didn't know what to say. "How can they do that?"

"When it's raining money," Frankie said, "sometimes your vision gets blurry. At these social media apps, it's *pouring* money. A once-in-a-generation typhoon of cash. And they don't care who it hurts."

Warren shook his head, searching for something to say. Finally, he stood. "I'm going to get you help. I wanted to see you today to pick your brain about a case I'm working on. But there's a VA assistance agency in Vegas and I'm gonna get you help."

There was a knock at the door. Frankie shot up, clearly worried.

"Don't get many visitors?" Warren asked. "Don't worry, I think I know who it is."

He'd forgotten to text Cole.

87

The man who opened the door didn't look like a Marine, at least not like the ones Cole had met. His shoulders were bent forward, hunched almost. He had a speck of blood on his left ear—maybe an earring malfunction. The apartment smelled stale, like no window had been cracked in years.

She was about to ask if she could come in when she met his eyes. They were wide, like he'd seen a ghost. His mouth was half open. He was searching for words. "I *know* you," he said finally.

She didn't recognize him. She glanced over his shoulder at Warren, who stood and gave her a side-out thumb indicating they should get out of there. The look on his face made it plain he hadn't gotten anything useful out of Frankie.

"Great to see you, Frankie." Warren scooched by him and joined her in the doorway. "I won't let you give in to this thing. I'll be in touch about the VA."

Frankie ignored him. His eyes roamed, his mouth still seemed to be searching for words. He snapped his fingers. "Matthew Cole. Matt Cole."

Cole stepped back. "What?"

"I was looking for the name. You were married to Matt Cole."

Her heart twisted. She scanned her memory, looking right into Frankie's face. Had she met him?

"You don't know *me*," Frankie said. "But I know all about you."

She put a hand on his forearm. It was cold and sweaty. He began rocking back and forth on his heels like a little kid who had to go to the bathroom.

"Frankie, you okay?" Warren asked.

Then, like he'd been struck by an invisible bullet, Frankie collapsed.

An hour later, Cole leaned on the railing of the rooftop garden and looked down on the empty pool and courtyard below. It wasn't much of a garden. Just a few potted plants and some plastic lawn furniture.

Warren had revived Frankie when he fainted. It turned out he hadn't eaten solid food for two days. Warren forced him to shower and shave while Cole ordered McDonald's and had it delivered to the apartment. Now, Frankie bit into a Big Mac and took long swigs from a soda. He seemed revived. Sort of.

Cole joined him at the table, which was surrounded by small potted trees, half of them dead.

"Feeling any better?" she asked.

"Little."

While Frankie was in the shower, Warren had told her about Frankie's new job. "You probably already know this," Cole said, "but you're suffering from post-traumatic stress. That was a panic attack you had. And it makes sense."

He waved her off. "Nope. I don't have PTSD. My grandfather was General Patton. He fainted once, too. It was just the heat messing with me."

It was around seventy degrees and a dry breeze played with the needles on the little trees. It wasn't the heat, but she let it go, contenting herself to nibble on fries while Frankie finished his food.

Warren stood a few yards away, arms crossed like he was guarding an important meeting. "At least you're lying again," he said. "That's a good sign. General Patton would be proud."

"How do you know who I am?" Cole asked the moment

385

Frankie popped the last bite of the burger in his mouth. "And how did you know Matt?"

"Third tour, woulda been six... no maybe four years ago. Rob, were you still in then?"

Rob peered down. "No, I was back home."

"That's right. You escaped early. I went back. Unit got partnered with a group near the Ghazni Province and—"

"What month was this?" Cole asked sharply. Frankie might have been a serial liar, but she sensed he was telling the truth. She didn't trust herself, though. She *wanted* someone to know about Matt's final days, and she'd already proved herself susceptible to wishful thinking. After all, Michael Wragg's promise of information had led her to make one of the worst decisions of her life. She'd be sure to test him on details she was sure of.

Frankie dipped a fry in BBQ sauce and left it there. "Woulda been January. I shipped out on New Year's Day and made it there a week later."

The detail checked out and Cole relaxed. He wasn't lying.

It took another hour to get the story, Cole prodding and Warren interjecting to keep him on track. He was jumpy and eager, but prone to lapse into moments of low energy and distraction.

In the end, his story rocked Cole to her core.

Frankie knew something odd was going on in Matt's unit right away. As the biggest BSer in the world, he'd developed a good lie detector. From the moment he arrived at the base in Ghazni Province, two of the men in Matt's unit had been standoffish, secretive. At first, he'd assumed they were simply unfriendly. After all, Frankie's unit had joined their party. They had seniority.

A week after he arrived, Frankie was out on a six-man patrol when he'd come upon the two men—Lopez and Morgan—behind a little restaurant in Zana Khan. As far as he knew, it wasn't their day to be on patrol, but he didn't know everything that went on, so he waved at them, hoping to win them over. They turned their backs. "Strangest thing," Frankie said, "was that they were talking to a tall, gangly dude who looked Asian. I'm no expert—coulda been Japanese, Chinese, Korean. Definitely not an Afghan."

It was the first East Asian guy Frankie had seen in rural

Afghanistan, not counting U.S. service-members. A week had gone by, and he hadn't thought much about it.

Then he'd met Matt. "It was dinner on a Tuesday night. Dudes I usually ate with were getting disciplined, so I sat next to Matt. I'd seen him around but we'd never talked. Quiet guy. Introspective. So I sit down and tell him, 'You look like a damn movie star. Way too pretty to be sitting out in a desert.' Told him I was the bastard son of Tom Cruise and Meryl Streep, that I was gonna go to Hollywood when this was over to get a new life. 'You should come,' I told him. 'You be the leading man, I'll be the hilarious sidekick.' Matt laughed, shook his head, and pulled a picture out of his pocket. A picture of you."

Cole sniffed and wiped her eyes. She knew the photo.

Frankie pulled the cold fry from the BBQ sauce and munched it, clearly uncomfortable with her tears.

She sniffed again and nodded. "Go on."

In the photo, he explained, she looked younger. Her cheeks more tanned, her hair a little shinier. She and Matt stood together, she in a New York Giants jersey, he in a Seahawks jersey, posing in front of a football field.

"We went to one game," Cole interrupted. "I don't watch sports, but he was a crazy Seahawks fan and wanted to start an inter-family rivalry. I played along that day. Still don't understand the rules. The Giants won, I think."

Frankie smiled. "When Matt showed me the picture, he said, 'Can't go to Hollywood, look what I get to go home to.' Something to that effect."

Cole's stomach turned. Her read on Frankie was that he might be embellishing some of the details, but she had no doubt the conversation with Matt had happened.

Frankie and Matt had hit it off and taken to eating meals together. "He had a way about him," Frankie said. "Affable, I guess. Every line I fed him, he pretended to believe. He'd ask me all sorts of questions, just playing along. Like when I told him I sang background for Beyonce—only white dude good enough to make her squad—he was all enthusiastic. He was like, 'Dude, amazing. Let's hear some vocals.' And when I told him my vocal coach actually asked me to re-enlist to get some time off from singing, to rest my voice, he just smiled. He liked my BS."

Warren finally took a seat next to him, his long legs bumping the table as he squeezed in. "Wait, have you known all along you were BS'ing everyone, about everything? We had bets going. Half the guys thought you knew you were lying, half thought you believed every word."

Frankie gave him a side-eyed look. "It was a damn war zone. Everyone needs entertainment." His face got even more sober. "I really *was* gonna go to Hollywood. Study screenwriting."

Cole thought Matt would have seen Frankie's lies not as lies, but as creative storytelling meant to entertain. Matt was good to everyone he met, and he would have liked the healthy version of Frankie.

"So we became buddies," Frankie continued, "as much as you can over there. Things were generally pretty calm. We weren't losing many men. That's one reason I took my vocal coach's advice to serve again." He rattled ice cubes in the cup, then sipped his soda. "One night, everyone was watching a movie and I ran into Matt near the bathroom. He pulled me aside and asked if I'd noticed anything weird going on with Lopez and Morgan. Those were the two dudes I'd seen with the Asian guy. Long story short, I told him everything I just told you. It was odd, but not a huge deal."

Cole leaned forward across the table. "And?"

"And nothing. He just kinda nodded and went to the bathroom. But he never came back to the movie that night."

"When was this?" Cole asked.

"All kind of a blur, but maybe a week or two before he died. Lemme finish, though."

"There's more?"

"Way more" Frankie said. "I was there when Matt confronted them. I know what they were up to."

Cole rocked back in her chair, speechless.

Warren said, "In Cole's business, that's called burying the lede. Tell us everything."

388

88

As he told the story, Cole grew numb. The far-off mountains and the skyline of Las Vegas faded. The sound of traffic below disappeared. Everything went black except Frankie Undercroft's freshly-shaven face, his mouth moving fast, then slow, then fast again. Her perceptions were distorted like she was in a dream.

But this was no dream.

A week after Frankie told Matt about the day he'd seen Lopez and Morgan with the Asian man, he'd come back early from a patrol. Heading for bed, he'd heard Matt's voice coming from inside a storage room. He crept to the door and listened. For a long time, the only voice he heard was Matt's. He was lecturing someone, but in his usual, friendly way. He explained why what they were doing was wrong, *really* wrong. He understood their financial needs, but they needed to stop.

Only after listening for a couple minutes did Frankie hear Lopez's voice. Sounding frustrated but not angry, he told Matt to mind his own business. He had the facts wrong, didn't know what he was talking about. Stay out of it. Then he'd heard Morgan's voice. More firm, more menacing. Morgan told him he'd never been to China, didn't know a damn thing about China, and had never met with any Chinese dude.

After that, there was a long silence. Next thing he heard was

Matt's voice telling them they'd get caught, and they needed to clear their consciences.

Cole interrupted. "What were they talking about?"

Frankie stood and walked to the railing, then walked back but didn't sit. He picked up his soda and rattled the ice cubes in the cup. "It's messed with me ever since. I don't know."

Cole stood and put her hands on his shoulders, her focus narrowing to only his eyes. "Look at me."

Frankie slowly raised his eyes. "I swear, I don't know."

"But you suspect something."

Frankie nodded, then shook himself free and sat. He turned to Warren. "I ever tell you about the time I won the Coney Island hot dog eating contest?"

Warren ignored him.

"Or the time I won the Texas barbecue championship? They still talk about my brisket down there."

Cole slammed a fist into the metal table, rattling it. "Tell me."

Frankie hung his head. Cole stood over him, and he wouldn't look at her. "Here's the thing most people don't get about wars," he said quietly. "People back home like to believe in the rules of engagement, like to believe things are neat and clean, right and wrong. They're not. Every man over there had to make his peace with killing another man. In some cases, it's not a man—it's killing women and children. I figure every soldier has had to make their peace with that." Frankie shook his head in a tight arc. "Not Lopez and Morgan. They were killers—had always *been* killers. I thought it was because they'd been over there longer than me, but the more I got to know them, the more I saw it didn't bother them. Don't think it ever had. One day they came back having shot two women. Said they were suicide bombers, and maybe they were. I don't know. But it didn't *bother* them. Shooting women. Didn't faze them."

Cole reached down and raised his chin so she could see his face. His lower lip quivered. He was afraid of Lopez and Morgan. They'd done something to Matt and they were still out there. He was afraid, but she didn't care. She wasn't letting him off the hook. "So what does that have to do with Matt?"

"If Lopez and Morgan were doing something wrong, something about China, something having to do with that guy I saw them with, and if Matt knew…"

390

"Wait a sec," Warren said. "You can't just accuse two Marines of murder."

"Not accusing, man. Just wondering."

"So you don't know what happened?" Cole asked.

"I heard the argument. Never saw them get into it again after that. Sometimes you have a feeling, you know?"

There was nowhere else to take the speculation, but Cole wanted to wrap up a dangling thread. "China? What could two Marines in Afghanistan have to do with China?"

"Drugs," Warren said, as though it was the most obvious thing in the world.

"They were getting high?" Cole asked.

Frankie chuckled. "Not those two. No way. They were on point. Cold as ice killers, but on point. No drugs."

"That's not what I meant," Warren said. "What's Afghanistan's number one export?"

It took her a moment. "Heroin?"

"Poppy. But China is where a lot of the world's heroin gets made these days." Warren leaned down and put his face right in front of Frankie's. "You talking garbage?"

"N-n-nah, man. No."

"Because if you're piling it high to entertain us and—"

Frankie kicked the chair back and stood. "Look at me, look at my life. The Marines were the only good thing ever happened to me. Only time I was anything close to happy. You think I'd make something like this up?"

Cole stood, too. "So what are you saying?"

"I don't know for sure...I...and I don't want to overstep here, but I think Lopez and Morgan were running poppy from Afghanistan to China, and Matt found out."

⊕

They took the stairs down from the roof to Frankie's apartment. Warren told Cole to stay in the hallway as he walked Frankie in. He wanted to try to convince him to accept help from the VA.

As the door clicked shut, she heard them inside, promising to stay in touch, exchanging numbers. Warren insisted that Frankie reach out if he needed anything. Frankie made a few half-hearted attempts to convince him to stay.

Cole leaned on the door, her mind racing, tumbling over and over every word Frankie had said, trying to commit them to memory. Then her mind went blank and the emotions hit her all at once. All the feelings she'd been tamping down since the moment Frankie said Matt's name.

She bolted for the elevator and smashed the button. The door creaked behind her. Warren came out, exchanging a final goodbye with Frankie. Her chest burned. She darted for the staircase and raced down, emerging into the residential neighborhood.

Staggering down the street, she played Frankie's story in her head. Matt always played by the rules, but he was also loyal. Had he found out two of his buddies were doing something wrong, he would have spoken to them directly, rather than going to superiors. In her mind she created images for Lopez and Morgan, imagined the conversation they'd had with Matt in the storage room, the pieces Frankie hadn't overheard. Filled in gaps with guesses. Clearly, he'd discovered they were involved in something illegal, or at least immoral.

He'd confronted them.

And they'd killed him.

Somehow, they'd managed to make it look like enemy fire.

She took off in a full sprint down the block, trying to outrace the twisted images of Lopez and Morgan that had taken over her mind. She turned a corner, then another, then another. She had no idea how long she ran. Time had stopped. She'd been transported to that storage room in Afghanistan and now it was all she saw.

She rounded another corner and crashed into Warren's muscular chest. He pulled her close.

Her tears wet his shirt as she buried herself in his arms. "What...what the hell is going on?"

"Jane," he said, "I'm so sorry."

"What is this world?"

He put his hand on the back of her head gently, but said nothing.

"What is this world?" she asked again. "What is this world?"

89

Warren stood at the window, staring north across the desert to the brown hills in the distance. Cole lay in bed, covers drawn over her head.

She hadn't spoken since they left Frankie's.

A cold vanilla latte sat on a round table next to the bed, along with a tuna melt and fries—his best guesses as to what might entice her to join him back in *this* world. That was exactly how it felt. Cole had fled the world during the conversation with Frankie. She hadn't responded emotionally during Frankie's tale. She simply asked question after question. Then she ran.

She'd said some pretty bleak things to him the first day they'd met and many times since. This was different. She'd entirely checked out. She'd ignored the lunch, ignored *him* as he left a series of messages for Takigawa, telling the FBI agent about his conversation with Skinny Pete and imploring him to fill them in on the "retirement party" for Sunny Lee. He'd hoped that news about the case would rouse Cole, but he *had* no news.

"Cole," he tried again. "Hey, Jane."

No response.

"Look, I know you're in a bad place. I've been there. Not exactly where you are, but I've been down a hole. I was there for a couple years. Eating might help. *Your* brain needs sugar to function." He tried to sound light. "I got you a latte."

He didn't think it would do any good. When he was in his darkest places, not much could pull him out. It had been his daughter Marina—the thought of losing her forever—that made him clean up his life. At the time, she was the only thing worth living for, the only thing that gave him purpose.

Cole poked her head out from under the covers. "Gonna go back to New York. Take the first job I can. This is over." Her voice was monotone, and again she disappeared under the blankets.

Warren took the latte and handed it under the covers. "Drink this. Please." To his surprise, she took the cup. A step in the right direction.

"I'm not going to argue with you," he said. "You want to head home, I'm in. We're not making any progress anyway, and chances are, we're not going to. It's almost dinner time and the cheese on your tuna melt is cold and congealed. It's gross. Let's go down to the casino and get a real dinner. Tomorrow morning we'll head back to New York."

She didn't reply, but the muffled sound of Cole sipping the latte emerged from under the blanket.

His phone rang, and he put it on speakerphone. "Agent Takigawa. I'm here with Jane Cole. You're on speaker."

"Mr. Warren. I got your messages. That was a curious conversation you had at Club Blue. And it *does* check out. The Truffle Pig was killed because of the old grudge, not his involvement in the nine murders plot. That was one of the theories we were already investigating."

"Okay," Warren said.

"As to the retirement party, we still believe Sunny Lee's in danger. We aren't certain it's connected, and I really can't tell you anything more than that. Of course, I can't involve you in any way. I'm sure you understand."

"Actually," Warren said loudly, pacing the room, "I *don't* understand. We handed those two NVM guys to local police and the FBI on a silver platter. Literally in a *silver* SUV. You all blew it. *Mistakes were made*, remember? The *least* you can do is let me in on the stakeout of the retirement party."

"I'm sorry, I really can't do that. Rules are rules."

Warren glanced at the bed. The top of Cole's head peeked out from the blankets. "Please," Warren said into the phone. "Maybe the two NVM guys are back in Vegas, maybe they're part of whatever crew is planning to take out Sunny Lee. We can help."

"I gotta go." Takigawa's tone was flat. "By the way, did you have any of the sliders at Club Blue?"

Warren stared at the phone. "What?"

"They're famous for their drinks, but they're supposed to have great bar food as well. They make these Turkish sliders, half pork, half lamb, with spices, yogurt dressing, pickled vegetables. I don't know what's in them, but, well, you really ought to try them."

Cole sprang from the bed and pointed at the phone. Warren was dumbfounded.

"Mr. Takigawa," Cole said, her voice strained. She cleared her throat. "Around what time would you say we should go for the best possible service?"

There was silence on the other end of the line. Then Takigawa said, "Hello, Ms. Cole. I'd say around seven to be safe. Beat the dinner rush."

90

They sat in white leather chairs on either side of a glass table in a corner of Club Blue. "Bottle service starts at nine," a handsome young waiter said, but you're welcome to hang here until then. "After that, it's a thousand dollars for most bottles. Mixers included."

"I hear the sliders are good," Cole said. "Can I get an order of those?" She'd swigged the cold vanilla latte in the hotel, but otherwise hadn't consumed anything since the fries on Frankie's roof.

The waiter turned his attention to Warren. "And for you?"

"Coffee, burnt if possible."

He gave Warren an odd look, then laughed and walked away.

"He thought you were joking," Cole said. "Nobody *orders* burnt coffee." She felt hollow inside, but ribbing Warren about his odd food and drink habits helped fill the emptiness.

Warren pointed to a camera in the corner, which moved slightly. "Facial recognition," he said. "If what I've been told is right, they've got your face and are matching it to your driver's license photo right now."

"How is that legal?"

He laughed. "It's not."

It was early for a place like Club Blue. The dance floor was empty and only a dozen tables were full. One of the hottest late-night destinations in Vegas, they served high-end bar food between five and nine to make money from people who wanted a hit of the prestige of Club Blue without staying up all night.

Warren nodded at a side door, where a group of women in evening gowns were on their way in. They didn't turn toward the front where the tables were. Instead, a man in a black suit led them to the back.

"Where do you think they're going?" Cole asked.

"Party? Special event? Noticed a banquet room this morning."

Cole scanned the bar. Silver sconces aimed blue light in all directions, striking the floors and walls at strange angles. "Wait, is that…" she gestured to a booth on the far side.

"That's Takigawa," Warren said under his breath.

"What's he doing?" Cole asked.

He sat across from a woman with long dreadlocks.

The waiter returned, placing water glasses in front of them, along with Warren's coffee.

Warren swigged his water. "Staking the place out. I saw two vans across the street on our way in. There's another couple behind, maybe one at the side door. Takigawa and the lady across from him must be their eyes and ears."

"Why do you think Takigawa told us where to come?" Cole asked.

"First I thought it was in case the two NVM guys showed up. So we could ID them. But they wouldn't be stupid enough to show up in Vegas again. And even if they did, we could ID them later."

"So why?" Cole asked.

"Guess he felt he owed us."

"You know, when he mentioned this place, I was about to come out from under the blankets. I'd decided to head back to New York and get a lawyer. Try to get Matt's records released. Try to find out what really happened. Lopez and Morgan. Their unit. Freedom of Information Act. Lots of rocks to turn over."

Warren gave her an odd look, eyes down, a slight shake of the head.

"What?" she asked.

"It's just…I don't know. I'd *never* tell you to drop it, but it won't be easy to get any information."

"So what was that look?"

Warren grimaced. "I know you have to keep looking, and I know how bad it's gonna get."

Another group entered from the side door and headed toward the banquet room. Three couples, all in suits and gowns. Takigawa noticed them, too. One of the women led the way. She had long blond hair and wore a black evening gown and pearls. Her movie-star smile lit up the club. She carried herself like she owned the place. "Sunny Lee?" Cole asked.

"Didn't get a look at her face," Warren said, "but I think so."

Takigawa lifted his arms and said a few words into his sleeve.

The waiter returned with the sliders. "We're famous for these."

"They smell amazing," Cole said, though she didn't smell anything. "Hey, can I ask you something? Is there a party in the back tonight? Seems like the place to be."

"There is!" he said. "Private function. That's our banquet hall. If you'd like I can bring you a brochure about renting it."

"That's okay," Cole said.

Another group joined the party. Then another. All were well-dressed and smiling. If Sunny Lee was about to get killed, there'd be a lot of well-dressed witnesses.

"If someone took out Sunny Lee, who would it be?" Cole asked after the waiter had left.

"Rival gang, maybe. Or someone lower down in the NVM. More likely the latter because..." He trailed off, frowning.

"Yeah," she said. "Something's not right here."

For the next half-hour, she ate her sliders and watched another dozen people enter through the side door and disappear into the back. As each new group entered, she became more and more convinced that Takigawa had it wrong. When the clinking of glasses sounded from the banquet hall, she stopped expecting to hear a gunshot. She dropped her napkin on her empty plate. "Rob, what if this is just a party? An *actual* retirement party?"

"A retirement party, not a *retirement party*." He used air-quotes to make his point. A look of recognition crossed his face. "Oh, damn."

He glanced at Takigawa, who stared, stone-faced, at an untouched salad on the table before him.

"He got an earpiece in?" Cole asked.

"Probably. Likely getting feedback from the vans outside. Guess is they've had wires on every inch of this club for a while. Maybe video. Which adds to your theory. Why would someone commit a murder here of all places?"

Another half-hour passed. No more guests arrived, but raucous laughter spilled out of the banquet hall at regular intervals. Warren got another coffee. Cole took a shot of tequila, and Warren stopped her when she tried to order another.

An hour passed and the club filled up with younger people, for whom the night had just begun.

A DJ appeared on a raised stage in the corner. Etheric string and horn music filled the club. Soon after, the men and women they'd seen entering through the side door began streaming out of the hall in small packs. One group came out, smiling and laughing, stopping only to take a group selfie with the club in the background.

"What the hell?" Warren asked.

The dreadlocked woman across from Takigawa left. Takigawa paid, then followed her out.

"What the hell?" Warren repeated.

Cole shook her head, paid the bill, and followed Takigawa out of the club.

⊕

Outside, Takigawa was talking through the front window of a brown van. As Cole approached him, he turned, "Hold on."

His head back in the van, he lowered his voice so Cole and Warren couldn't hear. After a moment, he joined them on the curb across the street from the club.

"Lemme guess." Cole's voice was pure snark. "Mistakes were made?"

Takigawa hung his head.

"You've gotta be kidding me," Warren said.

Takigawa stepped toward them, shooting a look behind him at the van. He wasn't supposed to be sharing with them, but he seemed as dejected as Cole felt. "It was an *actual* retirement party.

399

Sunny Lee officially passed the torch to Nathan Jackson. He's the new head of the organization. We don't know if it's real or not—I'm guessing not. Probably knew the club was bugged. They were careful not to mention anything illegal. But the party was…" He looked at the ground.

"An *actual* retirement party," Warren said. "We're nowhere."

A group emerged from the side door, led by the smiling blond woman in the black dress. Sunny Lee. She strolled right up to Takigawa and lit a cigarette, studying him as she inhaled.

She blew the smoke right in his face. "Thanks for coming to my party, Alan. Tell your interns to hurry up and start combing through my successor's Instagram account." She laughed and continued down the block, followed by her crew.

Cole let her head fall back, staring straight up into the dark. At least, for once, she and Warren were in total agreement. "We are absolutely nowhere," she said.

91

"I'm not going to London," Cole said. "I'm going home."

They'd been wandering the casino for an hour—past clothing stores and coffee shops and restaurants. They'd weaved through banks of slot machines and card tables, populated by a mix of twenty-somethings on their way to or from the clubs, sad-eyed gamblers with cigarettes dangling from their lips, and businessmen wandering around with drinks, looking for companionship.

Now they followed a red carpet that weaved through the center of the casino, back in the direction of the elevators.

"Hear me out," Warren said.

"You made your case, and I get it. The fourth murder happened in London. You want to keep going. I'm telling you it's not gonna happen. It's done. *I'm* done."

"Michael Wragg knew something about Matt. What he told you, coded as it was, matches what Frankie said. Go back to New York, get a lawyer...you'll be stonewalled for years. Go to London and—"

"Every detective in London is probably working this thing now," Cole said. "MI5. And who knows what kind of people the Saudis have flying to London right now to help?"

In their manifesto, the killers had announced nine murders. Cole's map had told the world which cities would be targeted. The story now led every hour on every news channel in the world and dominated the front pages of every newspaper.

Even the late-night shows were joking about it. One clip Cole had seen on a muted TV was a fake tourism ad for all the cities *not* included on the map. *Come visit Seattle: We're NOT on the map.* Or *See Beautiful Houston: NOT a target of deranged killers!* Tasteless, sure, but the image had spread far.

"I have an old professor in London," Warren said. "Expert on political history, terrorism, and extremist movements."

"How will that help?"

Warren went quiet for a minute, then said, "Might not. But if Wragg knew something, it meant he had access to files somehow."

"Wragg's dead."

"But the folks he was working with—or *for*—aren't."

A group of people in their twenties spilled through a door, followed by the heavy beat of electronic dance music. "It's two in the morning," Cole said. "Some of the clubs are letting out. This is why Matt and I never visited Vegas."

"Why?" Warren asked.

The twenty-somethings were drunk and staggering, some wide-eyed like they were on drugs. Two of the young women kissed, then one rolled an ankle, stumbled against a garbage can, and fell over. A young man pulled her up and she vomited on him. A security guard appeared out of nowhere and ushered them away. "That," Cole said. "The desperation. I already know enough about the sorry, desperate state of humanity. I don't need a closer look."

As they neared the elevator, Warren stopped. Cole followed his eyes to a short woman with light brown skin and black hair that was pulled back into a tight ponytail. She wore blue jeans and a black top, a silver and black laptop bag slung over her shoulder.

Warren stared for a long moment, then his face broke out in the widest grin she'd ever seen from him. "Gabby!"

⊕

They sat at a low table in a dark bar. Gabriella Rojas had taken a seat with her back to the wall and, as she spoke, she glanced past Warren and Cole, who sat opposite her. She struck Cole as living on a line between hyper-vigilant and outright paranoid.

"How'd you find us?" Warren asked. "And why?"

"The *how* was easy," Gabby said. "Credit cards. The why is a little more complicated. The last two years, I've been leaking NYPD documents to a half dozen news outlets around the world. Once I made it to JTTF, I gained access to a lot more info. FBI records. I started leaking them. Never anything that put a life in danger. Only things the public *needed* to know. Corruption. Incompetence."

Cole watched Warren take this in. He didn't say a word, just shook his head in disbelief.

"You're the Edward Snowden of the NYPD?" Cole asked.

"I guess, though I think he was out for his own reasons, too. I've lost everything."

"What do you mean?" Warren asked.

"That's why I'm here," Gabby said. "Someone caught wind I'd helped you. I had to disappear."

A waiter set down two coffees, plus a tequila for Cole.

"Mazzalano?" Warren asked.

"Nah. He had a side hustle protecting dropgangs. He oversaw Wragg's pickup of the nine rifles, but he didn't know anything about what Wragg was up to. Don't worry, that scumbag will hear from me soon. But this thing goes higher." She looked from Cole to Warren, giving her statement time to sink in. "*That's* why I'm here." She slid a large envelope across the table. "Passports. Tickets. Visas. I can't get out of the country right now. You two need to go to London."

"What?" Cole asked. "Why?"

"I have a theory, and you're in the best position to test it." Gabby held Warren's gaze for a moment, then turned to Cole. "Which is what you both want to do anyway."

Cole nodded. "What's the theory?"

"Killing these people—Ambani, Meyers, Diaz, now Mohammad bin Muqrin—won't actually achieve the stated ends of the group that claimed responsibility." Gabby chose her words carefully. "Killing them won't end digital globalization, won't make you or your kids any freer from the algorithms and AI models that have stolen your attention. The killings won't make international banks and tech giants any less predatory."

"True," Cole said. "But isn't terror the point of terrorism?

403

Even if it won't change anything long term, it'll still make their point."

Gabby sighed.

Cole shot her tequila, studying Gabby's eyes.

She seemed to be looking for the right words, as though she knew more than she wanted to say.

She glanced at Warren, who shrugged. He was probably still processing the revelation that, as Gabby had climbed the ranks of the NYPD, she'd been illegally leaking documents all along. Cole doubted this sat well with him.

"Michael Wragg was an old man," Gabby said firmly, as though she'd finally landed on an approach. "A good shot, maybe but no criminal mastermind."

"The manifesto mentioned a General Ki," Cole said. "Presumably he's the real mastermind."

"And I don't know who that is. Obviously, every law enforcement agency on earth has dug into that name—General Ki—and no one knows anything." She spoke slowly, firmly. The more she spoke, the more Cole trusted her. "*Someone* is organizing this thing. Someone smart. Someone powerful. But ask yourself this: What if a ragtag group of extremists *didn't* simply band together on the Internet under the leadership of the mysterious General Ki? What if the folks doing the killings and releasing the manifesto weren't capable of carrying out the most complex terrorist attack since 9/11? What if the stated aims of the terrorists, the mission they articulated in the manifesto, is just a sideshow? A diversion?" She tapped the envelope.

Warren picked it up. "Passports and plane tickets?"

Gabby nodded and looked at Cole. "Go to London, Jane. I'll be here looking into things as best I can, and I'll be in touch when I can."

Cole took the envelope from Warren. "Gabby, you know my situation, right? My husband?"

She nodded. "Warren told me a bit."

"At this point," Cole said, "all I want is to find out what happened to him."

"I can't help you with that," Gabby said, her tone matter-of-fact.

Warren added, "You're not likely to get the answers in New York. Like I said, too much red tape."

Gabby stood and scanned the bar like she was planning her escape. She looked down at Cole. "Honestly, if you figure out who's really behind this, it'll answer *all kinds* of questions." With that, she strolled out of the bar, ducked between two rows of slot machines, and disappeared.

Cole opened the envelope and examined the plane tickets. "Flight leaves at nine in the morning."

Warren took out the passports. "They look pretty real. *Very* real, actually."

Cole put the tickets back in the envelope. Warren added the passports.

Cole looked around the bar. Warren stared at the table. Neither said a word.

They both knew what they had to do next.

—End of Episode 4—

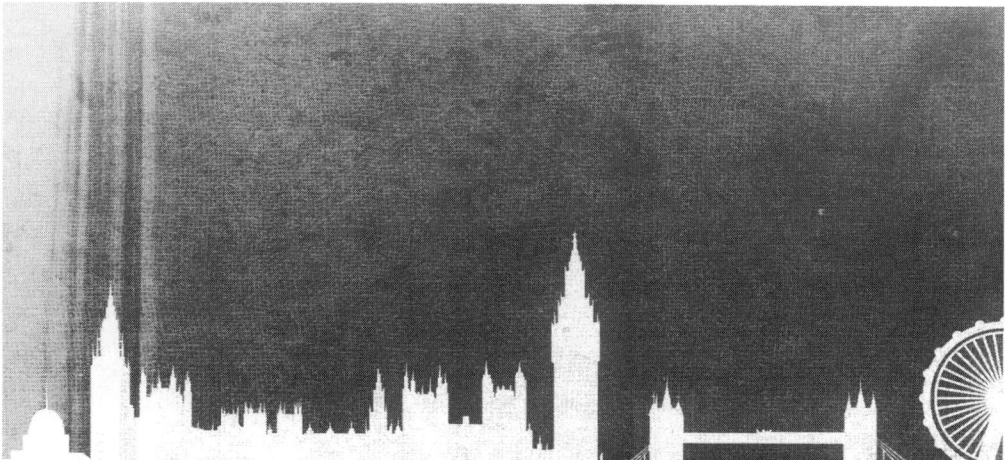

THE
CRIME
BEAT

EPISODE 5: LONDON

92

Tuesday

Cole rolled over in bed and rubbed her eyes. Where was she? A sliver of gray light peeked through a crack in the curtains, illuminating a neatly-made bed beside her. The room was otherwise dark. The bathroom door was open, but there was no movement.

Warren.

A hazy memory. She'd watched him wash his face through that bathroom door last night.

Hotel. London.

A screech of pain split her forehead. She groaned.

Hangover.

Her phone read six local time. No message from Warren.

Her first thought—a paranoid one—was that he'd ditched her. It was ridiculous; he'd been the one who'd convinced *her* to come to London. But she didn't see a note.

She went to the bathroom, splashed cold water on her face, then called room service for a pot of coffee and breakfast. She'd never spent money like this. She and Matt never had room-service money. She told herself the spending was only until she got to the end of... whatever this was.

Warren's stuff was on the dresser. Jeans folded carefully. Leather jacket hung on a hook on the wall. He hadn't ditched her.

408

And if someone had taken him in the night, they wouldn't have made his bed. She texted, asking where he was, and flopped into a stiff, modern recliner.

She'd lost a day on the way to London. The non-stop flight from Vegas had taken ten hours. She'd tried to sleep, but her conversation with Frankie, and the images it forced into her mind, haunted her. So she drank. First a vodka with tomato juice. Then a whiskey. Then a couple beers. She'd thought it would help her sleep on the second half of the flight. It hadn't. She vaguely remembered Warren cutting her off, and something about a pint of cider in the airport bar. There had been a taxi. And then she'd been in the room. At least she'd slept.

When her coffee arrived, she drank it while staring out a large window overlooking Trafalgar Square. Ant-like people hurried in all directions against a backdrop of a dozen shades of gray. Light gray stone buildings. A vast stone courtyard. And looming in the center, Nelson's Column, a 150-foot column of gray granite, topped with a bronze statue of the Square's namesake, Admiral Nelson, who won the battle of Trafalgar in 1805. Warren had lectured her on the military history as she lay in bed, her head spinning. For some reason, *that* memory had stuck.

She finished her coffee by seven and got to work. Warren would have insisted they work the nine murders case, but he wasn't there. He hadn't even texted back. She called Frankie in Las Vegas. There it was midnight local time—part of the reason she still felt groggy after three cups of coffee. Frankie picked up on the second ring.

"Hey, Frankie," she said carefully. "It's Jane Cole. How are you?" Warren had left Frankie with the number of a drug and alcohol counselor at the local VA, and Frankie had promised to call. Cole needed information, but she had no idea where his mind was. She didn't want to push too hard.

"Been sober sixteen hours." His voice was weary.

"Well done." It was a half-hearted congratulations. "That's something."

"I need to sleep," Frankie said. "You're calling about Lopez and Morgan, right?"

"Yeah."

"Figured you'd wanna track them down."

"I do," Cole said.

"Therapist today said I need to prioritize my own well being. My health and sobriety. Maybe quit being 'The Entertainer,' whatever that means. I'm out on this one. Last thing I need is you trying to drag me back in."

"Do you know if *they're* still in?"

A heavy sigh came through the line, followed by a soft thud, like Frankie falling heavily in an armchair. "Nah, they're both out."

"If I promise never to ask you another question, never to mention you to them, can you give me anything else? I *need* to find them."

Frankie let out a wet, heaving cough. "Like what?"

"First names for a start. Where they live. What they do."

"I don't know what they do. Always tried not to find out too much about the guys. Didn't know if they were gonna make it." He sighed. "Julio Lopez and Chris Morgan. That's it, though, okay?"

Cole wrote the names on hotel stationery. She didn't know how long he'd been an addict, but there was a struggle in his voice. If he'd been sober for sixteen hours, his body would rebel. She'd worried about her own drinking once or twice since Matt died. It was only on mornings like this, though, when the previous night was hazy and her head alternated between dull throbbing and sharp, electric jolts of pain.

Julio Lopez and Chris Morgan were common names. Not easy to track down. One more piece of information about each would go a long way to finding them. "Frankie, please. Gimme one more thing about these guys. Anything you've heard. Something they said about home, jobs, hobbies, wives."

"Lopez was the beta, Morgan the alpha. Heard Lopez went back to Texas. Morgan to California."

"Thanks." Cole walked to her laptop, which had somehow ended up on the small desk in the corner. "Get some sleep, Frankie. And keep in touch, okay? Warren worries about you."

⊕

It took her only an hour to locate the men.

She found Julio Lopez easily. He was a truck driver based in Houston and active on social media. His Facebook page indicated only three interests: the Bible, a soccer team called the Houston Dynamo, and his daughter, who'd been born recently. There was only one picture of the baby girl, and Lopez wasn't in it. His relationship status read "Single." Cole got the sense that he wasn't close to the mother of his daughter, but wanted to be. His posts had a loneliness to them—no pictures of himself with anyone, and multiple quotes from the Bible about redemption and giving oneself to God after a life of sin.

Guilt. That could be useful.

Chris Morgan was more difficult to locate. Social media offered nothing, but a public records search turned up a business in San Diego listed under the name Christopher Bruce Morgan. A puff piece in a San Diego newspaper named his contracting business the best in southern California for opulent homes. Diamond Luxury Construction specialized in beachfront homes for the rich and famous. An article in an upmarket real estate magazine had a photo spread with an image of Morgan standing in front of a beachfront "meditation cottage" in Malibu, high-fiving the stunning actress he'd built it for. He had short blonde hair, a nice tan, shiny white teeth, and a smarmy grin that made her want to punch the screen.

Cole walked a lap around the hotel room, which was decorated with modern furniture in white and black. She examined herself in a mirror, but looked away quickly. She shook her head, trying to shake off the hangover, but the sudden movement made it worse. Walking another lap, she sipped a cup of cold coffee, then stopped at the window. Thin gray clouds were backlit, the sun almost sneaking through.

Lopez would be an easier target. He seemed to be having difficulty in life, and vulnerable people were more likely to tell the truth. Frankie said he was the beta of the pair. If he *had* been involved in Matt's death, there was a chance he wanted to tell someone, even if he didn't know that yet. But how to get him talking?

As a reporter, she always had an excuse to initiate a difficult discussion. Most people didn't like it, but everyone understood it. "I'm Jane Cole from the *New York Sun*, do you mind if I ask you some questions?" Now, she had no opening, no angle. What was she supposed to do, send him a Facebook message? *"Excuse me, but did you kill my husband in Afghanistan four years ago?"*

She studied Lopez's Facebook feed again. For the last three weeks, he'd posted six to ten times a day. The content varied little —inspiring Bible quotes, score updates from soccer games, and the same picture of his daughter, re-posted multiple times. Sometimes the photo had red hearts drawn crudely around the picture, probably with some basic photo-editing app that came with his phone. His posts never got any reactions or comments. He was alone. Before three weeks ago, he'd posted once a day at most.

Something had changed three weeks ago.

She scrolled back in time. A few more soccer updates, and... then she saw it.

It was "Vaguebooking"—the practice of posting a status update that means a lot to the poster, but that most people don't have enough context to understand. Those sorts of posts annoyed the hell out of her and screamed Attention Seeker. Posts like, "*Oh, my God. I can't believe it!*" Or, "*How dare she say that to me?*"

Lopez had written, "Well, I guess its over." He'd left the apostrophe off of the "it's."

She scrolled back another week, then two, until she found a similar post: "Is it possible she'll take me back?"

She closed her eyes, allowing his posts to fill her mind. She used social media for work and work only. Some used it to connect with friends and family and to learn about the world. Others used it out of loneliness or even desperation. A whisper into the darkness. Free therapy, of a sort.

A timeline formed in her mind. Lopez had gotten someone pregnant, someone he wanted to be with. But he was away a lot, driving trucks. He'd tried to maintain the relationship, but it hadn't worked out. Maybe he'd cheated? Or hit her? He sought forgiveness from God, redemption. He'd wanted the relationship to work, but it ended abruptly.

She hated what she was about to do, but not enough to keep her from doing it.

With a burner email address, she created a new Facebook profile under the name Sandy Beltaggio. She found a dozen photos of a dark-haired model on a free stock image site and loaded a headshot as the profile picture, then filled out her profile with details.

Location: Houston, Texas
Interests: soccer, cooking, yoga, Bible studies.

Relationship status: single.

Facebook wouldn't allow her to backdate posts to build out her fake profile, so she'd have to build it over a few days. She started with a series of posts, designed to interest Lopez.

A beautiful image of a sunrise with a passage from John 3:18. *Let us not love with words but with actions and truth.*

A short post expressing excitement about an upcoming soccer match.

Another stock image of the model, now running on a beach.

A post about how she'd been divorced for eight months, and was finally ready to mingle again.

Another Bible quote.

She'd post again tomorrow to fill out the fake profile. It needed to be more convincing before she could approach Lopez. She'd also need at least a few friends with some interactions on her feed. She built three more fake profiles over the course of an hour, "friending" each of the fake accounts from the others, then liking and commenting on posts. It had to look real.

She let her eyes go soft, releasing the tension in her shoulders until they dropped. Her headache was fading.

There was a click at the door.

Warren entered, glistening with sweat. The front of his tight t-shirt had soaked through. "Decent gym in the basement," he said. "Not in the shape I was a few months ago, but…"

He went into the bathroom, leaving the door cracked slightly. He took off his shirt, exposing his strong back as he turned on the sink and let the water run over a washcloth. She watched him wash his face, staring longer than she intended. Longer than appropriate. Watching Warren reminded her of last night. Had she stared like this in her drunken stupor? Or done something even more embarrassing? She'd never been attracted to muscular guys, at least not *because* of their muscles. Matt had been in good shape, but lean. He didn't work out to build muscle mass. Warren was in the kind of shape she'd only seen on the cover of muscle magazines in grocery stores. His slim waist formed the bottom of a V that spread up his back into broad shoulders supporting a thick, muscular neck.

Cole forced her eyes to the floor, giving her head a little wiggle, erasing the image of Warren like an etch-a-sketch. She was just out of it. Hungover. When she looked up, he had on a new t-shirt.

"We should eat," he said on his way out of the bathroom. He wiped his forearms with a washcloth. "Found my old professor. He's willing to talk tonight."

She said nothing.

He pressed the washcloth into his face. "Cole?"

She took a deep breath, stood, and nodded at the empty plate. "I already ate, but I can eat again."

"Guy at the front desk recommended a breakfast place. It's near the site of the last shooting." He went quiet and Cole looked up. Warren was staring at her, his head cocked to the side. "You okay? You were pretty far gone last night. What were you doing while I was working out?"

"Yeah. Fine. Nothing." She was ashamed of what she was doing—the fake profiles, the Bible quotes—but couldn't stop herself from doing it. She *had* to find a way into Lopez's world. "Just… yeah. Let's eat, then check out the hotel where the Deputy Crown Prince was shot."

93

Cole stared at her plate of french fries, sunny-side-up eggs, and sliced tomatoes. The waiter had convinced her it was a respected hangover cure in England. She needed all the help she could get, but couldn't bring herself to dip a fry in the egg yolk, as the waiter had instructed. She pushed the plate away.

Warren noticed, scooped up one of the eggs with his fork, and ate it in a single bite.

"How do the London police work?" Cole asked. "Any way you can get a contact?"

"Don't know much about it. I doubt it. And it's not even the real issue. MI5 does domestic intelligence. MI6 does foreign intelligence. My guess is they're both in on this. That, and the Saudis are pissed. Saw a headline on the way over that they're sending investigators. And I'd bet they're sending people off the books, too."

Cole sighed. "How do we get close?"

Warren ate his spinach omelet in silence, his forehead creased in thought.

They'd walked by the site of the most recent shooting on their way to the restaurant. But standing in a crowd behind a police line a hundred yards from the hotel entrance had given them nothing. Mohammad bin Muqrin had been surrounded by four security guards when he was killed. He'd been out of his armored limo for six seconds. Police didn't yet know precisely where the sniper was when he fired. No weapon had been found. The only thing anyone knew for sure was that the assassin had been high up and far away. Same as the other shootings. Whoever killed bin Muqrin had known about the meeting, known he'd be there. But that didn't narrow it down much. At the scene, Cole and Warren had surveyed the area, heard locals and tourists speculate about where the shot had come from, taken a few photos, and given up.

Warren ate Cole's other egg.

Cole nibbled a French fry and broke the silence. "In New York, we were so close. Same in D.C. and Miami. Now..." She shook her head, then looked up and met Warren's eyes. He looked concerned. She didn't want that. "Don't look at me like that. I know you're worried about me."

"I am."

"Don't be."

"Can't help it," he said. "You scare me when you get bleak. Has it ever gotten this bad?"

"Has *what* gotten this bad?"

"You, your... whatever it is."

She leaned across the table, about to launch into a defensive tirade, but all the energy left her and she leaned back. She picked an ice cube from her water glass and crunched it. "When Matt died, it was bad. Now he's dying all over again. But it's worse this time. Because it's not just losing him. It's the *injustice* of the thing. If Frankie was telling the truth, and I know he was..."

"You don't have to finish that sentence. I know. I've worked with enough families of victims to know. You won't feel whole until you know what happened."

"Exactly."

"How did you get out of your funk before?" Warren asked. "I mean, the first time Matt died?"

Cole wriggled in her chair. "I don't remember."

"Yes, you do."

"I worked, okay? I took a month off and things just kept getting worse. Then I went back to work. I got promoted. I broke stories. I beat the *Times* and the *Post* on story after story. Unhealthy?" She shrugged. "Maybe. But healthier than sitting alone in my apartment and talking to Matt's mom and my therapist."

416

"And the drinking?"

"One time thing. I don't like flying and I overdid it." She drank her whole glass of water, avoiding Warren's stare. She knew he wasn't convinced. Neither was she.

"Before, did the work keep you from drinking?" He spoke slowly, and his voice conveyed a warmth she wasn't used to.

"Yes."

"So that's the answer."

"What?" she asked.

"You need to break this story. You need to do the work."

Cole put her hands flat on the table. "And how do you suggest I do that?"

"You're a reporter. Figure it out." He stood.

"What are you gonna do?"

"You're a reporter. I'm a cop—almost a detective—until you came along and screwed me." He said it playfully. It was now an unfortunate running joke.

She smiled weakly.

"I have no chance," he continued, "but I'm going back to the site. I'm going to investigate. Talk to cops, or people at the buildings across the street. Tonight I'll see the professor I mentioned. He may have insight into the motive of this thing, but I doubt it." He stared down at her long and hard, then frowned and nodded. "Do whatever you need to do to pull yourself together and find out what the hell is going on here."

Alone at the table, Cole called Gabby. Straight to voicemail, just like when she'd called her from the Las Vegas airport. "Gabby, it's Jane. Did you get my last message? I really need to hear from you. I'm in London with Warren and... well... I don't know what I need but I need something. A starting point. A thread to pull on bin Muqrin. Something." She paused, looking around the restaurant. Her heart wasn't in it, and it was coming through in her weary tone. "To be honest, Gabby, what I really want to know is whether you can tell me anything about a man named Julio Lopez. One child born recently—a daughter. Truck driver based in Houston."

Cole paid and walked outside where a cold wind bit her

cheeks. Sun peeked through the clouds and she squinted into the glare. She pulled up her collar and wandered down the street.

She'd told Warren the truth about how she'd gotten back to herself after Matt died. After a month off, she'd worked harder and longer than ever before because she had nothing to go home to but an empty bed and a Monkey Puzzle Tree wilting in the corner. Her therapist had said a hundred versions of "Take time to grieve," and "You can't just press through it. Emotions need time to surface."

She'd tried that and had only gotten sadder and sadder. So she worked. Reporting, and the occasional glass of tequila—that's what got her through it.

She stopped at the window of a pharmacy, studying a display of stocking-stuffers. Candy canes, Christmas-themed toothbrushes, miniature figurines from children's movies. Pens and pencils poked out from decorative gift bags.

Warren was right. She'd never been good at masking her feelings, and he'd seen right through her. If she couldn't overcome her grief, she *could* work her way through it.

She walked in and found the school supplies. The section was only a couple racks at the end of a long aisle filled with greeting cards. She grabbed a pack of notecards, a cork board, some thumbtacks, five highlighters in different colors, and a pack of the ballpoint pens she'd seen in the window. Finally, she found a spool of white string.

At the register, a woman gave her a wry smile. "You're either a teacher or you're purchasing the conspiracy-theorists starter pack. I'm guessing you're not a teacher on account of you're not buying the #2 pencils we have on sale."

Cole smiled. "You're right. Not a teacher."

"Gonna solve the nine murders or something?"

Cole slid her card into the reader. "Why? You got a theory?"

"Read in *The Guardian* this morning that MI6 thinks it's the Russians. Get that? The Russians killing people on our soil. Bastards."

"The Russians? Why would they kill Mohammad bin Muqrin?"

"That's what it said." She shrugged like she wasn't truly interested in the story.

Most people didn't process the news the way Cole did. This

lady had read a story—probably a factually-challenged opinion piece—and now repeated it to anyone who would listen.

Cole made a mental note to look up the article when she got back to the hotel, then stowed the cork board under her arm, took the bag, and walked out.

94

Back in the hotel room, Cole flicked off the lights, closed the curtains, and turned on a desk lamp. She set the cork board on the desk, leaning it against the wall so it faced her. Next to it she set the highlighters, pens, notecards, and string.

She closed her eyes and let her mind go blank.

Walking back from the restaurant, the cold air had helped clear her head. She'd scanned the article the clerk at the drugstore had mentioned—a wildly irresponsible piece of journalism that cited one anonymous source "close to British intelligence." Full of speculation and innuendo, and terribly written, the only significant claim came in the third paragraph. "According to the source, multiple Russian operatives (former KGB) are known to have been in and around London in the days before the attack on Mohammad bin Muqrin." The source didn't even claim to know that the Russians were involved. Only that "Russian operatives" were "in and around London." Stories like this were out there, being repeated by people all over the city along with a hundred other poorly-sourced theories. No wonder everyone was confused. And that's exactly how the people behind the killings wanted it.

She needed to shut out the theories and speculation, the noise of the 24/7-media shouting every story in every direction. She needed to blot out the world, descend into darkness, and see if she could drag out a sliver of light.

For over a week, she'd seen the murders the same way the world saw them. A group of extremists were killing world leaders, business leaders, and politicians in service of an extreme, anti-technology ideology. It was hard *not* to see things that way; she'd caught Michael Wragg and this had clearly been his motive. The manifesto sealed the deal.

She tried to set all that aside. What if something else was going on, as Gabby had suggested in Vegas? The rogue JTTF officer had said, "Someone is organizing this thing. Someone smart. Someone powerful. But ask yourself this: What if a ragtag group of extremists *didn't* simply band together on the Internet under the leadership of the mysterious General Ki? What if the folks doing the killings and releasing the manifesto weren't capable of carrying out the most complex terrorist attack since 9/11? What if the stated aims of the terrorists, the mission they articulated in the manifesto, is just a sideshow? A diversion?"

Cole made notecards for each person involved in the killings, along with each major question she needed to answer.

Chandler Price

In New York, she'd figured out that the reclusive businessman owned the townhouse Michael Wragg used to shoot Raj Ambani. Though owned by Martin, it was inhabited by his estranged wife Maggie Price, a socialite, Instagram star, and product endorser known in the NYC tabloids for her numerous trysts with younger men.

At the time of the shooting, Maggie had been out of town, shopping in Paris. Cole learned she'd left town at the request of her husband, who'd known in advance about the shooting.

Chandler Price had arranged for the townhouse to be available, but he'd also been unreachable since Ambani's murder. She and Warren had used computer experts at JTTF to steal his bank records, showing his payments for Michael Wragg's rifles. But she'd never printed this information. As far as the world knew, Price had nothing to do with the murders.

She'd called every number she could find and emailed the public relations contacts listed on the websites of his businesses. No replies.

She'd combed through his history and found no record of political activity, no extreme views posted online, and no evidence he agreed with the content of the manifesto. Besides that, if he *was* the mastermind, why pay for the weapons himself? Why leave that kind of trail?

She texted two business reporters she knew back in New York, asking for notes or links to stories about Price. Few reporters had gotten him on record, and the stories were boring interviews about New York real estate and his first love, the Yankees. Maggie was famous for searching out the spotlight. Chandler Price avoided it.

She added two questions on a notecard under his name:

Mastermind, patsy, or something in between?

Can I confirm he knew the sniper would use his roof?

She stuck the notecard into the cork board.

On another card, she wrote:

Marty Goldberg

The powerful K-Street lobbyist had been found dead the day after meeting with them in D.C. Cole doubted that was a coincidence. She posted the card on the board and, beneath it, tacked a series of cards—one for each company he'd lobbied on behalf of —Systems Key, Inc., Brown and Gunderson, LLC, Trulidia Systems Tech, Kane, Inc. Fifteen companies; fifteen notecards. Next, she made a card for each federal agency he'd lobbied, which was a list of five—USDA, FTC, DOD, ITA, and the BILA. She had to look up the last two—the International Trade Administration and the Bureau of International Labor Affairs. She didn't know anything about either, but the word "international" caught her interest. She pinned the cards to the board.

This thread alone could take days of research to unravel, and she didn't have that kind of time.

Where's Gabby?

Gabby had been leaking them information since the beginning. It turned out she'd been a mole within the NYPD and JTTF, leaking to reporters for years. She was a one-woman wrecking ball, bringing down corrupt cops, government employees, and the criminals they protected. She'd handed them plane tickets and passports, then disappeared. Warren wasn't concerned, but Cole feared the worst. After all, Goldberg had died the day after meeting them.

Next, she created a card for each victim, listing a few key facts about each, looking for connections.

Raj Ambani

Alvin Meyers

Ana Diaz

Mohammad bin Muqrin

She made a card for every connection between the victims, pinning them to the corkboard between the names and connecting them with string. Ambani was connected to Meyers through political donations. Bin Muqrin and Meyers were linked via the Saudi relationship to the U.S. government. And so on.

Stories in the Press

Multiple stories had appeared linking her and Warren to the murders. Someone planted them. Who and why? In her mind there were two options. The first: someone was after them specifically because they were investigating the murders. The second: someone realized they were on the case and simply wanted more misinformation floating around the Internet to confuse people.

The Money

"If you want to understand any problem in America, you need to focus on who profits from the problem, not who suffers from it." Years earlier, Cole had worked as a business reporter for six months, and her boss had taped this quote to her computer.

What Gabby said in Vegas opened up a new view of the killings, and it brought this quote to mind. People were capable of purely ideological killings and terrorist attacks. Recent history had shown that. But the more she thought about it, the less she believed the nine murders were purely ideological, as the manifesto claimed. She needed to get back to the oldest journalism maxim: *Follow. The. Money.*

It's what had led her to Chandler Price and Michael Wragg in New York. And it's what she needed to do now. A crime this big would almost certainly lead to business interests on the same scale.

She sat back and examined the large cork board, now pinned with dozens of cards connected by bits of string. She smiled briefly. Alone in the dark room, along with empty coffee cups and an unmade bed, she'd proven the drugstore clerk right. The place looked like the hideaway of a deranged conspiracy theorist.

Standing, she leaned over the desk and wrote one more card.

What Happened to Matt?

In Vegas, Gabby had said something that still resonated. "Honestly, if you figure out who's really behind this, it'll answer *all kinds* of questions." Gabby had a tendency of being direct most of the time, but maddeningly vague at others. Had she meant that solving the nine murders would unearth the truth of what happened to Matt? Or something else?

Cole wasn't sure and, staring at the card, she felt herself float away. Lopez's Facebook page. Houston. Morgan in Southern California making millions on high-end real estate.

She tore up the card and threw it in the trash. The thought of Matt wrecked her.

And she couldn't allow herself to be wrecked.

95

Warren used his phone to navigate the half-mile back to the hotel where Mohammad bin Muqrin had been shot. Something had bugged him since he and Cole stopped by on their way to breakfast. No video had emerged of the shooting, only its immediate aftermath. Investigators hadn't identified where the assassin was when he made the fatal shot. It should have been easy to figure out by this point. After all, bin Muqrin had died forty-eight hours ago.

The hotel was one of the grandest in London, occupying an entire city block and combining elements of classic and modern architecture. White and gray stone made up most of the lower floors, but shimmering towers of silver and black reached for the sky, like a crystal that had grown from igneous rock. The hotel had reopened, but the front entrance remained cordoned off by blue and white police tape, not the yellow and black stuff he was used to. He loved the film *Pulp Fiction*, and a scene popped into his mind—John Travolta explaining to Samuel L. Jackson that, in Paris, a Quarter Pounder with Cheese is called a *Royale with Cheese*, because of the metric system. The little differences between Europe and America, he thought. They had a different name for the greasy sandwich pressed between a bun.

Across from the hotel rose three tall buildings with smaller buildings filling the gaps between. The tallest was a hotel, the other two were drab office buildings, the sort found in any modern city. Judging by the signs out front, the office buildings had many tenants, providing a possible reason for the delay in locating the origin of the sniper's shot.

In a hotel, there would be a list of every registered guest, plus surveillance footage of everyone who'd come in and out. But that wouldn't be true of an office building. There would be *some* surveillance footage—London was the sixth most surveilled city in the world—but likely not as much. And instead of checking with the front desk for a list of comings and goings, investigators would have to check with each individual company. That could take days, even weeks.

Warren approached the police line, getting as close as he could to the entrance of the hotel where bin Muqrin had been killed. The OPEC meeting had been moved to a more secure location across town, but hotel guests streamed in and out, showing IDs to a pair of officers on the other side of the police tape. At the entrance fifty yards away, the red carpet had been removed, revealing bare cement that was out of keeping with the posh hotel and conference center. Two uniformed officers milled about chatting, looking at phones, and taking notes. Three men in dark suits examined the scene as well. Government investigators, he thought.

Turning back to the tall buildings across the street, he tried to judge the angles. For the shooting in Miami, The Truffle Pig had figured out the only angle from which he could hit Diaz over the wall of the beachfront compound. Warren had to assume bin Muqrin's shooter had planned similarly. The shooter would have known security would be tight, and that the Deputy Crown Prince would be visible for only a few seconds.

The angles from the balconies and windows of the hotel wouldn't allow for the shot. That meant the shooter had been in a window of one of the two office buildings. Both were possibilities, and the choice would have come down to which the shooter had easier access to and which had the better escape route.

A tour bus had stopped across the street and two dozen people streamed out to gawk at the scene. Terrorism tourism. The nine murders story had become an international phenomenon, and everyone was cashing in.

A family of four stopped beside Warren, posing in front of the police tape, their backs to the hotel. The dad pulled out a phone and shoved it in Warren's face. "Take a picture, mate?"

It was more an order than a question, but Warren had a soft spot for Australian accents, and he was in no mood for conflict. "You want a family portrait in front of a crime scene?"

A teenage girl sneered at him. "This is the new 9/11," she said. "But more, like, modern. 2025 vibes. This photo will be huge on Instagram."

Warren took the phone reluctantly. If these jackasses wanted a picture, fine. He held up the phone.

"Wait." The boy, maybe eight years old, brushed floppy blond hair out of his eyes. "Let's get on the other side of the police tape so it'll look cooler."

Warren began to object. "I don't think that's..."

The family was already slipping under the police tape.

They posed, smiling, as Warren snapped pictures. It was the "perfect" shot from a family vacation in London—posing for an Instagram photo in front of a murder scene.

He was starting to understand why Cole's outlook was so bleak.

As the mom, dad, and sister slipped back under the police tape, the boy walked toward the entrance, where the officers and investigators spoke in hushed voices.

"Hey!" It was an officer, Warren thought, shouting at the boy to get back. But all five people at the hotel entrance were looking away from the boy.

A man wearing a dark trench coat and sporting a shaved head was running toward the entryway. Everything around Warren slowed. Sound faded. His peripheral vision dropped away and his eyes focused like lasers on the man, who had bolted past the officer checking IDs. He wasn't fast, but he ran with purpose, straight for the entrance.

"Stop!" An officer's voice. "Stop!"

The boy entered Warren's view. Oblivious, he continued walking toward the entrance, calling for his sister to take a picture of him close to the hotel entrance.

Warren focused on the bald man's trench coat. It bulged on the sides and was too big for the size of his head, like a skinny teenager wearing his dad's suit.

Explosives.

Warren ducked under the police tape and sprinted for the boy.

The man in the trench coat reached the entrance.

Warren grabbed the boy from behind, swiveled on his heels, and dove back toward the police tape. In the air, he cradled the boy's head against his chest with one hand and used his wide body to shield him from the fiery blast exploding from the entryway.

The next thing he knew, Warren was on the ground, ears buzzing, knuckles burning. The boy had rolled out from under him. His parents were there. They snatched the boy up and hurried away, terrified.

The smell. Warren knew that smell. The acrid scent of explosives mingled with the horrid stench of burning flesh. He'd smelled it too many times in Afghanistan.

He sat up and looked toward the hotel entrance, now a caved-in shell surrounded by broken glass, chunks of rock, and metal fragments. Bodies and pieces of bodies.

In the distance, sirens wailed. The sirens in London were a little different, like the police tape.

Strange, the things he noticed.

Warren let his head fall back and opened his eyes wide. Staring into the sky, he let out a single scream, almost a roar, as though all his rage had been channeled into a single sound.

96

Curtains drawn, the desk lamp casting a pale glow over her laptop, Cole worked. She started with the victims, asking herself one simple question: Who benefits financially from their deaths?

She dug into the archives of every newspaper she could access. She read business magazines, political magazines, and a few dozen international publications.

She read every interview with Raj Ambani she could find. On YouTube, she found videos of him speaking at tech conferences on topics such as artificial intelligence, cryptocurrency and blockchain technology. He was a firm believer that the world was on its way to a single currency managed by an international financial council. At one point he even joked that he expected a spot on that council when all this came to pass in twenty or thirty years. "The rate at which the world is unifying is astounding," he said with quiet confidence. "Sure, we'll have some hiccups along the way, but the unity of all mankind is coming—governments, currencies, maybe even religions. This could mean the end of conflict, the end to war. And I'm happy to be alive for it."

She dug through the political history of Alvin Meyers. A moderate, he was known as a practical man who favored compromise over rancor. In his twenty-two years as a senator, he built a reputation for "reaching across the aisle" and "putting country over party."

He voted in favor of every U.S. military intervention during his tenure, and fought his party's every move away from the center. One phrase he'd repeatedly used struck Cole, and she jotted it on another notecard. "Incremental change leads to revolutionary results." After his time in the senate, he'd served eight years as governor of Virginia. Like any politician, he had his share of scandals, but nothing major. The only one that made national headlines involved a Chinese company that wanted to buy a locally-owned TV station in his state. According to reports, Meyers pressured the state legislature to allow the deal, despite objections from both Republican and Democratic colleagues.

Ana Diaz was tougher to research. On the internet, her name was often whispered, but she'd given no interviews. To Cole's surprise, three days after Diaz's death, a Miami reporter named Alexa Frias had released an excerpt of a book about the drug kingpin.

She'd been working on the project for a while and Diaz's murder brought the literary agents to Miami. After inking a six-figure deal for the book, set to be published next year, they'd released a teaser chapter to push pre-orders.

Cole read the chapter with rapt attention. It painted a picture of a woman who hungered for legitimacy in the world's eyes. Diaz wanted to be known as a businesswoman, not a criminal, and was willing to commit as many crimes as necessary to get there.

This was nothing new. Most criminals saw themselves as the good guys. Forced by circumstances and an unjust system into a life of crime, always one job away from going straight. Pablo Escobar amassed a drug fortune of $30 billion, ordered the murder of six-hundred police officers and thousands of others, but also built parks, soccer fields, and homes for the poor. Ana Diaz controlled the drug trade in Miami with brutal violence, but also gave small business loans to minority entrepreneurs.

The excerpt ended with an enticing quotation from Diaz. "Miami was built on crime and has become the greatest American city. If you build enough buildings, paint enough colorful murals, spawn sports stars and musicians... if you *contribute*... people forget everything else. They want to forget. They have to forget. If they love you enough, not only are they willing to forget where you came from, they *need* to forget." It was about Miami, but clearly about Diaz herself as well.

430

But how had Frias gotten the quote? Was it even real?

Cole had to contact the author, so she sent an email requesting a quick, off-the-record chat.

Next she combed through the Threads accounts of the few Middle-Eastern journalists who posted in English, looking for any mention of Mohammad bin Muqrin. The royal family had released an official statement of sorrow and outrage, promising to coordinate with American and European law enforcement to catch the perpetrators. Plenty of rumors floated around, but not much actual news. One problem was that Saudi Arabia lacked a free press and few foreign reporters were granted entry into the country.

But bin Muqrin had been on a campaign of persuasion in the United States for the last two years. In one of the oddest pieces of journalism she'd ever read, he'd partnered with a tabloid news-paper to produce a 160-page booklet about the history and culture of Saudi Arabia. The booklet was pure propaganda, and all of bin Muqrin's public appearances were polished and well-scripted. In New York City, on MSNBC, and at public forums on the future of venture capital in Silicon Valley, every word he spoke seemed designed to soften the ground as the Kingdom of Saudi Arabia moved more and more of its money into western compa-nies and investments. Saudi Arabia had an extra $300 billion and, eventually, the oil would dry up. Mohammad bin Muqrin was in charge of making sure that money kept growing in a diverse, international portfolio.

She stood, placing her hands on the back of the chair and staring down at her laptop, then up at the cork board. Something had to tie these four people together, but what?

The central claim of the manifesto was true—these three men and one woman were all powerful. All moved in circles of high finance and world events. All but Diaz had explicit pro-digital globalization stances. All had, in their own way, played a part in breaking down walls between nations using technology. Diaz was the smallest player, and a bit of an outlier.

Cole fell onto the bed and closed her eyes. She allowed the research to float around in her mind. There *had* to be something else. Something deeper. Gabby's words played over and over. "What if the stated aims of the terrorists, the mission they articu-lated in the manifesto, is just a sideshow?" The problem was that the targets *did* tie into the manifesto, they tied in perfectly, and she was having trouble *not* seeing the case that way.

Her phone rang and she bolted across the room to retrieve it from the desk. A number she didn't recognize but an area code she did. Pipo's gold chain appeared in her mind, the gold "305" encrusted with fake diamonds. Miami's area code.

"Hello?" Her voice was eager.

"Jane Cole? Alexa Frias returning your call from the *Miami Weekly Dispatch*."

Cole returned to the bed. "Thanks for calling me back. I know this is a little unorthodox, but—"

"Don't mention it, Jane. I applied to *The Sun* three times and you're the first person who's ever called me back."

"I... I'm not at *The Sun* anymore."

Frias laughed. "Oh, that was just a joke. But I really did apply to *The Sun*."

She wasn't sure how to proceed. She assumed Frias guarded scoops jealously, as she did herself. "Congratulations on the book deal," Cole said. "My max is five-thousand words. I don't know how you'll do it."

"Already have it half done. Don't know how I'll finish it. Before Diaz was killed, I couldn't get a publisher to give me the time of day."

Cole laughed.

Frias's tone turned serious. "I'd be remiss if I didn't ask, did *you* kill Ana Diaz?"

Cole nearly dropped the phone. "What?"

Frias didn't respond. It took Cole a few seconds to catch up. "You know I was in Miami?"

"Yes."

Cole's mind raced. "How'd you know?"

"Rumors."

"I was in the hotel just after Diaz was killed."

"I know," Frias said flatly.

"How?"

"Like I said, *rumors*. Did you kill her?"

"No."

"Didn't think so, but I had to ask. You know how it is. What a scoop it would have been if you'd said, 'Yup! I killed her.'"

"Ever gotten a scoop like that?" Cole tried to sound light as she tried to figure out what rumors Frias had heard.

"I know where you're going," Frias said. "You want my Diaz book. You were in Miami. You almost had the story."

"Off the record, deep background. I'll erase the call log, forget your name..." She let it hang in the air. "Is there anything you can tell me? I read the chapter your publisher released. Now I'm looking at possible connections between Diaz and the other victims."

The line was silent. Cole buzzed with anticipation. The unique situation might persuade Frias to give her something—after all, Cole wasn't a competitor anymore. She was something else. A subject, or potential subject. Frias had something to offer Cole, but Cole thought she had something to offer Frias as well. "Still thinking?" Cole asked.

"I think you can guess the calculations going on in my head right now."

Cole smiled. "Oh yeah."

"Then have at it."

Cole walked to the window and opened the curtains. She stared down at a park in a small square where a man threw bread to a bird. She gradually raised her gaze to the gray sky, allowing it to turn to static in her mind's eye. Then she closed her eyes, allowing the static to fill her. *Frias*, she thought. Frias, Frias, Frias. "You knew I wasn't involved in the Diaz murder before you asked, correct?"

"Correct."

"And you knew I was in D.C., and in Wragg's apartment. You Googled me and read the false smears about me and Warren?"

"Correct."

"So you know I'm close to this story?"

"Correct."

Cole thought for a moment, choosing her words carefully. "You know I'm good at this, and that I have a lot of information I haven't put in print."

"Correct."

Cole tilted her head to the side, eyes still closed. "You also have a lot you haven't written."

"A book full."

"You've been working on this book for—what—eight months?"

"Fourteen."

Cole opened her eyes. "At first you were thrilled that Diaz's death would raise the profile of your book. You signed a six-figure deal."

"Right."

"But any scoops you may have had are about to get investigated by every reporter with a pulse and a byline. If a hundred good reporters are on this story, your book may be irrelevant by the time it comes out. So your publisher dropped chapter one now to push pre-orders before the story passed you by?"

"Wait, wait, wait," Frias said. "That's not quite it."

"Well then?"

"I have things no one else has, or will *ever* have now that Diaz is dead. I have… *pieces*."

Cole knew what she meant by *pieces*, and she let the word hang in the silence. Frias had pieces that tied into the nine murders plot. Interviews, facts, documents. Things she had *before* Diaz was killed that made new sense in the context of the murders.

Frias continued, "I signed a two-book deal. My guess is that by the time we go to market with my Diaz book, the story will have passed me by. You were right about that. I might even change the nature of that book, depending on what happens. Instead of making it about her rise in the crime world, I could make it a story about the woman herself. Her motivations, her upbringing."

"Smart," Cole said. "The hard news angles will be eaten up, put online, but you'll be able to fill in all the color. There'll still be a market for that." Cole liked Frias more and more the longer she spoke with her. She was clearly a good reporter, smart and practical. "What about the second book?"

"That's why I'm considering telling you what I know."

Cole understood. "They signed your next book and you haven't set on a topic?"

Frias sighed. "Yeah."

"You know I know more than anyone else about the murders, and you want me to be part of the book?"

"Here's what I… no, lemme think for a moment." Frias was careful with her words, an attribute Cole appreciated. Finally, she said, "When an event is big enough, and when journalists play a special role in bringing that event into the light, books can be written about the role of journalism in the story."

"Watergate," Cole agreed. "*All the President's Men* is about reporting more than about Nixon."

"Exactly." Her voice had turned conspiratorial. "I have a feeling this may end up being one of those. The story, on its own, is huge. But if the press gets this story—if *you* get this story—as it's happening, there's a book there as well."

"A trade?" Cole asked. It wasn't really a question. Her tone conveyed understanding, and agreement.

Frias let it hang there for a moment, then said, with finality, "A trade."

97

The last thing Cole wanted was to be the subject of a book, but that's what she ultimately agreed to.

It took half an hour to negotiate the terms—terms that would never be written down or shared with anyone. In the course of negotiation, they got off topic a few times, but it wasn't accidental. They had to develop trust for this to work.

Frias asked about Cole's husband. Cole told her the circumstances of his death, and Frias looked up Matt's obituary while they were on the phone. Cole asked about Frias, who was Cuban-American. Her parents escaped Cuba in the late-seventies, and she'd been born and raised in Miami. She was divorced and had a son who was a freshman at the University of Miami.

The pact required total trust—either had the power to screw the other over. Frias would tell Cole everything she knew about Diaz, along with any possible connections to the nine murders.

Cole promised not to write a single word of it without meeting two conditions. First, it had to be connected to the larger plot of the murders. Second, she had to get approval from Frias, at which point Frias would release the "background" agreement and allow Cole to put it in the story. Most importantly to Frias, Cole agreed to credit her in any story she wrote that used her material. Frias agreed not to use any of Cole's information in any articles written before the eventual book.

For the book, Cole agreed to be interviewed—on the record—but only if she ended up playing a significant role in breaking the nine-murders story. Part of that agreement was walking Frias through the scoops that had led her from New York to D.C., to Miami and Las Vegas, and now to London.

"Here's what I'm thinking," Cole said, eager to get to the matter at hand. "I'll tell you what I know, then you tell me what you know about Diaz that might fill in some holes."

"Good. I'm recording now, alright?"

"Fine." Cole took a deep breath. "It started with nine rifles and a tip from a cop named Robert Warren."

It took an hour to summarize the events that brought her to London. She took her time, and told it slowly and carefully because she sensed Frias's mind at work. In journalism, sometimes the tiniest detail triggered a line of questioning that unraveled a story.

After another half-hour, she'd summarized her research into the victims and why she was doing that research in the first place. "So where I want to start," Cole said, "is what was Diaz up to that could have gotten her killed, assuming the motive in the manifesto *isn't* the real motive?"

Beginning with the drug kingpin's birth as Maria Battle, Frias told the story like a master. She was the illegitimate daughter of Miguel Battle Sr., who ran Miami's largest organized crime family, The Corporation. But Battle had wanted the best for his daughter. That meant she had to succeed in the legitimate world. He noticed early that she was smart, much smarter than his sons, both well known screw-ups around Miami. So he sent her to boarding school in the northeast for high school, then paid for her to get an economics degree from the University of Miami. There, she became a financial wizard, and in the early 2000s she began using an independent film production company to launder money for drug dealers. It was a smart move because the high budgets allowed her to funnel millions through the company without leaving a trace. Diaz wasn't working directly for her father at this time, but she must have had his permission because he controlled most of the drugs in Miami.

Around age twenty-five, things changed. Her inept brothers had pushed their father out of The Corporation and tarnished the operation and the family name. Maria Battle decided to take the business from her two brothers. She changed her name to Ana Diaz and began going as *Lady Chicharron*, a nickname that appeared after Diaz had a snitch thrown into a vat of boiling oil at a pork rinds factory.

Cole interrupted her story. "Warren told me she drove a car through a rival's storefront, too. A pizzeria or something. That true?"

Frias laughed. "He got that off her Wikipedia page, right?"

"Why's that funny?"

"Diaz had people edit her Wikipedia page. She *wanted* that information out there to cultivate an air of violence without admitting to anything *too* incriminating."

"So, did she do it?" Cole asked.

"Yeah, but that isn't the whole story, and it wasn't a pizzeria. C'mon, this is Miami. It was 2012. She and her brother Mikey were having a spat over a chain of walk-up empanada stands that were—in addition to being *legit* good food—used to launder coke money. It was a cool setup, if you're into the whole money laundering thing. Next to each empanada stand, they had a liquor store under a different name. In the back of each liquor store, a Western Union terminal. And that's how they made the money disappear."

"Wait, how?"

"Take in dirty money through the empanada stands, then walk next door to your liquor store and send it to various people via Western Union. Keep the amounts low enough per transaction and no one notices. Even if they do, you've got enough greased cops and politicians that it doesn't matter."

"Interesting," Cole said.

"*And* lucrative. At the time, Mikey was in a power struggle with Diaz's other brother, David, to take over sole control of what remained of The Corporation. She asked for a meeting, assuring Mikey and David she wanted to negotiate a truce between them, in her father's memory. He'd passed away by this point. She arrived late and plowed an Escalade into the front of the empanada stand. She did it herself. Bam. Shattered glass, exploded soda machine.

The whole bit. Meanwhile, three men from her crew walked in the back door and shot her two brothers in the face." She paused. "Closed casket. After that, well... she ran everything."

Cole swallowed hard, then put her phone on speaker and set it on the desk. She swung a leg onto the back of the chair to stretch her hamstring. She'd been researching for hours and the tension had translated into tight muscles. "What were her goals when she took over?"

"She was deeply involved in the Miami community. Charity, small business loans, and so on. But it was a myth she was trying to 'go straight.' That's what the movies and most cops don't get. People like her don't see it as *crime* versus *legit business.* That's not how they think. It's all just *business.* Of course, it pays to have a lot of legal sources of income, but make no mistake about it, she controlled the Miami drug trade. No one could do a serious trans-action without her handling the money. A billion dollars a year went through her hands, and she took fifteen percent. Politicians used her. Cops. Judges. Anyone with money they couldn't just deposit into checking."

Cole switched legs, stretching her other hamstring. "Damn. What about crypto? Was she wading into that?"

"Not wading. She dove head first."

"What do you mean?" Cole asked.

"She saw the future of the drug business as a technology play. Sure, it would be enforced by violence, but she believed whoever controlled the flow of money would control the drug trade. If you can't get large sums of money to and fro, you can't deal on any real *scale*, right? For the last two years she worked with a team of computer scientists plus—no joke—a currency expert who'd once worked for the world bank."

"To what end?"

"To launch a currency. *Her own* currency. An untraceable, end-to-end encrypted currency, like Bitcoin for drug deals, and only transactions of a million dollars or more."

"How can she do that?" Cole asked.

"A legit shell company, owned by another legit shell company, controlled by the board of directors of a third legit shell company, run—in secret—by Ana Diaz herself."

Cole stared off into space. Working the crime beat in New

York City, she'd seen some nefarious schemes, but nothing like this.

"If you ask me," Frias continued, "she got killed because of that, assuming this isn't about an anti-tech political ideology as the manifesto claims."

Cole dropped her leg to the floor and sat, grabbing her phone on the way down. Something in this story triggered a memory, something she'd read earlier in the day. "Say more about that. How'd it work?"

Cole's phone beeped. Call waiting from Warren. She declined the call as Frias went on.

"Say I'm importing ten million dollars worth of knock-off Fentanyl from China. I bring it in on a container ship and I want to unload it to a local crew for distribution. How much would it be worth to everyone involved to have a trusted third party handle the money?"

"A lot."

"It was going to be like PayPal for gangs. She'd collect the money from the buyer, pay the seller, and *guarantee the transaction* the same way credit card companies do. People trusted her. We're talking fraud protection, just like credit cards. But no one would have defrauded her because of her muscle. I mean, she'd had both her brothers shot in the face. It was brilliant. Without ever touching another drug, she could have collected hundreds of millions a year."

Cole saw it. Diaz was on the verge of becoming an internationally powerful criminal who could move the value of currencies and rival small countries. "She was starting an international banking operation."

"That was her goal," Frias continued. "Her dream. That's where she was headed—an illicit banking system for governments, businessmen, and high-value criminals."

98

Warren sat on the ground beside an ambulance, staring at the charred hotel entrance. Bodies and pieces of bodies had been crudely covered with hotel blankets. The bomber was dead. He assumed all five investigators were killed as well. Shards of broken glass, strips of metal and concrete, and a lone brown shoe lay scattered around the blast point.

Two female officers approached and stood over him. One glanced at her notebook. "You Mr. Warren? The American?"

Warren nodded.

"EMTs took your vitals? Checked you out?"

He slowly rose to his feet. "I'm fine." The pressure of the blast had pressed into him, but his injuries were mild—a slight ankle sprain and bloody knuckles from protecting the boy's head as they hit the ground. Now he'd limp with both legs, at least for a while. His prosthetic had come off, and it took Warren ten minutes to bend a small metal connector back into place. It wasn't perfect, but at least he got it reattached. A chunk of stone had hit him in the center of his back, scuffing his leather jacket and likely leaving a bruise. An EMT had cleaned and wrapped his knuckles.

"We reviewed the CCTV," the officer said, "but we'd like your statement. You saved that boy, y'know."

"Maybe."

"You did, Mr. Warren. If he'd continued even three more seconds trying to pose for pictures, he'd be dead."

"What happened to the five... I don't know... two officers, I think, and three suits?"

She looked at the ground. She wasn't going to confirm all five were dead, but her face did that for her. "This won't take long. Just walk us through what you saw."

The other officer took out a notebook and stepped forward.

Warren described exactly what he'd seen. The boy ducking under the police tape. No, he didn't think the family was involved. The man in the trench coat. No, he hadn't said anything. Warren had taken hundreds of statements. He knew what the police wanted to hear.

When he was finished, the lead officer asked, "What brought you to London?"

Warren didn't like lying, but they didn't know he was there to investigate the nine murders, and he wasn't about to get drawn into whatever this new wrinkle was, or was about to become. "Vacation."

"Well, we're sorry this happened. London is usually a very safe city." They took the name of the hotel and Warren's made-up departure date, and moved along to question more witnesses.

A moment later, a man in a fedora approached. "Greg Bailey from *The Guardian*. Couldn't help but overhear your conversation. Can I ask you some questions for my story?"

Warren turned and dialed Cole again, walking away briskly to get away from the reporter. News junkie that she was, he assumed she'd already heard about the bombing. He pictured her in the hotel, eyes jumping from social media feeds to TV news. She probably already knew more about it than he did.

"Bombing?" she asked when Warren told her. "Where?" She sounded distant, like she was barely listening to him.

"Turn on the TV. I was there."

"In London?" she asked.

"Damn, Cole. Are you *high* right now? Someone just blew up five people at the entryway of the hotel where bin Muqrin was killed. Took out some of the investigators."

There was a sigh on the other end of the call, then the sound of shuffling around the room. "Hold on. Putting you on speaker... Yeah, I see it now..."

"You online?"

"Yeah. Hey, there you are."

"What?"

There was a long silence, then Cole said, "You're about to get famous. Maybe not for-real famous, but Internet famous. There's a video. It's already viral."

That was the last thing he wanted. But there was nothing he could do about it. "The *bombing*. Is there anything about the bombing?"

"Wait… Here's something. It's from a site called *Aggression Storm*. Seems to be… Yeah, it's a note."

Warren held his breath as Cole read. How did she find everything so fast? Online searches that would take him an hour took her seconds.

"I don't know if this is real or not," she said. "But it looks like the bombing has nothing to do with the nine murders."

99

Warren walked against a wave of people who'd heard about the bombing and were rushing in to get a closer look. "What's it say?"

"Terrorist group—a *different* terrorist group—has taken responsibility for the bombing."

"Son of a—" Warren ground his molars together. "I almost got blown up and it's not connected? What was that bastard blowing people up for?"

The line was quiet as Cole read. Warren passed a pub, where a dozen faces stared at a TV on the wall. He stopped at the window and saw… himself. The back of his leather jacket flashed across the screen. He was looking at the boy, who was in the background of the shot. In the video, he ducked under the blue and white police tape and ran. Just before he reached the boy, the video went into slow motion. Every face in the pub was glued to the screen. He grabbed the boy and turned him away from the blast only a second before it detonated. For the first time, Warren saw his own face as he turned and dove away from the fiery explosion.

It didn't look real. It didn't feel real.

The scroll at the bottom of the TV read: **American Hero Saves Boy in London Terrorist Bombing.**

A man stopped at the window and stood next to Warren,

444

staring in. Warren pulled up the collar on his jacket to shield his face.

Walking on, he asked, "You still reading?"

"Yeah, it's… it's complicated," Cole said. "I've never heard of this group and don't really understand their ideology. I've made some other breakthroughs, though. Get back here and we can talk through it."

Warren pinched the phone between his ear and shoulder and pressed both hands into his thighs. "Gimme the short version. The CliffsNotes."

"Okay, lemme just finish reading."

He felt a group of people looking at him, or was he imagining it? He stepped into an alley between two brick buildings and leaned against a wall next to a dumpster. He understood why people wanted to watch the video. The bombing made them feel like crap, and it made them feel better to create a hero out of Warren. But he wanted no part of the five minutes of fame he was about to get.

"Basically," Cole said at last, "it's a group of exiled Chinese Christians, living in the west. U.S., UK, Italy, and Canada. They seem to be pissed that western democracies are placating China. Something about 'cooperating with the oppressor' and 'economic cowardice.'"

"Wait," Warren said. "They're pissed at China, so they're pissed at the countries that deal with China, so they blow up people who have nothing to do with either?" He stared at a long scratch in the wall, a spot where the back of the dumpster had ground up against the brick for years. Inexplicably, he wanted to punch a hole through the thick metal wall of the dumpster.

"That sounds like what they're saying," Cole said. "Wait… yeah… they even say here how they apologize for killing people, but they need to bring attention to their cause. Says here, 'Until the great democracies of the west recognize the persecution of Christians in China and unilaterally cut off all business dealings with China—"

"Save it," Warren interrupted.

"Why don't you come back here? This video of you is—"

"Nah." Warren pulled the phone from his face and checked the time. 4 PM. "I'm gonna go see the professor I told you about.

Says he understands the terrorists. Can help me understand. Meet me there?"

"I'm neck deep in research."

There was an awkward pause. "Fine," Warren said. "I'll see you later."

"Okay, see ya."

He was about to hang up, then said, "Ever think there's just no point to any of this? We solve these murders and what? Another group of crazy bastards I've never heard of—who think they're dissidents or something—blow up cops for... for what?" He swiveled and punched the dumpster as hard as he could. A metallic thud echoed in the alley. Pain shot from his hand through his arm and into his shoulders. Blood seeped through the mesh dressing on his injured knuckles.

"What was *that*?" Cole asked.

"Nothing."

Another long pause, then Cole said, "You're starting to sound like me, Rob. And just when I was feeling optimistic."

100

Cole hung up and sat in front of her laptop. She tried to focus on typing notes, but her mind kept returning to Warren. In their relationship, *he* was usually the less cynical of the two. Just as she was making progress on the case, he sounded like he wanted to quit.

Maybe it was a temporary lull in enthusiasm. After all, he'd been ten yards from getting blown up. Still, it concerned her. She assumed some of his optimism came from the fact that he'd gone through AA and faced down so many of his demons. What would happen if they resurfaced?

Her phone dinged with a text from Brian McPherson, one of the business reporters she'd contacted earlier. She'd helped him out of a jam with their boss his first week at the *Sun*. Her phone dinged again as she was reading the first text. Then again. And again.

Five, six, seven texts arrived, all from McPherson. The first was a long message, but the rest were images. She clicked one at random. At first she was confused. A pink-faced Chandler Price held a martini, his arm around a woman thirty years his junior. Next to them, sitting at a table in what appeared to be a fancy restaurant, was a man Cole recognized but couldn't quite place. Was it…

What?

The other man in the restaurant was Alvin Meyers, the former Vice President who'd been the second victim.

Her mind went blank, like something inside her had to make room for what was about to happen. She sat on a chair next to the window, which she opened a crack, letting in a freezing stream of air.

Texts were still arriving. More photos.

She read the message.

Jane,

This is absolutely off-the-record and confidential. But I trust you. Owe you. You asked re: Chandler Price, and I know something no one else does. Price is reclusive—I think you know. No interviews, etc. Six years ago he created an Instagram account under a fake name. Johnny Galt. I don't think the Atlas Shrugged *reference was an accident. Private account. I worked for him ten years ago and followed his Instagram before he made it private. Also under a pseudonym.*

Last six years I've spied on his posts, which he thinks can only be seen by his 20 or 30 followers. He uses the account to show lifestyle and network. Pure vanity. He deleted the account 10 days ago. When the Ambani shooter used his rooftop, I wondered about a connection, but couldn't find one. Then VP Meyers died. Look at the photos. I'm sending screenshots dating back to the beginning. A who's who of famous men and a few women.

I never have and never would use this for a story. It's given me some angles to research, but I'm out of my depth.

I hope you're not.

The photo of Chandler Price with the Vice President was from four years ago. She kept scrolling, past photos of Price with people she didn't recognize. All looked rich. Most were at dinner tables in fancy restaurants. She paused on the last photo. Price posed with an Asian man around forty years old. He was deeply tanned and looked unhappy to be in the photograph. His black hair cut short, he wore hip rectangular glasses. His handsome face was half-turned away from the camera, his eyes on Price as though asking, "Really?"

She recognized him, but couldn't recall his name. Luckily, Price had captioned the photo: "Sushi and sake with the legendary Ibo Kane."

Kane. The name set off alarm bells.

He was someone she'd considered briefly as a potential target of the killers. He had the stature of someone the assassins would

448

go after—he owned an AI company, was deeply involved in digital globalization, surveillance technology, supported a unified world currency, global banking, and international law.

She pored through her notes, scanning for the name.

Marty Goldberg, the D.C. lobbyist, had done work for Kane. A lot of work. In fifteen minutes she found a dozen instances when Goldberg had lobbied federal agencies in D.C. on behalf of Kane, Inc.

She looked back further, into her notes from the day she'd met Warren back in New York. Kane had been a business rival of Raj Ambani. Years ago, a newspaper article quoted him opposing a merger Ambani had tried to complete.

"Oh, my God." She stood, paced rapidly for a minute, then sat and looked again at the image of Kane with Chandler Price.

She found Kane's bio on the website of Kane, Inc. She read it twice, then his Wikipedia page and a profile in a business magazine. Like Chandler Price, Kane was reclusive. But unlike Price, he wasn't just a powerful New York City millionaire. He was a billionaire, and one of the most quietly powerful men in the world.

She read another bio, completing her picture of the man.

Ibo Kane was a half-American, half-Chinese businessman who founded a social media company, then a digital payment company, then a digital ad platform, then an AI company. He created hedge funds to legally manipulate financial markets and move money around the world, then used his enormous wealth to buy media and business entities throughout the U.S. and China. Kane also cut deals with the NSA and CIA. Brokered by Marty Goldberg in D.C., the deals allowed the federal agencies to use some of his data in exchange for paving the way to mega-deals with the FTC and other regulatory bodies. Forty-nine years old, he looked only forty. Kane was handsome, brilliant, powerful, and respected.

There was zero direct evidence he was involved. She didn't know how or why, but Cole was certain Ibo Kane was behind the nine murders. She knew it as much as she'd known anything in her life.

She'd heard people say social media would be the downfall of civilization. She didn't really believe that. To her, social media was like most new technological innovations: sometimes useful, but subject to abuse. If she was right, it would be the downfall of the bastards behind this crime. A stupid Instagram post by a drunk millionaire—Chandler Price—who didn't know a reporter was following him under an alias.

Pure ego would be their undoing.

She called Gabby—straight to voicemail. She called Warren. Five rings to voicemail. Unsure what to do, she sat down to write.

She checked her email for a message from Frias, who'd promised to follow up with an Ana Diaz interview transcript. She didn't know what it would be, but she was certain she'd find a connection between Diaz and Ibo Kane there.

She had an email from Frias, but not the promised transcript. The subject line read: *WTF*. The email was a link to an article on a website called *Crush Cycle*, a celebrity gossip site that blurred the lines between made-up tabloid journalism and accurate reporting. Their motto was *Crush Cycle: We CRUSH the news cycle*.

The article was only a few lines long and led to a video.

The video was surveillance-cam footage and it took Cole a moment to orient herself. Three people walked down a dark path, houses on either side. The shot was from above, as though a camera had been mounted high on the side of a building.

But the buildings on either side of the walkway weren't houses. They were too small to be houses. They were rectangular boxes, all the same height. Ten or twelve feet tall. Storage containers. Two men and a woman. Something about them was familiar.

They reached a door and one of the men opened it. She recognized that door. Now she recognized the people.

She nearly fell back in her chair. "Oh, no."

One of the men was Warren. The woman was Cole herself. The video was surveillance camera footage from Michael Wragg's storage unit in New Jersey.

"Oh, God, no."

101

Warren wandered through foggy streets, unsure where he was going. The late-afternoon chill had set in, and the sliver of sun that had peeked through the clouds earlier was gone.

He'd lied to Cole. He had an hour before his meeting with his old professor. Punching the dumpster had released some of his rage, but it was creeping back. He stopped in front of a coffee shop called *Calm Brews* and took a few deep breaths. His AA sponsor's voice echoed in his head, repeating one word over and over. "Trauma."

Warren inhaled the cold, coffee-scented air. He opened his eyes wide, scanning the buildings. "Trauma." He wasn't fond of the term PTSD, but that's probably what was going on.

He'd known right away that the man in the trench coat was a suicide bomber. He'd seen plenty of them in Afghanistan. Women, men, even a nine-year-old boy. A boy who'd strapped a bomb to his chest and killed one of Warren's buddies. He never thought he'd see the same thing in London.

His AA sponsor told him that recognizing trauma when it resurfaced was the first step in dealing with it. For Warren, trauma often came with rage. Historically, he'd either numbed the rage with booze, or tried to outrun it with coke. He didn't want to do that again.

He stepped into the coffee shop and ordered a black coffee. "Burnt, if possible."

The woman behind the counter gave him an odd look, like he was joking. "Two quid, ninety."

He was surprised by her British accent and immediately felt stupid. Of course she'd have a British accent. He fumbled with coins and paid.

She handed him the coffee. "American?" she asked.

"How'd you know?"

"You didn't give me enough." She reached into his hand and took another coin, allowing—or *making*—her fingertips brush his palm as she pulled her hand away. "We do take cards, you know."

Warren glanced up. Her eyes met his immediately. He hadn't been looked at this way in a while. "From California, originally. Now I'm in New York."

"*Fuhgeddaboudit.*" It was a ridiculously bad New York accent.

He smiled. "Where'd you hear that?"

"*Friends*, maybe. I can't remember. Do people actually say that in the States?"

"No one *I* know. White dudes from Jersey, maybe?"

"Where's that?" she asked.

"Across the water."

A man stood behind Warren, craning his neck to read the menu.

"You going to drink that here?" the woman asked. "I get off in an hour. I could show you around the city."

"Yeah, maybe…"

"You should stay." She delayed a moment before moving her eyes to the man in line behind him.

The woman was about ten years younger than him, pretty, and shockingly forward. He thought of Cole back at the hotel, then of Sarah. He'd dated a few women since Sarah made him move out, but nothing serious and nothing that didn't leave him feeling empty. The attention felt good, distracted him from his darker feelings.

His phone rang and he checked the caller ID. Cole. He sent it to voicemail.

The man who'd been behind him took his coffee and left. Warren leaned on the counter. "You get a lot of Americans in here?"

"A few. Hold on." The woman pulled a cellphone from her apron, sat on the counter, and leaned back, resting her head on Warren's shoulder. Before he knew what she was doing, she flashed a peace sign and took a selfie.

He stepped back. "Why'd you... oh, wait... did you see the video?"

"*Everyone* has seen it. They're calling you The Rock, Jr., ya know. Duane Johnson. He's huge on this side of the pond, and you look a little like him. Slightly darker, maybe, but you've got his build. I'm an aspiring TV host. You should get an agent."

Warren sipped his coffee. It was weak. And not burnt.

He threw it in the trash and walked out.

102

Studying the video, Cole recognized the greasy red hair of the young guy from the storage unit. Then Warren's face entered the frame. Then hers.

Watching herself gave her an eerie, creeping feeling. Hollow and full at the same time. Unreal and extra-real.

In the video, they reached the end of the hallway. Warren looked straight into the camera. Next to him, the kid tapped a code into the keypad on the door of Michael Wragg's storage unit. Cole stood with an intense look on her face, as though she could will herself into the storage unit. Did she really look like that?

As the door to the unit rose, the shot changed.

She recognized the location immediately. She knew what was coming. The footage was much clearer—a large hotel lobby, marble floors, a pale yellow runner leading to a section of colorful sofas and vases of flowers. The hotel in Miami where The Truffle Pig shot Ana Diaz. The video from the storage unit wasn't time-stamped, but this one was. It was shot only minutes after Ana Diaz was killed.

For an instant, she allowed herself to believe this wasn't what she thought it was, allowed herself to believe she'd see The Truffle Pig hurrying through the lobby. But she knew better. This video was a frame job. After a moment, Warren appeared. A second later, she appeared and followed Warren out a glass door. That's where they'd stolen the airport shuttle van to follow The Truffle Pig through southern Florida.

The shot didn't shift to an exterior of them stealing the van. Instead, the footage played again from the beginning. The dark path in the sea of storage units. But this time there was a voice-over.

"An international brotherhood, united by General Ki for a singular mission: to end the technological oppression, to restore the sovereignty of the individual, to birth a new era of freedom."

It was a woman's voice.

Cole listened once, then rewound fifteen seconds and listened again.

"An international brotherhood, united by General Ki for a singular mission: to end the technological oppression, to restore the sovereignty of the individual, to birth a new era of freedom."

She thought she'd seen it all. Heard it all. But the recording broke her. As though all the energy had left her body at once, she crumpled and fell to the floor.

The voice on the recording was her own.

103

Warren followed his phone's GPS, passing through multiple business districts before reaching a section of tree-lined blocks and row after row of three-story homes. His professor lived in a posh neighborhood called West Brompton, and the area looked as pretentious as it sounded.

Professor Simon Smith taught political and legal history Warren's freshman year in college, but now worked at a think tank in London. Smith had sparked Warren's fascination with history and, even though Warren had gone into law enforcement, he'd always told himself he'd go back to school to get a PhD in the subject. He knew he probably wouldn't, but it was the lie he told himself to keep going.

The home had a white marble facade and two black Mercedes parked out front, a station wagon and a convertible. It wasn't what Warren expected from the man he remembered as a wild-haired, wild-eyed, radical professor.

Warren's phone rang just as he knocked on the door. Cole again. He silenced it and shoved the phone back into his jeans as the door opened.

Simon Smith looked nothing like Warren remembered. Around fifty now, he sported short white hair and a dark brown suit. Expensive, but bland. Smith had been a pony-tailed thirty-

456

something when Warren knew him, always raving about "smashing the power structures that shape history."

Smith peered over his lowered glasses. "Come in, Rob. Punctual, as always."

They entered a small study—dark wood, brass fixtures, and antique furniture. Smith sat behind a desk and gestured to a small wooden chair. "Don't worry." He smiled at Warren's hesitation. "Oak, from 1721. Solid as they come, that chair! Three hundred years old. A slice of Europe's history."

Warren sat cautiously. A framed photo behind the desk showed Smith shaking hands with Boris Johnson. Smith flashed the same smarmy smile. "You're wondering what happened to me?"

Warren raised an eyebrow.

"Seems like things have changed," Warren said. "His and hers Benzes, Boris Johnson, that suit. What happened to smashing the system?"

Smith ran a hand through his hair. "I'm still doing that, Rob. The system's just changed. The good guys are now the bad guys, and the radicals like me? We've grown up." He smiled, then clapped his hands as though remembering something. "I didn't know when I took your call that I'd be welcoming a viral sensation into my home."

Warren looked away. "That was nothing."

"Nothing, he says. Look at your hand! You're a hero. And the bombing?" He shook his head. "Terrible thing."

Warren's phone rang, and he silenced it. "Sorry about that. Look, I don't have long. The saving-the-kid thing was nothing. Right place, right time. I didn't know there'd be a video."

"Humble, too? You're such an… *American*, Rob."

Warren decided to steer the conversation. "You have a theory about the nine murders?"

"You're investigating?"

Warren didn't want to get into it. "Sort of." He leaned forward. The chair creaked. "How do you make sense of all this?"

Smith stood and put his hands in his pockets. He walked to the bookshelf and cleared his throat. "Not long ago, America and the West celebrated the triumph of liberalism. The Soviet Union fell, and China—we all believed—would eventually follow a democratic path. Right?" He paused, smiled briefly at Warren, then turned back to the bookshelf. "Wrong. Look at Russia now. And the country with one-fifth of the world's population invented a new path. Their rise in the last thirty years is unprecedented. But it's not just economic power. It's the control they've built over information, technology, and data. Together with Silicon Valley, Chinese tech giants are the new oligarchs, dictating what we see, hear, buy, and think."

He spoke like Warren wasn't there, his voice affected, like an American trying to sound British.

"Unlike America," he continued, "where every election cycle is about the next fix, China has a system that can think long-term, and stay consistent. Meanwhile, here, in the West, we're losing ground. We've been sold convenience, surveillance has become normalized, and AI is quietly sorting us all into boxes."

"So, how would you define their economic system?" Warren asked.

Smith shrugged. "It's not comparable. They're merging state control with unregulated capitalism. Their tech companies are practically government agencies, controlling everything from speech to surveillance."

"The Beijing Consensus?" Warren asked.

Smith smiled, turning back to the bookshelf. "Very good, Rob. Mao's death started it. It's not a policy—it's just a way of life now: control, surveillance, efficiency."

"How does all this tie into the murders or the manifesto? Where are you going with all this?"

Smith paused and turned, eyes focused. "It's so different from what we have in the West. Here, too many competing interests are tearing us apart. The manifesto—that's about the battle between human freedom and algorithmic control. The terrorists? They're fighting the system that's been built to monitor, analyze, and categorize us. After the 2008 financial crisis, the West started to lose its grip. Wages stagnated, jobs vanished, and the power shifted to a handful of companies that own our data." Smith's voice lowered, more serious. "The twenty-six richest people own more than the bottom half of the world combined. And the tech companies, the banks, they're reshaping the entire global economy—without anyone asking. Some want to redistribute that power, others think it'll trickle down. But there's a larger group, the ones who've been left behind—they want to destroy the system entirely."

"So you sympathize with the aims of the terrorists?" Warren asked.

"Their aims? Yes. Their methods? No." Smith continued earnestly. "It pains me when people try to make sense of these assassins without understanding the bigger picture. Look at Europe after 2008. Austerity hit Greece, Italy, and Spain. Imagine you're a grandma in Tuscany, holding onto the quiet life you've known, then one day the EU tells you, 'This is over. The system we built for centuries is changing. And if you don't buy one of these thousand-Euro supercomputers we call 'phones,' you're going to be left behind.'"

Warren nodded.

"Look, is killing a handful of the tech and banking and criminal oligarchs going to fix things? Probably not. But I'm not the Frenchwoman who can't afford gas, or the Ohio factory worker whose job was outsourced to India. I'm not that grandma in Tuscany, wondering where her world went." Warren opened his mouth to object, but Smith raised his hand as though silencing a crowd. "I know I might sound like I'm siding with the killers, and I know you want to object, but before you do, put yourself in the shoes of that grandma in Tuscany."

Warren's phone vibrated with a new text. When Smith turned back to the bookshelf, he glanced at it.

Jane Cole: *I know who's behind the murders. Get back here.*

Smith was still going. "Is it any wonder you'd embrace an extreme, violent movement to destroy the whole damn system? Is it any wonder that, deep down, you'd support these terrorists— and they *are* terrorists—who say, 'Enough, we're taking our lives back.'"

He said it like a professor, a sort of open-ended question. But it was no question. Smith agreed with the group behind the murders. On the phone he'd told Warren he had a theory. This was no theory; it was a justification for their manifesto.

Another text arrived.

Jane Cole: *Also, I'm freaking out. PLEASE get back here.*

Smith noticed him reading the text. "The invention of those infernal devices is why I got out of teaching. I make a profound statement about the world and you're on your screen."

"Sorry… um, sorry. I—"

"I'm only teasing."

Warren read the texts again.

Jane Cole: *I know who's behind the murders. Get back here.*

Jane Cole: *Also, I'm freaking out. PLEASE get back here.*

He stood to leave. "Thanks for your time, Professor Smith. You've given me a lot to think about."

104

By the time Warren arrived, Cole had watched the video six times, closing her laptop each time and promising herself she wouldn't watch it again.

She'd called Gabby three more times, desperate to talk to someone who could tell her where the video had come from or how to get it taken down. The very idea was ridiculous—the video was already on a hundred websites and all over Threads and Facebook. It had passed "Viral" and gone straight into "Break the Internet" status. More than the previous articles, the video implied that Cole and Warren were connected to the murders.

After Warren called back, she'd gone down to the hotel bar, done a shot of tequila, and regretted it immediately. Sipping a cup of black coffee as penance, she watched the video again on her phone. Then she had another shot of tequila.

When Warren walked in, she ran into his arms.

He squeezed her tight. "What is it?"

"Watch the video on my laptop."

He let her go and she fell onto the bed. She listened, eyes shut tight, as he watched.

"Damn," was all he said. He walked to the bed.

She sensed him standing over her, but he didn't say anything and she didn't open her eyes. The moment seemed to go on for minutes, and all she wanted was for him to say something to make

461

it better. But he couldn't. She heard movement, sensed warmth in front of her face, like he was leaning in to kiss her.

She opened her eyes just as he inhaled deeply.

"Been drinking?" he asked.

"Two shots of tequila."

He took her hand and pulled her gently to her feet.

"What the hell?

"We need to get some air."

A walk wasn't what she had in mind, but she let Warren lead the way.

The sun had set and the air felt solid, like thin ice on her warm cheeks. Christmas lights decorated storefronts and happy Londoners stuffed packages in taxis and spilled in and out of pubs. As they walked a few laps around the hotel in silence, the bustling city heightened Cole's sense of unreality and panic.

Sometimes the content of the Internet felt more real than the flesh, blood, and stone of a living city. And when that content was a fake video using an AI-generated version of her voice, it was even more surreal that the everyday world went on around her as though nothing had changed. And when that video implicated her in a terrorist murder plot, well, the panic made sense.

"Why?" Warren asked. "Who gains from that video?"

"Confusion, most likely. First rule of propaganda. You don't have to convince people of a particular truth. If you can confuse them, convince them there are a dozen stories out there and any one of them *could* be true, they won't take action. Plus, if we're getting close, it means no one will believe what we say when and if we say it." She raised the collar of her jacket, shielding her face from a woman she was sure was staring at her.

"Breathe, Cole. You look like me when I'm about to explode." He pulled her forward and they crossed the street, sitting on a bench at a bus stop.

"How is it even legal to make fake videos like that using my real voice?"

Warren shrugged. "Remember your precious First Amendment?"

"I know, I know." Whoever created the video might have

broken the law in the process, and it was bad journalism to repost it, but it wasn't *illegal*. It was the same with leaked or stolen documents. If a government official stole documents, that was against the law. Handing the documents to a reporter, also against the law. But once the reporter had the documents, the law couldn't stop her from publishing them, except under the rarest circumstances.

And *Crush Cycle* wasn't known for having the highest journalistic standards.

Cole leapt from the bench, fists clenched. Her cheeks stung from the cold wind, but her chest was hot. She walked a lap around the bench. Then another. "I'm just so mad."

She stood before Warren. He touched her hand, which was balled up so tightly her knuckles were white. The slightest touch made her collapse onto the bench, as though all her energy had drained at once.

"I'm gonna say something now," Warren said, "and you're not gonna like it."

Cole opened an eye. The window of a pub behind him framed Warren's head. She felt outside her body, as though she was drifting out of herself into the pub.

"You need to sleep. I saw your empty bottle of Ambien in the hotel in D.C. You've been sleeping, what, three or four hours. Running on caffeine. Coming down with tequila. You're starting to worry me."

A sudden rush of energy caused her to leap up. "Worry you? Someone is trying to frame me, or us—"

"Maybe they are, or maybe they're just sowing confusion. A lot of people could have made that video."

She leaned in, almost shouting. "And I haven't even told you about Frias, Ana Diaz, Chandler Price, Ibo Kane. I haven't even... even..." She sat heavily on the bench. "I'm not making any sense. I can tell by how you're looking at me." She sighed. "And you didn't even tell me what happened with your old professor." She squinted, curiosity painted on her anxious face.

He put a hand on her forearm, but didn't reply.

Cole put her head on his shoulder. "China," she added. "There may be a China angle." She closed her eyes and everything around her faded into a dull buzz. "The video already has a million reposts." Her voice sounded like someone else's, the words appearing in her mind as though from outside. "When an online story grows that fast, the national news *has* to talk about it or they look like they're in on a coverup. CNN, Fox, MSNBC, BBC. Right now producers all over the world are figuring out how to present it, even though it's clearly fake. Doesn't matter."

"That's messed up."

"Do you ever sit back and look at the world and just think it's gone crazy?"

"Every single day," Warren said. "But not because of that. Out there is where things are really crazy." She felt him gesture with his free arm, but didn't open her eyes. "Threads, X. Facebook. The internet. That's *not* the real world."

"It's getting harder and harder to tell the difference."

He let out a long, slow breath. She immediately regretted what she'd said. He was thinking about the bombing, and she felt like a fool. "I'm sorry. You almost got blown up today—five people *did* get blown up—and here I'm worrying about a fake video and reposts."

"London police announced three arrests already," Warren said, "people connected to the bombing. It's official—it had nothing to do with the nine murders. A totally *different* group of nutjobs blowing people up. I don't need to go online to learn that the world is crazy."

They sat in silence for a long time, Cole's head on his shoulder. For the first time in days, she felt how tired she was. "You're right," she said softly. "I need to sleep."

"Your brain is the best tool we have at this point. It's not functioning. I've been there. I used to use coke to stay up, run on twenty hours of sleep a week. And I *always* thought I was doing well, the decisions I made in the moment seemed right. Looking back, I wasn't making good decisions. I was just high. You're high on caffeine and sugar, maybe on trauma. I mean, you found out about Matt two days ago. That must have been… I don't know. C'mon."

Warren pulled her from the bench and led her around the corner to a small pharmacy. They walked straight to the back and Warren approached a pharmacist, who was on his way out for the evening. "What's the strongest over-the-counter sleeping pill you sell?"

105

Wednesday

The sound of running water woke her. How long had she slept? An hour? A day? The sky was dark through the open curtains. She rolled over toward the bathroom, where steam escaped through a crack in the door. Instinctively, she reached for her phone and scanned the breaking news alerts.

Always in her mind was one question: *Has anyone else been killed?*

No one had. There were a hundred new theories on social media, and every major publication in the world covered the killings from every angle. The murder of the Deputy Crown Prince had escalated the story, especially in international circles. He was the first active politician or government official to be killed. That meant presidents and prime ministers, senators, kings and queens—all were potential targets. Judging by the coverage, that didn't sit well with the governments of the world.

Foreign Affairs and the *Washington Post* ran articles citing anonymous sources making remarkable claims: the intelligence agencies of the world—even those of rivals—were sharing information. That America and the UK shared intelligence was nothing new. The same went for Japan and South Korea. But if the reporting was right, hastily devised backchannels now conveyed intelligence between the U.S. and China, between Japan and China, and between Russia and the U.S. Most surprising of all were reports that Saudi Arabia was coordinating intelligence with its biggest rival, Iran. If true, it signaled unprecedented cooperation and coordination between usually distrustful nations. Had these nations suspected one another, they'd never cooperate. Ironically, the attacks fostered exactly the sort of global cooperation the manifesto had railed against.

On the desk, her laptop sat open. Warren had reviewed her notes after tucking her into bed the previous night. She stumbled to the chair. The screen glowed, open to an article from the *New York Post*: **NYPD Lieutenant Joey Mazzalano Arrested; Charged with Corruption, Sexual Assault.**

Head foggy, but feeling stronger than she had in days, Cole stared at the headline. An odd jumble of feelings hit her all at once. Happiness, guilt, shame, then satisfaction. He was a scumbag; she'd always known that. But she'd never known just how bad he was. Staying ignorant had better served her because he'd been her best source.

But of course he belonged behind bars. Before reading the story, she texted Gabby.

Cole: *You have anything to do with Mazz going down?*

She hoped this might tempt her out of hiding.

She found a huge paper cup and tasted the contents. Vanilla latte, and still hot. Warren knew her well.

As Warren continued to shower, she read the Mazzalano story, then searched the web for more information.

It had broken in *The New York Times*, but every other newspaper in New York followed up within hours. A spokesman for the NYPD appeared on a local radio show, then a local TV show. CNN picked up the story, then Fox News.

There were few specifics about the sexual assault allegations against Mazzalano. Cole had her own to add to the mix, but doubted it would be necessary. There were nine allegations against him, ranging from lewd groping to rape. Six allegations came from members of the NYPD. The usual stance of the NYPD was "Protect Our Own."

Not this time.

According to the reports, Internal Affairs had been investigating Mazzalano for months. Recently, an anonymous tip had helped them uncover his role protecting dropgangs in New York

City. She combed through every article, but none made the connection between Michael Wragg's purchase of the nine rifles and Mazzalano's racket.

She added a paragraph to her notes, explaining the connection.

By the time Warren turned off the shower, Cole was high. Partially on the vanilla latte, which had been especially strong and sugary, but mostly on the fact that her research was flooding back into her brain and connecting in ways she hadn't seen the previous day.

Most days, reporting was a tedious slog. A job with lots of slammed doors, unreturned voicemails, texts, and dead ends. Progress was incremental. A source would mention something tiny. Chasing it down took days—sometimes weeks—of painstaking work.

Yesterday had been a tsunami of revelation. Wave after wave of new information and miraculous connections. Now that she'd gotten enough sleep and caffeine, she saw the whole thing clearly. The entire story was in her head, in her bones, and every part of her tingled. She had something the whole world wanted to know.

Not even Warren knew everything she knew. Not yet.

She sat on the bed, waiting for him to walk out of the bathroom. She wiggled her toes, just to remind herself not to float away. She needed to stay grounded because she still had a lot of work to do.

He walked out, already dressed in jeans and a white t-shirt. "I have it," she said. "I have the story. At least, kinda. I think so."

He smiled. "You seem better." He nodded at the computer. "See the Mazzalano news?"

"Must feel good to you, right? Crooked cop goes down. I feel more… conflicted."

Warren frowned. "It wasn't your job to take Mazzalano down. When the NYPD turns on one of their own, they turn hard. He'll do real time."

She nodded. "Want me to tell you what I know?"

He stared at her. "No. I want to *read* what you know."

"Can I offer you the role of research assistant? There's a lot of work left to do."

He sat on the bed and his eyes widened in anticipation. "Just tell me what to do."

She started by researching connections between Ibo Kane and Ana Diaz. There was only one, but it was easy to find now that she knew what to look for.

Diaz's efforts to create a unified digital currency for drug deals and other high-level criminals directly conflicted with Kane's own digital currency ambitions. Kane got into the game earlier and came from a tech background, but there was no doubt her currency could have derailed his.

Once the Diaz connection was clear, other pieces fell into place, slowly at first, then rapidly. The entire story had been hiding in plain sight.

Combing over search results, reading interviews, and poring over financial disclosures for businesses and nonprofits, she put together the pieces of the puzzle. Often, she had a podcast interview playing on her phone while reading on her computer.

Ibo Kane was connected to everyone killed so far.

When he was shot, Raj Ambani's company had been on the verge of merging with X-Rev International, a firm specializing in high-frequency, computer-based stock trading. Cole felt like a fool when she found this because she'd *already* seen it once. Sitting in Warren's apartment, she'd found the article after Googling "Ambani" and "business rivals." Ibo Kane had been quoted in the piece, arguing that Ambani shouldn't be allowed to merge with X-Rev.

Cole found three connections to Alvin Meyers, the former Vice President. The key was focusing on the present day, not on his two VP terms. Meyers sat on the boards of two companies that rivaled Kane's, but killing Meyers probably wouldn't change much because another board member would simply replace him. It was the third connection that sealed the deal in Cole's mind.

Alvin Meyers had twin sons, Jacob and Michael. Twenty years ago, they'd graduated from the Wharton School of Business and moved to China, working in a series of firms, all related to the energy sector. No doubt they were bright and accomplished, but their rise in Chinese business had coincided with their father's time as Vice President. Cole found numerous articles questioning the appropriateness of their international business dealings, but no crimes had ever been discovered. Two years ago, they formed a company in China, along with two Chinese men, to create advanced AI models that would be able to predict the worldwide flow of money and, eventually, regulate all financial transactions from a single central location.

Using Google Translate, Cole found articles in which Kane had been quoted about their company. In short, he hated it. And he'd played two distinct cards in the media. "China allowing this company to exist is shameful. If a Vice President can get his spoiled, unqualified sons into business in China, what's next? Making Meyers himself the President of China?"

When that attack hadn't worked, he tried again in an article in the *Financial Times*. "Why should China allow privileged Americans to profit from Chinese technology, when Americans of Chinese descent are blocked?" He'd played the race card, but that hadn't worked either. Of course, Kane didn't mention that he had a competing company and hoped his ancestry would convince the Chinese government to give him a leg up.

The Deputy Crown Prince of Saudi Arabia was in charge of his country's sovereign wealth fund, which made him directly responsible for investing billions worldwide. His focus had been the United States, Europe, and China. And when you invest that much money, you can move markets, make or break industries, and pick winners and losers *within* an industry. And that's what Mohammad bin Muqrin had done.

A year ago, he'd gone against his family's wishes and invested $25 billion in a company called Above All. On the company's website, Cole learned that they were a player in 5G technology, and their plan was to compete with the Chinese companies already leading the way in this field. Companies in which Ibo Kane was a primary investor. She didn't know much about 5G, but the connection was clear: Mohammad bin Muqrin had put an obscene amount of money into a company fighting Kane for dominance in a key market in China.

Some billionaires give lots of interviews, appear on TV frequently, or make spectacles of themselves on the sidelines of the professional sports teams they own. Some become famous because the products they create affect people's daily lives. Ibo Kane was one of the most-powerful and least-known billionaires on the planet. He had his tentacles in every business that mattered, and every business that *would* matter over the next twenty years. Both in China and in the U.S.

If Cole was right, he'd somehow gotten an online extremist group to begin systematically killing the people in a position to slow his ascent. It was impossible to believe, even as the evidence piled up before her.

Warren watched over her shoulder as she turned the research into notes, the notes into sentences, and sentences into paragraphs.

First she recounted—step by step—how the story had taken her from New York to D.C. to Miami to Las Vegas, and now to London. Fighting every instinct to leave herself out of the story, she told her part, and Warren's. It would make her theory credible, make her harder to smear. Next, she carefully laid out her theory, piece by piece.

She cut and pasted paragraphs, wrote transitions, rearranged, and re-read. The goal was to weave her personal narrative into the theory so—taken as a whole—the piece would read like a mystery, she and Warren the protagonists, with the final revelations appearing at the end.

She lay on the floor. "Will you read it? I need to stare at the ceiling for a bit. Clear my head. There's something missing, but I don't know what."

Cole traced a small crack in the ceiling with her eyes, glancing at Warren every few seconds to make sure he was still reading. When he reached the end, he leaned back and laced his fingers together behind his head. "Motive."

"I've got a motive," Cole said. "Business."

"True, but he's already a billionaire. Sure this would make him *more* money, but I don't see an *ultimate* motive. Like, where does Kane want to be in ten years?" He walked past her on the floor, taking a spot at the window.

She sat cross-legged and stared at the back of his head. "What are you thinking?"

"Odd conversation with my professor. Used to be a wild-eyed radical, twenty years ago. Now, well I don't know what he is exactly, but he's sympathetic with the views in the manifesto. He's anti-globalization, anti-cellphone, anti-bank, and so on."

"There are a lot of off-ramps between those views and condoning international terrorism and murder."

470

He turned, holding up both hands defensively. "You don't have to convince me. Lemme finish. He had this whole spiel about China. I'm thinking anyone at the top of the business world would know all the dirty secrets about U.S.-China relations, know the way the businesses interact. Kane is an American citizen, but of Chinese descent. With a lot of business in both China and U.S. He—"

"Where are you going with this?"

"I don't know," Warren said. "It's like he was trying to tell me something without *telling* me. Or no, not that. It's like he himself didn't even know, but was trying to talk it out. Some way that the ideology of the terrorists relates to China."

Cole stood, walked a lap around the room, then sat at her laptop. "I hear you, but that's not anything I can put in my story."

"I know."

She scrolled to the top of her article. "How about you get us food while I take one more pass?"

106

Warren came back an hour later with a bag of food. "Fish and chips."

"I can smell the fries." She grabbed her phone from the night-stand. "Don't tell me you're stressed enough to eat carbs."

He opened the bag and held up a plastic container. A huge salad topped with grilled fish.

"Oh." She swiped open her phone, grabbed a couple soggy fries from the bag, and popped them in her mouth. She had a notification in her Signal app.

"What is it?" Warren asked.

She stopped chewing, eyes wide. "What in the hell?"

"Cole, what?"

She waved him over and he joined her. The message contained no text, only a one-page PDF attachment. The subject line read *Ibo Kane.*

In the near future, wars won't be fought with bombs or missiles, but in the digital realm. A single entity with control over communications, financial systems, social media, and data storage will hold power over entire nations. By 2030, digital currencies and AI-driven surveillance will control global economies and societies. Right now, China leads in this digital revolution, with a model of centralized control that the West can't match. While the U.S. and Europe struggle, China's head start gives them the upper hand.

There's an unseen war raging—one that will decide the future of global governance.

Kane, Inc. must win this war.

If China controls the digital economy, from cryptocurrencies to surveillance networks, they'll be able to dictate global trade, suppress free speech, and manipulate political outcomes.

The West, bogged down by fragmented systems, is too slow to react. Every moment spent in stagnation strengthens China's grip. They will have the power to reshape economies, censor ideas, and control resources—all through the networks they own.

Imagine a world where a single entity can control financial transactions, determine who gets to speak, and influence public opinion at scale. This is the future, and we can't let China or any other power dominate it. Kane, Inc. has the resources to take control of the digital infrastructure that will define the next era.

The West has failed to recognize the threat posed by China's digital rise. Kane, Inc. must act now, or we'll be left behind in the age of algorithmic control.

They read the document, then Warren sat on the bed and dug into his salad as Cole read it again. She hadn't asked anyone for help. Only five or six of her closest colleagues and sources had her contact information on Signal. No one but Warren knew she'd been researching Kane. And yet, someone *did* know.

"How could someone... someone hacked my laptop or phone. Someone figured out where my research was headed."

"You didn't tell anyone about Kane?" Warren asked.

She shook her head. "You know what's crazy? My very first instinct was to guard my scoop. If we're on to something, whoever has access to my computer can now leak it. Gotta get this out fast."

"But they *didn't* leak it."

"They did the opposite." She turned back to the document. She hadn't even noticed the stamp on the top-right corner, and she read it out loud. "*Kane, Inc., Internal Memo, Executive Committee Only.*"

"If this is true," Warren said, "Kane isn't just after profits— he's after *control*."

Cole nodded. "Dominate not just communications, but every- thing. If he controls the financial and information networks, he

473

controls economies, resources, even free will. It's more than business—it's global dominance."

Warren leaned back, processing. "This is worse than I thought. World domination through total digital control. And they're already halfway there."

Cole swallowed hard, her voice a whisper. "Total world domination."

⊕

In journalism, "the lede" was the opening paragraph, or "graf." It's where reporters stuffed the news, the thing that was *new*.

Neil Armstrong Walks on Moon.

President Kennedy Shot in Dallas.

She always wrote the lede last. Armed with the new information about Kane, Cole wrote hers.

It was 1 AM on Christmas Eve by the time she was ready to send the story to Alex Vane at *The Barker*. She attached the file and added a short note.

Dear Alex,

I've got a story for you. It's not "reporting" and it's not "guesswork." It's somewhere in between. It's 7,000 words. Get your art department going. You'll need photos of all the victims, plus Ibo Kane.

If you have my direct deposit information still on file, send payment.

- Jane Cole

She sent the email and sat on her bed. "I'm about to become the most famous reporter on the planet, or a laughingstock."

Warren laughed, then his face grew serious. He opened his mouth, but said nothing. Instead, he detached his prosthetic leg.

Cole watched his face eagerly. She was out on a ledge, and needed him to join her there. "This thing is dangerous. For me, for you. Our careers. Everything." She sighed. "And I'm way too close to it. I know that."

"You sent it, right?"

She nodded.

"Then take a sleeping pill," Warren said. "When will the story go live?"

"It's late afternoon in Seattle. Probably the end of the night—ten or eleven, their time."

"Grab six hours of sleep while you can. Like you said, you're

474

about to be the most famous reporter or a laughingstock, right? But I think you're missing something, and I'm surprised. Something about the way the news works now."

Cole squinted. What was he implying? The intensity of the day was still with her. The energy, the focus, and the drive to get at the truth. She had to slow her mind to see the bigger picture. Then it hit her. "Both." She laughed bitterly. "I'm going to be both."

"Exactly. Even if the story is right, the propaganda machines will kick in hard, discrediting you, making you into a joke. Ain't like the FBI will read the story and bust down Kane's door fifteen minutes later. Dude lives on a seastead half the time anyway. Private island country off the coast of French Polynesia."

He was right. The media ecosystem had changed in the last ten years. Part of her still believed the truth would rule the day. But that was rarely how things worked anymore. Most people got their news online, where echo chambers and curated news allowed them to hear what they wanted, or what someone else wanted them to hear. If Ibo Kane was as powerful as he appeared, he'd use that power to confuse, discredit, and lie.

They slipped under the covers in their separate beds, each staring at the ceiling. Cole said, "In the newsroom at the *Sun*, I used to tell my editors to keep pushing me until my lede made their face look like that one emoji—the shocked-face one—eyes wide open. Ya know that look?"

Warren nodded, rustling the bed linens.

"That's what your face looked like when you read my lede."

"I thought I'd masked it."

She chuckled. "You didn't. It was good?"

"Very."

"We're screwed, right?"

Warren laughed. "Yup. We are *absolutely* screwed."

She closed her eyes and the world went blank. Her mind buzzed with gray static, the caffeine battling the extreme fatigue. She played her lede over and over in her head, anticipating how it would land in the world.

The sleeping pill slowly overpowered the caffeine. Her thoughts slowed. The story faded.

Before she knew it, she fell asleep.

107

Thursday

Cole took a bite of a blueberry muffin and, for the hundredth time that morning, refreshed the homepage of *The Barker*. Her story wasn't live yet.

The restaurant was decorated in greens and reds, white paper snowflakes taped on the wall. "Today is Christmas Eve," Cole said. "Easy to forget when you're in something like this."

She checked her email. There was a message from a fact-checker at *The Barker*, a final question about her source for the details of the Ana Diaz murder. Cole explained that she was the source, that it was an eyewitness account. She'd already had two phone calls with Alex Vane, the owner of *The Barker*. He'd peppered her with a hundred questions, trying to ensure both the veracity of the story and the clarity with which it was communicated. It wasn't just Cole's reputation on the line, it was his as well.

She placed her phone face down on the table.

For better or worse, the story would break the internet. The young people at *The Barker* would make sure it did. That's what they did best. Her phone would blow up. Text messages. Emails. Calls. She'd be swarmed, digitally surrounded. The fake video would go even more viral.

She'd written big stories before, but they were big *locally*. They got her a few congratulatory texts from peers and—once or twice—five-minute hits on cable news when a story happened to have national appeal.

This was different. If her theory was wrong, it would be twenty-four hours of activity, followed by silence.

If it was right…

Warren pushed his empty plate aside. "Things are about to get weird."

"They've *been* weird. Things are about to… there's not a word for it. But you read my mind. One time, when Matt and I almost decided to have kids, must have been seven years ago, I asked his mom about it. What's it like? That kind of thing. She told me it's not describable, there's literally nothing that can prepare you. She said if you knew how much work and time and money and effort it took, you'd never have kids. Not that she regretted it, of course. Just that, until it really hits you, your brain can't project the future and imagine it. As she told me this, I got a feeling of being a small, fragile creature, fundamentally vulnerable and limited. Like there was a huge lifeforce outside me, coming toward me. Like when you arrive at the beach late at night and you can't see it but you can hear it and feel it. The immensity is there and you *know* it."

"I know the feeling. I didn't *know* I knew it until I got sober and realized one of the reasons I drank was to escape that immensity. Marina. She changed everything and I regret every day how I responded to it."

"You can still fix it," Cole said.

He put his hand on hers. "Maybe."

She looked at him and, for the first time in days, smiled. She was exhausted, but she'd done it. "I have that feeling now. Like I'm a tiny piece of driftwood on the beach, the enormity of the ocean nearby."

"Ready to wash you away?"

She squeezed his hand. "It's going to wash *us* away. You're in the videos. You're in the article. You ready for this?"

Warren squeezed her hand, then pulled away and sipped his coffee. "I'm not. I'm really not. Too late now."

"You warned Sarah?"

"Sent her an email earlier, yeah. I really don't think it's gonna be as bad as you think."

Cole let out a weak laugh, almost a whimper. "What's about to happen has never happened before."

"I've always wondered, when a story actually goes live, or is published or whatever, do they tell you? Do you get a notification or anything?"

"Nah, I just have to keep checking the homepage." She swiped open her phone. "Not up yet."

They sat in silence for a long minute, the downtime allowing another issue to move from the back to the front of her mind. "I created a fake Facebook profile. I'm going to reach out to Lopez." She acknowledged Warren's questioning look. "The guy Frankie told us about." She paused, but kept her eyes down. She didn't want to see the look of pinched disapproval she assumed Warren would be wearing. "Just need to build out the profile with a few more friends and posts, then I'll contact him. He's single, desperate, and I think he's ready to break. If I can get him to confess, I'll take him down, and Morgan too. If they killed Matt, I'll drag them into the desert, bury them to their necks in the sand, and stone them to death." She paused again, letting out a long sigh. "Just... thought you should know."

When she finally looked up, Warren wasn't frowning as she'd expected. She couldn't read his look. "That's cold. And probably not smart." He nodded. "But it's what I'd do."

She checked her phone. The headline on the homepage of *The Barker* was two levels tall, taking up her entire screen.

"NINE MURDERS" PLOT SOLVED
EXCLUSIVE REPORT FROM *THE BARKER*

December 24, 2023

By Jane Cole

She flashed the phone to Warren, who smiled and took it. "Things are about to get real."

"They are," she said. "Read me the lede graf. I want to hear it from outside myself, the way the whole world will hear it."

"Want me to use a fancy newscaster voice? Dan Rather or Brian Williams?"

"Just read it," she said.

Warren cleared his throat. "Eleven days ago, Raj Ambani was shot at the Metropolitan Museum of Art. Three days later, Alvin

478

Meyers fell, assassinated on the roof of The Watergate Hotel. Three days after that, Ana Diaz was killed in Miami. Later that day, the world found out why: a band of extremists had set out to terrorize the world, eliminating anyone who stood in the way of their aims. Three days ago, Mohammad bin Muqrin became their fourth victim. Now the world waits for victim number five, unsure who will be next, but certain of the motivations of the killers.

The world is wrong.

One man is behind the killings: Ibo Kane. He's the mastermind of a plot so wide it will stretch your imagination, a plan so sinister it will shock your conscience. We don't yet know the full extent of his diabolical plot, but we now know its outline. In the following pages, you'll learn how he did it, and why."

—End of Episode 5—

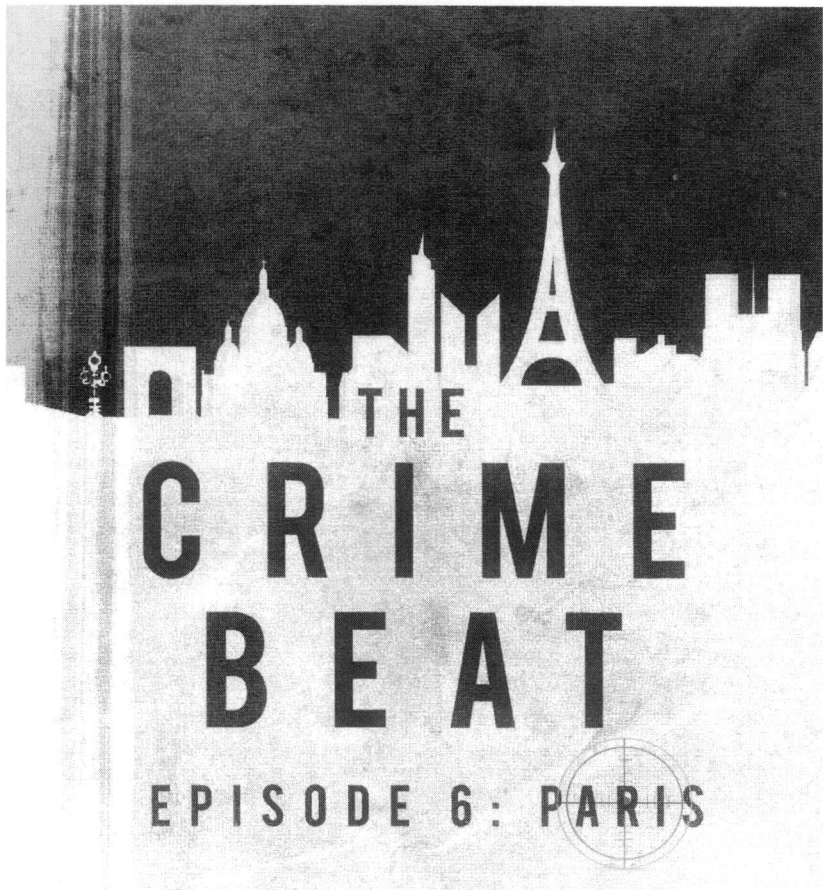

THE CRIME BEAT

EPISODE 6: PARIS

108

Thursday

"General Ki, the shot was not possible. *C'était impossible.*" The Shepherd pressed the phone to his ear, eager for a reply. He looked out the window. Snow fell softly, piling on the frozen lawn in front of the *École d'économie de Paris* across the street. The tracks of five men had left a path leading into the famed Paris School of Economics.

One of the five had been his target. The target he'd failed to kill.

He ran a hand down the barrel of the custom-made, .50-caliber rifle in his lap, petting it like a cat to give him comfort. A gust of wind blew through the small opening in the window and he shivered. "General Ki? Are you still on the line?"

General Ki spoke. "The target is inside?"

"*Oui.* As far as I know. He entered moments ago. There is movement on the fifth floor."

"Through windows?"

"*Précisément.*"

"Is there a shot?" Ki asked.

"No." The absurd modern architecture of the *École d'économie de Paris* blocked all lines of fire. The building had colorful, narrow windows, set at odd angles that left no clear view into the building.

That's why The Shepherd and his brothers had planned the shot as they had. The annual Christmas Eve brunch gathering of economic heavyweights never had much security. Until today. Around the world, men like David Fontes were afraid, and with fear came extra protection. "What do you suggest, General?"

While The Shepherd waited for a reply he mentally recited the words. *An international brotherhood, united by General Ki for a singular mission: to end the technological oppression, to restore the sovereignty of the individual, to birth a new era of freedom.* He felt no shame in failing General Ki. There was mutual respect between them. Not enough for The Shepherd to proceed on his own, but enough to report what had happened honestly and reassess the situation. He was a soldier awaiting the next command. But the long silence on the line worried him. Another icy breeze snuck through the window and he raised his jacket collar against the cold.

General Ki said, "Tell me exactly what happened."

The Shepherd explained. As expected, the limousine had been traveling south on *Boulevards des Maréchaux* and turned right on *Rue de la Tombe-Issoire*. That's when everything went wrong. His target hadn't slipped out of the limo onto the sidewalk and walked the thirty feet to the entrance. Instead, two men had gotten out, each holding a large umbrella. Then two more men, also with umbrellas. The four men stood close together near the rear door. The snow had come fast, landing on the umbrellas covering the four men. Further obscuring the shot was a large tree strung with Christmas lights that stood near the parked car. David Fontes had exited the limo and hustled into the *École d'économie de Paris*, a man on either side of him, plus one in front and one behind. Only the lower portion of his legs had been visible. "*C'était impossible,*" The Shepherd concluded.

"We can't deviate from the schedule. Security will only grow tighter."

"What would you have me do? There is simply no shot."

"Did you bring backup?" Ki asked.

A black duffel bag sat next to him. "*Oui.*"

"Then you know what to do."

The Shepherd considered as he glanced again at the blur of movement behind the colorful windows. "It's too uncertain."

"You'll have to go in."

A twinge of annoyance bubbled up within him. He'd argued

for a different location, and he'd been right. Damn modern architecture. As ugly as it was pretentious, and now it had cost him dearly. France really was going to hell. "I go in, I may not come out."

General Ki said nothing.

The Shepherd thought. That morning, he'd felt the first twinge of doubt when reading a new theory about the nine murders that had spread online. It had made its way onto French TV and, as he'd packed his duffel bag, he'd listened to the report. His cause was just and right, but that didn't mean others weren't benefiting from it as well. "The theories on the Internet, on TV. They are false?"

"All of them. False. I think you refer to one in particular."

The Shepherd was on high alert for a change in General Ki's tone, but the voice-modifier made his words sound similarly warped and tinny. "*Oui.*"

"False. Ibo Kane was one of the targets we considered. Hardly a mastermind. The reporter behind those lies will be, well…"

The Shepherd knew a threat when he heard it. He'd read the article, but hadn't checked the byline. If General Ki said he was coming for the reporter, then he was. And if he was coming for the reporter, there could be truth to what she'd written. But nevermind that. Whether or not there was truth to it, David Fontes deserved to die. "If I don't make it out, will you call my mother? I'm supposed to be there for church and Christmas dinner." Their tradition was a late dinner after Christmas Eve church services. Roast turkey with chestnuts, oysters, foie gras, and cheeses. For dessert, *Bûche de Noël*—rolled chocolate sponge cake.

"I will," Ki said.

"You'll take care of her?"

"I will."

Then it was decided. He'd storm the building. "I am The Good Shepherd. The Good Shepherd lays down his life for the sheep."

"Thank you, Shepherd."

The line went dead.

He stashed the phone in the duffel and pulled out binoculars, training them on the fifth floor of the building across the street. The largest conference room. The colored glass revealed movement, but no faces. He guessed there were seventy or eighty people inside, including the four security guards who'd led David Fontes in under the umbrella shroud.

⊕

There was no security at the front entrance. It made sense. This was a college of economics, not a bank or high-value target. The four flights of stairs were empty. Most of the school was on break. Security cameras monitored the stairwell landings, but he doubted extra security had been added. Had the head of the World Trade Organization been leading a gathering of world leaders in Geneva, or even participating in a regular council meeting, things might have been different. But this was a celebratory Christmas Eve brunch. The four umbrella guards had been deemed enough.

He cracked the door and peered down a long hallway that dead ended and turned right. He'd seen the blueprints. After the turn, the hallway continued for ten meters before reaching the meeting room.

Once he made that turn, he'd be committed. He let the door close and crouched on the stairwell landing, duffel bag in his lap.

He pulled out two handguns, a Glock 19 and a Beretta 93R. Two different weapons with two slightly different purposes, but using the same 9mm rounds. The Beretta was the older of the two, and the lesser weapon, but he was fond of it for no other reason than nostalgia. The first five or ten years protecting presidents had been some of his happiest. After leaving the *Groupe de sécurité de la présidence de la République*, he'd purchased the gun used for only fifty francs. It was a twin of the service pistol he carried during his fifteen years of service in the GSPR. Back then, he'd been Augustin Gustave Berger. Frenchman, patriot, hero, and he'd served France by protecting four presidents. Each had a code name, and he'd addressed them humbly at the time. When he'd been dishonorably discharged for posting negative comments about the French president on an Internet message board, everything changed. He now knew the men he'd once protected as François, Jacques, Nicolas, and Emmanuel. They were the men who'd given France away to the international tech giants.

He'd argued with General Ki that the last of these men, the current president of France, should be one of their targets, but the general had rebuffed him. Too risky. The president was a puppet

485

—better to focus on the leaders who pulled the strings behind the scenes. The men and women to whom he is beholden.

He stuck the Beretta in his belt and pulled a smoke grenade from the bag. He put on goggles. He left the duffel bag in the stairwell and cracked the door again. Still clear. Glock 19 in his right hand, held inconspicuously at his waist, he strode into the hallway.

After only a moment, the sound of heavy footsteps startled him.

He spun on his heels. Guards. The plan was already crumbling. But they weren't real police. Just losers in uniforms.

"*Qui êtes vous?*" one asked.

The other guard's eyes widened as he noticed the Glock, then shifted his eyes to the smoke grenade.

The Shepherd had two options. He could bolt for the corner and make it out of sight, but they'd likely be right on his heels. If they had the guts to follow him, they could shoot him in the back before he made it to the double door. Then again, only one of the two guards had a gun.

Even if he made it into the conference room before they reached him, they could cause problems. But if he dealt with them now, he'd be giving himself up. The shots would be heard in the meeting hall and he'd lose the element of surprise.

The guard on the left decided for him. He had no weapon, but he *did* have a radio. A kid of no more than twenty-five, he grabbed his radio with a trembling hand and raised it to his mouth as The Shepherd raised the Glock. He waited for the security guard's hand to reach his mouth, hoping he'd reconsider. The Shepherd met his eyes, shaking his head slightly as if to say, *Don't do this.*

As the guard touched the radio button with his finger, The Shepherd fired.

The high-velocity hollow point round knocked the kid back. A single shot through the heart. He was dead before he hit the ground.

The other guard was older, with ruddy cheeks and a round face that made him resemble a dumpling. He didn't reach for his gun. The Shepherd guessed that he never had. Instead he took off down the hall and The Shepherd shot him in the back. He took a few strides forward and fired another round into the back of his head to be sure.

Noise erupted from the meeting room. He turned and jogged down the hallway, pulling the pin from the smoke grenade as he rounded the corner. Ten meters ahead, the double door swung open. Two of the umbrella guards stepped out. One reached for his weapon.

The Shepherd lobbed the grenade underhanded, leaping to the right as he did. He hit the wall with his right shoulder, aiming the Glock as he fell to the ground. The canister rolled to their feet, releasing gray smoke that rose around their bodies. As they disappeared, he shot six times into the smoke, aiming for the spots where their chests had been.

A woman screamed, then two heavy thuds sounded.

He'd dropped the two guards.

He pushed himself up and darted through the smoke. He dropped the Glock and pulled the Beretta from his belt.

He had to shove one of the dead guards out of the way to get through the double door. Inside, people screamed and ran for the emergency exit on the far side of the hall. His eyes moved to the stage, where the other two umbrella guards stood on either side of a short, black-haired man. His target. They had him by his elbows, practically lifting him off the floor as they rushed across the stage.

The one on the right was larger; The Shepherd dropped him with a double-tap in the back. The other one turned and got a bullet in the forehead.

The target turned, hands up. "You cannot do this."

Around him, people streamed toward the exits. The Shepherd had taken out the four guards who'd led Fontes in. He doubted any Econ students or professors would try to be a hero. He'd enjoy this one. "David Fontes, for your role in selling out the people of France, I condemn you to die."

He aimed and pulled the trigger. *Click.*

Nothing happened.

He fumbled with the weapon. The spent casing hadn't ejected after his last shot. The slide was half open with a half-seated round. An instant of panic overwhelmed him before his training took over. He tapped, racked, and cleared the malfunction in less than a second.

Not fast enough.

When The Shepherd looked up, Fontes was on his knees

holding a gun. He'd rolled behind the motionless body of the larger of his two security guards. Before The Shepherd could fire, a bullet hit his chest. It felt like a hard shove, followed by the most intense, searing pain he'd ever experienced. He looked down. Blood appeared through his white shirt. He heard a sucking sound, air leaving his lungs.

He fell back and crumpled to the ground, blinking furiously through the pain as Fontes jumped down from the stage and pushed for the exit.

The Shepherd's vision blurred. He rolled onto his belly and closed his left eye, trying to focus on the black suit. The black hair. *I am The Good Shepherd. The Good Shepherd lays down his life for the sheep.*

The screams around him faded. The world closed into a square patch of black, his target's suit, and an oval patch of black, his target's hair. Using a last gasp of strength, he clicked the selector switch on the 93R to three-round burst. He pulled the trigger.

Two bursts did the job.

David Fontes hit the floor. The shots had connected with his upper back, probably hitting a lung. Or both lungs. He'd die slowly over the next five or ten minutes.

The Shepherd rolled onto his back and stared at the ceiling. He moved into the lights.

When he closed his eyes, the lights stayed with him, filling his mind. He *was* the light, had been the light all along.

It was odd. He didn't feel one way or another about accomplishing his mission. He'd thought it would feel different. Better.

As the light filled his whole body, he wondered whether General Ki would take care of his mother, as promised.

109

"I can't believe I didn't see it." Cole shook her head slowly. "I never thought I'd say this, but thank God for internet mobs digging up old information."

Warren leaned his head against the window of the train and let out a long sigh. "It's not proof. Just another theory."

The world outside had gone dark when the train entered the Chunnel. Now they were two-hundred feet beneath the surface of the water, halfway between London and Paris. The train offered good wifi, so Cole had spent the last hour reading reactions to her Ibo Kane story. There were a lot of them. Articles and research were appearing faster than she could keep up with. One theory in particular, hatched by a blogger named *1-Der*, had struck a chord.

"It's proof," she insisted. "General Ki *is* Ibo Kane. The *Ki* is his online name. His initials, backwards. IK. KI."

"Might be, but—"

"No," Cole interrupted. "Read."

She handed him her phone, open to an article about Kane's first social media company, *SmartFace*, which had grown huge in the mid-2000s before Facebook eclipsed it. "His screen name was Ki back then, too. People get attached to their early online personas. He thought all evidence was erased when SmartFace went belly up, but... obviously not."

Warren glanced at the article. "The Internet is forever."

Cole looked out the window, trying to pick out seams in the dark tunnel walls. She imagined the weight of the water above them—the Strait of Dover—pressing down and shattering the tunnel. If that happened, she'd drown like a rat.

A new article about her theory appeared every few minutes online. Next to the shootout at the *École d'économie de Paris*, it was the number one trending story in the world. Even some TV networks had picked up her theory, though most had yet to vet it. A worldwide manhunt for Chandler Price was underway. As far as she knew, Ibo Kane was not yet being investigated. Despite the irrational fear of drowning, she felt safer in the tunnel. The French media would probably be waiting for her when she emerged in Paris. "The screenshots showing Kane used 'Ki' as a screen name don't *prove* my story right, but they're damn good evidence."

Warren shook his head. "All the stuff I read about your article basically said, 'Yeah, but…'"

"I'll write a follow-up, but it'll take a day. I honestly didn't see David Fontes or the WTO as a target, and I don't know how Kane benefits. I'm sure it's there, but it'll take time." She sighed and stared again into the darkness.

Warren broke a long silence. "This morning while you were in the shower, I called Sarah."

Cole turned, eyebrow raised. "And?"

"Back in the day, she and I talked about going to Paris. Said we'd go when Marina was old enough to remember it." He shrugged. "Maybe seven or eight. Feels wrong to be going now, with you, to look into a murder."

Cole shook her head. "More of a slaughter this time. The fifth murder, with a half-dozen bonus murders. Sloppy. Getting more desperate?"

Warren shrugged. "Or security is tightening, which they had to anticipate."

There was irritation in his tone. Cole got the sense he wanted to talk about Sarah. "Sorry, what did Sarah say? She see the video of you saving that kid?"

He nodded. "Said, 'Stop trying to be a hero. Marina misses you.'"

"What'd you say?"

"What *could* I say? She's right. Instead of being a dad I'm… I don't know what I'm doing."

Cole brought up the Facebook App on her phone, then remembered something. "You didn't ask her about Bakari Smith, did you? She know you figured out they're dating?"

"I held back," Warren said. "*Wanted* to bring it up, but..."

"Good. That would have been... not good. Want some free advice?"

Warren raised an eyebrow.

"You want Sarah back, right?"

He nodded.

"Even though she's been with Bakari, possibly others?"

His face grew pinched, but he nodded slowly. "I can force myself to get over that."

"Good. Most women want to be with the father of their kids unless they're real scumbags. You've been sober for a long time now. Four years?"

"A little over."

"Right. You got your life back together." His frown told her he didn't agree. "Well, not exactly *together*, I guess. No job. Traveling around the world with a crazy reporter. But you're sober, you love her, and you love Marina. When you get home, don't tell her. Show her. Put everything you have into being stable and being there for Marina." She paused. "I doubt she's fallen in love. No offense to Bakari, but he isn't *in love* material."

Warren cracked a small smile.

The train's trajectory shifted as it began its ascent. Light appeared ahead and they exited the tunnel.

"France," Cole said. "Never been. Matt and I..." She trailed off. "Speaking of love." She was back on Facebook, adding new posts to her fake profile.

Warren looked down at her phone. "You're not gonna..."

"I am."

She scrolled through Julio Lopez's latest posts. More quotes from the Bible and a selfie at a soccer field that depicted him sweaty and smiling. Behind him in the photo stood a dozen men and women dressed in shorts and soccer cleats. The caption read, "Lucky to have a sunny day for our weekly game. No game next week, but come join us in the new year."

The location tag indicated Memorial Park in Houston. A perfect opening. She sent him a friend request, then composed a private message:

Hey there! I'm new to Houston and, totally randomly, met someone who said you organize co-ed soccer at Memorial Park on weekends. I played in high school, but want to get back into it. I hear you're an incredible keeper.

Cole looked up when she felt Warren's eyes move from her screen to her face. "What?"

"Keeper?"

"It means *goalie*." Her tone took on a defensive note. "It's how real soccer fans talk. I looked it up."

He shook his head. "You have no shame?"

"If he was in on killing Matt, no. Hell no. If he wasn't"—she paused to consider—"still no." She sent the message.

"Ask me," Warren said, "totally wrong approach. Guys—unless they're a rare breed and truly full of themselves, truly confident—are skeptical when a hot woman shows interest. Look at his profile. He knows he's damaged goods. You need to be damaged too if you want him to buy it."

She chuckled. "Damaged goods? Me? That won't be hard to pull off."

Warren smiled. "I'd have chosen a less attractive woman for your picture." He pointed down at the beautiful, black-haired woman on her profile. "No way Lopez believes a woman that hot messages him about a soccer game."

Cole turned off her phone. "You could be right. But I think most men are led around by their desire to be noticed by attractive women. They can't help it."

"You think that's what I want?"

Cole studied his face.

He squinted, half frowning.

She squinted back. "Hmmm."

A smile broke out over his face. "You tryin' to read me, Cole?"

"I *am* reading you."

"And?"

"No." Her voice grew serious. "Most men never mature. You did. Maybe Afghanistan. Or losing half your leg."

"It was losing Sarah. Marina. Forced me to look at myself."

She nodded. "In any case, you're no Julio Lopez. He won't be able to resist the possibility—no matter how slim—that a beautiful woman wants to play soccer with him. Bet I hear back in a couple hours."

"What then?"

She shrugged. "I chat with him. Make him comfortable—get him to confess."

"Just like that?" Warren looked skeptical.

"Yeah."

"If it doesn't work?"

"Plan B."

They rode in silence along the coast as the English Channel drifted by outside the window to their right. The train turned southwest, passing through frozen countryside and small towns. They were almost to Paris.

"Another thing," Warren said. "Your theory was basically that Ibo Kane is behind these murders for business reasons, not political reasons. If that's true, and it's also true he's *the* General Ki…" He cocked his head to the side and trailed off.

He didn't need to finish. Cole had been wondering the same thing. Though she was certain she was right about the fundamental facts, there were dozens of unanswered questions. And one stood out. If Kane's motivations had nothing to do with the politics espoused by the extremists carrying out the murders, how had he convinced them to join him? Were they all in on it, or had he manipulated them?

The train arrived at the *Gare du Nord* station in Paris half an hour later. Cole handed Warren his bag from the overhead rack. "You reserved a place to stay?"

"Hotel. Three nights. I figure you go check in while I go to the Embassy. Maybe they can tell me something."

He'd explained that a few Marine Security Guards were stationed at the U.S. Embassy in Paris. He hoped to get information about the Parisian shooter—possibly even a contact within the Paris police department. If he could somehow connect the dead shooter to Ibo Kane, it would be further proof of Cole's theory. It might break the story wide open. If Kane could be clearly implicated in masterminding even one of the killings, that would be enough to force world governments to act.

"Think you'll get anything?" Cole asked.

Warren shrugged. "Got a better idea?"

Cole pulled her bag from the luggage rack and stood in line in the aisle. "I guess I'll return some of the media inquiries. Someone might have something to trade that'll advance the story." She'd gotten hundreds of pings since her story went live on *The Barker*. She hadn't responded to any. The more she said, the more the story would evolve until it was about *her*, rather than Kane. A spotlight on her would only make her job harder.

The line began moving and Warren joined her in the aisle. Cole glanced out the window and stopped short. Two uniformed officers stood by the door, peering in as if waiting for someone. One was tall and slightly built. His eyes were narrowed on Warren, who fumbled with his bag. As Cole watched the officer, her stomach turned. His eyes moved from Warren to her. A look of recognition passed over his face. He nudged the officer next to him, who stepped forward.

"Warren." She elbowed him gently in the side, eyes still on the officers. "They're waiting for us."

Warren shot a look behind him. The aisle was packed with people and luggage.

"We're not escaping." Cole pointed out the window behind them, where two more officers guarded the rear door. She and Warren dutifully inched forward as the line moved. "What do you think they want?"

Warren shrugged, his look stern—maybe fearful, too.

They reached the door and stepped onto the platform, where the slender officer approached and took Warren by the forearm. "Mr. Robert Warren?" He had a thick French accent.

"Yes," Warren said. "What is this about?"

The officer ignored the question and turned to Cole. "Jane Cole?"

"Yes."

Another officer stepped forward and put a hand behind her elbow, barely touching her but clearly indicating that she was to come with him. She flinched. Sweat beaded on her forehead. Her hands felt clammy. She and Warren had shown their passports to get on the train in London. Cole expected they'd have to show them again in Paris, but tourists with American passports didn't require a special visa to visit Paris.

Warren looked focused, but calm. She figured he'd been in situations much worse than this. "I'm sorry, what is this about?"

"I am Capitaine Abbé Bisset. You are being lawfully detained.

494

We will explain. Come." He nodded down the platform definitively.

Cole and Warren walked side by side with the two officers down the platform, up an escalator, and into a small room through a door marked *Police*.

Bisset pointed at two chairs behind a small desk. "Sit."

They sat.

"I know my rights," Warren said firmly. "What's the problem here? Do you need to see our passports? Are we under arrest?"

Bisset sat across from them. "You are *not* under arrest. Not... exactly. You're being held on the basis of a diffusion notice." His accent made him hard to understand, and his voice was thin and wispy, like a trail of smoke from a chimney that could be dissolved by a slight wind.

Cole looked from Bisset to Warren, dumfounded. "What the hell is a diffusion notice?"

"Interpol." Warren's eyes dropped to the floor. "A red notice. Some country issued warrants for our arrest."

"What country?" Cole asked.

"Don't know. Could be any Interpol country other than France."

"Why other than France?"

"Because if it was France, we'd already be under arrest."

110

Bisset leaned forward and rested his elbows on the small table. He had big, hollow eyes and the skin was tight over his bony face. "You are a journalist?"

"I am." Cole tried to sound calm, but her insides roiled.

The other officer had stepped into an adjacent room, though his voice was audible through the door. He was younger than Bisset and spoke French rapidly in a soft voice. Even had his voice been loud enough to make out individual words, Cole wouldn't have understood them.

Bisset turned to Warren. "And you?"

"NYPD. Retired Marine." Warren's words had even more edge than usual.

Bisset smiled. "There is no need to be confrontational, Mr. Warren. I am just doing my job."

"And your job in this case is?"

"As I said, a diffusion notice has been issued. France is encouraged"—Bisset raised a finger—"though not required, to comply. You are being lawfully detained as we contact the proper authorities." He leaned back and laced his hands behind his head, seemingly content to take it easy as the other officer dealt with the phone calls.

Warren pointed at the other officer, visible through a window in the door. "What's he doing?"

496

"Interpol is a complicated system. He is figuring out what to do."

Warren put his hands flat on the table. The veins in his temples popped. "As a veteran, I have the right to contact the U.S. Embassy. I am formally requesting permission to make such a call."

Cole put a hand on his thigh under the desk. She needed him to stay calm.

Bisset undersold it when he said Interpol was a complicated system. Any country in the system could issue a Red Notice, essentially an international warrant for arrest. Partner countries could choose to honor the notice and extradite the suspect. If she and Warren had arrest warrants issued by an Interpol country, the last thing they needed was for Warren to commit a crime in Paris by leaping across the table and assaulting Bisset.

A voice came through Bisset's radio and he stepped to the corner of the room. As he spoke, Cole whispered to Warren, "What the hell is happening?"

Warren shooed her away. He was listening to the conversation between Bisset and the man on the radio.

"You speak French?" Cole whispered.

"No. I heard '*École d'économie de Paris.*' They're talking about the latest shooting."

The other officer returned from the adjoining room and whispered something to Bisset, who rubbed his chin, then sat.

Before Bisset could reply, Warren stood. "I understand you're short staffed because of the tragedy at *École d'économie de Paris.* We are journalists, in Paris legally, writing about the nine murders case. Interpol can't arrest us on a Red Notice, and we've committed no crimes in France. I'll give you the name of the hotel we're staying at. You're free to monitor us there. But I *demand* a call to the U.S. Embassy."

Bisset spoke into his radio and sat, then waved an arm at Warren's empty chair. "Mr. Warren. Please."

Warren sat.

"Ms. Cole, Mr. Warren. I am required to inform you that a diffusion notice has been issued by Chinese authorities for your arrest. A diffusion notice is a country-to-country notice. China is seeking your arrest for—"

"China?" Warren stood again, squeezed the desk with both

hands, and leaned in. "China? The reason they issued a diffusion notice and not a red notice was to fool idiots like you into detaining us illegally." He glanced at Cole. "A Red Notice goes out to all 194 Interpol countries. A diffusion notice is on the down low, from one country to another. Whoever is behind this knew we were coming to Paris. They didn't want other countries to see it because they *know* it's bogus." He turned back to Bisset. "Captain Bisset. I'm telling you, give me a call to the U.S. Embassy. I promise you won't regret it."

Bisset walked to the next room where he whispered in French to the other officer. Cole only made out two words of their conversation. *"Américains stupides!"*

Eyes still on the officers, she said, "Ibo Kane. You think he has enough sway with Chinese authorities to get them to issue a diffusion notice?"

Warren nodded. "Or he has people in China who did it without him even asking. Jane, look at me."

She drew her eyes slowly from the two French officers. Warren's face was hard, but his eyes pleading. "We *cannot* allow ourselves to be sent to China. If we are, that's it. They'll hold us there for weeks, months. Eventually, they'd let us go. Or maybe no one would ever hear from us again. My guess is Kane—or people who work for him—saw your article and are trying to make us disappear. Getting us into China is the best way to do that. If they have enough clout with the French authorities, they can get us shipped to China before anyone notices."

Bisset returned carrying a white land line telephone. "Make your call."

"You'll let us go?"

"I did not say that. Make your call, and if the Embassy sends representation for you, they can discuss this with my superior, who is ready to take the call."

Cole watched the back of Warren's bald head. He'd been on hold for five minutes after being transferred around and around the U.S. Embassy. No one he knew was there, and he agreed to be transferred to someone who held the title "Diplomatic Liaison."

She wanted to tell him to relax, but his hand gripped the phone so hard his knuckles were white.

A few notices were pinned to the wall, written in French. A cork board similar to the one she'd used in London was pinned with surveillance images of wanted men and women. Through a small window, a large Christmas tree with white lights and silver bulbs was visible in the center of the train station. More lights were strung along a railing. People came and went with luggage and packages. Christmas Eve in Paris.

She stared again at Warren's head and let her eyes go soft. The tension and immediacy of the moment faded. Assuming she didn't get sent to China today, she'd wake up tomorrow to Christmas Day in Paris. She'd always wanted a Parisian Christmas, but not like this. She'd dreamt of coming with Matt. They were never big shoppers, but they'd talked about spending one day in the fancy Paris shops. They'd each make one extravagant purchase. A $1,000 purse for her, maybe. A $3,000 linen suit for him. One ridiculous expense they couldn't afford, just to say they'd shopped extravagantly in Paris.

From the corner of the room, a security camera stared down at her. The two officers watched fixedly. Without warning, an unfamiliar feeling gripped her. She looked from the camera to the officers, then back to Warren. He stood motionless, coiled like a tiger, ready to pounce when someone came back on the line. For the first time, she realized how vulnerable they were. Even when she'd been held at knifepoint in New York and chased through D.C. and Miami, she'd felt in charge.

Now, paranoia crept in. There was nothing she could do but hope for Warren's success. Hope someone at the U.S. Embassy cared enough to work a little magic. She was at the mercy of an international legal system she didn't understand and didn't believe was on the up and up. If things went poorly, she'd be in a Chinese prison on Christmas.

"Yes." Warren's voice brought her back. "Right, okay." He turned to face Cole. "Mrs. Fires. Yes... yes this is Robert Warren... Kandahar, no but I served in... yes, that's right."

His face relaxed and his eyes softened. His shoulders dropped. Warren expressed his emotions through his body more than anyone she'd ever known. She didn't need to hear the other end of the call. Something good was happening.

"That would be excellent," he said. He listened again, cracking a smile. An actual, ear to ear smile. "Yes, ma'am. Improvise, adapt, and overcome."

He hung up the phone and handed it back to Bisset, then sat. "She'll be here in half an hour."

"Who?"

"Carolyn Fires. She's the RSO."

Cole's face was blank.

"Regional Security Officer. Special Agent of the U.S. Diplomatic Security Service."

It sounded important, but Cole couldn't make heads or tails of all the different agencies and roles within the military and state department. "What does that mean?"

Warren sat next to her. "She's a badass, and she's coming to help."

111

Carolyn Fires burst through the door like she owned the place, a leather padfolio in one hand, a giant plastic cup full of iced tea in the other. "Who's in charge here?" she barked.

Warren stood to greet her. "Thanks for coming."

She shook his hand and turned to Cole, who also stood. "Thanks for coming."

"Where are they?"

Warren nodded toward the adjoining room, where the two French officers had scrambled to their feet.

Fires set her iced tea on the desk next to Cole. "Wait here."

A commanding woman—and not just because of her large stature—Fires wore a navy blue skirt suit, her chest pinned with medals. Among them was a bronze star. She'd dressed to intimidate.

Fires met the French officers at the door, nearly knocking them over. Forcing her way into the adjoining room, she closed the door behind her.

"What do you think she'll say?" Cole asked.

"She'll find out what this is all about. Technically, they don't have to tell her, but they will. They don't want to piss off the U.S. Embassy without a *really* good reason."

"We're not a good reason?"

Warren shrugged. "Hope not."

For five minutes, they watched through the small pane of glass in the door. They couldn't hear her words, but every so often a single word was shouted loud enough to slip through the door.

"*Abhorrent.*"

"*China.*"

"*First Amendment.*"

"*Reporters.*"

Fires gestured as she spoke, like a defense attorney making a closing argument. The back of her head bobbed, her bright red hair swaying as she pounded the air with her fist. Sometimes she waved the leather padfolio, and once or twice Cole heard it *thwack* onto the desk. After a few minutes, Bisset handed her a phone, into which she began shouting.

"Damn," Warren said.

"I know, right? She's a Marine?"

"And a lawyer. Utter badass."

"Why's she helping us?" Cole asked.

"Few reasons. The Marines connection doesn't hurt. And it's embarrassing to America if two of its citizens get sent from France to China on a diffusion notice. My guess is she Googled us. Your name is trending because of the article. If you disappear into China, it'll be an international incident. You can see the headlines, right? *American journalist detained by oppressive Chinese government.*"

"Americans love hating on reporters, right up to the point where one gets detained by China. Then everyone loves us again."

"I'm not touching that one." Warren shifted in his seat. "Part of it could be that Fires is bored of paperwork. You'd be amazed how little action there is at the Embassy."

Fires emerged suddenly, grabbed her iced tea, and drank half of it in one long pull from the straw. "Stand up. We're leaving, but first we need to talk."

They stood.

The French officers tried to follow Fires in, but she slammed the door in their faces and held up a hand apologetically as if to say, *Please, give me a minute.*

She turned back to Cole and Warren. "Got any enemies in China?"

"I wrote an article about Ibo Kane. He's of Chinese descent, but American. Any way he could—"

Fires held up a hand. "Ding, ding, ding. The way this crap

works is, some billionaire can get to Chinese police and make them issue a notice. Guess is, Kane had a Chinese national do it on his behalf. Putin does this kind of thing all the time to harass his enemies abroad. It's his hobby. The reason they used a diffusion notice instead of a red notice was to keep it on the down low. Didn't want all the Interpol countries to know about it." Fires raised her eyebrows. "Good instincts to call the Embassy, Rob."

"What's the bottom line?" Warren asked.

"They're letting you go under my supervision, but you have to surrender your passports until we get this straightened out. I'll talk to the chief of police later today, but it'll be tough to get anything done. Christmas. Might have to wait a couple days in Paris. In addition to the French police, I'll contact my counterpart in China. Always have to connect with the issuing country on these things. See if I can squash it." She faced Warren. "Improvise, adapt, and overcome."

Warren offered a warm smile. His demeanor had changed around Frankie in Las Vegas, and it was different now. Something in him relaxed around other Marines. "They already have our passports," he said, "so we can live with that."

"One last thing," Cole added. "What were you saying about reporters in there?" She pointed at the adjoining room. "We overheard."

"Told them I'd leak a story that French police were detaining a famous American reporter if they didn't let you go."

Cole smiled. "Thanks."

Fires opened the door to the train station. "You want to stay at the Embassy while we get this sorted out? Three hots and a cot?"

Warren laughed. "We have a hotel."

"Reminds me," Fires said. "I told these losers I'd let them know where you were staying." She tossed Warren a notepad from the desk, and he wrote the name of the hotel on it.

Fires tossed the paper in Bisset's general direction. It fluttered to the floor as they walked out of the office into the busy *Gare du Nord* station.

Fires stopped them as soon as they got a few yards from the office. "Jane, do you mind if I talk to Warren for a sec?"

Cole glanced at Warren, who nodded.

Cole saw a small gift shop. "Sure. I'll do some Christmas shopping." She left her bag with Warren and approached the shop, but turned back to watch their discussion instead of going in. She assumed they'd want to reminisce pleasantly about the Marines, but Warren wore his *intense-listening* face. Fires was telling him something important. Before Cole could guess what it might be, they were done.

Fires slapped him on the arm with her leather padfolio, then strolled out of the train station.

112

A swarm of reporters and at least three TV camera crews blocked the entrance of the Grand Hotel du Palais Royale. Cole wasn't surprised, but she'd hoped they'd get lucky. "Damn."

The driver double parked and glanced back. "Celebrities stay here sometimes."

Warren said, "We might *be* the celebrities this time."

The driver didn't get it. "You are famous?"

"Not exactly."

Cole knew what he meant. "The police screwed us?"

Warren handed the driver twenty Euros. "That's my bet. Your story is everywhere now. Combine that with the diffusion notice, China, and the latest shooting. This thing is bigger than Beyonce. I bet Bisset called every reporter in Paris before we were out of the train station. Just to screw with us." He nodded toward the entrance. "You ready."

"I have a choice?"

"In ten minutes we'll be up in the room."

Cole took a deep breath. "I ever tell you how much I hate reporters?"

Warren chuckled. "Tell me about it. Not nearly as fun when *you're* the one being written about, is it?"

She grabbed the door handle and sprang out, waited for

Warren to follow, then wrapped her arm around his and stepped onto the curb. Five or six reporters rushed toward them.

"Ms. Cole," one asked in a thick French accent, "what are you doing in Paris?"

She tried to sidestep him, but ran into a large woman holding a camera. "A picture, please?" She said it while snapping dozens of pictures, but the question made Cole turn long enough for the woman to snap a dozen shots of her face.

Warren tugged her toward the hotel entrance, which was blocked by a large luggage cart. Two porters were pulling it inside as another tried to shoo away the mob.

"Why are you in Paris?" someone yelled.

"Are you here to investigate the murder of David Fontes?"

"Did you kill David Fontes?"

"Ms. Cole, are you planning a follow-up article?"

"Who will be the next victim?"

"Where did you find the map?"

"Are you and Robert Warren lovers, Ms. Cole?"

This last question got her to turn. The woman who'd shouted it was short, around thirty years old, and she shoved a cell phone in Cole's face.

"What did you say?" Cole asked.

"You and Mr. Warren chose to come to Paris at Christmas. Are you lovers?"

Cole opened her mouth to speak, but Warren pulled her around the luggage cart and into the hotel. Behind them, the staff blocked the reporters from entering.

<hr>

Their small, elegant room overlooked a large square with a fountain. In the distance, the top half of the Eiffel Tower peeked out over an apartment building.

"It just struck me." Cole fell onto the plush bed. "We're now *stuck* in Paris. No passports. I'm not someone who likes being stuck."

Warren was changing in the bathroom, door half open. "Even in Paris?" he called.

"There could be another murder any minute." She sighed.

506

"Even if we have no chance of actually getting close to the story, I have to be where the action is."

Warren came out, wearing black jeans, a white t-shirt, and his brown leather jacket, still scuffed from the bombing in London. Gray stone dust covered the jacket's right shoulder.

She stood and examined it. "In action movies, the hero never brushes the dust off his leather jacket after he goes down. That your strategy for attracting French women?"

He looked down at the front of his jacket. "What?"

She brushed the dust off of his shoulder. "Got it for you."

She walked to the window and looked out. The day had cleared after the morning snow. All the roads were driveable, but a thin layer of powder still covered roofs and awnings. "It's more beautiful than I imagined." She turned quickly. "Wait, why'd you change clothes?"

"In the train station, Fires gave me a lead."

Cole raised an eyebrow. "Bet that's not all she wants to give you."

Warren shrugged. "Seriously? It's not that. She has a constant rivalry with the French. She heard something she can't act on."

"And she'd love you to break something before the French authorities do?"

He walked to the door. "Exactly. We're allies with the French, but let's just say she has a friendly rivalry with... well, literally every law enforcement and military officer in this country."

"You're not gonna tell me what the tip was?"

"Long shot. I'll call you if I learn anything."

With that, he slipped out the door, leaving Cole alone.

The desk clerk had assured Warren that reporters wouldn't be allowed inside. All he needed was to avoid the front entrance. He took the elevator to the basement, where a small gym had been fashioned out of an old storage room. He examined the gym equipment—he always scoped out potential workout locations when he traveled—then found a hallway that led to a kitchen. Probably where they filled room service orders.

He walked casually through the swinging double door and

across the kitchen to the employee entrance. The door led to a flight of stairs, which took him up to an alley on the side of the hotel. *Perfect.*

At the end of the alley he found a taxi. "*École d'économie de Paris.* As fast as you can."

113

Cole opened Julio Lopez's Facebook page. He'd updated it three times since she last checked.

A bible quote. A photo of a Tex-Mex, stuffed-crust pizza with the caption: "Mmmmmmmmmmm!!!" A score update from a Houston Texans football game.

On her Sandy Beltaggio profile, she posted a link to an article about the playoff chances for the Houston Texans, then found a Tex-Mex cooking class offered in Houston in January and posted a link to it with the caption, "I'm thinking of going. Anyone want to join?"

She logged off, then back on using another fake profile. She commented on Sandy Beltaggio's posts, then logged off. She did this three more times, making it look as though Sandy Beltaggio was a popular woman with friends who couldn't wait to engage with her posts.

Finally, she logged back on as Sandy Beltaggio. She had a new message, which must have just arrived. She perked up. Lopez had replied to the message she'd sent on the train.

Lopez: *I'm an okay keeper. Not in the shape I was before but I do alright. We play once a week at Memorial Park. Saturdays at noon unless it's raining.*

Cole took a deep breath. Studying how to read people had taught her one important truth: when people are excited, or nervous, or lying, their bodies give them away, not their words. Humans are betrayed by their physiology much more than they'd like to believe. A reddening face, a flushed cheek, or a hand to the neck, which had been Maggie Price's tell.

Cole's heart had started racing the second the little red "1" popped up on her private messages. Now she tapped her foot nervously. She hunched tightly over the phone, as though trying to fold herself into a package small enough to disappear into the screen and reappear in Lopez's living room.

This was her chance to talk one-on-one with one of her husband's killers. She was nervous, excited, and full of rage.

As much as she wanted to come right out with it, she had to go easy. She took another breath, sat up straight, and typed.

Cole: *Thanks for writing back. I bet you're better than just "okay." I'd love to join the game.*

Lopez: *Great. Meet at the north field at noon.*

She needed to keep this going, and took a moment to contemplate. Warren had said she should come across as damaged or Lopez wouldn't buy it. She decided to play the ex-husband card.

Cole: *See you there. Ugh, my ex NEVER wanted to play sports. You into football?*

Lopez: *Grew up calling soccer "football" and calling football "American football." Dad was from Mexico and that's how they call it down there. So soccer is my first love but I watch the Texans every Sunday.*

Cole: *I'm in the NFL betting pool at work. Winner gets an extra day off and I NEED that day, you know?*

Lopez: *Hear ya. We all could use an extra day off. I drive trucks for a living and sometimes my eyes go numb.*

Cole: *Ha! Seriously, though.*

Lopez: *What do you do for work?*

Cole: *Insurance sales. Boring as hell but decent money. Texans gonna make the playoffs this year?*

Cole waited as Lopez typed out a long reply. He'd given this serious thought, apparently. When the reply appeared, she scanned recent articles about the team and faked her way through a brief back-and-forth.

From football, she moved the conversation to stadium food, then cooking in general, then to favorite foods, which led to Tex-Mex. They'd been chatting for half an hour by the time she asked

Lopez to join her at the cooking class. She didn't want to come on too strong though, so she added:

Cole: *Not a date, or whatever… might be fun, ya know?*

As expected, he'd already clicked over to view her recent posts.

Lopez: *Saw that class on your page. I used to make a mean enchilada sauce. I'm in.*

Cole: *My ex never wanted to try anything new, either. Probably all the regimen and discipline from being in the service.*

Lopez: *I'm a Marine. Retired Marine. Where'd your ex serve?*

She did some quick Googling to find a believable story.

Cole: *2nd Battalion, 503rd Infantry Regiment. Wardak province, Afghanistan.*

Typing it out, she felt guilty for the first time. Matt told her once that one of the worst things someone could do was lie about military service. It disrespected the men and women who actually served. Most civilians didn't know the difference, so they were easy to fool. Of all the lies she'd told, this was the only one that gave her pause. But she'd live with the guilt if it helped her break Lopez.

Lopez: *Served in Afghanistan, too, but never made it to Wardak.*

Cole: *Any chance you knew him? Michael Beltaggio?*

Lopez: *It was a big war. Didn't run into him that I can remember.*

Cole: *Assumed not.*

Lopez: *What happened? You cheat while he was away?*

This was unexpected. If she could see his face she'd be able to interpret a tone behind the comment. He followed up quickly.

Lopez: *Sorry, too personal. That happened to me and it sucks.*

Cole: *Sorry to hear that. No, nothing like that. Honestly it was an okay divorce as divorces go. Just grew apart. He's remarried now. Actually I'm friendly with his new wife so it's kinda cool.*

Lopez: *That's cool.*

Cole: *Gotta run but I'll see you Saturday.*

Lopez: *Later.*

As much as she'd wanted to go in for the kill, she had to establish rapport, get him to trust her. Next time she'd go all in.

But first she needed a costume and a little help from Frankie in Las Vegas.

114

Warren arrived at the *École d'économie de Paris* just before dusk. The soft light made the thin layer of snow look pinkish gray. On any other day it would have been beautiful. Now, police cars surrounded the college and all Warren could think about was the shooting. At least eight dead, including the shooter.

In New York City, they'd tracked down Michael Wragg, who'd jumped to his death rather than being caught. In D.C. and Miami, the shooter had been a hired assassin, The Truffle Pig, who'd been executed by members of the New Vegas Mafia during his escape. Warren still had no idea who the shooter in London had been.

Something was different about the Paris massacre, though. The killing was at close range and there'd been multiple casualties. Warren had briefly considered whether the people killed in the *École d'économie de Paris* had been murders five through nine, but that didn't make sense. Other than David Fontes, the victims were of little international importance. There were still targets in Tokyo, San Francisco, and Los Angeles. And there still hadn't been a murder in Las Vegas. Everyone believed the head of the WTO had been the real target of the massacre. The others just ancillary casualties.

The scene was no longer busy. Yellow and black police tape

surrounded the entire building. *Barrage de police. Ne pas traverser.* But it wasn't the scene he was interested in.

The killing of David Fontes was different, and he wanted to find out why. As he'd done in London, he studied the buildings around the crime scene. There were no tall skyscrapers, but there were plenty of spots from which a sniper could have taken the shot. So why had the murder been done up close?

He put himself in the mind of the person planning the killing. Newspapers had reported the name of the shooter: Augustin Gustave Berge, a former member of the French police who'd gotten into radical politics after his firing. Warren shook his head. Berge would have known what sort of security Fontes would have. He wouldn't have planned the assault the way it happened. Rule number one of combat, never give up the high ground. Around here, Berge had *plenty* of high ground.

No, he must have been in one of the buildings across the street, similar to the snipers in the earlier killings. The two buildings each took up half a block. The police tape blocked neither of those, but he had to believe investigators had checked them out.

The building on the right was completely dark, likely an office closed for Christmas Eve. The one on the left was an apartment building. Half the windows were lit. In a few he saw people preparing meals and talking. Faint music drifted down from an open balcony door.

Fires had told him the U.S. State Department owned a block of apartments there, which they used to house Embassy visitors. A day ago, a U.S. Congresswoman had noticed a cleaning van parked in the back lot for the third day in a row. Also for the third day in a row, she'd noticed that no cleaning was taking place, just a guy in the van smoking cigarettes and reading a newspaper. Not illegal, but suspicious. After the shootout, the Congresswoman called Fires from the airport. Fires, instead of calling the French police, passed the tip around the Embassy, which sent out a couple DSS Special Agents to investigate. Finding no van, stonewalled by French investigators, and eager to get home for Christmas Eve, they'd given up.

The building had plenty of windows that would have worked for a sniper. Something must have gone wrong. More security than Berge expected, or maybe a faulty rifle—but Warren doubted

513

that. Berge likely had one of the nine, and they were top of the line.

Warren stuck his tongue out a little and wrinkled his forehead in concentration. A snowflake touched his tongue.

That was it.

He pulled out his phone and opened up the homepage of *Le Monde*, then *Le Figaro* and *Les Échos*. He didn't find what he was looking for. Next he loaded *Libération*. There it was. A photo of the crime scene, which had tastefully excluded the dead bodies. The photo showed the interior of the meeting room—desks and chairs flipped over, a buffet table sitting sadly in the corner. In the foreground, three large umbrellas. Fontes had been shielded by umbrellas as he walked in. Probably because of the snow, but they could have served as another element of the increased security. U.S. presidents usually entered and exited buildings under canopy cover—Secret Service protocol. It made sense that world leaders like Fontes would have similar protection at this point, given that any one of them could be the next target.

He began to cross the street, figuring he'd wait for someone to leave the apartment building, then grab the door before it locked. Or he might be able to gain access to the office building through a shared basement.

He stopped in the center of the street.

On the seventh floor of the office building a light had flicked on. A single bright window in a sea of darkness.

He watched. For a full minute he stood in the road. He couldn't discern any movement, but the light stayed on.

A pair of scooters turned onto the street and he stepped back to the curb, eyes fixed on the window.

Then someone was there. He couldn't tell if it was a man or a woman. A figure of medium height and build, dressed in dark clothes, maybe a jumpsuit of some sort, had appeared at the window. The figure wiped the window with something, then got on his knees. Whoever it was, he moved like a man. He was cleaning the floor now, scrubbing it with something.

Warren scanned the street. Nothing. No one.

He jogged around the side of the office building. In the back, he found a large parking lot shared by the apartment building and the office building. In the far corner sat a van. It had a cartoonish picture of a woman vacuuming a carpet with an industrial carpet cleaner. Stenciled on the side: *EXPERT DU NETTOYAGE LE TAPIS.*

A cleaning van. At five o'clock on Christmas Eve. And he happened to be cleaning only one office that was perfectly situated for an assassin with a sniper rifle. Along with the tip from Fires, this was enough. The van belonged to an accomplice of Berge.

Thinking quickly, Warren raced to a dumpster behind the apartment building and rifled through the trash. He didn't see what he needed. To the right of the dumpster, he found an old radio with a bent, two-foot metal antenna. He broke it off and sprinted for the van, shooting a look at the back door of the office building.

The "cleaner"—Warren was sure that word described the man—was there to erase any evidence of the shooter. He'd be out and in the wind the second he finished.

He bent the skinny end of the antenna into a fish-hook shape and stopped at the far window of the van so he couldn't be seen from the building. He wedged the antenna down through the window and tried to tug at the lock. It slipped.

A door creaked across the parking lot. Through the van window, Warren saw movement at the back exit of the office building.

Squinting in the dark to see the lock, he pressed his face into the frosted window and tugged with the antenna. This time the lock popped.

He slipped through the door, re-locked it, and shoved the antenna into the inside pocket of his jacket, bending it down as he did so. He closed the door softly behind him. The van was largely empty, but in the back on the right side was a huge wheel of thick orange hose—the sort that attaches to carpet shampooers.

The crunch of snow got louder as the cleaner approached. Warren had two options. The first—and smarter—was to position himself behind the driver's seat and grab the man as soon as he sat. The second was riskier, but more likely to yield useful information.

Moving quickly, he duck-walked to the back, careful to step only on the thick raised ridges of the metal floor to avoid making a sound. The side door slid open just as he wedged himself between the massive spool of hose and the side of the van.

His breaths were long, slow, and silent. In everyday conversation he could lose his cool. In moments like this, he was ice.

Something rattled as it hit the metal floor. The side door slid closed. Then the driver's side door opened and closed. The van started with a gentle rattle and eased out of the parking lot.

The van turned right, then left. He heard two shrill rings.

The first voice came through the car's speakers. "Is it done?"

"It's clean."

115

Warren pressed his feet into the floor.

There was a long silence before the driver continued, "He left little trace. He did the best he could under difficult circumstances. If he'd stayed to scrub the site, he might have missed his chance."

"Yes."

"I've been thinking…"

"Thinking what?"

"Added security almost saved Fontes. The next targets will certainly have increased security."

"We've planned for that. Tokyo and San Francisco are prepared." The man's voice was hard to make out from the back of the van. He spoke in short, crisp sentences and his words were clipped, almost robotic. Warren didn't know Ibo Kane's voice, but he had to believe it was him on the line, running the call through some kind of digital anonymizer.

"I know," the driver said. "But I can help."

"Help how?"

Warren had never seen an interview with Kane but could picture him. Since Cole's article was published, his face had been all over the Internet. He closed his eyes and allowed an image of the billionaire to fill his mind. Handsome but severe, with short black hair, a sharp nose, and eyes like black ice.

"Los Angeles will be difficult," the driver said. "We've known this from the beginning. It'll be more difficult now. I had no idea how big this would get."

"I did. Please, Dorian. Make your proposal."

"Take me to America."

Warren's mind raced, but he made a mental note of the driver's name. Dorian. It likely wasn't his real name, but it was still worth remembering so he could pass it along to French police. He considered using an app on his phone to record the call, but doubted it would capture the sound clearly. It wasn't worth the chance that he'd bang an elbow into the side of the van, drop the phone, or make another unintended sound.

The man Warren was now thinking was Kane finally spoke, "Be on the roof of the Gregor Building, Champs-Elysées. One hour."

"The roof of… why?" Dorian sounded confused.

"That's when my helicopter leaves."

"You're in Paris?"

Kane said nothing.

"You'll let me travel with you?"

"You served twelve years in the Special Forces?" Kane asked.

"In Pau, Pyrénées-Atlantiques, yes."

"And you were dishonorably discharged?"

"For refusing an order. An order that violated the French Constitution and put our sovereignty at risk. I would not see France become like the rest of Europe."

"Be there in an hour. I could use someone like you in the final phase."

"Final phase?"

"There are things you don't yet know."

"Somewhere else?"

"Not some*where* else, some*thing* else."

The words floated to the back of the cold van as though Warren could see them, taste them.

Not some*where* else, some*thing* else.

Warren didn't know what it meant.

Neither, it appeared, did the driver. "I… I—"

The line went quiet. Warren listened to the low whoosh of the tires. Sirens from a passing ambulance wailed.

"Don't worry," Kane said. "I'll explain when you arrive."

The call ended.

Warren's knees burned from crouching. He shifted his right leg, careful to keep his body pressed up against the hose to avoid clanging the wall of the van with an elbow or shoulder. Pulling his prosthetic into place, he sat cross-legged. Slowly, he pulled his phone from the inside pocket of his leather jacket. Shielding the screen with his body so the light wouldn't be visible, he texted Cole.

Warren: *Gregor Building, Champs-Elysées. Kane will be on roof in one hour. Call local police. A cleaner broke into the apartment building across from the site of the shooting. Name=Dorian. I think he scrubbed evidence.*

He sent the text, double checked that his phone was on silent, and stowed it. It might not be enough to get a rise out of the local police, but it was worth a try. Cole's story had taken off in the media, but French police couldn't arrest someone based on a theory from a blog. And Warren knew from experience that there were two systems of justice in the world. One for men like Kane, one for everyone else. When a billionaire was accused of a crime, there were no police raids busting down his door at 3 AM. No, if Kane was ever questioned, the chief of police would show up with flowers and chocolates, humbly requesting the privilege of an interview. Unless there was overwhelming evidence that Kane had committed a crime in France, he was above the law.

So the question was—why was Kane in Paris, and had he committed a crime? Local police would ask themselves those two questions. If Cole relayed the message—and if Warren was lucky —they'd immediately escalate the situation to federal law enforcement, which would likely coordinate with the MI5 in London and an alphabet soup of U.S. agencies who were working on the nine murders.

Loud classical music filled the van. A string quartet, tinny but melodic. It sounded terrible through the cheap stereo, the sharp notes burrowing into his skin as they echoed back and forth off the walls. The smell of a lit cigarette wafted into his nostrils and there was the whoosh of a cracked window.

For ten minutes they rode. Warren's entire world was smoke and classical music and a thin stream of cold air on his face. The Eiffel Tower appeared through a side window, bedecked with sparkling white lights. Soon they'd cross the Seine, only a couple miles from Champs-Elysées.

He had to make a move.

Stretching his legs out before him, he readied himself. He inched his head out from behind the roll of vacuum hose and glanced at the rearview mirror. If the driver looked as Warren crept to the front of the van, he'd be visible. He decided not to creep.

The van passed over a seam in the road—a quick *thud thud*—followed by an uphill climb then a slight descent. They'd crossed the bridge.

Warren peeked again. Out the side window, all was darkness.

He quickly looked at his phone.

Cole: *Where R U? Made the call. Police said they'd check. Called Fires at Embassy. Said she'd alert a contact in the CIA.*

He opened the audio recording app on his phone and pressed the red button, then shoved it back in his pocket. He stood slowly, crouching awkwardly to keep his head from hitting the ceiling. He took a vacuum attachment about four inches long from a holder bolted to the floor. Made of rigid white plastic, he hoped it would feel the same as the barrel of a 9mm handgun when pressed into Dorian's side.

The van approached a stop light.

Warren took three slow breaths. In, out. In, out. In, out.

When the van stopped for the light, he sprang forward, head slouched down. Dropping to his knees between the two front seats, he rammed the plastic into Dorian's ribcage. "Keep your hands on the wheel."

Dorian turned his head slightly.

Warren pressed the pointed plastic harder into his ribs. "*Eyes. Forward.* When the light turns green, you're going to pull forward. Then you're gonna turn onto the side street and park. Nod if you understand."

Dorian nodded. "Who are you?"

"I didn't tell you to speak."

The light changed. Dorian followed Warren's orders, parking in front of a fire hydrant in the center of the block.

"Keep your hands on the wheel and don't look at me. The nine millimeter pressed between two of your ribs might not kill you, not immediately. The first shot will crack both ribs. The second will tear through the lower portion of your lungs."

The man's eyes shifted toward Warren, but his head didn't

move. "*Amerloque Noir*," he muttered. His voice dripped with disdain and his eyes burned with hatred.

Warren didn't know the phrase, but he thought "noir" meant "black." This wasn't going to be a friendly conversation. "I'm going to ask you a series of questions. If you fail to answer me, I'm going to shoot you."

The man said, "I'm prepared to die."

Warren believed he was. He knew when an enemy was afraid. This one wasn't. "Is Dorian your real name?"

Nothing.

"Was that the apartment where the shooter was supposed to kill David Fontes?"

Dorian smiled, but said nothing.

"Why are you meeting Ibo Kane?"

A twitch in the man's eyes. A moment of confusion. Then it hit Warren. This man didn't know General Ki was Ibo Kane. Either he hadn't read Cole's article or, more likely, he'd assumed it was a lie. This was his way in.

"Your beloved General Ki is the *international* businessman Ibo Kane. He's one of the richest men in the world. Richer than Raj Ambani, richer than Ana Diaz *and* the Deputy Crown Prince. He's *using you* to kill those who threaten his business interests."

He waited, gauging the man's response. The twitch in his eye told Warren this was new information, but the man showed no other reaction.

"Do you read the papers?"

"They lie. Controlled by evil powers." Dorian's voice was cold and steady.

"I was in the room when Michael Wragg jumped to his death. One of your"—Warren paused for emphasis—"*brothers*."

The man blinked. "T-Paine?"

"His screen name, yes. He was an old nut living in New York City, above a fried fish place. It helps to be honest with yourself about who your friends are. Who *you* are."

Dorian said nothing.

"I don't think Wragg would've wanted to help Ibo Kane," Warren said. "And I don't think you do. You've been duped." He let it hang in the air. "The Paris murder was botched, likely because of the snow. I'm guessing Fontes was covered with umbrellas when he got out of the car. So The Shepherd went in,

521

guns blazing, and you were sent to cover the tracks. You know, Kane—I mean *General Ki*—doesn't give a damn about you or your cause. He is using you. This whole thing has been a setup. He duped a bunch of fools like you to eliminate people for his benefit. You think you're serving a cause. You're serving *his* cause. And his cause is literally the opposite of yours. Kane wants total world domination, a file of digital activity on every human being, one world currency, a global government beholden to international business. And *he* wants to run it."

Warren studied his eyes, which stared blankly through the windshield. He wanted the man to break. Needed him to break. "You can still stop this. Save at least four lives. Las Vegas. Tokyo. San Francisco. Los Angeles."

Dorian's eyes dropped. He opened his mouth to speak.

Lights flashed through the rear windshield.

Police lights.

They both glanced back at the same moment. But Dorian grabbed Warren's "gun" as he turned, pushing it up into Warren's chest. Then he looked down at it. A smile appeared as he realized it wasn't a gun.

Warren grabbed for his jacket just as Dorian lunged at him, striking him in the cheek with a violent forearm. A second later, Dorian leapt out of the van.

Warren jumped out the passenger side and raced after him. He heard shouts from behind and, looking back, saw two officers getting out of the police car.

116

Cole tried calling the French police again, hoping to reach someone different, someone who would promise action. Instead, she was transferred to the same person, a detective who spoke broken English and didn't seem to understand the significance of the fact that Ibo Kane was in Paris.

Next, she called Fires again. The call went straight to voicemail.

She hadn't heard from Warren since his text twenty minutes ago. She considered heading out to Gregor Tower, but something stopped her. Warren told her to call the police. Not to head down there. He had to have a reason for that. What good could she do, anyway? It's not like she could stroll up to Kane and ask for an on-the-record interview. Still, she was going nuts waiting.

She paced the room for a few minutes, then took the elevator to the lobby and got coffee.

Back in the room, she paced nervously, trying to figure out how Warren had learned about the cleaner and about Kane being in Paris. She ran a series of searches, but there was nothing on Kane being in France.

Out of options, she returned to the follow-up article she was writing for *The Barker*. Watergate, she told herself, wasn't one big story. It was a trickle of dozens of stories over two years. She needed to get something fresh out there and hoped other reporters and law enforcement officials would use her work as a starting point to investigate further.

Her new article tied Ibo Kane's business interests to the death of David Fontes. It wasn't hard. Turned out, Fontes had been working in opposition to a deal that would allow U.S. and European tech companies a freer path into Chinese and other Asian markets. Markets Kane desperately wanted to reach. Next, she tried to answer one simple question: *Who's Next?*

As she had in Miami, she tried to put herself in the mind of the killers: what sort of people would they want to kill? Now the range of victims was narrower. Not only did they need to be appealing targets to the extremists carrying out the murders, their deaths also had to benefit Ibo Kane. Running a series of searches, she created a list of potential targets in Las Vegas, Tokyo, San Francisco, and Los Angeles.

From there, she narrowed her list to the five most-likely victims from each city, writing one paragraph for each. She hoped the article would move the public's consciousness to a new place. Even though her piece on Kane made a big splash, most still believed the extremist motives espoused in the manifesto were the real reason for the killings. In this article, she wanted to show how any of these twenty targets could fit into the motives of the manifesto. More importantly, she wanted to show how the death of any of these twenty leaders would serve Ibo Kane's personal interests.

When she finished, she emailed the story to Alex Vane at *The Barker*, along with a note.

Alex,

My gut feeling is that the next victim will be in Tokyo. Fei Mingkang is there right now, and only for forty-eight hours. If you want to make a splash, edit the piece a little to make it more of a prediction. The right headline will make it go viral—JANE COLE PREDICTS NEXT KILLING IN NINE MURDERS PLOT—something flashy. You all know how to sell it.

Any chance you can get expedited media visas for Robert Warren and me? We don't have our passports, but we're working on it.

-Jane

As written, the article didn't come right out with the prediction that Fei Mingkang would be next. Cole's journalistic instinct was to be conservative with predictions. But she knew how Alex would respond.

Mingkang was the Deputy Governor of the People's Bank of

China, in Tokyo for a long-planned meeting of Asian banking leaders. For years, she'd blocked Kane's efforts to establish a foothold in the Chinese financial system. If Cole was right, he'd love to see her go so he could persuade her successor to be more accommodating.

Closing her laptop, she texted Warren again.

Cole: *Where R U?*

117

The shouts of the officers faded as Warren turned the corner. He was fifty yards behind Dorian, but gaining.

Dorian took a left, then a right, and disappeared down an alley. When Warren skidded into the alley, Dorian was halfway up a fire escape ladder. The ladder was attached to a four-story brick building. With his upper body strength, Warren could take the rungs three at a time.

The metal was cold on his hands, but he gained on Dorian as they ascended.

Dorian reached the top of the ladder and disappeared onto the roof. Seconds later, Warren fell onto the snowy roof, breathing heavily. If *he* was breathing heavily, Dorian must be gasping for air.

He stood too quickly and slipped in the snow, falling backwards and smashing his hip on the curved handle at the top of the ladder. His cell phone fell from his jacket pocket and dropped into the alley below. The two officers had turned the corner. They'd seen him, but as he turned back to Dorian, he doubted they'd catch him.

Dorian leapt from one rooftop to another. Warren followed, running as fast as he could without slipping. He easily cleared the two-foot gap between buildings, despite a tentative takeoff. He chased Dorian across another roof, then another, and another.

Dorian slowed and paused, now only twenty yards ahead.

He'd reached the end of the block. The cross street meant a sixty-foot gap between roofs. He had nowhere to go.

Dorian turned to Warren and smiled, then turned back to the empty space at the edge of the roof and jumped. Warren heard a faint thud. Oh no. His mind flashed on Michael Wragg, who'd chosen to kill himself instead of being taken alive.

He skidded to a stop at the edge of the roof and glanced down. At first, he saw nothing. An awkwardly angled floodlight blinded him. The sidewalk below was under construction.

He blinked rapidly, then saw Dorian on the ground rolling, then standing. He'd landed on something. A pile of dirt or gravel? Somehow he'd survived the four-story drop.

Eyes adjusting, he saw what it was. Dorian had landed on a bank of large plastic garbage cans. Three of the cans had toppled when he hit them, but there were still four more upright.

Without a thought, Warren jumped. The cold air rushed past, stinging his face as he fell. He flailed his arms to keep himself upright, but overestimated how his body would rotate in the air, so instead of landing on his butt, he landed on his knees and toppled to the ground. His left shoulder slammed into a block of concrete. He cried out, then leapt to his feet. Leaning to the left and hugging his injured arm close to his body, he continued the pursuit.

Dorian was a hundred yards away and Warren was slowed by the pain in his shoulder. His prosthetic had come loose, too, so he had to favor it to keep it from coming off. He couldn't take the time to re-adjust. At the next corner, Dorian turned onto a main road, then slowed to a walk and ducked into a building.

The building was a high rise, roughly twenty stories, with a large canopied entrance.

Warren slowed. Was this a trap? Why had he gone inside?

Then everything clicked. It was the Gregor Tower in Champs-Elysées. Dorian had led Warren straight to the spot where he'd agreed to meet Ibo Kane.

Warren sighed, relieved. He didn't need to catch the guy. Cole had made the call and the police would be there waiting. At least he hoped so.

He jogged to the entrance, shoving past two valets and a group of women on their way out of the building. In the two-story marble lobby, he stopped. No police. He looked left, down a long hallway. Straight ahead, a concierge spoke on a black phone behind a desk. To his right… there he was.

Dorian stood before a gold elevator door, his head tilted toward the digital numbers. The elevator was on its way down. *Nine. Eight. Seven.* Dorian looked over his shoulder at Warren. He held his gaze for only a second, then smiled and inched toward the elevator door.

Six. Five. Four.

Warren didn't need to hurry. He had him. If the police weren't there, he'd follow him into the elevator. He approached, stopping two feet behind Dorian. If it came down to a fight, the guy stood no chance.

Three. Two.

An elderly couple joined the line for the elevator.

One.

"*Monsieur, quel est votre numéro de chambre?*"

Warren turned. The uniformed concierge who'd been talking on the phone now stood beside him. Warren shrugged and locked his eyes on the back of Dorian's head.

Ding.

The concierge put two fingers on Warren's forearm. "*Monsieur, quel est…* erm… I'm sorry, sir, what is your room number?"

A group of people exited the elevator.

"I…I…" He pointed. "That man is part of the assassination of David Fontes. He is here to meet Ibo Kane, who—"

A man pressed in on Warren's other side. He didn't carry a gun, but he was Warren's size and wore a scowl across his face. He didn't say a word. The concierge said, "*Monsieur*, if you are not a resident or the guest of a resident, you will have to leave."

Dorian walked into the elevator, followed by the elderly couple.

Two security guards came up behind Warren, each touching one of his elbows lightly. They didn't speak, but the message was clear.

The concierge said, "Sir, turn and leave this building right away or we will be forced to call the police."

Warren stepped forward. The men at his sides gripped his biceps, but didn't pull him backwards. It was a show of dominance. They were telling Warren, *Don't move another inch, or we will throw you to the ground. Just go quietly.* They didn't want to make a scene in the lobby.

Dorian winked at Warren as the gold door slid closed.

Warren shook his arms loose and walked out.

118

She texted Warren one more time, then opened her fake Facebook profile on her laptop and messaged Lopez.

Cole: *You around? Just got home. Bored.*

Lopez: *Chilling. Leave for a quick trip tonight.*

Cole: *Where to?*

Lopez: *Hauling a truck of salsa. Houston to El Paso. You know they make it in a factory outside Houston, then ship it to El Paso to put the labels on. No idea why.*

Cole: *Weird. Been meaning to ask you, you served in Afghanistan, right? Ever end up near Ghazni Province?*

Lopez: *Sure did, why? Your husband was there?*

Cole: *No, not that. Another military wife I know. Husband was a Marine. Died there.*

A minute passed without a reply from Lopez, and she wondered if she'd gone too far. She was tired of waiting, tired of laying a trap. She was going all in. Finally, his response came in.

Lopez: *Lotta brothers and sisters died there.*

Cole: *Maybe you knew him. Matthew Cole?*

She pressed "Enter," holding her breath as the words appeared in the chat. She half-expected the chat to end immediately, but his reply popped up right away.

Lopez: *Didn't know him. Lotta Marines went through there. Sorry your friend's husband passed away.*

530

She'd expected a denial. That's why she'd called Frankie for help. She dragged a photo from her desktop and pressed "Enter." It appeared in their chat.

Cole: *That's crazy because she sent me this photo and, totally random, I thought the dude in the picture with Matt Cole looked like you.*

The photo showed Frankie next to her husband and four or five Marines she didn't recognize. They stood in front of a mountain range with bright white clouds dotting a picturesque blue sky. On the far edge of the photo was Lopez.

Again, she expected him to end the chat. She didn't think her story was believable, even as she spun it. After thirty seconds, his reply appeared.

Lopez: *Oh, Matty Cole. Yeah now I remember. His unit got folded into ours for a week or something. Didn't know him well, but we met.*

Cole: *Sure you didn't know him better?*

Lopez: *Like I said, met a lot of people over there.*

This was the moment of truth.

Cole: *According to your partner Chris Morgan, you pulled the trigger on the gun that killed him. Julio, I know you want to shut your phone off and delete the app right now, but don't. I'm with the FBI. We will initiate a video call in thirty seconds. Answer it, and you might be able to stay out of jail. We have cars on each end of your block and a helicopter on the way. Ignore the call and we'll have no choice but to believe Chris Morgan's story.*

She let out a long, slow breath and sat with her back to the wall. She adjusted the camera on her laptop so it captured her face perfectly. Earlier, she'd purchased a black business suit in the boutique in the hotel lobby. Lopez would only see her upper half, so she'd thrown the skirt in the trash and now wore the white collared shirt and black blazer. Her hair was loose at her shoulders. She looked professional. No one smart would believe she was an FBI agent, or that an FBI agent would engage a suspect on Facebook Messenger. But Lopez wasn't smart.

She started the call.

Lopez's face appeared on screen, slightly pixelated. His expression was blank. "Sandy?" he asked weakly.

Cole held her ID up to the camera for a second, but not long enough for him to read it. "Gretchen Blacker, FBI field office in San Antonio."

"Oh, damn."

"That's right, Julio. *Oh. Damn.*" She paused, shaking her head like a disappointed mother. "My colleagues are down in San Diego, questioning your pal Chris Morgan right now. He's already told us everything, said it was your idea from the start and that you pulled the trigger."

"He's lying, he—"

"Hold on, Julio, just calm down. I don't want you to say anything to incriminate yourself. You have the right to speak to a lawyer, and I suggest you do so. But I want to tell you the situation and instruct you on how you *might* stay out of jail. You have a young daughter, right?"

He nodded.

"I don't like seeing fathers separated from their daughters. I don't want to see that. So, here's the thing. Chris Morgan is in a locked room in our San Diego office trying to pin this on you. What he doesn't know is that we *know* he was the alpha in your racket. We know about the drugs. We know about China. He was the mastermind. We know you were a follower. I'd like to believe you were an *unwitting* follower and—"

"I was, I was, I—"

"Please be quiet and let me finish. We asked Mr. Morgan to give up his contacts and he tried to push it all onto you. Made you out to be a real drug kingpin. A criminal mastermind like Lady Chicharron or El Chapo. You're not a drug kingpin, are you, Julio?"

"No ma'am."

"Didn't think so. I will ask you one time and one time only, before we run with Mr. Morgan's version of events: Who pulled the trigger on Matthew Cole?"

"Chris."

"And it was because Mr. Cole learned of an operation—run by Marines—to export heroin from Afghanistan to China?"

"Yes, except…"

"What?"

"It wasn't *run* by Marines. We were only security… hired help. We offered safe passage to a crew of Chinese drug runners. They traveled to Ghazni Province to pick up product. We made sure no one messed with them when they did. That's it, I swear."

"Who was in the Chinese crew? Who led it?"

"Don't know."

"C'mon, Julio. Morgan is telling us it was your operation and you're telling us it was a magical Chinese drug-running crew with no names?"

"I swear, I…"

"A name, Julio. Give me a name."

He looked down, shaking his head. "William Wei. Tall dude. Rail thin. We called him Dubya Slim. Spoke perfect English, but looked Chinese. I think he was from Texas because he pronounced the Dubya with an accent, like the former president, ya know?"

"George W. Bush, you mean?"

"Yeah, ya know? *Dub-ya*."

"Was William Wei the mastermind?"

"No, he answered to someone. Don't know who, but he called him The Boss. Made it clear we 'Shouldn't disappoint The Boss,' or 'The Boss was pleased.' Ya gotta believe me, Chris *made* me do this. I told him we shouldn't."

"I believe you, Julio. How'd you get paid? What was your end?"

When Lopez looked up, he had tears in his eyes. He looked left, then right, then down again. The call went black.

Cole glanced around the room. She could barely believe it.

She grabbed her phone and ended the recording she'd made of the conversation. She saved the MP3 and emailed it to herself as a backup.

119

After being escorted out by security, Warren stood on the curb, listening for the sound of a helicopter.

Rich-looking men and women in fancy coats strolled by, some carrying Christmas packages, others swaying drunkenly back and forth. Two teenage girls shared a pair of earbuds and sang in French, the white wire swaying between them as they walked arm in arm.

Warren stared into the luxurious lobby he'd been thrown out of, shaking his head. It wasn't a race thing. It was a wealth thing, a power thing. He'd been thrown out because men like Kane have the power to have men like him thrown out of lobbies. Other than Cole's article, there was little evidence Kane was involved. He wouldn't be the first billionaire to get away with murder.

Warren reached for his phone. The pocket was empty. Cursing, he recalled that it had fallen out.

There was a pay phone at the end of the block, probably one of the last ones in Paris. He walked over, but it only took pre-paid cards. No coins, no credit cards.

He wandered down the block until he spotted a diamond-shaped sign for a TABAC. It was a small cafe that also sold newspapers, beer, and tobacco products. He stopped in front of the beer fridge, studying the labels. They had both French and American brands. He'd never been a big beer drinker, but the glistening

534

brown and green bottles called to him in a way they hadn't in years. His leg hurt where it attached to the prosthetic, his shoulder throbbed with pain, and he was both freezing cold and sweating profusely.

He turned on his heels and bought a twenty-Euro phone card.

Back at the phone, he dialed the hotel, which connected him to Cole. When she picked up, he didn't wait for her to speak. "I'll be back soon."

"What happened?"

"I'll tell you the long version sometime." He heard the dejection in his own voice. "Short version: Kane is in Paris. His helicopter is on the roof of an apartment building. I assume he has a place there. Call the police again and see if they give a damn. My guess is, they don't."

"I tried the police and—"

He hung up before she could finish. What was the point?

Next he dialed Sarah. Eight in the evening in Paris meant it was two in the afternoon back home. He assumed she'd have the day off for Christmas Eve.

"Hello?" Her voice was questioning and delayed by a second or two.

"Sarah, it's Rob. Merry Christmas."

"Rob, I... Merry Christmas. Two calls in one day, huh? You must be feeling guilty. You're in London still?"

"Paris."

"People are saying you look like The Rock in that video."

"How's Marina?"

She avoided the question. "Why are you in Paris?"

"Hard to explain. How's Marina?"

After a long pause, she said, "Marina is good. You know, she misses you. I was going to explain where you are, but then I realized I don't know where you are. Or why you're there. Rob, I'm *tired* of explaining. I got tired of explaining a long time ago." She sighed. A quick, loud breath. He recognized that sigh. Not defeated, but decisive. A mix of exasperation and decision. "Rob," she continued, "whenever you get back from your adventure, we need to talk. I've been offered a job in D.C. and I think I should take it."

His hand went loose on the phone. He stepped back like he'd been pushed. He hadn't planned on mentioning Bakari Smith, his

535

one-time friend whom he'd learned was dating his wife. "D.C.?" was all he could think of to say.

"I want to talk about moving there, whether you'd come visit Marina. I don't want to deny you, or her, that. But I need to—"

"How could you screw that guy?" It came out despite his best efforts to keep it in.

"What? Who?"

Warren said nothing.

"You know about me and Bakari?"

Warren's cheeks grew hot. He was ready to explode, but not at Sarah. She'd done nothing wrong. His anger lacked a target. As calmly as possible, he said, "Yeah."

"It just happened, and I don't know where it's gonna go... Look, that's not why I want to move, but—"

"Can I talk to Marina, wish her a Merry Christmas?"

"She's next door. Playing with Olivia."

Warren sighed and closed his eyes. He wanted to make the world disappear. Instead, he saw a moving van, parked out front of his old apartment. Bakari Smith loading boxes of Sarah's things. Marina's things. Or even some of *his* old things. Like the desk he'd put together from Ikea for their home office, or the old baseball glove he'd planned to give Marina when she was old enough.

His body ached. His skin crawled. "Merry Christmas. I'll try Marina tomorrow. Please tell her I love her."

"Goodbye, Rob."

He hung up, walked back to the Tabac, and bought two bottles of Stella Artois. He found an alley, popped the caps on the side of a dumpster, then froze.

What the hell was he doing?

He'd been sober fifty months. Once he'd committed, it hadn't been too hard to stick with it. He knew people who struggled every day, but not him. He'd decided it, then done it. It hadn't been *easy*, but it had been manageable. And he wasn't the kind of person to slip up. Not anymore.

He thought of Marina, tried to picture what's she'd look like at the neighbor's house, playing with Olivia. An iPad game, perhaps. Or Legos. Maybe soccer in the tiny patch of grass in the backyard, but it was too cold in New York for that.

He heard the pulsating blade slap of a helicopter taking off.

Looking up, he saw it. Its shiny black belly was illuminated by spotlights from the rooftop.

He drank the first beer in five long sips and tossed the empty bottle into the dumpster. He chugged the second faster and dropped the bottle on the ground. Returning to the Tabac, he bought two more beers, then hailed a taxi to take him to the hotel.

120

"Merry Christmas, Jane Cole."

Matt had said her full name that night, something he only did when he wanted a moment to be special. In their everyday conversation he called her "Jane," if he used any name at all. Usually his tone was enough to tell her he was talking to her. But when he'd led her into Central Park, blindfolded, to reveal the Monkey Tree strung with twinkling Christmas lights, he'd said her full name.

Four years ago.

She sipped her wine. She wasn't a wine person, but the man behind the bar in the hotel lobby had said something about the Rhône Valley. That it was in Southern France was the extent of her knowledge. The wine was good. She couldn't say why, but it was better than she was used to. She took another sip.

Four years ago she and Matt had been in Central Park. Soon after, he'd left for Afghanistan. Everything after that felt like an empty space.

She sipped her wine again. Then—in one dreadful moment that felt like a black hole opening up inside her—she realized something. This wouldn't get better. *She* wouldn't get better. Even after getting Lopez to admit the murder, nothing had changed.

She'd tried messaging him twice since coming down to the hotel bar. No response, and she didn't expect one. He wasn't smart, but probably knew enough to get a lawyer. She assumed that's what he'd done the moment the call ended.

She tried swirling the wine in the glass like she'd seen on TV. She stopped after almost spilling it twice. Only three other people sat at the bar. An elderly man reading a newspaper—an *actual* newspaper—and a young couple, maybe late-twenties, leaning in and exchanging laughing whispers. The woman put a hand behind the man's head and pulled him in like she was going to kiss him, but instead whispered something. His eyes lit up and he slid a hand to her thigh.

Cole finished her wine and the bartender appeared with the bottle. "Another?"

"Please."

She checked her phone. It was nearly ten o'clock. She'd expected Warren by now. There was no message from him but, to her surprise, she had a new Facebook message.

Lopez: *Ms. Beltaggio, or whoever this is. Julio killed himself. When I got home he was on his computer. He locked himself in the bathroom and shot himself. His Facebook was open to this chat. I will be turning it over to the local police, who just left with his body. If this is actually the FBI, I thought you should know. If this was a sick prank or something, now the police know.*

Michael (Julio's roommate)

Cole read the message three times, the panic rising with each word. Her mind danced between options. At first she believed it was Lopez himself, trying to throw her off. But he'd admitted to the whole plot and couldn't possibly think she was stupid enough to believe a fake suicide. The more she read it, the more she believed it was real. The desperate loneliness he'd displayed in his Facebook posts, the guilt he likely felt about Matt, the thought of his former partner ratting him out to the FBI. Those were forces strong enough to make even the most stable person look for a way out. The more she thought about it, the surer she was that he was dead.

And she was responsible for it.

Warren appeared beside her and touched her elbow, but his gaze was toward the hotel entrance. "Damn reporters. Hounding me out front like I'm Elvis. Should have taken the kitchen entrance." He slid a stool out from the bar and sat.

Cole was tipsy. The memories of Matt and the night in Central Park had gotten hazier and further away, crowded out by the thought of Lopez shooting himself in an apartment bathroom in Houston. She wasn't ready to tell Warren, though. Not about any of it. She tried to sound light, though her mind swirled with anxiety. "Reporters are the worst, right?"

The bartender appeared. "The lady is having a *Château de Beaucastel Châteauneuf-du-Pape* from the Rhône Valley. Shall I pour you a glass, sir?"

"He doesn't drink," Cole said. Her speech was loose and her words sounded far away.

"Yes," Warren said. "We'll have a bottle, actually."

"I can't drink a whole bottle."

"It's Paris," he said firmly, "I can have a few glasses."

As the man turned to get the bottle, Cole sat up, trying to clear her head. She locked in on him. He wouldn't meet her eyes. "You've been drinking already, haven't you?"

He pressed his hands into the wooden bar and looked up. "We're prisoners in a posh Paris hotel, waiting to find out if we're gonna get sent to China on trumped-up charges. I just chased a member of Kane's gang through Paris before being unceremoniously escorted out into the night, where I realized that French police have my phone and my wife might be taking my daughter to D.C. to shack up with my former friend." Warren sniffed a deep breath through his nose and frowned. "Been a rough day." He flashed a mocking look of shock. "Oh yeah, and terrorists are murdering people around the world and we can't do a damn thing about it." He looked down at the bar, then back at her. "Just... lemme have this."

His eyes were glassy. Any objection would likely do little. Already half drunk herself, she liked the idea of him joining her there. She didn't like that she liked it, but she liked it.

"Sparkling water," she said to the bartender as he set down the wine. "A large bottle to share. And can we order food at the bar?"

121

Two hours and two bottles of wine later, Cole took Warren's hand and pulled him up from the stool. Their third plate of oysters lay decimated on the bar, next to a basket of bread and a half-eaten charcuterie platter. The bar had grown crowded, but she hadn't noticed until standing.

She grabbed the third bottle and handed it to Warren. Pulling him from the bar area, she called over her shoulder, "Bill it to our room."

They headed for the lobby, but Warren redirected their route to the elevators, where they followed the path he'd taken that morning. Into the basement and through the kitchen.

They staggered into the night, swaying drunkenly arm in arm, and passing the bottle between them.

Sometime later—Cole didn't know how long they'd walked—they stopped on a side street. Their conversation had been like a dream, composed of scenes of bright color that jumped to others without rhyme or reason. Most of it was forgotten as soon as it ended.

"Talked to Lopez." Cole leaned on a bench and stared off into space. Her feet hurt. "He admitted it."

Warren leaned up against a streetlight poll and took a long pull from the bottle of wine. "Huh?"

"Killed himself right after. Where'd you get that wine?"

"What?"

She stumbled forward, turning into an alley that looked like an appealing place to rest. She sat, attempting to land on a wooden crate. She missed and landed in a shallow puddle. Laughing darkly, she scooched out of the puddle then lay on the ground, staring up at the few visible stars. "Think Ibo Kane is in the drug business? China? Afghanistan? The Marines?"

"Huh?" Warren sounded as out of it as she felt.

"Dubya Slim…"

Warren stared at her as she closed her eyes. He wasn't sure what she'd been saying. Something about Lopez and George W. Bush. And where *had* this wine come from? They'd been walking—that much he knew. A few blocks at least. Maybe a few miles? He remembered the bar. Oysters. And he'd eaten a whole loaf of bread.

Had they stopped in a Tabac for the wine? It didn't matter.

His head spun. The buildings rotated and closed in like a tornado moving toward him.

"Dubya Slim," Cole said.

At the end of the alley, a large moving truck stopped. Ten or twenty people exited, all wearing bright blue vests.

"Cole." He nudged her. "Blue vesters…"

He lay on the ground, his head turned at an awkward angle to watch them. They seemed to be doing something important— moving things, speaking French with urgency. He blinked. Their movements blurred together into a blue fog.

"Blue vesters are French protesters," Warren said to no one in particular.

He sat up, head still spinning. His curiosity brought a little clarity. It was the middle of the night, Christmas Eve. The men and women in vests were setting up a barricade. "Stay here." He wobbled to an uneasy stand, then crashed into the dumpster.

Cole heard Warren say something, but none of it made sense. Something about vests?

She just wanted to sleep. She remembered she was in an alley in Paris, but everything else was gone.

Staggering down the alley, Warren caught the eye of one of the blue vesters, an old man with a thin white beard. "What're you protesting?" Warren asked.

The man shrugged and went back to setting up a barricade. Maybe he didn't speak English. The blue vesters had been protesting for a while now. They'd originally come together as a reaction to social media's role in controlling public discourse, digital surveillance, and the growing wealth gap. While they had no unified political philosophy, their message resonated with various groups across the spectrum—some focused on income inequality, others on tech monopolies and privacy violations.

A young woman approached him. "Are you here to help?"

"Why are you here?" He tried to speak clearly, but his words were slurred.

"We're shutting down the streets today," she said. "One store at a time. People have to wake up to how the system is rigged—big tech, surveillance, they're all part of the problem." She looked him over, then added, "You shouldn't be drunk if you're planning on helping."

"Okay. But why *are* you here?"

The woman was about twenty-five, with short brown hair framing a kind face. She grabbed his arm to steady him. "The rich keep getting richer while the rest of us struggle. This isn't just about shopping; it's about reclaiming our lives from the digital systems that control us. The working class is paying the price for everything, and we're tired of it."

Warren stumbled back, then lurched forward, nearly knocking her over.

"You shouldn't be here drunk. This is serious."

"Augustin Gustave Berge," Warren said. "He killed people."

"We're not him. We don't condone violence. We're non-violent. We're fighting for freedom." Her words blurred in and out. "We're fighting against the data mines, the surveillance, the systems that control us like puppets."

"Macron?" Warren asked, his vision still spinning.

"We hate Macron. He sold out to the globalists. It's not about the left or the right—it's about taking control of our own lives again. The system has failed us, and we won't stand by while it continues to grow stronger."

Warren turned away, staggering toward Cole, still lying in the puddle by a wooden crate.

"Everyone thinks they have a good reason to commit crimes," he muttered to himself, then shouted it down the alley toward the blue vesters. "Everyone thinks they have a good reason to commit crimes."

"Cole."

"Cole!"

She opened her eyes. Warren stood over her, as tall as a giant.

He reached down to pull her up, but she pulled him down on top of her, laughing. He rolled to the side and lay on his back next to her.

The brief nap had helped. She felt clearer. "I was dreaming," she said. "Weird dream. About my old boss."

"Did you see the blue vesters? Everyone thinks they have a good reason to commit crimes."

She turned to him, resting on her elbows, and took his face in her hands. His cheeks were hot. "I don't care about them."

He smiled. "Me neither. What did you dream about?"

"No one has ever worked on a story like this. It's never happened. But there was one that was in the same ballpark, and that's why I was dreaming about my boss. The story was about a city councilman who had a stake in a shipping container scam. Red Hook Terminal. Underage girls. Russia, Ukraine. Reported on it for a month. Sick stuff. Matt was away. The time he never came back. By the end I was frazzled, afraid, burned out. Boss pulled me into his office and said, 'Jane, break the story before the story breaks you.'" She laughed and let go of Warren's face. "This time, I broke the story and it broke me anyway."

Cole weaved through the lobby and found the elevator, Warren right behind her. It took three attempts to press the button for the eighth floor.

Warren stumbled and ran into the brass railing at the back of the elevator. Cole laughed. "You're hammered, Rob."

He laughed. "I was a drunk for a long time, but never a fancy wine drunk. Beer, liquor, but never *Château de Beaucastel Châteauneuf-du-Pape*."

"Nice pronunciation." She leaned her head on his shoulder as the elevator beeped its way up.

"I did ask the bartender what kind of wine it was, like... six times."

"Think we annoyed him?" Cole asked.

"Two loud Americans getting hammered at his elegant bar? Of course not."

She laughed. "I'll tip him well when I pay the bill."

The elevator door opened and they poured out, Cole leading the way.

In the room, she opened the curtains and cracked a window. The cool air felt good and she reached out her hand. Something hit it. Cold and wet.

"Rob. Snow. Turn off the lights."

He flicked the lights off and joined her at the window. Outside, streetlights illuminated a few flakes drifting down from the black sky. They stood, watching in silence for a long minute.

Without a word, she reached out and squeezed his hand. "I'm happy we're doing this."

"Doing what?"

Her head swam. "Just, *this*. I don't know."

"You're drunk."

After another silence, she said, "You're not gonna get back into booze, right? I don't want it to be my fault."

"One time thing. Paris. Rough day. That's all."

It didn't sound right, but she was in no position to argue. She took him by the bicep, pressed herself up on her toes and kissed his cheek.

He looked down at her, then out the window, then back at her. "You want this?"

His words were wet and deep, like he was speaking through muddy water.

She took his hand. "I do."

He leaned down and kissed her on the mouth. She pulled him toward her, and they tumbled backwards onto the bed.

122

Friday

The Boeing 787 9 Dreamliner was over the Atlantic Ocean when Ibo Kane logged on. Through the anonymous Tor browser, he found DogLoverSupplies.Com, then navigated to the site's invisible backend. It one in the morning, GMT. Christmas Day. Time to roll out the final phase of the plan.

Dorian Boucher sat in the large leather recliner facing him, drinking coffee and watching his every move.

General_Ki: *My brothers, we have reached the final phase of our great plan. An international brotherhood, united by General Ki for a singular mission: to end the technological oppression, to restore the sovereignty of the individual, to birth a new era of freedom. Are we all here?*

Kokutai-Goji: *Here.*

Gunner_Vision: *Here.*

Tread_on_This!: *Here.*

No_Surveillance_State: *Here.*

8/15/47: *Here.*

General Ki: *Good. All are accounted for.*

Tread_on_This!: *Rest in peace to our friend **Freedom_2023**. May I say a few words?*

General_Ki: *Please.*

Tread_on_This!: *We knew him as **Freedom_2023**, but some of*

547

us also called him by the name, The Shepherd. He was a religious man. I knew that about him, though I didn't know much more. I guess we all now know his name was Augustin Gustave Berger, French patriot. He did what he had to do and all of France will honor him for fighting for their freedom. I believe he would be happy to know that we are carrying on without him.

8/15/47: *Rest in peace.*

Kokutai-Goji: *And we thank him for his service. Just as we thanked* **T-Paine**, *both for doing his part in New York, and for destroying himself before the pigs could get to him.*

Tread_on_This!: *RIP,* **T-Paine**.

No_Surveillance_State: *And thank you for your service.*

General_Ki: *Thank you,* **T-Paine**, *and thank you, Shepherd. Now, I have something important to tell you.*

Gunner_Vision: *Wait, where is our Parisian brother,*

End_the_Digital_Panopticon. *Do we know if he made it back?*

General_Ki: *He is with me. I was in Paris and collected him after the cleanup.*

8/15/47: *What?*

Kokutai-Goji: *What?*

Kane looked up from his laptop screen and met Dorian's eyes. He looked nervous and shifted uncomfortably in his seat. He'd had four cups of coffee and the flight was only three hours old. Beads of sweat formed on his forehead.

Kane understood. To Dorian, watching the scene must have felt like seeing the Wizard of Oz behind the curtain. For months, he'd corresponded with a mysterious General Ki, a man of brilliance with seemingly unlimited access to information. Four hours ago, in a helicopter on the way out of Paris, he'd learned that General Ki was in fact Ibo Kane.

Luckily for Kane, Boucher had believed his explanation. Now he had to make the rest believe it as well. He returned to the keyboard.

General_Ki: *Please, brothers, let me explain. I was in Paris on business. You see, from the beginning, I have kept my true identity private, both to protect myself and to protect you. To protect the integrity of our mission. We are a band of brothers, of patriots who love our countries and our freedoms. Despite racial and religious differences, we united behind a singular mission, and that mission is almost complete. You may have seen speculation in the news that I am a businessman named Ibo Kane. That speculation is correct, but almost everything else you have read is incorrect.*

548

My name is Ibo Kane and I am one of the richest men in the world. I am a man who, if you met me on the street, you might want to kill. According to the lying news, I hatched this plan to win control over business and politics. That is false. I hatched this plan for the exact reason we all know: To end the technological oppression, to restore the sovereignty of the individual, to birth a new era of freedom. We are well on our way to doing that, and we must not let anyone distract us from that mission. As I said, I was in Paris. When The Shepherd's original plan broke down, he improvised at my direction, and carried out his mission. Our other Parisian brother, **End_the_Digital_Panopticon**, *stepped in to clean up the mess. I am taking him with me to Los Angeles. I will need him to help with the final phase. As you know, The Shepherd was scheduled to make the trip on his own, but because of his sacrifice he cannot. Now, I will answer questions until you are satisfied.*

Kane took a deep breath and stared at the screen. He wasn't anxious, not exactly. He was utterly confident in his ability to keep them in the fold. Getting men to kill for you is easy if you have enough money. And getting men to love and trust you is easy if you have enough information about them and their enemies. Getting men to do both took a special set of skills and circumstances, but he had both. He hadn't expected to be identified publicly, but now that he had… well, he had to turn it in his favor. So he wasn't anxious, just eager to see how these men convinced themselves to believe.

Tread_on_This!: *I saw the article when it came out and dismissed it. I have to admit, it's surprising.*

No_Surveillance_State: *I for one do not care. The mission is the mission. The dead men and women were parasites. That's all.*

Gunner_Vision: *I have questions.*

General_Ki: *Please.*

Gunner_Vision: *I had heard of Ibo Kane, heard of you, long before now. When I was brainstorming targets, your name made my list. I think you can understand that. The companies you founded are a great part of the problem. Social media, world currencies, the digital products made by China that may soon run our lives. One simple question: why? Why did you do all this? Why have you built these evil companies?*

Kane snapped for the flight attendant, who brought a large can of Red Bull and refilled his glass. "Ice spheres, three."

She returned to the galley and reappeared a moment later with three perfectly spherical balls of ice in a black bowl. She placed them in the glass with silver tongs, causing the Red Bull to fizz.

Kane took a sip and returned to the keyboard.

General_Ki: *It's a fair question, one you must all share. And there's a simple answer. I have amassed all this power so I can walk away from it when it will do the most damage to the system. In addition to the killings we've all taken part in, I have been planning to cripple the world's business systems, its technological systems. But one can't do that with assassinations alone. I've taken control of world powers so I could walk away from them. This, along with our other actions, will truly fulfill our mission. Do you understand?*

Kane was glad he'd had a chance to test his lie on a shocked Dorian in the helicopter. The story had worked then, and he'd done an even better job spinning it the second time.

Gunner_Vision: *I believe I understand, but I have another question. How can we be sure you will relinquish power? I understand your need to deceive us, and I do not question your wisdom. Now that I know, I see that you had to be a hugely influential man in order to gain the travel plans, security plans, building schematics, and so on. Everything we have used. But how can we be sure you will not grab power when this is all over?*

General_Ki: *It's a good question. Other than my word, which is gold, here is what I can offer you.*

Kane scrolled to a document, then cut and paste a large section of text and numbers. He pasted it into their chat box.

General_Ki: ***Kokutai-Goji*** *(#3448791),* ***Gunner_Vision*** *(#3448792),* ***Tread_on_This!*** *(#3448793),* ***No_Surveil-lance_State*** *(#3448794),* ***8/15/47*** *(#3448795). These are accounts in the Cayman Islands Bank of the Caribbean. Each account has ten million dollars in it. I ask* ***Kokutai-Goji*** *to access the system to verify this. I had similar accounts set up for T-Paine and The Shepherd, and* ***End_the_Dig-ital_Panopticon*** *will receive his from me in person.*

Gunner_Vision: *You're bribing us? You think this is about money?*

General_Ki: *Not at all. When this ends, you will need money to hide out. Access your funds and do so. Then, one month after Los Angeles, we will reconvene in this chat, where I will announce phase two of our mission. Phase one will cripple the world's power apparatus. Phase two will ensure that it stays crippled. If this is not enough, then I'm sorry. I need to hear from all of you. Are you satisfied?*

There was no phase two and there never would be. But Kane thought that the promise, along with the money, would convince any holdouts to continue with the plan. One thing he'd learned about poor people was that most of them were naive enough to believe that men like him would act in their interest, even when the opposite was clearly true.

Kokutai-Goji: *Yes.*

Tread_on_This!: *I am surprised, but satisfied.*

No_Surveillance_State: *Honestly, I just can't wait to hear about phase two.*

8/15/47: *I'm in.*

Kane was worried about **Gunner_Vision**. He didn't know his entire backstory, but the man was a former Navy officer, dishonorably discharged for breaking the arm of a superior officer. Younger than most of the men in the chat, he was more likely to show spirit when being manipulated. Kane had expected them to fall in line when money was dangled in front of them. Most people—whether political ideologues, religious zealots, or any other kind of fanatic—were quick to abandon principles when ten million dollars was on the line.

Gunner_Vision: *I'll ask Kokutai-Goji, have you confirmed the money?*

Kokutai-Goji: *Doing so now.*

Kane had made sure that the bank he stashed the money in would be easy to hack. For someone with Kokutai-Goji's skills, it wouldn't take more than a few minutes. He glanced at Dorian, who sipped a French beer, which seemed to calm him. "I'm telling them about the money, and phase two. Would you like to look over my shoulder?"

Dorian walked behind his chair and read through the chat thread. "Excellent."

"Yes," Kane said. "Like you, they see the necessity of my deception, which, again, I do apologize for."

"Couldn't be helped." He sat again across from Kane. "When will we arrive in Los Angeles?"

"Five or six more hours."

A new message popped up in the chat.

Kokutai-Goji: *I have confirmed the money is there. Easy bank to transfer money in and out of, or to cash out.*

Gunner_Vision: *Then I'm in, but not because of the money. We all need to stay alive and out of jail to finish this and get to phase two. The money will help us.*

General_Ki: *Then it's settled. I must rest now, but there's one more* *thing. The woman who wrote the article, Jane Cole. She's in Paris with Robert Warren. They are the two who tracked down T_Paine and forced him to jump. They've been on us since the beginning. I've had to take actions to keep them at bay. Interpol is helping, but it may not last. Now, I need your help. Find them and kill them.*

8/15/47: *Where are they, exactly?*

General_Ki: *Hotel in Paris. But we have no men in Paris. Not anymore. If they are extradited to China, as I've tried to arrange, all will be well. If not, my guess is they'll travel to Tokyo after the events of Christmas Day.*

Kokutai-Goji: *My turf. I'm on it.*

General_Ki: *Then it's settled.*

—End of Episode 6—

THE
CRIME
BEAT

EPISODE 7: TOKYO

123

Friday

Samuel DeLunge would need all of his three-hundred pounds to bust through the door. His first attempt had cracked the frame, but not broken through. He stepped back, lowered his shoulder, and tried to summon the violence. He'd played linebacker for the Navy football team and before every play he'd uttered a mantra: *Find the violence*. Twenty years older and softer now, he had to believe he still had it in him.

He bounded forward. Four large strides, right shoulder aimed at the spot just above the metal strike plate. A deep *thud* sounded as he rammed into the door, followed by a sharp *crack*. He wiggled the doorknob, then pushed. It gave but didn't open. A crack marred the paint next to the plate, but it held. He hadn't found enough violence.

DeLunge knew that the best way to break down a door was to kick it in. A single, well-placed front kick was more effective and easier on the body. But with only two toes on his left foot, his balance was suspect. He had to resort to the more-brutish method.

He stepped back, ready to charge again. In the stillness before the charge, he listened. It was an oddly *loud* silence. Perhaps it was the bones of the old church speaking to him. Or maybe the act of committing a crime in a former house of God on Christmas morning made his mind louder than usual.

A noise broke his concentration and startled him—an electronic hum from around the corner. Instinctively, he pressed himself into the wall, trying to make himself small. Barrel-chested and standing over six feet tall, shrinking was useless. He'd never been good at hiding. Only fighting.

The sound grew louder—almost like the whir of a vacuum mixed with the high-pitched whine of a water pipe.

No one was supposed to be here. He and his brothers had confirmed that Club God would be closed on December 25th and 26th. It was the calm before the flurry of preparations for their annual New Year's Eve party, one of the most expensive affairs in Los Angeles. If Kokutai-Goji had done his job, the security cameras and alarms had all been disabled. Kokutai-Goji *had* done his job. DeLunge had strolled, unimpeded, into the most exclusive club in Hollywood through the back door. He'd taken the stairs into the basement where a commercial kitchen prepared overpriced tapas. Along the way, all doors stood unlocked and every security camera was dark. The entire place relied on digital locks —except the one room he needed to enter to get the job done.

DeLunge left his duffel bags in the hallway and retraced his steps, approaching the sound as quietly as possible. As he reached the corner, it stopped.

He froze and cocked his head. No footsteps, no voices. Nothing.

The hallway smelled strangely clean. He'd worked in restaurants as a teenager and they'd never smelled this clean. The sound resumed and he inched toward it, cautious as he rounded the corner.

When he reached the kitchen doors, he paused. The windows in the swinging double doors were dark. The sound was probably a piece of kitchen equipment. But what if it was something else? He pressed his ear to the crack between the doors and listened. The sound stopped again.

In the silence, all the doubt he'd ignored since the last chatroom session landed with a thud in the front of his mind. For a year, he'd worked with his online band of brothers to plan the great strike against the powerful puppet masters of the world. He'd even learned how to use the Internet, something he'd proudly avoided for most of his adult life. Real men, he'd always thought, didn't use chat rooms. He'd adopted the screen name **Gunner_Vision**, a nod to his Navy career as a Gunner's Mate. He liked to say he'd forgotten more about weaponry than most learned in a lifetime. And what was he using it for? The doubt pressed into his forehead, throbbing like a hangover.

Someone could walk around the corner and catch him any second. And for what? To help Ibo Kane make his next billion? He pushed the thought aside. Kane's potential profits aside, their mission remained a virtuous one. Many terrible people would die. But then a worse thought occurred to him. Had his brothers turned on him? When they'd learned their beloved General Ki was actually Ibo Kane, Gunner had been the loudest, most skeptical objector. They wouldn't hesitate to take him out if they thought he jeopardized their plan. This was his paranoia. He knew he had that issue. He was always the first to detect danger—always had been—but sometimes the danger was imagined.

The sound began again.

He was once less paranoid. Sometimes he wondered how his life would have turned out had he never had "the incident." His JAG lawyer had insisted he use that term—had even drilled and tested him on it. When his commanding officer got drunk and challenged him to a fight over a stupid argument, he could have refused, but he didn't. And when he'd broken the guy's arm, well… what had he expected? DeLunge outweighed the other man by forty pounds and had two years of MMA training before joining the Navy. Two months after the fight, he'd been dishonorably discharged, and his view of the integrity of the U.S. armed forces had degraded little by little ever since.

He slipped a flashlight from a loop on his belt, turned it on, and swung the kitchen doors open. "Who's there?"

Nothing.

He trained the light in the direction of the sound. The small circle of light illuminated a bank of three industrial stoves, their glimmering stainless steel contrasted in the sharp light by black burners. Above the stove, an exhaust fan hummed and whined. The kitchen crew had left it on. Most likely it was clogged with grease and needed servicing.

He let out his breath and returned to the half-broken door.

His nerves calmed, he found the violence this time. His meaty shoulder led the way as he charged the door. When it struck, pain coursed down his arm and into his hand. The door broke open and he tumbled into the storage area.

Before Los Angeles went to hell, the building that housed Club God had been the United Church of Christ. For forty years, this basement had been used for Bible study. Ten years ago, dwindling attendance forced the pastor and the board to sell. Over the objections of a small group of protestors, the church had been renovated and transformed into one of the most exclusive clubs in the world. Celebrities, athletes, business leaders, and even politicians made regular appearances.

DeLunge found a panel of switches and flicked them up one by one. A dozen wall sconces revealed a room of roughly three-thousand square feet, exactly what he'd expected. Spaced every thirty feet or so were wooden columns connected by wide cross-beams that supported the floor above. Along the walls hung dozens of metal storage racks, heavy with boxes of high-end booze, jars of olives, pearled onions, as well as maraschino cherries, boxes of toothpicks, and cocktail napkins. Everything needed to throw the most exclusive New Year's Eve party in Los Angeles. Along the wall to his right, an entire shelf was stuffed with boxes of edible 24 karat gold leaf. Club God was famous for their gold-wrapped *hors d'oeuvres*. Kobe beef poppers, lobster mac-and-cheese bites, mini vegan asparagus soufflé—all wrapped in sheets of edible gold. The thought was enough to erase any lingering doubts he had about blowing up every person entitled enough to feel welcome here.

He grabbed the eight duffels from the hallway and went to work, first climbing onto a chair to remove a panel of the drop ceiling. He slid a bag into the ceiling and replaced the tile. He repeated this seven times, placing a bag in each corner of the room and a couple in the middle for good measure.

A hundred pounds of **RDX** was more than enough to kill every person on the floor above. He had a hundred and twenty.

As he walked past the broken door, he stopped. He needed to make this look like a robbery. Searching for high-value targets, he took everything he could carry: a case of Johnny Walker Blue, a dozen small boxes of the gold leaf, a magnum of Cristal.

Back at his car, he stashed the stuff in his trunk and messaged Kokutai-Goji. He didn't know what time it was in Tokyo, but he counted on his Japanese brother to relock the doors and get the security cameras up and running again.

Leaning on the hood of his car, he listened to the sounds of Los Angeles and lit a cigarette. It was less than a week before the explosives would shred the bodies of many of the greatest criminals in the world.

124

Jane Cole yanked the curtains open as loudly as she could. The metal rings screeched against the rod, a noise that *should* have awakened the dead. Passed out atop the blankets, Warren didn't move. She cracked the window and took in the view of the street below. Bright morning sunlight was already melting the thin blanket of snow. A shard of light split her head as the sun peeked over a building.

Warren was still wearing yesterday's clothes. She remembered kissing him by the window, falling on top of him in the bed. Then other memories came. Earlier memories. Lying in the street. Eating oysters at the bar. Talking to Julio Lopez.

She was reluctant to wake Warren up directly—unwilling to shake or talk to him—though there was no reason not to. She turned on the TV news, hoping that would wake him. She couldn't understand a word of the French broadcast. She frowned, stabbed the mute button, and threw the remote on the bed near Warren's feet.

She didn't know what to feel because she barely remembered what had happened. Large sections were missing from her recollections, though she was sure they hadn't slept together. Even if Warren *hadn't* been fully clothed, she could tell from the way she felt.

She remembered her hands on his shoulders. She'd been next to him on the bed when he'd passed out. She'd shaken him once or twice. She remembered wanting him. Or had she just wanted *someone*? It didn't matter now. Immune to her charms—or just dead drunk—he'd begun snoring after a minute, even through her continued shaking.

She closed the bathroom door loudly and she splashed cold water on her face. Her cheek was smudged with sap or oily dirt, some substance that didn't easily come off. The memory of lying cheek-down in an alley drifted through her mind. Had Warren gotten into a fight with blue vesters? Had she told him about Lopez killing himself? The recording she had? She ran warm water over a washcloth and scrubbed the grime from her cheek.

When she left the bathroom, Warren was sitting up in bed, rubbing his forehead with a thumb. His eyes were puffy, his bald head freckled with mud on one side. He grunted something inaudible, his mouth not opening wide enough to say a full word.

Guilt hit her—not in the form of a thought, exactly. It was more of a full-body realization that she'd done something terrible. Had she encouraged Warren to drink? She didn't think so, which helped a little with the guilt.

She'd asked Warren if he'd already been drinking when he showed up at the bar. He had, but she shouldn't have participated. He'd been sober for four years. She had no idea whether last night had opened something new in him or whether that something had been open all along.

"Water," he croaked.

She filled two glasses from the bathroom faucet and handed them to him. He slid his back up the headboard slowly and drained each glass. He closed his eyes as she took the empty glasses and set them on the desk.

"What happened?" he asked.

It wasn't really a question as much as an acknowledgment that many vaguely-remembered things *had* happened and were likely regretted.

"Lots of things."

He looked around the room, pausing on the window, then the desk, then the door, as though connecting dots in his mind. "What happened?"

"You came back to the hotel. You'd been drinking." She cleared her throat. "We *kept* drinking."

560

"My legs are sore as hell. I chased… where's my phone?"

"You told me last night the police have it, but not how that happened."

He wrinkled his forehead, closing one eye. "Fell from my pocket. I chased a guy. Kane got away."

"I know." Cole's head throbbed gently, but she was certainly doing better than Warren. The hangover was easier than expected. She'd lost count of how much wine she'd had, but knew it had been good wine. A hangover from good wine was easier than one from the cheap stuff.

She sat at the foot of the bed. "Remember what I told you about Lopez?"

He looked down at his feet. His shoes were by the door but he still wore his socks. "No. I mean… sort of. You talk to him yesterday?"

"He's dead."

Warren frowned. "Yeah, I think you told me that."

"I confronted him, pretended to be FBI. He admitted everything and then killed himself. Here." She got her phone from the bedside table and opened it to the recording she'd made of Lopez. "Listen."

"Wait." Warren pushed the phone away when she held it in front of him.

"What?"

"Did we sleep together?" He ran his hands down his chest like he was trying to remember whether his shirt had been on all night.

"What's the last thing you remember?"

"Bread," Warren said. "I binged on carbs. Not sure if it's that or the beer and wine making me feel this bad."

"I'd bet on the latter. What else do you remember?"

"We walked around. Lay on the street. I remember a young woman. Blue vest. Some protest." He shook his head. "You know the last thing I remember? I said something to the woman about The Shepherd killing all those people and how everyone thinks their ideology justifies violence. It seemed like a profound thought at the time." He let out a long sigh. "Damn. Four years sober. Gone."

"You'll get it back."

He bit his lower lip. Cole knew the look of someone trying to hold it together.

"Did we sleep together?" he asked again.

"Listen to this recording and I'll tell you." She pressed play and put the phone on his lap.

While he listened, she made two cups of coffee in the coffee maker in the bathroom. She added two sugars to hers and gave a cup to Warren, who drank his black. He'd sat up in bed and, though he still looked like he'd been hit by a liquor truck, he'd perked up slightly. As it was with her, only the work kept him sane. He reached the part of the recording where Lopez named Chris Morgan as the mastermind of the plot to use Marines as security for Chinese drug runners in Afghanistan.

A furious look cut a swath through the haze on his face. "Coward," he whispered into the mug.

In the next part of the recording, Lopez gave the name of the man who'd organized the operation. William Wei, a tall Chinese man who'd lived in Texas. They called him Dubya Slim.

Warren took a tentative sip of coffee when the recording ended.

She retrieved her phone. "What do you think?"

He sipped his coffee, finishing the cup in three long swigs. "This is bad."

"The coffee or the recording?"

"You impersonated a federal officer. That's a serious crime."

"But I did it on French soil, so I didn't commit any crime in the U.S." She didn't believe it as it left her mouth. It was more of a wish than a serious legal argument.

Warren frowned. "You serious? That's not how any of this works."

"Setting aside how much trouble I might be in, what else?"

Warren let out a wet, throaty sigh. "I mean..." He blinked rapidly a few times, as though the caffeine had just kicked in. "It implicates Lopez and Morgan and William Wei—if that's even a real person. But it also implicates *you*. Just because you got a confession doesn't mean the Feds won't prosecute you if the recording goes public. If I were you, I'd delete the thing."

"His roommate messaged me after he killed himself. The chat with me was one of the last things Lopez did. Roommate said he was turning it over to local police."

"That's bad."

She sipped her coffee. It wasn't sweet enough. "How bad?"

"Depends. Chance they ignore it if they're sure it's suicide. Chance they alert pals at the FBI. Either way, I'd get rid of that recording and, if you're still on your crazy scheme to get closure on this, I'd look into William Wei separately."

He was probably right, but she wouldn't delete the recording. Not yet, anyway.

He turned to her. "So?"

"What?" she asked.

"What *happened* last night? Between us. I have my clothes on. I have a memory of getting dressed and going down to the lobby, but that might have been a dream."

"That didn't happen."

"So what *did* happen?"

There was a loud knock at the door. Cole shot up, but Warren didn't budge.

"Mr. Warren, Ms. Cole?" A French accent. "This is Gregory from the front desk. The police are here to see you."

125

Ten minutes later, Warren wobbled down the hallway, struggling to put one foot in front of the other. He followed Cole into the elevator and leaned on the brass-paneled door after it closed. The cool metal felt good on his head.

"Don't lean on the door," Cole chided. "You'll tumble out when it opens."

He raised his head slowly. "My mother told me that once."

He'd changed clothes and splashed cold water on his face, taking full advantage of the ten minutes Cole bought them when she told Gregory they needed a moment to get dressed. The coffee and cold water had helped, but he still felt like a zombie. "What's your guess?" he asked between the throbbing pulses in his temples.

"Public intoxication? Aiding and abetting blue vesters. Chasing random terrorists across French rooftops?" She laughed bitterly. "We've committed enough crimes between the two of us, could be damned near anything."

The elevator opened. Across the lobby, Gregory chatted with two men in dark blue suits who looked as though they might be detectives or other high-ranking French police. Carolyn Fires stepped into his line of sight.

He let out a relieved sigh. "Did you know Fires was here, too?"

"Nope. This could get weird."

The two men in suits introduced themselves as the detectives they so clearly were. One stood at Warren's height, his crooked nose too large for his face. The other was short, with blotchy pink cheeks. Warren forgot their names immediately. He could barely remember his *own* name. In his mind, they were *Tall Guy* and *Pink Cheeks*. He and Cole followed them to a lounge off the hotel lobby. Gregory excused himself to return to the desk, and they sat.

"What's this about?" Cole asked.

Warren was fine letting her lead the conversation. The pain in his head and legs had subsided just enough for the regret to kick in fully. Four years of sobriety, gone. The sense of loss left him speechless.

Tall Guy leaned forward, elbows on his bony knees. "We've been communicating with Ms. Fires." He handed Cole an envelope. "Your passport." He smiled as though he'd done something deeply generous.

Cole stuffed it in her belt purse.

Warren held out his hand.

Fires gave him a concerned look. "Sorry, Rob. Bad news."

Warren glanced from Fires to Tall Guy, who wasn't holding another envelope. "What?"

"I'll let Ms. Fires tell it," Tall Guy said.

Fires put a hand on his knee. "Short version, Rob. You'll get your passport back at the airport."

Pink Cheeks cleared his throat. "You're being... how do you say it in English? Evicted?"

A fire rose in Warren's chest. Despite his baby face, Pink Cheeks spoke haughtily, like a parody of old French royalty. The fire subsided. He didn't have the energy for a fight. "The Interpol thing?"

"We got that squared," Fires interjected. "That's over, and Cole is free to go."

"But you, Mr. Warren," Pink Cheeks said, patting a padded envelope he'd pulled from somewhere. "You've broken numerous French laws."

Warren tried to scowl, but his face was sore and numb. He didn't know if it communicated the look he intended. "What's in the envelope?"

Fires shifted in her chair, turning her back to the officers. "Your phone, Rob. Bottom line, we're heading to the airport and you're leaving Paris today, or you'll be arrested. The Interpol thing has been squashed, but you're really not supposed to break into vans and chase guys across rooftops."

"If these guys had done their jobs"—Warren pointed—"they wouldn't need guys like me to—"

Fires held up a hand like she was trying to block his words before they reached the detectives. "Rob, stop." Her voice was stern and invited no rebuttal. "We can talk about it on the way. I'm telling you, this is your best option."

He turned to Cole, who nodded. "Fires has your back. If she says this is the thing…"

Warren glared at the French detectives. "You know that the man behind the nine murders is in Paris right now? Or *was* in Paris. Probably long gone." His temples throbbed, both the sharp throb of anger and the dull ache of a hangover. "The guy I chased across the rooftops was cleaning up the room where The Shepherd was posted before he killed half a dozen people. Half a dozen innocent people dead and you couldn't care less, am I right?"

Pink Cheeks gave Warren a condescending smile. Warren's legs tightened like he was going to stand, but Fires grabbed his arm. "Let's go, Rob."

126

It was only as Warren disappeared through the door of their hotel room that Cole realized she was alone and hungover on Christmas Day in Paris. To her surprise, she didn't feel any self-pity. She still felt some guilt that Warren fell off the wagon, even though it hadn't been her fault.

Online, there was a good amount of discussion about her articles, but the most recent one had been buried in an avalanche of theories and nonsense. There were also a half-dozen articles about her personal life. Not *articles*, exactly—she wouldn't elevate them that high. They were smears on questionable blogs, spread by armies of fake accounts and bots on social media.

"Jane Cole is a slut," one claimed, "known for sleeping with police officers she was supposed to be covering." They even had the name Danny Ronan, the guy she'd broken up with recently. At least they didn't have a quote from him.

"She's a lying alcoholic," another wrote. "Fired from the *New York Sun* for drinking on the job, creating sources out of thin air, and lying to the public." Of course, this was a complete falsehood. She'd quit; she hadn't been fired. And she'd never had more than a drink or two on the job.

In her email, she found a handful of death threats. She forwarded them to Alex Vane at *The Barker*, but doubted he could do anything about them.

She was about to listen to her recording of Lopez again when a new text lit up her phone. Then another. They were from reporters back in New York City, both telling her some version of, "Turn on the TV."

As she reached for the remote, her phone buzzed, displaying a 305 area code. Alexa Frias, the Miami reporter she'd cut a deal with when she was in London.

"Hello?"

"Are you watching TV?"

"Trying. My French is not great." Cole turned on the news. "What happened?"

"Two more murders. Las Vegas and Tokyo."

A name Cole recognized was on the screen—Nathan Jackson.

Jackson was the new head of the NVM, the one who'd taken over for Sunny Lee at the retirement party they'd staked out in Vegas. He and the NVM had ties to drugs coming in from China —heroin, Fentanyl, and new exotic smart drugs—sex-trafficking from Eastern Europe, and a franchisable drug business that used Dropgangs and Crypto. She and Warren had been right that NVM would be a target. They'd been a few days too early. "I'm in France. What happened to Jackson?"

"Shot with one of the nine rifles." Frias's voice crackled with excitement. "Apparently he had added security, so the shooter had to get close. Ran up to him outside one of his clubs. The Blue something?"

"Club Blue. I was there." Cole recognized herself in Frias. The intense high of breaking news quickly overwhelmed shock, grief, or compassion.

"Anyway, shooter missed his mark. Hit Jackson in the chest but missed the heart. His guards beat the shooter to death. Three have been arrested. Jackson himself died of his wounds an hour later."

"Who was the shooter?"

"No word yet."

Cole sighed. "And Tokyo?"

"Your last article was right. You're about to be a damn legend."

As Frias spoke, the name popped up on the screen. Fei Mingkang was the head of the Industrial and Commercial Bank of China—the largest bank in history. The last piece she'd written for *The Barker* had offered a soft prediction she'd be the next victim. Cole had known that Mingkang would be in Tokyo at a long-planned summit of Asian financial leaders, and her connection to Kane had been easy to find. He'd been trying for years to break into the Chinese financial markets, but their centralized government and Mingkang's efforts had stopped him.

"How'd they get her?" Cole asked.

"Shot through the window of a glass elevator when it stopped at her floor. Four rounds. Shooter broke the glass with the first, took out a couple security guards with the next two, and nearly blew Mingkang's head off her neck with the fourth."

Frias kept talking, raving about how there had never been a murder predicted in a respectable journalistic outlet, at least not that she knew of.

Cole could barely listen. She walked to the window. The brief sunshine of the morning was gone, the sky now a pale gray. Alternating waves of pride and shame battered her. As much as she liked being right, it hurt her to take pride in predicting someone's death. Adding to the embarrassment and grief was the fact she hadn't been able to stop it. She'd done everything she could, but the deeper she got into this story, the clearer it was that just being right wasn't enough. Her prediction had done nothing, helped no one. In the never-ending tsunami of online content, the truth didn't have the impact it once had.

"Cole, you still there?" Frias asked.

"Yeah."

"I was saying…"

She tuned Frias out again, struck now by urgency and purpose. Her prediction would change the way everyone saw the murders, saw her work, and saw her. She had to use that. "Hey, I need to cut you off," Cole said.

"What? Why? What's up?"

"Keep your TV on. I'll probably be on it soon."

127

A cold wind numbed Warren's cheeks as he extended his hand. "Thanks. I guess it could have been worse." He and Fires stood on the curb of Charles de Gaulle Airport, where her driver had taken them after Warren was given five minutes to gather his belongings and say a hurried goodbye to Cole.

Fires pulled a scarf up around her chin. "Much worse. One night won't destroy four years of sobriety. Don't let it." She sipped from the straw in a plastic cup of iced tea. "This isn't goodbye. I promised French police I'd make sure you got the hell out of their country."

Warren chuckled, but his eyes were narrow. "I'm really that popular here?"

"They saw the video of you in London, and let's just say they weren't crazy about the rooftop chase. I can get you a ticket." She raised her leather padfolio. "I've got your passport and cellphone." She tapped on the window and told her driver to wait, then trailed Warren into the airport.

As they waited in line at the ticket counter, Warren had a dark thought. He heard the words leave his mouth before he could stop them. "Are the French police protecting Kane?"

"The French? No. C'mon, man. You're smarter than that."

Warren inched forward in line. "What do you mean?"

"You chased a guy through Paris after seeing him exit the

building where the shooter had been planning to take a shot from, right?"

Warren's temples throbbed. He was getting angry. "Not only that. I heard him talking to Kane about the attacks."

"You're in law enforcement. You know that's not enough. To get a guy like Kane you need—"

"What?" Warren demanded. "What do you need?"

"Hey, calm down. I'm not the enemy." She sighed and leaned in, continuing in a whisper. "He's well beyond juiced in. He lives in a different stratosphere." She cocked her head. "Think about what you *actually know*. A speculative article from your pal Jane, a phone call you only heard because you illegally broke into a vehicle. Remember Jeffrey Epstein? Known pedophile and criminal for two decades before he got got. He wasn't a tenth as powerful as Kane. You know what would happen to a random French detective if he tried to arrest Kane or one of his associates based on what you have? Those blue-suited bastards are trying to make a living and get home to their kids alive, ya know? Not everyone wants to be a superhero."

Warren clenched his fists. "But—"

"No, Rob. C'mon. Go back home and get your life together. You're way too close to this thing."

"Do you think we're right about Kane?"

"Sure, but it doesn't matter what I think. Put yourself in their shoes. Imagine you're walking your beat in New York and a French officer shows up, breaks into the van of an American citizen, then chases him through the city. How kindly are you gonna look at that?"

She was right. Warren had acted like he was in an action movie and it had gotten him nowhere.

The line cleared and Fires stepped to the counter, then turned to Warren. "Where to?"

He opened his mouth, but nothing came out. At the hotel, everything had happened too quickly to think it through. The right answer, he realized, was *New York*. But something in him couldn't stand the thought of going home.

He heard himself say, "D.C. Heading to D.C."

Fires studied him for a moment and raised a disapproving eyebrow, but said nothing. She turned to the ticket guy and

571

handed him a credit card. "Next flight to Washington, D.C. One passenger."

They stopped at the security checkpoint. "Promise me," Fires said, "you're gonna get on the plane. I said I'd watch you get on, but I got stuff to do."

"I promise, but you have to do something for me?"

She smiled skeptically. "Have to? I've done a lot already."

Warren put a hand on her arm. "And I appreciate it. But... one more thing. Check on Cole. Make sure she gets out of the country."

She gave him an odd smile. "You're protective of her."

"She's even more reckless than I am, and I just chased a dude across Paris rooftops."

Fires nodded.

"Seriously. Will you check in on her? Make sure she gets out safely?"

Fires finished her iced tea. "I will. And if you ever get over your wife, look me up." She winked.

"Huh?"

She turned and began walking away, rattling the ice cubes in her empty cup.

"Wait," Warren called. She stopped. "I know you went out on a limb for me. I appreciate it. Might be rotting in a Chinese jail right now if not for you."

She walked back to him, took him by both shoulders and met his eyes. She was tall. Not as tall as him, but probably six foot. "Rob. You're a handsome guy. A smart guy. A good guy. You don't need to be so severe all the time. You're acting as though you *are* in a Chinese prison. And you shouldn't act that way because there are a lot of people who *actually* are." Her voice filled with emotion and cracked. "I know some of them." She shook her head. "I don't know if it's guilt because of your troubles when you got back from Afghanistan, something from your childhood, or if you're just an uptight guy. But you're *not* gonna save the world. Stop trying." Her face relaxed a little. "Enjoy your life. Go back and win your wife back, or don't. Either way, find some relaxation and enjoyment that doesn't involve booze." She smiled at him. "And, like I said, if you *do* get over your wife, look me up."

After buying a new charger and a traveler's packet of aspirin, Warren sat at a cafe. He had three hours before his flight boarded.

He drank black coffee after black coffee, watching people pass hurriedly in all directions and glancing occasionally at a TV mounted on the wall. A few times he picked up his phone to call Sarah and Marina, but something stopped him. Calling might make him feel better temporarily, but it wasn't going to help them.

He liked Fires—her confidence and her directness. All his life, his intensity and ability to focus had served him. In the Marines, he'd become a leader. When he got home, he'd put the same intensity into being a drunk. Or maybe being a drunk was his way of dealing with the intensity. Either way, Fires was right. He'd never found another way of relaxing. One of the first things he'd learned in AA was that high-functioning people often don't learn how to relax without alcohol. And one of the worst parts of sobriety, for some, was the realization that they couldn't function at the same high level because they no longer had a way to unclench.

Warren, full of confidence, had rejected this mentally, but it had proven true. Without coke and booze, everything was just mediocre. The chase across the Paris rooftops had given him the same high, the same adrenaline rush. And he'd needed to come down, to bring himself back to normalcy. Without thinking, he'd gone to the bottle.

His talk with Sarah had factored in as well. The thought of her taking Marina to D.C. shredded his insides.

A young man darted across the cafe to stand in front of a TV. A young woman followed. Warren scooched his chair to get a better view. The chyron on the bottom of the screen scrolled slowly. TWO MORE KILLINGS IN NINE MURDERS PLOT. LAS VEGAS AND TOKYO TARGETED.

Images of Fei Mingkang and Nathan Jackson appeared, along with bullet-pointed bios in French. Warren didn't need to read them.

His first instinct was to call Cole. Instead, he stood and watched the screen over the shoulders of the young couple. A waiter turned up the sound as a small crowd gathered. He only understood every tenth word of the report, but he got the gist.

The head of the New Vegas Mafia had been assassinated and Cole had been right about the Tokyo target. Exactly right.

He shook his head and returned to the table. They'd been so close in Las Vegas. He needed to revisit everything they'd done, to tie up loose ends and figure out if they'd missed anything important.

He had just over $3,000 to his name. He needed to return to New York, find a job in private security, and get his life back in order. When he'd decided to fly back to D.C., two things had been in his mind. Bakari Smith and Blue Lightning, the '69 Cougar he'd been forced to abandon.

Now he had a third thing.

128

The valet pulled the door open and stepped aside as Cole strode through. She looked up and down the block in front of the hotel. The throng of reporters was gone, likely back in their newsrooms covering the new shootings. Others might be covering the blue vest protests that had shut down parts of Paris.

A young woman approached, shoving a phone in her face. "Ms. Cole, do you want to comment on the two murders that happened today?" She spoke English with a British accent.

"Damn right I do. But first, can you do me a favor?"

"Um…"

"What's your name?" Cole asked.

"Rebecca McKnight. I work for *The Guardian* in London."

"You're far from home."

"Not as far as you."

Cole smiled. "*Touché. The Guardian* sent you from London to Paris to talk to me?"

"*And* to cover the shooting."

"Here's the favor. I want to say some things. Can you call or text any reporters you know, especially TV people, and get them here?"

"What's in it for me?"

Cole considered. "Did you read my article in *The Barker*?"

"Which one? I read them both."

"The second."

"You called that one—Fei Mingkang." A glint of grudging respect made its way into the reporter's expression. "Why do you think I'm camped in front of this hotel on Christmas while everyone else ran back to their newsroom? Your piece is date stamped. You knew beforehand. Either you're in on it"—she smirked and a subtle eye roll made it clear she'd dismissed the idea—"or you're gonna be a legend."

Cole shifted her weight from foot to foot, rocking slightly. "You're right—I'm *not* in on it, and I doubt I'll end up anything more than a freelancer looking for gigs. But here's what's in it for *you*. If I figure out who's next, I'll give you the scoop. All my research. You just gotta write it."

McKnight's babyface—round and pink-cheeked like it rarely saw the sun—pinched in skepticism. "Why in the names of Harry and Meghan would you do that?"

The valet hovered too close for comfort, so Cole leaned in. "I have reasons not to want to be associated with this story anymore. Not that I can get away from it, exactly. But more importantly, it'll be better coming from you, printed in a more old-school newspaper. You want the deal?"

The young reporter had already pulled out her phone. "Sure, I want it. Lucky for me"—she flashed a coy smile—"*and* for you, I'm on a group text with a dozen of the best journalists—and biggest gossips—in Paris."

An hour later, Cole stood on a small footstool before roughly twenty reporters, including teams from a French news channel and CNN, a Paris-based reporter from the *New York Times*, and a stringer from the *Washington Post*.

While waiting, she'd downed two coffees, three aspirin, and three glasses of water. Her hangover was fading.

"I'm Jane Cole, former reporter for the *New York Sun*. I was assigned the story of the Raj Ambani shooting in New York because it happened a couple miles from our newsroom. Since then, I've followed this story around the United States and the world." She paused, looking from face to face, trying to meet their eyes. She tried to project confidence, but truthfully, she was gath-

576

ering strength for what she had to say next. "I solved the nine murders case." Her cheeks flushed as she said it. Like most reporters, she was more comfortable behind a laptop than in front of TV cameras. And she was more comfortable speaking truth in print—backed by research and evidence—than she was making blanket declarative statements aloud. But she needed to engage in a way that would turn the world's attention and her article—though a decent start—hadn't done it. "I published an article with the name of the mastermind. His name is Ibo Kane. A couple days later, and using the information I've collected through the course of my investigation, I predicted the identity of the seventh victim, Fei Mingkang. She was murdered this morning. I've invited you all here—members of the press—to ask me questions. It may be too late to stop what's happening. I don't know. But I'll stand here until every question you have about my research and this case has been answered."

The stringer from the *Washington Post* held up a hand like a defense attorney ready to make an objection in court. An older black man, he wore a tan fedora and old-fashioned aviator-style glasses. During her monologue, he'd stroked his bushy gray beard skeptically. "Ms. Cole, bold declarations aside, and with all due respect to the work you did, don't you think—as journalists—we should leave it up to police to declare a case 'solved'?"

Cole locked eyes with him. "No."

"May I ask why not?"

"We can leave it up to police to call cases closed or under investigation or whatever. That's their business. My business is the truth. *Your* business too, I'd imagine." She raised her eyebrows in challenge. "It *should* be." He gave a small nod and Cole continued. "In this case, my job was to figure out what happened. I tried speaking with police sources and got very little. So I figured it out myself." Her mind flashed on Warren. He deserved credit, too. But public acknowledgment was the last thing he'd want at this moment. "Others helped me." She thought of Alex Frias and Gabby. "A lot. I won't name them right now, but they know who they are and if they want to step forward, they know where to find a newsroom."

The man shook his head. "But Ms. Cole, yours is one of a hundred wild theories out there. Surely you know that more evidence is needed."

She gave him a hard, stony look. "More than predicting the next murder in print?" The man leaned away slightly, demurring. She had him. "Look," she continued in a friendly tone, "I was a beat reporter for a long time. Trained to write the facts, cultivate police sources, and so on. Last thing I wanted was to throw out a story that was too long for most people to read that included lots of speculation. But what I wrote is correct."

She held up her phone, open to the article she'd written for *The Barker*. "It's all here, people. I know reporting is hard and gossip is easy. It's easier for you all to throw out a bunch of crap, a bunch of theories, instead of digging deep into the powerful people. But for God's sake, do your job. At least two more people will die if you don't."

For the next three hours, she took questions. Questions about her reporting. Questions about her husband. Questions about her personal life. And question after question about Ibo Kane. Most of the questions were basic information she'd covered in her story. Many were stupid. Some were insulting. The only thing she didn't go into was what she'd recently learned about her husband's death —Chris Morgan and Julio Lopez and Willian Wei and Afghanistan. That would remain off the table as long as she could keep it off.

Other questions, however, dug deep and elucidated pieces of the story Cole herself didn't know. Luckily, McKnight knew some of the top reporters in Paris. They'd read her pieces, along with hundreds of others about the murders, so they asked nuanced questions about the killings and her research.

One by one, reporters took their turns. Some left after getting their answers, but others arrived to take their places. Some tourists even stopped and took a video of her, probably streaming it on Threads or Facebook.

As the crowd thinned, McKnight asked a question. "Jane, assuming you're right, what needs to happen next? What is a good outcome, from your point of view?"

The unexpected question hit Cole hard. She hadn't even thought about it. She'd been like a dog with a bone on this story.

In her mind, breaking it had been the final step. Now she was in new territory.

Across the street, an old black Peugeot was double-parked. She hadn't noticed it arrive, but now a man wearing a black jacket and jeans sat on the hood. He stared straight at her and, from the look on his face, he'd been doing so for a while. He smiled. It was a strange, cold smile. He'd been watching her. For a chilling instant, she imagined that one of the last two rifles could be trained on her.

"Jane, are you going to answer the question?"

She shifted her eyes back to the baby-faced reporter. "I know what I wrote isn't enough for law enforcement, but I have to believe they have more information than I do. Much of what I found is in the public record. If law enforcement can't—or won't—do their jobs, then others should."

McKnight frowned. "But what does that mean, practically? What would you have people do?"

"Research, call your politicians, call your law enforcement. I don't know. But if Ibo Kane can get away with this…"

She trailed off, not wanting to finish the thought and also distracted by the man across the street, who'd just gotten into his car. He started it and drove away without another glance in her direction. She tried to suppress the fear that she was being watched, followed. There were so many people who might be watching her that she almost laughed. Then almost cried. All while keeping her face stoic.

When the last question had been answered and the last reporter had wandered off, she thanked McKnight, took her number, and collapsed on a couch in the lobby. Her hangover was gone, but she was too tired to go up to her room.

She scanned her texts, which included a dozen messages from friends and colleagues telling her they'd watched her press conference. CNN International had taken a piece of it live. Other networks had run her opening monologue during segments on the killings.

Next, she opened her email and found the one from Alex Vane.

Jane,

Your two stories on the nine murders are our two biggest pieces of the year. By far. The story you wrote predicting Fei Mingkang is going viral in ways

579

we've never seen. We had to double our server capacity. Consider this email a blank check. We'll triple your price per word and pay for unlimited travel anywhere you want to go. We'll print anything you send us after throwing our best editors at it. BUT KEEP SENDING US STORIES. This could be retirement money for you if you keep it coming.

Now, practical stuff. As you requested, I got you and Robert Warren press visas to Tokyo. They're waiting for you at the airport. First-class tickets. Already paid for. There are half a dozen flights there today, so just get there as soon as you can.

One more thing: next time you want to do a live press conference, call me and we'll stream it on our site.

Anything else, call me, text me, whatever.

And stay safe,

Alex

She tapped out a quick reply, thanking him and telling him to cancel Warren's ticket and visa. She'd be taking the next leg of this journey on her own.

129

DeLunge logged onto the chatroom. His brothers were spread out among several time zones, so he was never sure who'd be present. Tonight most had already logged on. They knew what he'd been doing, knew that the final phase of the mission hinged on him.

He scrolled through the chat log. The last half-hour had mostly been small talk and speculation about the status of his mission. Nothing from their General. His leader was still 'General Ki,' but sometimes the name Ibo Kane moved to the front of his mind instead. This caused an odd buzzing sensation, like an alarm sounding. He'd held it at bay long enough to complete his task, but it was becoming more difficult to ignore.

The comments in the chat seemed nervous, superficial. His outburst during their last chat had likely left his brothers worried about whether he would carry out his task. And yet, he had.

He leaned over the keyboard, tapping out his message slowly with two fingers.

Gunner_Vision:

9/9

Initiated

(Los Angeles Elites)

An international brotherhood united by General Ki for a singular mission: to end technological oppression, to restore individual freedoms, to birth a new era of digital liberty.

He pressed "Enter" and walked to the fridge. He'd tossed the Johnny Walker Blue off the Ballona Creek Bridge, along with the other things he'd stolen, but beer never tasted as good as it did after completing a difficult mission. He opened one and took a long swig. Why did it taste bitter and unsatisfying?

Dexter, his orange and white tabby, leaped up from under the desk and rubbed his sides against the warmth of his computer screen. DeLunge sat again and Dexter found his lap.

The replies were all congratulatory, but something was wrong. He didn't feel like he was supposed to.

Kokutai-Goji: *Well done, my American brother.*

Tread_on_This!: *New Year's Eve fireworks!*

8/15/47: *I only wish I could be standing there when it happens.*

Tread_on_This!: *But then you'd be dismembered or burned alive.*

One brother had a question.

No_Surveillance_State: *Was the setup as expected?*

DeLunge knew the man behind the screen name—an architect and ex-hippie in San Francisco who wanted to destroy the system, but for very different reasons than DeLunge. He was the kind of guy he'd hate in real life, but he'd acquired the plans to the building and he deserved an answer.

Gunner_Vision: *Your plans were spot on, No_Surveillance_State. Only issue was a locked door, not on the digital system. I broke through and staged it as a robbery.*

No_Surveillance_State: *Damn. Sorry about that. Sounds like you did the right thing.*

Gunner_Vision: *Question for Kokutai-Goji. Will the party still happen as planned? If they suspect anything after they discover the door, then…*

Kokutai-Goji: *Many of the men and women have extra security. We anticipated that. But that will be for entering and exiting the building. And the doors of the party will be monitored as well. My guess is that no one is expecting anything other than another sniper-style event. I will monitor communications from the club. If anything changes, you will be the first to know.*

Gunner_Vision: *Good.*

He didn't mean it and he wasn't sure why. He'd seen the guest list and genuinely wanted every person on it dead. He'd said prayers for the waiters, bartenders, and security personnel who would die as well. He took no pleasure in those deaths. But that's what happens when you serve the wicked. Every war had civilian casualties, after all.

He stroked Dexter, who looked up briefly. Why wasn't he happier about this?

Sometimes memories struck DeLunge at the worst times. Now, in his moment of triumph, all he could think about was that long-ago argument and the resulting fight. The sound of his CO's arm snapping. To that point, he'd loved his service. Then everything went wrong.

These men on the screen, most of whom he'd never met and never *would* meet, were his new unit. The tone in the chat had turned more celebratory since he posted his success. So why couldn't he celebrate with them?

He shut down the computer without signing off. Beer in one hand, Dexter pressed between his chest and his massive forearm, he walked to the bedroom.

The window beside the bed was cracked and, as he sat, a cool breeze blew off the ocean and hit his face. It was almost dawn.

Roughly ninety-six hours before a button tapped on his phone would trigger the fuse on the RDX and shred the bodies of many of the most famous people in the world.

130

Saturday

"First time in Tokyo?" The taxi driver spoke English haltingly, but well enough to be understood. It came as a relief after Cole's failed attempt to figure out the public transportation system.

"Yes. How far to the hotel?"

"One hour. Maybe half. Business or pleasure?"

Mount Fuji loomed over the skyline to the west. She'd caught a glimpse of it from a special observation deck at the airport, but it had grown more magnificent as the sun rose. She'd heard about beautiful hotels and luxurious resorts around the mountain. She wished she was headed to one of those. "Not pleasure... but not exactly business."

After her press conference, she'd somehow summoned the energy to pack and hurry to the airport, where she'd caught a red-eye from Paris to Tokyo. Alex's email had mentioned a "blank check," and he wasn't kidding about the first-class ticket. She'd collapsed into her seat and slept most of the flight, waking refreshed, but not exactly looking forward to the day ahead.

Her eyes dropped to her phone. She'd received so many texts and emails over the last day that she couldn't read them all. Instead, she scanned the names of the senders, looking for one in particular.

Warren: *I'm in D.C. Call me when you can.*

She smiled and cracked the window. Just like Warren to get straight to the point after all they'd been through. "You mind if I make a call?" she asked the driver.

He shrugged and she dialed. He turned on the radio, cheesy love ballads that reminded her of top-40 radio in the U.S., though the lyrics were all in Japanese.

"Cole, you in Tokyo, or...?" Warren sounded tired and far away.

"Tokyo, yeah. Just got here. D.C., huh?" She thought she knew why but, like any good reporter, she tried to ask open-ended questions.

"Gotta deal with Blue Lightning. And Marty Goldberg. I figured I'd look into that angle more, at least find out if the cops are looking into whether Kane had anything to do with his death."

"Not a bad idea. I figure my work on this story is basically done. Now I need to do everything I can to bring people's attention to what's already out there."

Warren sighed. "I'll let you know if I find anything."

"Sounds good."

"Good."

Cole closed her eyes. The amount unspoken between them weighed on her, but she didn't know how to bring it out.

"Cole?"

"Yeah?"

He sighed. "I don't know."

There was another silence, then she said, "Don't kill Bakari Smith." Warren laughed, and it was good to hear. "I mean, seriously. Maim him if you *have* to, but don't actually kill him."

"I won't."

"That's the real reason you're in D.C., right?" Cole asked.

Warren said nothing.

"You'll get it back, you know. Your sobriety."

"I know."

"*Do you?*"

"I do," Warren said. "There are different types of drunks. Some, when they relapse, it's a slippery slope. Things go from bad to worse and they end up back in rehab—or dead—a year later.

585

Not me. I'm the other type, who has a relapse and never goes back. That was it."

He sounded sure of himself, but he was good at sounding sure of himself when he needed to. She hoped he was right, but doubted it.

"You and me," she said, "as a couple. We'd be a disaster." She laughed quietly. "I mean, an *absolute* disaster."

"We've got some redeeming qualities."

"What? No. Honey, we're a dumpster fire topped with sprinkles."

Warren chuckled. "I guess we're each enough of a disaster on our own. Together, yeah…" He paused. "Probably why you married Matt. Sounds like a stable, upright guy."

"He was. And you probably married Sarah for the same reason."

"Opposites attract," he said.

"They do."

After another pregnant silence, Warren cleared his throat. "For the life of me, I can't remember what happened the other night."

"We didn't sleep together, Rob. You passed out. That was that." Cole listened to the quiet hissing of tires on freeway. Out the window, the Tokyo skyline grew closer. Dozens and dozens of skyscrapers of white and gray and brown stone, framed against a clear blue sky. "So this is gonna be it for a while, huh?"

Warren didn't say anything.

"Lemme know if you find anything new on Goldberg."

"I will."

"I hope you get Blue Lightning back. Sorry we had to leave her in the snow."

"I'll get her back," he said.

She liked that his confidence had returned, even if he was forcing it a little. "What then?" She figured Warren was avoiding New York, avoiding Sarah and Marina. This was her way of bringing it up. She pictured Warren's temples popping out at the question.

"I don't know," he said.

"Just promise me you won't kill Bakari Smith. Remember what I said. He's not *in-love* material. You want some free advice?"

"No."

"Too bad. Find Blue Lightning, drive her north, and show up for Marina. We've done all we can."

"You're in Tokyo doing more."

"You chased one of the perps through Paris and they deported you for it. You don't owe the world anything. Go be with your family."

"I'll think about it," Warren said.

The driver took an exit into downtown Tokyo. "Five minutes," he said.

Cole listened to faint static on the line. "Gotta go."

"Bye, Cole."

"Bye, Warren. Be safe."

After checking into the hotel, Cole bought a selfie stick at the gift shop, attached it to her phone, and started a FaceTime call with Alex Vane. As she wandered out of the hotel and into a large street market, Alex's tech person got on the line and talked her through what he was doing. She understood none of the details but got the big picture.

The Barker had set up a special section of its website for the nine murders. In a few minutes, her video would be streamed live there, a sort of inside look into her investigation. The whole thing felt corny and overly dramatic, just as her press conference had. She knew of no other way to bring attention to the story, though, and trusted Alex and his people to make it go viral.

In the distance, she saw the towering office building where Mingkang had been shot. She headed towards it and began to address the world.

131

Hirota Sanada scanned the crowd from behind black sunglasses. The reporter's head was visible just below her phone, which hovered a couple feet above her head. The day was unseasonably warm, but he pulled up the collar of his leather jacket nonetheless. For a moment, he imagined himself to be Robert Warren, saving the little boy outside the conference center in London. People compared Warren to The Rock, one of Sanada's favorite actors.

At five and a half feet tall and a hundred forty pounds, Sanada was no action hero. He felt guilty about his love for American films and the buff stars who made them shine, but he couldn't help it. He'd chosen the screen name Kokutai-Goji. Kokutai meant "sovereignty" or "national identity," a concept dating back hundreds of years. The prevalence of American cultural products damaged Japan, he knew, but he loved them anyway. Something about the massive American stars made his heart race.

He opened a blank webpage on his phone and navigated to Cole's livestream on *The Barker*. Holding the device in front of his face, he kept an eye on the back of her head as she navigated the crowd, listening to her words through his AirPods as he walked.

"The crowd is huge," she said, "and it's odd. It's like nothing happened here. Average Tokyo residents and tourists are going on as though everything is the same. The concierge at the hotel pointed out to me that the New Year is the biggest holiday in Japan. *Shogatsu*. The festivities start days before and, apparently, this street fair is part of it. I think I'm only a few blocks from the building where Mingkang was murdered. Now, let me tell you a little about why she was killed, and why I predicted it in advance."

He muted his phone. He'd had enough of this woman. It would be a pleasure to kill her, he told himself. He wasn't quite sure he believed it, though. Most of his online brothers had military backgrounds. T_Paine had been a sniper in Vietnam. Gunner_Vision and The Shepherd both had military backgrounds as well. He'd spent his life bathed in the glow of screens and bent over circuit boards.

He tried to visualize it as he fingered the knife in his pocket, a CS20A cold steel hunting knife. Guns were almost impossible to find in Tokyo. Even carrying the three-inch blade in his pocket was a criminal act. He pictured himself plunging it into her chest, slashing her throat. It made him feel powerful, but also afraid. Like he wasn't supposed to be this powerful. Jane Cole was famous now, so her death would spark an investigation the likes of which Tokyo had rarely seen.

The crowd thinned as people left the market. Before them, dozens of towers dominated the sky. He knew she was headed to the sixty-story Nishimoto Japan building. Its curved base straightened as it reached the tenth floor, making it look like the base of a tree emerging from the ground.

He turned the sound back on as she reached the building. "I'm approaching the Nishimoto Japan building, hoping to give you a glimpse of the site where it all went down." She went quiet. Only her breathing was audible in the silence. Sanada figured the delay was likely two to three seconds. After all, her signal had to travel from her phone to a cellphone tower, then to Seattle where *The Barker* was housed, then bounced to a server farm somewhere in Texas, most likely.

She stopped and pointed. What a fool. Her hand extended past the selfie stick so no one could see where she was pointing.

In the planning stages, he'd scoped out the building for over a month, using every excuse he could to study it. He knew every store and noodle shop within a ten-block radius.

"Duh," she was saying, turning the phone so it took in the

building. "You can see there's a heavy police presence at the base of the tower. I'm going to see how close I can get. While I walk, I really need to say something." Cole glanced at the camera as if trying to make eye contact with millions. "Why the hell am I doing this? Because the world needs to wake up. It's not like we don't know what's happening. We just need to pay attention, and if me pulling this stunt can bring a little more attention to what's going on, then I guess that's a good thing."

In the movies, men with murderous intentions followed their targets until they were alone, then pulled them into alleys and stabbed them. He'd been quick to volunteer to kill the reporter, but it wouldn't be as easy as he'd hoped. There were police everywhere. Japan had about ten gun deaths per year. No one of Mingkang's status had been murdered in decades. The New Year and the warm weather weren't helping. The streets were even more crowded than usual. Her hotel, no doubt, would be packed as well.

Sanada was no fan of Ibo Kane. In fact, the Chinese-American businessman was loathsome. His business tentacles reached all over the world, including into Japan. It was the latter Sanada cared about. He'd first heard of Kane in the early 2010s when Sanada had been fired from his job at a prominent computer manufacturer when the operation relocated to Mexico. In front of his computer screen, alone in his small apartment outside of Tokyo, Sanada had read about the chain of events that led to the move. The company had been purchased by a larger computer manufacturer, which had then acquired a massive manufacturing plant in Mexico. It had taken two years to get approval to move the construction, but one day it happened. The man behind the company was Ibo Kane. Still, as much as he loathed the businessman, he'd made peace with the fact that Kane had turned out to be General Ki. Sometimes God used imperfect messengers, he told himself.

He turned off the reporter's livestream, but kept an eye on her. This was going to be more difficult than he'd thought.

132

"The building is stunning." Cole felt like a fool talking into her phone, her arm outstretched before her like the tourists she once made fun of in New York. "Looks like a tree trunk rising from the earth. I'd love to go inside, but—" she angled the phone toward the perimeter of the building, where hundreds of officers ringed the edifice—"obviously that's not going to happen. I'm getting the sense that violence like this is rare in Japan. *Very* rare. Festivities are going on as normal—New Year's Eve is a big deal here—but... I don't know. The response to the attack seems more coordinated, more..." She couldn't find the words.

She'd never been to Japan and she regretted that her first trip had to occur under these circumstances.

She turned the phone back on herself. "Okay, folks, what do you want to see next? Should I walk the perimeter?" Alex had given her three tips for live-streaming. Be yourself. Keep talking. And don't worry about being boring. Alex had once been a reporter, too. He'd transitioned to running the online magazine *The Barker*, but his warning to not worry about being boring had spoken to her. As a reporter, she was trained to be economical with words. Her editors would tell her, "You have six-hundred words to tell this story. Make every one count." Online streaming was different. It was all just "content." Whether it was interesting or good wasn't exactly the point. It just had to attract eyeballs.

She walked around the edges of the building describing the scene, the architecture, and the police presence, which was like nothing she'd ever seen.

"That's the building," she said. "My bet is you all want to hear what I think will happen next. We all know that, after today, two cities remain. San Francisco and Los Angeles." She laughed bitterly. "Half of me wants to check my phone to see if there's any news out of those cities. If you go back to my first article on *The Barker*, you'll see the types of people I believe are under threat. Between San Francisco and L.A., there are literally hundreds of people who might be next, and I imagine those people are taking extra precautions. Okay, I'm beating around the bush here. Who's next?"

She sat on a wooden bench with a view of a beautiful courtyard. Trees were decorated with lights and people walked hurriedly across, talking on phones or carrying shopping bags. "*Media.* I don't have a name, but I think the media is next. What do I mean? If I wanted to take over the world, what would I do? Bribe politicians? Sure. But I'd also want control of the financial system. Kane's desire to do *that* is why I'm in Tokyo right now. But none of this works without an ability to control the media, to control how people think. And despite the fact that most of the media have moved to digital, there's still value in TV stations and newspapers. *Old media.* Kane already controls much of the social media you use every day. So if I were him, I'd be trying to buy the *New York Times*, CNN International, the *Times of London*. But they aren't selling, and we're talking San Francisco and L.A. So, I don't know. There's the *LA Times*, the *San Francisco Chronicle*? But those are likely too small-time for him. Great papers, but I don't think they're enough to move the needle for a guy like Kane."

Cole stood and walked across the courtyard, the phone trained on her face. "I do my best thinking while I'm walking. I don't know how many of you are watching, but here's what I want you to do. Get in the comments section on this video and share your research. Maybe we can crowdsource this thing. I've tried to share how I think about it, but there are too many options, especially in LA. Share your theories and let's see if we can keep someone from getting killed."

She ended the video and turned back toward her hotel. As she turned, a man's head dropped quickly. He'd been staring at her from across the courtyard. Not too surprising, given the way she'd been carrying on. Still, it made her uncomfortable.

Her phone rang. She answered as she turned back away from her hotel, hurrying across the courtyard. "Hello?"

"It's Alex. You did awesome."

"Hold on a sec." She glanced over her shoulder. The man wasn't following her. He'd turned away as well. "Sorry, Alex. Just paranoid. What were you saying?"

"Peak views hit five point four million?"

"Is that good?"

Alex laughed. "Yes. What's next?"

"Back to the hotel. I'll get into the comment section and see if we can figure out who's next."

133

Warren stared at Bakari Smith's house, gripping the steering wheel. He relaxed his hands, then tightened them around the cool leather. He repeated the action again, then again. Tightening and relaxing. Somehow this soothed him.

His hands were at home on the wheel. Blue Lightning gave him some version of the relaxation Fires had told him to seek. He thought back to the times he'd felt at home after getting sober. Most had occurred behind the wheel of his beloved car while cruising the streets of Brooklyn at night with the windows down, listening to the sounds of the city. Or the time he'd driven to Jersey and smelled the salt marshes outside Atlantic City.

Getting his car back had proven easier than he'd expected. After three phone calls, he'd been directed to the right impound lot. The $650 fine made him curse under his breath as he paid it. They'd matched his ID to the registration information in the glove compartment.

Finding Bakari Smith's house had been more difficult. He'd tried Gabby first—two calls and a text—but she was still in the wind. His calls had gone straight to voicemail; the text remained unanswered. He'd called the FBI, but they wouldn't give out Smith's address. As a last resort, he'd done a public records search on his phone. Turned out Smith had hosted a fundraiser for a

Virginia State senator last year. His address was in the public record.

A stone townhouse in Arlington, it was a nice place, and not far from his FBI office.

He'd been waiting two hours when Smith arrived in a silver SUV. His former friend's white button-down was tucked in, and the fat hung over his belt, jiggling as he stepped onto the curb.

Warren took three deep breaths, tried to relax the muscles of his face into something resembling a smile, and stepped out. "Bakari."

Smith stopped on the sidewalk. Recognizing Warren, he stepped back. "Hey, hey. What the hell are you doing here?"

Warren raised both hands. "Not here to cause any trouble. This isn't about Sarah."

Smith looked skeptical. He sighed, took off his round glasses, then put them back on. "If I ask you inside, you gonna kick the crap out of me?"

Warren took a tentative step forward, hands out, palms up, and shook his head. "I'm gonna give you a tip that will make you famous."

Smith's place was nicer than Warren expected. The furniture was new, the wood floors sparkled—every corner was clean and tidy. The place smelled like money and Warren paused to consider whether the agent was corrupt. He discarded the notion; Smith had jumped from the NYPD to the FBI for a lot more money and, unlike Warren, he hadn't blown his paychecks on coke and booze.

They sat across from one another in the living room. Smith folded his hands in his lap, waiting for Warren to speak.

"I've been in London and Paris," Warren said.

"I saw the video. Stupid as hell, you ask me."

Warren's cheeks tightened. "Why?"

"Back before you got canned, how did you like it when average Joe's played hero? We have processes—*procedures*—and they're there for a reason. I'm sure the cops in London and Paris agree."

Last time they'd seen each other, Cole had to restrain Warren. Smith had been afraid, then. Now they were on his home turf and he was much more comfortable. He made the same argument Fires had made, and Warren couldn't disagree. Still, he wished Smith appreciated what he'd tried to do.

Warren closed his eyes, trying to find some calm. Clenching his fists, he opened them. "When we were here before, we met a lobbyist named Marty Goldberg. Did you read my friend's article?"

"Read it. Bunch of speculation. Like a lot of crap in the news these days."

"There's *some* speculation." He said it as calmly as he could. "But she's also *correct*. You heard about Tokyo?"

"I did."

"She predicted that. In writing."

"Did she?"

Warren let out a long sigh. He had to remember that not everyone was following this story as closely as he was. The case was important, but Smith was likely working on half a dozen others that were just as important, if less sensational. "She predicted Mingkang would be the next victim. She—"

Smith leaned forward, waving a hand dismissively. "Probably a lucky guess."

"Her theory is right!" It came out louder than he'd intended. Warren took a breath, trying to stay calm. "Let me get back to what I was saying about Goldberg." He paused until Smith raised his eyebrows as if to say, *Get on with it.* "Right after we met Marty Goldberg, we got tailed. In her first article, Cole connected Goldberg to Ibo Kane. You've at least heard of *him*, right?"

Smith nodded. "If you ask me, it was wildly irresponsible to print that story without proof. Probably why it wasn't in the *Post* or the *Times*. I work the media all the time and I've never even heard of—what was it?—*The Barker?*"

Warren ignored the jab. "Goldberg *was* working for Kane. Was his personal lobbyist in D.C. He knew too much. Kane suicided him. Goldberg was sleazy as hell. He's a lobbyist, after all. Guess is that Kane knew he was sleazy, knew he'd flip on him if a better client or a better offer came along. Or, if the FBI showed up asking questions."

Smith sighed and looked at his watch. "This isn't my case, Rob. I—"

"Let me finish. You're in a unique position to prove Kane

596

committed a crime on U.S. soil. Imagine for a moment he's guilty. Imagine he's behind this. What would that do for your career if, say, you're the guy who busts him? FBI's already on this case. Could be they're already pulling the thread I'm offering you. But maybe they aren't. I'm guessing not. They've been a week behind us the whole time. If they still are, could be you're the only one looking into this angle."

"I'm *not* looking into this." Smith stared at him, chewing on his gums silently. Warren had seen him do it before; it meant he was interested. He always had his eye on the next promotion, the next pay raise. And even if his old friend thought he was crazy, the thought of cracking this case had to turn him on.

Warren needed to seal the deal. "You know me, man. Am I a crazy conspiracy theorist? Would I have come back to D.C. if I *didn't* have something real?"

"I thought you came to beat the hell out of me over Sarah."

Warren pressed his feet into the floor. "Don't say her name again and you and I will be fine."

There was a long silence. Warren watched him think.

Smith had an annoying habit of taking his glasses off his face and buffing the lenses on his shirt, then putting them back on and doing it again.

After the second round of lens buffing, Smith crossed his legs and leaned back. "What's the tip?"

134

Cole spent the afternoon engaging with readers in the comments section of *The Barker*. She also responded to emails and texts from reporters, providing updated quotes and details that hadn't made it into her stories. Journalists were now writing to her from major newspapers, TV stations, and tiny blogs all over the world. She fielded multiple requests for podcast interviews and co-hosting opportunities, even an invitation to appear on a Japanese game show.

Her story was getting out there, and that made her happy. She had the truth; all she could do now was amplify it as loudly as possible. If enough of the world took notice, law enforcement would be compelled to pay attention. Someone would be able to nail Ibo Kane for a specific crime. Or maybe someone would get one of his "brothers" to flip. If she could funnel the attention of the entire world onto him, someone, somewhere would bring Kane down.

In the online conversations about her work, one name came up over and over: Chandler Price. Price's townhouse had been the first story thread she'd pulled in New York. It seemed like years ago, but it had been mere weeks since she'd begun looking into the reclusive businessman who owned the building Michael Wragg used to shoot Raj Ambani. He'd used one of his bank accounts to purchase the nine rifles, and Cole assumed he'd known in advance about the shooting.

A week earlier she'd spent hours poring over his history and found no record of political activity, no extreme views posted online, and no evidence he agreed with the nine murders manifesto. But a business reporter had sent her photos of Price with Ibo Kane that had helped her break the story. Now, she and much of the online community wondered just how deeply Price was involved.

She'd tried to reach him. Vague reports had surfaced that a worldwide manhunt for Price was underway, involving the NYPD, the FBI, and the law enforcement and intelligence agencies of multiple U.S. allies.

One photo had emerged just hours earlier, purportedly of Price. Taken through the windshield of a car stopped at a red light, the photo depicted a man said to be Price in the front passenger seat wearing a brown suit jacket with a blue button-down. A beard obscured his face, making him harder to identify. Most photos of him were easy to recognize because of his pink, dumpling-like cheeks. Despite the beard, it *did* look like him. The eyes gave him away—heavy folds of skin above bright blue irises.

She leaned back in her chair and looked out the window. The sky over Tokyo had darkened and the city had come alive. Colorful lights sparkled in all directions from high rises, billboards, and festival decorations.

She logged onto her fake Threads profile and—pushing her hesitation aside—replied to the Price photo post with photos of her own, the ones sent to her by the business reporter. Price with Alvin Meyers. Price with Ibo Kane. She sent another reply with speculation about his Instagram name: Johnny Galt.

Finally, she posted screenshots of Chandler Price's financial records—the ones that proved he'd paid Michael Wragg for the nine rifles. Because she'd gotten the records from JTTF agents who'd obtained them illegally, she'd promised herself she wouldn't put them out in public. It could get her in trouble, and get them in *big* trouble. But the time for playing by the rules had passed. The financials might spark some interest from the police if they didn't already have them. Maybe they'd go viral and someone would spot Price in the wild.

Either way, her work for the day was done. She hadn't eaten

and had no energy to go downstairs for food. She ordered room service, flopped onto the bed, and turned on the TV.

Flipping through channels, she reflected on what she'd just done. Sending photos and speculation from a fake Threads account was the height of journalistic irresponsibility. Posting the illegally-obtained financial records of Price broke every rule she'd learned in journalism school.

Two weeks ago, she could have given a Ted Talk on how people who did things like that had ruined journalism in the digital age. Within a fortnight, she'd become what she loathed. The only way to forgive herself was to tell herself she'd tried to follow the rules and gotten nowhere.

Would Matt approve? He was a by-the-book guy, so she doubted it. It was hard to imagine him condoning unethical behavior, even if the end result meant solving, or perhaps stopping, murder.

Tap tap tap.

Room service had been much quicker than she expected. Or maybe she'd lost track of time in her musing. "Just a sec," she called.

She straightened the blankets and pushed the chair into the desk, wondering whether the room service guy would understand her English. For some reason, she always wanted the room to be a little neater than it was when accepting a room service order.

She opened the door and froze, confused. No room service cart. No guy holding a tray. The man in front of her wore a bitter scowl, his short black hair in a bowl cut, his eyes burning with hatred. She tried to slam the door but his foot jammed in the opening.

He shoved her back into the room, stepped in, and closed the door. Her eyes dropped to his right hand, where dancing light from the TV flashed off the polished metal of a silver blade.

He lunged forward as she stepped back, but she was too slow.

As he buried the knife in her belly, he shouted a single word: "*Freedom.*"

135

Bakari Smith shifted heavily on the couch, his head cocked and his lips pursed as he eyed Warren. "What's the tip?"

The man was interested, Warren thought, but the issue of Sarah still hung over them like a black cloud. "How closely have you followed the case?" he asked.

"Not very. I know it pops in the news, but we've got other important cases."

"Fine. So here's the tip. In New York, where the first shooting happened, we looked into a man named Chandler Price. Rich dude, real estate. The first shooting took place from the roof of *his* townhouse. Long story short, we acquired his bank records. He purchased the rifles used in the shootings so far."

Smith raised both hands. "Wait, wait, wait. *Acquired?* How'd you get the bank records?"

Warren sighed. "We got them in a way we shouldn't have." He waited for Smith to absorb the admission, then continued. "Now, Price is in the wind. Disappeared. But we already know that he paid Michael Wragg for the weapons."

Smith removed his glasses and polished the lenses absentmindedly with his shirt. "Why didn't you give this to the NYPD from the beginning, Rob?"

"We gave them a lot of what we had. There was a corrupt cop

named Joey Mazzalano. It went nowhere. Either got dropped or buried. Then Price disappeared."

"And no one has heard from him?" Smith asked.

"That's right. Photo surfaced online that says it's him, but who knows these days? Could be photoshopped or whatever."

Smith tapped his foot. "I'm still not hearing a tip."

"More I think about it, the more I think there are three levels to this. At the top, there's Ibo Kane. Maybe he's smart enough— or *powerful* enough—to shield himself from any crime that could stick. As sure as I am that he's guilty, everything that's happened in the last few days has me thinking it doesn't matter. I mean"— Warren's eyes flashed as if to challenge Smith—"would *you* have the guts to arrest him?"

Smith ignored—or perhaps hadn't noticed—the slight. "There'd be a lot of politics involved, but if we had him on something real? Murder? Then, *hell* yeah. Guys like him can get away with a lot on the financial side. But murders?" The agent scowled as if he'd tasted something unpleasant.

"That's good to hear. One level down from Kane, I think, is Chandler Price. Someone has to do the dirty work, and it's him. Pay for the guns, the transportation. Someone to move money around who has more power than the saps at the bottom. A level below Price are the guys doing the hits—or in some cases taking money from Price to *hire* hitmen. I'm talking about the disgruntled radicals Kane duped into this whole scheme."

Smith's face grew pinched, like he was getting impatient.

Warren leaned forward, his elbows on his knees. "Just listen. This dead lobbyist, Marty Goldberg, *will* connect to Chandler Price somehow. I'd bet anything on it." He stood, walked to the window, and laced his hands behind his head, his eyes fixed on Blue Lightning parked across the street. "Think about it. Me and Jane Cole come to D.C. and talk to Goldberg. Then we get tailed. Then Goldberg gets suicided. You think Kane himself arranged it? Doubtful. Just like he wouldn't have left fingerprints linking the nine rifles to himself. Chandler Price's wife Maggie knew we were on to him. We were in her damn townhouse. She told Chandler and he probably arranged the tail. At least, one of them. If the FBI—if *you*—look into Chandler Price, you're gonna find that, somehow, he's involved in the murder of Marty Goldberg in D.C. Not that he pulled the trigger, so to speak, but I bet Kane had him do it. You can get into his financials—with a court order, of course—and prove it. You do that, you can use the financials to figure out where he is. Bring him in for questioning… well, he's an old guy. I think, a *weak* guy. He'll give up Kane."

Warren returned to the couch and sat. He studied Smith, but couldn't read his former friend's reaction. From a legal standpoint, the argument was weak, but the FBI had investigative powers Warren didn't, powers he hadn't had even when he worked at the NYPD. If they got a court order for Price's financial records, they could bring him down. If they got to Price, they'd get to Kane.

"Here's my question," Smith said. "I don't get why Price hasn't already been brought in if you connected the nine rifles to him through financials."

Warren stifled a frustrated sigh. "I told you. We got the records illegally, just for our own purposes. My bet is other agencies are looking into him and just haven't gotten enough. We know for sure more attacks are planned. You could get a court order for his financials expedited because there's an imminent threat."

For the first time, Smith smiled. He didn't possess the same drive to uncover the truth that Warren did. He was a career guy who played it safe and played by the rules, but he recognized his own self-interest. "I could do that."

"But *will* you?"

Smith walked to the window. "That Blue Lightning out there?"

"Yeah."

"Kind of a gas guzzler. Not environmentally friendly."

Warren stood and stared at the man's back. "Don't screw with me, Bakari."

Smith turned and winked. "Take her for a drive. Come back in two hours. Not promising anything, but I'll see what I can do."

136

At first she didn't feel anything.

Cole stumbled back onto the bed, a mixture of shock, confusion, and horror flooding her as she stared at her belly. A rose-colored blossom stained her shirt. She pulled it up to look and her ears filled with a piercing scream. It took a moment to realize the shriek was her own. A long, deep gash tore the flesh on the right side of her abdomen. She saw inside herself—a thin white lining of fat laced with crimson blood. It left her feeling disembodied, as though seeing herself from outside. Blood slowly seeped from the wound and coursed down in a red stream over the waist of her pants.

Her vision blurred and she couldn't hold her head up without swaying. She feared she might faint. Strangely, the wound didn't hurt. There was no sensation at all.

She closed her eyes and thoughts of Matt filled her mind. Unlike Cole, Matt had believed in heaven and hell. Lying there, bleeding, she wondered whether he'd been right, and whether she'd soon see him in one of those places. She'd rather be in hell with him than in heaven without him. With her luck, she'd probably be the one to wind up in hell, leaving him alone in heaven.

Her grip on consciousness was slipping. She was blacking out as she did twenty minutes after taking a sleeping pill. She would pass out at any moment.

With horror, she realized her attacker was still in the room.

⊕

Stabbing her had been easier than he thought. And different. Sanada's entire life, he'd viewed Japan as an all-powerful entity. Something outside him, larger than him. But a nation that had rusted and atrophied over the years. Japan was now a fallen God, controlled by a few giant companies in America, Europe, and China. He'd just committed his first violent crime on her soil, and it had been easy. He'd simply walked to the hotel, taken the elevator up, and knocked on her door.

Why had he thought it would be harder?

The hem of her shirt was soaked with blood and rolled up, exposing the gash in her belly. She seemed to teeter in and out of consciousness. How many cuts did it take to kill someone? He wasn't sure. He urged himself to slit her throat, but after a couple piercing screams, she'd gone quiet. Now, lying there on the bed, breathing and bleeding, she looked peaceful. Blood loss and time would be enough to end her life.

"Japan is the victim," he said, more to himself than to her. "Cut her throat," he whispered.

He stepped forward, knife tight in his hand.

"Wait," she said, her voice weak.

⊕

It was all she could think of. "Wait."

It worked. The man stopped. Somehow, the knife at his side had no blood on it. Had he wiped it on his pants? "Can you tell me why?" She barely recognized the sound of her own voice.

"To save Japan."

"From what? From who?" Thoughts of Matt still drifted in and out of her mind. Random images of him, scenes from their life. A soft touch in the kitchen, a spilled cup of coffee. A hug at the airport. Had they been coming or going? Moments long stored in her flesh were surfacing at random.

"From…"

"You want to save Japan from men like Ibo Kane. Yet you're killing for him. Don't you see that?" Her own words sounded like

605

they were being played on low volume from a speaker far away. Only then did she realize she was trying to stay alive. She was trying to convince him not to kill her.

She lay with her back on the bed, but her legs dangled off the bottom, her feet flat on the floor. He stepped toward her and his shoe landed on her bare foot. He pressed his weight down. Hard. A toe knuckle popped. It hurt more than the wound in her belly.

"The last two targets," she said. "At least tell me who they are."

Sanada pressed his heel into her toes. He'd seen the movies. The victim always jumped up and, with one last heroic effort, turned the tables on the killer. In the elevator, he'd told himself he wouldn't let that happen. He could see the strength draining from her. Maybe he wasn't The Rock, but neither was she.

He'd also seen the war movies. The ones where the soldier is faced with a moment of conscience after coming upon an unarmed foe in the jungles of Vietnam or a forest outside Normandy. In the quiet elevator ride to Jane Cole's floor, he'd told himself only one thing: he wouldn't be that soldier.

He'd be the one who killed without conscience.

His heel on her toes, he tried to work up the courage to take three large steps around the side of the bed and slit her throat. Instead, he said, "There aren't two more murders." He needed someone to know, even if that someone would only know for a few minutes before she died. He wanted credit.

"Seven, eight, nine," she said.

"No. Seven, eight, then hundreds and hundreds."

Her eyes opened wide. The look of shocked horror on her face evoked in him a pleasurable feeling—a *powerful* feeling. He wasn't sure how he felt about Japan anymore, and he wasn't sure whether what he was doing would save the people who'd built the country he once loved. What he knew now was that he quite enjoyed power. At this moment, he had it.

He eased his heel off her toes and walked around the side of the bed.

Tap tap tap.

A knock at the door.

606

He swiveled, knife raised in front of his face.

✛

Tap tap tap.

Cole watched as her attacker turned.

"Room service!" a loud voice through the door.

He turned back to face her, knife held close to his face. Fear filled his eyes.

As though she'd been forcibly thrust back into her body, the pain came all at once. A sharp twinge followed by stabs of screaming intensity.

Between waves of pain, she rolled onto her left side toward the man, swinging her right leg up and kicking him in the stomach. "Help!"

She rolled off the other side of the bed as the man stumbled.

An unintelligible shout came from the hallway.

She lunged for the door, but the man with the knife was at her back.

She felt a pinch, like a violent pinprick. Turning, she saw the handle of the knife sticking out of her shoulder. She screamed again, then whirled and kicked and punched at the same time; both her hand and foot connected with something meaty and hard. Her attacker stumbled back again and she opened the door, then dove into the hallway.

She tumbled across the room service cart that blocked the door, sending metal trays clanging and tipping plates of French fries and cups of soda across the carpet.

The last thing she saw before passing out was the room service guy falling atop her as he pulled the cart down as a shield against the attacker.

137

When Warren returned two hours later, Smith was waiting by the door. "You're not going to believe this."

Warren followed him to the living room. Night had fallen while he drove. Warm recessed lights now lit the room and gleamed off the hardwood floor.

"What?" Warren asked as they sat.

"Taskforce had already been set up. JTTF in NYC plus six agents down here—one of whom is someone I play squash with on Sundays."

"And?" Warren asked.

"They'd already sucked up the investigation into Goldberg. And *he'd* already been under investigation for six months. It's D.C. Crooked lobbyists are a dime a dozen. But apparently he was also laundering drug money *through* his lobbying firm."

"Wait, wait, wait. What's that got to do with Price or Ibo Kane?"

Smith smiled. The glee on his face wasn't because of a break in the case. It was because the information gave him power over Warren.

"Get that stupid grin off your face and tell me," Warren said.

Smith frowned. "Your girl was right about Kane. Marty Goldberg was laundering money for Ibo Kane, using his lobbying firm to do so. Most of Goldberg's clients were fake. He took in millions in cash from drug deals—he even paid taxes on some of it, wrote it up as legit business. Some of the money was paid back out to Chandler Price."

"Wait, Goldberg's lobbying firm *paid* Chandler Price?"

"For 'consulting fees rendered.'" Smith scoffed. "These bastards. Goldberg took in money, cleaned it, and paid Price. Price, we think, paid some of *that* money to your boy Michael Wragg. They're working on the rest of the money trail. But we know Price is in San Francisco now and—"

Warren sprang from his seat. "And you know that—"

"San Francisco is supposed to be one of the targets? Yes." He shook his head and shot Warren an *I'm not an idiot* look. "They already knew that too, of course, and were in touch with field offices in SF."

Warren walked a lap around the couch. "Wait. If Goldberg was using laundered drug money to pay Price, and Price was using *that* to buy weapons and fund the operation"—Warren frowned and shook his head—"where was the drug money coming from?"

"That's what I meant—your girl Jane Cole was right on Kane. Had a beef with Ana Diaz in Miami. Feds were looking into her for a year but never made anything stick. I guess they had some high-end turf war going, battling over the drug trade in and out of China. You believe that? Two American citizens—one with Cuban heritage and one with Chinese—battling to control the flow of heroin from Afghanistan to China and from China to the U.S?" He shook his head. "Ibo Kane has a ton of legit business, but augments it with billions in straight up drug money, too."

A cold wind blew through Warren's mind, clearing it out. Then a name appeared. William Wei. "Any chance the name William Wei came up? Alias 'Dubya Slim.' A middleman in the heroin trade."

Smith lost the smug smile he'd been wearing. "How the *hell* did you know that?"

"Tell me how he's involved."

The agent slouched and sighed, like a balloon losing air. "William Wei *worked* for Ibo Kane. He managed his drug business. Dead now. One of the last things Ana Diaz did before she got shot was to have Wei killed while he was bringing a shipment from China into the Port of Miami. Part of the turf war."

Warren's mind flashed on Cole. Had she deleted the recording of Lopez from her phone? Had she figured out that William Wei was connected to Ibo Kane, and Kane, therefore, was connected to the death of her husband?

He'd call her as soon as he finished with Smith.

"Now, Rob," Smith said. "You said this was a tip for me, right? Ya gotta promise me you're not gonna fly off to San Fran and try more of that superhero business on Chandler Price."

Warren stood. "I'll drive back to New York in the morning." It was a lie. He felt a little better knowing there was a taskforce all over Kane and Price, but there was no way he was backing off now.

"Good." Smith gave him an odd look, like he both wanted and didn't want to say something.

"What?" Warren asked.

"After your first visit, I looked into what happened up in NYC. You got a raw deal, man, and I'm sorry it happened. There's nothing I can do to help. Not from down here. But it has to feel good knowing the judge got taken down."

Warren was about to agree when he realized he had no idea what Smith was talking about. "Judge?"

"Guy whose face you bashed in. The judge on his case."

Warren stepped back. He'd almost forgotten. When he'd spoken with Gabby, she'd encouraged him to back away slowly, implying that the judge who heard the case had a history of going easy on sleazebags like the one he'd assaulted. He'd taken her advice, chalking it up to bad luck. "Start from the beginning?" he said firmly.

Smith cracked a condescending smile. "Surprised you haven't heard. Too busy galavanting around with that reporter to keep an eye on your own cases?"

"Not my case." He shook his head. "Not anymore."

Smith shrugged. "The judge who heard the case of the guy you roughed up is dead. Yesterday morning, his entire search history got leaked online. And his emails. Someone caught him with child pornography years ago, then someone flipped him. CIA, I'm guessing. He was somebody's source, so they let him keep operating."

Warren's stomach turned. "They let him... *what?*"

"Hundreds of pages of emails. Looks like he got caught, but he was a well-to-do judge. CIA flipped him, made him promise to

610

lay off the porn in exchange for information. Hard to tell exactly, but this was about ten years ago. None of this was in the emails, but reading between the lines, it's pretty clear. So he spends the next ten years going light on sentences."

"And he's dead?"

"Within hours of the stuff getting leaked, they say he killed himself."

Warren's first thought was of Gabby. He closed his eyes, trying to recall the details of the conversation. She'd said something like, "If this judge is what I think he is, he's gonna get got. But not by you. I'll do what I can." He was sure she'd leaked his emails and search records. Could she have killed him, too?

"You still here?" Smith asked.

Warren opened his eyes. "Yeah, it's just…"

"It's possible the judge or someone who owed him a favor pressured the department to get you gone," Smith said. "Maybe now… Look I don't know. Could be things are different. Maybe you can get your job back."

"You just trying to help me get my job back so I'm not tempted to follow Sarah down here?" The question had come out without his permission.

Inside him, there was a conflict. One piece was like a wild, jealous wolf. He wanted to leap across the room and rip his old fat friend to shreds. That would be easy enough.

Another part of him knew that he was to blame for his marriage falling apart. This piece couldn't blame Sarah for seeking out another, more stable man. This part also knew Marina was the one who mattered most. And if Marina found herself in the same situation with a man in twenty years, he'd want her to do exactly what Sarah did. He had no claim to his wife anymore. The problem was, these two pieces were not at peace. And as much as he tried to let the rational part of him win out, sometimes it lost. He worried this would be one of those moments. If Smith was smug or entitled, he didn't know what he would do to him.

Instead, Smith looked perplexed. "Follow Sarah… where? D.C?"

"Follow her down to D.C. When she moves here."

Smith's face was blank. "I have no idea what you're talking about, Rob."

Warren left Blue Lightning in the long-term parking and bought a standby ticket to San Francisco. He'd called Cole three times while driving from Smith's house to the airport. Each time it had gone straight to voicemail.

He'd even pulled up her social media accounts and *The Barker*, but she hadn't posted anything new on either.

While he waited for his flight, he did his best to search for her name on every social media platform he could think of, but the most recent thing he could find about her location was her livestream from Tokyo. That had been eight hours ago. He tried to watch part of it but it wouldn't load on his phone and he wasn't about to pay for airport wifi.

He stashed his phone and strolled around the terminal drinking decaf coffee and thinking about Sarah. That she wasn't moving to D.C. for Smith gave him some peace. They *were* dating, but she hadn't even told him she was moving.

He could move down when this was all over. Get an apartment. Hell, maybe Smith could get him something entry-level at the FBI. He could start over. If Sarah wasn't moving to D.C. for Smith, he had to support her. He'd go, not with her but *beside* her. For Marina.

In his pocket, his phone buzzed. The number on the caller-ID was longer than normal. An international call. "Hello?"

"Rob? It's Cole."

"Hey, we gotta talk. I just learned something about—"

"Rob, wait. I'm okay, but I'm in the hospital in Tokyo. Got stabbed. Twice."

138

The pain came in waves of varying intensity. Sharp twinges rippled along the surface of her skin and dull pounding came from deep inside the wounds, echoing through the rest of her body.

Back in the hotel room, it had come slowly. A nurse had explained that delayed pain was common after a stabbing. If the knife was sharp enough, it could enter and exit without much tearing. Then the endorphins kicked in, interacting with the opiate receptors in the brain to reduce the perception of pain, like natural morphine.

She'd awakened in the ambulance, unsure how she'd gotten there. Her memory after falling over the room service cart was a blank, empty hole. The ambulance ride had been the worst of the pain. Every bump in the road increasing the agony until her entire body rang with pain. It was better now, but even with the morphine drip, she could barely stand the sense of *wrongness* she felt.

Talking didn't help. Holding the phone to her face caused the pain to shoot from her belly into her chest. But she had to hear Warren's voice.

"I got stabbed. Twice." She let the phone go, pressing it into her shoulder. It felt a little better to have her hands down by her side.

"What happened?"

"Can't explain now. Really, I'm okay." She coughed, causing the pain to explode from her back into her arms and making her dizzy. "Well, I will be."

"One of Kane's guys?" Warren asked.

"Don't know. Police just left. Said he was a known member of the Nippon Kaigi."

"Heard of them. Ultra-nationalist Japanese organization. Right up the alley of the rest of these bastards."

The silence felt good. Knowing Rob was on the other side of the line felt good. "I don't have anyone to call but you."

Warren wasn't much for sentimental moments; she'd said it partly because it was true and partly to mess with him.

He changed the subject without acknowledging her comment. "Can I tell you something important?"

She scooched up in the hospital bed, steadying the phone with a hand. "Sure."

"Bakari Smith—"

"You didn't kill him, did you?" She laughed, which somehow hurt even more than coughing. Maybe the morphine drip wasn't so bad. She felt warm and somehow peaceful, the way she sometimes did after two shots of tequila.

"Just listen, okay?" He paused and she closed her eyes, letting everything fall away but the sound of his voice. "I don't know. I told him I was there to give him a tip. I sort of was, but really I was trying to get information from him. And I did." He let out a long breath. "William Wei worked for Ibo Kane. Marty Goldberg wasn't *only* a lobbyist. He laundered money for Kane. Drug money from heroin run through China."

She opened her mouth, but it was dry and the muscles of her face hurt. Nothing came out.

"Kane was in competition with Ana Diaz. Drugs and money laundering. My guess is it goes even deeper. This is what Smith found out in *two hours*. Feds have been on them for a while, but... well, I don't know everything."

She tried to speak. Again, nothing came out. Her cheeks suddenly felt cold. Tears were drying on them. She hadn't realized she was crying.

"Cole, you still there? Say something."

"Still here."

"I'm guessing it hurts to talk. Not to be a jerk, but the pain will get worse. Under the stitches. You have stitches, right?"

"Eighty, I think they said."

"The next few days will be hell. Don't try to do anything. Don't be tempted to follow me."

"Follow you where?" Cole asked.

"That's the last thing. Price is in San Francisco."

"Why?"

"Don't know for sure, but I'm going. Maybe he's hiding, or he's part of whatever comes next, but…"

She stopped listening. Words tumbled from the back of her mind like they were trying to break through her forehead, but they dissolved before reaching her lips. Something had happened. Something important. She tried to focus, but the morphine drip had numbed her senses as much as her pain.

Warren had said, "Whatever comes next."

She opened her eyes. "Next."

"What?"

"Something happened."

"You got stabbed."

"Not that," Cole said, fumbling for her words. "In the hotel room. Guy said something…"

A nurse came in and checked the various monitors on the wall behind her. She smiled at Cole, then took a few notes and left without saying a word.

"'There aren't *two* more murders.' That's what he said." Recalling the scene made her whole body tense. The police officer who'd visited had told her she was in shock, and there was no need to try to remember all the details now. He'd be back in the morning to speak with her again.

"What do you mean?" Warren asked. "Oh. Oh, *no*."

She allowed her body to go soft and the pain recessed slightly in the stillness. "'Seven, eight, then hundreds and hundreds.' That's what he said."

"Anything else?" Warren asked.

She felt her mind turning off. She was falling asleep. She was also hungrier than she'd been in years.

"Jane?"

"Seven, eight, then hundreds and hundreds. I don't know what it means. I bet Chandler Price does. *Tell* people."

"Tell people what? Jane?"

"Tell them what he said." Was she slurring her words? "Then hundreds and hundreds. Warn them."

"I will."

"I'm huuuuungry, Rob." The phone slipped from her hand as she tried to say goodbye, but had the word come out of her mouth or had it only echoed in her mind?

Her last thought before falling asleep was that, before they dragged her to the ambulance, she should have grabbed some of the fries that spilled onto the carpet from the room service cart.

—End of Episode 7—

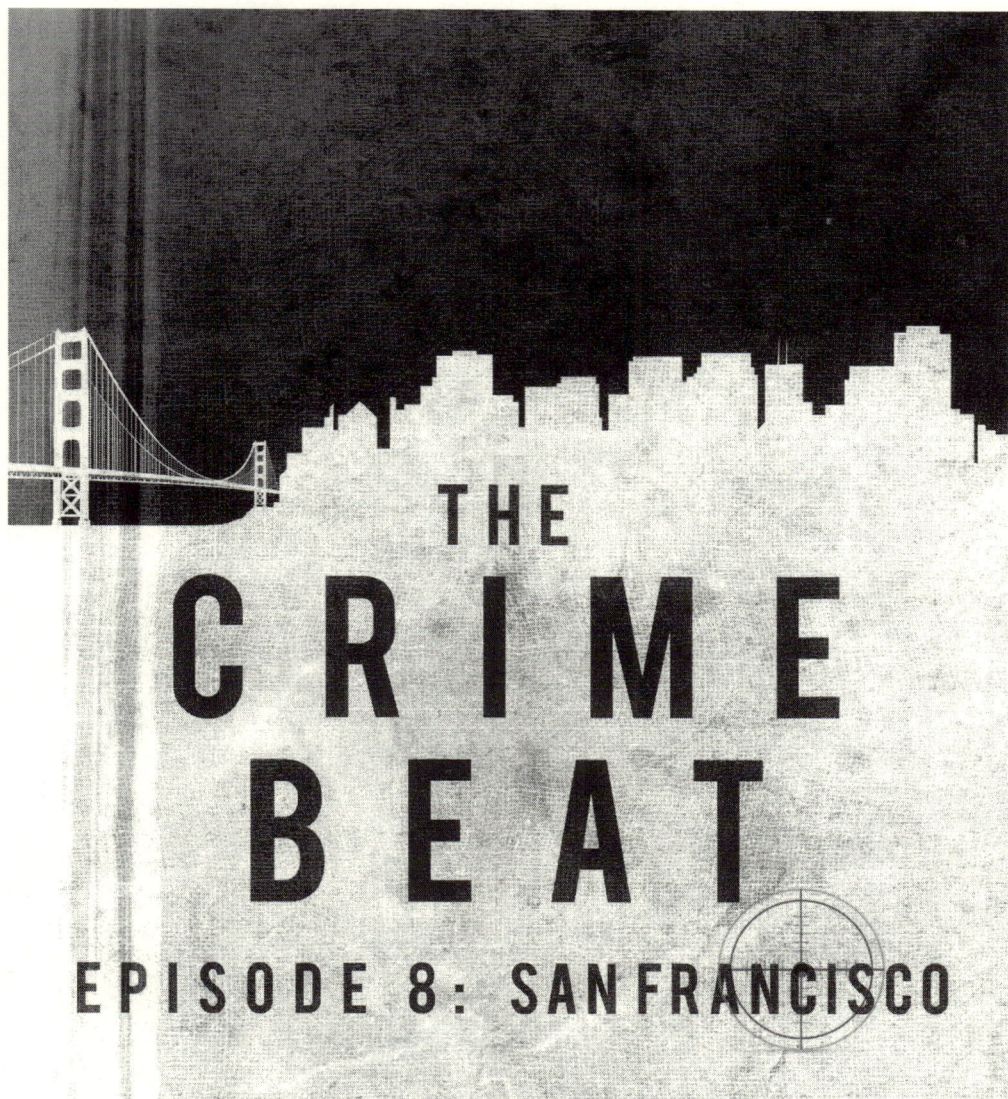

THE
CRIME
BEAT

EPISODE 8: SAN FRANCISCO

139

Sunday

"You awake?"

Cole recognized the voice, but it wasn't one of the nurses. Her vision was cloudy and her eyelids nearly caked shut. She rubbed them with one hand and reached for the dilaudid 'Patient Controlled Analgesic' button with the other. She pressed it three times, though she'd been told it would only release one dose every ten minutes.

"Jane?"

She blinked rapidly, trying to force the world into focus. Each blink shot a loop of pain around the side of her face to her temples, then back across her forehead. Her whole body ached. She pressed the button again.

She blinked once more and a dark shape came into view. A woman dressed in black hovered over her bed. She had straight black hair and looked vaguely familiar.

"Jane, it's me. Gabby."

Cole tried to mouth the name, but her lips were dry, her tongue like sandpaper. Where the hell had Gabby been? Why was she now in Tokyo?

Gabby stepped forward and the blurry edges of her face came into focus. "You look like hell, Jane. Does Rob know?"

Cole couldn't tell if she'd moved her head when she tried to nod. Odd, blurry memories swept through her mind, adding to her confusion.

"I can tell you're out of it. Dilaudid drip. You've probably been in and out of sleep. The doctors say you're gonna be fine, though. Out of here in a few days. Week or two of bed rest after that and, well, a full recovery sounds likely."

Cole opened her mouth to object—there was no way she would stay in bed for the next couple weeks—but her mouth was too dry. Her vision came into focus and she lifted her head a couple inches from the pillow. Gabby stood over her, face frozen in a severe frown. She wore blue jeans and a black top, and a silver and black laptop bag was slung over her shoulder. It was the exact outfit she'd worn when they met in Las Vegas. It felt like a lifetime ago.

Gabby let out a long sigh. "You're wondering why I'm here and how I knew *you* were here, right?"

Cole nodded weakly. She wanted to add a question, *And where the hell have you been?* But not badly enough to try to speak again. Her head swam with shadowy memories. The hotel, her room service order, the man who'd stabbed her. A conversation with Rob. Had that been real, or a dream? The opiates were affecting her sense of reality, but knowing that wasn't the same as knowing which of her memories were true and which had been dreamed.

Gabby put a hand on her shoulder. "After I met you and Rob in Las Vegas, I had to disappear. Go dark. Turns out the NYPD doesn't look fondly on ex-cops going rogue and leaking information to journalists straight, or to the internet. Neither does the New York State Unified Court System." She frowned. "And neither does the CIA. Especially not them."

Gabby went quiet as Cole's mind slowly worked. In Vegas, Gabby had told them about leaking NYPD info. And she'd helped take down Joey Mazzalano. But Cole didn't understand the CIA reference.

Gabby filled in the details. "The judge assigned to the case of the pedophile Rob roughed up? He was a pedophile—a child rapist—and had a history of letting suspects off easy. Turned out, he was a CIA asset, which is why he was able to get away with it. Got flipped decades ago. Fed the CIA all kinds of stuff. Now, he's dead."

Cole felt her eyes open wide. Gabby was ruthless, but Cole never suspected she was a killer.

Gabby pulled the curtains closed to give them more privacy. "*I didn't kill him,*" she said, as though reading her mind. Without the bright lights of Tokyo flickering through the window, the room was darker, lit only by sconces on the wall. "I told Rob I'd look into him, and I did. Some of his secrets leaked onto the internet, and he took matters into his own hands." Gabby walked from one side of the hospital bed to the other, inspecting the wall-mounted devices monitoring Cole's vitals. "Ask me," Gabby continued, "we're better off without that guy. But after I found out about him I knew I had to disappear. CIA doesn't like people ruining decades of their work."

With great effort, Cole reached for a paper cup of ice on the table beside the bed. She crunched into a piece and let it melt down her throat, then said, "London? That document? Kane?"

"Try not to talk too much, Jane. You need to regain your strength." Gabby handed her a lemon glycerine swab from the bedside and Cole ran it through her mouth, unsticking her teeth from her cheeks. "But, yes," Gabby said, "I was the one who sent you the document in London."

The document had tied Ibo Kane into all her other research. It was *the* document most crucial to her breaking the story. She suspected Gabby was the sender, but she could have sent it only if she'd been spying on her. Cole found Gabby's eyes. "How did you know?"

"When we met in Las Vegas, I didn't know Kane was behind this. Barely knew who the guy was, actually. I was on your laptop while you were in London. Tracking your searches. Once I saw you were onto Kane, I knew I'd be able to get something you wouldn't."

Been on my laptop? How? The question faded as quickly as it arose. She didn't want to know.

"You probably have a lot of questions," Gabby said. "But we don't have time to do everything now. We just don't." She let out a long sigh, a departure from her usual businesslike, unemotional demeanor. "I got it from an FBI source that Ibo Kane has been questioned. Your work is being taken seriously. He's been questioned and released. There's no solid evidence that he's involved. Nothing tying him to this—and I've looked everywhere I can."

Questioned and released? In her mind, Cole pored over all the work she'd done. She'd found connections to dozens of his businesses and learned how the deaths of the victims would benefit him. She had his old screen name, which was the same name used by the assassins in their manifesto. She had a decent amount of circumstantial evidence. More importantly, she knew Kane's motive.

Again, as though reading her thoughts, Gabby said, "Everyone knows the work you did. Everyone knows he did it, *is doing* it. But he's smart and there's just no *evidence* he's involved. Not enough to meet the kind of legal standard needed to arrest a guy like that."

Cole pressed the PCA button again and this time, the machine beeped. The relaxation came immediately. She fought sleep. "So, what do we do?" she asked softly.

"The best chance is to get someone to flip on him. Someone with something to lose. There are rumors, and I think they're true, that Chandler Price has resurfaced in San Francisco."

Warren had said something about that, Cole recalled, assuming that conversation had actually happened and wasn't just a drug-addled dream. "Warren. Going to San Francisco. Said something about..."

"Makes sense. It's all over the internet that Price was spotted there. Probably helping arrange the eighth murder. I watched your livestream, and I think you're right—the next target is in the media. I wasn't gonna say anything, but I have an idea who it might be."

Cole was about to press the button for more pain medication, but a phrase appeared in the front of her mind like a flash. *Seven, eight, then hundreds and hundreds.* The man who'd stabbed her had said it, and the look in his eyes made it clear he was telling the truth.

Something much bigger was planned. She got the phrase out with great effort. "Seven, eight, then hundreds and hundreds."

140

"What?"

Cole closed her eyes and her thoughts grew hazy.

"Jane, what did you mean, 'then hundreds and hundreds'?"

She tried to scooch up, but her body felt like a melted marsh-mallow. Gabby put a hand on her lower back and helped her sit.

"What is it, Jane?" Gabby leaned in and turned an ear to Cole's mouth.

His voice was in her head, clear and cruel. Angry and certain. "The man who stabbed me. He said there aren't *two* more murders. Seven, eight, then hundreds and hundreds. Fei Mingkang was seven. Maybe the eighth has something to do with why Price is in San Francisco. But there isn't a ninth murder. There's something bigger."

"He said that?"

Cole turned her head to meet Gabby's dark eyes, then she nodded. "When he thought I was going to die."

Gabby's eyes widened, but through her mental haze, Cole couldn't tell whether it was surprise or recognition. The rogue cop walked a lap around the hospital room and stopped at the window. She opened her eyes and Cole followed her gaze. She was on a high floor and the lights of Tokyo sprawled out before her.

"What time is it?" Cole asked.

Gabby didn't turn from the window. "Around nine. Took me

almost a day to get here and the doctors told me you slept for almost the entire time."

"What are you thinking?"

"In Vegas, I told you I'd left JTTF—left the NYPD, gone rogue. It's funny, in some ways I'm after the same things as the terrorists. Some of the people they took out were real sick bastards. Corrupt politicians, drug dealers. But the *way* they're doing it." Still staring out the window, she shook her head. "It's just wrong, and honestly it's got me questioning how *I* go about things."

"You use the truth to bring people to justice outside the system. They're just murdering people. It's not the same."

"It's not, but still…"

"This about the judge?" Cole asked.

Without turning, Gabby nodded into the window. The reflection of her face looked worn and tired.

"You feel bad that he killed himself?"

She turned quickly. "You see the stuff I leaked? No, of course you didn't. You've been here. I don't feel even a moment of sadness that he's dead. I'd have killed him myself. You would too if you'd seen what he'd done. But still…"

"What?" Cole asked.

"How the hell do you know who's right and who's wrong? The judge deserved to die, sure. But there's a real chance the CIA was using him as an asset for something good. Don't get me wrong, could be they weren't, but I don't *know* that. And the nine murders. They're killing all these powerful people, some"—she shook her head—"terrible people. And it's still wrong to kill them but…"

Cole had experienced moments of moral relativism. Moments when nothing added up, when she didn't believe in her work. Moments when the complexity of the world made her want to give up. She caught Gabby's eye and waved her over.

Gabby pulled up a chair and sat. Cole let her head fall onto the pillow and Gabby tilted hers to meet Cole's eyes.

"In Paris," Cole began, "Rob got drunk. Wasted, really. So did I, but that's… par for the course. He said something about how everyone thinks they have a good reason to break the law. He was talking about a blue vest protest, but he was also talking about this." She took a few deep breaths, gathering her strength. "From the perspective of the terrorists, they have good reason to kill the people they're killing. Ibo Kane thinks he's got good reasons, too. No one ever thinks *they're* the bad guy. Everyone is the hero of their own story." The narcotic had fully kicked in and the pain, though not gone, somehow didn't trouble her anymore. As loopy as she was, the temporary break from the pain gave her energy. "I didn't make the connection at the time, but right after I met Rob, he said something else. He said the law enforcement system, as screwed up as it is, is the best thing we have. 'Literally the *best thing we've got*,' he said." She closed her eyes. Her own voice seemed to be coming from someone else. "For Rob, that's how he makes sense of the world. Follow the rules. Believe in the system. For me, it's writing, reporting. I don't need to know what's morally right or good. I just write the truth and let the chips fall where they may." She shook her head. "I don't know if it's a *good* way to be, but it's the way I am. Old editor told me once to break the story before the story breaks me." Wet tears slid down her cheeks. "I'm broken now. This one has almost killed me."

Gabby put a hand on her shoulder. Cole got the sense she didn't know what to say. Gabby wasn't a sentimental person. Wasn't one for deep conversations.

"Matt, my husband, he made sense of the world with religion, with good acts. He was a good person, a..." She drew a deep breath. "He..."

"He what?" Gabby asked.

The mention of Matt brought the conversation with Warren to mind. It *had* happened. He'd spoken with Bakari Smith while in D.C. William Wei worked for Ibo Kane. Marty Goldberg wasn't *only* a lobbyist. He laundered money for Kane—drug money from heroin, run from Afghanistan into China. Kane was in competition with Ana Diaz. "We need to get out of here," Cole said.

"You can't leave for at least another day."

"I don't know how you got in, or how you even knew where I was. Fake IDs, hacking the Japanese hospital system? Doesn't matter. You're gonna do whatever the hell you need to do to get me out of here. And you're going to get me to San Francisco—get *us* to San Francisco—and we're going to finish this thing."

Gabby was silent for a long moment, then stepped back from the bed, giving Cole room. "Can you stand?"

Cole took a deep breath and tried to slide her back up the

mound of pillows, but she had no energy. She threw the pillows to the floor, then scooched so her back was against the headboard. Pressing her feet into the bed, she pushed herself up slowly. Hot rivets of pain overwhelmed the opioids running through her system. "Aaacccckkkk!"

Gabby winced. "I'll go to SF. You rest a couple more days, then join us."

"Couple more days I might be too late."

"Too late for what?"

It was a good question. How much impact could she have on what happened next? The truth was, she just *had* to be there. There was no reason other than an overwhelming sense of sheer necessity. Gabby and Warren were trained to stop crime; she was trained to write about it. It was a subtle but real difference. For her, the high came from being where the action was, from being an observer to history.

She didn't answer Gabby's question. Using her hands to assist her weakened legs, she shoved them over the side of the bed. Her feet dangled a few inches off the floor. "Will they let me out?"

"They have to. Unless you're a danger to others or are being held involuntarily for mental health reasons, they'll let you out." She swept a hand out before her, as though offering up the floor space, daring Cole to try to stand.

"The IV. My pain meds." She waved at the clear tubing that ran from her arm to a bag of fluids.

"I wondered when you'd remember that." Gabby sat next to her and cocked her head to the side, a concerned look spreading across her face. Cole was about to get a lecture. "Look, if you want to come, then fine. But are you willing to let me be in charge?"

Cole nodded hastily. "Fine, fine."

"No." Gabby locked eyes with her. "I *need* to be in charge. I told you to go to London. Gave you the damn tickets. That led you to Kane, then to Paris, then here. And you got stabbed. By rights, you should have been killed. The guy who stabbed you is a deranged fanatic. Michael Wragg, too. But Ibo Kane *isn't*. He doesn't get off on killing people. Doesn't want revenge. His only ideology is power. The murders are a means to an end." She shook her head. "I almost feel bad for all these saps. Kane used their ideologies to make them kill for him. Amazing how easily powerful men can manipulate people's emotions."

Cole grew impatient. In her mind, she was already on a plane to San Francisco. "I wrote the damn article, Gabby. I know what Kane is doing."

"Jane, listen. I can go to the doctors and talk you out of here. I'll get you pain meds. We'll pick them up on the way to the airport. I'll have your back." She sighed. "Your research and reporting broke this case when I couldn't. When *no one* else could, and everyone owes you. But I'll be damned if I'm gonna let you get shot. Or worse, bleed out thirty thousand feet over the Pacific."

Cole chuckled, causing a lance of pain to stab her ribs. "Would it really be worse to bleed out over the ocean than to get shot by a sniper?"

Gabby put a hand on her forearm. "Having done neither, I dunno. My point is, if I get you out of here, I'm in charge. There's a reason I stay in the shadows. I come out of them, it's on my terms."

Cole looked into her eyes. Gabby didn't look afraid, just deadly serious. It struck her then, that she and Gabby were from two entirely different worlds. Gabby *had* killed people, she was sure. She'd brought down Mazzalano, probably others. She was a fugitive.

"You're in charge," Cole said softly.

Gabby's serious look remained for a moment. Then she smiled. "Gimme half an hour. I'll talk you out of here. That doesn't work, I'll use a fake state department ID."

141

Monday

Samuel DeLunge stared at the endless vista of low lights that made up Los Angeles. For the first time in years, indecision paralyzed him. His orange and white tabby cat, Dexter, purred in his lap. DeLunge stroked his fur. The cat gave him comfort and quieted the questions that swirled through his mind. But not even Dexter's reliable love could silence them.

Since planting a hundred and twenty pounds of RDX in the basement of Club God, everything had gone wrong. First, there was the empty feeling he'd had while celebrating with his online "brothers" in their group chat. He'd posted the message as planned, starting the clock on the final, explosive phase of the plan. He'd accepted their congratulations. But nothing had felt the way he'd expected.

The next morning, he'd hopped in the chatroom again, only to learn that something had gone wrong with the eighth murder, the last act before the finale. Security had been tightened everywhere, especially for the rich, famous, and powerful. They'd learned Roberto Santos had a team of ten guards, all former members of the *Comando de Operações Especiais*, Brazil's elite special operations force known as *C Op Esp*. They were the best-trained military personnel in South America. DeLunge despised the man they guarded but was smart enough to respect the abilities of the men guarding him.

Santos's trip to San Francisco had been planned for months. DeLunge and his brothers had anticipated tight security. Security efforts were expected to increase with each murder. But Santos was taking extreme measures. He'd canceled or re-arranged some planned tourist activities. He'd switched email addresses, possibly after learning they'd been hacked, and so far they'd been unable to access his cell phone. Other than the conference on media ownership keynote, they couldn't be sure where he'd be, or when. At the conference, he'd been untouchable. Security had been increased tenfold. In the chatroom, his brothers were on edge. Kane—still chatting as 'General Ki'—had demanded a solution.

DeLunge had agreed to take the next flight to San Francisco. Instead, he'd sat on his bed, petting Dexter and staring out at the Los Angeles skyline as the sun rose.

The burner phone he'd ordered on Amazon rang. He'd only shared the contact information with one person: Chandler Price.

"Chandy!" He said the name with fake enthusiasm.

"Sam. You know I don't like it when you call me that. My older brother called me that. Hated that bastard."

"Okay, Chandy." He'd been on the same team with this guy for a year, but DeLunge hated rich people reflexively, as a matter of principle.

Price sighed. "You in SF yet?"

"Still in LA."

"What? Why? You said—"

"I had second thoughts, Chandy. I'm not sure we're approaching this thing right. Why do we even need Santos? We have New Year's Eve."

Price stammered something he couldn't make out. DeLunge loved the thought of the little old dumpling of a man getting angrier and angrier, his face turning beet red. Pissing off rich people was a sport. "Calm down, Chandy. Why don't you take Santos out yourself? You're a tough guy, right?"

"You know I can't do that, I'm—"

"Old, rich, and fat?" DeLunge asked.

"What the hell has gotten into you, Sam? I mean *Gunner Vision*. I thought we were in this together."

A bird landed on the windowsill and Dexter perked up.

DeLunge stroked his back until the bird flew away. What the hell was he doing? Picking a fight with an old millionaire just to be a jerk? He sighed. "Look, Chandler, I'm sorry. I'm all over the place right now."

Price didn't say anything. There was so much unspoken between them, and yet DeLunge couldn't find the words. After a long silence, DeLunge said, "Where are you staying?"

"Dunmore East."

"Sounds fancy."

"What has that got to do with anything?" Price asked.

DeLunge looked around his tiny bedroom. Clothes spilled from the closet and a single lightbulb dangled over the bed. His view of the L.A. skyline and Dexter were the only nice things he had. He hated the thought of Price ordering room service in a hotel that probably cost a thousand bucks a night. Then it hit him. He wasn't mad at Price. The old man, despite his shortcomings, had kept up his end of the bargain at every turn.

They'd needed a rooftop in New York City, and he'd come through. They'd needed custom rifles, and he'd purchased them and organized distribution in D.C., Miami, London, Paris, Vegas, and Tokyo. He'd disappeared, said nothing publicly. Price had done nothing wrong. The man DeLunge was angry at was Ibo Kane. He couldn't shake the feeling he was being manipulated. Chandler Price was a millionaire, but his wealth still put him closer to DeLunge himself than either were to the *multi-billionaire* Ibo Kane. That made Price a fellow soldier. And he couldn't abandon a comrade in the middle of a mission.

"I'm sorry, Chandler. Can I level with you?"

"I'd rather you get on a plane to San Francisco."

DeLunge stood and grabbed his backpack from the floor. "I will. Leaving now. Next flight out."

"Good. What is it you want to say, Sam?"

"Did you know Kane was behind this from the beginning? I just can't shake the feeling that we've been played."

"Absolutely not."

"You're in this for the right reasons?" DeLunge asked.

"Same reasons as you, Sam." His voice dropped slightly. "*To carry out a singular mission: to bring an end to the technological oppression, to restore the sovereignty of the individual, to birth a new era of freedom.* I was as pissed as you when I learned about Kane. But what we are doing is *good*. Sometimes God sends imperfect leaders to carry out perfectly righteous missions."

DeLunge reached his front door. "I'll be at the airport in thirty minutes. Should be in SF by late morning."

"Good."

"And Chandy?" DeLunge paused. "You better be telling the truth. Last time someone with authority pissed me off, I broke his arm. And that was *while* I was trying to use some restraint. When I still had something to lose."

He snapped the phone in half without ending the call. At the curb, he dropped the pieces in the storm drain and got into his car and peeled out, glancing at his tiny stucco house in the rearview mirror. As he turned the corner, something tugged in his heart. A certainty struck him—he'd never see Dexter again. *I should turn back and take Dexter and drive to Mexico and never look back.*

But he didn't.

As he entered the freeway, the feeling faded and his head once again filled with the excitement of a mission, the excitement he'd only known on the eve of battle.

142

Warren's brothers stood on the curb of the Oakland airport, standing shoulder-to-shoulder like two linebackers waiting to tackle an oncoming running back. Warren felt like crap, but couldn't suppress a smile. It had been over a year since he'd been home, and being around his brothers made everything feel right, if only for a moment.

He darted toward them, jutting left, then right, pressing his duffle bag into his side like a football. James, his younger brother, squared on him, ready to make the tackle. They both slowed just enough to turn the collision into a hug. James was taller and thinner than Warren, though still muscular.

Warren let him go and gave a one-armed bro hug to Malcolm, his older brother who still made him feel small. The same height as Warren, Malcolm was over three-hundred pounds. A layer of fat covered his massive muscles.

"What the hell are you doing home?" Malcolm asked as they walked to the curb, where they'd double-parked a black SUV.

Hand on the door, Warren inhaled deeply. It was around sixty degrees and sunny. Despite the fumes from the cars all around, the air had that familiar Bay Area scent. He couldn't describe it, but knew it right away. His shoulders dropped. "What's the smell?"

Malcolm looked to James, who was folding himself into the

back seat. He was the youngest and always got the back seat when the three of them were together.

Warren took the front seat. "The Bay Area smell. The Oakland smell. The more time I spend other places, the more I notice the smell of home."

Malcolm peeled out like he'd heard a starter pistol. "Probably the salt water from the Bay, mixed with traffic fumes."

James punched his shoulder from the back seat. "If your dumb ass hadn't moved somewhere where it's frozen half the year..."

His brothers always gave him hell for leaving the west coast. It had become part of their routine, a way to avoid weightier topics. They rode in silence for a minute, Malcolm weaving in and out of lanes like a racecar driver.

James spoke from the back seat. "Seriously, though. Why you in town?"

His tone carried a touch of sarcasm, and Warren thought he was being made fun of. He glanced back, trying to read his brother's tone.

"I mean"—James shrugged—"Hollywood is eight-hundred miles south, and if you want to capitalize on your fame, that's where you need to be." Slowly, a smile spread across his face and he let out a howl of laughter. "The Rock *is* getting older."

Oh, God. They'd seen the video from London. Of course they had.

Malcolm laughed, too. "What in the hell are you doing saving little Australian kids in London? I mean, seriously, what the *hell*?"

Warren laughed and shook his head. "Wrong place, wrong time, and I'd rather not say why I'm in town." He changed the subject. "That Vietnamese restaurant on the corner still there?" Food was a topic they could always agree on.

"Hell yeah, it is," James said. "Why you think Malcolm's carrying an extra thirty pounds."

"Thirty? I was thinking more like sixty." Warren laughed. "I'll call in an order and we can pick it up on the way to mom's."

He'd forgotten to restart his phone after the plane landed. He waited while it powered on, then grunted. He had a voicemail from a number he didn't recognize.

Pressing the phone to his ear to prevent his brothers from eavesdropping, he listened. "Rob, it's Gabby. I'm on a plane six miles over the Pacific Ocean. Jane's with me, but she's sleeping. Codeine knocked her out. We're headed to SFO, and I hear you're already in the area. We know Price is there, and we might know who the next target is. I can take calls on the plane via WiFi. The following number will bounce around a few satellites and take longer to connect, but it's secure. Don't want to say much more in a voicemail. *Call me.*"

He wrote the number on his hand with a pen he found in the glove compartment. The call didn't shock him, but maybe it should have. Gabby had disappeared for over a week, ignored dozens of calls and texts, then, just like that, she was on a plane with Cole. She must have figured out where Cole was, or maybe set up a name-ID hack that pinged her when Cole was admitted to the hospital. However Gabby got her information, it was damned impressive.

"What was that about?" James asked.

"Nothing."

"Sarah take you back yet?" Malcolm always got straight to the point.

Warren didn't want to talk about it. "No."

His older brother gave him a concerned look. "That lady you've been gallivanting around with? Anything there?"

"Nope."

"Still sober?" Malcolm asked.

Warren swallowed hard. This was turning into an interrogation, and the last thing he wanted was a lecture about sobriety from his mom and brothers, even if their hearts were in the right place. They'd supported him when he was at his lowest four years earlier. He didn't know if it was because he feared they wouldn't support him again, or if he was just guilty, but he couldn't tell them the truth.

He stared out the window as Malcolm took the exit into East Oakland. "Sober as a judge."

Three hours later, Warren sat on the bed in his mother's guest room. When he was a boy, it had been his bedroom. He dialed the number Gabby left him, but it went straight to a voicemail box that hadn't been set up and didn't accept messages.

He'd eaten two orders of lemongrass beef with extra vegetables, and was beginning to feel more like himself. It had been three days since the night in Paris, and he missed how strong he'd been before falling off the wagon.

He lay back on the bed, his feet dangling off the end, and stared at the ceiling. As a boy, he'd covered the walls and ceiling with posters—mostly sports stars from the Oakland A's and San Francisco 49ers, but also some musicians and a few classic cars. Now they were gone and his mom had painted over the tack holes he'd left behind.

He closed his eyes.

What he'd learned in D.C. had shaken him. He knew the world was screwed up; the things he'd seen in New York had convinced him of that. Child molesters, murderers, rapists. But this plot was a level of corruption and criminality he'd believed didn't exist. *Couldn't* exist. He'd *needed* to believe it, in fact. Criminals were everywhere, but fundamentally, at the top, the system itself was good and decent. Believing this had allowed him to sleep at night.

The thought that, while he was busting dudes for dealing weed in New York, Ibo Kane and Ana Diaz were engaged in a turf war over the heroin trade from Afghanistan to China and from China to the U.S. was bad enough. That they'd used *Marines* to protect the product was too much to comprehend. Marty Goldberg, the corrupt K Street lobbyist, had laundered drug money for Kane and used some of it to pay Chandler Price. Price was the key, and high enough in the plot to have access to Kane himself. But not high enough to avoid doing some dirty work. Price had used drug money to pay Michael Wragg and probably others. He'd probably paid The Truffle Pig—maybe even hired him.

The buzz of his phone jolted him. "Hello?" He sat up.

"It's Gabby."

He heard faint white noise in the silence after she spoke. "Are you still on the plane?"

"I am."

"And Cole?"

"Still sleeping."

"Lemme guess," Warren said. "It was her idea to get out of the hospital, but you made it happen?"

"Good guess. Doctor resisted for a while. Had to tell them I was State Department and she was part of an important government operation. We signed a bunch of release forms."

Warren smiled, then he remembered something. "The judge. The one overseeing the case of the dude I bashed. That was you?"

"I don't know *what* you're talking about," Gabby said.

Warren detected mischief in her voice. "I thought you said this line is clean."

"*Mine* is," Gabby said. "Don't know about yours."

He walked to the window, which looked out on a tiny square of grass his mother watered and trimmed so religiously it looked like a putting green. "Good point." He paused, then said, "I'm glad the judge got got. *Whoever* leaked his records."

"Me too, Rob."

"When will you be here?" he asked.

"Six more hours. I want you to do something. There's already a task force in SF hunting for Price and watching for the next killing."

"I know. I was in D.C with Bakari Smith. He says it's FBI, local police, and more."

"Right, so we're not going to do much they're not already doing."

"Then why are you coming here?" he asked. "And speaking of that, why didn't you convince Cole to stay in the hospital? There won't be anything she can do here. There's not—"

"That's what I'm saying, Rob. We already did something."

"What?"

"We figured out who the next target is."

143

DeLunge recognized Chandler Price's doughy face immediately as he stepped through the sliding glass door at SFO. Price sat in the back of a black Mercedes wagon, and had rolled the window down just enough to make eye contact.

It was odd meeting a man for the first time after working with him for a year. So much had passed between them—said and unsaid—mostly in a chatroom with a dozen other men. He joined Price in the back seat, his knees bumping against the driver's seat.

Price pressed a button on the door and a glass divider rose, blocking off the driver. He offered DeLunge a strange smile. "You're bigger than you sound on the phone."

Price looked older and even less healthy than his photos online. In the photos, he was pasty and pale looking, his face like flappy, uncooked pizza dough. In the flesh, he was sweating despite the cool San Francisco weather, and he seemed out of breath.

DeLunge smirked. "Thanks, I guess. You know I used to play football."

Price smiled. "I used to watch football." He gave DeLunge a questioning look. "I notice you limp. Why?"

They drove from the airport onto the highway. DeLunge watched the signs. He'd been to the Bay Area once but didn't know his way around. They rode in silence until the driver merged onto another freeway toward Marin/Sausalito. "Where we headed?"

Price wiped his forehead with a handkerchief. "I rented a place. It's secure. You didn't answer my question. Why the limp?"

DeLunge nodded toward the driver. "He can't hear us?"

Price raised his voice. "Hey, Brian!" The driver didn't turn his head or glance in the mirror. "Satisfied?"

DeLunge nodded, then wiggled the one remaining toe on his left foot. "I only have one toe on my left foot." He said it firmly. He didn't like talking about it.

Price either didn't pick up the signal or didn't care. "What happened?"

"Landmine."

Price licked his lips, as though the thought of the injury somehow excited him.

DeLunge gazed out the window, where a body of water had come into view. He guessed it was the San Francisco Bay. "Luckily the toe I got left with is my big toe. Balance sucks now but I've got a contoured footplate that makes it okay."

"Tough guy, huh?"

DeLunge turned back to Price, whose face had turned glassy, like he was half-dreaming. "What's wrong with you? You're sweaty, zoned out, getting off on my toes being blown off. And where the hell are we going?"

The driver tapped on the divider and Price rolled it down.

"Three minutes," the driver said.

Price raised the divider without responding. "I have a surprise for you."

DeLunge clenched his fists. Could be Price was on drugs, maybe painkillers or muscle relaxers. The businessman didn't smell like liquor, but he might have been drinking. Either way, DeLunge began to regret coming. He thought of Dexter, probably watching for birds out the window of his messy bedroom.

Price looked down at DeLunge's clenched fists. "Don't worry, Sammy, it's a *good* surprise.

The car turned down a private road leading toward the water. They passed through a security gate and entered a parking lot, which ended at the water and a row of what appeared to be houseboats.

The driver got out and opened the door for Price. DeLunge followed them across the lot, staying a few paces behind. As they walked onto a long, wide dock, Price glanced back and waved for him to catch up.

This was getting weird. First Price's odd demeanor, now this. With his MMA training, DeLunge could kill Price in seconds. The driver was a larger and younger man, but not as big as DeLunge. Unless he was trained, he could break the driver easily. So it wasn't fear for his safety, it was something else. Something felt odd. Wrong.

He caught up to Price, who nodded toward a white houseboat trimmed with brass at the edge of the dock. "Rented it through a shell company. Totally private and secure. That's our home base for finding Roberto Santos."

DeLunge watched as the driver led the way onto the boat, unlocked it, and led them in. Inside was a small living room, where two men and one woman sat hunched over laptops. They glanced up, then refocused on their screens. DeLunge didn't recognize them, but they weren't threatening. They had the look of hired tech help.

"Why here?" DeLunge asked.

Price held up a hand and addressed a woman with a laptop. "Miriam? Anything?"

"We're getting close, Mr. Price."

"But he's in the area?" Price asked.

"Yes."

DeLunge looked from Price to Miriam, who was a woman of no more than twenty. She had short hair, dyed a bright silvery gray, and a nose ring that matched. She looked like the kind of young woman he'd often see through the window of the hip Los Angeles cafes he never entered. She stood and looked over the shoulders of the other two men. Pointing at one of the laptop screens, she said. "Signal just pinged on the Bay Bridge."

"That's the one from Richmond to San Francisco," Price said. "Good, keep at it."

"What's going on?" DeLunge asked.

Price smiled and took his forearm, leading him through a small galley kitchen and out onto the deck of the boat, where the air was briny and moist. From there, they climbed a small flight of outdoor stairs to the second floor, the entirety of which was taken up by a ten by ten room, a cube of windows with a bed in the center.

"Amazing what you can rent on Airbnb," Price said.

But DeLunge was no longer listening. Sitting on the bed was a man with black hair and a healthy tan. A man he recognized immediately.

Ibo Kane.

DeLunge swallowed hard, trying to keep his cool. As loopy and out of it as Price seemed, Kane was the opposite. His black eyes were focused like a laser. He looked calm, confident, and fully in control. "Have a seat." Kane waved at a chair.

DeLuge sat and allowed his voice to take on a hint of aggression. "What the hell is going on?"

144

Warren had been listening to the police scanner for an hour when he finally heard something of interest.

He was about ten minutes from SFO, sitting in his brother's SUV, staring across a parking lot at a decrepit McDonald's. For the last three hours, he'd listened in on the familiar chatter. He'd missed the sound of it—the rhythm, the different voices appearing then fading away, punctuated by little bursts of static. He'd heard about a car crash downtown, a homeless guy stealing coffee from a Starbucks, and a suspicious car driving by someone's apartment over and over. Apparently, the SFPD had moved to digital scanners a few years back, so one could no longer just buy a police scanner and listen in. But Gabby had found a way to access the digital network. She'd set it up and emailed him a link. It probably wasn't legal, but he imagined Gabby had covered their tracks. He hoped so, at least.

The first interesting interaction started with a young, panicked officer. "Three-seven-two, I've got shots fired, Lincoln and 14th."

"Ten-four, three-seven-two."

"Suspect driving east on 14th. I'm pursuing."

Warren listened for the next ten minutes as a chase played out. Three cars converged on a road, blocking it before the suspect could reach it. He was taken alive, but, minutes later, it was reported he'd been fleeing a convenience store he'd just robbed. The clerk had resisted and been shot and killed.

Not the eighth murder.

Warren went back to listening to the scanner while doing research on his mom's old laptop. Gabby had given him the name Roberto Santos. He still didn't know how she and Cole had determined he was the next target, but Cole hadn't often been wrong.

Apparently, Santos was one of the most powerful media moguls in the world. He got his start in the Brazilian stock market, squirreling away five million Brazilian Reals by the age of thirty, and using that to start a conglomerate that would eventually touch nearly every market and every country in South America. Steel and iron in Brazil, tobacco and coffee in Mexico, silver and gold mines in Chile. And those were just the early years of his expansion.

After a string of lawsuits and some big losses in Venezuela, Santos got serious about media ownership. He made money off them, sure, but he also needed them to shape public opinion about him. Santos knew that the cleaner his image was in international markets, the easier time he'd have doing business in them. He bought TV stations, newspapers, blogs, social media networks, and radio stations throughout South America, giving them a fair amount of editorial independence, but also getting a clear message across: *Don't write or say a bad word about Roberto Santos*. With the media handled, his businesses expanded, and by 2010 he was the sixth richest man in the world, according to Forbes. That's when he started investing in U.S. media properties. Foreign ownership laws made it more difficult to take complete ownership, but over the next decade he acquired partial stakes in forty American newspapers, including three of the largest.

Warren was no expert, but Santos appeared the most powerful of the targets. Richer than Raj Ambani, he was more connected than the former Vice President or the head of the WTO. Santos was a South American version of Ibo Kane himself.

Gabby said Santos was originally scheduled for a conference in San Francisco, and she thought he was staying on for sightseeing, business meetings, and his sixty-fifth birthday celebration. She'd also said he had more security than most presidents.

A burst of static over the radio made him look up. By the way the officers chatted, they seemed freed by the fact that police radio had gone private and digital. When Warren was an officer, it was always in the back of his mind that reporters with scanners, and the occasional hobbyist, could be listening in. It pissed him off, but that was the price of freedom.

He shut the computer when an officer reported a potential suicide. For thirty minutes, he listened as a woman with stage IV cancer stood at the edge of her balcony, threatening to jump. Every 30 seconds or so, like clockwork, the officer on the scene reported back to dispatch. In between check-ins, he talked to her calmly through a megaphone five stories below, reminding her of her grandchildren and promising to help her find medical treatment.

Then, as if someone had turned off the program, the frequency went silent. Not another word.

Fifteen minutes later, the same officer checked in from the hospital. "We've notified next of kin." His voice was flat.

Murders make the news, suicides don't. Warren learned that early on. But many of his early calls as a new officer were responding to suicides or suicide threats.

The scanner conversations reminded Warren of the parade of misery that went out over the radios every night. Crime and police activity happened during the day, too, but nights were worse. Especially warm nights in New York City. When people were out, drinking and crime always spiked. Since his suspension, and especially over the last couple weeks, he'd wanted nothing more than to get his job back. Now, it wasn't actually a *desire*. He recognized it for what it was—another *addiction*. He craved the action, needed the rush. He needed it like he'd needed booze.

As the full realization sank in, a calm settled over him. A fresh sense of mental sobriety told him one thing for certain: he'd never be a police officer again. To stay sober and stable, to have any chance of getting Sarah and Marina back, he had to find a new line of work. Something simple. Something safe. Something that supported his sobriety. The immensity of the acknowledgment put him near tears.

He wanted the rush so badly, but he wanted his *family* more. He had to walk away.

Between domestic violence calls, suspicious person reports, and check-ins, officers occasionally made bawdy jokes or said things they otherwise wouldn't. Two officers began a back-and-forth about the worldwide murders.

"Ask me, some of the people had it coming," one said, his voice gruff.

"Don't say that," came a woman's voice.

"I'm not *condoning* it. But c'mon. You know what I mean."

There was a long silence, the gentle white noise of the radio filling the car. Then another male voice. "Speaking of rich bastards, you hear about the dude who tried to have us shut down the bridge?"

"Which one?" the man with the gruff voice replied.

"Golden Gate."

"No, I meant which rich bastard?"

"Oh, I don't know. All the same to me."

The woman chimed in, "They're not all the same. Some give to charity, some…"

She was interrupted by a call to respond to a potential domestic violence situation in the Mission District.

Warren checked the clock on the dashboard. He had an hour before Cole and Gabby arrived. He leaned back in the seat and turned the speaker down so that it was still audible, but didn't demand his attention.

He wanted to rest before they arrived.

145

"Tell him," Price said to Kane.

DeLunge looked at the old man, still sweaty and red-faced. "Tell me what?"

Ibo Kane flashed an icy look at Price, silencing him with a glance, then steadied his gaze on DeLunge. "You're aware of the importance of this target?"

DeLunge nodded. "Roberto Santos. He's trying to buy up American media companies." As much as this angered DeLunge, he couldn't help wondering whether Kane would care about this if he wasn't in competition with Santos on a dozen business fronts.

"And you're aware that our plans have gone awry?" Kane asked.

"Sure." DeLunge scowled. Of course he knew. That's why he'd agreed to come to San Francisco in the first place. "I know everything."

"Not *everything*," Kane said.

DeLunge had expected at least a 'thank you' for the work he'd done in Los Angeles. That had been the most important phase of the plan. Instead, Kane treated him like a child. He stabbed a finger at the wealthy businessman. "I'm leaving unless I get answers right the hell now."

Kane's eyes narrowed. "You haven't asked any questions."

"Did you ever believe any of the reasons for doing this?

Breaking the international technological cabal? Ending technological oppression? Restoring the sovereignty of the individual? Birthing a new era of freedom? More I think about it, more I think you're actually the problem, and we've just helped you consolidate power."

Kane stood and walked to a wall of windows, which overlooked a small bay. In the distance, the towers of downtown San Francisco were visible. To their right, the rust-red Golden Gate Bridge.

DeLunge pressed his feet into the floor, steadying himself, reminding himself this was real. He was in this room with Ibo Kane, and he'd just asked him whether he actually held any of the ideals he and his brotherhood had killed for, and died for.

Kane laced his hands behind his head as he stared out the window. "No."

He didn't even turn around to look DeLunge in the eye as he said it.

DeLunge stood. "No?"

"No to all of your questions. The technological oppression is an unscientific, retrograde, conspiracy theory designed to make you feel better. I don't believe in national sovereignty. We're headed toward a one-world government, whether knuckle-draggers like you know it or not. I don't believe in individual freedom —other than my own—and even if I did, we're certainly not headed toward any 'new era' of it."

DeLunge shot a look at Price's expressionless face. He felt ready to spring up, to tear through Kane. But something stopped him. Why would Kane tell him this? He took a breath. "So the articles about you have been right all along?"

Kane turned and sat again. "Mostly, yes. I'm doing this for my own benefit. Though I really do believe that what benefits me will benefit the world. We are inevitably heading toward one unified world government with round-the-clock digital surveillance, one currency, and a set of international laws that govern us all. Might take thirty more years." He let out a paternal sigh. "Might take fifty. Lot of people will die in the process. No avoiding that. The only question is, who's at the top of the new pyramid once it's constructed." He smiled. "I'd vote for me."

DeLunge had heard enough. "What makes you think I won't lunge forward and crack your neck right now." He nodded toward

Price, who still stood in the corner. "You think that marshmallowy troll will help you?"

"In a manner of speaking, yes."

DeLunge looked from Kane to Price.

Price stepped between them. He'd picked up a backpack from the corner. He shoved it onto DeLunge's lap.

It was heavy, maybe seventy pounds.

"Open it," Price said.

DeLunge slowly unzipped the backpack. He didn't need to open it all the way to recognize what it was. A vest of stretchy white fabric, cordoned off into sections. The sections were filled with nails, ball bearings, and random bits of metal. Wire ran between the sections, all terminating in an explosive pack the size of a paperback book. It was a suicide bomber vest.

Kane said, "As you might have heard from Miriam and her team downstairs, we have information that Santos will be out and about today. Nothing on his public schedule. They're guarding that closely. But we believe we know where he'll be."

DeLunge stared at the vest, still trying to grasp why they would have put it together, and why they would have given it to him.

Kane continued, "Our team accessed the phone of someone on his team and we believe he's going to make a stop today. Out there." He pointed at the Golden Gate Bridge in the distance. "The thing is, it's too windy to get a shot, and we have no snipers left, anyway. You know our plan to take him out at the conference didn't work."

DeLunge set the bag on the floor. He knew enough to know it wasn't at any risk of exploding, but he set it down gently nonetheless. "You want me to strap that thing on and take out Santos? After telling me that this whole thing has been a con from the beginning? I have half a mind to strap it on and blow the two of you up." He stood. "I'm out of here."

"Wait," Price said. "We have something that might change your mind." Price handed him an iPad. "Press play."

DeLunge did so and a video began. The shot was a wide angle from high up, like surveillance footage. He watched himself walk into the frame. He knew right away the video had been taken outside of Club God. The shot changed to an interior view of DeLunge walking down a hallway inside the club. Then another shot, from a different angle, of DeLunge breaking the door to the storage room where he'd planted the explosives. Kokutai-Goji had disabled the surveillance cameras at Club God. At least, that's what he'd thought. DeLunge dropped back into the chair. "He set the cameras to record and send the video straight to him? Why?"

"In case a situation like this arose," Price said. "We need you to use the vest to kill Santos. If you don't, we will release these. *After* the explosives go off, of course."

DeLunge clenched a fist. "You think I care? I'm proud of it. I'll be proud when they're dead."

"Will your sister and her kids be proud, too?" Price asked. "Your nieces and nephews?" He grabbed the tablet from DeLunge and tapped a few times, then handed it back.

DeLunge gripped it tight. "What?"

"Press play again."

"You son of a bitch."

"Press play," Price repeated.

Lump in his throat, DeLunge pressed play. The video was drone footage, high in the air above a farmhouse. Around the house, yellowing grass encircled an old well. A broken down Ford truck sat in the yard. Three kids entered the video as the drone dropped down. They ran up the steps of the old house and disappeared onto the porch. "You sleazy mother—"

"Stop," Price said. "Don't bother."

DeLunge looked back at the screen. It was his grandparents' old house, now inhabited by his sister, her husband, and their three kids. They ran a small almond farm in central California. Since DeLunge had embraced more extreme views, their relationship had grown strained, but he still saw them once a year. He loved those kids more than anything. When it came down to it, he was doing all of this for them. All he wanted was for them to have the freedom he'd known as a kid. Having no children of his own, his sister's kids were everything to him, even if their father didn't want them to have much of a relationship with their radical uncle.

Kane had been quiet when Price stepped in with the suicide vest and the videos. Rich people always let others do their dirty work, DeLunge thought.

The betrayal complete, the mogul sighed, as though the whole proceeding bored him. "We'll drive you to the spot and, when Santos appears, you'll do what needs to be done. The videos will be destroyed and the two men eating lunch at the diner down the road from your sister's farm will be called off. Your nieces and nephews will be *fine*." He smiled. "Do what we require of you and the syringes of arsenic won't be injected into their juice boxes after all."

146

Cole hobbled through the sliding glass doors to the curb, standing as tall as possible, despite feeling as though she might collapse. Gabby followed, carrying their bags and probably readying herself in case Cole fell backward.

"What's he driving?" Gabby asked.

"How the hell would I know?" Cole's own tone surprised her.

Gabby raised an eyebrow.

"Sorry. I think the pain meds are wearing off."

"You're not supposed to have any more for another hour."

Cole was itching for more medication. She'd slept through most of the flight, but somehow the pain had slowly grown worse. Now, her belly throbbed and new hotspots of aches and bruises had sprouted all over her body.

Cole turned at the sound of a shrill whistle coming from the road. Warren poked his head out of a black SUV. His face broke into a wide grin, and her pain subsided into the distant background as she smiled in return. It surprised her how good it was to see him again.

He jogged over, grabbed the bags from Gabby, and threw them in the trunk. He leaned in to hug Cole, but she leaned away.

"Right," he said. "No hugs. How are your wounds?"

Cole raised her shirt, revealing an abdomen wrapped in white bandages.

"I leave you for a couple days and you go and get stabbed."

He was trying to play it light, but Cole knew he was the type of person who'd blame himself. The protector role came naturally to him, and she had no doubt he'd view her injuries as his failure.

"There's a more important issue." Her smile faded. "More important than all of this."

Gabby gave Warren a quick hug and appraised Cole skeptically. "What?"

"Yeah, what?" Warren added.

"Did you get Blue Lightning back?" Cole asked.

Warren smiled and nodded. "Damn near broke the bank, but she's at the airport in D.C. I'll head back and get her when this is over."

"And Bakari Smith is still alive?"

Warren nodded. "You don't remember? He's the one who told me about William Wei and—"

"Move along!" A man in uniform stood next to the SUV with a ticket book open. "This is for loading and unloading only."

"Let's go," Cole said. "It'll be good to sit."

"Nothing," Warren said. "I listened to that damn scanner for hours and I got nothing." He scowled. "Except depressed."

Cole sat in the back, leaning between the two front seats. Gabby occupied the front passenger seat. Outside, bumper to bumper traffic inched forward along the freeway that led away from the San Francisco airport.

She wanted to grill Warren about his conversation with Bakari Smith. She wanted to ask Gabby what she should do with the recording she'd made of Julio Lopez admitting his role in Matt's death. But some instinct within her prevented the words from leaving her lips. If she picked up that ball, she might drop the one she was running with.

They rode in silence and she figured Warren and Gabby had come to the same realization she did: they were stymied. Chandler Price was in town, and one of the next two murders would likely take place here. They *thought* they knew the target: media mogul Roberto Santos. But they had no idea where he was. They also knew that multiple law enforcement agencies had formed a Task Force to investigate.

But Ibo Kane had been questioned and released. Now he had free reign.

Cole scrolled through her phone, ignoring dozens of messages about her stories—some positive, some death threats—and the well-wishes from people who'd heard about her stabbing. She found the Instagram account of Roberto Santos. "Seems like billionaires just can't resist acting like a tool on social media these days. Part of 'branding' or whatever."

Gabby looked back at her. "It's the new social media reality. Doesn't matter what people say about you as long as they're talking. I spoke with a powerful CEO once—this dude was the face of a packaged food company. You know—chips, candy, snacks. He said he could track in real-time how sales spiked when he was more active on social media. Dude had a couple million followers. As long as he didn't touch the third rail of politics or religion, it was like juicing the cash register. Tweet a cute cat dressed in a hat made of potato chip bags? That's nine thousand in sales. A viral Instagram post with a snarky comment about some football players needing to recharge with one of his protein bars, forty grand in sales." She shook her head.

Cole laughed and scanned Santos's Instagram. She swiped past photos of him getting on his private jet in Brazil, then landing at SFO, then a post about how his company had just closed a deal to buy ten small, midwestern newspapers. Santos was smart, though, and surely knew he was a potential target. He only posted photos with location information *well after* he'd left that location. "Lots of photos, but nothing that says where he'll be, or where he was. At least, not until after he's long gone. He's too smart to give away anything about his location."

Warren mumbled angrily and the knuckles of his hand paled under what appeared to be an iron grip. She remembered how he'd driven from New York to D.C., and around D.C. itself. Blue Lightning was like his own personal racecar. Sitting in holiday traffic was driving him nuts.

"Gabby," Cole said, "is there any way to get onto his phone? Location tracker or anything?"

"There would be, if he was dumb enough to use a garden variety smartphone. "

"What does he use?"

Gabby reached in her bag and handed Cole a phone. Thinner than her iPhone, it was also heavier, with sharp square edges and a back of glossy white metal. "EchoPhone," Gabby said. "Santos uses the same phone as me."

Warren glanced back. "What's so special about it?"

"The most expensive set-up includes privately hosted servers that generate ephemeral encryption keys. Every single individual communication is locked into a sealed vault, essentially. It even installs bespoke versions of apps, not available to regular consumers. So let's say you use WhatsApp or something for communications. It installs an encrypted version that's much more secure. Plus, it's got various blockers to keep it from being hacked even if you are in possession of the phone. Jane, remember when we met in Las Vegas?"

Cole handed her back the phone. "Sure."

"And remember where you set your phone?"

Cole thought. "No. I mean, probably on the table or... in my pocket? I don't know."

"Right. You set it on the table like most people do. I had my laptop in my bag, hacking your phone via bluetooth while we were sitting there. There are other ways to do it, but bluetooth is easiest. That's how I knew where you were. And that's how I got onto your laptop in London. I mean, you don't make much of an effort."

Cole shook her head. "I guess not."

"With an EchoPhone, even if I handed it to you, you couldn't get in. It was created by Israeli entrepreneurs. Used by some governments, top business people, intelligence agencies."

Cole reached out and took the phone back, looking at it more closely now that she knew the details. "How much?"

"They cost three hundred thousand dollars."

Cole nearly dropped it. "What?"

"*I* didn't pay that much, but that's what they cost. Year or two there'll be a consumer-level version. Maybe five to ten grand."

"How'd you get yours?" Warren asked.

"Know the creators. I'm helping them test it."

Cole shrugged and handed it back. "Don't suppose there's anything on there that will help us track Roberto Santos?"

"Nope," Gabby said. "Totally untrackable."

The traffic had cleared and Warren took an exit toward the bridge. "Didn't you tell me once that *nothing* is untrackable?"

"Technically, yeah, but this phone is as close as you can get. If I had a hundred guys in a warehouse for a month, maybe we'd find a way onto his phone. But even that might require access to the physical object, and since all we want to know is where the guy is…"

Warren curled his fingers around the steering wheel so tight his knuckles popped. "Damn."

"*Damn* is right," Cole said. "We're nowhere."

Warren said, "How do you find a billionaire who doesn't want to be found, in a city of ten million people?"

"Like I said," Cole repeated, slumping down in the seat, "we're nowhere."

"We're *not* nowhere," Gabby said. "We know the target, we know the city. We just need to know…" The positivity faded from her voice halfway through the sentence and she trailed off. "Okay, we're nowhere."

147

Warren leaned back in his chair, studying a colorful mural on the wall of Ana's Taqueria. Painted in rich browns, bright yellows, oranges, and reds, the mural depicted the Mexican city of Veracruz. The Tampico Bridge connected Veracruz's homes and tree-lined streets to another city across a river.

They'd stopped at a Mexican restaurant in the Mission District for tacos and *agua frescas*. For an hour, their conversation had circled the difficult task of locating Santos. Gabby and Cole had done their thing on their phones and computers, but when a man as powerful as Santos wants to remain anonymous, it's not hard for him to do so.

Cole's head was buried in her phone and she had a piece of lettuce on her cheek. He worried about her. Her face was pale, her eyes glassy. She grunted when she stood and grimaced when she moved. *She shouldn't be here.* "You've got a piece of—" He gestured, but she didn't seem to understand. He brushed the lettuce off her face.

"Thanks." She squinted and returned to her phone.

Gabby said, "Jane, I found the password on the Dark Web of Hector Ramos. Was that the name of the security guy?"

"Yeah, but it was from a year ago. No idea whether he works for Santos anymore."

They'd hit multiple dead ends and were now trying to figure

out who Santos's close friends and most immediate staff were. If they could locate one of his assistants, attendants, or security guards—any of whom might be easier to hack than Santos himself—maybe they could get a line on the billionaire's location.

"Hold on." Gabby typed furiously on her laptop. "I'm on his Gmail." She scanned the screen. "Yeah, no. From this, it looks like he doesn't even work for Santos anymore. Where'd you find that name, Jane?"

"Old article. Year ago, at least."

"It was a good idea, though." Gabby shrugged. "My bet is the security team won't be stupid enough to give up a location. Has he got a private chef, or assistant or something?"

Warren was out of his league. He stared at the mural, listening with half of his attention, contemplating their predicament with the other half. "Why don't we just call Santos? Warn him."

Cole nodded at Gabby. "She did that while you were in the bathroom. I couldn't get his personal cell, but we called a ton of business numbers, left messages with secretaries, left voicemails. He's scarce—he knows he's a target. But what's he gonna do?"

"Yeah," Gabby added. "This is one of the richest, most powerful men in the history of the world. You don't get to where he is in life by locking yourself in your house. One secretary I reached thanked me for my concern and reassured me he's surrounded by the best security detail in the world."

Warren pushed the uneaten rice and beans around on his plate. "Then what are we *doing* here? Shouldn't we head to LA? The thing Cole heard in Tokyo. Seven, eight, then hundreds, or whatever? Maybe we need to accept that SF is out of our hands and head to LA. See if we can... I don't know."

Gabby and Cole ignored him and went back to their devices. The longer he sat across from them, the more certain he was about not going back to being a cop. If this sort of technological myopia is what investigations required, he was out. He stared at the mural, focusing on the Tampico Bridge. There was something about it...

"Maria Machado," Gabby said loudly.

Cole looked up and blinked. "Who's that?"

"Maybe an assistant? A bodyman?"

"Where are you getting that?" Grimacing, Cole leaned over Gabby's laptop as she shoved it to the center of the table.

"Santos made an appearance at the Conference of South American Media four months ago," Gabby said, "well before this thing started." She rotated her laptop so Warren could see the photo. Santos was a handsome guy around sixty-five years old, with dark hair and firm cheeks that looked like they'd been tightened with botox injections. Standing next to him in the photo was a young woman, maybe thirty years old, and pregnant.

"Okay, so what?" Warren asked.

Gabby turned the computer back to herself and Cole. "I ran a facial recognition on the woman next to him, figuring she was a secretary or something. Her name is Maria Machado."

Warren cocked his head. "Facial recognition?"

She patted her laptop like it was the head of a friendly puppy. "Same one that half of police forces now use. Take any photo and it runs it through a database of every single online photo. Facebook, Instagram, regular websites, and so on."

Cole shook her head like she was about to object to the practice, but she said nothing. This wasn't the time for a philosophical debate about privacy.

"And it works?" Warren asked. "We didn't have that in the NYPD yet, but I knew it was out there."

Gabby smiled. "It works. Took this pic of Machado and ran it through. She has no social media herself, but someone else posted a photo with her in it on Facebook. From there, I figured out her name and got into her Gmail."

"That easy?" Cole asked. "Damn."

Gabby shrugged. "Ninety million Gmail passwords are on the Dark Web."

"So where is she?" Warren asked.

Gabby tapped her laptop. "Searching her emails now. Wait, here… she's seven months pregnant now and… boom! Yeah okay, so she's Santos' secretary and… apparently, his lover as well. The kid is his, according to this email to her sister."

"Is there anything about his travel plans?"

"It's her private email, so…" Gabby trailed off, reading.

Cole set her phone on the table.

Warren said, "You look like hell, Jane."

"Thanks."

"I mean, you should get some rest."

"I'm fine."

Gabby closed her laptop. "Machado is smart. There's almost nothing personal in there about Santos. One small thing about trying to arrange a birthday surprise for him while he's in SF. He's turning sixty-five today."

"What kind of surprise?" Cole asked.

Warren let out a long sigh and leaned back in his chair. "How is this what we're doing? Parsing birthday surprises for a billionaire from hacked emails from his secretary-slash-lover? How is this police work?"

"It's not," Gabby admitted. "We're not cops anymore." She returned her attention to Cole. "Something about walking across the bridge for his birthday. Apparently it's a thing."

"I've heard of that," Cole said. "People walk across the Golden Gate on their birthday."

Warren nearly fell back in his chair.

"What?" Gabby asked.

"The scanner. When I was listening to the scanner." He racked his brain, trying to piece together the conversation he'd been half-listening to. "They said something about some billionaire trying to get them to shut down the Golden Gate Bridge."

148

They parked in the lot on the north side of the bridge. To their left lay Alcatraz Island and the East Bay. To their right stretched the expanse of the Pacific Ocean. Diamonds of sparkling light flashed off the water as they approached the bridge's walkway.

A gust of wind chilled Cole's face. "If Santos *is* coming here, which I doubt, and if they know, which I doubt even more, there's no way they're gonna get him with a sniper rifle."

Warren stopped abruptly, licked a finger, and stuck it in the air. "Yeah, this is brutal. Maybe fifty miles per hour." He licked his finger again and held it up. "North, northeast. But… damn, the wind is all over the place." He looked north, back in the direction from which they'd come. A bank of low hills rose to the same height as the top of the bridge. "Not even The Truffle Pig could make a shot onto the bridge from there. Not in these winds."

Cole pointed up at the famous towers. Their dark red frames almost glowed in the bright sun. "It's about five hundred feet from the top to the walkway."

"Possible," Warren said.

Gabby had been walking slowly behind them while looking at her phone, but she skipped forward to catch up. "Only one problem—there's no one there." She pointed. "Or on the other tower, or dangling from any of the cables." She put a hand on Warren's forearm. "No sniper would try him here."

658

"I know he's gonna be here, though. I *know* it."

Cole sighed. On the ride from the taqueria, Warren had gone over everything he remembered about the conversation on the scanner. It wasn't much, but he'd convinced himself Santos would be there. She'd never believed in cop instincts. In her years as a crime reporter, she'd heard dozens of cops claim they'd nabbed a guy based on "gut instincts." But they never shared how often their gut instincts turned out wrong. More often, what they called gut instinct was just unconscious bias or a random guess. "Maybe I should head back to the car," Cole said. "I should be doing research. Something."

"Do what you want," Warren said. "I'm gonna look for Santos."

He picked up his pace and Cole was happy to hang back with Gabby. They walked slowly, watching Warren from behind. Cole said, "Let's stop for a minute."

They sat on a bench halfway across the bridge, watching Warren disappear.

Cole watched the clouds move slowly across the sky, their pace out of keeping with the swirling winds. Gabby scrolled through various apps on her phone. Cole cleared her throat. Gabby looked up. "There's something I want to talk to you about."

"William Wei? Afghanistan?"

"Right," Cole said.

Gabby cocked her head to the left. "How much of the conversation do you remember?"

"From the hospital?"

Gabby nodded. "Yeah. You told me you'd talked to Warren about it."

"He said William Wei worked for Kane, and that Kane was indirectly responsible for Matt's death. And you know about Julio Lopez. I have a recording of him admitting his involvement. Plus a guy named Chris Morgan, who runs a luxury construction place down in San Diego."

Gabby set her phone on her lap and gave Cole an odd look. Not condescension, more like pity.

"What?" Cole asked.

"Look, I know you covered crime for a long time. You're no amateur. But I don't think you want to know what I know."

"Yes," Cole said, "I do."

Gabby pointed at Warren, who'd made it to the end of the bridge and stopped to chat with a security guard. "Probably grilling him on whether Santos has been around." She chuckled. "Warren loves old-school police work. Knocking on doors, we used to call it."

Cole turned and put a hand on Gabby's knee. "Tell me anything you know. Tell me what I should do."

"You shouldn't have to deal with this. And you already know most of it. Here's what I don't think you get. At Kane's level, there's not a difference between illegal and legal. He operates between countries, between legal systems, and has his paws all over shaping the laws where he operates. He—quite literally—wants a single, unified world government that *he* largely controls through ownership of the tech, media, and financial sectors. There are only a few things that could get him in real trouble. Co-opting a group of Marines is one of them. You said he was 'indirectly' responsible for Matt's death." She nodded toward Warren, who was now only a hundred yards away. "Kane likely ordered Wei to do whatever it took to cover up the operation. And Wei probably told Lopez and Morgan to do the same. People like to convince themselves the people at the top of the pyramid are businessmen, or women—that they keep their hands clean. Maybe they *let* people get killed from time to time, but they leave that to the people lower down to do the dirty work."

"Yeah, and?"

"How do you think they get to the top of the pyramid to begin with?" Gabby asked.

"What do you mean?"

"Occasionally, it's genuine merit. Intelligence"—she shrugged —"hard work. But in a case like Kane, it's ten percent intelligence, ten percent hard work, and eighty percent ruthless violence that stops at nothing to acquire power."

"What are you trying to tell me?" Cole asked.

"Erase that recording of Lopez from your phone. Don't pursue this. Even if you prove Kane was behind it, you'll regret it. Even if you win, you'll lose. You know the truth now, just let it go."

Warren stopped in front of them. "Nothing. No sign of them and the security guard said they never close down the bridge for celebrities." He frowned. "He didn't know anything about Santos."

149

The limo wound through San Francisco's narrow streets, up and down steep hills, following signs to the Golden Gate Bridge. Sweat soaked DeLunge's chest and back under the explosive vest.

Next to him, Price took tiny, nervous sips from a tumbler of Scotch. He'd offered DeLunge a glass when they'd first gotten into the car. DeLunge spat in his face.

For the last two hours, he'd tried to think of a way out. Back on the houseboat, he considered rushing Kane. It would have taken him mere seconds to kill the man, assuming the billionaire had no training. And Price—he glanced at the pasty old man and couldn't keep himself from grunting in derision—he could have killed Price with a single punch to the throat. There was still time and opportunity for that. But he hadn't done it, and wouldn't. Not now.

Instead, he'd stayed calm and asked Kane questions. It had taken only a few minutes to remove all hope Kane was bluffing. It was no bluff. Two of his men waited near his sister's farmhouse in California. He'd stared into Kane's icy black eyes, and though rage nearly consumed DeLunge, he saw the killer in Kane—a killer who wouldn't hesitate to kill again.

He observed Price, who stared out the window. "Chandler, remember when we spoke on the phone and I asked if you were for real?"

150

Sitting at gate B32 in the San Francisco airport, Cole whipped out her phone, selected all the photos she'd taken, and emailed them to Rebecca McKnight, the babyfaced British reporter she'd met in Paris. She'd promised McKnight to send her a scoop, and these photos fulfilled Cole's end of the bargain.

She tapped out a quick message.

Rebecca,

These were taken about three hours ago on the Golden Gate Bridge. Only photos, as far as I know, of one of the nine murders as it took place. The big dude wore a suicide vest. You've probably already seen it on the news. But you're the only one who will have these photos. Before the bombing and after. High winds made a sniper shot impossible, so I guess they changed plans.

I don't know what's next, but I imagine it's in LA. Consider joining us there.

Jane

Gabby sat down and handed her a coffee. "Warren says you like it sweet. I put in four sugars."

"Thanks."

"How are you feeling?"

Cole lifted her shirt. The bandage was dotted with blood. "Turns out that running on the bridge and snapping pictures was a bad idea. Next pill is when?" She bit back a grimace.

"You just had one."

667

"Gimme a half?" Cole pleaded, hoping she didn't sound like a drug addict.

Gabby broke a Vicodin in two and Cole washed it down with a swig of coffee. "Heard from Warren?"

"He texted. Just finished with the police and will be here soon. We'll see if he makes the flight."

Cole began a text to Alexa Frias, the reporter who'd given her the backstory about Ana Diaz that connected Diaz to Ibo Kane. Another reporter she owed.

Alexa,

You're probably following what happened on the bridge in San Francisco...

She set her phone down and looked out the large, angled window. A plane taxied and stopped at their gate. Part of her wanted to drop her phone in the trash, change her flight to one for Mexico or Costa Rica, and never look back. But she owed Frias, and she couldn't break her promise, no matter how much she regretted it. In exchange for Frias sharing her Diaz information, Cole had agreed to speak on the record for a book. More than that, she'd agreed to be the *subject* of a book.

Every once in a while, a story got so big that the news itself wasn't enough to satisfy readers. People want to know *how* the story had been broken. Woodward and Bernstein became famous for breaking the Watergate story, but their book, *All the President's Men*, was as much about doing journalism as it was about the downfall of President Nixon. Alexa Frias wanted to do *that* kind of book, and Cole would be its subject.

She returned to the text.

In note form, here's what I saw on the bridge. If you ever write the book, this may well be the finale. On my way to LA now—you should join us there —but I doubt we'll find anything. This whole story is too far gone. Anyway, here it is...

In the note, she recounted how Gabby had learned about Maria Machado, leaving out Gabby's name, of course. Then she told how Warren had figured out Santos would head to the bridge. She sent the text and, when she looked up, Warren stood before them.

"Glad you made it," Gabby said. "Police grill you pretty hard?"

"They were decent. Medical had me for an hour or so.

Concussion, but no wounds. Security guard on top of me died. If he hadn't been pinning me to the ground…" He crouched between them, then sat cross-legged on the floor. "Anyway, I was lucky."

"Did you tell them how you knew he would be on the bridge?"

"Nah," Warren said. "But they knew who I was. Even asked about you." He nodded at Cole. "They might call you at some point."

The plane began disembarking, releasing a steady stream of tired-looking travelers.

Cole sighed. She was tired and her whole body ached. The Vicodin made everything feel softer, but didn't seem to dull the pain. "Los Angeles is a city of twenty million people. There are more possible targets than we could come up with in a year." She looked from Warren to Gabby, then back to Warren. "Chandler Price—the one guy who might have given up something—is dead."

Gabby sipped her coffee and handed it to Warren. "Black, no sugar. You want some?"

Warren took a swig and handed it back.

Gabby said, "Price dead, plus Santos, his pregnant mistress, and three security guards."

Warren shook his head and stared at the ground for a long time. Without looking up, he said, "When the detectives finished questioning me, they passed me over to a couple FBI guys. Didn't want to tell me much, but I figure they were from the joint Task Force. At first they were all tough. You know, 'How'd you end up on the bridge? What do you know?' Stuff like that." He took Gabby's coffee and finished it, then handed her back the empty cup. "Sorry, I'll buy you a refill. Anyway, after they figured out we're on the same team, their tone changed."

"To what?" Cole asked.

"Pleading. They wanted to know what I know. I told them about the 'hundreds and hundreds' thing. They weren't about to tell me anything, but I got the sense…" He trailed off, shaking his head.

"What?" Gabby asked.

"That they *knew*. They exchanged a look. Man, I don't know. My brain doesn't feel right."

Cole tapped his knee with her foot, trying to comfort him. "You said yourself, you had a concussion."

"It's not that, though. I think somehow they'd already heard the next attack might not be a single, sniper-style killing."

"Maybe," Gabby said. "But that doesn't help us much, does it?"

Cole was confused. "If they had any indication something bigger was planned, why wouldn't they have released that information to the public?"

"Could be a lot of things," Gabby said. "Might not have confirmation. Might not want to cause a panic." She leaned back and squinted. "I see that look in your eyes, Jane. Not everything is a conspiracy."

A boarding call came over the speaker system for first-class passengers.

Warren said, "You guys are off on a whole tangent. That's not what I was saying."

He looked exasperated. Cole folded her hands in her lap dramatically. "Then what *are* you saying?"

"I told them this could be a bigger attack. They already knew that. At least I *think* so. If this is something major, some grand finale... think about it. That means it just got a lot easier for us to figure out where and when the final attack will be. We need to get to work."

—End of Episode 8—

THE
CRIME
BEAT
EPISODE 9: LOS ANGELES

151

Thursday

In the one-bedroom suite in the Tannerman Hotel in Los Angeles, the chaos was getting to Cole. The pain in her belly wasn't as sharp as it had been yesterday, but it was a consistent, intense ache that carried memories with it. Every throb of pain contained a vision of the angry man who'd stabbed her.

She sat on a loveseat, looking out at the Los Angeles skyline framed by a clear blue sky. At the desk along the wall, Alexa Frias worked the phones. The Cuban-American reporter had flown in from Miami, as Cole had suggested. On the couch beside her, Rebecca McKnight spoke quietly into her Bluetooth headset while simultaneously scrolling on her laptop. The British reporter always did two things at once.

For a day and a half, the three had worked tirelessly without a single breakthrough.

Gabby and Warren worked separately, but no less intensely. An hour earlier, they'd closed themselves off in the bedroom, taking only Gabby's laptop, phone, and two salads topped with grilled salmon. Like Warren, Gabby avoided carbs.

What was it about rogue, ex-NYPD officers and their carbs?

Cole had a plate of fries, cold and half-eaten, sitting on the end table next to her. She'd enjoyed the first couple bites, but the sight of them brought memories of the hallway and the toppled room service cart screaming into her mind and through her body. She'd shoved them aside to eat later.

Cole looked from Frias to McKnight, closed her eyes, and thought. Each of them had tried desperately to figure out where the next attack would take place. Each went about it in her own way. McKnight was from London and didn't have many sources in Los Angeles, so she studied large public gatherings—concerts, sporting events, conferences. Of course, there were hundreds of them, so her next tactic was to cross-check major events with public appearances by celebrities, politicians, and financial leaders. This was slow going, and so far she hadn't found more than a few weak options.

Frias, on the other hand, had worked in L.A. for two years after college and had dozens of contacts in the city. Her way of asking questions was much like Cole's. She dug into each source, getting the most information possible without letting the source know what angle she was working. Cole had considered quitting journalism more than once in the last couple weeks. Knowing reporters like Frias were out there reassured her she'd be leaving the profession in good hands.

"Alexa," Cole said when Frias ended her most recent call. "You getting anything?"

Frias sat on the couch next to McKnight. "Not much. I'm hearing all sorts of good rumors, though. Word around the city is that a lot of people suspect something big tomorrow. It's New Year's Eve. There are some basketball games and—"

"Yeah," McKnight interrupted in her quick British accent. "Staples Center has a game at five. And a college game earlier in the day."

"Sure." Frias ran a hand anxiously through her black hair. "But sources are asking why they'd attack a big random crowd, and I agree. I don't know if we're on the right line of attack here."

Cole agreed, too. They'd spent the better part of the last thirty-six hours chasing their tails and getting the runaround from FBI and local law enforcement agencies. With great effort, she stood and walked a lap around the loveseat, then sat. "There are endless celebrities, bankers, and former politicians here. How do we find out where *they'll* be? Focus on the targets, not the locations."

McKnight closed her laptop. "That's the issue. Most of the guest lists are private anyway, but this year security is way tighter. Looking into big public events, I did find some possibilities—parties and whatnot. But I don't know the wheres and whens. People aren't sharing plans on social media like usual."

Cole sighed. "So there's no database of where the rich and powerful are spending New Year's Eve?"

"No," McKnight and Frias said in unison.

A large TV on the wall played local news on mute. Along the bottom of the screen, the scroll read: LOS ANGELES ON HIGH ALERT AS NINTH MURDER EXPECTED. CITY DEFIANT. UNDER TIGHT SECURITY, NEW YEAR'S EVE PLANS GOING FORWARD. RUMORS OF A WIDER ATTACK.

The last portion—RUMORS OF A WIDER ATTACK—had been leaked by Cole herself. After speaking with the police and FBI, she'd called a half-dozen reporters to leak what the deranged man in Japan had said. If they weren't able to stop a potential attack, at least she'd done her best to warn the public.

"What about big public gatherings?" Cole asked. "We do Times Square in New York. Is there an equivalent in LA?"

"I don't think so." Frias tapped at her laptop. "Nothing *that* big, but... hold on."

Warren's deep voice rose from behind the door and she wondered what he and Gabby were up to. They'd been quiet about their lines of research. Cole figured it was because Gabby was comfortable operating well outside the law and didn't want to get her wrapped up in her efforts. Cole appreciated it. One way or another, this would soon be over, and she hoped it wouldn't end in a prison cell with Gabby.

Frias said, "Here's a list. Looks like there are dozens. Hundreds. A couple outdoor things, a million hotels and rooftop bars and parties. But there's not *one big thing*."

"Los Angeles *is* decentralized," Cole agreed.

McKnight sat cross-legged on the floor. "Whatever happened to your research into the weapons? They didn't use one in San Francisco. I'm no weapons expert, but how are you going to kill hundreds and hundreds of people with a sniper rifle? Your original reporting said they bought nine rifles. Why buy nine rifles if you only need seven?"

Cole frowned. She'd considered the weapons issue, but hadn't yet taken the thought all the way to its logical conclusion. "We assume the original plan was to shoot Roberto Santos with the eighth rifle at the conference in San Francisco, but security was too tight, so that was scrapped. They likely improvised the suicide vest idea as a backup."

McKnight tracked Cole as she paced the room. "Okay, but what about the ninth?"

Frias agreed. "The guy in Tokyo said there would be hundreds and hundreds more—how can that be the plan with just the one rifle left? Even the best sniper couldn't do that."

"Lemme think." Cole leaned against the wall to the bedroom. Warren and Gabby spoke loudly enough for her to hear their voices, but not make out distinct words.

She ground her teeth. The research she and the other two reporters were pursuing was going nowhere. Los Angeles was too big a city to figure out a location. And the weapons angle, while interesting, involved too much speculation. She turned to the two women and spoke in a tone of finality, eager to end this line of research. "The last rifle could be a decoy. Maybe they figured we'd find out about them and then everyone would be trying to find the ninth victim and therefore miss the larger scheme. Maybe they simply changed plans after they bought the rifles, adding the plan for 'hundreds and hundreds more' *after* they saw how well it was going."

"But"—McKnight stretched her legs out in front of her—"and maybe this is just my Britishness speaking, that's so *untidy*. There's no way they plot this thing out for a year, hack all these powerful people's travel plans and schedules, buy *exactly* nine rifles, announce *exactly* nine murders, then *don't* use the ninth gun. I understand San Francisco. That makes sense. Obviously the plan wasn't to blow up Roberto Santos along with Chandler Price and"—she frowned—"do we even know who the bomber was yet?"

"No," Cole said. So far, news had reported that it was a large man, but that his body had been so damaged they hadn't yet identified him. Gabby had assured her they'd have his name from dental records within a couple days, and they might successfully track down the limo driver who fled the scene. "But even if we find out who the guy was, how will that help?"

McKnight moved deftly into a downward dog pose. "My point

is, I'd bet anything there will be a ninth shooting. Maybe it'll only be *part* of something else, but these dudes are fanatical. Precise."

"Maybe," Cole said. "But how does that help us? Without knowing a target, how does that help us?"

She walked back over to the love seat and flopped down. Her movements had been too quick and she winced with pain as she sat.

"You okay?" Frias asked.

"Not really. Is it noon yet?"

"It's eleven. Why?"

"Gabby said I can't have my medication 'til noon." Cole closed her eyes and let her head rest on the couch. She was supposed to be leading the two younger reporters, but they were getting nowhere.

A door creaked and she opened her eyes.

Warren stared down at her. "You solve the crime?"

She smiled sarcastically. "Colonel Mustard. Billiard Room. With the revolver."

"That's actually not too far off." Gabby sat on the floor in front of her. "How you feeling?"

Cole grimaced. "Any chance I can have my pill early?"

"No." Gabby had busted her out of the Tokyo hospital only after Cole agreed to follow her orders. And Gabby was always happy to give orders.

Frias and McKnight were again buried in their laptops. Warren took the last chair and looked from Cole to Gabby, then back to Cole. He raised an eyebrow pointedly. "Did you miss it?"

"What?" Cole asked.

"Gabby just told you, you were close."

"Close to *what*?" The pain meds were wearing off and it made her irritable. She didn't like the feeling, but couldn't control it.

"Well, her name isn't Colonel Mustard," Gabby said. "But she *is* ex-military. Topped out at sergeant, I think. And a sniper rifle is *kinda* like a revolver. And though I'm not certain of the location, it might have a pool table."

Cole's eyes opened wide. "What?"

"All in all, a pretty good guess," Gabby added.

A faint knock came from the door. The three reporters perked up at once.

Cole looked to Gabby, who smiled. "Don't worry."

She stood and walked briskly to the door, followed by Warren. Before opening it, Gabby pulled a firearm from her belt. Cole was too stunned to say anything. She hadn't known Gabby concealed a weapon under her long shirt. She said to Warren, "Don't think it'll be an issue. She knows who I am. Knows you're here. Just in case. You open."

Cole stood to get a better look as Gabby got into position and Warren grabbed the doorknob. He swung it open and Gabby aimed. The woman stood about a yard back, arms out, palms up. Resting across her forearms was a skinny black bag. She held it out as though making an offering.

Gabby lowered her gun, took the bag, and waved the woman inside.

She walked in, her stride slow and hesitant, and shut the door behind her.

Cole sat back on the couch as Gabby set the desk chair next to it. She waved the woman into the chair and sat on the floor, draping the bag across her lap. Cole waited for someone to speak, staring at Warren, then Gabby, then the mysterious woman.

Everyone stared at Gabby, who sat cross-legged, inspecting the bag. She unzipped it, revealing a barrel of cold black metal. Cole's mind flashed back to the hotel room in Miami where she and Warren found The Truffle Pig's weapon. This rifle was the exact same model, with the same matte black color, large scope, and thick barrel.

Gabby inspected the weapon carefully, turning it over in her hands as a half-smile spread across her face. "This is one of the finest weapons I've ever seen."

Cole sat in stunned silence for a moment, then said, "What the hell is going on?"

152

Cole had been so focused on the weapon, she'd barely noticed the odd appearance of the woman who'd delivered it. She had a wide forehead, blue eyes and a sallow face, like her cheeks hadn't seen the sun in a while. Her straight blonde hair nearly touched the floor. She wore brown, military-issue pants and boots that flaked dried mud onto the carpet. The pockets of her red vest bulged as though stuffed with supplies. Cole thought she would have been pretty if she didn't look so unhealthy and nervous. She kept cracking her knuckles and flashing nervous glances at Cole and the other two reporters in the room.

Gabby finished inspecting the rifle and spoke. "Everyone, this is... well, let's call her Colonel Mustard for now. Her real name isn't important."

Cole's gaze was fixed on the woman. Her shoulders had dropped a little when Gabby gave the fake name, which made Cole think she'd come against her will. Why would she have shown up to a meeting with three tenacious reporters *without* the assurance her name would be kept private? Somehow, Gabby had *made her* show up.

"Gabby," Cole said. "What the hell is going on? Just tell us straight."

Gabby turned toward the nervous woman. "*Colonel*, tell them what you told me in the chat."

an online rabbit hole of radicalization, first blaming the Olympic Team and their toxic politics, then the government, then the social media companies that had allowed word of her cheating to go viral, to make her a pariah.

She grew angry at everyone and everything. Newly unable to get prescriptions for the beta blockers for competitions, she started buying them on the street, along with opioids to numb the emotional pain.

When Price showed up at her door, she'd reached a low point, but still not low enough to agree to his insane scheme. She didn't recognize the man in the picture and didn't need the money that badly. She rejected Price's offer.

A few days later, he'd shown up again with a political argument rather than a financial one. He'd seen her online comments and posts about the Olympic Committee and the international order and thought she might agree with their ultimate aims, though at the time he was quite vague about them. He spoke in terms of "digital globalization," and the "international technological cabal," and "the freedom of individual citizens." Sarah had dabbled in online conspiracy theories and made a few comments she regretted, but ultimately found Price's arguments weak and nonsensical. She'd turned him down a second time.

Another week passed, and this time he returned with two men —one white and one black—both large and scowling. Neither said a word, but she knew why Price had brought them. Intimidation. At this third meeting, the two men stayed outside as Price laid out his demand. Take the shot as he'd suggested, or die.

She'd asked why the man wanted to be shot in the leg, but Price wouldn't answer. Then she'd asked why he was so set on *her.* There were other good shots out there. Why not find someone else to do it?

At this, Price had frowned, almost as though he'd been embarrassed at the answer he was about to give. "You're the most accurate shot in the world, and the man I work for chose *you.* He gets what he wants. Please understand this isn't a *threat.* It's a statement of fact."

She tried to laugh it off, but Price had called the two men into her house and destroyed it. Ripped pictures off the walls, broke vases, even busted the stock of one of the classic rifles hanging on her wall.

Next time, they said, they'd do the same to her. She'd agreed to Price's plan and he left, saying he'd be in touch when the time was right.

"Did you think about going to the police?" Cole asked.

Sarah frowned. "That's what got me in trouble. I was terrified. Didn't know what to do. That night I called a friend who had a brother in the LAPD. I didn't tell him much. It was more me just feeling out my options—'If I wanted to talk to someone about something important, what would I do?'—that kind of thing. Next morning, I walked out of my house and the two guys who'd been with Price were there. They threw me in the back of a van, blindfolded me, and took me to a cabin somewhere outside the city. They had bugged my phone." She closed her eyes. "Held me there in isolation for… what has it been? A few weeks now. Told me I was still going to make the shot, and they'd let me go after."

Cole's mind raced while she tried to take this all in. How had Sarah escaped? Had she learned anything else about the men who abducted her or their plan? But one question above all stayed at the front of her mind. "Why the hell would Ibo Kane want you to shoot him?"

She tossed the picture of Kane onto the carpet between them. "I'm telling you, I barely even know who that is?"

"You don't read the paper?" Cole shook her head. "I mean, the internet?"

Warren said, "She's been in isolation the whole time, has no idea what's going on. Kane has been rich for years, but wasn't a household name until your story came out."

Alexa Frias had watched Sarah closely during her story, casting an occasional glance at Cole. "I can tell you why," the reporter said. "Kane knew he'd be a suspect from the beginning. He knew he'd be on the list of potential targets." She smiled. "If *he's* the ninth victim, it puts him in the clear."

Cole waited for Frias to elaborate, but noticed Warren staring at her. He looked like he wanted to say something, but he stayed quiet.

Before she could say anything, Rebecca McKnight chimed in, speaking briskly in her British accent. "Exactly what I was thinking. Kane was smart enough to know someone would connect him to these murders eventually." She nodded at Cole. "*You* were smart enough. Getting shot gives him an alibi of sorts."

684

"And I was supposed to shoot him in the fleshy part of the thigh," Sarah said.

"That would still do massive damage, wouldn't it?" Cole asked.

Sarah nodded. "Absolutely. But assuming I did my job, and he had immediate medical attention, it's definitely survivable."

Cole picked up the photo of Kane and crouched next to Sarah, who seemed to have settled down as she told her story. "Did Price say anything about hundreds and hundreds dying, or this being part of some larger plot?"

Sarah shook her head. "They kept me in the dark. Locked away."

Cole looked up at Gabby, who was tapping something on her phone, then turned back at Sarah. "How'd you escape?"

Sarah buried her head in her hands and Cole looked back at Gabby. "How'd you find her? How'd you get her to come here?"

Gabby had her phone in front of her face. "No time for that now. We need to get out of here."

154

If a lie is big enough—and you tell it boldly enough—people find it more credible than a simple truth. Ibo Kane counted on the men in the chatroom to believe one more big lie. To fall in line.

There was little doubt they would.

He leaned back in his office chair, catching a glimpse of the Hollywood Hills before turning his attention to the screen. Only moments ago, he'd informed them of the plan to get himself shot. He'd explained how he and Chandler Price had "hired" Sarah, knowing he'd eventually be tied to the string of murders. Being targeted himself was the ultimate alibi. What he didn't tell them was that he'd planned for Sarah to miss him and kill *Price*, not him. That way, he could claim to have been a target without actually taking a shot. And he would have eliminated his number one accomplice at the same time.

Tread_on_This!: *Um, okay, so what now?*

8/15/47: *Yeah, what now? The important thing is that the main target is still taken out, despite what happened to Gunner_Vision.*

Tread_on_This!: *What DID happen to him? We know he's gone, but what happened?*

Kane thought for a moment, then tapped out another lie.

General_Ki: *As you know, after initiating the final stage, he went to SF when Santos changed plans. I met with him and tried to convince him not to, but he demanded that he sacrifice himself for the cause. We found him an*

686

easier way, but it wasn't enough. He wanted to be sure. Suicide vest was the only way to be sure.

Tread_on_This!: *RIP hero.*

8/15/47: *We won't forget him.*

The thing about lies, Kane knew, was that the content doesn't matter much. Most people don't think critically. They don't test statements against reality. Instead, they orient themselves emotionally towards believing or not believing something, and once they've decided, they filter all information through that. If he told these idiots the sky was red right now, they'd applaud him for his insight.

General_Ki: *Yes. We will never forget him. And I've already taken care of his sister and his nieces. They live on a small almond farm in California, and will never lack for anything.*

Tread_on_This!: *Good man, General_Ki.*

They hadn't blinked an eye.

He'd been worried about the interaction, but only briefly. These men were now his puppets. If they hadn't abandoned the plan when they'd found out he was behind it, they weren't going to abandon it now.

Sarah had escaped—Kane still didn't know how—so they'd been forced into yet another backup plan—one he dreaded. But after being questioned and released by the FBI twice, he needed to end this and get off their radar.

General_Ki: *Who's closest to Los Angeles?*

Tread_on_This!: *I'm in Phoenix. Can leave now and be in LA by 7 or 8 PM.*

General_Ki: *Good. Leave now. What kind of weapon do you have?*

Tread_on_This!: *What kind of weapon DON'T I have?*

8/15/47: *This is no time for jokes, Tread_on_This!*

Tread_on_This!: *Okay. I've got everything, but I'm no sniper. Will have to go close range.*

8/15/47: *A .22 is the safest bet. Outside section of the thigh, away from the femoral artery.*

Kane winced. Even if that was the safest place to get shot, it didn't sound especially appealing.

General_Ki: *Good. Leave now, Tread_on_This!*

Tread_on_This!: *Will do, boss. No offense, but getting shot by a fifty cal was a dumb ass idea. Woulda turned your leg into mincemeat. Maybe blown it clear off.*

687

General_Ki: *I know that now. Bad idea.*

Of course, he wasn't going to tell them that he never actually planned to take the bullet. That bullet would have ended up in Chandler Price's head had things not gone sideways in San Francisco and with Sarah McNeeley.

General_Ki: *The detonator. Is our backup plan set?*

8/15/47: *I'm ready. 10:30 exactly. Kokutai-Goji gave me the codes to log on and detonate before he was arrested.*

Their Japanese brother had done his duty. Their tech expert since the beginning, Kokutai-Goji had taken it upon himself to try to kill Jane Cole. Life in prison would be his reward. Kane already had sources within the Japanese legal system to find out in advance if there was even a whisper that he was going to flip. Of all the men he'd conned into this plot, Kokutai-Goji may have been the truest believer. He wouldn't flip.

General_Ki: *Yes, that means, Tread_on_This!, you need to be there by 10:15, got it?*

Tread_on_This!: *Sir, yes sir. Over and out.*

Tread_on_This!'s screen name went gray as he left the chat.

No_Surveillance_State: *Anyone see this yet?*

Following the message was a video, and Kane recognized it right away. He'd tried to figure out exactly what happened on the bridge. They'd achieved their mission, but Price getting caught in the explosion had forced the change in this evening's plan.

The video attached to the message was cellphone footage that started with a beautiful, panoramic shot of the hills and water around the Golden Gate Bridge. It scanned left, taking in the massive red towers, then the walkway and road across the bridge.

A limo appeared in the frame, then stopped. DeLunge emerged, dragged Price out with him, and darted across a lane of traffic. The video wobbled as it tracked toward DeLunge, but ultimately lost him. Then, everything shook and the shot went black.

No_Surveillance_State: *First video I've seen yet. What the hell? Was that Price with him?*

General_Ki: *He was supposed to drop him off. I don't know what happened.*

He knew exactly what had happened. Killing Price had been DeLunge's small act of defiance. A final "screw you" to Kane.

No_Surveillance_State: *He's dragging him. What the hell? Damn.*

This wasn't good. The last thing he needed was a mutiny.

General_Ki: *I don't know what Gunner_Vision was thinking. But, like I said earlier, he did his duty and we should all be thankful. 8/15/47, are you 100% sure you're ready?*

8/15/47: *I'm sure.*

General_Ki: *Okay, gentlemen, logging off. One last time:*

9/9

Initiated

(Los Angeles Elites)

An international brotherhood united by General Ki for a singular mission: to end technological oppression, to restore individual freedoms, to birth a new era of digital liberty.

Initiated

9/9

(Los Angeles Elites)

The men echoed his refrain before Kane logged off for the last time.

By the door, his assistant waited. He was a short man Kane called "Kid" because he had a young face, despite being ten years older than Kane himself. "We leave here at 9:45, Kid. Call the chopper for pickup across the street at 10:20. Got it?"

"Understood, Mr. Kane."

"And get my doctor. Have him on the helicopter ready to treat a minor gunshot wound."

"Mr. Kane… I…"

Kane leveled a gaze at him and his subordinate dropped his eyes.

"Yes, sir."

"Remember this, Kid, if a lie is big enough—and you tell it boldly enough—people find it more credible than a simple truth."

Kid backed away, not raising his eyes. A minute later, Kane heard him making his calls from the other room.

He took a long swig from a Red Bull and leaned back, examining the skyline. Soon it would be over. Soon the world would be his.

155

"Wanna tell me how your people found these two locations?" Warren asked.

Over the last four hours, he and Gabby had sipped black coffees in a cafe across the street from Club God. He'd tried to get into the building multiple times, but two security guards were posted at each door. It was only late afternoon, so he assumed there'd be even more bouncers by the time guests arrived. Across town, Cole, Sarah, and Frias circled Hotel Nine in a rental car.

"Not really," Gabby replied. "For your own protection. Unless you wanna be in what I'm in, better you don't know."

Warren didn't answer right away. Gabby had a team of ex-cops, intelligence analysts, and military people working with her, but she was reluctant to say much about them. Warren figured she was willing to risk her own safety, but not theirs. Even though he trusted her, he had to know why they were staking out these two locations. "Tell me this, at least: without naming names, what is it about these two spots?"

She gave him a look that said, *Not my funeral.* "Once we found Sarah, I figured there would be one location where Kane would be *and* where the final attack would be." She nodded at Rebecca McKnight, who sat at a nearby table scrolling on her phone. "I sent them all the various locations McKnight and Frias came up with. He created a quick AI to comb the web for historic data of celebrity and politician appearances on New Year's Eve in LA. These two locations were what he got."

"That *sounds* great," Warren said, "but what's your confidence level?"

"High. This guy is disgruntled NSA. He's *good*. And it's actually not *that* hard. Basically, he scanned the web for mentions of celebrities and politicians and financial leaders with about a hundred LA locations. All from *past* years. Then, he factored in social media mentions, which is easy enough to do, in order to figure out the most likely spots people would be tonight."

Warren waved a hand and grimaced. He didn't buy it, but what did he know? A lot of things he didn't understand were proving integral to police work these days. It was just one more reason he didn't belong in the business anymore. Hunches were proving less and less valuable than computer skills. Still, he had a hunch he needed to get off his chest. A thought nagged at him since the moment Alexa Frias figured out Ibo Kane was setting himself up to get shot. Why did Kane have faith he'd survive a .50 caliber rifle round, even one precisely aimed in the safest possible location? No matter where it hit a person, a .50 caliber left one *hell* of a hole.

Gabby had called in their location to an FBI contact, along with the other location, where Cole, Sarah, and Frias waited. Her contact promised to check it out and pass it along to the LAPD, but they were so overwhelmed with tips—not to mention already being understaffed and stretched thin by hundreds of different V.I.P. New Year's Eve plans—that he wasn't confident they'd follow up. He soothed his conscience by telling himself that if nothing else, at least they'd *tried* to do the right thing, but that excuse was wearing thin from overuse.

Mostly, they'd been silent, but every half hour one of them walked a lap around the massive former church, scoping things out, chatting with caterers and other staff—most of whom ignored them—trying to figure out what was happening.

Now, he couldn't hold back the thought any longer. "Gab, a fifty cal turns bones into mush and shreds flesh. Even if Sarah *could* be perfectly accurate, it could paralyze him, or kill him if it hits the right artery. I had a friend get hit with a fifty cal shell while wearing body armor. The shock crushed his organs, and he died later that same night." Gabby was listening carefully, head cocked to the side. "What I'm *saying* is, Ibo Kane is not a stupid man. No way in hell he's stupid enough to hire someone to shoot him with a fifty cal unless the alternative is certain death. There's just no way."

Gabby shifted her eyes to the sprawling exterior of Club God, visible through the cafe window. "Agreed. I didn't want to get into it in the hotel, but... *yeah*. I trust Sarah, but I think they must have had some other plan. Something ain't adding up."

Warren waved McKnight over and nodded toward the club. "Wanna try?"

"Sure. What do I say?"

Warren shrugged. "Dunno. Just... be a reporter, I guess? See if anyone'll give you anything. Guest list, start times, musical acts. Just get them talking and see if you can find anything we can use to find out who's gonna be there and when."

The reporter nodded, pulled out her notebook, and left.

"Think it'll work?" Gabby asked.

"Cole says she's good, but no, it won't work. I just wanted her out of here. Don't think I'll ever be comfortable with reporters ever again."

Gabby laughed. "Me neither."

Warren watched as McKnight crossed the street and strode up to a security guard out front. She spoke to him for a few minutes, then disappeared around the side of the building. The sun was setting, the sky fading to an orange-brown. One way or another, this ordeal was about to end.

Warren turned to Gabby and she waited until she met his eyes. "I'm done being a cop."

"Yeah?"

"Gonna head back home, try to get back with my wife, with Marina."

"Sure you don't want to join me?" Gabby asked.

Warren frowned and shook his head in a tight arc. "More than sure. I'm done with this. We're pushing against a tsunami of evil in this world. I'm gonna find myself some peace and let all this go."

The look Gabby gave him was strange.

"What?" he asked.

"You say that, but you're sitting here, still trying to stop this thing."

Warren laughed at himself. "Good point. But seriously, what the hell is Kane doing? We know Sarah's telling the truth, but there's just no way in hell he was ever going to go through with it."

McKnight appeared from around the other side of the building. Her shoulders were slumped and she looked a lot less peppy than she had when she left the cafe. They waited while she returned from across the street.

Gabby said, "I've been puzzling it out, and here's my best guess: the two guys who held Sarah captive? Neither of them was Chandler Price, the guy who set it up. If I were Kane, I'd want everyone to think I was a target, I'd want to take out my closest associates—like he did with the lobbyist in D.C.—but I *wouldn't* want to risk taking a fifty cal, even to the fleshy part of my thigh."

"Yeah, so what do you do?"

"I give Sarah another picture on the eve of the job—one of Chandler Price. I have her shoot *him*, maybe even kill him. I could still claim I was the target."

Warren considered this. It was possible, but a stretch. "Could be, but with Price dead, we'll never know."

A bell chimed as McKnight burst through the door of the cafe.

"Nothing?" Warren asked.

"Not nothing." She held up a piece of paper. "I got the guest list from the bouncer on the back door."

156

For the last few hours, Cole had been sitting next to one of the most accurate shooters in the world, circling the block around Hotel Nine in a rental car. The hotel was one of the nicest in Los Angeles, with multiple ballrooms and a rooftop bar and party area famous for its views of LA. "Tell us how you escaped."

In the back seat, Alexa Frias leaned forward, notebook in hand.

Sarah shot her a look, and Frias sat back, setting the notebook aside.

"None, and I mean *none* of this can be public, okay?" She opened her mouth to speak, then went quiet and rolled down the window. She inhaled deeply. To Cole, it smelled like moderately dirty Los Angeles air, but Sarah seemed to enjoy it.

"Must be good to feel the wind on your face," Cole said, trying to move her back to the question.

"Was in that cabin so long. It was so dark, dank." Sarah inhaled again. "Never thought LA air would smell this good."

Sarah had been through hell, that much was clear. Cole didn't yet have all the details, but the woman appeared profoundly shaken. She didn't want to push her, but she needed answers. "No pressure, but it might help to know how you escaped. I'm a reporter—" She paused. "Well, I *used* to be a reporter. Worked the crime beat in New York City for years. Don't know what the hell I

694

am now, but I have a knack for picking important details out of stories. There might be something in your escape that helps us."

"I don't think there's anything in my escape that will help. Before I competed, I was in the Army. Not very long, never saw any action, but enough where I was well-trained and in pretty good shape. Mentally, I mean. My mind was in good shape. Couple weeks in the cabin with those two guys and I learned their routines. Learned their blind spots."

Cole flashed on Joey Mazzalano. "They ever try anything with you? Nothing… you know."

"No, thank God. And they could have. Guess they were under strict orders. I mean, they wanted me to take the shot. Probably knew that wasn't gonna happen if they assaulted me while we were waiting."

Frias chimed in from the back seat. "So how'd you get away?"

"Long story short, they locked me in my room at night, so that wasn't an option, but they let me out an hour a day to practice with the rifle. They needed me to be good, and damn, that was a fine weapon. Only thing that kept me sane. When I shot, they both watched, guns on me. If I'd have turned and tried to take them out, they would have killed me. So yesterday I missed on purpose, missed over and over and asked for more bullets. I knew they had them back in the cabin. So, that's how I got the first guy to leave. They made me put the rifle back in the bag before I could turn around. But while he was inside, I pulled the target forward and showed it to the other guard. It made him happy to see how off my shots had been. And I played it up. I was all, 'Can't believe how off I am today,' really down on myself. As he examined the target, I swiped the rifle up and cracked his jaw with the butt. Blow was softened a little by the bag, but still. Knocked him back enough. Then I ran." She pulled one of her feet up, holding her boot like a trophy. "Ran through a muddy creek and a stand of trees or two, but hit the highway within five minutes. Car picked me up."

Cole turned left, then left again. A team of security guards was surrounding the hotel with a red velvet rope. They couldn't completely close the sidewalk, but they were creating a nice perimeter around the building.

Frias asked, "How'd you connect with Gabby? Why didn't you go to the police when you escaped?"

"I *really* hate reporters," Sarah said. "No offense."

"None taken," Frias laughed.

"I *did* call law enforcement. The friend I have. He said 'don't go to the LAPD' and connected me with Gabby in a secure chat."

Cole shook her head. "That woman has tentacles all over." She stopped at a red light and turned to Frias. "You should write your book about her, not me."

Frias chuckled. "Doubt she's dumb enough to agree to that."

"What else?" Cole asked Sarah. "Any other details that might help?" The light changed and Cole turned, again passing in front of the hotel. For the first time, she noticed there was no building directly across the street from the hotel, just an empty crater where a construction crew was halfway through building the foundation of what was likely a new skyscraper. She thought of all the other murders, with shots that had been meticulously planned. "What about the shot itself? They'd given you the target. Did they say anything about distance or angle? Maybe that would help us narrow down the location."

"I asked about that and they wouldn't say much, but…" She trailed off, thinking, then stuck her head halfway out the window. "Pull over!"

Cole double-parked and Sarah hopped out.

Cole heard a buzzing in the back seat. Frias said, "Just got a text from McKnight."

"What is it?"

"An image. Still loading."

Through the window, Cole watched Sarah spin around, examining all the buildings around the main entrance to Hotel Nine. She walked a few yards down the block, studying angles, then returned to the car. "It can't be here."

"Why not?" Cole asked.

"They wouldn't tell me much about the shot, but they only let me practice on one slope, about twenty degrees above the target. Said it was what I needed to stay sharp on. Across the street, there's nothing. A hole. And there are no buildings with an angle on the front entrance that work. This can't be the site."

"It's not," Frias said. "McKnight got a guest list for Club God. And Ibo Kane is on it."

157

As night fell, they waited. Cole and Warren sat in the rental car's front seat, Cole behind the wheel. Alexa Frias sat in the back.

Just barely visible a block away was Gabby, who had reluctantly agreed to let McKnight shadow her. Through binoculars Gabby had given her, Cole watched them, a yard apart. Gabby paced while McKnight scribbled in her notebook under the short glow of a streetlight.

They were about half a block from the front entrance of Club God, which was roped off and flanked by a dozen security guards and three doormen who were just as large and just as intimidating. They stood under a black tent-like canopy that stretched from the sidewalk all the way to the entrance, almost eliminating the possibility of sniper fire.

"Anything?" Warren asked.

Cole moved the binoculars from Gabby to the front entrance. The doormen each held clipboards, chatting amongst themselves. "Nothing." She looked at Warren. The interior dome light of the car lit the side of his face. His cheeks were tight, his lips pursed in worry. "Isn't there anything else we can do?" she asked.

"Gabby called it in to everyone she could think of. Problem is, there are a dozen credible threats on a normal New Year's Eve in LA. Tonight there are hundreds," he said.

Sarah had been quiet for a long time in the back seat. "We can't just sit here doing nothing. Why don't we go to the roof?"

"We went over this," Cole said.

"We need to hold our position and be ready to react," Warren added.

When they'd arrived, they'd immediately found the location they assumed was the spot where Sarah was supposed to have taken the shot. But with her and the ninth rifle out of the picture, Cole and Warren had convinced her there must be some new plan now. They'd agreed to get two good angles on the building and watch for Kane's arrival.

With binoculars, Warren scanned the area. "There's something." He handed the scopes to Cole and pointed at a white limousine pulling around the corner.

Cole followed the limo as a driver stepped out, followed by two beefy men in black suits. They opened a door, glancing side to side as a tall man in a fedora stepped out, a blonde woman on his arm. A photographer appeared from behind a car and snapped a few pictures before being shoved away by a security guard. The couple approached the doormen, who checked the list and waved them inside.

"Not Kane," Cole said, "but I guess people are arriving."

Sarah asked, "What do we do when we see Kane?"

Cole looked at Warren, who shrugged. "Gabby said to call if we see him, and she'll… I don't know. She'll do something. She always does."

Halfway down the block, a large truck stopped. Two men wearing gold chains and baseball hats got out and Cole followed them through the binoculars as they approached the club. "Who are they?" She handed Warren the binoculars so he could get a look. "I think I recognize them."

He peered through the device. "One of them is Downtown Jake. Rapper. He was on the guest list. Don't know the other."

The list—which McKnight had gotten by flirting with a security guard who'd been mesmerized by her British accent—was a Who's Who of Los Angeles celebrities from music, sports, and entertainment. More importantly, though, it was full of names from the worlds of business, tech, and finance. There were dozens of new money millionaires from California and New York who were richer and more powerful than the athletes and musicians on the list, but who wanted to rub shoulders with the real stars. There were no fewer than fifty names who would, in one way or another, tie into Ibo Kane's business plans.

Cole said, "Rob, you want to try one more time? Maybe approach the guests individually?"

They'd already tried to warn the security guards and called the venue, but had been rebuffed. The party was safe, they were told. "Probably the safest place in Los Angeles tonight," one of the guards had insisted.

"Nah," Warren said. "Let's wait."

"Don't have to wait," Sarah said from the backseat. "That's him. They told me to watch for the limo."

She'd rolled down the window and was pointing at a black SUV limousine with license plates that read: KANE.

158

Inside the limo, Kane finished a tumbler of Red Bull and set the glass on the mahogany bar. The LED lights on the side paneling made the glass glow an other-worldly blue.

"Is everything set?" He asked the question into his bluetooth earpiece, making him look as though he was speaking to himself.

"Yes, General Ki." The thin Indian accent was that of the man he knew as 8/15/47. The man's real name was Suresh, the leader of an anti-technology Hindu nationalist group in Southern India.

"It's ten after ten."

"Yes, sir. Twenty minutes."

"I'll leave the line open," Kane said.

"Good."

Without ending the call, Kane turned his attention to his assistant. "Are you ready?"

Kid pointed to a low rooftop across the street from Club God. "There, right?"

"Right."

The assistant handed him three small white pills. "This will numb the pain some. But, sir..." Kid shook his head. "This will be no fun." He smiled.

Kane laughed. "You ever been shot?"

"No. I've heard it hurts."

Kane swallowed the pills with a bottle of water. "Make sure you have more of these on the helicopter."

The assistant nodded. "And Dr. Bryan will have morphine."

Kane pointed to a corner. "Start there, and make sure you're not so close it looks staged, okay. It's gotta look like I'm just going to the club and you're a loser fan."

The limo stopped at the corner and Kid got out.

Alone in the limo, Kane paid special attention to the sensations of his body. He didn't feel the codeine kicking in yet, but he almost regretted taking it. He'd worked for this for years and he didn't want his senses numbed when he was so close to the finish line. Excellence required sacrifice. Pain.

His whole body coursed with excitement and tingled with anticipation. He doubted three codeine pills could take that away.

He tapped a button and a sliding glass divider retracted. "I'll be getting out in about five minutes," he told the driver. "Drop me halfway between where you dropped Kid and the front entrance."

"Will do, boss."

"And when you drop me off, head home for the night. I'll be leaving on the chopper."

159

Cole watched the man get out of the limo as Warren started a call. "Gabby. Yes, you saw the limo?… yup. Guy hopped out and… yeah."

The man wore a black suit and took a long drag from a vape pen before stashing it in an inside jacket pocket. He leaned on a post, scrolling through his phone, then cocked his head and watched the limo move slowly down the street. "Rob, what do you think he's doing?"

She handed him the binoculars and took them back after he'd taken a moment to scan the scene.

"Seems to be just chilling," Warren said.

The limo stopped halfway down the block. Cole's eyes darted from the limo to the man on the corner. "What the hell is going on?"

Sarah said, "I've got half a mind to jump out of the car and tear that guy a new one."

"I know," Cole said, "but we have to wait."

The man now had his phone out in front of him, as though taking a picture. Slowly, he walked down the block toward the club entrance.

"What the hell?" Warren asked.

The rear door of the limousine opened and a figure stepped out. His back was to them, but he wore a dark blue suit and his black hair was visible in the lights that shone from the side of the massive former church.

Cole pointed. "It's Kane."

Warren nodded. Cole drew a breath, her eyes moving from the young man with the phone to Kane, who'd paused just outside the canopy leading into the club.

Then, everything seemed to happen at once.

The man with the phone picked up the pace, then jogged toward Kane, phone trained on him.

Warren's phone buzzed.

Another figure emerged, Cole didn't know from where. He had a gun. Not a rifle, but a small handgun.

Cole leapt from the car as she heard a *CRACK*.

Kane dropped to a knee, holding the back of his thigh, but making no sound.

Security guards rushed at the shooter. Gabby sprinted from her position down the block toward the melee.

The man with the phone, inexplicably, was smiling. He raced toward Kane as the security guards swarmed the shooter. Then he lifted Kane by the arm. Hobbling and favoring his leg, Kane allowed himself to be led across the street.

Warren and Sarah now stood next to Cole on the sidewalk. Gabby was arguing with security, trying to get into the club. McKnight scribbled furiously in her notebook.

"Rob," Cole said. "I…" Her mind was moving faster than her words could form.

He met her eyes. "I think I know what you're thinking."

"He had a guy film him getting shot. He never intended to go into the club. You, join Gabby, get people out of there. Sarah, come with me."

Sarah reached through the open window into the back seat of the car and grabbed the rifle bag. Warren took off towards Gabby.

Cole dodged traffic as Kane and his assistant reached a building across the street.

160

Warren and Gabby exchanged a look that let him know she'd figured out the same thing Cole had. Kane never planned to enter the club. He'd set up the whole thing to make it look like he was a target. That meant the real target was the club itself. They didn't have much time.

The security guards broke protocol when the shot was fired, and Warren took advantage of it. Grabbing Gabby's hand, he raced around a row of potted trees as they subdued the shooter, then burst through the doors into the Club.

Despite the disturbance outside, inside the club was a sort of organized chaos. Apparently, the patrons hadn't heard the gunshot over the electronic string music playing through speakers hidden in every nook and cranny. Waiters in white shirts and black bow ties carried silver trays of hors d'oeuvres from person to person. Celebrities and other rich-looking partiers populated a few dozen individually roped-off tables.

Gabby moved to the wall and McKnight darted away, though Warren had no idea where she was headed.

He jumped on the bench of a booth. "Everyone," Warren shouted.

"Whooooo, party!" someone yelled back.

A few dozen people shouted drunkenly. They seemed to think he was the hype man for the party.

He looked for Gabby, who was busy inspecting behind curtains along the wall. That's when it hit him. She wasn't scanning for a shooter. She was looking for explosives.

"Everyone!" he shouted. "Stop! We believe this club is going to come under attack as part of the nine murders plot."

A few people looked up, but others went along with their drinking and conversations as though Warren were a performance artist they wanted to ignore.

"Seriously, people! There's a credible threat that the very rich and important people in this club are being targeted. Please get the hell out of here right away."

A few people moved toward an exit at the rear of the huge, open space. A man approached and took his arm. "Sir, get down from there. We've called security and they—"

Warren shook his arm free. "They're busy responding to the *gunshots* outside."

The man was older and appeared to be some sort of a manager. A twitch of fear moved across his face, then he said, "We haven't heard anything about *that*."

Two security guards shot through the door and ran for Warren. "Everyone, seriously, get the hell out of here." He turned his eyes to Gabby, who was still quietly examining the perimeter of the room.

The two men grabbed him. One turned to the manager. "Shooting outside, sir. The suspect has been apprehended and we're waiting for police, but there's no threat to—"

"There is!" Warren shouted, and they tightened their grip around his biceps.

He scanned for Gabby, but she had disappeared. McKnight was nowhere to be found.

"Just let me explain," Warren pleaded. "I've been working on the nine murders case and we believe there's going to be an attack on—"

"We heard," one of the guards interrupted. He was a beefy Asian guy, maybe Warren's size, with a holstered firearm clearly visible. "LAPD told us there have been tips." He turned to the manager. "We checked it out. Nothing."

"Get him out of here," the manager said.

The guards began tugging Warren toward the door.

"Wait!" It was Gabby's voice.

Warren turned. She and McKnight stood across the room.

"There are bags of explosives in the basement!" Gabby shouted.

As if she'd disturbed an anthill, everyone began to stir. Some ran for the exits, others looked around with confused, blank looks, unsure whether it was a prank.

McKnight ran toward Warren and the guards, holding out her phone. It was open to a picture of a duffle bag, half open, full of what Warren was sure was RDX. She swiped, showing a wider view of the duffle bag in context, nestled in the drop ceiling. Then another of a storage room full of luxury goods, the open drop ceiling barely visible.

Gabby said, "Right now, in your basement."

Finally, the manager understood. So did the two security guards. The grip on Warren's arms went slack.

"You need to evacuate everyone," Warren said. "Now."

The manager stood on a nearby chair. "Everyone, we're sorry, but please exit the building in an orderly fashion."

Warren waved toward the back exit. "Hell with orderly. Everyone get out!"

161

The pain coursed from Kane's thigh into his hip and across his pelvis, but it wasn't as bad as he expected. "Did you... get it... Kid?" he asked his assistant. He was trying to keep his voice steady, but the words came out in a peppered staccato between heavy breaths.

"Like Scorsese."

They reached a metal staircase that led up four stories to the roof of an abandoned building. Slowly, Kane tackled the steps, each more painful than the last. "I wanted... it to look like a fan's video... not Scorsese."

"People are stupid. They see what you tell them to see. They'll love it. We'll tell them to see a botched assassination and that's what they'll see."

The distant sound of the chopper approached through downtown Los Angeles. Right on time.

Kane spoke to Suresh, still on the line in his earpiece, "8/15/47... you there?"

"Here. Three minutes."

"Good."

At the landing after a flight of stairs, Kane paused and looked back at the club. A swarm of security guards had detained the shooter. Many others were rushing in and out of the club.

Then he saw her. A woman with straight black hair was at the bottom of the stairs, looking up at him. Who was she? He thought he recognized her, but before he could place the face, Kid was pulling him up.

The helicopter had grown loud.

"It's landing," Kid said. "Let's go."

⊕

Cole waited for Sarah to catch up, then bounded up the fire escape.

Sarah yelled something, but the churning roar of the helicopter was deafening. "I can't hear you." She looked back at her as they passed the first landing, but knew Sarah couldn't hear her either.

Kane and the young man were a flight ahead of them and Cole tried to pick up the pace, but tripped on the top step of the second landing. Sarah leapt over her without missing a beat and, by the time Cole was on her feet again, she was a flight ahead.

By the time she reached the roof, Kane was climbing into the chopper. The wind from the propellers startled her, nearly knocking her backward. At first, she didn't see Sarah, but then noticed her on the ground.

On her lap lay the rifle bag.

⊕

Kane strapped on the belt and shouted at the man in the cockpit. "Go, go!"

"What?" It was the voice in his ear. 8/15/47.

The helicopter lifted off. Kane looked at the scene below. People were rushing out of the building in waves and no one seemed to be rushing in. "Now," Kane shouted.

"It's not time yet—"

"Blow it now!"

708

162

Cole dropped to the ground and lay still, watching as the helicopter rose into the night sky.

"Ready." Sarah flipped onto her belly and aimed the rifle. But the helicopter had risen too quickly, making the angle impossible.

Quickly, Sarah maneuvered her body into a cross-legged sitting position, balancing the rifle on her knee. As she leaned back, Cole spoke directly into her ear. "Please don't shoot Kane. I have some things I need to say to him."

She rolled behind Sarah, who tilted her body to a point where her back was almost parallel to the rooftop. As she did, she raised her knee and pressed the rifle butt into her shoulder. Suddenly, a massive *CRACK* broke through the sound of the helicopter, which was now about forty yards above the rooftop.

Then she heard another sound. A deep boom. No, a *series* of booms. For a confused instant, she wondered how Sarah had gotten off another shot so quickly. Then a yellow glare reflected off the falling helicopter.

"I took out the fuel tank," Sarah yelled.

Cole turned toward the church. The sky was orange and yellow. She scooched forward toward the edge of the rooftop as another *BOOM* broke the sky.

Below, there was a crater where the side of the church had

been. Fire jumped from the center of the building and smoke shrouded the whole scene.

Terrified shrieks mingled with the *thwapping* sound of the descending helicopter. On the perimeter of the cloud of billowing smoke, people emerged, running from the building and collapsing into the street and onto cars.

A crash of glass and metal erupted and Cole turned to see the wrecked helicopter skidding to a halt twenty yards away from her.

Sarah was still on the ground, lining up another shot, but Cole wrestled the rifle from her hands and ran to the helicopter. The driver was unconscious in the cockpit and she found Kane, eyes closed, forehead bloody, still strapped into his seat in the back. The glass and metal around him had busted out and smoke ran from the side of the chopper. In the back seat, two other men were strapped in, also unconscious.

"Kane!"

He said nothing, but his eyes flickered open.

She raised the rifle. "Ibo Kane!"

His face was expressionless. He was either concussed or more stoic than any man she'd ever met.

"My name is Jane Cole. The reporter who figured you out. I broke the story."

Still, no expression.

"You and Marty Goldberg and Chandler Price worked with a man named William Wei to move drugs from Afghanistan to China. Marines. You used *Marines*. My husband was one of them. You had him killed."

The blades of the helicopter had stopped and an eerie quiet had fallen, pierced occasionally by shouts from below.

Kane's eyes were wide now. Fully alert. He offered a noncommittal shrug. "Doesn't sound like something I'd do."

His voice was weak, but just as arrogant as she'd expected.

"Matthew Cole. You knew he'd found out about the operation and then you had him killed."

Kane smiled. "You have me confused with someone else."

"Say his name. *Matthew Cole.*" She raised the rifle from his chest to his head and gripped a finger on the trigger. From the corner of her eye, she saw Sarah approaching. "Admit it and I'll let you live."

All she was aware of was Ibo Kane's face and the feel of the curved metal under her finger's subtle pressure.

Kane frowned slightly. "Matthew Cole? I swear to you, I've never heard that name in my life."

She watched his eyes, cold and clear. His face showed nothing. Either he was the best liar she'd ever met, or he was telling the truth.

"But William Wei? Afghanistan?"

"Yes, I did all that. But I never ordered, well, anything like what you said." He closed his eyes. "You honestly think I have time for that?"

Then it hit her, of course he hadn't directed anyone to kill Matt. He'd left that task to someone else. To middle management. To William Wei, probably, who would have known better than to bother his bosses with the silly problem of an uppity Marine who needed to get murdered. Throughout history, men like Kane had forced other people to do their killing for them. Wasn't that what Kane had done with his entire plot? Conned other men to do his killing? Her husband had been no different.

The metal trigger warmed where it touched her finger, and she wanted nothing more than to press it. But she didn't. The desire for short-lived vengeance wasn't as powerful as the desire to see Ibo Kane hauled into court, questioned, and humiliated for months, maybe even years of trials. More than anything, she wanted to watch as his crimes were proven publicly, his businesses dismantled piece by piece while he stood by, helpless.

Sarah had inched to within a yard of her and Cole nodded for her to join them. In one swift motion, Cole released her finger from the trigger, swung the rifle down to her side, and handed it to Sarah. "Point this rifle at his heart until the police show up to drag his ass to prison."

"Gladly." Sarah nodded. "By the way, the recoil on this thing would have broken your shoulder if you'd squeezed off a round."

To Kane, Cole said, "This is Sarah McNeeley the woman you had Chandler hire. If you move, she'll shoot you. She's a two-time Olympian. I doubt she'll miss."

Cole walked to the edge of the roof and looked down. A crowd had gathered in front of the smoldering church. Fire trucks raced down the block. The building had caved in completely, but the size of the crowd outside made her hopeful that most of the people had escaped.

Four stories below, a man came around the side of the building, trailed by two, smaller figures. She recognized Warren's brown leather jacket and slight limp. The other two were Gabby and McKnight. Warren stopped and lifted his head.

She couldn't tell if he was looking at her, but she thought so. Hoped so.

She waved and nodded, acknowledging him, then watched as he walked toward the throng gathered at the entrance of the burned-out church.

163

Two Days Later

Diamond Luxury Construction was located in a large office in an industrial park only ten minutes from the San Diego Airport. It had its own building, the smallest in the development, but large enough to house an office and a facility for constructing custom cabinetry, doors, and other high-end wood projects.

Cole had picked up Susan Cole, Matt's mother, an hour earlier. Now, the two of them waited in her rental car. It was eight in the morning and they expected Chris Morgan, the company's owner, to arrive any minute. "You too cold?" Cole asked.

Susan looked straight ahead. "I'm fine, dear."

Cole cracked a window and a cool, salty breeze filled the car.

"San Diego is beautiful, don't you think? So much *warmer* than Seattle. Must be—what?—sixty degrees already." Susan had been a chipper, cheery woman before Matt was killed. Fundamentally positive about people and the world—the opposite of Cole herself. But Cole had always liked her mother-in-law. After Matt died, they grew closer, often talking for hours about Matt, or about nothing at all. In the first few months, sometimes they'd stayed on the phone for hours, allowing long silences to fill the space between shared memories of Matt. Now Susan's positivity was rare and seemed forced.

"There!" Cole pointed to a silver BMW convertible that had just stopped in a spot marked: *Reserved for THE MAN.* A blond guy around forty years old sprang out and walked quickly inside.

"Was that him?" Susan asked. She spoke in a loud whisper, her voice full of fear and urgency. Cole hadn't been sure it was a good idea to bring her. Now she was sure it had been a *bad* idea.

"That was him, but… uh… why don't you stay in the car?"

Susan brushed aside a curl of shoulder-length brown hair, reached up, and took Cole by the chin. "Jane, I'm doing this. Yes, I'm afraid, but I *have* to do this."

Cole nodded once and they stepped out of the car and walked across the parking lot.

From her hotel in San Francisco, Cole had called Susan and told her everything she'd learned about Lopez and Morgan. She'd described Ibo Kane's drug business, and how his middleman William Wei had used the Marine unit in Afghanistan to move drugs through China and into the U.S. Through tears, she'd explained how Matt had gotten involved. She'd also played her the recording of Lopez's confession. Chris Morgan, the man who'd pulled the trigger, was the last loose thread she needed to tug.

In the lobby was a black desk where, Cole guessed, a secretary usually sat. It was empty now. Cole led Susan down the hall, checking an office here and there along the way. "Let me do the talking, okay?"

Susan didn't respond.

"There," Cole said. Near the end of the hallway, she stopped a yard short of a large office, the only one with a light on. A set of wide double doors opened into a huge workshop next to the office. Buzzing, banging, and sawing noises came from behind the doors.

Without knocking, Cole walked in and stopped in the middle of the room. "Chris Morgan?" She tried to sound polite.

He stood, dropping a car magazine on the desk. "I… yes? Did we have an appointment I forgot about?"

"No, I'm Jane Cole." His face didn't change. The name didn't mean anything to him. "And this is Susan Cole. May we sit?"

He waved at a couple chairs and they sat.

"Sorry my receptionist wasn't there this morning. We don't get a lot of walk-ins. How can I help you?"

"There's something I want you to hear." Cole set her phone

on his desk, then looked up. Before pressing play, she wanted to get a read on him. He wasn't a large man, standing maybe five foot eight and leaner than she expected. His face was taut, not unlike Warren's, and her read on him was that he was emotionally explosive. Cool on the surface but always a moment away from rage. "Do you remember your pal Julio Lopez?"

He shrugged. "What's this about?"

She stood, hands firm on the desk. Susan faded away, the room faded away. Everything but Morgan's well-tanned face and blue eyes. "He's dead. He killed himself right after admitting that you and he killed my husband."

Morgan's face quivered, his left eye twitching against his will. Without taking her eyes off Morgan, she pressed play.

"Sandy?" It was Lopez's voice.

Judging by the way Morgan's forehead wrinkled nervously, he knew it, too.

Cole: *Gretchen Blacker, FBI field office in San Antonio.*

Lopez: *Oh, damn.*

Cole: *That's right, Julio.... My colleagues are down in San Diego, questioning your pal Chris Morgan right now. He's already told us everything, said it was your idea from the start and that you pulled the trigger.*

Lopez: *He's lying, he—*

Cole: *Hold on, Julio, just calm down. I don't want you to say anything to incriminate yourself. You have the right to speak to a lawyer, and I suggest you do so. But I want to tell you the situation and instruct you on how you might stay out of jail. You have a young daughter, right?*

She paused the recording and met Morgan's blue eyes, now filled with fear. "Do you understand, Chris?"

His hands were on the desk, fists clenched. His left eye twitched again. All he said was, "Play the rest."

And she did.

Cole: *Please be quiet and let me finish. We asked Mr. Morgan to give up his contacts and he tried to push it all onto you. Made you out to be a real drug kingpin. A criminal mastermind like Lady Chicharron or El Chapo. You're not a drug kingpin, are you, Julio?*

Lopez: *No ma'am.*

Cole: *Didn't think so. I will ask you one time and one time only, before we run with Mr. Morgan's version of events: Who pulled the trigger on Matthew Cole?*

Lopez: *Chris.*

Cole: And it was because Mr. Cole learned of an operation—run by Marines—to export heroin from Afghanistan to China?

Lopez: Yes…

Cole stopped the recording and leveled a vicious glare at Morgan. "It goes on from there."

Morgan stood quickly, glanced at the door behind them like he was going to make a dash for it, then fell back into his chair. He took a few deep breaths, regaining his composure. "It's illegal to impersonate an FBI agent."

He was trying to sound smug, Cole thought. Confident. But it wasn't working. The twitch over his left eye was his body telling her he was scared.

"What do you want?" he asked.

Before Cole could speak, Susan stood. "We want you to turn yourself in. To walk into a police station today, admit what you did, and stand trial under military justice for the murder of a fellow Marine." When she'd finished, she sat and folded her hands in her lap. Cole had never heard such a firm tone from Matt's mother.

Morgan appeared to consider it for a moment, then his face broke out in a wide, phony grin. His eye stopped twitching. Condescension oozed from him. It was the look of a man who'd gotten away with everything his entire life. The look of a man who'd gotten away with murder. "I just realized something. You're here to try to get me to confess because the police won't do anything with that recording. It's illegal, even if it was real, which it *isn't*." His voice was growing louder, like he was raising it for a nearby microphone. "You're probably recording this right now, aren't you? Hoping for a confession."

Cole said, "I'm not recording this."

"I bet you *are*, and I'll just say for the record, I have no idea who you are, who that recording was, or why you'd want to create a fake… whatever that was."

"I'm not recording this." She leaned across the desk, her face now only a foot away from his. She smiled so wide she wondered if she looked deranged. "And I know you won't confess. Have you heard of Ibo Kane?"

"Sure, nine murders thing. Wait, are you the reporter who…"

"I am," Cole said. "And I know you don't know this, but you were working for him."

He leaned back, his eyes wide, but he said nothing.

"I just wanted to be the one to tell you that. Right now, Kane is under arrest in San Francisco. He'll be charged with so many federal crimes it'll be a full-employment program for lawyers. Law school courses will be created to cover the depth and breadth of his criminality. One of those crimes will be using a man named William Wei to hijack a Marine unit and run drugs. Kane will have the best lawyers on earth, but Wei is dead, so they can't pin it on him." She lowered her voice to something just over a whisper. "Who do you think Kane's lawyers will try to pin that one on? After all, Kane was never even *in* Afghanistan. How do you think your fellow Marines will look at you once they know you murdered one of your own?"

Morgan closed his eyes for a long time, as though he could make this all disappear by shutting off his own perception.

Cole glanced down at Susan, who nodded at the door.

They left together, leaving Morgan's door open as they strode into the hallway hand-in-hand.

164

Saturday, One Week Later

Cole and Warren were on their second lap around the Harlem Meer when Warren said, "I've got a surprise for you."

It was an unseasonably temperate January day and the brisk walk through Central Park had warmed her. Cole unbuttoned her jacket. "What?"

"It'll be here in ten minutes."

Cole gave him a little shove. "I don't like surprises. Well, usually not."

The last surprise she'd had in Central Park had been the night Matt brought her to a spot about a mile south. It had been Christmas eve before his final deployment, when he'd decorated the potted Monkey Tree for her. He'd gone back to Afghanistan soon after and never returned. The Monkey Tree had slowly faded, until now. She'd been back in New York for a week and had watered it, cut off a dead branch, and moved it into the sun on her windowsill. The little evergreen was showing some signs of improved health.

They sat on a bench by a small grassy field, looking out over the 11-acre pond. Cole watched Warren's eyes follow a bird as it flew from a tree and landed on the water. When he looked up, she asked, "Heard from Gabby?"

"Kind of. Got a message on some app I didn't even know I had. I guess she downloaded it onto my phone when I wasn't looking or something. Anyway, it was an anonymous message."

"What did it say?" Cole asked.

Warren pulled out his phone, swiped, and handed it to her.

The message was white text on a black screen and contained no sender information.

War Dog,

I'm disappearing for a while. Maybe a long while. It was a risk coming out of hiding to do what we did, but it was worth it. Just know that I'll be trying to do the job in the way I can. If you need anything, you can message me here. It'll ping through six countries and three different encryption systems before it reaches me. I hope things work out with Sarah. You deserve to get her back. And my hunch is she needs you.

-G

Cole read the message twice and handed him the phone. "Have you seen her yet?"

"Sarah?"

"Yeah."

Warren looked out at the water. "Heading there after this."

"That's good news, right?"

He shrugged.

"Warren, c'mon. Be honest."

He looked at her, his eyes less intense than usual, his face softer. "I'm… I don't know."

She crossed her legs on the bench and turned to face him. His hands were folded in his lap and he kept turning them like he was kneading invisible dough.

"Makes sense. Does seeing Sarah feel kind of like a first date?" she asked.

"Kinda."

"You've been through hell, man. You found out she was seeing a former friend. You were nearly blown up, shot at, chased through God knows how many streets. You sat through five days of questioning by LAPD, FBI. You've been lauded as a hero by some and vilified by a lot of others. You saved maybe three-hundred lives and now you're sitting on a park bench with a crazy reporter staring at the ducks. You've got a right to be a little discombobulated."

Warren chuckled. "It's not just that. I'm *nervous*."

"Nervous?" Cole asked.

"Feels like this is my last chance. And… I fell off the wagon in Paris."

"One-time thing. You gotta forgive yourself for that. You deserve a get-out-of-jail-free card, given the hell you just went through."

"I know," he said. "But that doesn't mean I deserve Sarah and Marina back."

Warren's eyes shifted down the pathway and he stood suddenly.

Way down the path, a figure moved slowly, limping. A dog scurried along by his side. "Who's that?" Cole asked.

"That's the surprise."

"What?" Cole asked.

"Remember I told you about the retired cop who finds homes for dogs rescued from crime scenes?"

She thought back. "Liberty?"

Warren walked down the path without answering, but, as they came into view, she knew she was right.

The dog had the face and body of a bulldog and the black-and-white spots of a dalmatian. She'd been too freaked out to notice at the time, but he was one of the cutest dogs she'd ever seen. And he looked healthier than the last time she'd seen him, which made sense because the last time she'd seen he was starving and clearly neglected by Michael Wragg, the man who'd killed Raj Ambani.

"This is Brandon." Warren introduced an old man with a thick gray beard.

"You Liberty's new mama?" He handed her the leash.

"I, um…" She looked at Warren.

"You don't have to," Warren said. "But this is the surprise."

Brandon sat in the center of the bench, Warren and Cole on either side of him. "Couldn't find him a new owner, but honestly I didn't look hard. Wanted to nurse him back to health first. Warren called me a few days ago and said you might be interested."

"Did he?" Cole raised an eyebrow. She held out a hand, which Liberty approached cautiously. He sniffed, then gave it a few licks and lay down, resting his head on her foot.

Brandon slapped his knee. "He likes you. I can tell."

Warren said, "No pressure, now. You don't have to take him. But, I don't know. I thought you might want to."

She thought of the Monkey Tree, which she'd nearly let die from neglect over the last few years. "I can barely keep a houseplant alive, Rob."

"When Marina was born, me and Sarah constantly worried whether she'd survive."

"Was she sick?" Cole asked.

"No, we just... *worried*. There's this whole other person there and you have no idea how they're gonna survive. I used to wake up in the night just to see if she was still breathing. Turns out, most of this stuff takes care of itself."

"But—"

"There's something else," Warren interrupted. "You rise to the occasion."

"He's right," Brandon added. "Got three kids myself, each one terrified me in their own way, but you rise to the occasion."

Cole looked down at Liberty's belly, rising and falling. "He looks healthier than before."

"Gained a few pounds," Brandon said. "Been feeding him, walking him. He wasn't treated well. Not for a while." He looked at his watch. "So, want him?"

Cole reached down and pet the dog's head. It felt like a terrifying leap. She was good at a lot of things, but taking care of another living being wasn't one of them.

As if reading her thoughts, Warren put a hand on her knee. "You'll rise to the occasion."

***

The door opened before Warren had a chance to knock.

"Daddy!"

Marina was in his arms before he knew what was happening. He lifted her into a hug, squeezing her tight as Sarah appeared from the living room and joined them on the porch.

They lived in a one-bedroom apartment on the first floor of a three-story brick building. Warren had only been here a few times, but he'd imagined it a lot over the last few days, usually with moving trucks parked out front.

He set Marina down and knelt. "How are you, baby?"

"Good, I got a new Lego set, wanna see?" She grabbed his hand and tried pulling him into the house.

He met his estranged wife's eyes. "Okay with you?"

She nodded inside, and he followed them into Marina's room.

For the next hour they played Legos, Marina leading the way, asking for advice on which color to make the fortress and which wheels were better for the battering ram she made to knock it down.

Sarah brought coffee—perfectly burnt—and stood in the doorway, watching but saying little.

He felt her there, though. Not judging, exactly, but observing carefully. When Marina got up to go look through another Lego box in the living room, Warren said, "She seems good. You're a good mom."

His eyes were still on the Lego project and Sarah said, "Hey, look up."

He turned to where she stood, leaning in the doorway.

"You're a good dad, too," she said.

"No, I'm not."

"I said 'good,' not 'great.' But... you've got potential."

He smiled. It was all he'd wanted to hear.

"We're gonna go to D.C. You should come. Not to *live* with us, but maybe near us. Maybe we get together more regularly. Maybe, well... I don't know."

He stood, watching Sarah carefully. He heard Marina rummaging around in a box of Legos and singing quietly to herself. "I'd like that," he said. "I'm done being a cop, but I can find something down there. Private security. Consulting for police work, maybe."

She gave him a little shove. "Know what I think you should do?"

He smiled playfully. "Hollywood?"

She laughed. "I was gonna say, go back to school. History. Police and military history. You've always been interested in that. Maybe it's time."

"No better place than D.C. to study that stuff. I'll look into some programs."

She put a hand on his forearm. It wasn't a grand gesture, but it was kind. She met his eyes. "Rob, no promises, okay? But I'm willing to give this a shot."

For the first time in years, his whole body relaxed.

That was all he'd wanted to hear.

Cole rolled down the window as she merged onto the Taconic Parkway. She was forty-five minutes outside of New York City in her rented Honda Civic, and now the scent of trees and the cool air mingled with the smell of minty air freshener.

In the back seat, Liberty perked up at the noise and the wind.

"Don't worry," she said. "It's just wind."

Next to her in the passenger seat, the Monkey Tree was belted in. A small shovel lay on the floor mat.

She saw a good spot, a turnout next to a low hill, but it was too late. She was already halfway past by the time she noticed it. After another dozen miles, she pulled off at a rest area and got out.

She handed Liberty a treat from the bag Brandon had given her. He'd also given her a bag of food and a printed sheet of instructions for dog owners. Some were from a list he gave to everyone, he said. The ten things every dog needs. Exercise, food, attention, and so on. But he'd added some items specific to Liberty. He loved this particular kind of treat that came in a yellow bag. They had black lines on them to show that, as the package promised, they "tasted like real grilled steak."

She walked about fifty yards off the road and found a small clearing. Liberty tugged at his leash, so she tied him to a nearby tree and gave him another treat. She dug a small hole, pulled the Monkey Tree out of its pot, and planted it. Liberty watched her for a minute, then lay in a pile of dried leaves.

As she shoveled dirt back over the base of the small tree, she thought of Matt. For the first time in a long time, she wasn't hit with a series of painful memories and unanswered questions. He came to her more like a feeling, a general presence of warmth and love that was just... there.

She also thought of what she'd do next.

She was done with journalism—at least for a while. The newspaper world she'd expected to inhabit for life was dead. It had still existed for most of the 2000s, faded quickly in the 2010s, and in the 2020s been replaced by an explosion of social media, disinformation, and chaos.

And she didn't know her place in that new world. She'd had offers from TV stations, newspapers, and magazines. Alex Vane at *The Barker* had offered her a full-time job, too. But nothing had enticed her. She had enough money to last a few months, and she'd figure something out.

She patted the last of the dirt onto the Monkey Tree and emptied a large jug of water at its base. She took a picture and sent this and a pin drop to Warren with a text message, asking him to check in on it and give it some water if he passed through. The sky was a pale blue and the wind carried a wave of dried leaves past her.

She gave Liberty another treat, worried she was spoiling him already, and led him back to the car. She stowed the shovel, the empty water jug, and pot in her trunk next to her suitcase.

All she knew about what came next was that she would drive her rented car across America to Seattle to spend time with Matt's mom. She'd stop at pet-friendly hotels along the way, and see a few sights. She stowed her phone in her suitcase so she wouldn't be tempted to check the news while she drove. She took a deep breath as she thought about it. There would be a *lot* of news. The headlines would be relentless. But it wasn't her problem.

Not anymore.

She would head north a few more miles, then merge onto Interstate 84 West. From there, she'd enter Pennsylvania, merge onto Interstate 80, and continue west through Ohio, Indiana, Illinois, and Iowa. Eventually she'd turn northwest and, in five or six days, she'd arrive at Susan's house in Seattle.

She didn't know what she'd do when she got there.

All she knew was that she had to go.

—The End—

Thanks for reading! If you enjoyed *The Crime Beat*, you'll love my mystery series, The Thomas Austin Crime Thrillers and FBI Task Force S.W.O.R.D.

A NOTE FROM THE AUTHOR

If you enjoyed this book, I encourage you to check out my two big series: The Thomas Austin Crime Thrillers and FBI Task Force S.W.O.R.D. The books in each series can be read as standalones, although relationships and situations develop from book to book, so they will be more enjoyable if read in order.

I also have an online store, where you can buy signed paper-backs, mugs, t-shirts, and more. You can also get a free E-Book copy of my cookbook by joining my newsletter!

Every day I feel fortunate to be able to wake up and create characters and write stories. And that's all made possible by readers like you. So, again, I extend my heartfelt thanks for checking out my books, and I wish you hundreds of hours of happy reading to come.

D.D. Black

MORE D.D. BLACK NOVELS

The Thomas Austin Crime Thrillers

Book 1: *The Bones at Point No Point*

Book 2: *The Shadows of Pike Place*

Book 3: *The Fallen of Foulweather Bluff*

Book 4: *The Horror at Murden Cove*

Book 5: *The Terror in The Emerald City*

Book 6: *The Drowning at Dyes Inlet*

Book 7: *The Nightmare at Manhattan Beach*

Book 8: *The Silence at Mystery Bay*

Book 9: *The Darkness at Deception Pass*

Book 10: *The Vanishing at Opal Creek*

Book 11: *The Secrets of Second Beach*

FBI Task Force S.W.O.R.D.

Book 1: *The Fifth Victim*

Book 2: *We Forget Nothing*

Book 3: *Widows of Medina*

Book 4: *Beneath Hemlock Skies*

Standalone Crime Novels

The Things She Stole

The Crime Beat

ABOUT D.D. BLACK

D.D. Black is the author of the Thomas Austin Crime Thrillers, the FBI Task Force S.W.O.R.D. series, and other crime novels. When he's not writing, he can be found strolling the beaches of the Pacific Northwest, cooking dinner for his wife and kids, or throwing a ball for his corgi over and over and over. Find out more at ddblackauthor.com.

73035050R00427